WINDS of CHANGE

Also in the Series

WINDS
of
CHANGE

Jane Hatton

Copyright © Jane Hatton 2019
First published in 2019 by RaJe Publications
Garth Cottage, Little in Sight
Mawnan Smith, Falmouth, TR11 5EY

Distributed by Lightning Source worldwide

British Library Cataloguing in Publication Data
A catalogue record for this book is available from the British Library

ISBN 978-0-9554508-9-1

Typeset by Amolibros, Milverton, Somerset
www.amolibros.com
This book production has been managed by Amolibros
Printed and bound by Lightning Source worldwide

Author's Note

I have been writing this series for many years now, and all of them are set in my homeland, the beautiful West Country that runs along the southern coast from Dorset via Devon to end in Cornwall. At one point, my then publisher elected to christen the first books "The Nankervis Family Chronicle", but as time goes on, this has become less and less accurate – yes, it all began with the Nankervises but as I began to know them better, I realised that there was a lot more to them than a simple family story – they had friends, as people do – they had a past, and gradually this began to become apparent, at first in the background, but then gradually working the way into the foreground, but the important point here is, the people in all the books know each other, they have history together, they are often good friends, and even if the Nankervises themselves have settled in Cornwall – well, for now, they have, who knows? I certainly don't! – a lot of their friends and their past lives are in Dorset, which is where several of both the earlier and the later books have been set. But it is all part of the same overall story, and it is important to bear this in mind.

Which brings me to my present problem: I began to write a book which was planned to follow on after *Full Circle*, but for some reason, couldn't seem to get it off the ground. This is unusual for me, as generally words flow like tap water once I get going, but I began this one back in 2013, and by the beginning of 2018, it was still run aground on Page 45! Then all of a sudden, it dawned on me what was blocking it. There would soon be characters introduced who first appeared in *Things that go Bump in the Night* and *A Dream of Dragons* among others, but at least one of these had never been properly introduced. As he was now going to take a leading role, this was obviously a problem, as it left far too much to be explained, and as I thought about it something else dawned on me too. What I had done, in fact, was to miss out a whole book, possibly even two books, in my eagerness to get to the Dragons and to the archaeology that comes third on my list of passionate interests (after writing books and sailing). I know what happened in the interval – nobody else will. There was only one answer. So here it is, and some old friends with it.

And while I am writing this, I shouldn't omit to include a Very Big Thank-you to my good friend Pat Slater, who happily took on the tasks of checking the continuity for me and the grammar and spelling at the same time, and encouraging me if I ran aground again, making me keep the plot flowing so that she could find out what happened next – she and me, both! I needed her! It is very easy to get either carried away or lost in the jungle when things are going well, and writing this book has been like doing a very large jigsaw puzzle with no picture to guide me and invisible pieces! It comes between the two I already mentioned, but it also runs parallel to *A Different View* – ouch! So thank you, Pat, what would I do without you?

Jane Hatton
Cornwall, 2019

About the author

Jane Hatton was a child during World War II, and grew up in the unpermissive fifties, when career options for women were largely confined to Secretary, Nurse, Teacher, Physiotherapist. She opted for the first, thinking the skills required would be useful in her preferred career as a writer, but has also worked in hotels, as a sailing instructor, in a craft workshop and as a cookery demonstrator – a remarkably unstructured career – while continuing to write whenever there was a spare moment: sometimes there were not many! She has had two children's books published in the mainstream (a while ago now), followed by three novels in the genre of "literary fiction", plus The One Too Awful to Mention – which we don't mention – and has also independently published a long series about the Nankervis family and their friends and  relations, all set in various areas of the West Country. Apart from writing, her interests include sailing, painting – including at one time scenery for the local pantomime – archaeology, photography and cooking. She lives in Cornwall, on her own these days, with a small black cat for company and a background of family and friends.

I

Edward Freemantle closed the door behind his departing guest and stood for a moment with his back against it, trying to get his thoughts into some kind of order. That had been a bad half hour or so…he squeezed his eyes shut in a further attempt to clear his brain and then opened them abruptly at the sound of a departing car revving up on his drive and roaring off into the distance. The impossible situation had to be faced, standing here agonising wasn't going to help. He walked back to his drawing-room door to rejoin his aunt, Henrietta Chillingworth, who waited there staring out of the window in much the same state of painful confusion as his own. She turned round as he re-entered the room, and he could see tears on her cheeks, but she left it to him to make the first move.

'So, what did you make of all that?' he asked; a neat but cowardly way of passing the buck.

'I'm really not sure.' His Aunt Henry looked troubled, as well she might. 'She must have had some motive for telling us, but I can't work out what it is. She didn't ask anything of us. I thought she might.'

'I think she was leaving that for us to think about. But I know what I think we ought to do. Somebody is going to have to go and see him, and sort it all out face to face. Would you be up for it?'

'No,' said Henry, without equivocation. 'I think it's a job for your generation, not for mine. You were children, he can't blame you, he could be right to blame us. And you were his friends back then.'

'That's the rub. "Back then" – you don't realise how meaningful it is, until you hit this kind of thing. He would be quite justified in throwing the elected envoy over the cliff – and I recall that as being rather high.' The wonderful Jurassic Coast, he remembered it well. Part of a golden past.

Henry said, thinking it out, 'I don't think it's a job for Peter or Tom, even Peter was only about nine when they last met. And certainly not Ros, she was a year older, but she was far too much in puppy-love with him back then, she'd over-react and make bad, worse. And all three of them are too lightweight for the job. This is a misunderstanding of monumental proportions, Ed. I think it's a job for you or Michael.'

'Ergh?' said Ed, before he could stop himself. He took a breath. 'Well thank you, Aunt Henry, for that vote of confidence! And how do you suggest we approach the problem? Write him a letter? He wouldn't read it. He never read the ones Mike and Ros sent him before.'

'You mean, he never answered them. You don't know that he didn't read them.'

'That's exactly what I'm trying to say. If he'd wanted us, he's known where we were all these years. The inference is obvious to me. He didn't.'

There was a silence between them. As family misunderstandings go, the one they were facing was in a class of its own. Even trying to think about it made both Ed and his aunt feel slightly sick.

Brought down to basics, over twenty years in the past, Henry's only brother, a married man and father to a son, had fallen for the charms of a young girl with two children, twin girls, of her own by an unknown father. She had married, in panic when she ran from her home and an angry father and found herself on her own, a man who had turned out to be a violent bully who beat her, and presumably the children too although history didn't relate that. She had run again, a twin under each arm, to Christopher Chillingworth for help, as the only person she knew in London (apart from his mother, father, sisters etc. whom she had apparently overlooked in her panic). Christopher had found her a cottage to shelter in close to his wife's Dorset farm while he apparently planned to elope with her, leaving his own wife and son to deal with the fallout, but before he could carry out this plan the girl was murdered, and one of the little twins brutally attacked along with her – where the other one had gone, nobody knew at the time unless Christopher did, and he had never said.

The murderer was never identified. A grief-stricken Christopher had confided to his own father that he believed his son Francis, then sixteen, had done it and the shutters had come down between the west country side of the family and the far greater contingent in London. Ed and his cousins had never seen their cousin Francis again. They had all been close friends and allies, and nothing was ever explained: it was as if Uncle Chris, Aunt Mary and Francis, and the lovely old house and farm down in Dorset where they had spent so many happy holidays, had fallen off the planet.

They had all been young, of course – Francis himself was the oldest of them, then their cousin Michael Stacey, then Ed himself. The rest of them had been several years younger still. Children grow up: if they had ever given their cousin a thought it was with regret and affection, but resignation too. Life goes on. They didn't know the backstory.

But now, the twin who was supposed to be dead along with her mother had turned up out of the blue, bringing a wind of change in her wake that threatened to turn into a howling gale. For Francis had not killed her mother, he had always believed that his own mother had done so, just as she believed it of him. Neither of them had spoken out, even to each other, how could they, realistically? They had apparently just buried the grief and got on with life as best they could – and then the other twin, Kim, had turned up out of the blue and the whole tissue of lies and misunderstandings had collapsed and the debris was lying all over Dorset! The murderer had been identified, the mother and son who had believed each other to have committed the crime had been vindicated and proved disastrously mistaken in the same breath.

Ed knew that he really, really didn't want the job of taking all this up with his cousin, but Henry was thinking back over the recent interview, trying to identify something that she had seen at the time and then filed to concentrate on what was being said – filed so thoroughly that she was having trouble recalling it now. And then it came back to her. The Will! Diana Carey/Tamsin, renamed by her adoptive parents in the absence of any identification, knew about the terms of Chris's infamous Will! Christopher had been killed in a car crash the year following the murder and left all his money in trust to his son, cutting his betrayed wife right out of it and imposing conditions that made it difficult, if not impossible, to challenge.

And there was only one conclusion to reach about that. Diana Carey knew Francis a lot better than she had let on.

So where did that leave them?

'It's a mess,' she said.

'Perhaps we should think about it for a bit, before we do anything else,' Ed suggested.

'Why? Or are you just trying to put off the evil day? It's got to be faced sometime, Ed – we let him down. We may not have done it on purpose, or even realised that we had done anything in the first place, but the fact remains. We did. And the sooner we put the strength of that old friendship you all had to the test, the sooner we can rule a line under the problem and sleep at nights again. It either won't be one any more, or there isn't anything we can do about it.'

'Shouldn't you or Mum make the first approach?' Ed suggested, trying not to sound as if he was pleading with her. His Aunt Henry gave him a look that told him exactly what she thought of this tactic.

'Talk to Michael,' she said. 'See what he thinks. We won't tell the others yet, let's see what happens.'

Ed looked glum, but he said, 'I think he'll be in the office tomorrow. I'll catch him at lunchtime, if he hasn't an appointment with someone.' Hopefully, Michael would have. He often did. And if that only put off the evil day for twenty-four hours, at least it would be a breathing space. More than anything, Ed didn't want to throw them all in off the deep end. While they didn't know what Francis thought of them, or even more, what he and his mother had been through, it wouldn't hurt them. When they knew, it well might. What was that thing about sleeping dogs, again?

'You do that,' said Henry. She got to her feet. 'Let me know what happens. And now, my brave little nephew, if you don't want your wife to divorce you, you had better hurry off to Sunday lunch with your in-laws, and I must get back to town. Keep in touch, don't forget!'

When his aunt's car had vanished down the drive in Diana Carey's wake, Ed did not immediately follow to his wife's parents' house for the ritual of Sunday lunch. Instead, he went back into the drawing room and opened the photo album that he had taken out to show Diana. He stood by the table for a few minutes, turning over the pages – it had not been opened for such a long time that some of them were sticking together and he had to pull them apart, which was sad, but the photographs were unharmed. All of them were there, the merry crowd of cousins who had shared so many good times together, sailing boats, building sandcastles, exploring rock pools (particularly in Francis' case, he remembered), riding on haycarts and playing with dogs and cats, stooking hay in the fields at harvest…they should have been happy memories, but they made him sad. Could you ever go back to the happy relationships of the past?

Well, they would find out. Ed closed the album finally and headed for the door.

Unfortunately, Michael was in his office at the family business, Chillingworth Investment & Banking Services the next morning: Ed could have done with more time to think. He couldn't do lunch, he said in answer to Ed's reluctant invitation, but he could manage a quick drink later if Ed liked? He was looking at him very carefully, Ed realised, and hoped his chaotic state of mind wasn't as obvious to the rest of the Bank's employees. His palpable uneasiness prompted Michael to say, 'Everything all right, Ed? No problems?'

He meant business problems, of course, Ed realised. There was no point in leaving his cousin in too much perturbation, so Ed said, against his better judgement, 'No, business is fine. Going well. No, this is family stuff,' and added, although he didn't mean it, 'and it'll wait until later, no problem. I'll see you around six?'

'Fine,' said Michael, and filed it at the back of his mind for later on. Families were always a problem. Tom, or more likely Peter, was probably rocking the familial boat, for what business it was of theirs, there was precedent for it. At least Tom wasn't a married man. He put the whole thing out of his mind, called up his PA, and immersed himself in the day's financial business.

Shortly after six o'clock, the cousins met as arranged in a handy pub around the corner from the Bank's offices, where they frequently met to discuss things that they didn't want the Bank's employees to overhear. But not things like this, as Michael realised the moment Ed spoke his first sentence, when they were seated, a comfortable pint in front of each of them and the subject of their appointment still a blank sheet between them.

'So, what's the problem this time?' Michael asked, casually, and Ed replied, 'One of those twins of Sarah's turned up out of the blue and dropped us in the shit!' He hadn't meant to put it quite like that, and looked down at his pint so that he didn't have to see his cousin's expression. But Michael was more astonished than anything.

'Can you run that past me again, slowly?' he asked. 'I don't think I can have heard you properly.'

'I think you probably did,' Ed muttered.

'Then fill me in. Why? Why did she turn up? And what shit has she dropped us in? Trying to take us all to court over Sarah's death?' He sounded grim. It was a random guess, but a possibility he supposed. But Ed said, 'No. Worse than that.'

Could anything be worse than that? Michael wondered, and very shortly found that yes, it could. Ed didn't mess around, there was no point. He plunged straight into the mire.

'She came to tell us that Francis didn't kill bloody Sarah. Neither did Aunt Mary. The man who did, who was Sarah's husband, has been identified but unfortunately can't be jailed for the rest of his bloody life, because he's conveniently already dead. And you can see without me spelling it out exactly where that leaves us.'

'Whoa there,' said Michael. 'Can we just run this by a bit more slowly? How does she know this? And do the police know it too?'

Ed took a large gulp of his beer. It didn't make him feel calmer. Going over all this again was having the predictable effect of making him furiously angry – with Uncle Chris, with Aunt Mary, with his grandfather, with everyone concerned. Even Francis, who could have trusted them, surely?

Michael took a moment to sort out his thoughts, and then asked the obvious question.

'So why did Aunt Mary say Francis did it? And why shouldn't Francis say that he didn't? I'm sorry, I haven't quite grasped the plot here.'

'Lucky you,' said Ed. 'Aunt Mary said it because she believed it, and Francis didn't deny it because he thought that she did. Think about it.'

Michael thought about it, and came up with the second obvious objection.

'So how did this girl who turned up out of the blue know this? If she's one of Sarah's twins, she was a toddler at the time! And I'm presuming this is Kim, we're talking about? The other one was killed with Sarah at the time, wasn't she?'

'Apparently not. Or if she was, she was a pretty substantial ghost. It was Tamsin who came to us – well to Aunt Henry. She shanghaied her at that big Charity Auction thing – can you imagine poor Aunt's reaction?'

'That doesn't answer the question. Stick to the point, how did she know? How could she know? Technically, nobody knew who she was at the time, so how could she know it now?'

Except our grandfather and Uncle Chris, who are both now dead, Ed thought bitterly. He tried to explain, but as he didn't have it clear even in his own head, it all sounded a bit far-fetched. 'She ran into Kim, who was, or even is, living in that cottage. Mark Eliot was still in the area. Obviously, he saw them together and drew his own conclusions.'

'The cottage that belonged to Uncle Chris?' said Michael, trying to orient himself. 'This is the one where Sarah died, I suppose? So how…he didn't leave it to her, or anything, we would have known…come on Ed, you're going to have to explain.'

'I wish I could. But as far as I can understand it, Kim came over from New Zealand – she was kidnapped, or something, by Rod Ford from the garage in Emberton – remember him? – and his wife, with Uncle Chris's connivance, as far as I can understand it, but no doubt we will learn what really happened one day. And I didn't get the impression that she actually owns the cottage, I think she must rent it. As a holiday cottage, or something.'

'So who does it belong to now? – no, don't try to answer that. It doesn't matter. Go on with what you were saying.'

It hadn't occurred to Ed to ask himself this question, but it did now. He said, slowly, 'I suppose there's every chance that it belongs to Francis. I doubt if anyone would have wanted to buy it, after what happened there.' It was a disquieting thought. He could see that Michael was thinking much the same, but his cousin only said, 'Let's get back to the plot. Mark Eliot, you said – that's Sarah's husband?'

'The very man. He had been there all the time – not under that name, of course, but there. And when Tamsin and Kim turned up together he must have lost the plot. And they seem to have met up with Francis somewhere too, which must have made it worse.' He filled a pause with another gulp of his beer, and then sat twirling the glass between his hands, looking at it to avoid looking at Michael. 'We haven't got the full story here, but Tamsin said that he tried to murder Francis…he must have lost it completely, poor man.'

'"Poor"?' Michael queried.

'Yes, I think so. Tamsin certainly does, and I don't know quite why, but I tend to agree. All that trouble Sarah dragged him through, the lies she very likely told about him, setting everyone against him – and then having to live all those years with the guilt of what he'd done. I think he probably did pay, even if he was never identified until the very end.' Diana Carey would have liked to hear him say that, he thought as he spoke. She didn't condone what he had done, of course she didn't, but she had known the man and that had made a difference, he supposed.

'Let's get back to Francis,' said Michael. 'You said Mark Eliot tried to murder him?'

'So Tamsin says. He didn't succeed, obviously.'

'Obviously.'

'We don't know how, of course,' said Ed. Now they were coming to it. 'I expect he'll tell us, if we ask.'

There was a long pause. To fill it, Michael picked up his own glass for the first time and took a long swig. Then he put it back down on the table, very carefully.

'Explain,' he said.

'The clue is in the word "tried",' said Ed, without looking up from his glass.

'You know I didn't mean that. Francis obviously survived, skip that. What I'm asking is, how come he's likely to tell us? We haven't had any contact with him for the last twenty years. Why now?'

Ed said, mumbling, 'Tamsin seems to want us to start building bridges.'

'Bugger Tamsin! Why should we? He hasn't bothered with us!'

Ed finally raised his head to look straight at his cousin.

'You haven't been listening,' he said. 'He thought his mother was a murderer. And Grandfather thought he was. And Uncle Chris thought she was, and she thought he was – that's Francis, not Uncle Chris.'

Michael took a moment or two to unravel this, understandably. Then he said, 'Oh my God!' and went very quiet.

'You see the quandary?'

Michael was thinking about it. He said, 'And is Aunt Henry going to grasp the nettle?' thinking that he already knew the answer.

'No,' said Ed. He paused to let this sink in. 'She says it should be one of us – that's you and me.'

'She's right.' Michael looked up and met his cousin's eyes across the table. 'Toss you for it.'

'You mean you agree with her?'

'It looks like a no-brainer to me. The others were too young, the aunts are a different generation. Doesn't leave a lot of choice, does it?' He felt in his pocket and took out a coin, placing it carefully on the back of his clenched fist. 'I'll toss, you call – loser takes all.'

'Loser?'

'It's a bugger of a job. Neither of us wants it,' Michael explained. 'Ready?'

'Ready.'

'Call, then.'

'Tails,' said Ed, and Michael tossed. The coin fell neatly into his palm and he looked at it.

'Oh shit,' he said.

It was to be some time, however, before Michael found a window of opportunity to go down to Dorset, even in this impossible situation the Bank had to come first, and it was obvious that he would need to give the problem his full attention. In the meantime, he and Ed had agreed, that they would say nothing about any of this to the others, not even Ed's sister Freda from whom he generally didn't keep secrets.

'Because there's no telling what one of them might do to bugger things up still further,' Ed had said. 'Ros, particularly is too impulsive, and the brothers aren't much better. Let's find out if the plan is going to work first − if Francis doesn't want anything to do with any of us, they'll be no worse off if they don't know about it.' Michael had agreed to this, but running into Peter or Tom at the Bank, as neither of them could help doing occasionally big though the business was, put a strain on both of them. Michael was thankful when a Friday afternoon appointment with a client in Dorchester finally allowed him to head south-west into the downlands of Dorset and stay overnight without having to make excuses, to his wife or anybody else. Which is not to say that he was looking forward to it.

'Give me a ring in the evening, when you've seen him,' Ed told him. 'I shall be wondering. So will Aunt Henry, we won't last until Monday.'

'That'll be if I do see him,' Michael pointed out. 'He might slam the door in my face, I wouldn't blame him. Or he might not even be there, we don't know. I can hardly ring up and make an appointment.'

'Then you can tell us that. At least we'll know something then.'

'Even if it's nothing at all?'

'Oh, very funny! I'm glad you can laugh about it.'

'I'm not laughing. I'll give you a ring, OK, but it might not be early, so I wouldn't hold your breath. Farmers work very unsocial hours, particularly at harvest time, which I have a feeling it might be.'

'Don't know,' said Ed.

'He might run me down with a tractor. I'm not sure that I'd blame him. I don't have to tell you, I'm not looking forward to this meeting.'

'Just make sure he puts it away first, before you talk to him,' Ed advised him.

So Michael drove off to Dorset on Friday, on both the Bank's business and his own, and that evening, there was no phone call. Ed tried ringing him, but Michael must have had his mobile phone switched off. His wife, when Ed phoned his home, said he was planning to be back sometime on Sunday, there had been a problem with the client apparently.

If you believed that, Ed thought cynically. But there had certainly been a problem somewhere. He just hoped his cousin wasn't in A&E, after being beaten up. Or run over by a tractor...

Unlikely.

On Sunday afternoon, on his return with his family from a day out in the country, there was an answerphone message. 'Hi Ed, I had an interesting weekend, tell you about it over lunch tomorrow?

Damn Michael!

Michael was in his office on Monday morning, and it didn't look as if anybody had hit him. In fact he looked smug, if anything, Ed thought, but he refused to say anything then.

'Not the place, not the time. I'll tell you over lunch – I presume you can get away for an hour?'

'Believe me, nothing will stop me.'

'No need to sound so grim. I'm sorry about not being in touch, but I didn't get home until mid-afternoon yesterday, and then you were out.'

'You said you'd ring Friday evening.'

'I meant to, but it was very late – and anyway, I was more than a bit drunk. I couldn't get any sense out of myself, you certainly wouldn't have got any.'

'Just tell me this. You did see Francis?'

'Yes. Quite a lot of him in fact, but I can't tell you now—' The phone on his desk rang, he reached out for it. 'See you lunchtime.' Then he spoke into his phone, half-turning his shoulder towards his indignant cousin. 'Michael Stacey.'

So convenient, Ed thought, as he made his way back to his own department. But he had sounded cheerful enough. And he had seen "quite a lot" of their cousin, which was hopeful too. Probably hopeful. He found that he was feeling happier, and more positive than he had at any time since Diana Carey's revelations, and entered his own office smiling, much to the relief of his assistants. He hadn't done a lot of that just lately.

They met for lunch at the same convenient pub where they had their first discussion, but Michael refused to say anything until their pasties had been brought and they could reasonably expect to be uninterrupted.

'So now,' said Ed, opening the batting. 'Tell me what happened. You saw Francis, I presume?'

'Certainly did – although at first, I admit I didn't recognise him. He's changed…' He looked momentarily pensive, then broke into a smile. 'For one thing, he's about twice the size I remember him – over six feet tall, wide across the shoulders like a caber-tossing athlete, and dark and unsettling as an Italian mafioso! I wouldn't like to get on the wrong side of him!'

'He was always rather good-looking as a teenager,' said Ed, remembering. 'So what happened?'

'Nothing happened, he just grew up like the rest of us. And spends his time wrangling cows, driving tractors, and sailing fast boats. I expect we've changed as much, it's just that we got used to each other gradually. But he looks exhausted Ed, I think he's having quite a bad time right now. Eat your pasty, and I'll tell you what he told me.'

'He didn't throw you out then?'

'Well, obviously not. I thought he was going to at one point, mind you, but he thought better of it, and we were able to talk. We talked a lot. And then I took him out to dinner and we talked some more. And killed several bottles of wine. And now shut up and listen.'

So Michael talked, and Ed listened, and at the end of it Ed said, 'So what do you think we should all do now?'

'First of all, we must tell the others what's happened, which might be interesting. We have to convince our Cox-Hamilton cousins that they can't just jump in with both feet – particularly Ros, who has always been…shall we say, impulsive? Better leave her to me, you can have the brothers. And Freda, of course, but she won't be a problem. But we must make them all see that the next move is down to Francis, not us. Jumping in with both feet isn't going to help. The same applies to the aunts, particularly Aunt Clara, but Aunt Henry can deal with her. This is one time when rushing in with open arms isn't going to help. I can't emphasise too much, Francis is a stranger to us. We need to make friends again, and we need to do it gradually. He's had enough.'

11

'What do you think he'll do?'

'He's already promised he will come up to London and see Grandma. After that, we shall just have to see. But I think we restrain Aunt Clara from organising a big family reunion. Slow and steady wins the race…'

'Softee, softee, catchee monkey? I get the picture.'

'Some monkey! More like a gorilla – here, have a look at this. I took it while we were out on that appalling farm I told you about.' He felt in his pocket and took out a photograph, passing it over the table to Ed, who looked at it and raised his eyebrows.

'See what you mean. But rather good looking for a gorilla, wouldn't you say? For God's sake, warn Ros off!'

'Ros is a grown-up now, and she loves Andrew. She'll toe the party line all right. But let me tell her first, then we'll tell the others. We don't want Peter and Tom wading in.'

'True.' Ed looked again at the photo in his hands. A man close to middle-age, darkly handsome, beautiful even, although that was an odd word to apply to a man, but looking, as Michael had said, utterly exhausted. A man who had reached the end of what he could take and was still facing more. He laid the picture face-down on the table beside his plate, it was making him feel uncomfortable. As maybe they all should…he said, because it came into his head unbidden, 'He never married?'

'No,' said Michael. He added, 'But don't get the wrong idea. I don't think he's lived the life of a monk, he gives off the wrong vibes.'

'So long as he didn't do a Peter, and go after other men's wives,' said Ed, not with approval.

'I very much doubt that. He knows better than anyone where that can lead, think about it.'

There was nothing to say after that, so a pause ensued while they both ate some of their lunch. Then Ed said, 'Aunt Henry thinks that Tamsin has the hots for him.'

Well, look at him. Would it be surprising? But I didn't meet her, of course – she's a bit young for him, I would have thought.'

'He didn't mention her?'

'No he didn't. Look, Ed—'

'I'm listening,' said Ed, after a pause.

'Just, let's leave telling the rest of them until I've seen Ros. You could warn her maybe, without giving too much away that is, but tell her to keep it to herself until I've spoken to her: she's the one it's going to mean the most to – the one of us, I mean. And if we tell the aunts, except Aunt Henry of course, then Aunt Clara will tell everyone. What do you think?'

'I think, they've not known anything for so long that a little longer won't hurt them,' said Ed, after thought. 'But don't leave it too long. Once things are known, even just to one person, information is liable to slip out without anyone meaning it.'

'I have to go to Oxford one day later this week. I'll drop in on her then.' He put down his fork and raised his glass. 'Here's to conspiracy! Long may it flourish!'

'Here's to it then,' said Ed, and they clinked glasses.

II

Michael drove across Oxfordshire to his cousin's home much exercised in mind as to how he should approach his mission. Ros had been deeply involved with her older cousin when she was young, in fact she had a monumental crush on him if he was honest – she must have been around twelve at the time, Michael estimated, and Ed had said that when he told her over the phone that Francis had re-surfaced in their lives, even if not exactly in person, she had been nearly in tears – but although she was no doubt prepared for a discussion on the subject, she would not be prepared for what he was actually going to have to tell her. It wasn't, he reflected with a despairing twist of his lips, the kind of news one relayed over the phone. He had merely said when he rang her that business was bringing him out her way, and would it be OK if he dropped in for coffee around ten o'clock? And Ros had said that yes, that would be lovely, and had he talked to Ed lately? And he had said that yes, he had. End of conversation. Ros had made no comment on the situation over the phone, and he had been happy to follow her lead, but he had no doubt that she had read between the lines.

But now, here he was about to turn down into the lane where she lived with her husband Andrew and her two children, who thankfully would be busy at work/in school respectively, and God alone knew how she would react to what he had to say. Ros had always been a sentimental idiot – well, that wasn't quite fair he supposed, but he did hope she wouldn't weep all over him. And here was the gate. Michael took a deep breath and turned between the posts; he had never realised that being the bearer of good news could be so stressful! Although there was a good deal of ground to clear before they reached that point...

Ros, however, greeted him calmly – he had been afraid she might throw herself into his arms but she showed no sign of it, merely kissing his cheek lightly and inviting him into the kitchen.

'It's warmer in here, and I thought we could sit out in the conservatory and drink our coffee looking out at the garden,' she said, smiling. 'It's getting a bit autumnal now, but that's OK, isn't it? Lovely colours, gentler than the summer rainbow...' She was fussing with the percolator and two mugs as she spoke, her back turned to him; she lifted the mugs onto a tray, added a plate of home-made biscuits, and turned to face him, the tray in her hands and a smile on her face. 'You go first, then you can open the doors for me.'

The conservatory opened straight out of the kitchen, and contained several comfortable chairs and a wicker sofa. Ros set the tray down carefully on a small table, turfed a tabby cat out of the best chair, and invited him to sit down. When they were both seated with mugs in their hands and the cat had stalked off in a huff, only then did she broach the subject that hung in the air between them like a fog.

'I suppose you've seen Ed, and talked to him properly?' she said. 'He only told me the bare bones on the phone, that girl – Diana or something, was it? – turned up out of the blue and told them some horrendous story about that murder...' Her voice tailed away into silence, and she pulled herself together with an effort to continue with a challenge in her voice, 'The one that caused all the trouble. Bloody Sarah Crawfurd! I always believed it had to be Sarah – she really buggered up our lives, didn't she?'

Michael said, getting it over quickly, 'You're right, it was Sarah, but she didn't quite deserve being murdered and left to pass into limbo with no identity, wouldn't you say? Grandad believed that Francis had done it, Uncle Chris told him that – but he didn't.'

'I never thought that he had,' said Ros, defiantly, and not entirely truthfully. Even if nobody had told them outright, they weren't stupid. They had none of them known for a fact about Sarah's death, they had – the older ones anyway – wondered, if only because of the subsequent attitude of their elders, snatches of overheard adult conversation, a general feeling. They had none of them asked, they wouldn't have been told anyway. Michael gave her a gentle look.

'No need to shout at me. I found it hard to believe too. But something happened, and he was caught up in it. What Diana Carey did was to put the record straight. What we do now is up to us. And to Francis of course.'

'How does she know, anyway?' asked Ros, trying to keep resentment out of her voice. Michael looked down at his coffee.

'Because she's Tamsin,' he said. Ros put her own mug down with a slightly shaky hand.

'She can't be. The other twin vanished completely, but Tamsin died too – I couldn't believe…I couldn't believe Francis would do a thing like that to a child, but…'

'You were right, and he didn't,' said Michael firmly, there was no point in allowing this to turn into a melodrama. 'And Tamsin lived. Nobody knew who she was, because Uncle Chris didn't tell anyone who Sarah really was, and eventually she was put for adoption as nobody had claimed her. And that's how she came to be Diana Carey.'

'But if nobody but Uncle Chris – and Aunt Mary and Francis, presumably – knew…' Ros was getting lost here, and Michael gave her a twisted smile.

'Somebody did. You aren't going to believe this, but she ran into Kim, quite by chance. And it gets weirder than that. I'd better begin on page one…'

'I think you had,' said Ros.

Michael took a minute for thought, and then he said, 'Do you remember the man who ran the garage? Ford, his name was – appropriate, I always thought. He was mates with Uncle Chris.'

'I remember him,' said Ros. 'His wife used to give us sweeties when we were small – later on it was biscuits.' She glanced down at the plate on the tray. 'Would you like one now?'

'In a minute. Rod Ford and his wife emigrated to New Zealand, and they took Kim with them.' He paused. 'Look Ros, this is going to be hard to swallow, but take a deep breath and try. Uncle Chris and Sarah were to follow with Tamsin – she thought they would attract less notice with just one child, the pair were pretty noticeable. They were just going to disappear into the blue, which would have been pretty hard on the rest of us…but of course, they never made it, and Kim wasn't ever told that she once had a twin. She says that she dimly remembered some child she used to play with when she was tiny…but she was never told the truth because where would be the point? Tamsin was dead, and their mother with her, and Uncle Chris told his friend Ford to sit tight and say nothing.'

'So how did they meet, then?' asked Ros, a challenge in her voice that Michael took as a warning. He said, 'Listen Ros, this will be much easier if you don't bite me.'

'Sorry. Go on.' She bit her lip instead. 'When do we get to Francis?'

'In a moment. But listen first. Kim was renting that cottage – the one where…of course, she knew nothing about what happened there, not then. And Tamsin came down for a sailing weekend with a boyfriend that went a bit pear-shaped…and they ran into each other. She filled in the details for us before she left us, Aunt Henry asked her – more as an afterthought than anything, but it's odd…look, Ros, I'm not making this up so don't interrupt me. Tamsin's car ran off the road in a fog and ended on the verge outside that bloody cottage.' He looked at her helplessly. 'You knew everyone said it was haunted after…well, what happened there?'

'No,' said Ros. 'How would I? We never went back – thanks to Uncle Chris and his bit on the side. We hadn't been back for a good year before she died, and then he…' She stopped.

'He died in a road accident in that very place,' said Michael, making it easier for her. 'But what we weren't told until Tamsin told Ed and Aunt Henry is that Francis was with him at the time…and Ros, don't look like that. Because he wasn't hurt, except superficially, not then, but of course it was a tremendous shock.'

'Poor Francis…oh, poor Francis! And we never knew, we couldn't be there for him…oh Michael, how cruel!'

'It gets worse,' said Michael. 'You see, he thought that Aunt Mary did it – killed them both – and she thought that he did. Presumably she thought that he – Francis or his father, who knows? – was trying to commit suicide.'

'Oh my God,' said Ros, and thought about it.

'And that's why it was arranged that we never saw Francis again,' Michael finished.

'But we wrote to him – you did, and so did I…'

'He says he never got the letters,' said Michael, and left her to draw her own conclusions.

Ros thought about this. After a moment, she said tentatively, 'He says? You've seen him?'

'Ed and I tossed a coin as to which of us made the first approach – I lost, so it was down to me.' He made a face. 'Although, maybe I didn't lose. It was…interesting…how times change.'

'Is he still at Vachells then?' It seemed unlikely, given the circumstances as she now knew them, but Michael answered, 'Yes. He didn't have much choice, did he?'

'But he never meant—' Ros stopped, and ended lamely, 'He was meant to go to University. He wanted to read Marine Biology…'

'Yes, well, there are several good reasons why that didn't happen, and at least one of them should be obvious.'

Ros was silent. After a few minutes, Michael said, 'Don't let it get to you too much Ros. He made himself a different plan. He's run Vachells for his mother, and he's a very successful cattle breeder among other things. And he sails one of those Moonrakers, they had a fleet at Emberton, if you remember – pretty successfully too from the little he said, he's a member of the Yacht Club in the town, and the Sailing Club at Emberton…and the Chillingworth genes have worked well for him, come to that. He's not had a wasted life, don't think it.'

'But such a disappointment! And why do I feel that it sounds…well, lonely? As you tell it, it's all being best at everything, making more money, and not having any friends, you didn't mention any…or am I getting that wrong?'

'I think you're pretty close to the truth. Or up until recently, you're pretty close to the truth. I think things are changing for him – for one thing, all the cards are on the table now. He's free.'

'That's a very telling thing to say,' said Ros, narrowing her eyes at him. She thought for a moment, and then said, 'But what a shame. He was brilliant, and breeding cows…well…'

'Yes.' Michael looked down at his hands, thoughtfully, spreading his fingers and studying them as if they were of great interest. 'I think he and Aunt Mary have had twenty-plus years of pretty bad times…it's going to take a bit of time to get things back on an even keel…if that's even possible. A lot of very troubled water has gone under that particular bridge. But if it's any consolation to you, I think the cattle give him great pride – and pleasure, too. He wins cups and trophies and things with them at shows, and exports them all over the world…if it helps?' He ended on a question, and Ros shook her head.

'I'm not sure that it does. Did he show them to you?'

'No. It was getting dark and they were all out in the fields, and anyway, we needed to talk. There was a lot of ground to cover and believe me, it was pretty rough territory.'

'So how deep did you dig?' asked Ros, looking at him perceptively.

'As deep as I was allowed, which I suspect wasn't very. Then we went out and got drunk.'

'Sounds like a plan. And are we now back on his Christmas Card List?'

'Probably. I think that's down to us though.'

Ros was silent for a minute or two, mechanically sipping at her coffee but not looking at it. Her eyes held shadows as she stared out at the changing colours in the autumn garden. After a while, she said, 'So how is he – Francis? And what changed things? I'm assuming that they have changed?'

'They found the murderer, and after all these years. Tamsin and Kim turning up like that was a sort of catalyst, things started happening again.' He paused. 'There was an attempt on Francis' life. Fortunately, It didn't succeed. But it blew the whole thing apart.'

Ros took a deep breath. 'Was he hurt – Francis?'

'A bit, but he's been through worse and come out on the other side. And he's still very much alive, so don't get upset about it. It's in the past, thank God. All of it.'

'Except for the fallout,' said Ros, sombrely. 'How will they manage, Mike – Francis and Aunt Mary? They were such good friends once – before all this.'

'They have sensibly agreed to let the wind blow between them,' Michael told her, pleased to be able to say something positive. 'They were both wrong, after all, which makes the score even. Francis is moving out quite soon to make a different life for himself, and one of his cousins is going to take over Vachells for Aunt Mary. Not one we ever met. Cosmo?'

Ros wrinkled her nose.

'Wasn't he a baby or something? The name sounds familiar – it's not one you can easily forget.'

'He's not one now. Any more than Francis is fifteen, Ros.'

'I know that. But they're still on speaking terms – Francis and Aunt Mary?'

'Since they accept that they were both barking up the wrong tree, they will eventually be able to be – let's hope, anyway. After all, they were close once – when we knew them. And now we've got that out of the way, would you like to hear about something more cheerful?' There was a lot more to say, in fact, but he didn't feel up to it now. He felt in his jacket pocket and pulled out a bundle of what looked like photographs. 'I went to visit a farm while I was down there – have a look.' He handed them over and Ros took them, but didn't immediately look at them.

'Is this relevant?'

'Look and see. And while you're looking, I should tell you that we all have a standing invitation to visit with our kids in the summer when it should be a bit more fit for human habitation, and let them enjoy the kind of holidays that we remember – sea and sun and animals and boats and picnics along the beautiful coast – take a look.'

Ros turned the pictures over in her hand and looked at the top one. It was of a sprawling house, low to the land, built of dirty yellow brick or maybe stone, and with dormer windows in the roof, more than a bit run down and looking in need of some serious TLC. She said so.

'It looks a wreck. A good sneeze out of place, and it would probably fall down.'

'It is a wreck, but not an irreparable one. Look at the next one.'

The next one was of a wide vista of downland rolling away into the distance, ending in a distant line that looked like the very edge of the land; there was a glow on the sky that looked like reflected sea-light, Ros remembered it well and recognised it; Vachells had been on that same stretch of coast, although not so far inland. She said, 'This is still in Dorset, isn't it?'

'Yes. That's the view from the front of the house. It's even better from the upstairs windows, he told me, but he won't have the key to get in until completion. Go on. Take the next one.'

The next one was of a section of exceedingly scruffy farmyard, and contained, apart from a tumbledown barn, a load of rubbish and a spreading heap of manure, a tall man with broad shoulders and dark hair wearing scruffy jeans, a black sweater over a blue checked shirt and working boots, and with him a black and white dog, both with their backs to her as they investigated the tip. The dog looked to be the more thorough of the pair. The one after that was of the inside of a gloomy barn with more rubbish in it, and surprisingly, given the backdrop, a big and shiny-looking tractor beside a selection of implements, also shiny – well, shiny-ish, anyway – that looked out of place in the dusty gloom. Ros wrinkled her nose.

'It doesn't look the sort of farm where I'd want to take my children,' she said. 'There's a heap of cow shit the size of Mount Everest out in that yard!'

'It'll be put to use, I have no doubt. Keep going.'

The next one was of the same man sitting on a mounting block, fussing with the dog who was demonstrating great enthusiasm and rather stealing the show. Once again, the man's face was half-hidden, but Ros was beginning to get a picture now.

'He's another Vachell, isn't he?' she said, screwing up her nose as she considered. 'They all have that dark, mafioso look I remember. Francis had it too, but a bit more class with it.'

'He could be,' said Michael, hiding a smile. He had expected Ros to be quicker in the uptake than this, but decided to go with the flow. 'Try the next one.'

A beautiful tithe barn in need of serious attention: the dog, fussing round the empty doorway. No human life visible. Then a view of some overgrown fields and a thick, tangled wood with fallen branches and deep undergrowth. And last of all, the dark man again, leaning on an open stable door and reaching down for the leaping dog. But this time, his face was clear to be seen, and although he looked tired with shadows under his eyes, he was very good looking indeed. Scarily so, Ros decided.

'Wow,' she said, with approval. 'He's some looker! Is this Cosmo?'

'No. Look again. He's too old to be Cosmo anyway, think about it.'

'He's one of the Vachells though, isn't he – this man?' She tried to remember their names, the ones she had met. 'He looks as if he was making a bit of a night of it quite recently!'

'You could say that. And for your information, he had – been making a night of it. We both had.' He was smiling openly now. Ros looked at him, her mouth half open, and then back at the picture. Yes, she had been right, the man was very nice indeed to look at, but she didn't think she had ever seen him before...or had she? She said, slowly, not quite believing it, 'Is this Francis?'

'Certainly is.' Michael smiled at her bewilderment, but with sympathy. 'And before you say anything, I wasn't sure either when I first set eyes on him, and I was in his bloody office!'

'But he's beautiful!' said Ros. She shook her head. 'And how did he get to be so big? He wasn't like this when we were young!'

Heredity?' suggested Michael. 'He's a Vachell after all, some of them were pretty tall, as I remember – look at Aunt Mary, just for starters, and it's over twenty years since any of us have seen him. And anyway, he's only about six foot two, I've seen worse.'

'But the breadth of him! He's gorgeous!'

Michael laughed, with real amusement.

'That's the third time you've said that,' he pointed out. 'And don't get excited, coz – I'm pretty certain that he's already spoken for. And anyway, Andrew wouldn't like it.'

'He never married.' It was a statement, not a question. She sounded sad. Michael said, 'Not so far. Watch this space.'

Ros didn't question this; probably she realised that he didn't really know any answers. Or maybe she had worked it out, he corrected himself, she was far from stupid. Instead, she looked back to the photograph and said, 'Who's the dog?'

'Sacha. You'll meet him.'

Ros took a deep breath; all of this was proving difficult to edit into common sense, she decided. She settled on the most obvious anomaly in the muddle.

'Did you mean it – that we have an open invitation to visit? With the children? In the summer?'

'Yes,' said Michael, watching her. 'The house has five or six bedrooms, if it doesn't collapse in the meantime, and there's a cottage too out on the land somewhere, although there's a tenant in it at the moment.'

'So is he going to carry on farming, then? You said "out on the land". And it's all in such a mess…some of it has practically reverted to nature!'

'You can say that again! To be honest, I don't think he knows what he's going to do, it's a bit of a work in progress. And I think that he needs a challenge right now, too. But don't get in a state over it, remember he's a Vachell as well as a Chillingworth, and I already told you about the cattle.'

Ros shuffled the photos and pulled out the view of the downs. 'So where is it? This looks sort of familiar, somehow.'

'Oh come on, Ros! Downland is downland, it all looks pretty much the same. But since you ask, the farm – it's called Burnthouse, by the way, and the house is Grade II listed like Vachells – adjoins the Ravenscourt land around Ravenscourt Place. So it's out at Shearwater. Does that answer your question?'

'Good place,' said Ros with approval. She shuffled the photos back together. 'Did he mind you taking all these? Did he even realise?'

'Yes, of course he did. And he accepted that it was a necessity – not just for us, but more particularly for Grandma. She's grieved for him long enough.'

Ros held out her hand with the pictures. 'You'd better take these back then.'

Michael brushed her hand aside. 'No, those are for you, I've printed them out for all of us. We need to get used to the idea. He's a stranger who isn't really a stranger, we have to catch up with the passage of time.' He grinned at her, but the grin was a bit lopsided. 'Believe me, there's a lot of leeway to make up.'

And there was one bit of it that he was going to have to address right now.

'Look, Ros...'

There was something in his voice that made her look up from the photos that she was shuffling through for the second time, a sudden arrested look on her face. She said, 'What?' abruptly, feeling a change in the atmosphere.

'Put those down for a minute – no, you've got to listen properly, no distractions.' He waited until she had laid the photos beside her empty coffee mug. 'Ros, you remember that I said that Francis wasn't much hurt in the murder attempt – or no, he was hurt, but it wasn't desperate, not that time, thanks to Tamsin. But...'

'There was another time,' said Ros. It wasn't a question.

'Yes, there was – and before I tell you about it, just remember what you see in those photos and don't over-react. It won't help.'

Ros gave the photos a brief glance where they lay beside the mug, and then looked back at him.

'Go on then. What happened to him?'

'I'm not really sure, because he doesn't actually know – no, don't interrupt me. Just listen.'

Ros let out the breath she had drawn to object to this incredible statement. Instead, she said, 'I'm listening.'

'He thinks that he was probably quarrelling with Aunt Mary – it was when he was in his early twenties, I suppose, he didn't specify exactly, but it was around when the Trust that Uncle Chris set up until he came of age was being wound up and there was a lot of argument because the provisions of the Will were manifestly unfair; Francis got everything. I stress that he doesn't know this is what it was all about for a fact, but given the circumstances it sounds a reasonable conclusion to draw. But anyway, whatever was happening between them, he thinks they were almost certainly having a noisy row – and the estate manager came bundling in thinking there was murder being done.'

'Still speculation?' asked Ros, sceptically.

'Reasonable speculation. Francis thinks he probably had his hands on Aunt Mary, trying to shake sense into her, and the manager acted from pure instinct and lashed out with the stick he was carrying – apparently the two of them never saw eye-to-eye anyway. Only he had been out in the barn dealing with vermin, and the stick was weighted…he caught Francis on the left temple. Hard.'

'Oh God,' said Ros. There was a silence while Michael gave her time to think about it, and then he continued quietly, trying to be rational about it so that Ros would be the same.

'It was an accident. I think there's no question about that. But it put Francis in a coma for the next almost-three-months, some of which I suspect may have been induced to allow things to settle. He had some bleeding into the brain, apparently – almost like a stroke I gather, although it was due to an outside cause rather than high blood pressure or something. But it had some of the same result as a proper stroke, in that it affected his speech and took all the feeling out of his right arm. He was in therapy for quite a long time.'

Ros drew a breath, trying to get her thoughts in order. She said, 'So, Aunt Mary—'

'History doesn't relate what Aunt Mary did,' said Michael. 'Francis doesn't know, except by deduction, he wasn't there. Look – do you remember, when we were children, that family who used to come down in the summer and stay in a cottage in Emberton? They came most years, we knew them well – two boys and a girl, our ages, and their parents and a small dog?'

'The Bartons, wasn't it?' said Ros, nodding, although she still felt as if someone had punched her in the stomach from shock. 'The girl – Barbara – was about my age, we hung out together. Are you telling me he was with them?'

'There's a hospital near where they live that specialises in that kind of injury and has a marvellous reputation. They stepped in and gave Aunt Mary an opportunity to think. But in the end, Francis tells me, he was with them for four years before he went back.'

'I'm surprised he ever did!' said Ros, suddenly angry on her absent cousin's behalf.

'No. Think about it. He didn't have much choice. The manager had to go, of course, he was lucky he didn't end up in court. And Aunt Mary was running the place on her own with no capital behind her, and even then she wasn't exactly young. Francis…well, as he says himself, if she was a murderer, he was her son. He couldn't accuse her, he had no proof, and even if he had…well, let's not go into that. He realised, as soon as he could think at all, that he would have to go back, later if not sooner.'

'But he never wanted to be a farmer – he wanted to be a marine biologist—'

'Well, he couldn't be that anyway. He shouldn't do deep-water diving after that head injury, he was told, so he gave up on University and went to Agricultural College instead, and learned everything they could teach him and then a bit more on top…and then he went back to Vachells.'

Ros said, in a tight voice that she tried to keep normal, 'So he recovered – so far, anyway. Except for the thing that really mattered to him.'

'Sort of,' said Michael. 'Mentally, he seems to have pulled it together OK, but then he always had enough intelligence that he could spare a bit—'

'Michael, please don't make jokes about it! Tell me – what happened to him.'

'Don't look like that, Ros,' said Michael, very gently for him. 'He got away with it pretty well, except for that one thing—'

'The one that mattered the most to him,' Ros interrupted.

'Well, maybe. Maybe not. But it left him with a speech impediment, he has a bad stammer, particularly under stress. And, again under stress or if he's overdone things, his right arm and hand give out on him occasionally and he can limp a bit too. But he was lucky, Ros. You must believe that. It could have been so very much worse. And he's made himself a good life, given the circumstances. You must believe that.'

Ros began to cry. Michael silently passed her a tissue from a box on the coffee table. After a moment, he said gently, 'Don't do that, Ros. It was a long time ago. And Tamsin has given us back to him, and him to us come to that, and we can all start again. Things can only get better.'

Ros blew her nose and sniffed, crumpling the tissue.

'Yes. Tamsin. What about Tamsin? Is she who you meant when you said…?'

'That, I'm only guessing. But there is somebody. Only, Francis being

Francis, he won't offer whoever-it-is damaged goods. I tried to make him see he was being unfair. People should be left to make their own choices.'

'But you think it is Tamsin?'

'She seems the obvious candidate, on present evidence.'

'She's much younger than him.'

'Believe me, Ros, he needs young.'

Ros said nothing to this, relapsing into thought. But thinking got her nowhere, it was all too much to take in. She got to her feet abruptly.

'I don't know about you, but I need something stronger than coffee after all that. You? Fancy a whisky or something, to take the taste away?'

Michael knew just how she felt. He said, 'Just make it a small one. I'm driving – and theoretically, I'm working, too.'

'So long as you don't have to make it to an urgent appointment,' Ros threw over her shoulder as she left the room. He heard her moving about in the kitchen, and after a few minutes she reappeared carrying two glasses half-filled with amber fluid. She handed one to her cousin and flopped back in her chair. She took a sip. Michael was pleased to see she had gathered her self-control about her again, and they sipped in thoughtful silence for a few minutes. Then Ros said, 'So what happens now?'

'Nothing, until after the quarter-day, there's too much to be done down there. But between the quarter-day, when he will leave Vachells, and the completion date on Burnthouse there's a small window of opportunity when nothing can be done at all. He said he'd come up then and see Grandma. We'll take it from there.'

'How do you think the rest of them will take it? – are taking it, I imagine they all know what's going on?'

'They soon will. But what happens after that, Ros, I think is more down to Francis than us. He must feel that we let him down pretty badly.'

'It wasn't our fault. Uncle Chris and Grandpa were calling the shots…' Her voice tailed off. 'We were children, Mike. And we did write – we did.'

'Yes, we were children – but children grow up, Ros, and we've all been grown up for a long time. Which one of us ever made a move back towards him?'

'We didn't know what had gone on. We thought he had outgrown us, just couldn't be bothered any more after Uncle Chris died.' And that had hurt, if she was honest. She had adored Francis when they were teenagers. She said, in a small, lost voice, 'I can't believe that nobody told us…not when he was so hurt…what if he'd died, Mike? It sounds as if he very easily could have.'

'Leave it, Ros, please. I feel as bad as you obviously do, so does Ed – probably Peter and Tom too. And Freda, although she was much younger. But there's nothing to be done about it now but go forward. It's too late for anything else. Just be thankful for Tamsin, who has at least given us the chance to do that, which we will take, obviously. It's up to Francis what he does himself.'

'I feel so awful…' said Ros. She brushed a finger under her eye, caught Michael's expression, and hurriedly dropped her hand. 'Sorry. I'm not going to be a watering can, Mike, I promise. It's just it was so…sudden. And unexpected. I thought losing people was what made you cry all over the place like this, not getting them back.'

'I totally agree with you.' Michael reached out to put his empty glass on the table. 'And now, I'm sorry, but I'm going to have to leave you. Will you be OK?'

'Yes, of course I will – but does it have to be right now? You couldn't just stop a little longer and talk a bit, now it's all out in the open?'

Michael glanced at his watch, and shuddered. 'Sorry Ros. No. I'm supposed to be lunching with one of our wealthier private investors at half-past twelve, and I'm twenty miles in the wrong direction. But you can ring me at home this evening, if you haven't thought it all through by then.'

'I'm sure I will have. But thank you anyway. And thank you for coming.' She hesitated. 'Do you think Francis would like us to get in touch with him?'

Michael hesitated too, that was a hard one. He went with his instinct.

'I think, leave well alone until we meet him face to face. He's got a lot on his plate right now. And he knows that we're here.'

But leaving well alone turned out not to be an option. Other forces were now in operation, and shortly after this conversation a huge storm, real this time, not metaphorical, hit the west country, breaking branches, blocking roads with fallen trees and floods, and more significantly, bringing down a huge oak tree, more than four centuries old, to crash down on the roof of a small, scruffy, single-storey cottage that stood by the side of the coast road that ran westward from the town of Embridge, and all the parameters altered.

III

Diana woke early: in spite of the disastrous and latterly, unbelievably amazing twenty-four hours that had preceded this cool dawning: she hadn't slept that well, she had been too hyped up by events that had, if she was honest, gone beyond belief. Particularly that last one...She felt herself smiling, and her left cheek twinged in objection. It had certainly been a day to remember. And a night, of course. Unfortunately, not in that order. Shame, that.

First, a huge oak tree had landed on the roof of Kim's rented cottage in the early hours of the morning, completely destroying the roof and ceiling above their bedroom, and they had had to crawl out just in their pyjamas, with a very random handful of miscellaneous clothing items that Kim had grabbed from the only accessible drawer of the chest as they left – that bottom one, where nothing actually wearable is ever put. At one in the morning there didn't seem a lot to be done about it, so they had put on what clothes they had, which was barely enough, and then sat in the combined kitchen/living room of the tiny cottage, hoping the roof wouldn't cave in here, too, and watching water run down the walls. They could have phoned for help, she realised now for the first time, her mobile phone had been in her bag, and that was safely with them in the kitchen, but at the time neither of them had thought of it. Shock did strange things to your brain. She considered this for a minute. Shock, she thought with a quiet smile had played quite a large part in the events of yesterday, both the bad and ultimately, the amazing. On balance, hooray for shock! But instead of doing anything sensible, they had spent the time gathering up anything that was worth saving and putting it by the door ready for their escape in the morning, when people would be awake to help them. There hadn't been a lot. Most of Kim's furniture had been secondhand crap, and anyway, it wouldn't have gone in her car...

She yawned, and turned over without thinking so that her left cheekbone, cut by flying glass when the tree came down, twinged again, more painfully this time. She sat up abruptly, and almost banged her head on the top bunk above her, reminding herself for the first time of exactly where she was. She was immediately fully and irretrievably awake. Oh well, at least she would get first go with the shower before her twin's boyfriend, Val, who had come roaring down from London to the rescue the previous evening, used up all the hot water, as he probably would in her experience of the male sex. She swung her feet to the floor, and ducking her head carefully, stood up and went to the window, drawing back the curtains to look out on the dawn.

Well, perhaps it was a bit more than dawn, it was fully light. Below her, a small courtyard full of tubs of flowers, fading a bit now in late September, was surrounded by a high stone wall and a distant view of fields. To the left, there was a space with her car parked in it, she could just see its roof, and then what appeared to be a barn, or maybe somebody's garage; to the right, the top of a small tree in the yard next door peeped at her over the wall. Strange ground. This lovely holiday home that Kim's horrified landlord had found for them at short notice was in the middle of the village of Emberton, not right out in the country. But at least that little tree peeping over the wall from next door wasn't big enough to fall on them!

Diana quietly gathered up her weird selection of salvaged clothes; a long cotton skirt, a T-shirt from the village shop, a pair of briefs – Kim had managed to save three pairs of these, fortunately, so they could share them – and a bra that rightfully belonged to Kim that had been conveniently drying on the kitchen stove – they had tossed for that – and crept out of her bijou bedroom onto the tiny landing. The door to the larger double room opposite was still firmly closed, it must be the first time ever recorded that she had woken before Kim – but then Kim, whose love-interest had elected to stay overnight, had probably gone to sleep later than she had. Her own love-interest had gone home; he had cows to look after. Shame.

Downstairs, she crept quietly into the kitchen, said hello to the black and white collie who was sleeping there on an old hearthrug, and wondered if she should let him out, and if so, where to? Out at the back was the pretty paved yard, out at the front, the village street. Checkmate. Sacha didn't seem bothered so she left the problem for Kim and Val later and shut herself into the bathroom.

The bathroom! A real bathroom, not a tiny stone outhouse at the bottom of the garden, with dubious access to a cesspit somewhere and a hand pump to take water up to the overhead cistern, and for other needs, the stone sink in the rudimentary kitchen and a kettle on the stove. Bath, shower, proper washbasin, all with running hot and cold – Diana prepared herself for a happy half hour.

One glance in the mirror over the washbasin brought her back to earth abruptly. She had a magnificent black eye, her cheekbone was black with bruises too, and across this devastation wandered a thin crimson streak decorated with three conspicuous white plasters. Reality came back with a bang, and her stomach churned. Yesterday, she and Kim had near-as-nothing been killed, or at least seriously injured. There might never have been last night with its amazing main event, never have been a golden future to which she could look forward. She might never have woken up this morning knowing that, just like Kim, she was firmly engaged to the man of her dreams. She might never have woken up at all, and she hated to think of what that might have done to Francis, it was his cottage, after all, although not his tree. He had been upset enough when they had survived. What if they hadn't?

Best not to think about that. Instead, she turned on the shower. Time to wash all that stuff away and concentrate on what might happen today.

One thing that must happen, she decided as she got dressed, was a trip into the nearby town of Embridge to buy some clothes. She and Kim had nothing but what they stood up in, except for one spare pair of knickers between them; something had to be done, not least about the knickers.

When she went out into the kitchen again, Kim was standing there yawning, and staring, empty-eyed, at an electric kettle that was singing to itself on the worktop. Good idea. Diana wished she had thought of it herself, a cup of tea was just what was wanted. She said, 'Good morning,' and Kim jumped, and swung round.

'Goodness! What are you doing, all up and dressed?'

'Couldn't sleep.' Diana yawned, and Kim said, 'Did you let the dog out?'

'Where to? I thought one of us could take him for a walk when we were dressed.'

'You are dressed,' Kim pointed out. 'His lead is on the table. Take him up that field behind us, while Val and I use the bathroom.'

'Is Val awake?'

'Almost. I got up quickly before he actually opened his eyes, we have things to do today.'

'Shopping,' said Diana, with satisfaction. 'I love a good shop.'

'It can't be that good, I've only got my wages – and before you say anything, no. I won't take anything from you, I've taken enough already with the car, and everything. But there's something else we have to do first, Val says, and that's go and see his mother and let her see for herself we're OK. He says she didn't believe him when he rang yesterday. She was all for coming steaming over from Shearwater to sweep us back with her.'

'I'm glad she didn't,' said Diana, hiding a smile.

'I bet you are.' Kim grinned at her. 'But fair's fair. Val said he'd drive us over there, and on to Embridge and treat us both to lunch to celebrate our miracle survival.'

'I hope he doesn't mean to come shopping with us,' said Diana.

'I don't think wild horses would make him. He said we could ring him on his mobile when we were ready to come home. He said he'd go down to the Yacht Club, there's an big race scheduled tomorrow, and they're sure to be able to find him something useful to do to get organised for it if everyone else is at work. Now for goodness' sake, take that poor dog out while we get dressed!'

Diana picked up the lead, and Sacha immediately came and sat at her feet, looking hopeful. The two of them went out into the still-early morning to look for a gate into the field behind and, not finding one, compromised with the foreshore. The tide appeared to be coming in; the evidence would soon be gone Diana told herself, and hopefully nobody was watching. There was no way she was going to pick it up unless she absolutely had to, and not even then with her bare hands, which was all she had with her! Then she let Sacha run up and down until he lost interest, encouraged him to paddle to get rid of some of the mud he had collected, and took him back to the cottage. By this time, Val was in the bathroom and Kim had started to get breakfast. Her twin's fashionably torn denim jeans, combined with the pink T-shirt from the village shop that had fallen to her lot, didn't go that well with her flaming red hair. Yes, definitely time to shop!

'He said he wouldn't be long,' said Kim, doubtfully, looking at the bathroom door.

'He's an accountant. Can you believe him?'

'Oh, come on!' Kim grinned at her, like her twin she was singingly happy this morning. 'They're not all shysters! It's supposed to be a respectable profession – where've you been with that dog? He's filthy. And he's all wet.'

'He went paddling.'

'Then you'd better fetch his rug from the kitchen before he lies on that nice clean one. We don't want to leave this lovely house in a mess.'

'Odd, isn't it, how we've both ended up in the financial sector?' said Diana, as she obediently fetched their old hearthrug. She spread it over the one already laid in front of the fireplace and perched herself on the arm of the big cushiony sofa that went with their new lair. 'I know Francis isn't an accountant, but his father's family is even worse. They're bankers or something. He must have inherited some of those genes from them, wouldn't you think?'

'I'm very sure that he has,' said Kim, who had heard things about Francis Chillingworth that maybe Diana hadn't been listening to properly.' She broke off. 'Oh, hello Val! That was quick, I expected you to be hours yet.'

'Oh, ho!' said Val. 'We've got a lot to get through today – is that ready? I'll just take my stuff upstairs and fetch my bag down, give me a minute—' He vanished up the stairs, and Diana looked at Kim, raising her eyebrows.

'He's not staying, then?'

'No. Not tonight anyway. He says there's no point in upsetting his mother when she's upset enough already. She doesn't really approve of extra-marital sex, and she thought he was still in London last night and drove down this morning.'

'Mothers generally don't,' said Diana, who had some experience of this. She had met Valerie Harries, Val's mother, and she didn't think she would actually disown her son if he spent a night away under the circumstances, even if she guessed what he was up to. It wasn't as if it hadn't happened before. She was about to say something to this effect when Val came back down the stairs, his overnight bag slung over his shoulder, and a grin on his face.

'I don't want to spoil your breakfast, Diana, but there's a very posh car just pulled up outside, and a rather smart chap just got out of it and seems to be heading for the door.'

Diana gaped at him for a second and then ran to the door, wrenching it open just as Francis was about to knock on it. She fell straight into his arms as a result. Kim and Val applauded.

'Put that woman down, and come in,' Val invited, and Francis said, as he stepped inside, 'Th-that's two days running we've g-got a round of applause—' He broke off to repel Sacha, who, muddy paws from the foreshore and all, was about to leap on him. 'G-g-good God dog, where have you been? You're f-filthy! Get d-down!'

Kim and Diana by this time had taken in exactly what had visited them at this early hour; not the usual scruffy farmer in jeans and muddy boots driving a muddier 4x4 that they were by now getting used to, but an elegant gentleman in an open-necked white shirt, very smart khaki trousers, a beautifully tailored casual jacket and smart, polished loafers; the only thing missing from this elegant ensemble was a tie. Through the open door, Diana caught a glimpse of his silver-grey Mercedes blocking their gate.

'We were about to have breakfast,' Kim told him. 'Fancy a coffee?'

'N-no thank you, I can't stop. This is just a f-flying visit – you s-said you were going into t-town this morning to d-do some sh-shopping—'

'That's right,' said Diana, with a speaking gesture towards herself and Kim, 'You can see that we need to—' She was about to go on, when Francis interrupted her.

'I s-spoke to the Insurers yesterday, th-they ph-phoned me back last n-night. There's no d-doubt that s-somebody will have to p-p-pay out, so if you can c-come in with me, I can s-s-see you right for money – d-don't look at me like that -K-Kim – I'll get it back. B-but you need it today, and I have to go into town anyway.'

This was too true to argue with, the pink T-shirt/red hair combination said it all for them. Kim looked at Val. 'Can we leave your mother until later, do you think?'

Val looked dubious. 'I don't know if we should. She's been worrying herself sick.' He turned to Francis. 'You say you're headed that way yourself?'

'I've an ap-p-pointment with Jerry Nankervis in thirty-five minutes. I s-suppose I could meet you afterwards b-but I have to see an architect at eleven th-th-thirty. It would have to be quick.'

'No chance of you meeting us for lunch, then?'

'No. S-sorry about that.'

'Well then.' Val thought swiftly. 'There's a coffee shop more or less slap-bang opposite Jerry Nankervis's office. We'll meet you there…oh, about ten fifteen? That do you?'

'I m-might be late. B-but I'll come. And now I must do the opposite and g-go, if I'm to catch the Bank first.'

He grabbed Diana, gave her a quick kiss, and was gone before any of them got their breath back. They heard the full-throated roar of his car pulling away.

'Breakfast,' said Kim.

'I feel as if I've just been hit by a tram,' said Diana, as they sat down. Val grinned at her.

'You chose him. I must admit though, I never saw him in business mode before, either.'

'A chameleon man,' said Kim, pouring coffee. 'Get this down you, both of you, and eat your toast. We need to hurry up if we're not to upset Val's mum, she's not going to be happy when we rush straight off as it is.'

Diana surreptitiously slipped a piece of her toast to Sacha, under the table. 'What do we do with Sacha? He might lie on the sofa or something if we leave him here, and it's a strange place too.'

'We'll take him to Mum and Dad with us,' proposed Val. Penny won't be at work, it's Saturday. She'll look after him.' Penny was his younger sister.

'Maybe she'd give him a bath for us?' suggested Kim. 'I don't know what Di did with him this morning, he looks like a mudlark. I thought he was going to put his dirty feet all over Francis's beautiful shirt.'

'Eat, don't chatter,' Val ordered. 'We can put the washing-up in the sink and do it later—'

'I love that "we",' Diana remarked, as if to the milk jug.

'Don't get clever with me, young lady!' Val grinned at her. 'You know what I meant.'

'That's what I'm afraid of—' She ducked, but his swipe at her had no force behind it and he was grinning.

They tumbled out of the cottage a frantic ten minutes later and set off in Val's car bound for Shearwater, four miles away and a bit further inland. Diana was interested to see it in daylight, she had only seen it in the dark so far, and that was only the Ravenscourt Arms car park really. This was where she would live with Francis when she married him. She wondered exactly where? She would have liked to be able to ask Val's mother where Burnthouse Farm was, but thought she had better not. It might give too much away, and her own parents – not to mention Francis's mother – had a right to be the first to know their intentions.

To their relief, Valerie didn't make too much fuss, perhaps Penny had been lecturing her. She did ask them if they would perhaps sooner come and stay here rather than be on their own after such a terrible experience, but accepted their refusal with equanimity.

'So long as you're happy about it. And you know where we are if you need anything, or change your minds.' She looked at them with concern. 'Did you lose everything, you poor darlings? You look as if you've dressed from a Charity Shop!'

'It's the pink shirt,' Diana explained. 'The skirt and the jeans are mine. It's just the…the accessories,' and Valerie laughed.

'You must go and have a good shop,' she said, which gave Val the perfect cue to say, 'They're going to. But we have to meet with Francis first, there'll be an insurance payout eventually, he said he'd give them a sub meanwhile.'

'That's nice of Francis.'

'I think he feels responsible,' said Diana, looking down at her hands.

'And so he should! You might have been killed!'

'It wasn't his tree,' said Val, quietly. 'And he's seeing them right, he found them the new place and he'll make sure Kim is fully reimbursed. Be sure.'

'I'm glad to hear it.'

They made their escape soon after that, making their way to Embridge and the designated coffee shop with five minutes to spare. Francis was not yet there, so they ordered coffee and sat down to wait for him. Val chose them a table where they could see the door of the Solicitors' Office a few doors down on the opposite side of the street and could watch for him coming. They had hardly spoken since they had left Shearwater in the car, but now Val said, 'We got through that pretty well, I think.'

'She's blaming Francis,' said Diana contentiously. 'It isn't fair, he didn't push the tree over!'

'Well, don't you blame her, it could be argued that she's got a case. He admits himself that he'd been on to the farmer about it.'

'If it had a Preservation Order on it, there wasn't much he could do,' Diana pointed out.

'True. But Francis needn't have let the cottage to Kim in the first place.'

'Whose side are you on?' Diana asked indignantly.

'It's not about taking sides, Diana. You know that. It's the facts.'

'Don't squabble, you two,' ordered Kim. She glanced out of the window. 'And shut up, both of you. He's just coming now.'

Francis came through the door, and straight over to them. He carried a briefcase, which he laid down on the table and rubbed a hand over his eyes. He looked shattered, and Diana's heart turned over.

'Everything OK?' she asked.

'Yeah. OK.' He dropped his hand and looked at her. 'B-but it's a right m-mess, to be honest.'

'Can you tell us about it, or is it sub judice?' Val asked.

'I can t-tell you, but keep it to yourselves for now, if you w-wouldn't m-mind. It'll be in the papers soon enough.'

'Why?' asked Kim. 'A tree came down in the wind − that's just bad luck, isn't it? And it's already been in the local news yesterday morning, so surely that's it?'

'Not in this case, it t-turns out.'

'Explain,' said Val.

'I asked H-harold if I could see the r-r-report from the Council's t-t-tree expert. I p-picked it up this morning on m-m-my way in, after I left you.'

'And?'

'He was quite r-r-right. She did say it was s-s-sound. And it d-did have a Preservation Order. S-so t-t-technically, it isn't Harold's f-fault.'

'Nor yours either,' said Kim, quickly.

'M-maybe not, b-but I c-c-could see that it was rotten. I t-t-told him so.' He looked at Kim. 'I'm s-s-sorry. I should never have l-l-let that place t-to you. To anybody.' It was what Val had just said. Nobody spoke for a moment, then Val said, briskly, 'Well, you did, and nobody died. It's too late now anyway, it's done,' He moved on quickly. 'So what happens now? Does your insurance pay, or does Harold's, or what?'

'J-Jerry Nankervis says Harold m-must sue the Council. And so should I, b-because I let the place in good faith. I kn-knew about the report, you see. He says it doesn't matter that I didn't b-believe it, she was the Council's expert.'

'Then as I see it, that lets you out,' said Val firmly. 'If the woman was supposed to be an expert, and she said it was safe, then that seems to me to be that. What you think is another thing. You don't claim to be a tree expert.'

'I w-wish it was as easy as that.'

'Make it be. You've enough on your plate at the moment without adding more.'

'That's what J-Jerry said.' He turned his wrist and pushed back the sleeve of his jacket to look at his watch – not his usual heavy-duty black affair, Diana noticed, but a Rolex on a broad leather strap. 'And now, I sh-should be going, or I'll be l-l-late for my next appointment.'

'Will we see you later?' asked Kim, when Diana didn't.

'I d-d-don't know. I d-d-don't know what I shall be d-doing.'

'I tell you what,' said Val, watching him. 'You go off now, and these two can go shopping, and I'll go over to Mario's and book the four of us a table for dinner tonight, we can celebrate your engagement to Diana, what do you say? They should be fit to be seen in public by that time.'

'Th-that reminds me,' said Francis. He opened his briefcase, took out an envelope and handed it to Kim. 'Split it b-between you. And have fun.'

It was a fat envelope. Kim took it and squeezed it experimentally.

'Unless this is all in fivers, it's an awful lot of money,' she said.

'Th-then make the most of it.'

'And I book a table for dinner?' said Val, as Francis stood up. He hesitated, then caught sight of Diana's carefully blank face.

'Sounds like a p-plan t-t-to me,' he said. 'T-time?'

'I'll try for a table at eight o'clock. Be at Romans for seven-thirty? We can travel in one car from there.'

'F-fine. See you then.'

He was gone. Diana looked at the other two.

'He didn't even have any coffee,' she said.

'I think it might have choked him,' said Kim. 'Don't worry about him, Di. He's a big boy now, and he's seen a lot worse in his time. It's just because it was you – us – but mostly you. He really loves you.' She lifted the flap of the envelope she held and peered inside, hoping to change the subject. 'My God!' she said.

'What?' asked Val, watching her face. She dipped into the envelope and pulled out the corner of a £20 note.

'It's stuffed with these.' She poked around a bit. 'There must be thirty or forty of them, at least…he's given us near enough a thousand pounds!' She sounded horrified.

'And so he should,' said Val, watching her. 'Think about it Kim. You lost everything you had with you from New Zealand, you have to start from scratch. Even your phone went, you say. Diana doesn't have so much of a problem, if push comes to shove she can slip home for more stuff, she's no doubt got wardrobes of it, but you can't.'

Kim had to admit that this was true, but the money still felt as if it was burning her fingers. She said, 'We can't walk around Embridge carrying a thousand pounds in loose cash. Someone'll mug us! Or arrest us for suspected theft.'

Val laughed outright at this, although he did see her point, it was a bit of a responsibility. He said, in a calming tone of voice, 'Then pay it into Diana's bank, whichever that is, it's bound to have a branch in the town, and use her debit card. You're in this together, after all. And you can keep a note of what you spend and then she can give you the change – if there is any!' He got to his feet. 'And now, ladies, I'm going to do a Francis and leave you to it, and get me down to the Yacht Club. I'll get some lunch there, you two will do better on your own Give me a ring when you're done and I'll meet you at Bordens or somewhere else conspicuous.' He stooped to kiss Kim's cheek. 'Now stuff that in Diana's bag, before someone sees it and sends for the Police to tell them you've robbed a bank. And have a nice day.'

A minute later and he, too, was gone. Diana and Kim looked at each other.

'Right,' said Diana. 'Bank first, then a phone shop, get the boring bit out of the way. Then we can go to that big department store and buy enough decent everyday clothes to make ourselves fit to be seen, and then we can have lunch and think about where to go next. How's that for a plan?'

'Sounds good to me.' Kim decided to let the day take its course and enjoy it anyway. 'Let's get the show on the road!'

Shopping proved to be good therapy. Once they had the money safely in the Bank, they found a phone shop and bought Kim a new phone and had it set up. Then Diana said, 'Now for the good bit!' and made a dive in the direction of Bordens, the town's biggest department store. The first thing they did there was to buy each of them a pair of decent jeans and a smart top, pay for them, get the checkout girl to cut off the price tickets for them, and return to the changing rooms to make themselves fit to be seen. After that, they both felt a lot better. They still had their own outer jackets, which fortunately had been in the kitchen and living area at the cottage, so they were both decent and warm enough.

'I feel halfway human again,' said Diana with satisfaction, stuffing their discarded clothing into the now-empty Borden's plastic bag. 'Now we can really enjoy ourselves! But let's get ourselves some lunch first, we hardly had any breakfast and I'm starving! There's a restaurant upstairs here, and then we can come down refuelled and hit the underwear department and put your boobs to bed – Val can't take his eyes off them! And if we're going out to a posh restaurant tonight, we need to plan for that as well, isn't life great?'

Over their lunch, by mutual but unspoken consent, they avoided discussing the brief talk with Francis in the coffee shop, and tried to concentrate on happier subjects.

'We could have a double wedding,' said Diana, happily, as they ate, but not meaning it; she wanted her wedding day to herself but it was something uncontroversial to start a conversation. The atmosphere was a bit touchy this morning, she thought, and it wasn't all Francis's fault.

'We could, but let's not. I want my wedding day just to myself,' said Kim. She grinned at Diana over their salad – they had resisted anything too substantial, as Mario's Italian restaurant was famous for its wonderful food, and they needed to be hungry again this evening. 'So do you, don't kid me. Val's mother will probably suggest it, but we can talk her out of it. Anyway, Val and I have decided to postpone ours until Spring. He'll need time to settle into his new job – if he gets it, that is – before we can concentrate properly.' She followed Diana's lead with relief, she felt much the same as her twin.

'Anyway, it would be too confusing – four different families, four different sets of friends—' Diana said.

'Three sets of friends,' Kim corrected her. 'My friends over here are yours too. And yours aren't necessarily mine.'

'I keep forgetting.' Diana looked thoughtful. 'I think...I think it's because I feel, somehow, that you've always been there beside me. Isn't it odd?'

Kim was still thinking too, however. She said, 'Actually, I think most of Francis's friends are probably friends of Val too, but just like us, Val's aren't all his.'

'I don't think Francis has a lot,' said Diana. For a moment, a shadow seemed to pass across the sun. 'I wonder why?'

'Not had the time, or the inclination to make any?' suggested Kim, hoping to get away with it.

'A bad reputation, I think,' said Diana. 'All those stories that mutter in the background – and the Sailing Club in Emberton asked him to resign because of all that business with his mother, someone said he was walking out on her and leaving her in the shit, which he isn't…' She broke off. 'I wonder how they knew about that? And who put that twist on it?'

They looked at each other, each of them aware that they had touched a nerve somewhere.

'We could ask. Someone will know,' said Kim. She laid her knife and fork together on her plate, abandoning the remains of her salad, and reached for her coat. 'Come on, we need some more therapy, we're getting morbid again! Knickers, here we come!'

They ransacked the underwear department, went back to the clothes department and ransacked that for the second time, but more thoroughly this time, and kitted Kim out with some warm but smart trousers and a couple of sweaters for the coming autumn and a few similar items that Diana didn't need, but liked, and then Diana said, 'I spotted a rather nice clothes shop as we came in, just over the road from here. Let's go and suss it out.' So they did that.

"Sophia" was indeed a rather nice clothes shop: it was also a very expensive one, but hey, they had a thousand pounds to spend between them, and it rather went to their heads. Diana's particularly, but Kim, too, was beguiled by a rather beautiful dress and a pair of pretty high-heeled shoes, both of which would go down well at Mario's that evening.

'I don't generally wear dresses,' she admitted, but this one was rather special. It made her look both sophisticated and elegant, and the really great thing about it was that it wasn't, in any way, pink. The assistant produced a necklace and earrings that went with it nicely, and Diana said, 'Go on – it's a once in a lifetime chance to splash out without a guilty conscience.' She laid her own choices, even more expensive, on the counter beside Kim's, and added, 'But we'd better stop there. We must both be spent out, I should think, but I admit that I haven't been counting.'

They went back to Borden's well laden and returned to the restaurant upstairs, and Kim rang Val on her new phone. Switching it off at the end of her brief conversation with him, she said, 'He'll pick us up in half an hour outside the main door, and should he borrow a trailer?'

'Cheek!' said Diana.

Kim fumbled in the depths of the new shoulder bag she had just bought to replace her old bumbag, which had been lost, unregretted since it was showing its age, in the tree disaster. She meant to pull out her receipts for a cashing-up session, but as she did so, a new and scary thought came into her head.

'Oh, my God!'

'What?' asked Diana, surprised by the shock in her voice.

'I just thought. My passport! It was in my camera bag! I shoved it under the bed last night, I always do – oh my God! And I thought losing the camera was bad enough!'

'Oops!' They looked at each other, Kim in shock, and Diana with speculation. Finally, Diana ventured, 'Maybe Francis knows someone with a digger who can excavate it?'

'It'll be a sodden mess, even if it was found.'

It seemed there were to be no end to the problems that now beset them. Diana said, 'Perhaps it won't be, but even if it is, it isn't the end of the world. You'll be coming up to London with me sometime soon, I hope, to meet my parents. You can go to your Embassy, I'm sure there is one somewhere. They'll sort it out. Or you can marry Val very, very quickly as you originally said, and be a British citizen. And in the meantime, you don't need it. You aren't going anywhere.'

'I do need it. My visa will expire, or something, and they'll deport me! And I'm not certain I can marry Val without it.'

'Rubbish. You just need to get some advice somewhere – you could ask Val's father, perhaps, he's a Police Superintendent or something. Or Francis's solicitor, he sounds like a good bloke. And that reminds me – we should have bought you a new rucksack. You've nothing to put things in when we go to London.'

Kim took a deep breath, her sudden panic beginning to subside. Of course, there were all sorts of things she could do, she told herself thankfully, she wasn't the first person in the world to lose a passport, and at least she had a convincing reason for it. She spread out her receipts on the table with fingers that almost didn't shake.

'I'm not sure I can afford it.'

'Yes, you can. You lost everything, I lost not a lot, in the general scheme of things. So most of the money is yours anyway, and even if we spent it all, which I shouldn't think we did, quite, the balance was my money, on my things. Don't get stroppy with me—' she had read Kim's expression very accurately, '—it's true. Just think about it before you bite my head off. And a rucksack isn't going to break the bank, I think they might sell them downstairs in the sports department, we can look on the way out—'

'Diana—'

'Shut up, you! If it helps, just think of all the birthday and Christmas presents I've never given you, and say "thank you" for this one, that I will have.'

'I haven't given you any, either.'

'No, but you've given me free accommodation for the whole summer, so just shut up. If Val's going to be half an hour, we could have a piece of cake with this tea. What do you think?'

Kim said, 'I think that all four of us have spent today on the verge of quarrelling, and you're right. We do need sweetening. But if you're going to buy me a rucksack, I buy the cake. Come with me up to the counter and choose what you want.'

'It's just reaction,' Diana told her, as they got to their feet and headed off to the counter.

'I know. But I wish all difficult problems could be solved by cake.'

Maybe the cake wasn't as enjoyable as it should have been, but they ate it anyway and then went back to the floors below.

'Actually,' Diana said, 'a rucksack isn't really what you need, you aren't going backpacking any time soon. We can get you a nice holdall, or a suitcase or something. Give you a bit more style.'

'I don't need style, I'm not a stylish person,' Kim said, controversially, but Diana's response was a simple, 'Oh, shut up! What is the matter with you today?' and then realised, from the mental echo of her own voice, that it was the matter with her, too, and added. 'Sorry.' They looked at each other. Kim took a deep breath.

'Let's go and buy a holdall,' she said.

'We can put some of these bags in it, and then Val won't kill us,' said Diana, and they exchanged a rueful smile.

Val was already waiting at the main door when they appeared, and greeted them with a lift of his eyebrow as he took the new holdall, full of shopping, from Kim. There were still a few bags that hadn't fitted in, which Diana was carrying.

'I see you've been having a good time,' he said, and as the words left his mouth, realised that he could have chosen them better, for all he got back was two identical subdued smiles. 'Come on,' he said, 'I found a space to park in the Square, it's only a step,' and turned to lead the way.

It was a quiet drive back to Emberton, and Val, feeling an atmosphere, didn't try to break it. They were tired after all that shopping, he told himself, and probably the shock had caught up with them. What they needed was a good rest before they all went out to dinner this evening, which wasn't quite what he had in mind. Oh well.

When they were back in the house, Diana said, 'I think I'm going to take all my stuff upstairs and have a bit of a lie down. I feel like shit.' Her face was hurting, for one thing, but she hadn't mentioned that to Kim. The rest of her felt like rolled-out pastry – flat.

'I'll sort it out, and bring it in a minute,' said Kim, looking at her. 'You go'

Diana went. Kim and Val were left looking at each other.

'Not the best day you ever spent?' asked Val.

'It was a lovely day – but it had it's downside…we kept almost-quarrelling…I think we're both tired, and probably still in shock if we're honest…and Francis didn't help, really.'

'I feel very sorry for Francis. He must feel terrible,' said Val, and Kim said, 'Yes.' A silence fell. Kim picked up a couple of the bags and peered into them, setting one to the left of the sofa, the other to the right. Val watched her.

'Look,' he said, 'You are tired, I can see. How about, I go home and placate Mum, and bath the dog or something, and you do like Diana, get some rest? I can come over before seven and make sure you're both awake.'

It sounded a wonderful plan, but Kim said, 'We won't be. Awake, I mean. Our alarm clock is under all that debris—' and burst into tears. Val put his arms around her and she wept into his shoulder for a minute or two, then drew herself back. 'Sorry.' She rubbed her hand over her wet eyes, making her appearance even worse. 'Excuse me – I'll get some kitchen roll—'

Val followed her into the kitchen.

'Did you buy that phone?' he asked her, and when she nodded her head without looking at him, he went on, 'Then find it in all that muddle, turn it on, and take it upstairs with you. Get some rest, you look as if you need it. I'll ring you at a quarter to seven in case you're still asleep by then, that should give you time to be ready by half-past. But give me the number, for I won't know it otherwise.'

He drove away ten minutes later, wondering if his bright idea of going out to dinner had been the best one he had ever had. All three of his chosen companions seemed to be on the verge of disintegration, they would all have been better at home with a bowl of soup and an early night. Oh well, too late to change it now. He didn't even know how to get in contact with Francis anyway, if he was still in town.

He drove on, thinking.

IV

In spite of Val's misgivings, the evening turned out well. He rang Kim on her new phone, as promised at a quarter to seven, and she was already awake, which was a good start, and sounded much more like her usual self which was even better. The first thing she said after their greeting was, 'I forgot about the dog. What do we do with him? I don't want to leave him alone here, it's all a bit…well, posh.'

'Mum says he can stop here,' said Val. 'He can spend the night, you two won't want to be bothered with him when you get back late and all poshed-up. I'll bring him over in the morning. He seems to have bonded with Penny, he'll be OK.'

'Did you bath him?' asked Kim, meaning it for a joke, but Val said, 'Actually, Penny already had – he was in a bit of a mess, you have to admit. Now go and make sure that twin of yours is awake, and I'll see you in half an hour—'

Kim switched off her phone, and looked across at Diana, who was in the room rootling in the new holdall for the Sophia bags.

'The dog's had a bath,' she said, and Diana said, still rootling, 'Great. Will you have the shower first, or shall I?'

'You can, and make it quick. I'll sort out the stuff, you're just making things worse – go! You can have ten minutes!'

Sorting out the stuff was soothing, Kim found, she needed soothing. She was still ashamed of the way she had broken down in front of Val, although she did feel better after a couple of hours surprisingly deep sleep. They all needed to take a deep breath and start again, the only one of the four of them who was holding it together was Val – but then, he had been only superficially involved. He hadn't even seen the debris at the cottage, so far as she was aware. They hadn't gone that way to Embridge, and on the way back they had passed it so quickly…she gave herself a shake. Don't think about it. Unpack your new underwear, you're going to need it in a minute – and that beautiful dress and shoes Diana talked you into, so your lovely, long-suffering man won't recognise the miserable watering-pot he saw last.

Diana came out of the shower after twelve minutes, which was pretty quick for her, and gathered up her share of the now-sorted bags to take upstairs, and Kim dived in. Even so, she was still upstairs putting on the unfamiliar sheer tights Diana had insisted she buy, with the equally unfamiliar dress hanging on the wardrobe door, when Val arrived to find the downstairs rooms empty – they had left the door on the latch for him. He yelled up the stairs.

'You awake, up there?' Two voices yelled back, 'Of course we are!' and 'Yes!' respectively, and then Diana leaned over the stair-rail and said, 'Give us ten minutes. I'm just polishing Kim.'

Whatever that meant. Val sat down in an armchair and waited, looking at his watch. Nearly half-past already, he hoped that Francis had remembered, among all his other problems, that he was meant to be going out to dinner with them.

Ten minutes passed with nothing of note but the sound of a lot of laughter from upstairs, and Val looked at his watch again. Twenty-five to eight. They were going to be late. He was about to yell up the stairs when two beautiful girls appeared at the top of them. For a moment, he thought he was seeing double; he had never seen either of them wearing a dress and high heels, except for once at a dance, which had been different, and he had never seen Kim wearing make-up fit for an evening out in a posh restaurant – which was hardly surprising, since Kim had never seen it herself. The two of them walked slowly down the stairs like a pair of catwalk models and arrived at the bottom, laughing at him.

'What do you think?' asked Diana, pirouetting, and Val said, 'Wow! You both look amazing.'

'Pity about Kim's old jacket, but she'll be taking it off when we get to the restaurant. We forgot about that when we were in Embridge,' said Diana, grinning at him. She added casually, 'No Francis yet?'

'Not so far,' said Val, resisting another glance at his watch.

Diana went over to the sofa and sat down, crossing her legs with conscious elegance. She made no comment, but it was as if a light had dimmed a little. Kim went to the cupboard under the stairs, where their coats hung, and unhooked them putting them over her arm. Diana's wasn't exactly evening-smart either, but at least it was expensive. She made a face into the dark of the cupboard, and then shut the door, and as she did so, she heard the sound of a car turning into the space beside the house where Diana had left hers, pulling up behind it. There was the slam of a car door, and the "beep" of an alarm setting itself, and footsteps on the path.

'He's here,' she called, and opened the front door as Francis reached it. 'You're late,' she greeted him.

'I kn-now. I'm sorry.' He gave no explanation. Val got to his feet.

'Come on then, now we're all assembled, we should be on our way!'

Francis was busy greeting Diana, so it was Kim who said, 'Should you ring the restaurant? Say we'll be a few minutes late?'

'That will make us a few minutes later.'

'But polite, don't you think?'

'You can do it as we go along. Here – the number's in the contact list. Chillingworth, put that woman down, I've spoken to you about that before! We're late enough as it is!' He handed Kim his mobile and headed for the door.

The four of them went out to Val's car, laughing. 'We'll sit in the back,' said Kim, opening the rear door to suit the action to the word. 'Francis will never get his long legs into it – it would be a shame to crease him.'

'Th-these trousers are c-crease r-r-resistant,' he told her. 'B-but thank you anyway.' He had shed the morning's business mode for a more relaxed black-jeans-and-a-blazer look with a blue shirt that, whether he realised it or not, showed up the blue of his eyes to great advantage, but he still looked expensive. Val, in similar mode, looked more smart-casual ordinary bloke. Mario's, Kim concluded, wasn't that posh, and was glad. Posh wasn't really her style.

Mario's, in fact, was an Italian restaurant that served fantastic food and didn't operate a formal dress code, but offered a more easy-going approach in keeping with its bistro image; clean and tidy was fine. Looking around her as they went in, Kim decided that the four of them had struck exactly the right note, and that she liked this place. When they had been shown to their table and been handed a menu each, she liked it even more. She had fallen in love with the food of Italy on her recent travels around Europe, and here it was again. Lovely!

'You're smirking,' Diana told her.

'I love Italian food.'

'Then you're in just the right place,' Val told her.

When they had made their choices and ordered two bottles of Italian wine to start with, there was more time to look about them.

'This is nice,' said Diana appreciatively. 'I love the pictures—' they were of famous Italian landmarks, mixed with reproductions of famous Italian paintings, '—and all the white walls are very Mediterranean. You almost feel you're actually there.'

'I think that's the general idea,' said Val, leaning back in his chair and picking up his wine glass. He raised it in a toast. 'Here's to us. May we all come out winners.'

The meal was delicious; between that and the wine the atmosphere between the four of them, which had started off a bit on the sticky side, both Kim and Diana had thought, began to mellow. Val had got over their unpunctual behaviour, the restaurant had been very understanding which helped, thanking Kim for their courtesy in letting the staff know. Whatever had delayed Francis, if it wasn't congenital unpunctuality, which none of them actually knew, he had obviously filed it for now, and the atmosphere of the place was conducive to pleasant relaxation. Over the antipasti, their conversation became easier.

'What a great place this is,' Kim said, looking around her. 'I'm glad you chose it, Val – I always feel uncomfortable in very formal places. Probably comes from growing up among sheep – they feel the same way.'

'I b-bet they do,' said Francis, with a sudden smile in her direction, there, and gone in a flash, 'How w-would you like to be r-roast lamb w-with mint sauce?'

'Hmm – see what you mean,' said Kim, although privately she had just had a bit of a shock. She had never, she suddenly realised, seen Francis smiling quite like that, rarely seen him smile at all come to that, it had been a bit of a revelation just for that split second. She took her next mouthful thoughtfully.

'It's about the best in town,' Val was saying. 'There's one or two other good ones, of course, a great Indian one, and a couple of standard English that aren't too bad, and the usual burger-bars and Chinese takeaways, and pubs. A couple of good hotels. But Mario's, yes, is about top of the heap.'

'Mmm.' Diana had her mouth full, but nodded her approval. She swallowed her mouthful to say, 'Indian is good, too, though.'

'We'll try that next time,' Val told her. Nice to think there would be a next time, Diana thought, smiling her agreement, and Francis put in with, 'How did your sh-shopping trip go? S-s-s-damn!'

'Very successful indeed,' Kim told him. 'Just look at us now, if you want a confirmation! I think we spent you out, and it was great so we have to give you a great big thank-you!'

'G-good.' He took a swig, from what was by this time his second glass of wine, 'and y-you shouldn't look at it like th-that you know, Kim. You're entitled, you l-l-lost everything due to s-somebody else's negligence. You'll g-get a lot more than th-th-that in the end.'

'My clothes weren't even worth that much,' Kim objected.

'It's n-n-not just about clothes. You were put at unacceptable r-risk, you should get c-c-compensation for that. And th-there's your furniture—'

'Most of that survived,' objected Kim, and could have added "so did we", but didn't. 'It was only the beds, and the chest of drawers, they weren't worth much – well, Diana's bed was worth a bit more, but—'

'N-no, it didn't,' Francis told her, interrupting. 'B-by the time I g-g-got back with Harold in the evening, the d-d-damp had brought the c-ceiling down in the other r-room too. Everything was b-buried.'

Kim felt herself go white. She remembered herself and Diana sitting waiting for the sun to rise, and suddenly her delicious plateful didn't taste so good. She caught Diana's eye, and knew she was thinking the same.

'Ouch,' said Diana. Francis looked contrite, he could see that he had upset them both and mentally cursed himself, he didn't think he was usually that maladroit. He hoped not anyway.

'I'm s-sorry. I shouldn't have b-brought that up t-tonight.'

'I think really it was me that brought it up,' said Kim.

There was no point in changing the subject too abruptly, it would only make things worse; it would have to be discussed some time anyway. Val said, 'So whose insurance gets the final bill, Francis? You, Harold, or the Council?'

'Jerry says, the Council.'

'Then that seems to me to let you off the hook. Now tell us, when are you going to sweep Diana off to a jewellers' and buy her a great big flashy diamond ring?' And that had been really abrupt. They all seemed to be suffering from foot-in-mouth disease tonight. To his relief, Francis took the change of subject in his stride, perhaps he felt the same way.

'B–bit early for that, wouldn't you s–s–say? We should m–maybe r–run it past her m–m–mother and f–father first.'

'They don't even know he exists at the moment,' Diana added.

'Oops! So when are you going to break it to them?' Val asked, smiling at her.

'I thought I'd ring them tomorrow morning, when all the dust has had a chance to settle—' Diana broke off and bit her lip, it seemed that none of them could say the right thing tonight. She went on quickly, to put the mistake behind her as soon as possible, 'They're likely to be home on a Sunday morning, and have time to talk too.' The next obvious question was "and will you tell them everything?" but nobody asked it. Instead, Val said, 'And when are you planning on introducing them all?'

'God knows.' Diana had given this some thought, obviously, but had come up with no sensible answer. 'He's so tied up at the moment, it's hard to spot a window of opportunity. I suppose they'll have to come here, really, but my father has a full schedule too, so who knows when it'll be?'

Unexpectedly, Francis cut in here before Val could make any comment.

'Actually, in a couple of d–d–days, I won't be tied up with anyth–thing until the c–c–completion date on Burnthouse. And I p–promised t–to go up to t–t–town soon anyway, to see m–my grandmother. W–we could c–c–combine the two.'

The other three looked at him, but it was Kim who asked the obvious question.

'How come?'

'I l–l–leave Vachells on the qu–quarter day. Th–that's the twenty–n–ninth. Completion isn't until the sixteenth of October.'

'So what on earth are you going to do in the meantime?' asked Val, before he could stop himself after all, it could be argued that it was none of his business. 'Stop in a hotel, or what?'

'N–no. I shall m–move in t–t–temporarily at Sh–Shortlanesend with Ernie and B–Bennie. I b–believe you m–m–met Bennie.' He said this last to the twins, who both nodded – like a pair of nodding dogs, Kim thought, catching sight of her twin's simultaneous action. She said, 'Yes. I did, not Diana. You'd swept her off to the surgery by the time she called round.'

'She seems to make a business of re–homing the homeless,' said Diana, with a smile at him.

The waiter came at that moment to clear the plates and to bring the main course, so it was a while before the conversation between them could be resumed, and then Val changed the subject completely, or at least, he changed it's direction.

'So, tell us about your new place,' he said. 'I know where it is, of course, I've passed the gate when I've been visiting Mum and Dad – in fact, we passed it this morning come to that – but I've never actually been up the lane.'

'Did we?' Diana sat up straight. She hadn't noticed. How awful, the way she felt about Francis, it should have leapt out at her!

'We certainly did. Only the name board seemed to have fallen off, so you wouldn't have known.'

'Th-that sounds about right,' said Francis, with a rueful look. 'The whole p-place is a t-tumbledown mess.'

'Are we to be allowed to see it?' asked Kim, curiously. After all, it would be her twin's home eventually, and thus play a part in their lives.

'W-when it's mine, of c-course you are. I haven't g-g-got the key right now. J-just access to a barn to store f-farm equipment and s-s-stuff meantime.'

'Is it liveable-in?' Val asked. 'I know someone was living in it, but Merlin reckons it's about to fall down.' Their mutual friend Merlin was one of the Ravenscourts of Ravenscourt Place, and therefore lived more or less next-door to Burnthouse, give or take an acre or two of farmland. He was also a partner in the boatyard opposite to Romans and, like both Val and Francis, sailed a Moonraker at the Ember Valley Sailing Club in Emberton.

'I r-reckon he's not far wrong. B-but if it's d-d-dealt with soon, it should be savable.'

'It'll be a huge job,' said Val. 'Can you get someone in that quickly?'

'Oh y-yes. The R-R-Ravenscourts want it d-done. So it w-w-will be.'

'Handy,' commented Val. 'Don't they mind that when you buy it, even more land locally will belong to your mother's family and not to theirs?'

'N-not enough to m-m-matter. Most of it b-belongs to the-them anyway, it was only r-r-rented. W-which is great, because they're c-c-cleaning their fields r-r-ready to r-r-rent them to me, which s-saves me a job.'

Diana put in here, because she rather felt it might concern her, 'So if the house is crawling with builders, where are you going to live? Still at Shortlanesend?'

'N-no. I n-n-need to be there while the w-w-work is going on.' He smiled at her, wickedly Kim rather suspected. 'I sh-shall live in the f-farmyard. In a c-caravan. Is that OK w-w-with you?'

Diana would have lived with him in the barn alongside the tractor, but she didn't say this. Instead, she said, 'Make it a posh one then, please. And big enough so you don't keep banging your head on the ceiling!'

'I w-wasn't thinking of a camper van, exactly,' he told her. 'It c-could be m-months b-before even j-just one end of the house is f-f-fit to live in.'

'As bad as that?' Val rejoined the conversation.

'Oh, definitely. The r-roof l-leaks everywhere, th-the inside all needs r-repair or r-r-redecorating, and the p-plumbing is V-V-Victorian. The r-roof will have to b-b-be done first, of course, and the whole p-place re-wired, th-then the k-kitchen end will b-be done to give me – us – s-somewhere to l-l-live indoors.'

'So long as it gives us a bedroom as well as a kitchen,' said Diana, thinking about it with wonder; this was her future home they were talking about.

'Oh, it'll g-g-give us m-m-more than that. We shall have th-three bedrooms and a b-b-bathroom upstairs, and the kitchen and a d-dining r-room d-downstairs. W-we can use the d-dining room f-f-for a s-s-sitting room m-meanwhile.'

'Sounds positively luxurious,' Kim commented. 'So, when do you expect that bit to be finished, so you can move out of the caravan?'

'Probably about th-three months b-before any of it is hab-bitable, w-w-with everything else that has to be d-d-done. B-but th-that end of the house has g-g-got to be all f-finished by the m-m-middle of January at the latest, b-because th-the builders n-n-need to start converting the t-t-tithe barn for a manager to live in, and anyway, th-th-the p-previous owner gave the University permission for an archaeological dig on that old B-Barrow over on the b-boundary overlooking the r-r-road, and ac-c-commm…damn, l-lodging f-for the s-s-site directors was part of the d-d-deal.'

'That'll be fun,' said Kim, without defining to which part of this speech she was referring.

Diana was looking pensive. It looked, from where she was sitting, as if her accustomed hedonistic social life in London, with its parties and shopping and – well, expensive luxury, be honest – was about to be turned abruptly on its head. Did she mind? She thought about it for a brief second, and came up with an answer. No, she didn't mind, and she quite liked the sound of an archaeological dig. Perhaps they would let her help, while Francis was busy doing whatever he did all day with cows and tractors and things? That might be interesting.

'Doesn't sound as if you're going to have much time for sailing next season,' Val commented.

'I w-wasn't going to anyway. N-not racing. I've sold the boat to P-Pete.' Pete had been his crew in the Moonraker, and Val had known that anyway, he had — well, been fishing, he admitted to himself. After all the fuss at the end of last month, he found he didn't want to see Francis just walk away and let the Sailing Club Committee win.

'But you won't be giving up sailing altogether? That would be a pity.'

'I shall get s-s-something a b-b-bit bigger than the M-m-moonraker when the w-w-work is all finished and th-there's time again. T-Tamsin will like that better.'

Diana thought of her father's expensive gin-palace, at present spending the winter somewhere in the Mediterranean, waiting for next summer and another luxury trip around Italy, or the Greek Islands or somewhere even more exotic. Her father had spoken about Africa…She gave herself a mental shake, and asked the million-pound question.

'Sail or motor?'

He gave her a gentle, understanding look.

'Sail of course. B-but it'll h-have a r-r-reliable engine. And be a d-d-decent size.'

'Promise?'

'Promise.'

'I'll make do with that, then,' said Diana happily.

The waiter came back now to clear away more plates and offer the dessert menu for their inspection, and Val ordered another bottle of wine. The conversation took a different turn after that. But it had been interesting, Kim thought, watching her twin's animated face across the table. Diana might not realise it herself, but she was opening her petals in the sun by the minute. And come to that, she now realised, Francis had done similar. Telling them about his decrepit farmhouse and his plans for its immediate future had brought him alive; she thought she had never seen him so animated. It made him less beautiful, somehow, but a lot more accessible.

She had meant to put out a feeler about the putative fate of her passport tonight, but she decided now to leave it until tomorrow; it would be a shame to spoil this new atmosphere; the start of the evening had been dodgy enough. She thought again that today, none of the four of them could consistently say the right thing, no need to start it all off again, and on purpose this time. She picked up her refilled glass and took a sip, listening to Val and Francis, now discussing sailing. Diana seemed to have gone off into a dream, and Kim sympathised. She had been given a lot to dream about.

Francis, remembering his night on the tiles with his cousin Michael, had turned down a third glass of wine, the hangover the next morning that time had been spectacular and he had no wish to repeat it He had enough headaches at the moment without asking for more, and in any case, he had to get himself back to Vachells quite soon. He had gone quiet now, just listening to the other three talking together about this and that, but when they finally got up to leave, he said, 'I'll take Sacha with me, when we g-get back to Emberton. He'll be all right w-with me for a couple of d-d-days, he d-d-doesn't really f-fit in there. N-nowhere for him to run.'

'He isn't there at the moment, you'll have a job,' Val told him. Francis looked surprised; his late arrival at Romans had meant that they had all gone out the minute he got there, and before he had time to notice his dog's absence. He said 'W-where is he, then?'

'Spending the night with Penny, and Val's parents,' Kim told him. 'We thought it wasn't a good idea to leave him on his own, it's still a strange place to him, poor darling.'

'He's had a bath,' added Diana.

'Hmm. All r-right, I'll pick him up t-t-tomorrow m-morning, when V-val brings him back. I p-presume he's planning to?'

'Not too early,' Val told him. 'These two look as if they'll sleep the night away and get up at around mid-morning, and come to that, very probably so shall I.'

'L-lucky old you!'

'But it's Sunday,' said Diana, without thinking.

'T-tell th-that to the cows,' said Francis.

Val grinned. 'Poor Diana is on a very steep learning curve.'

They were back at his car by this time, he unlocked it and they had all started to get back in as before, when Francis said. 'You -g-go in the front, Kim – put the s-s-seat forward, I'll be OK in the b-back for that sh-short dist-t-tance.'

So Kim travelled back to Romans with Val close enough to her for her to be able to touch him, and Diana travelled with Francis's arm around her and her sleeping head resting against his shoulder. There could only have been one better end to the evening they had just spent, but unfortunately it was off the menu for tonight...

V

Ringing her parents, Diana realised as soon as she had taken time to consider this properly, was yet another of those problems, like Kim's passport and the best thing to do with the dog, that needed to be approached with a certain amount of care. Although she had known him for several months now, her parents had never so much as heard Francis's name; this made it potentially controversial to announce that she was going to marry him and live with him in a caravan, not necessarily in that order. Her mother made no secret of the fact that it was the dearest wish of her heart to see her daughter married to a wealthy man, preferably with a large country estate, but did a farmer thirteen years her senior with a farmhouse that was falling down around him come under that heading? Still less, would the falling-down farmhouse fit in with her mother's treasured concept of an elegant country mansion? And that was before she even started on what her father might think.

Even so, this mountain had to be climbed. Breakfast over, and even the washing-up done simply because it put off the evil hour, Diana went reluctantly upstairs to her bedroom with her mobile phone, shut herself in, and sitting on her lower-bunk bed, pressed the right buttons and took a deep breath before diving off the high board into a sea of explanations, that would be further complicated by the fact that she had not yet informed her parents about the falling tree on the cottage either. She sincerely hoped that unfortunate incident hadn't made the national press: it had featured in the local paper, she knew, but hopefully, on a wider scale it was small beer,

They'd have rung if it had. Or come straight down to Dorset.

Perhaps they were on their way even as she rang them now.

Ouch!

They weren't. Her father picked up the phone, and recognising the number on the little screen, said, 'Hello, stranger. To what do we owe this pleasant surprise?'

'Hello to you too, darling Daddy.' Diana took a deep breath; where to start? She jumped straight in, the only way. 'I should have rung you yesterday, but so much was happening – Daddy, nobody's hurt, I promise, but in that storm the night before last, a big tree came down on Kim's cottage and squashed it flat, and we've had to move out—' She broke off, and there was a pause. When Sir Charles spoke, it was in a voice she didn't recognise.

'Just run that past me again, will you? A tree fell on your cottage? Were you there at the time? Please tell me that you weren't.'

'Well, it was the middle of the night, so we were. But we were all right – well, I got a cut on my cheek from flying glass, but it's not serious. It only destroyed one half of the cottage, the rest held up all right.' Then – but she needn't tell him that. It was a piece of information that she wished she didn't have herself.

'I'm finding this very difficult to take in,' said her father. He couldn't recall when he had felt so deeply shaken: he felt an impulse to shout at her for keeping this from him and her mother until now, and smothered it, it would do no good. 'This tree…did you know it was unsafe? Did anyone know?'

'No,' said Diana, which was true, she told herself. Francis hadn't known, not for a fact; he had only wondered. She went on, 'It was a big old oak tree, right on the boundary, with a Preservation Order on it. The Council had passed it as sound.'

'Then I hope your landlord plans to sue the Council concerned until they scream for mercy,' said her father grimly, and Diana said meekly, 'Oh, he does.'

'So, what did you do?' asked her father. 'You got out safely, you say, and I presume you then called for help – you still had your phone, I hope?'

'I had it in my bag,' said Diana, which was essentially true, although misleading at the same time; Kim had used the phone at the village pub, early the following morning. 'Lots of people stopped to help. And we had my car, Daddy, that wasn't hurt. We went to the Two Pigeons, that's the pub in the village, where Kim works, and they gave us a bed for what little was left of the night. And while we were asleep, our landlord came to the pub, and left us the key to a lovely holiday home he had found for us to move into, right in the village and rent free, and had generally seen we would be looked after.'

'Well, good for him, he has my thanks. You must have had the fright of your lives!'

'We did. And we lost a lot of our stuff too, we had barely enough clothes left to be decent.' She tried to make a joke of it, but her father, she could feel without him saying a word, wasn't deceived. She went on, talking for effect and too fast, 'We bought a couple of emergency T-shirts in the village shop – Kim's was pink, it looked dreadful, her hair is the same colour as mine—' She stopped. Too much information; she could almost hear her father thinking. She ended, 'We had to buy everything new...' and thought that she sounded pathetic.

'I hope your landlord plans to reimburse you,' her father said, not sounding in the least amused.

'He already has. He gave us a thousand pounds against the eventual insurance payout and told us to let him know if it wasn't enough.'

'I begin to like the sound of your landlord,' said her father, grimly. It was too good a cue to ignore, even if the timing was bad. Diana said, before she could stop herself, 'That's good, because he wants to marry me, Daddy. And I want to marry him.'

It was like turning off a radio, or something, Diana thought: that same sudden, completely empty silence that you got when you did that. She said, 'Daddy?' She actually heard him drawing in a deep breath over the phone.

'All right,' her father said, pulling himself together with an effort. 'Let's start on page one, shall we? Who is he? That would be a good start.'

'His name is Francis Chillingworth, and he's a—' She stopped herself before she said "farmer", wondering, for the first time, if that was actually true in the purest sense; she settled for '—cattle breeder. He breeds prize cows – and bulls, of course – Ayrshires, I think somebody said. Or they might be Herefords.'

'And you met him because this cottage is on his land?'

'No. It isn't, actually, not on the main estate. We met him down at the local sailing club, and it was quite a while before we realised that he was our landlord.' Which was all true, and sounded good, but was actually misleading, the word "met" being the operative one. You meet many people without actually knowing them other than by sight, but her father needn't be told that. She wondered momentarily how many other

58

equivocations surrounded her chosen man: that was three in the same number of sentences.

Well, that didn't sound so bad. Sir Charles began to relax a bit. He made a small joke, 'No relation to the Banking House, then,' but to his astonishment, Diana replied, 'I think his grandfather, or maybe his great-grandfather, may have been the founder.'

There was a pause, while her father thought about this, chasing vague fragments of knowledge through his, admittedly startled, mind. Old man Chillingworth, he recalled, had three daughters, whose sons were now directors of the bank, but had he had a son, too? Sir Charles had an unidentifiable feeling that perhaps he had. But his name hadn't been "Francis", and if it had been, he would be far too old now for Diana... the name "Christopher" drifted into his mind and out again. Whoever he was, if he had been part of the Bank, it hadn't been for very long. He said, 'So when are we going to meet this young man you plan to marry?'

'Quite soon. We hope to be able to get up to London next week sometime. I don't know exactly when, Francis has some business to tie up first.' No need to go into details on the phone, it would only further confuse the already confused issue. 'He has to come up anyway then, to see his grandmother. She's very old now, and she hasn't seen him for quite a while.' Understatement of the year.

'Then we shall look forward to that. And now, perhaps you had better speak to your mother, don't you think? Break it all to her gently.'

He took the phone through to his wife, sitting reading a magazine in the drawing room.

'Diana,' he said. 'She's got some news for us.'

'Good or bad?' asked Eloise, accepting the phone with a smile.

'Bit of both, at least I hope so. I'll be in the study when you bring the phone back.'

He went back into his study himself, and sat down heavily at his desk; he felt he needed a strong drink, but it was a bit early. The indigestible mixture of falling trees, cows and Chillingworth's Investment Bank was almost too much to take in. Perhaps he would prosecute a few enquiries in the City tomorrow, spy out the land. Given Diana's past record, it all sounded a bit too good to be true...

Diana spoke to her mother, who was deeply shocked and threatened to drive down and bring both her and Kim back to London, and had to be calmed down before any sense could be talked to her, and then thankfully turned the phone off, and took herself downstairs where she found that while she had been wrestling with her parents, Val and the dog had arrived.

'Val's rung Francis,' Kim told her. 'He said he'd come past around lunchtime and he'd pick Sacha up then. I've packed his stuff ready.' She nodded towards the dog basket by the door, piled up with dog food, dog toys, dog dishes, dog lead, and with their old hearthrug rolled up and laid on the top. Diana thought that it was a sad sight. The collie had been with them for several weeks by this time, ever since Francis had brought him for Kim to take care of, after somebody unknown at Vachells had tried to poison him. He had never found out for certain who, and if he had any ideas on the subject, had never shared them.

'We're going to miss him,' said Diana, stroking the narrow black and white head that nuzzled now at her knee. 'He's become like part of the furniture. I love him…'

'Cheer up,' said Val. 'You'll be sharing a caravan with him before that long. That'll be fun. In wintertime, too, there'll be a pervasive smell of wet dog, to remind you how lucky you are!'

'Is it safe to take him back to Vachells, do you think? Suppose whoever-it-was has another try?'

'I don't think Francis means to let him out of his sight,' said Kim. 'It's only for – well, I suppose by now it's only for another forty-eight hours.'

'He should have left him with us.'

'Not with all that lovely mud, so tempting to roll in, out on the foreshore,' said Val, with a grin.

A silence fell, during which the question that both Kim and Val longed to ask seemed to hang in neon lights in the air around them. Finally, when Diana didn't say anything, Val asked it.

'How did it go with your parents? Did they hit the roof, or do you think you got away with it?'

'They hit the roof over the cottage,' said Diana, with unintentional appropriateness, and after considering how comprehensive her answer should be 'At least, Eloise did. But she does tend to over-react…' She never referred to her mother as "Mummy" these days, she wasn't absolutely sure why this was, but Eloise didn't seem to mind. 'Daddy just muttered about suing everyone in sight, but I told him that was all in hand.'

'And Francis? How did he go down?'

'His name made Daddy sit up a bit. And they were both impressed that he had looked after us so well. Not sure about the cows…but obviously, they want to meet him as soon as it can be arranged – then they'll tell me what they really think, I expect.'

'You didn't tell them how old he was?' said Val, with a lift of his eyebrows.

'They'll find out, soon enough.'

Kim got to her feet. 'That's enough, Val. I'm going to make some coffee, do you both want some?' She went into the kitchen, and Val leaned back in his chair and looked at Diana, with what she described in her head to herself as "a measuring look".

'Kim and I are going down to the Sailing Club when Francis has picked the dog up,' he said. 'Want to come with us? Maybe Francis will come too, we can ask him.'

'No he won't,' said Kim, from the kitchen. 'He hasn't been down once since they asked him to resign.'

'He didn't resign. Technically, he's still a member.'

'That isn't the point.'

'What was it all about, anyway?' asked Diana. 'Did anyone ever find out?'

'I don't know for a fact, of course, nobody seems to – but the general view is that somebody close to the family talked too loudly about all that commotion at Vachells – the word seems to be that Francis is walking out on his mother, and taking all the capital with him, leaving her in the lurch. It has to be someone close to one of them, or they couldn't have known the details. And of course now – somehow – it seems to have passed into common knowledge – or belief, anyway.'

'They don't know the details,' Diana pointed out.

'They think they do, somebody has seen to that. And whoever it is must really have it in for Francis. But I can't give you a name.'

'They certainly got the committee all riled up,' said Kim, coming back in with three mugs clutched precariously in her hands.

'I think it has to be somebody on the Committee,' said Val. He took his mug before Kim spilt it, and set it on the coffee table. 'Fortunately, Francis has the Ravenscourts on his side. And one or two others who pack a bit of punch, too. But the atmosphere is still stormy, and I honestly don't think his staying away is going to cure anything. It just makes certain people nod knowingly.'

'What do they say at the Yacht Club?' Kim asked. 'You were there yesterday – and there was certainly something going on when we went to that Regatta Dance – Francis walked out.'

Val said, carefully, 'At the Yacht Club, the current Commodore is Francis's solicitor. I imagine there have been some warnings handed out about ill-informed gossiping, where it seems appropriate. But he hasn't gone back there, either. I asked while I was there yesterday.' He caught Diana's eye. 'Don't glare at me – only if anyone had seen him lately. They hadn't.'

'He's got a lot to see to right now,' Kim pointed out, when Diana said nothing immediately.

'That's what I told them.'

'So what it amounts to,' said Diana, having thought about it, 'is that they asked him to resign because of conduct unbefitting an officer and a gentleman, that was none of their business in the first place?'

'I believe their exact words were "actions unacceptable in a senior member of the Club,"' said Val. 'But something like that, yes. And before you ask, I got that in private from Merlin Ravenscourt, who is actually on the Committee, since he's the Membership Secretary. Obviously he voted against the proposal, but it was approved by a majority. And went to a special enquiry, as you know.'

'Do we know what Francis had to say when they acted on it?' Kim asked, trying to imagine it.

'Apart from, he declined to co-operate, no. Merlin didn't tell me, and I didn't ask. But as you know, he is still a Club member.'

'So he won the day?'

'I think it was what they call a Pyrrhic Victory,' said Val. 'And he hasn't helped his own case, selling his boat like that Some people are saying he can't face them.'

'Drink your coffee, it's getting cold – that's both of you,' ordered Kim, picking up her own. 'It sounds like a problem that only time will cure to me. Poor old Francis, what a position to be in!'

'He's had a lot of practice at that lately,' said Diana, with unintentional bitterness. She wrinkled her nose in thought. 'There was a farm that the vendor wouldn't sell to him back in the summer, there was poor old Sacha here, now this – there must be a common factor there somewhere, if only we could put a finger on it. It almost feels as if it's personal.'

The other two looked at her, and Val said, 'Unlikely, I would have thought. It's just the general effect of ill-natured gossip, Diana. Nothing more.'

'But who is doing the gossiping?' Diana asked, pertinently. 'And where do they get their ammunition? The Vachells don't seem to spread their private affairs around, and Francis certainly didn't.'

'So you're postulating, personal spite? Come on, Diana – he doesn't make close friends easily, I grant you that, but he doesn't make enemies either. He's doesn't make waves, not like some…' He paused, and thought about what he had just said, and added, 'And personal spite implies personal knowledge, in this instance. Who could have that?'

It was just a different way of saying what she had just said herself. Diana said, 'Or envy. Or both.'

'She's right,' said Kim. 'It makes sense, Val.

'Which brings us back to where we began,' Val pointed out. 'Who would have the knowledge, or the malice, to do such a thing? I don't know, you two don't know. End of discussion, really.'

'Francis may know,' said Diana.

'And I'm certainly not going to ask him. Leave it, Diana. Talking gets us nowhere, and time heals all things – or so "they" tell us.'

'That's just an easy get-out!'

'Show me the alternative, then,' Val replied, and Diana was silent.

Francis turned up just before one o'clock, when they had practically given him up. He arrived on the doorstep in working mode, and the muddy 4x4, plus a trailer, waited in the road outside. He seemed to be in a hurry.

'C-can't stop, I'm running late.' He paused at that point to give Diana a quick hug and a kiss before turning his attention to the dog-heap by the door. 'Is this everything?' He swept it up into his arms as if it weighed nothing at all, which Kim and Diana, who had carried it through from the kitchen between them, knew that it didn't. Sacha, recognising that his belongings, and probably himself, were on the move leaped around barking.

'There may be the odd lurking tin of dog food,' Kim told him, and Val said, although they all knew already that there was little point in it, 'We're just going down to the Club now – any chance of you joining us later on?'

'S-sorry. Too much to do, I m-move out tomorrow, t-t-time's running out.' He was already halfway through the door, Sacha jumping round his feet, and Diana seized the dog and the chance he offered together.

'You go on ahead – I'll bring the dog, before you break your neck over him.'

All three of them vanished through the door, and Val and Kim looked at each other.

'Told you he wouldn't,' said Val, although it was actually Kim who had said it, and Kim said, 'That's one very stressed-out man. Let's leave him to Diana, just like you said, for a minute.'

Out by the gate, Francis dropped the dog basket into the trailer, which appeared to be fairly full already with empty tea chests, and opened the back door of the car for the dog. Once Sacha was safely inside and the door shut again, he turned to Diana. She looked at him, a long, measuring look, and came to the same conclusion as her twin.

'That was a bit abrupt,' she suggested, without confrontation.

'T-true, though. There's a van coming to p-pick up all my f-f-furniture and s-s-stuff f-first thing t-t-tomorrow and take it into st-store. It'll take m-me the rest of the day to g-get it organised.'

Momentarily sidetracked, Diana asked, 'Do you have a lot of furniture, then?'

'No-no.' He flashed her a sudden smile. 'M-mainly b-b-books, but they have to be p-packed up.'

Well, that probably explained the tea chests, or some of them. There seemed to be quite a lot. Diana asked, because it would obviously concern her eventually, 'You said "mainly". Much else?'

Francis gave her a grave look, that she sensed had a certain amount of amusement behind it which was a relief after the last few minutes. He said, 'S-some bookcases, a d-desk, three p-p-pictures and a g-grand piano. P-plus m-m-most of the stuff in the f-f-flat.'

It took quite a lot to render Diana completely speechless, but at least one item on that short list managed it. She just looked at him, wide-eyed. Francis took advantage of the pause to say, 'I d-don't know if I'll get t-t-to see you this evening, b-but I'll g-give you a ring later anyway. I'll be t-tied up for the next c-couple of days, b-but after that I c-c-can spend some t-t-time with you.'

'That'll be nice,' said Diana. She added, 'Val is off back to London this evening, and Kim is back to work at the pub tomorrow, so I'll be on my own a lot of the day. If there's anything I can do that's useful, just ask me, I shall feel a bit at a loose end after the last few days.'

'I'll r-r-remember that.'

They looked at each other for a minute, and then Francis took her in his arms.

'N-no school bus this time,' he observed, and Diana giggled. Their engagement kiss, which had taken place on a bench down by the foreshore, had been witnessed by a busload of secondary-school pupils on their way home for tea, and had been accompanied by cheering, catcalls and applause. This one took place more quietly, but was equally satisfactory.

'I must go,' said Francis, regretfully, at the end of it.

'Ring me. Please. I shall miss you.'

'Only a couple of days. M-m-maybe I'll g-g-get a chance to see you anyway.'

'I hope so.'

One more kiss, quicker this time, and then he opened the door of the car.

'Do you really have a grand piano?' asked Diana, still thinking it had been a joke and laughing as she said it.

'Yes,' said Francis. He slid in behind the wheel and slammed the door, winding the window down as he did so.

'And do you play it?' asked Diana.

'N-now and then. S-s-see you.' The engine roared into life and he drove off, waving to her out of the open window and with Sacha's face pressed against the rear one, his tail a blur of joyous activity. Diana stood there until he was out of sight. Then she said, to the empty air, 'What have I let myself in for?' before turning to go back into the house.

'Right,' said Val, getting to his feet. 'If you're both ready, shall we be on our way?'

Diana gave voice to the thought in the forefront of her mind. 'He says he has a grand piano.'

'Well…people do,' ventured Kim, and asked the same question her twin had asked. 'Does he play it?'

'So he says, although where he finds the time, I can't imagine.'

'Come on,' said Val, making for the door, 'you can discuss it in the car if it's that important to you. I need a drink. And if he's telling the truth, I hope he also has a big, big farmhouse to accommodate it!'

And so do I, Diana thought, to both of those, and then, for the second time, 'What have I done? What else don't I know about this man I mean to marry?' and naturally enough, found no answers. Which was not to say that there were none, and before long she would be finding a few, but that was still in the future. There was another scene to play out before events reached that point, and the curtain was already going up even as they walked to the Sailing Club – it was too close to be worth taking the car, and Kim insisted the walk would do them good, and look, the sun was shining!

Francis parked the 4x4 and its trailer in the enclosed courtyard in front of the house, which he didn't normally do, but a lot of the books he had mentioned to Diana were in the office inside the main house, where estate and household financial affairs were alike conducted, only the day-to-day farm business being done in the smaller office adjoining the stables in the yard. Which was not to say that said books were entirely about agriculture and finance; they were not. Some of the tea chests needed to be put in this office, and there was no point in hauling them all through the house from the back door, and so it happened that he came through the front door well laden, with Sacha dancing at his heels and overjoyed to be home again, and by coincidence, happy or otherwise remained to be seen, ran into his mother in the hall.

To say that Mary Vachell-Chillingworth was startled, would be seriously to understate her reaction. She stopped in her tracks.

'Good gracious!' she exclaimed. 'Isn't that Sacha?'

Francis lowered his burden of tea chests onto the tiled floor; he had been prepared for this, but times had changed lately; the goalposts had been moved a considerable distance. He said, 'Yes,' and waited to see what happened next. Sacha was bouncing around in front of Mary, delighted to be home and to see her again; she stooped and stroked his head with such obvious affection and relief that even if Francis hadn't done a lot of re-thinking lately, he would have done some now.

'I'm so glad,' said Mary. 'I thought he had died, and I was sorry for it. He's a good dog. Sit, now!' This to the dog, who obediently sat at her feet.

'He n-n-nearly did,' said Francis. She straightened up from patting the dog and looked him straight in the eye.

'You blamed me, didn't you?' she said.

'I w-w-wondered. It d-d-definitely happened here.'

'You should have known I would never do such a thing!'

'I d-d-do now,' said Francis.

'So, where did you take him? The kennels?'

'T-to a s-s-safe place.'

There was a pause there, while they both did some thinking. At one time, they had each of them jumped to a wrong conclusion, and not for the first time; they knew that now, but there had to be a right one this time, too. Mary spoke first, but without absolute conviction.

'It must have been someone on one of the farms, putting down rat poison. He must have caught a poisoned rat. Did you ask?'

'No.' Francis was at least sure on this one, although about nothing else. 'No, farmers d-d-don't use arsenic-b-b-based poisons th-the-these d-days. It's illegal.'

'And this was arsenic-based?'

'S-s-so the vet said.'

There was another pause then. Mary hesitated to say what had immediately leapt into her head, which she would have classified as an unthinkable thought if she hadn't found herself thinking it now. Francis was only a step behind her, even without her particular knowledge: he had other evidence in his own recent experiences, only needing a confirmation which he had intended to ask for anyway when the time was right. Perhaps that time was now. He asked, 'D-do you remember? D-d-did anyone else c-c-come here that day? N-not the p-postman or s-s-someone l-like that. Some v-v-visitor.'

'Yes,' said Mary, slowly. She paused for a moment, wondering if she should say the name, but there was nothing to be gained from holding things back, he would only ask her housekeeper. She said, 'That tiresome woman, Jennifer Carruthers came, wanting to talk some rubbish about the Arts & Crafts Exhibition in town.' She stopped. Francis asked as if casually, but she could see that he was ahead of her already, 'D-d-did she come alone?'

'Her son drove her,' said Mary: once more, there was no point in holding back the information; again, he had only to ask, and Francis said, 'Shit!' It was exactly what he had expected to hear and hoped not to. Sacha, sensing an atmosphere, had got to his feet and stood alert to the echo of his master's angry expletive, and there was an electric pause. Mary broke it.

'Francis, don't jump to conclusions here! All of that was twenty years and more ago, and you can prove nothing.' She had to say that, even if she knew that it was seeds of discretion sown on stony ground, and his immediate response confirmed that.

'W-while he was here, d-d-did he leave the -r-room at all?'

'He asked if he could take a look around the garden while we talked. It was reasonable, Jennifer is very boring and he was not concerned with the Exhibition.' A small part of her wished she hadn't had to say that. She said, and heard her own voice, crisp and authoritative and winced inside, 'Francis, don't do anything hasty, please? You can prove nothing, I repeat, and Sacha survived.'

But Francis was thinking back. There had been that fiasco at the Regatta Dance back in the summer: Jennifer Carruthers had instigated that. There was the present unresolvable stand-off with the Ember Valley Sailing Club: Max Carruthers was on the Committee, he was the Sailing Secretary, and now there was this, the worst of all: the attempted murder of his best friend. It was all too much to be coincidence.

Well, he had known for a long time that Max Carruthers was a slimeball and a liar; he had known it for years, and had said so on one memorable occasion, and with cataclysmic results. That was at the root of all this trouble he was having now? A teenage quarrel?

It was like watching an approaching thunderstorm, Mary thought now, watching him. Quick flashes on the horizon, and an occasional distant warning rumble, a heavy threat in the air. Time to take sides, and not before time. She said, with more decision than she actually felt, 'Francis, please don't act before you have thought this out properly. I suggest that you gather some firm evidence before you do, or say, anything at all.' Or better still, leave it alone, but she knew he wouldn't do that; at least one reason was now sitting warmly on her feet.

'And h-how d-do you suggest I do th-that?' He sounded dangerous, but at least he had asked.

'Talk to your solicitor,' said Mary, firmly. 'Jerry Nankervis will advise you what you can, and can't do with impunity. Or better still, talk to his ex-wife, Benita knows her and can introduce you. Jennifer Carruthers has been destroying her reputation along with yours, don't think you are the only sufferer, the woman is poison and seems to believe she's so important that she can say what she likes. But whatever you do, don't go on a crusade. It will only make things worse!'

Francis seized onto one phrase in that speech, she hoped he had listened to the rest of it too.

'Y-you kn-know about this witch-hunt?'

'My dear Francis, I, too, am a long-standing member of the Yacht Club, if you recall. Of course I have heard all about it, and Jennifer Carruthers was at the back of that, too, I understand.'

'M-m-more like, in the f-front,' said Francis. Jennifer Carruthers had been standing in the entrance foyer, he recalled, talking in a loud voice to her friends about things that it wasn't her business to either know or to advertise if she did somehow know them, exactly like the present situation at the Sailing Club. He had stormed out, he remembered, for what that had achieved, and spoiled Tamsin's evening and made her cry. He had not been a witness to the sequel, since he had already left, but Merlin's wife, Julie-Anne, had apparently set about the Carruthers hyena with American forthrightness, and being married to a Ravenscourt, had got away with it and won the encounter. He had almost wished he had stayed to see it when Merlin had told him about it. He thought about that now.

At least he had apparently paused to think, Mary thought, watching him, although about what, exactly she couldn't be sure: he still looked stormy. She followed up on her advantage. 'Talk to Benita, you will see her tomorrow,' and then she remembered exactly why he would be seeing Benita tomorrow, and her heart clenched. What a mess they had got themselves in, even this present talk, in which they were − more or less, anyway − on the same side, had an undercurrent to it. Would things ever improve between them to the point where they were back with their old, happy, relationship as mother and son, or had Christopher and his spoilt-brat behaviour destroyed that for good? For goodness' sake, she had been trying to push him around right now − although that had been from necessity, he had looked as if he was about to launch out on a suicide mission! She drew a deep breath. Thinking back to the past had reminded her of another high-handed decision she had taken it upon herself to make. She wondered whether to mention it now, or to let it slide into oblivion and hope he would never find out. That was if he didn't already know…

Because she was, had always been, an honest and forthright person, Mary decided to go for a clean sweep; they could not rebuild a relationship if there was still debris on the site. She would like to rebuild, she had known this for weeks now, and it would be good to have everything in the open before he finally left. It was time to change the subject anyway; she just hoped she wasn't about to do it with a bomb.

'Do you still see Tamsin?' she asked, as lightly as she could manage, which wasn't very.

The abrupt change of subject had knocked Francis off course. He simply stared at her blankly. He said the first thing that came into his head. Unfortunately, it wasn't also the best one.

'H–how d–d–did you find out th–th–that I ever had?'

Mary said, more sharply than she had intended, 'I wasn't spying on you, if that's what you're thinking. It was common knowledge, Francis. She was seen with you in your car, she was seen with you in the Ravenscourt Arms, she was riding your horse, do you think people don't notice these things?'

'And is this Jennifer Carruthers at work again?' He sounded dangerous. Mary, knowing from experience how easily she could pick a fight with him these days, answered softly.

'Jennifer did mention it, but so also did others. You didn't make a secret of it, the whole family knew! And they were pleased to see it, Francis. You keep yourself apart too much – and before you tell me why, I already know! We have travelled that road, let us not go there again.'

'You t–t–told Kim about me. W–why?' He sounded fierce, but this time it was his mother's turn to be caught on the wrong foot.

'Kim?' she said. 'I have never, to my knowledge, seen Kim since she was a baby! She went to New Zealand with Rodney Ford and his wife…' She broke off. 'That was Kim?'

'Th–they're identical t–twins.'

'I thought that was Tamsin. It was Tamsin who came here one day, looking for you.' She hesitated. 'I assumed it was.'

'Th–that time, it was. N–n–n–not the second. And you h–haven't answered m–m–my question.'

Mary took a deep breath, and momentarily closed her eyes. Quite suddenly, she was aware of a burning need to get every card on the table before he was finally gone. If she did that, there might be a future other than the emptiness that she saw ahead of her now. She said, 'I didn't think that you would ever tell her yourself, and that if you did not, then you would never ask her to marry you.'

Francis said, in a voice she didn't recognise, 'Kim thought you were warning her off.'

'Then Kim was wrong. And now, if you plan to finish packing your library today, you had better take those tea chests into the study and get on with it.' She had begun to turn away, but what Francis said next stopped her in her tracks.

'I am going to marry her. I hope th-that's all right with you.' It was a challenge, she heard it in the tone of his voice and made herself speak calmly.

'I have never believed in visiting the sins of the fathers upon the sons. Nor yet the sins of the mothers upon the daughters, as in this case. Sarah was happy with older men—' she tried to keep the bitterness out of her voice and almost succeeded, '—Tamsin is her daughter, and heaven knows who her father may be. I will look forward to knowing her better.' She turned away towards the door of the drawing-room, and Francis, after a brief hesitation, picked up a tea chest and headed for the study, his dog at his heels. He went back for the other two, and then closed the study door and leaned against it, cradling his right hand in his left and mentally reviewing what had just taken place. Whatever it had all been about, he realised ruefully, it was going to be some while before he should pick up anything valuable. Fortunately, books didn't break if you dropped them. He pushed himself upright again and set one-handedly to work. Work at least stopped you thinking too much.

Mary, who also had things that she ought to be doing, sat down in an armchair and stared at the wall. She felt a hundred years old after that encounter, instead of her actual seventy-seven, and only time would tell what she had actually done. There was no guarantee that the last hope she had uttered would ever be fulfilled. A horrible feeling that time was running out, and the last drops of her life were running away with it, swept over her.

She had no idea what would happen next, and tomorrow, when her – yes, her beloved only son might be gone away for ever, loomed over her like a dark cloud.

So this was what it felt like to have a broken heart...

VI

The visit to the Sailing Club had turned out to be rather a mixed blessing. People came up to ask Val why he hadn't been racing over the weekend, and when he said that he had been busy, said things like 'What, on a Sunday?' in a disbelieving way, so that in the end, they ended up telling people about the tree falling on the cottage, which it turned out that most of them knew about already, having driven past it,- although not all of them had known that Kim and Diana lived there. Of course it did answer the question of why Val had been too busy to sail, but it did pose others, less easy to answer. There was a lot of concerned sympathy for Diana's bruised and cut cheekbone to begin with, but the discussion obviously wouldn't stop there.

'Who does that place belong to, anyway?' asked Val's regular crew, Rob Lambert. 'I hope you mean to take him to the cleaners, putting you in danger like that!'and there was a murmur of agreement round the bar, where they happened to be standing at the time.

'Probably Harold March,' said somebody else. 'Isn't it part of his farm? But he'll be insured, presumably. Not that it excuses him.'

Kim hesitated. It was obvious that Diana wasn't going to answer these pertinent questions, but in the present climate of opinion, it would be unfair to throw Francis to the lions in his absence. She had no idea who, among those around them, was on what side, and Val wasn't helping her either. And then the solution, which was conveniently buried in her subconscious, came back to her; according to the details on her lease, Francis didn't necessarily own the cottage personally; he had signed the lease, yes, but on behalf of...who? What? Some company...she groped about in her memory. She said, slowly, 'I'm trying to remember...I think it belongs to some company or other...I rented it through a letting agent in the town...' It came back to her complete as she was speaking, and she ended thankfully, 'Vachell Farm Holdings, something like that. But it wasn't their tree that fell.'

'Oh God, it had to be them!' said somebody else, and added, 'I thought all their land was to the west of here.'

'Don't ask me,' said Kim, shrugging her shoulders. 'I was only the tenant.'

'Pity Francis isn't here, we could ask him,' said somebody else, in a lazy, don't particularly care, sort of voice that for some reason made Kim turn her head to look at him. A slim, fair man with already-thinning curly hair, maybe in his mid-thirties, she had seen him around before, she recalled. Wasn't he on the Committee, or something? She didn't think she had ever heard his name, or if she had, she couldn't recall it. 'Anyway, I thought all the Vachell properties were individually owned?' He made it into a question. 'Isn't the Company a tax dodge, or something?'

'Is it relevant anyway?' Val asked. 'Kim says it isn't their tree. And in any case, the Council had passed it as safe.'

The Council appeared not to interest the fair man. He just smiled and said, 'Then that's all right, isn't it? They'll have to pay up. Good thing too.' He moved away then, with a nod in their direction, and their friends closed in on the gap that he left.

The brief exchange had left a bad taste behind it, for some reason. Kim thought that Val thought so too, and Diana had been very quiet throughout. She was glad when Merlin Ravenscourt appeared at her elbow, pint in hand, and whispered in her ear, 'Don't worry, Kim. All the heavy artillery is ranged alongside Francis. We'll defeat the enemy, don't doubt it.'

'Was he the enemy? That slimy man?' The adjective jumped into her mouth unsought, but it only made Merlin laugh.

'Max Carruthers. Our revered Sailing Secretary. He seems to have it in for Francis just lately…' He let the statement tail off with an accompanying shrug of his shoulders. 'You should tell Francis, when you see him, that it would help his case if he showed his face occasionally. I know he's busy right now, but when he gets a break, maybe? When does he move out of Vachells, do you know? I know when he takes over Burnthouse, but I have an idea it isn't straight away, so maybe then he could make the effort? We've still got all his cattle at the Place for a while yet, so he won't have that much to do.'

'He has to go up to London some time,' said Kim, evasively, and Merlin said, 'OK, but just pass the message on, would you?' He moved off to talk to someone else, and Diana appeared in his place.

'I'm wishing I'd stayed at home,' she said bluntly. 'What was that man getting at? Not Merlin – the one making nasty innuendoes.'

'I have no idea, but I get a distinct impression that he hasn't got it all his own way; probably, he should duck below the revetment while he has a chance. Come on, let's go and talk to Penny – look, she's over there – at least she won't need to question us about the tree! We can leave the men to their sailing talk.'

Penny was sitting at a table with two of her friends, they shifted up to make room for the twins.

'We're having some Girl Time,' Penny explained, but it wasn't to be for long. Very shortly, Val, Rob and Merlin and his wife, Julie-Anne, came to join them and they had to push two tables together.

'But I shall have to go home to lunch quite soon, or my mother will shoot me,' Rob remarked, and Penny said, 'Mine too. Although I did warn her the Moonrakers were racing at ten o'clock.' She looked at Val. 'She asked me if you would be sailing today?'

'Next weekend. And I did tell her that, before I left this morning.'

'Are you going straight back to London from here?'

'More or less. Later on though.'

Penny grinned across at Kim. 'I see. And what will Diana do? Walk the dog?'

Diana was about to say that the dog had gone home to Vachells, but stopped with her mouth open ready to speak. An odd little shiver crawled up her spine; who knew who might be listening? Then she gave herself a mental shake. Stop it, Diana! You're getting as bad as Kim with her premonitions and things! You'll be seeing ghosts next thing you know! 'I shall read a book,' she said, instead, and Penny asked, '"Fifty Shades of Grey"?'

Altogether, there had been more successful visits to the Club for a Sunday lunchtime drink. They all three of them thought it as they walked back to Romans, but none of them said it. Only Kim said, as they reached the front door, 'It'll be odd without the dog to greet us,' and pushed it open on quietness and silence.

It was even worse when, some time later, Val took his leave of them and set off for London in his car. The twins were left looking at each other.

'It's going to be a very quiet evening,' said Kim. 'What's Francis doing, did he say? Will you be seeing him, do you think?'

'He said he'd ring sometime. I think he's packing stuff – a lot of it is going into store for now. Caravans come fully furnished.'

'You shouldn't let him live in it on his own, not on an empty farm,' said Kim, voicing a thought that was not new. 'It'll be horribly quiet and lonely in the evenings when the builders have gone, and at night – a bit like the cottage was, and we had each other.'

'I know,' said Diana, who had obviously thought about this too, but found no immediate solution; she rather thought that, if there was one, it had to come from Francis.

Kim walked across to the television and switched it on, simply for company and the sound of a human voice. She said, 'What will you do tomorrow? I shall be at work from eleven until three. You'll be all on your own.'

'I might drive into town and do some more shopping,' said Diana, but listlessly. 'Francis has my mobile number if he wants me. I couldn't just sit here on my own, I'd go mad! At least at the cottage, you could go out and dig the garden.'

'You could weed the tubs,' suggested Kim, with a grin.

'I might pull out the plants,' said Diana, and they both laughed. It made them feel better. Kim switched on the electric fire, for the evenings were getting chilly this late in September, and then put on the lights as well, although it wasn't anywhere near dark yet. Then she headed for the kitchen.

'I'm going to make some coffee. Fancy a sandwich with it? We didn't get any lunch, unless you count crisps – Val did ask if I wanted a sausage roll or something, but I didn't fancy it—'

'That sounds like a plan.' Diana reached for the TV Times and flipped it open. 'I'll check what there is to keep us entertained while we eat it, shall I?'

Or we could talk to each other, Kim thought as she opened the fridge for the milk, although what we would talk about is a good question. The grand piano? Why do I feel that's only the tip of an iceber? She peered into the chilly depths and called, 'Cheese, Egg, Ham, Tomato. Which?' and Diana called back, 'Ham – with French mustard. With a tomato on the side.' and the atmosphere slipped back on the words to normal-in-the-cottage mode. It's just this posh house that's thrown us, Kim decided, we're more used to slumming it. And the Vachells, whoever they are, suddenly breathing down our necks. But it'll be all right. It has to be.

They ate their sandwiches and drank their coffee in front of an entertaining quiz show, trying not to look at the empty hearthrug where a black and white collie was used to lie.

Francis didn't ring.

He didn't immediately ring in the morning, either, and Kim went off to work leaving Diana sitting listlessly on the sofa, turning the pages of a magazine without bothering to do more than glance at them.

'I'll be back about three,' said Kim, as she prepared to leave. 'Leave me a note, if you decide to go out.'

'Will do.'

Kim looked at her for a moment, but there was really nothing to say that hadn't been said already, so she said 'See you then,' and left.

She was barely through the door, when Diana's mobile broke into song. She looked at it, but didn't recognise the number – which might be a good sign, she realised. She picked it up eagerly.

'Hello?'

'T-tamsin! I thought you m-m-might have g-gone out.' No apologies for not having rung last night, she noticed.

'No, I'm here.'

'L-look – did you mean it yesterd-day? When you s-s-said you'd lend m-me a hand?'

'Of course I did!' She paused. 'I take it, you can do with one?'

'If you've the-the time, I n-n-need someone to m-m-meet me at Shortlanesend and th-then drive me back here. I h-have to get both cars over there, and I c-can only drive one at a t-t-time.'

'I've the time, but where's Shortlanesend? You'll have to give me directions.'

'P-put the p-p-postcode in your Satnav. I t-t-take it you have one?'

Diana had, she told him, and he gave her the code, which she wrote down on the open page of her now-to-be-abandoned magazine.

'I'll m-m-meet you there in about half an hour, th-then.' End of conversation.

Since Diana had no idea how long it would take to drive to Shortlanesend, or even where it might be located, she wrote a swift note to Kim in case she wasn't back before three, and went out to her car. It was amazing, she thought in amazement, how one moment you could be glooming over a boring old magazine, and the next be dancing on air. She entered the code, started the engine, reversed carefully out of the parking slot, and obeying the instructions from the Satnav, headed off for the main road, and although she didn't realise it at the time, took the next step up what was to turn out to be a very steep learning curve, of which the grand piano had been only the beginning. She had never met any of the Vachells before, except for Clare, that was, who helped Francis with his horses, but she was only about eighteen and hardly counted. There was going to be a lot to learn, probably on both sides. She made a face at the windscreen.

Shortlanesend lay about midway between Shearwater and Emberton, and turned out to be a mellow golden farmhouse of venerable age with mullioned windows and a beautiful pillared front porch, tucked snugly under the rolling downs. A sprawl of buildings stood round a gated yard to the east, to the west were what looked like orchards; it was all very clean and cared-for. There was no immediate sign of either of Francis's cars, so Diana parked her own in front of the house and went over to the yard gate to see if he had parked in the yard, but he hadn't. There was a tractor there, and a horsebox, but no Discovery, no Mercedes – although, come to think, didn't she recognise the number plate on the horsebox? She was wondering about this when a woman came out of what seemed to be a stable block to the right of the yard, and came over to her, smiling.

'You must be Tamsin – you're the living spit of Kim! Hello, I'm your new landlord's wife, Benita.' She held out her hand for Diana to take, but leaned over the gate to kiss her cheek as well. 'Lovely to meet you – come in – hang on, I'll open the gate.' She added, as she did so, 'Francis isn't here yet, but he shouldn't be too long, they were still loading when he rang. Come on in.'

Diana went through the gate, and Benita Vachell closed it behind her. 'Come over to the house – we can have a cup of tea while we wait for him to get here, and get to know each other.' She gave Diana a quick, friendly smile. 'It seems we're going to need to do that anyway, we might as well start right here.' She was leading the way to the back door while she was speaking, and when they reached it she pushed it open and led the way inside, Diana stopped on the threshold with a gasp, for the kitchen was a beautiful old period piece, wooden dresser, beautiful china to decorate it, wooden cupboards, big kitchen table, the whole works, it was like a set for an historical TV series. The only slightly more modern touch was a big old Aga, sitting under the huge arch of the fireplace.

'Good gracious,' she exclaimed, before she could stop herself, and Benita grinned at her.

'Great, isn't it? Really inconvenient of course, but at least it has electricity, we don't have to use candles! And there is some more up-to-date stuff lurking in the scullery, we don't still use a mangle, for instance. Not sure that they didn't at Burnthouse, mind you – don't just stand there. Come right in and sit down.'

'You know Burnthouse?' asked Diana, accepting the invitation and pulling out a chair. She sat down, and Benita said, while moving a kettle onto the hotplate of the Aga, 'Yes, but it was some years back. I don't suppose it's improved in the meantime, but I won't spoil it for you by trying to describe it. You have to see it for yourself really to appreciate it!' She reached two mugs down from the dresser and ranged them on the table. 'Tea or coffee?'

'Either – I'm not fussy, whatever you're having yourself.'

'Tea then.' Benita busied herself with teabags and hot water, vanished for a minute through what was presumably the scullery door, and returned with a jug of milk. Only then did she sit down, a mug of tea in front of each of them and the jug in between.

'Now tell me all,' she invited. 'How did you meet Francis? – which incidentally, was the best thing that has happened to him for years, and the whole family is applauding!'

Like the kids at the bus stop, Diana thought, and hid a smile. She said, 'I didn't think they knew anything about me,' and Benita said, much as Mary had done earlier, to Francis, 'Oh, come on, Tamsin! You neither of you made much of a secret of it! Apart from Clare running to and fro from Vachells with eggs and lettuces and stuff, you were seen in his car, on his horse, in the pub in Shearwater, at the Regatta Dance, you even drove him to the hospital that time he tried to break his neck – we've all been holding our breath, hoping for a happy ending. It's time the poor man had a bit of luck, life has dealt him a really, really shitty hand so far!'

'Goodness,' said Diana, not sure if she liked this revelation, for if the

Vachells had noticed what had been going on, who else might have done the same?

'We weren't spying on you,' Benita assured her, reading her expression. 'It's just that neither of you seemed to be making the least attempt to hide it.' She paused to take a breath. 'Tamsin, if I ask you a really, really, impertinent question, will you promise to forgive me?'

'That depends on what it is, doesn't it?'

'It's this. If Francis asked you, would you marry him?'

Diana gave up. If this was to be the Vachells attitude generally, things were looking good. She said, 'He has, and yes, I will. But please, don't tell the whole world just yet. My parents have only just heard that he even exists!"

'Wo!' said Benita. She raised her mug in a toast. 'Here's to you, the bravest woman in Dorset!'

'I can drink to that,' said Diana, clinking her own mug against Benita's. They smiled at each other.

'We must have a really good talk together,' said Benita, with satisfaction. 'I'm sure that Francis hasn't told you the half of it – but not now, it isn't the moment! I just heard an engine roaring, out in the yard.'

Diana nearly choked on her tea, and Benita grinned at her.

'Off you go then, I'll forgive you.' She took a sip of her own tea and smiled, and Diana made a dive for the back door. 'Fetch him in here,' Benita called after her. 'I'll put the kettle on again—' Diana had already gone; she smiled to herself and rose to her feet to move the kettle.

Out in the yard, Francis and another man were unhitching the trailer from the 4x4 and pushing it into an open barn, with Sacha trying to trip them up, weaving round their feet. There didn't seem to be much in it this time; a couple of suitcases and some cardboard boxes that, from their printed sides, should contain a computer and a printer respectively, and a small wooden filing cabinet. Probably the last trip, then.

Francis hadn't noticed her yet; Diana waited until he turned round, the boxed computer in his arms, and saw her before she spoke to him. She didn't want to startle him so that he dropped anything valuable, or tripped over the dog or something, although Sacha had now gone off, sniffing round the stable block with enthusiasm.

'Hello,' she said, then.

'I s-saw your car outside.' He smiled at her. 'Th-thank you for c-c-coming. J–just let me get this inside, and I'll s-s-say hello p-properly.' The other man – well, not much more than a boy really, from his slightly scruffy appearance possibly one of the farm workers, grinned and said hello, hefting the suitcases out onto the ground before turning back for the printer. Francis had headed for the back door, Diana picked up the smaller of the two cases and followed him, the boy bringing up the rear.

Once the computer was safely on the kitchen table, Francis kept his promise and swept her into his arms, regardless of the audience, and kissed her soundly before turning back to the door. 'I'll j–just fetch in the r-r-rest…' He and the boy disappeared again, and Benita met Diana's eyes with a rueful smile.

'No finesse, my husband's cousin, you notice?' she said. 'Is there much more? He's taken over a whole loose box and a henhouse already. And that's without even bringing us a horse to look after.'

'Another box and a filing cabinet. And another suitcase. Oh, and a dog.'

'He'll never get a filing cabinet upstairs,' said Benita. She looked around her helplessly. 'It had better go in the scullery, it might fit between the vegetable rack and the fridge…it's only for a couple of weeks, after all.'

Diana asked, curiously, 'So what did he put in the henhouse?' It seemed a strange place to store one's worldly goods, but Benita answered, 'Hens, of course.'

Of course. Diana decided not to follow that thread right now. She said, 'Should we go and check the space in the scullery?'

'You do that – I'll take this suitcase out of the way upstairs.' Benita picked it up and staggered a bit, mostly for effect. 'He can carry the computer through to the office himself. I wouldn't be responsible for dropping it!"

Diana went through into the scullery, which was large, airy and well-equipped with essential electrical goods, feeling slightly out of breath. There was a whole new atmosphere in this place, and she had already realised even in that short encounter that Francis, for all he looked as if he hadn't slept properly for a week, was different here, too.

Interesting. She added the impression to those she had already garnered and turned her attention to the vegetable rack.

The filing cabinet safely squeezed between the fridge and the vegetables, and the rest of the items banished elsewhere, Benita offered tea again, but Francis was in a hurry to be off.

'Pity,' said Benita, but not arguing with him. 'I was just getting to know Tamsin – look,' She turned to Diana, 'why don't you come back this evening, and have supper with us? Then we can get to know you properly, and you can meet Ernest too – we'd like that. It'll just be the four of us – the kids will have tea when they get back from school, they always come back starving, I don't think they can feed them properly, and be off upstairs with their homework by then – maybe with their homework, you never know your luck! Will you?'

Diana looked at Francis for guidance, but he was looking enigmatic and didn't help her. She made her own decision; Kim would just have to live with it. 'Yes, I'd like that. Thank you. What time would you like me to come?'

'Make it about half-six – I'll have cleared the children away by then. And Francis, you can leave the dog here if you want – he'll be all right, and the children will be back soon, and presumably so will you. Tamsin won't want him slobbering all over her nice car and I promise I'll watch him.'

The drive back to Vachells was a silent one. Diana drove, and Francis, having run the front passenger seat back as far as it would go to accommodate his six-foot plus, appeared to have gone to sleep. It wasn't until they were turning off the main road for Emberton, that he spoke.

'M-my mother w-w-would like to m-meet you before you go back to Romans.'

'What?' Diana missed the gear she was just changing, and it made an awful scrunching noise with which she entirely sympathised.

'W-we talked yesterday.'

'But she hates me! She tried to warn me off!'

'Sh-she says n-n-not. She s-says she w-w-wanted you to know the t-t-truth b-because I w-wouldn't tell you. And she was r-r-right.'

When you were driving a car wasn't the best time to hear things like this. Diana's thoughts were whirling so that she nearly missed the turning in Tildown, screeching round it abruptly and then stepping on the brake so hard that she stopped the car altogether, and stalled the engine. She took a deep breath and started the car again.

'Is there no end to the pain your father and my mother caused between them?' she heard herself asking, such anger in her voice that she almost made herself jump.

'W-we must be about th-there, I w-w-would think.' He was looking at her, she could feel it even without turning her head. How could he be so cool about it? But then, she thought, of course he's had time to think. Probably he's known this since yesterday...and that's why he didn't ring last night. It must have shocked him rigid, too.

'She must hate me,' she said, for the second time.

'N-no – m-mind the t-t-turning – she doesn't hate you.'

They screeched round another turning, and Diana said, trying to lighten the atmosphere, 'You're going to be sorry you asked me for a lift...I'm sorry.'

'S-so is my m-m-mother. S-so am I, c-c-come to that. Speak to her T-tamsin. P-please.'

'I will then, if you think I should. But it won't be easy.'

'N-n-not for any of us, b-b-but we need to t-t-try,' said Francis, but left it there. Diana managed to make the turn into the narrow lane that led only to Vachells without further incident, and the silence came back until they were approaching the farm gate.

'G-go into the c-c-courtyard,' Francis told her, 'it's easier to t-t-turn.'

The last time she had been in this courtyard, was the night he had nearly been murdered; Diana, acutely aware of this, obediently drove through the gates and parked alongside his Mercedes, outside the beautiful house, once again built of the golden stone that seemed to be the thing round her, that he would never now inherit. His cousin Cosmo would do that. She wondered if he was thinking the same thing, and if he minded but didn't ask; it had been his own idea, after all. There was something more important – immediate – to say.

'Francis, I can't do this – to her, or to you. She must hate me – my mother stole her husband, ruined her relationship with you, ruined her life, caused all that misery...how can she want to even set eyes on me? It'll be like turning a knife in an open wound, every time she has to see me...her grandchildren will be my mother's too – oh God, Francis, what are we doing?' Her voice broke, she turned her face away from him so that he wouldn't see the tears in her eyes.

Francis sympathised, both with Diana and with his mother, but it was true that he had been granted the time to think this one out. He said, 'W-we're b-building a b-b-bridge, T-tamsin. W-we have t-t-to, or it w-w-will r-ruin the rest of our l-lives along with w-what's alr-ready gone. M-my mother s-s-said she w-wouldn't visit the sins of the f-f-fathers on the s-sons. She m-meant me – and you, too. It c-cost her to s-speak to Kim th-that time, however m-much of a m-m-mess she made of it – d-don't w-w-waste that. Please. And I l-love you.' He opened the door of the car. 'C-come on. W-whatever happened in the p-p-past w-w-wasn't your d-d-doing, you were th-three years old. Just r-r-remember that.'

Diana opened her own door, and reluctantly followed him across the courtyard to the front door of the house. She really, really didn't want to do this, and was shamed by the courage and – yes, the generosity – of both Francis and his mother. But they were right, of course they were. If she intended to marry Francis, as she most certainly did, then she would have to pay the price, or…she realised that she had not got that right. If she intended to marry Francis, as she most certainly did, then his mother had to pay the price, or lose her son finally. She would be wrong to think otherwise, and put like that, and remembering too what Benita had told her only this afternoon, it all became suddenly easy.

Mary had seen the little red car pull in through the gate from the hall window, she did not relish the thought of the coming encounter, but like Diana, and Francis too, she knew that it had to be done. She stiffened her back and walked out into the hall to greet them as they came through the door. For a moment there was deadlock, none of the three of them knew what to do, or to say, then Mary stepped forward, her hand held out in welcome.

'Tamsin. How good to meet you at last, I have been hearing so many rumours about you and my son here!' She tried to put a laugh into her voice, and almost succeeded. Diana took the outstretched hand and then, by mutual consent, they released the clasp and stepped back, assessing each other. Francis's mother looked as shattered as he did himself, Diana thought, and felt sorry for her. Mary thought, she's not so very like Sarah after all: same colouring, but far more character in her face. She has lovely eyes, like a lion's, Sarah's were that insipid grey colour. Someone had to speak though, and it was unlikely to be Francis, who was simply standing there, being a man. Mary said, trying to put a smile in her voice, 'Francis tells me that you are brave enough to marry him. I hope you will be very happy together,' and thought that she sounded as if she was reading the words from a rather boring script.

'Thank you. I'm sure that we will.'

She had a good speaking voice, Tamsin: she had been gently brought up, that was obvious, maybe some of it would rub off on her own son? Mary began to relax just a little. She turned to her the son in question,, changing the direction of the conversation, if you could call it that, to more practical matters. 'I have asked Mrs Fairburn to strip the pillows, the quilt and the blankets from your bed and to pack them up for you to take with you, you will need warm bedding if you persist in living in a caravan in midwinter. And I have asked her to look out some bed linen and towels from the linen cupboard to tide you over until you can move into the house, when Tamsin will no doubt wish to buy new. There is plenty here to spare.'

Francis looked taken aback, so Diana replied for him. 'That's very thoughtful of you, Mrs Vachell-Chillingworth – men never think of things like that for themselves, do they?'

'This one you've chosen certainly doesn't,' said Mary, with grim humour. 'And please call me Mary – Mrs Vachell-Chillingworth is such a mouthful, and I daresay we shall be meeting again.'

'Thank you – Mary,' said Diana. 'I'm sure that we will.'

Francis found his voice at last. 'Th-thanks. You're r-right, I hadn't thought.' He looked at his watch, although he had no immediate need to know the time. 'I should get on – th-there's still a f-f-few things in the f-farm office I n-n-need to sort out f-for Cosmo—'

'Off you go, then,' said Mary, undeceived and privately relieved, 'and I expect Tamsin wants to get off home, you've taken up her whole afternoon with your affairs!' She smiled at them both, almost with warmth, and moved away towards the stairs. Diana and Francis looked at each other.

'That wasn't easy, but it seemed to go off all right,' said Diana, but quietly, not wanting to be overheard.

'It w-was a start anyway. C-come on, I'll s-s-see you to your car.'

They walked together back across the courtyard to the car. Diana opened the door.

'Goodbye then.'

'I'll s-s-see you this evening, at Sh-shortlanesend,' he reminded her, and bent his head to kiss her; she had thought he might not be going to and kissed him back warmly. 'And thank you,' he said, but whether for the lift, the kiss, or the brief interlude with his mother just past wasn't clear.

Diana slammed the door, started the engine and drove away. He had already gone out of sight by the time she reached the courtyard gates, and she drove back to Emberton very thoughtfully.

Kim had been home from work for some time by now, she was sitting on the sofa much as she had left Diana that morning, leafing through the same magazine. She looked up as the front door opened.

'Hello stranger, I thought you'd left the country!'

'Why, what's the time?' Diana glanced at her watch quickly. 'Oh goodness, I didn't realise! Francis asked me to drive him back from Shortlanesend so he could pick up his other car – and I got sidetracked after that—' She broke off, and sat down beside Kim. 'Kim, we've been a bit stupid, I think.'

Kim laid down the magazine to look at her properly.

'How, stupid? Mind you, I'm not saying we haven't been, but how exactly, this time?'

'We've been so busy worrying about the Chillingworths and what they had been made to think, we completely overlooked the Vachells – I've had the most interesting afternoon, you won't believe it!'

'Try me. I'm listening,' said Kim, and Diana told her. All except for that last bit at Vachells itself, which she needed to think about before she mentioned it.

'So, what you're saying,' said Kim, when she had finished, 'is that the Vachells have been tracking you all over the countryside, have I got that right?'

'Not tracking me, exactly, but they're a big family who mostly live and work round here, and in the same line of business too, and they've been concerned about Francis – I suspect, for years – so they've been keeping an eye out once they suspected something. And from what Benita said, they're all thrilled to bits, although that may be a slight exaggeration because she is herself.'

'Even so, it does make things look a bit different, doesn't it?' Kim thought about it. 'What are they like, these Vachells? Someone – I don't remember who – said that they were "county", but they sound more plain country to me. They're all farmers and stuff, from all accounts. Vachells is the big one, and even that seems to be a lot of farms, and Val described Francis to me as a farmer when we first met.'

'Actually, I've been thinking about that, and I don't think it's strictly true.' Diana wrinkled her nose in thought. 'I think he's more some sort of working estate manager – I haven't asked him, but that's the impression I get.'

'Well, you've seen more of him than I have,' said Kim. She paused. 'So what you're saying is, that Francis isn't exactly alone against the world, as we thought, but has a large family solidly behind him, if he'd only had the sense to trust them?'

'Something like that – except that he couldn't, could he?'

'Couldn't? Couldn't what?'

'Trust them. He thought his mother was a murderer.'

'Oh God, yes. And the same goes for her. She couldn't trust them either, because she thought...so we're back at square one.'

'No. We're not. Because they both know they were wrong thanks to us, and the family never knew anything at all...do you see what I'm getting at?'

'Yes...' Kim looked thoughtful. 'Yes, yes I do. Both families, the Vachells and the Chillingworths, are back in the game...'

'...and all we need to know now, is who's behind all that unpleasantness at the Club!' ended Diana, triumphantly.

'That might be a tricky one. And why is another question that needs to be answered. It's obvious he – Francis, that is – must have really upset someone.'

'We'll have to keep our eyes and ears open, and see what we can come up with.' Diana got to her feet. 'I'm going to have a shower. I've been invited out to supper at Shortlanesend, and after driving all over the shop, and wrestling vegetables and stuff, I feel a mess!' She paused. 'Oh Kim, I'm so sorry, I never thought. You'll be all on your own here.'

'Think nothing of it. I shall watch the telly with my feet up. And how much time did you spend on your own at the cottage, while I was living it up with Val?'

'Yes, and I didn't even have the telly.' Diana paused. 'Oh Kim, isn't it great to think that we're going to be living so close to each other for ever and ever?'

'Yeah. All we need is for Val to get a job down here, and we're away.'

'What if he doesn't?' Diana paused on her way to the stairs. 'You're definitely buying that house you looked at, aren't you?'

'We shall live in it at weekends, and in Val's London flat in the week. Or we'll stay here, and he'll commute – he could, just. There's a through train from Embridge to Victoria or somewhere. We shall see – now go and get your shower, for goodness' sake. I want to watch Pointless.'

Diana went on upstairs on dancing feet, thinking how great it was to have everything out in the open, no more shocks and surprises, nothing more to learn apart from the obvious one, and even that might well get up and go away with time!

Except that she was wrong. She was still only half way up that learning curve, and although shocks and unpleasant surprises were off the menu right now, disbelief and astonishment were not, and the speed of ascent was accelerating.

She still had a few things to learn.

VII

This time, when Diana reached Shortlanesend, she knew immediately that Francis was here before her, his Mercedes was parked to the side of the porch, but there was no sign of the man himself. She got out of her own car, and stood for a moment wondering whether she should ring the front door bell or go round to the back as before, and while she was hesitating, two children came rushing up, apparently out of nowhere, and danced in front of her; a girl of about nine, and a boy a couple of years older, both of them dark, sturdily built and beautiful in what seemed to be the Vachell default mode; their cousin Clare was similar, although Mary, a handsome woman still, could never have had that sturdy build, not even when she was younger, which must, at least partly, be the reason why Francis, of those Vachells she had met so far, seemed to have missed the square gene. Of course, he must take after the Chillingworths, too, at least in that respect. Ed Freemantle had been tall, his Aunt Henrietta too.

'You're Tamsin,' the girl told her, 'Mummy said we were to look out for you. I'm Maisie.'

The boy stopped jumping up and down and gave her what could only be described as a measuring look. He said, 'And I'm Clive. You're to come with us, Mum said,' before turning to lead the way to the yard gate. Diana followed obediently, Maisie skipping at her side, still chatting happily.

'You're Francis's girlfriend,' she said; it seemed to be a habit with her to tell people what they already knew. She unexpectedly slipped her hand into Diana's. 'We're all really, really pleased you're here!'

'Shut up, Maisie, said Clive. He caught Diana's eye and grinned. 'It's true, though. Come through.' He held the gate for her, and Sacha came rushing out of nowhere to jump up with his dirty paws on her clean top, barking and flailing his tail from side to side, obviously a very happy dog. The clamour brought Benita to the back door.

'Hello Tamsin, did these two ambush you OK? Come in, I'll get you a drink – and you two, it's time to come in too, now, and go up to do your homework – no, Maisie! No arguing, and please go upstairs quietly. And keep your music down, Clive, for once.' The children stampeded through the kitchen, and she called out after them, 'Quietly, I said, not like a herd of elephants!' She waited until the children had vanished, now on tiptoe and hushing each other, and then turned back to Diana. 'Sorry about that. Hello, sit down, and do you prefer red or white?' She picked up a couple of bottles that sat at the nearer end of the table together with four glasses and held them up invitingly. The far end of the table was laid ready for a meal. Benita pulled out a chair invitingly. 'Sit.'

Diana sat, and said, 'What will we be eating?' There was a wonderful smell in the air. She sniffed it appreciatively, and Benita grinned at her.

'Beef casserole, couldn't you guess? Red, then?' She poured two glasses and sat down opposite to Diana. 'Oh – there's a dog under the table, I didn't see it come in.' She bent to peer underneath. 'Oh yes – that dog.'

I saw that Francis's Merc was here,' said Diana, with a lift at the end that almost made it into a question. Benita made an expressive face.

'Oh yes, he's here, safe and sound – only he went upstairs for a shower and a change of clothes – both of which he desperately needed, I may say – and sort of flopped onto the bed while he was getting dressed again, and lost consciousness. When he didn't come down, I went up to check he was OK and there he was, dead to the world, so I thought I'd leave him there, he looks wrecked, poor man. We'll let him sleep until I put the potatoes on, then you can go up and wake him.' She laughed. 'A bit like the Sleeping Beauty, only the other way around – you can wake him with a kiss.'

'Sounds like a good idea to me,' said Diana, thinking about it.

'But Ernie will be down soon, you can meet him. He just got in from the farm, so he's having a shower too but probably he will manage to stay awake.'

Diana looked down into her glass, swirling the wine around as she spoke. 'And did leaving Vachells go off all right? It must have been a bit of a wrench, he's put a lot into that place.'

'Well, it was, I imagine, but he's got a new life to look forward to – you, and Burnthouse, and a whole lot of new ideas that he will no doubt run past you. He didn't say anything, if that's what you're asking.'

She had been, of course. She took a sip of the wine, it was a good one. 'Oh well, what's done is done. Life starts here.'

'He has been away before,' Benita said. 'He went to Public School – at least until his father was killed in that accident, he did. Did he tell you about that?'

'I heard. He had a breakdown, or something.'

'Yes, he did. And then he was away for four more years when he had that accident.'

Some accident, thought Diana, with bitterness. Brutal assault was a better description, but she didn't say that, it appeared that the Vachells in general might not know the details there. She said, 'But I wasn't thinking of stuff like that. I was thinking, that lovely house and estate should be his inheritance and it must be a bit hard, wouldn't you think?'

Benita gave her a shrewd look. 'And has he ever let you think that he wanted it?'

Before Diana had to answer that one, there came the sound of footsteps on wooden stairs, and a moment later a dark, square-built man, essentially Clive grown up, appeared in the doorway with his arms held out in welcome.

'Tamsin!' He bent down and gave her a huge hug that nearly smothered her, before straightening up to reach for the wine bottle. He poured himself a generous slug and grinned at her. 'Has Bennie broken it to you that your newly-betrothed is sleeping with another woman?'

Diana's mouth dropped open of its own accord, and Bennie said, 'He means his cat – and this is Ernest, by the way. This is what you end up with if you marry a Vachell, so be warned.'

Only one question came into Diana's head to ask right then, she felt as if she had been caught in a high wind; Ernest Vachell had that effect on a lot of people, had she but known it. She asked, 'Whose cat?' and felt bewildered.

'His cat – Francis's cat,' said Benita. She saw Diana's expression. 'Didn't you know about the cats?'

"Cats" in the plural, now. Diana shook her head, partly to clear it. 'No,' she said. 'Francis has cats?'

'You make them sound like a communicable disease,' said Ernest. He took a gulp of wine. 'Don't you like cats?'

'I love cats. I just think of Francis as more of a dog person.'

'Francis is an animal person,' said Ernest. 'And fish…and octopuses and squid…prawns…probably birds too, they seem to just gravitate towards him. I reckon when he did the thesis for his Master's degree, every time he went out on the Bornhope Rocks the mussels sat up and clapped their shells.' He took another swallow of his wine and picked up the bottle again to top up his glass. 'Ah, that's good!'

'The cats were on the farm out at Vachells,' said Benita, brushing this diversion aside. 'He brought two of them away with him, the ones he was particularly fond of. The other three stayed on the farm, no doubt they'll bring the numbers back up soon. Birdie and The Boss went to the cattery in Emberton, but they pined – being outdoor cats, they hated being shut in. So we told him to bring them here. It was a bit of a gamble, but they fitted in all right with the residents – The Boss has lived up to his name, in fact, but little Birdie seems to fancy a new life as a house cat, she loves Francis, and she must have sneaked up while he was in the shower. I left the bedroom door ajar for her when I came back down – which is why I told the children to be quiet, for once. Little Birdie was all snuggled up with him, I hadn't the heart to disturb either of them!'

Which was all very well, Diana thought, but too much information designed, she rather thought, to cover up the main theme. Thesis? Master's degree? Mussels? She felt as if she had strayed into a bog. She said, tentatively, 'Francis wrote a thesis on the Bornhope Rocks?'

Ernest grinned at her, 'Actually, I believe he wrote it on his computer, but I get your point.'

'I thought they were under water – he said he couldn't dive.' She heard her own bewilderment in the statement.

'He shouldn't. Part of the reef is above water at low tide.'

Benita said, quietly, 'He hasn't told you?'

'He told me he studied with the Open University. He didn't say what.'

'Actually, it was by distance learning, with a university that had an excellent record for Marine Biology,' said Ernest. He looked at her thoughtfully. 'What else don't you know?'

'Ernie…' said Benita. He switched his eyes momentarily from Diana to his wife.

'Someone has to tell her. It doesn't seem as if it's going to be Francis – the poor girl will have a heart attack the moment she picks up the post'

'Even so, he should be the one to tell her.'

Diana could bear this no longer. She said, 'Tell me what? You'll have to tell me now, I can always pretend I don't know, if he ever gets round to it himself. What will give me a heart attack?'

'Dr Francis Chillingworth, BSc, MSc, PhD,' said Ernest. 'All Firsts, he's a clever bloke is Francis, not like the rest of us hayseeds; it got him some stick at Sixth Form College, I should tell you! That, and the Public School. The dumber ones didn't appreciate it. Have some more wine.' He held out the bottle, but Diana shook her head. She felt slightly stunned. Maybe she should follow that up with Ernest some time – but not this time. It wasn't the moment, if she could get him on his own it would be better.

'I won't right now, I have to drive home later,' she said, to excuse herself. Ernest grinned.

'You could always stay the night. Bennie will lend you a nightie, and I'm sure we could find you a bed.'

'Ernie!' said Benita, but she was laughing as she said it. 'Behave yourself, for God's sake!'

'Tamsin isn't offended – are you Tamsin?'

'I ought to be,' Diana told him, sternly, but there was no real intent there. She said, 'So he could have been a marine biologist? So why…?'

'Two reasons,' said Ernest. He had pulled himself together now. 'Sorry Tamsin, I was way out of order there, I shouldn't tease you when I hardly know you. Now, marine biology…what fascinates Francis is the deep, deep water stuff – all those neon things that float around in odd shapes and sizes looking like something from Outer Space, you'll have seen them on the telly no doubt. There's still a lot to be learned about them, and that's where his main interest lies – lay, I should say. But as things are, he's stuck with the shallow water stuff that's pretty well documented already.'

'You said, two reasons,' Diana reminded him.

'The second one should be obvious – anyway, you know it for yourself. Vachells. For some reason that none of us could fathom, he seemed to feel duty bound to work Vachells for his mother. What suddenly changed his mind now, we don't know either.' He looked at Diana steadily as he spoke, but Diana, who of course knew the answers to both these questions, said nothing. He shrugged his shoulders. 'OK. But however that goes, he has now changed his mind. Perhaps you should think about that?'

'I'm not sure I understand you,' said Diana, who didn't.

'The sky's the limit?' suggested Ernest.

'But the new farm…Burnthouse…?' The bog was getting stickier, Diana realised. 'He still has the cows, they're at Ravenscourt Place…'

'And they're part of the future for you,' Benita told her, giving up; if Ernie was determined to clear the undergrowth, he was probably not wrong. 'Ernie didn't tell you this bit, but Francis has a PhD in Bovine Genetics, not Marine Biology. But, and it's a big "but", out at Burnthouse there is a beautiful old tithe barn, which he intends to apply for Planning Permission to convert into a house. Think about it.'

Diana thought about it, but came up with nothing beyond a vague feeling that Francis had mentioned something about this himself. 'So?'

'If it's to be a house, presumably someone is going to live in it?'

'So, who do you think? This is not my country.'

'A farm manager, something like that? To free him up a bit? And he's planning to buy a yacht, which presumably he intends to use?'

'I know about that,' said Diana, pleased at being able to admit to some knowledge, at last. She hadn't properly considered the implications though. She did so now.

'So we can assume that he plans to sail it to somewhere from time to time?' said Bennie, watching her, and Diana let out a long breath that she hadn't realised she had been holding.

'So we probably can,' she agreed.

'There you are, then.' She didn't define where "somewhere" was, and looked at her watch. 'And now, I'm going to put the potatoes on, so off you go and wake the sleeping beauty. I mean the cat, of course…'

'In a moment,' said Diana. There was something she wanted to know more about, while there was yet time to ask. She turned to Ernest. 'What did he actually do on the Bornhope Rocks, anyway?'

'As I understand it, he did an intensive study of a rock pool,' he told her. 'Tides, weather, the effect of the moon, what lived there, what grew there, the seasonal changes, the lot – he was out there in some filthy weather; one of the fishermen went out with him and stood off in the boat while he worked – there's nothing to tie up to out there, safely anyway. He – Francis, I'm talking about now, not the fisherman – he had an underwater camera that would take pictures under the overhangs, where he couldn't see. The exposure must have been amazing, it's dark in those places and he couldn't use flash.'

'Was it safe?' Diana was privately horrified; she had seen the Bornhope Rocks close up on one memorable occasion.

'The fishermen go out there at low tide when the weather's good, collecting shellfish. So yes. If you take care and know your tides.'

Diana thought about this, it didn't sound as if Francis had taken particular care: "filthy weather" was the clue there. She said, 'I'd better go and wake him, then.' She got to her feet. 'Where do I find him?'

'Up the stairs, turn left, the door is slightly open, mind the cat,' Benita told her. When Diana had gone, she looked at Ernest.

'You stuck your neck out a bit there, didn't you, my darling?'

'Somebody had to. The poor girl was dancing in the dark.' he defended himself. 'Francis has known her for the best part of six months, and apparently hasn't said a word. It's hardly fair, wouldn't you agree?'

'I don't know…maybe he had other things to think about – something's been going on, don't you feel it?'

'Oh, definitely. But I get the feeling that whatever it was, it's run its course.' He put down his wineglass and turned for the scullery door. 'I'm going to look for a beer – if I drink any more of that stuff, I might say anything,' and Benita said, 'You already have, don't you think? And go steady. There's the rest of the evening to get through yet.'

'Don't be such a wife,' he said. 'And thank God for Tamsin, the best thing that's happened for years! She knows, whatever it was, Bennie, so he's safe. I'll just get the beer, and we can drink to it, we don't have to drive home.'

Diana found her way upstairs feeling stunned, more than anything else. It wasn't, she now realised, that Francis hadn't told her anything, in a way, he had. She had known he had studied with a university, although he had given no details of which, or of what, and she had certainly known about the yacht. She knew more than Benita and Ernest, she was fairly sure, about the events of the past years. What she hadn't known, and that partly because she had never asked, was what he planned to do next, and she still didn't. He had never set out to be a farmer – another thing that she knew. The new knowledge that he was Dr Chillingworth, rather than Mr Chillingworth, was a bit disconcerting, which was stupid as technically, he had been so since long before she first met him, but no doubt she would get used to the idea. She pushed at the door that was ajar, as instructed.

Immediately, she saw just what Benita had meant. "Abandoned" was one word that leapt to mind. "Sprawled" was another one. It was quite obvious that he must have given up and keeled over while attempting to put on his socks; one of them lay under his relaxed right hand, the other one was on the floor. The cat, who was small and black, was curled up in the curve of his midriff, she was the only one of the two of them who acknowledged Diana's arrival, opening yellow eyes to size her up and then closing them again. Diana took a step forward, holding out a hand to make friends.

'Hello, beautiful,' she said, but it was a step too far for the cat. She opened her eyes again, wide this time, gave Diana a look, jumped down and headed for the door, and Francis said, in a voice slurred with sleep, 'W-w-was that f-f-for me or th-the c-cat?'

Diana took the cat's place on the edge of the bed. He wasn't really awake, she realised; with a tiny bit of encouragement, he would be flat out again. 'Are you awake?' she asked loudly, just checking, and he said, 'N-no,' without moving.

She just sat there and simply looked at him for a minute; he was a pleasing sight, and all hers unless you counted the cat! He didn't have the stocky Vachell build, but he had their dark, Italianate good looks, and thick black hair, worn a little long for a man of his age in his case, and with a heavy wave in it and, seen this close up, with a few silver hairs too, particularly on the left temple where the scars must be. No sign of thinning, or receding – Ernest was getting a bit thin on top, she had noticed. She loved him until it actually hurt, but this wouldn't do; the potatoes would be done before he found his second sock at this rate!

'Wake up,' she said, more loudly. 'Dinner's nearly ready!'

That time, his eyes flew open and he actually looked at her, a step in the right direction; blue eyes, all the Vachells she had met so far had brown eyes, probably including Mary, although she hadn't been close enough to her to check. This blue was from the Chillingworths, Edward Freemantle had them too she remembered. Which set of genes would finally triumph? Anybody's guess! She realised that she had been staring at him when he said, 'Tamsin? Wh-what's up?' and sounded concerned.

'Nothing,' she said hastily. 'I was just thinking how much I loved you – don't you dare close your eyes again! I'll set Maisie on you!' He laughed, and reached up for her, pulling her down beside him to kiss her soundly.

She mumbled through the kiss, 'and don't change the subject. Get your socks on, you're only half-dressed.'

'I didn't th-think I was changing the-the s-subject.'

'Benita just put the potatoes on,' she said. She picked up the sock from the bed, paired it with the one from the floor, and handed them both to him. 'And you need to put these on. Where are your shoes?'

'G-god knows. In th-th-the holdall? Ov-v-ver there, by the w-window?' He smothered a yawn, and reluctantly sat up, sitting on the edge of the bed and groping for the first sock. Diana found the shoes and handed them to him.

'Get these on, and then put a comb through your hair, you look a tousled mess! And stop yawning!' She yawned in sympathy as she spoke, and he gave her another hug. The phrase "drunk on freedom" slipped into her head, and out again. But it was true, this was a man she hardly recognised, there was a lightness to him that was new and unfamiliar, she had noticed it yesterday but it was even more in evidence today. She filed the idea to consider later, there wasn't time now. She could hear Benita along the passage, chivvying the children to get ready for bed. 'You can play on the computer, or watch a DVD until nine – one of us will come up and put the lights out then, and you had better be tucked up ready!' Francis heard her too. He looked at his watch.

'Hell – Tams-sin, how l–long have you b-b-been here?'

'Since half-six, as instructed. She grinned at him. 'It's all right. I've been getting to know your cousins.'

'G-god knows what th-th-that will m-mean,' he looked apprehensive. Along the passage, Maisie's voice could be heard, complaining, 'Can't we say goodnight to Tamsin? We like Tamsin.'

'You'll be seeing her again. Now, get yourselves organised, please!'

'And we had better do the same,' said Diana. She ran her eye over him. 'You look tidy enough now – come on. Those potatoes must be done by now, I hope your cousin Ernest is keeping an eye on them.'

Supper was a pleasant meal, eaten at the kitchen table with Sacha underneath it, lying on his master's feet, and a huge tabby cat watching them from the dresser – "The Boss", Ernest introduced him. 'Our own farm cats are wilder, they don't come indoors – at least, they aren't meant to – but Francis's two have ideas of their own. He's spoiled them.'

'Th-they may have, b-b-but they learned them h-h-here,' Francis told him, ignoring that last sentence.

'So, where's Birdie?' Diana asked, and Benita said, 'Asleep on the sitting-room sofa,' and sighed, but smiled as she did so.

The beef casserole, accompanied by potatoes and vegetables grown on the farm, was delicious, only slightly marred for Diana when Ernest asked her, 'And are you a good cook too, Tamsin?' It had to be Ernest, he seemed to have a gift for disconcerting her; she wondered if he was actually trying to do so but that was probably imagination.

'I do a brilliant fried-egg sandwich,' she said, which was the literal truth. She added, quickly, 'I thought I might take lessons.'

'Well, that's breakfast taken care of,' said Ernest cheerfully, 'Francis, my man, are you sure you know what you're doing here?'

'Is there a cookery school in Embridge?' Benita asked. Nobody knew.

'We can look in Yellow Pages,' Ernest suggested, and began to get to his feet then and there, but Benita stopped him.

'Ernie – not right now, for goodness sake! Anyway, they can always have a housekeeper or something. Mary does.'

'A housek-keeper in a c-c-caravan?' asked Francis, with a grin, and Ernest said, 'It's that, or being permanently eggbound. Think about it!'

Diana raised a forkful of potato to her mouth and chewed it thoughtfully. They all seemed to be assuming that she was going to be living in that caravan, or at the very least spending some time in it, which was good – up to a point. There were one or two queries that came into her mind, however, not the least of them being warmth, light, and cleanliness. If they were rewiring the house, presumably there would be no electricity. Winter was on its way, time for further enquiry. She said, 'I can open a tin of beans with anyone – so long as there's something to heat them up on. Aren't they going to turn off the electricity when they rewire the house?'

'W-w-we'll use the g-g-generator,' Francis told her, 's-s-same as on a yacht. Y-you should know.' He smiled at her, and she felt her mind go blank. She was sure there was no generator on her father's gin palace, she would have noticed. Ernest caught her eye, and obviously read her thoughts, which seemed to amuse him.

'They call it "the engine" on a boat,' he told her kindly. She met his eye without flinching; Ernest thought he could get away with too much, she decided.

'Of course they do,' she said.

'So you'll be able to sit and watch the telly, and do your knitting in the warm,' he told her kindly, and she kicked him under the table, hard. 'And you'll have running water on tap, ha-ha, and plumbing – of a sort, anyway. Francis can empty the doings in the cesspit. He'll enjoy that.'

'Th-thanks for that th-thought,' said Francis, and Benita said, 'Please – not while we're eating!' and they all laughed.

It was so odd, Diana found herself thinking, as the meal progressed from stew to sticky toffee pudding, it was as if Francis, in this company, was a completely different person from the one she knew from the Sailing Club. There, he was always very quiet, wary even, and kept himself largely apart from the crowd – that's when he was there at all. Here – yes, with his family, it was a completely different story. She had loved him anyway, and for some time now, but tonight she could feel herself falling in love all over again. She wondered if the Chillingworths would have the same effect on him? Well, she would find out soon enough, they were talking about that right now.

'So, when are you off up to London?' Benita had asked, and Francis looked at Diana.

'Up to T-tamsin – and Kim. Th-they'll be c-c-coming too. C-completion on B-burnthouse isn't until th-the t-tenth so m-maybe this w-w-weekend w-would be favourite, I'll b-be a bit busy after that.'

'He has to meet my parents yet,' Diana enlarged on this. 'They haven't met Kim, either—'

'At least they know what she looks like,' said Ernest, with his ready grin. 'What they'll make of Francis is something else again—'

'—oh Ernie, do shut up!' said Benita, but affectionately. 'You never did know when to keep your mouth closed!' She directed her attention to Diana. 'So, where will you all stay? With your parents?'

'Kim will. She'd like to stay with Val – that's her fiancé – but my parents have invited her, so we'll go with that this time. And Francis will stop in a hotel – he could stay with his grandmother and his aunts, but he's chickened out.'

'Don't blame him – I remember his Aunt Clara! She stayed at Vachells on one memorable occasion. So, all very diplomatic and respectable then,' said Ernest, irrepressibly, but added, 'but probably a good idea, given the circumstances. No need to push the boat out, until you've checked the gear.'

'Exactly,' said Diana.

There was just one more thing to be learned, before she shot off the top of that learning curve and sailed off to the stars, and it was, as it happened, something that she had half – or maybe a quarter- suspected already. The subject came up over the coffee that followed the meal, drunk sitting companionably round the now-cleared table, and it was Benita, not Ernest for once, who brought it up.

'So, when does Cosmo get here to take over?' she asked casually, and Francis replied, 'End of October. He has t-t-to w-work out his n-notice.'

Benita nodded as if she had expected that, but Diana said, before she could stop herself, 'But will your mother be able to manage things all right on her own for that long?' and immediately wished that she had kept her mouth shut. It was, after all, arguably none of her business, but it did seem a monumental task for an elderly lady to take on single-handed. Ernest raised an eyebrow at her, but it was Francis who replied.

'H-hardly "on her own" T-tamsin.' He was laughing at her, she realised. 'It t-takes m-more than one m-m-man to w-work t-twelve-hundred acres. Even if he's m-me.'

Of course it would. Diana felt a fool, and wished the floor would open and swallow her up. What business had it been of hers, anyway?

'No Francis, it was a fair question,' said Ernest, coming unexpectedly to her aid. 'She doesn't know how these things work, how could she?' He turned to Diana. 'Francis managed the estate for her, he does know how to drive a tractor and plough a field and all that, but mostly, the men do that. He did the brain work, except for his cows and at harvest time.'

Diana had seen Francis driving a tractor, not exactly ploughing but raking grass, or something, she hadn't been studying the process at the time, other considerations had got in the way. This, of course, was what had misled her, and now it was pointed out to her, it was obvious; she had even wondered about it, she recalled. She had also, on the couple of occasions she had visited Vachells in the past, seen other men around. She said, 'So that's what your cousin will be doing? Managing the estate?'

'He's the manager's assistant on a big estate up in the Midlands somewhere,' Ernest told her. 'Doing well for himself, but he jumped at the chance to come home. Only, obviously he couldn't just drop everything and come straight away, they needed time to find a replacement. Mary will manage for a month, she's had to do it before, she knows the ropes. And Francis isn't going far, even if the rest of us weren't here to help if necessary. She'll be OK, don't you worry.'

Francis added, 'B-but th-thank you for d-d-doing it, anyway,' and smiled at her.

'Any more coffee, anyone?' asked Benita, 'No? Then shove the cups over here and I'll put them in the sink. They can go in the machine tomorrow.'

Diana looked up at the clock on the wall above the Aga. 'And I should be going. You all have to get up at dawn, or something, tomorrow. It's been a lovely evening, and thank you all so much for inviting me.'

'Oh, we shall probably do it again,' Ernest told her.

Francis stood up, and Sacha immediately came out from under the table and stood in front of him expectantly.

'I'll c-come out to the c-car w-w-with you,' he said. 'S-S-Sacha n-needs a r-run anyway.' He went to the back door and opened it for her. Benita and Ernest both gave her a hug and a kiss, and said how nice it was to have met her.

'And I'm not even going to say, we shall hope see you here again,' said Ernest, grinning. 'We know damn well that we will, and you're welcome any time.'

As soon as the back door had closed behind them, Francis slipped his arm around her shoulders and walked with her to the car, but slowly, spinning it out.

'Y-you'll have a t-talk with Kim about the w-w-weekend?' he said, when they finally reached it.

'My parents too. Yes.'

His other arm slipped round her shoulders too, and she put both her own round his waist and rested her cheek against his shirt. They stood close for a moment. The dog had run off.

'I'll see you t-t-tomorrow. You w-w-will be at Romans in the morning?'

'I'll make sure of it.'

'I'll s-s-see if the agent will l-let me have the k-key t-to the house for a c-couple of hours. Sh-show you what you're l-l-letting yourself in f-for.'

'That would be interesting.'

A long kiss. Goodnight. Into the car. Diana started the engine and reversed round ready to drive off. Francis blew her a kiss and turned away. As she drove to the gate that led into the lane, she saw him in the rear view mirror, leaning on the yard gate, watching her leave and stupidly, her heart felt as if had turned right over.

★

Kim was still up when she got back to Romans.

'I thought I'd wait for you to get in,' she said. 'See how it all went.' She took in her twin's starry eyes and slightly dishevelled hair. 'All right, I see.'

'Very all right. But Kim...it was a...a very instructive evening.' She thought about that; it could have been phrased better, she realised.

'In what way?'

'Move up on that sofa, and I'll tell you.'

She recounted to Kim all the interesting things she had learned in the course of the evening, and Kim listened and nodded her head from time to time.

'So,' she said, summing up when Diana had finished, 'You now know a lot of things about Francis that you didn't know before, and he seems to be someone quite different with his family, so how does that make you feel about him now?'

'I love him even more.' Diana heaved a sentimental sigh. 'I loved him before, but I did wonder...well, what I was taking on. I still don't know, but the difference is, I don't believe any more that it's anything I need to fear.'

'Did you fear it?'

'Oh, not Francis himself. The...the history, I suppose. But it turns out to be not what I thought – do you see what I mean?'

Kim did, of course, they were twins after all.

'So what do you think he means to do now?'

'I have no idea, but I'm looking forward to it!'

'I've got some news too,' said Kim, after a pause.

Diana had half-known it; there was some of the same excitement about Kim as she felt herself, only her own affairs had taken centre stage for the moment.

'OK, so what have you been getting up to while I've been gone?' she asked, laughing.

'Well, mostly things like watching that new chef on the telly – the Cornish one with the motor bike and the pub—'

'I know the one.' Diana nodded. 'His name is Mawgan Angwin, I've seen him a couple of times – peculiar name – actually, I need someone like him right now. I really must learn to cook more than fried-egg sandwiches, Kim.'

'I think he may be a bit advanced for you at the moment,' said Kim, hiding a smile. 'But apart from that, Val rang – and guess what!'

'Tell me.'

'That accounting firm in Embridge that he wanted a job with – remember? They wanted a prospective partner, but they weren't going to hold interviews immediately, they wanted to make a Short List first. Alex Hetherington Associates?'

'I remember. You both talked about it.' Diana nodded her head. She guessed where this might be going, and it was only fair. Kim was her twin, they should share good fortune together.

'Well, they start interviews at the end of next month – and Val is on their Short List! How's that?'

'Brilliant! Oh Kim, I do hope he gets it! It would be perfect.'

'Once things start going right, sometimes they just snowball for a bit – what next, I wonder?' Or is that our allowance for now?'

'Time will tell – and now, Kim, what are you and Val planning to do at the weekend? Because we have a plan…'

VIII

By the following morning, some of the euphoria had evaporated and had been replaced by more practical considerations. It had been very late by the time they went to bed, and neither of them had wished to discuss the boring stuff at that time of night, but by the time they met over a rather late breakfast, they had each of them used some time for thinking. Diana kicked off the discussion, over their coffee and toast: she was interested in their plans as they would concern her, too. Kim and Val were in the process of buying a bungalow on the cliff here in Emberton, and it would be great if it all coincided with Francis moving to Burnthouse. But perhaps that was too much to hope for?

'If Val actually gets this job, what are you planning to do? You're getting married when your parents come over in the Spring, you said now, so where is Val planning to live until then? Surely not with his parents!'

'Well, no. If he gets it, we shall move into the house – our house, that is; it will be ours by then, so we might as well. We shall have to get some furniture for it anyway – his flat is an unfurnished let, but it isn't that big so he doesn't have that much – but even if he does get it, the chances are he won't start until New Year and he'll still be in London during the week until then. We've got this place until the beginning of April if we need it, I checked with Benita Vachell that day she came here – so you'll be OK.' She met Diana's eye, and added to that, 'If you need it.'

'I'm not sure about that,' Diana confessed. 'I may know for certain later today, of course – but last night, everyone seemed to be assuming I'd be living in a caravan on a building site long before then. With two cats, a dog, and maybe a few hens for company. I'm not sure about the cows, they may be scheduled to arrive later.'

'Well, if you will marry a millionaire, you'll have to get used to being taken for granted – I believe they do an awful lot of that kind of thing.'

Millionaires were outside Kim's personal experience, but she read a lot, and had her own ideas. Francis didn't strike her as typical. Even as she thought that, Diana echoed the thought.

'Funny – I can't think of him as a millionaire.' Diana's own adoptive father was also a millionaire as it happened, although that, she never really thought about; it was, had always been, just there in the background. But like a lot of things, they came in all sizes, and with Francis, for some reason, she found it impossible to feel the same way, in fact she had a feeling, not necessarily a good one, that he might leave her father standing in that respect. It wasn't anything he had said, or done, or even was, apart from the name "Chillingworth" itself, and the fact that he had been his fathers's sole heir, but she had heard people say things, not necessarily to her, but meaning her to hear, notably at the town Yacht Club on one memorable occasion. She fiddled with the spoon in her mug, stirring her coffee when it didn't need stirring, and watching the swirl it made. 'I think some people may, though – there's a feel to that spite campaign someone's been waging down at the Club, and jealousy is a strong motive for some people.' She looked up, straight at Kim. 'I think, if I asked, Ernest Vachell could point the finger, there was something he said last night…but I don't know if it would help. Accusations are all very well, but it would be better if it all came to the boil on its own…I think so, anyway.'

'You might be wishing for the moon, there,' said Kim, sceptically.

'I know this may sound silly – stupid, even. But I keep wondering about that story that keeps cropping up – the one where he's supposed to have beaten up another boy at Sixth Form. Jealousy certainly came into that – but would somebody hold a grudge over it for…well, it must be nearly a quarter of a century by now?'

'I think that depends on what really happened,' said Kim. She added, 'And who to. And exactly why. Some people just love to bear a grudge, and the other side of that coin is that even Francis admits that he did something, don't forget that. So, will you ask Ernest?'

'I might. I don't know.'

'Stick it in the pending file, then. We've more immediate problems to think about right now. I rang Val this morning before he left for work, and while you were still snoring – he said he's OK with staying up in town over the weekend. So you need to ring your parents when you've finished torturing that piece of toast, and check it out with them.

Then it's all systems "go" – I'm assuming Francis will sort out his own grandmother?'

'If she doesn't sort him out first,' said Diana, with an involuntary giggle. She dropped the crumbling toast crust she had been fiddling with back onto her plate. 'He's stayed away for long enough to upset her seriously, if she cared about him – and Henrietta Chillingworth says that they all did.'

'Hmm.'

Diana forbore to ask exactly what "hmm" was supposed to mean. Instead, she said, 'You are happy about the arrangements? Only Daddy and Eloise really wanted you to stay with them – and me, of course – so they could meet you properly. But they don't know about Val...well, except that he exists, of course.'

'I'm fine with it, Val will survive. And it doesn't do to try and cross your bridges before you get to them, anyway. We can take it a step at a time, it's all complicated enough as it is.'

'I'll ring home then.' Diana picked up her phone from where it lay, beside her plate in case Francis rang her, and found the number she needed now in its directory. 'Don't bother with the washing-up – I can do it – oh, hello Eloise darling!' She turned her attention to the phone, and Kim began gathering up the debris. She placed no reliance on Diana's offer to do the washing up, and carried it through to the kitchen to see to it herself.

Diana joined her when she was halfway through the drying up, and without comment, began putting things away.

'That's all OK, they'll expect us some time on Thursday, I said I'd ring when we were on our way.'

'Are you driving us?'

'I shouldn't think so for a moment, but we shall see nearer the time. Francis will want his car in London, I should think. I'm easy.'

'He's a brave man, then,' said Kim, who had spent a brief time in London on her way down to Dorset, and wouldn't have driven a car there for a fortune.

'I don't think bravery comes into it. It's just a man thing.' Diana pushed the cutlery drawer closed and looked at her watch. 'I don't really know what to do now – he said he'd see me today, but he didn't say when.'

'Then I would say "wait,"' said Kim, grinning at her, and almost as she spoke, Diana's mobile played it's opening tune. She rushed back to the dining table and snatched it up. Yes!

Kim stood at the kitchen door and watched her. Up until last night, she had felt that her twin's relationship with Francis Chillingworth had an edge to it, a slight uncertainty that had kept her wondering – which Kim had not necessarily considered a bad thing; Diana was too used to getting her own way too easily. But yesterday, all of that seemed to have melted away, and it was almost certainly, she now realised, because Francis could now see his way clear for the future. That, and the fact that the Vachells' attitude had given Diana confidence in her own future, too. The rules had changed. Well, good, they had needed to in Kim's opinion.

Diana was saying, 'Yes…yes, that's fine with me…yes, I'll be ready – what?' And then she blew a kiss into the phone, laughing, and switched it off. She looked, Kim thought as she turned around, as if a light had been turned on. "Shining with happiness", a cliché for every occasion. She said, 'They wouldn't give him the key, but someone is meeting us out there at eleven o'clock. He said he'd pick me up at half-past ten.' She paused, her eyes dancing with amusement. 'He said to bring my wellies. Can I borrow yours?'

'You've time to slip across to Crowe's and buy your own,' said Kim, looking at their clock on the mantelpiece. 'Come on – I'll come with you – you're going to need some anyway if you're planning to live on a building site!'

Crowe's was the village hardware store, it sold everything from garden seeds to camp beds and all the stops in between, including wellie boots, although not smart, fashionable ones in pretty colours; working boots, designed for close encounters with a lot of mud.

'Appropriate,' said Diana, slipping one on to try for comfort. It felt surprisingly good. 'These'll be fine.' She picked up the pair and carried them to the counter. The man serving them was a stranger, the owner, George Crowe, hadn't been seen here since his wife had been killed in a hit-and-run, and Tim Wakeley, who had been his assistant, was also gone now. Their stepfather…she felt a crawling sensation up her spine. The man who had killed their mother, and tried to kill Francis, but failed and met his own death instead. She wished they hadn't come in here, it was bringing it all back.

She paid for the boots, and they walked back to Romans without speaking. Only when they reached the front door and Kim was opening it, did either of them say anything.

'It had to be done, Di, sooner or later. Both of us are going to be living round here, we can't go dashing off to town every time we need a packet of screws – I can't anyway, it would be stupid. Think about it.'

'I know, I know! It just needs getting used to.' Diana dropped the boots by the door, and Kim said, 'Aren't you going to take the price ticket off?' and they both laughed. Kim looked down at her twin's feet, bare, with painted toenails and pretty sandals, just the thing for a muddy farmyard.

'If you go up and rootle around in my top drawer, you'll find a pair of thick socks. And hadn't you better put on some more practical shoes?'

'I've got boots now—' Diana began, but Kim said, 'You can't go round the house in them, even if it is falling down. The agent won't like it. And who knows what else you'll be doing before you get home again? You certainly don't!'

Diana went upstairs to look for Kim's wellie-socks and her own very slightly more practical slip-on ballets, and Kim stood at the window looking back up the street, her mind making pictures against her own will. You couldn't actually see Crowe's from here, but she could see it in her head, and she knew exactly how Diana had felt, in spite of her practical approach. Everywhere round here was full of memories, but on the credit side, a lot of them were good ones too. And there would be more, probably in both categories. She had got no further in her thoughts than that, when a shining, cream-coloured Discovery slid into view and pulled up outside. She gave it a second look, not quite believing what she saw, then went to the foot of the stairs.

'Your taxi's here,' she shouted. 'Or I think it is – he seems to have washed it, it looks almost unrecognisable!'

Diana appeared at the head of the stairs, wearing one shoe and clutching the other, together with a pair of socks.

'I'm on my way. And I can't think why, if that farmyard is all it's cracked up to be!'

Francis, Sacha and Diana all reached the door together, and greeted each other, variously. When that was over, Francis and the dog turned their attention to Kim, and greeted her too, in Francis's case slightly less exuberantly. The hands of the clock stood at exactly ten-twenty five, Francis threw it a glance and grinned at Diana.

'N-never thought you'd m-m-make it in t-time,' he said.

They left, the dog leaping around them, and Kim went back to the kitchen to finish tidying up. She had to be up at the pub in an hour for the lunchtime shift, and she had no idea when they were likely to be back, she hadn't had a chance to ask – if they even knew. She just hoped Diana had taken her key.

Francis drove to Shearwater down a series of narrow, twisty lanes that Diana had never set eyes on before, emerging unexpectedly at the eastern end of the village, close to where Val's parents lived, turned right for Embridge, but within half a mile dived down yet another narrow lane, this one with a sagging and broken gate at its entrance, and Diana began to wonder if she would ever find her way home when she lived here. This lane wasn't even tarmaced; it was two tracks of dirty chalk with grass and weeds growing down the middle and tangled heaps of brambles and miscellaneous weeds to either side.

'Home,' said Francis. 'W-what d-d-d'you think?'

'You really don't want to know,' said Diana, looking about her. To the left, beyond the tumbledown wall, she saw a low green, rolling hill with some scraggy trees on the top and a smaller mound below it, in an overgrown green field that seemed to have some sort of building on the far side; it could be a cottage, but equally, it could be a barn. What was beyond the far end of the field was obscured by some thick woodland – very thick woodland, it looked close to impassable to Diana's park-accustomed eyes. To the right, there were two very overgrown fields full of ruts; one had another sagging gate, the other just had a gap in the wall with rusty hinges sticking out. These fields could once have been plough land, but now they were just a weed-grown wilderness. On the far side of the second one was a wall, and beyond that the gabled, moss-grown roof of a house. The roof, Diana decided, did not look happy. The whole depressing scene had a wonderful backdrop of the downs, golden and green and with purple shadows cast by the sun. Beautiful.

'This is it?' she asked, trying to sound neutral. They were slowing up now alongside the end wall of the house, which was yet again of the local golden stone, with a lot of damp-looking moss to decorate it. One window in this wall was smallish, square, probably quite modern and cracked from top to bottom, a second one, set back a little on the upper floor, was too high to see properly, but it looked as if it was mullioned like the front windows, and was therefore likely to be original. Francis watched her looking at it, and seemed to be amused. Then he put his foot down again and drove into the farmyard.

The first impression here was of dirt and rubbish and the world's biggest manure heap, occupying a large area of a square courtyard surrounded on three sides by old stone farm buildings, including a beautiful old two-storeyed barn straight ahead of them, with holes in its tiled roof where the tiles had slipped, or even fallen off: the tithe barn, presumably. Three gates led out of this yard, one, straight ahead, onto what appeared to be a continuation of the approach lane, the one to the left into another, smaller yard with what looked like stables and – possibly – a mounting block along its visible side. The third, adjoining what could – again, possibly – be a back garden to the house, the rear of which could be seen from here in all its tumbledown entirety, led into yet another unkempt-looking field. Francis opened his door and jumped out, coming round to Diana's side to give her a hand down, although she didn't really need it, and with difficulty restrained Sacha from following. He indicated the last gate while wrestling with his dog.

'Th-through there is w–where the carav-v-van will be p-put.'

'I see,' said Diana. She took a deep, unpleasantly fragrant, breath. 'Isn't it a bit close to the manure heap?'

'Oh, th-that will be gone, d-d-don't worry about it.' He looked down at her feet. 'G-g-get th-those s-smart new b-boots on, and I'll sh-show you r-r-round out here while we're w-waiting.' He was wearing heavy lace-up shoes himself – forewarned is forearmed.

Putting on the boots entailed opening the back, and Sacha made another determined attempt to join them, which once again failed. 'W-we'll take him up on the d-downs later,' said Francis. 'G-give him a r-r-run – th-this is no place for a d-d-dog r-right now,' and Diana could only agree. It was no place for her, either.

Francis walked her round the stable yard, which contained more rubbish and had weeds growing in the cracks in its concrete surface, plus, in the case of the stables themselves, a quantity of dirty straw in every one of its four stalls that looked as historic as the stables themselves. Diana kicked at some of it with the toe of her new boot.

'Didn't they ever clean up anywhere?' she asked in disgust.

'Th-they d-d-didn't have a horse,' Francis told her. 'J-just a donkey th-they k-kept in the field b-by the house. Th-they j-j-just dumped everything on top of this, l-lazy buggers – I imagine th-they r-rented it w-w-with the f-farm and just left it – these st-st-stalls were full of old b-b-boxes and st-stuff. You should have s-s-seen it! W-well, you can s-see it, come t-t-to that. It's all in the main yard n-now.'

The barns in the main yard had at least been swept – sort of, anyway, although they were still remarkably rich in cobwebs and dirt around the roof and the edges. One of them had obviously been a cowshed, which would explain the monster manure heap. The tithe barn had a big padlock on the door, so they couldn't look at that, but the general aspect looked in keeping with the rest. Only the last building, adjacent to the field gate, was different. Francis did have the key to that one, and when he unlocked the brand-new padlock and slid one of the big doors across, Diana could see why; it was full of farm machinery. Not the kind that Noah used on Mount Ararat, as she had half-expected; shiny up-to-date stuff, clean and tidily ordered, Even the barn itself was swept completely clear, and had no cobwebs hanging like arras from the rafters. Which was not to say that there weren't any at all, but the ones there were looked of recent date; one or two even had live spiders sitting in them.

'This is all yours?' said Diana, making it a question.

'I had to put it s-s-somewhere. Th-the landlord agreed to t-to r-rent me this b-barn until completion.'

'So who cleaned it? The landlord?'

'M-me. Who d-d'you think? You've s-s-seen the rest.'

Diana was about to voice her admiration, when another car drew into the yard behind them, a sleek new Audi with an equally sleek new man driving it. He got out of his car jingling a bunch of keys and smiling.

'Sorry if I kept you waiting, something came up just as I was ready to leave.' He shook hands with Francis first, and then with Diana. 'And you are?'

'Diana Carey,' said Diana, without qualification.

'Ah. Pleased to meet you, Miss Carey.' He gave her a speculative look but made no comment. 'Well, shall we do the grand tour, then?' Diana looked down at her boots, they were now far from clean. Francis saw her looking.

'B-be a good idea t-to ch-change b-back into your shoes,' he said. Then he added thoughtfully, 'F-for what it's w-w-worth,' leaving Diana wondering.

They left her boots in the car, after another quick tussle with Sacha, and walked round to the front of the house to get in, going through a small, rusty gate to access the predictably overgrown front garden and the front of the house, and the moment that she saw the house properly, Diana realised why Francis had decided to buy it. It was long, low, and potentially beautiful, the way in which it had been allowed to decay was criminal. She fell in love at first sight.

''What do you think?' the agent asked, watching her.

'It's beautiful – or it could be. However was it allowed to fall apart like this?' She sounded indignant, and Francis raised an eyebrow at her.

'Grade II Listed, and too expensive to put in order for most people to want to take it on,' said the agent. 'Shame, really. I think the owner may have hoped it would fall down and be condemned, so he could develop the site, but don't quote me on that, it's just an impression.' He fitted a large, slightly rusty old-fashioned key into a large, slightly rusty lock, and turned it with difficulty. 'Could do with a bit of WD40 here,' he remarked, and pushed the door open, standing back to let them past.

The hall into which they stepped was chilly, and also dim, only partly because the beautiful mullioned windows either side of the door were dirty; they were set into a stone wall that must be almost two feet thick. There was a flagged floor that looked as if it hadn't been washed for some time, although it might have been swept if you gave it the benefit of the doubt; an empty tea chest sat in the middle, and some crumpled newspaper and wisps of straw blew about in the draught from the open door. A graceful, but battered staircase curved up to a balustraded landing above. It all had a desolate, unloved air, and a considerable accumulation of dust and, it had to be faced, dirt, in all the corners. The agent saw the expression on Diana's face and pushed open the big door on the right. 'And this is the drawing room,' he said, and stood aside for Diana to go in. Francis, of course, had seen it already; he waited by the door. Diana stepped inside.

It was a big room, the full depth of the house and beautifully proportioned, and had big mullioned windows at each end, and smaller windows in the end wall of the house, high on either side of what looked like the original medieval fireplace: predictably, the wide hearth was unswept and sooty, with a small, rusty, modern fire basket full of grey ash sitting forlornly in the middle. The wooden floor of the room was worn, splintery in places, and showed signs of woodworm, it had last seen polish about a hundred years ago, Diana estimated, perhaps unfairly. It was not just dusty, yet again it was downright filthy, and the same could be said for the panelled walls. The stone-mullioned windows themselves were both crusted with dirt round the edges and in places, cracked; the room looked and felt as if hadn't been used for some time, simply been ignored. The beamed and plastered ceiling was cracked and cobwebbed, but maybe it could be restored? If it could all be put right, the room could be beautiful, it was beautifully proportioned and fortunately, it was plenty big enough to take a grand piano...

The agent ushered her back into the hall, where Francis waited for them, prodding experimentally at the front door frame with a finger nail, and suggested that they went upstairs next.

'Then we can go through the dining room to the kitchen, and you can see the store rooms on the way out through the back door,' he said, smiling.

'Where does that door at the back go to?' Diana asked, with a gesture to the rear of the entrance hall, and he told her, to a cloakroom, and lobby leading to the door out into the vegetable patch, and also to the cellar. 'But you won't want to go down there,' he said, smiling. Diana caught Francis's eye, and he gave a slight shrug of his shoulders. They followed the man upstairs.

There was a wide landing at the top, with a very beautiful stained-glass window tucked under the eaves to the front of the house, a window in keeping with those downstairs but smaller at the rear and a bank of cupboards against one wall, plus five bedrooms and a scarily antiquated bathroom of enormous size, with a rusting old bath in the middle of the floor, a cracked sink and an ancient chain-pull lavatory with an overhead cistern; it also, rather surprisingly, had a fireplace with a rusty, obviously long disused, grate in it.

The biggest bedroom was to the right of the landing; it too had a fireplace, and a gabled window looking out over the front garden and the field, with another narrow bedroom, that could well have been a dressing room originally, tucked in behind it. Because the roof didn't come quite so far down at the back of the house, the window here was set quite low into the bedroom wall, the ceiling sloped away above it. The scary bathroom was the other side of the landing, to the back and opened off a short passage that served all the rooms on this side. In the two smaller front bedrooms here, one had a gabled window, the other, slightly wider, had its main window in the end wall of the house, but also a small round one tucked low, under the eaves at the front. The fifth bedroom, adjoining the bathroom, had a similar window to the possibly-a-dressing room, and another fireplace which must share a chimney with the bathroom and, presumably, whatever lay below. All the rooms were of respectable size, but it was all in extremely poor decorative order, and again, not very clean – and that was putting it politely, Diana reckoned. She already could see where at least one of the putative millions might find a purpose in life and she hadn't seen everything yet.

Downstairs again, the door at the foot of the stairs led into a good-sized rectangular room, smaller than the drawing room, with a window looking to the front of the house, and another door in the rear wall, leading into a back room with a window overlooking what might once have been a vegetable patch behind the house. This, said the agent, would make a study, or perhaps a sewing room – this with a smile at Diana, who mentally replied some chance. The dining room had another of those huge fireplaces, and another door, presumably to the kitchen, beside it. Neither of the doors in here was near to the front wall, leaving a rectangular space where perhaps a desk could stand, or even a small table. Beyond, lay the kitchen, which was enormous, and only a very little cleaner than the rest of the house.

Flagged like the hall, it had yet another fireplace, backing onto the one in the dining room and still with its original bread oven; it was sad and empty. At the opposite end of the room was the cracked window they had seen from outside, beside a second fireplace that had been bricked up, and an equally sad-looking electric stove, obviously at the end of its useful life which would be why it hadn't been taken, with a cheap Formica kitchen cupboard falling apart to either side, but under the windows that looked out to the front of the house, was a long range of old-fashioned wooden cupboards and a Belfast sink, all in rescue-able condition, which looked a far better bet. There appeared to be no back door here, but a door in the long wall opposite to the windows led down a shallow step into a narrow flagged passage, with opening off it, a big, empty larder, a scullery with another big old-fashioned ceramic sink and more of the wooden cupboards, and storeroom big enough to take a number of useful modern appliances, if only it had any electricity connected. Beyond this room, the passage took a turn to the right, long enough to make the house L-shaped and forming part of the vegetable garden wall. There was a door to either side of this short turning; one of them led into a smallish, rectangular room, with the cracked window Diana had seen from outside. This room, from what was still pinned to its panelled walls, had at one time been used as a farm office, and the other door opened into an antiquated and unhygienic lavatory with another of those rusted chain-pull cisterns and a dirty and stained sink with – wonder of wonders – an ancient immersion heater above it and a suspicious smell. And even more wonderful, Diana realised, looking through the now-open back door, conveniently handy for a caravan parked in the field on the other side of the vegetable patch, or at least, in the daytime it would be. Well, that was the first priority sorted – modernising this and making it workable!

The two men had gone on ahead, and were standing beside the agent's car, talking. Diana pulled the back door to behind her and went to join them, sparing a glance as she went for the vegetable patch, which she could see through its small, wrought-iron gate as she passed. It had a stone shed at the far end, a broken greenhouse, and a lot of run-to-seed cabbages, or something. And weeds. And wind-blown rubbish, probably from the heap in the yard. Who was it, Diana found herself wondering, who was set to cleaning the Aegean Stables? Hercules, or someone? They could do with him here!

The agent turned as Diana approached, holding out his hand and smiling.

'Well, Miss Carey, I hope you're not too put-off by all this!' he said. 'I'm just going to lock up now, and then I'm off back to town. I hope all goes well with the completion, and that you'll be very happy here.' He shook hands with Francis and headed off back to the house, jangling keys. Diana and Francis looked at each other.

'Well?' he asked, with a hint of a smile. 'W-what do you th-think n-now?'

'That you're barking mad,' Diana told him. 'But it could be lovely, I can see that.'

'It w-w-will be, I p-promise you.' He caught sight of Sacha's face, pressed appealingly against the window of the Discovery. 'And t-talking of b-barking, we'd better t-t-take pity on the p-p-poor dog.' He opened Diana's door for her. 'In you g-get. B-B-Bennie gave us a picnic, we'll h-h-have it up on th-the d-d-downs, we c-can g-give him a good run up th-there.'

'A picnic?' Diana asked, as he climbed in beside her. 'It's October tomorrow! Or had you forgotten?'

He waved a hand towards the window as the car started to move.

'The s-s-sun is sh-shining, w-what's the problem?'

The agent was walking back from checking the front door, he saluted as they went past. Diana smiled and gave a small wave in return, before turning back to – well, to the tough outdoors-man beside her.

'The problem is, the wind is straight off the Arctic!'

'We'll f-find a sh-sheltered spot.' He was heading off into the hinterland again: Diana sat back in her seat, they couldn't talk properly while he was driving on these narrow lanes, and there was a lot that she wanted to say – to ask, indeed, her mind was full of so many questions that they kept bumping into each other and giving her a headache! He had something on his mind too, she could tell by the offhand manner in which he kept switching the subject, first to the dog, then diverting her still further with the picnic. And there was me, thinking of a nice snug soup-and-a-sandwich, or something, in the nice warm Ravenscourt Arms, she thought ruefully. Oh well, go with the flow.

A serious talk might just turn out to be illuminating. And now, it probably wouldn't hurt to give some equally serious consideration to that house she had just been looking at, for he was bound to ask her again what she thought, and this time she had better have a proper answer ready.

She sat watching the countryside spin past the window, and thought about what she would say.

IX

Francis, who seemed to know every path, trackway and lane in the area, drove them to a point up on the downs where, having parked the Range Rover on the verge of a narrow track, they could exercise the dog while enjoying a fabulous view over the farmland below them, all the way to the distant sea shining under what was by now very much an Autumn sun, rather than a Summer one. It was chilly up there in the wind, but chasing after Sacha and trying to keep up with Francis kept Diana warm enough for her to agree to eating their picnic sitting out on the grass on Sacha's car rug, where they could continue to enjoy the glorious view spread below them with Sacha, temporarily at rest, beside them. It was only then, as they shared Benita's gift of home-made pork pie, pickled onions, home-made rolls with cheese and fat red tomatoes, followed with home-made cake and apples, that Francis again raised the subject of Burnthouse. Benita had included two cans of beer and a water bottle in the cold bag she had packed for them, he pulled the tag on one of the beers, and said, 'W-w-well? You've had t-t-time to s-sort out your impressions n-now, t-tell me the worst.'

Diana replied only after a pause, because she was still thinking this out: she sensed it was important what she said. 'I thought, it must have been beautiful in its heyday,' was what she eventually settled for, '—but it's in such a state! What had they been thinking about – those tenants? It was criminal neglect, and with such a great house too.'

'N-not a l-lot, if rumour d-d-doesn't lie. Th-they were away w-w-with the f-fairies half the t-time, a l-load of junkies p-playing at organic f-farming – w-which ent-tails a l-lot of b-bloody hard w-w-work, which th-they w-weren't b-b-bothering t-to do. S-s-successive landlords aren't b-blameless either, and that's over decades, not j-just years – hence the way it's all d-d-deteriorated so far.' He sounded disgusted: Diana agreed with him.

'Such a shame.' She thought about this. 'And the last owner, presumably, did nothing about it, because if that man was right, it suited him fine if they trashed the place?'

'S-something like that, I imagine. It c-c-certainly l-looks as if he didn't care. It w-w-was only when the l-locals threatened t-t-to call the Police over th-their behaviour in the v-v-village that he g-got an eviction order. Th-then he had to c-c-call the Police t-t-to m-make them leave. And if you w-w-wonder how I know all that, M-Merlin f-f-filled me in, when he t-told me it was f-for s-s-sale.'

'He being the landlord? So the locals must be overjoyed to see you!'

'Th-they think he hoped th-they'd set fire t-to it w-with all their r-r-rituals, so th-that he could collect a m-m-million on the insurance. If he could have, I w-w-wouldn't know about that.'

'So he must have been really upset, when you walked in and made an ordinary offer based on the state it was in?'

'W-we c-c-can hope s-so. Now s-stop changing the subject.'

Diana thought, not wholly amused, that the soon-to-be-ex-landlord would now be another person with a grudge to nurse. She said, 'I'm surprised he didn't set fire to it himself, if he felt like that.'

'W-well, m-m-maybe he d-didn't. It's only g-gossip anyway. N-now st-top d-ducking and d-diving, please. W-will you l–like to live there?'

'All right. Yes, then, I can see it has huge potential. And I love the position. But I shall be interested to hear your plans for making it fit to live in, because at the moment I wouldn't put a pig in it!'

Francis smothered a laugh. 'D-d-don't traduce p-pigs, they're n–no w-w-worse than th-the rest of us if th-they're c-c-cared for p-properly.' He bit into an apple, and chewed thoughtfully. Finally, he said, 'It h-has to b-b-be an on-going operation. St-stage one, the roof. Stage t-two, an arm-my of in-ind-indus- them, anyway, all th-through the house f-from th-the b-beams that hold up the r-r-roof t-t-to the cellar f-floor. Th-then we have t-to d-deal with the w-woodworm and d-dry rot. M-meanwhile, you-c-can b-be p-planning w-what you w-w-want to d-do with it w-when all that's d-done, b-but th-there are l–limitations, r-remember, b-because it's l-listed.'

'I can be planning?'

'It's your d-d-department, I sh-shall be d-d-dealing w-with outside.' He flashed her an amused look and took another bite of his apple, continuing after a pause to chew it. 'Th-there's the m-m-manure heap to sh-shift for one th-thing, and w-w-we sh-shall need at least four b-big skips for the rubbish, p-probably more. Th-that's b-b-before I even start on the st-state of the f-farm buildings or the f-f-fields.'

'You're never going to attack all that on your own! You'll kill yourself!'

'N-no, of c-c-course I'm n-not' He gave her a lazy smile that not for the first time, made her heart turn over. 'Once we c-complete, I c-c-can employ p-p-people t-to help. Th-think about it.'

Diana thought. It made her feel very strange.

'So, what you're offering me is technically a business partnership?'

'Among other th-things. And of one k-kind or another.'

'Don't smile at me like that. I can't think!'

'D-do you n-n-need to th-think?'

'Not really. It's a no-brainer, and yes, I hereby accept the challenge! But I should warn you that my interior-decoration skills are as yet untested.'

'Th-they can't be w-w-worse th-than mine. C-come here, and s-s-seal the c-contract.'

They did that, and when she had got her breath back, Diana picked up her cake again – she had dropped it on the rug in the encounter, and only just beat Sacha to it. It was amazing how he had woken up on the instant, he couldn't possibly have heard it fall – could he?

'So, you fill me in now. Will you move over here as soon as you complete, or what?' She was fishing, she realised, for a definite confirmation of his intentions towards herself in that respect, not liking to ask outright in case she had read him wrong.

'I sh-shall be at Sh-Shortlanesend for a c-couple of weeks m-more after the c-c-completion date, it won't be f-f-fit f-for human h-habitation out here before th-that. Then I'll move the v-van on site, w-when the y-yard is clear.' He stopped there, and Diana turned her head to look at him, but he was looking out to the sea and didn't meet her eyes. 'I h-hope you w-w-will come out here w-with me th-then. B-but it won't be exactly luxurious. You don't have t-to.'

Diana caught her breath, that shot had come out of left field and caught her unprepared. She said, trying not to stammer worse than he did himself, 'Yes I do. For all sorts of reasons, not least because how can I plan what to do with the house, since you've landed me with it, if I'm not there on site to see what's going on and talk to the contractors?' She was talking to give herself time to think, but really, this was another no-brainer. She finished, with a gentleness that surprised even herself, 'but most of all, and far more important, I can't think of anything I'd like to do more.'

He turned then, and met her eyes, and what she saw in his expression removed the last possible doubt from her head, heart, and every other relevant body part. She caught her breath, which was fortunate as she had no opportunity to catch another for several minutes: it was an entirely different animal of a kiss from the one that had sealed the work contract. When they finally let each other go, for a moment she couldn't breathe at all.

They sat there for a while in the slowly-cooling afternoon sunshine, Francis with his arms around her and she with her head on his chest. As the sun went round, the wind was getting up; she snuggled closer for warmth and felt his arms tighten round her. Then he said, 'Did you want th-that l-last beer, or are you ha-happy with the w-w-water?' and they both sat up, the spell abruptly broken.

'You have it,' Diana said. 'I'd sooner have a hot coffee, to be honest. This wind has a bit of a nip in it, don't you think?'

'W-we'll g-go and f-f-find one in a bit.' He reached for the second can and pulled the top off, but then sat with it in his hands, looking out to the sea once more rather than at her. 'I n-n-need to t-t-talk to you first. I th-think I do.'

'About anything particular?' Diana asked cautiously, when he said nothing more. He didn't answer her directly, but continued his study of the horizon as he said, 'Ernie t-t-told me he w-was shooting his m-m-mouth off a bit l-l-last night.'

'He did a bit, yes. I can forget what he said, if you want.'

'N-no, don't d-d-do that. I sh-should have told you m-myself c-come to that. I d-d-did mean to. It j-j-just never seemed t-t-to come up.'

'You did sort of tell me, I knew you'd done a university course. I just didn't have the details.'

'W-well, now you have.'

'Yes.' She wondered momentarily where to go from there, but realistically, there was only one direction. 'I just assumed you'd studied something agricultural – as a follow-up from Agricultural College, maybe.'

'I d-did.'

'Don't split hairs, I know you did – in the end. But before that...if I understood what Ernie said correctly, you are a qualified marine biologist.'

'I've n–never worked as one, it's j–just b–been a hobby. You kn–know w–w–why.'

'Yes, you were stuck with the family seat.'

He said nothing to that, just took a swallow of the beer and continued to study the horizon, because both of them knew that wasn't the only obstacle. To break the silence, Diana said, 'You must have done all that studying for some reason. It must have taken years!'

'It helped to pass the t–t–time in the evenings, when I w–w–wasn't taken up w–with the estate. And it's s–s–something th–that I f–find interesting. It wasn't g–going to l–lead anywhere, n–not th–then, anyway – and face it, n–nobody's ever g–g–going to want m–me on an under–w–w–water survey team.'

'I'm not sure that's true,' said Diana, thinking about it; she had watched a few wildlife and nature programmes in her time. 'Don't they have those submersible things these days, that you can go right down to the bottom of the Mariannas Trench in, or something?'

'Th–they do. Yes.'

She had missed something there, Diana realised. She re-ran the brief conversation through her head, and this second time, she spotted it.

'You said "not then",' she said. '"It wasn't going to lead anywhere, not then." So tell me about "now".'

He said nothing for a minute, and then, when he did speak, it sounded like a complete change of subject. 'H–he t–told you about the t–tithe b–barn too, he s–said. Ernie.'

'Yes – or actually, Benita did, but yes anyway. Are you changing the subject, Dr Chillingworth?'

'N–no.' He did look at her then. 'Any ideas w–w–why I m–might do that?'

'Benita said you could put a farm manager in it.' Diana was beginning to see a pattern here; she liked the look of it – if she was on the right track, she liked the look of it. She took the bull, appropriately enough, by the horns. 'Are you telling me you plan to let someone else feed the cows and plough the fields, and go off and do ...well, something different?'

'I m–might be.'

'Don't tease,' said Diana, and he laughed.

'All r–r–right, then. It's a b–b–bit of a work in p–progress r–right now, f–first thing is t–t–to get the house and th–the f–f–farm up to speed, that w-will take us until th-the end of n-next year, probably. I've p-put out f-f-feelers for s-s-someone to help w-w-with the f-farm side – I w-w-was at c-college w-with him, b-but we k-kept in touch. I th-think he'll c-come, he and his w-wife. W-when we c-can m-move into the house, th-they'll take over th-the caravan while the barn is c-converted. Th-that won't be immediately, w-w-we need p-planning permission f-first, b-before we c-c-can do anything.' It was a long speech for him, and ended abruptly.

'Sounds good so far,' said Diana, encouragingly, when he spun out the pause with another swallow of his beer.

'I t-told you th-the next bit alr-r-ready. I m-m-mean to b-buy a yacht.'

'What kind of a yacht? A swanky gin palace like my father's, or what?'

'N-not a g-gin palace, n-no. S-s-something with sails.' There was something in the way he said that, that made Diana ask, 'Any ideas what?'

Francis said, slowly as if he was thinking it out as he spoke, 'There's one d-d-down in the M-Marina now, it b-b-belongs to an acquaintance of m-mine – m-my solicitor's s-stepdaughter, actually.' He paused there for another swallow of beer, and after a moment, Diana said, 'And?'

'Her m-m-marriage c-c-crashed earlier th-this year – n-n-not surprised, the m-m-man was a complete t–tosser.' He gave her a brief glance. 'You m-m-may w-well meet him, if V-val gets this j-job he's after; he w-works for Alex H-hetherington. D-don't look f-f-forward to it.'

I'm assuming that's relevant?' Diana prompted, when for a minute he said nothing more.

'I th-think so. Th-the yacht m-may well be a c-c-casualty in the d-divorce. S-susan has m-moved t -t-to C-Cornwall, her s-s-sister lives there, her b-brother t-t-too. Sh-she has t-two young children, she m-m-may n-not f-fancy s-sailing such a big b-boat on her own.'

'But if she has family there -?'

'D-debbie runs a s-s-sailing school, she w-wouldn't have t-t-time. And Oliver – w-well, he c-couldn't either.'

'So she may be up for sale – this yacht? But she isn't as of now?'

'S-something like th-that, yes. I t-t-told B-bob and Merlin to l-let me know if th-th-they hear anything. I'd r-r-really, really l-l-like to own her. She's b-b-beautiful.'

'Wouldn't the husband want her?'

'Ap-part from th-the fact that he c-c-couldn't sail a plastic b-boat in the b-bath, he p-probably c-couldn't m-m-maintain her without S-Susan's input; wooden b-boats eat money. So h-h-hopefully n-not.'

Diana realised that she had inadvertently side-tracked the discussion, not for the first time. She said, 'So if you could buy her – or any other yacht, failing that one – then if you had a reliable manager, you would be free to go cruising and stuff? Racing maybe? That kind of thing?'

'N-n-not exactly, no.' He looked at her directly for the first time. 'I'd t-t-take her to the M-Mediterranean.'

'Whoo!' said Diana, before she could stop herself. 'That sounds like a plan!'

'M-more of a plan than it s-s-sounds, actually.' He paused: 'I d-d-don't know if you'd be up f-for this.'

'Try me. You never know your luck.' She smiled at him, but he didn't smile back; he looked serious.

'Y-you'll have h-heard about c-c-climate change, of course, b-but I d-don't know h-how ecologic-cally aware you are in detail, s-s-so bear with m-me. Th-there's a lot of p-pollution in the M-M-Med. S-sewage from b-boats, g-general r-rubbish, all k-k-kinds of cleaning ch-chemicals th-th-that get into the d-drains and f-flush out to the s-s-sea. It's h-having an effect on th-the s-sea life, f-fish st-stocks are d-d-declining and th-there are ch-changes along th-the shoreline, and in th-the sh-shallow w-water. I w-want to d-do a detailed st-study in the sh-shallows, where I c-can work, and m-maybe write a p-paper on it for the University. Or even wr-write a b-book.'

'You'd be safe to do that? If you can't dive…'

'I w-wouldn't have to. Snorkelling won't hurt me, and p-paddling around in pools certainly won't.' He paused. 'W-when you g-get tired of s-sunbathing on the b-beach, you c-c-could come with me. And p-people w-will alm-most certainly c-come out to join us for h-holidays. K-kim and V-val, I expect, and m-my cousins. And Merlin and J-Julie-Anne. M-maybe even S-susan and her kids, if she actually s-s-sells me the b-boat. B-but if n-not th-that one, th-there'll be another. W-what d-do you think?'

'I think it sounds an amazing idea! When do we start?' If she was honest, it had taken her breath away – and for more than one reason.

'F-first we n-n-need a base t-to w-w-work from; if S-silver Spirit isn't a g-goer, w-we need to find another, w-we'll need t-t-to be able to move around. And w-we won't g-get out to the M- Med next year, th-there's too much t–to do here. The f-following s-spring, we should be g-good to go.'

'And in the meantime, you can teach me to sail properly.' She paused there, not before time, she realised. There were questions arising; at least one of them was important. 'You're not planning to cross the Bay of Biscay twice a year, are you?' She sounded apprehensive, and he grinned at her.

'N-no. I'll l-lay her up out there for the w-winter, w-wherever we end up, we'll b-bring her back when I f-f-finish the s-survey, in a couple of years maybe. You don't have t-to worry.'

'So, would I be right in thinking, we're going to spend quite a lot of time out there?'

'You could b-be. Yes.'

Diana looked at him. Even just talking about it, she saw, had brought more animation into his face than she had ever seen before, it set him alight. She hadn't guessed how much his love for, and fascination with, what went on in and under the sea had meant to him. Maybe there was more yet to learn. She said, 'And there was me thinking I was going to be a farmer's wife!'

'I h-hope you're not d-d-disappointed.'

'Oh, desperately! I was really looking forward to mucking out the chickens.'

'Oh, y-y-you'll get p-plenty of chance to do th-that. W-we can't be out th-there all the time, there is s-s-still the farm to l-look after, even if th-there's a m-manager here: it can't all be done by computer. You're shivering.'

'The wind's getting up. I know you're a hardy outdoors-man, but I'm not, I'm just a feeble female who's led a sheltered life!'

'OK then. We'll go and find that coffee, shall we?' He began to sweep the debris of their picnic together and to pack it back haphazardly into the cold bag. Sacha jumped to his feet and stood wagging his tail, obviously expecting another run. Diana said, 'If you get off the rug, I'll put it back in the car – he's getting ideas!'

After giving Sacha another brief run, he was reluctantly persuaded to jump into the back of the car and they set off back through the winding lanes. When they regained the proper road that led through Shearwater, Francis set off in the opposite direction.

'Now where are we off to?' asked Diana, with interest. It had already been an amazingly instructive day, she wondered with apprehension what was in store for her now. She had never, she realised, spent a whole day with Francis before; on present form it was going to be unexpectedly stimulating living with him.

'T-town. Th-there-s a coffee shop on th-the s-s-seafront; w-when we've w-w-warmed you up a bit, we can w-w-walk to the M-M-Marina.'

'And look at this yacht you've got your eye on?'

'W-wouldn't you like to?'

'I'd like to very much. But don't set your heart on it too much, will you? If it's not even for sale…'

'N-no, Auntie.'

The coffee shop was indeed on the seafront, although the wrong side of the road for it to have an uninterrupted view of the harbour, and sold fancy coffee in enormous cups; after she had downed a cappuccino that was almost too hot to hold, let alone to drink, Diana began to feel warmer, although still mildly bewildered. The speed the day was going, she reflected, only half in amusement, she would be glad when it came to an end and she could think about all the new things she had learned and all the new impressions she was still receiving. It was all good, of course but it needed digesting; she had been parachuted abruptly down into a land where she neither fully understood the natives nor was familiar with the customs. Exciting, yes, but it would be nice to stand back and consider the implications, some of which, she admitted to herself, were disquieting.

For just one of these, the courage that Francis must have shown to get through all those years of…yes, of virtual imprisonment, must have been heartbreaking; the change in him already, in just twenty-four hours, told its own tale. It was true, too, that whatever lay in the future, a lot of what he had lost could never be returned to him; youth, perfect physical fitness, ambition…or maybe she wasn't too sure about the last. His mother too, must have lived a nightmare, for it had been obvious to Diana, on the one occasion that they had met, that she had loved her beautiful only son, and no doubt been proud of him once upon a time, and had high hopes for him, so how much had those lost years cost her, too? How much could be healed or retrieved, for either of them? A wave of fury against the two who had been the cause of it all, her own mother and his father, swept over her out of nowhere and nearly made her drop her cup. She had never seen it so clearly as she was seeing it now; she wondered if Kim had ever done so.

'You've g-gone very quiet,' said Francis, watching her.

'I feel very quiet. You've given me a lot to think about.'

'N-not having s-s-second thoughts, I hope?'

'Certainly not! It's just an awful lot to take in all at once.' She put down her finally empty cup on its saucer. 'Come on then, you were going to show me a boat.'

They collected Sacha, from where he was attached sulking to a ring outside the door of the coffee shop, and walked together along the seafront. The huge new Marina had been constructed about halfway along, they had to walk through a small car park and past the Marina Office to get to the steps that led down to the first long pontoon; nobody took any interest in them although there were one or two people about – no more, not on an almost-October Monday.

'It's all very lush and expensive-looking,' Diana said, looking about her. She had had in her head, she realised, a picture of a small family-sized sailing yacht, much like the ones she had seen on flotillas when she had been out in the Mediterranean on her father's motor yacht; there was nothing like that here. Or if there was, she corrected herself, they were all much bigger in close-up. Not for the first time today, she wondered what she was letting herself in for. And then they stopped, and she knew.

Silver Spirit wasn't the biggest boat in the Marina, but she was still big compared to most of them: even the foreshortened view from the pontoon was enough to convince Diana of that. She was also both elegant and beautiful, Francis had certainly been right about that, and she was long enough to have two masts, plus a bowsprit that soared up at the bow.

'This is it?' she asked, not sure if she hoped for an affirmative answer or not, and Francis said, 'Y-yes.'

'I don't think I was expecting anything quite so...so big. What is she, a schooner?'

'A ketch. And y-you'll be g-glad of the size if we're l-living on her, b-believe me. I c-c-can t-take up a lot of r-r-room.'

'I'd already noticed. I'm really looking forward to the caravan – not!' They exchanged a quick smile, and then she returned her attention to the boat in front of her. 'She's like Burnthouse – beautiful. But hopefully, in better condition.' He liked beautiful things, she realised now; the house, his car, his horses, his cows presumably, if they won him prizes, cats, now this lovely yacht. Me? she found herself adding, and then, I hope so! and couldn't help letting a giggle escape which made Francis grin at her.

'I w-w-won't ask you what you w-w-were th-thinking just then,' he said. He put his arm around her shoulders and turned her round; they walked back up the pontoon together with Sacha trotting behind them. It was too cold to stand around for long; the sky had clouded over while they drank their coffee, there was even a spatter of rain in the wind now.

When they were back at the car, Francis unlocked the door for Diana to climb in while he stowed Sacha in the back, before slipping in beside her. He put the ignition key into its hole, but didn't turn it; instead, he turned with his hand resting on it and looked at her.

'W-what d-d-do you want to do n-now?' he asked her. 'I c-c-can t-take you back to Romans, if y-you w-w-want to spend a b-b-bit of t-t-time with Kim, or you c-could come back with me. It's going to be too w-w-wet to do anything m-much.' Which was true, the rain was already harder than it had been while they were at the Marina, and picking up speed by the minute.

'Kim may not be there,' said Diana. 'I was out with you, so as she's got the car, she said she might go over to Shearwater to see Val's mother between shifts. I think Valerie wants to talk about weddings and things – although it's a bit early yet, I would have thought. Six months, now they've changed the date! But I suppose they have to liaise with New Zealand… she'll be back later, but her shift at the pub starts at six.'

'Sh-shortlanesend, th-then?'

'Got to be better than sitting alone, watching the rain come down.' She smiled at him.

'Hmm.' He engaged reverse and backed out of their parking space out onto the road that ran past the harbour, but he didn't turn back the way they had come. Instead, he headed off back past the Marina. Diana had never been along this way before; she asked, 'Now where're we off to? This is a real magical mystery tour you've taken me on today!'

'W-where I said – Sh-shortlanesend. Haven't you been this w-way before? It goes p–past the commercial d-d-dock and out th-the other end of t-town.'

Diana looked about her with more interest; she had known, of course, that there must be a fishing quay somewhere, because there were fishing boats around on the water, both in the harbour and out on the sea: it had never occurred to her to wonder where it was. Now she saw it, a big, solid stone enclosure reaching out into the waters of the harbour. There was one fishing boat moored against the seaweedy outside wall, with a couple of men heaving lobster pots around, and a few more against the quays inside, plus a couple of yachts and a bigger boat that looked as if she might be used for commercial diving. Sheds and buildings on the far quay were probably offices or storage sheds, or both.

'It doesn't look very busy,' she said.

Francis had slowed down so that she could have a better look. 'It's not,' he said. 'Th-the fishing fleet is a l-l-lot smaller than it used t-t-to be b-b-because of f-f-fishing quotas and d-d-diminishing fish stocks. M-more y-yachts use it in th-th-summer these d-d-days. Th-the M-M-Marina g-gets p-pretty full in July and Aug-g-gust.'

'At least that will keep it alive. That's got to be good, surely?'

'F-for yachtsmen, and p-people on holiday.'

'Not for the fishermen. I see what you mean.' She looked around her at the buildings on the opposite side of the road. 'This is definitely the lower end of town, isn't it? All those blocks of posh flats at the other end, and all these little fishermen's cottages and corner shops along here! Is this end of town the original bit, then?'

'P-pretty m-much, I s-s-suppose. It grew up r-r-round the f-fishing originally.' He indicated across the road, to where a seedy looking pub lurked in the now-much-heavier rain. 'Th-that place is about th-the same age as B-burnthouse. In about th-the same s-s-state too.'

'Shame. Have you ever been inside it?'

'Only th-the once. Th-that was enough, it's a d-d-dive.'

'The Duck Inn,' said Diana, as they left the forlorn building behind. 'So, do you have to? Duck, that is?'

'I d-did. You w-w-wouldn't. And it's th-the D-Dock Inn.'

'Oops! That sign is almost illegible.'

'L-l-like everything else. The C-council w-w-want to knock it all d-d-down and b-build more apartment b-blocks.' He didn't say what he thought about that, but she thought she could guess.

They had, by this time, left the shore road behind and begun to climb through a narrow street of terraced houses and B&B signs, again, the houses were all much older than the buildings in the centre of town but obviously in good repair, so it wasn't all bad news around here. Diana looked about her with interest: it could be a completely different town. Shame about that poor old pub, it really let the side down, and from the look of them, the houses immediately adjacent had been thinking about joining it!

They were going downhill again now, emerging finally on the familiar road that led from the town, but turned off before they reached the cottage – thank goodness, Diana thought, she didn't want to see that, thank you – and onto a road that ran up into the foothills above the back of the town, that now dropped away behind them to be replaced by fields golden with autumn and fiery hedgerows with brilliant foliage bowing under the rain.

'You certainly know your way around,' said Diana, only half in admiration; she was completely lost again.

'I h–have l–lived here all of my l–l–life.'

'Is all this your family's land?' Diana asked, looking at it with interest.

'N–no, we're further to the west. This is Ravenscourt t–t territory. The p–posh end.' They dived down another narrow lane, that looked almost too narrow for the Range Rover to pass down and had a surface composed largely of wet mud, and after a hundred yards or so, slithered out onto a road Diana recognised, the one leading to Shortlanesend. She looked at her watch, it was half–past three.

'It's Kim's last night at the pub, tonight,' she said. 'She signed on until the end of September, they probably won't need her after that. And if they do, they know where to find her. But I did say I would try and get down there some time this evening. Is that OK with you? Because you'll have to drive me back – or I suppose I could get a real taxi.'

'D–don't be daft, of c–c–course I'll d–drive you.' He paused to negotiate the farm gate. 'C–come to that, I was p–planning to t–take you out for a m–m–meal tonight anyway. We can have f–fish and chips at the T–two Pigeons, and annoy K–kim. N–not quite what I h–h–had in m–mind, but th–there'll be other n–n–nights.'

They parked the Discovery in the yard, and while Francis closed the gate behind them, Diana released Sacha from the back, and they all three made a dash for the back door and went through it more or less together. Inside, they found Ernest sitting in one of the big wing chairs that flanked the Aga, with a huge mug in his hand, and Benita sitting at the table with a smaller one, holding forth about something with considerable indignation. The second wing chair was occupied by Birdie. Asleep. Benita broke off what she was saying in mid–sentence as the back door opened. She said,

'Oh, hello, did you have a good day?' and drew a breath to continue her diatribe, but Ernest interrupted her.

'Give it a rest for a second, Bennie, and get these two some tea. They must be frozen. Then you can tell us all again.' He gave a grin to the newcomers. 'Bennie went to a committee meeting of one of her charities this morning. It turned out to be a bit more exciting than it generally is. Sit down, take your coats off. She'll tell you.'

'It's not "my" charity, it's one I got shanghaied into by that hyena Jenny Carruthers! And if it happens again, in future, they may have my donations, but they do not get my time!' She took Diana's wet coat from her and threw it over the back of a chair. 'Move the cat, and sit down. I'll make some more tea.'

'I wouldn't have the heart,' said Diana, pulling out a chair at the table and sitting down. 'I daresay Francis will, though.'

'T-t-too r-right!' He scooped up the sleepily indignant cat into his arms and looked across at Diana. 'You sure you're OK th-there? It's w-w-warmer by the Aga.'

'It's warm in here anyway. You take it, it's a better size for you.'

'God knows how he'll fit into a caravan,' said Ernest, stretching his legs out luxuriously. 'You sure you don't want this chair, Tamsin?'

'Don't nag the poor girl. She's already said,' Benita told him.

'Just being polite,' said Ernest, grinning.

Benita made two mugs of tea, and Francis settled down in the wing chair with the cat on his lap, where she promptly purred herself back to sleep, and Sacha threw himself disgustedly at his feet, where he lay with his head on his paws and his eyes on the cat. 'S-s-so what h-happened?' Francis asked, and Ernest groaned.

'You've done it now! She really will tell you!'

Benita drew out a chair beside Diana and sat down, her mug between her hands.

'Jenny's been bitching for ages, trying to oust Dorothy Nankervis – that's Francis's solicitor's ex-wife, Tamsin. He walked out on her, I'll tell you why in a minute. Anyway, she – that's Jenny, not Dorothy, has always wanted to be the chairman of the committee herself – the stupid cow is power crazy! She's not had much luck until now, but what happened this past year gave her some ammunition, and she hasn't been slow to use it—'

'Hold on a minute,' Diana interrupted. 'I'm a stranger in these parts, remember. What did happen?'

'Oops – sorry. Dorothy's daughter – that's Debbie, not Susan – got herself involved with an ex-con, a rough-as-rats Cornishman who reputedly ran some sleazy village pub down in Cornwall, and Dorothy, so gossip has it, told her she needn't come home until he was history – which of course is why her husband finally took off – although gossip has it that had been on the cards for a while. But on the face of it, she deserved some sympathy – I wouldn't want that for my daughter, after all.' She paused, and Diana asked, 'What did he go to prison for?'

'Manslaughter,' said Ernest, and took a sip of his tea.

'Ouch! She had a point then.'

'Except, as it now turns out, that isn't necessarily the case,' said Benita. 'For one thing, although he did serve a prison sentence, the conviction was recently squashed on appeal—'

'Not exactly the technical term, but you know what she means,' said Ernest.

'Ernie, shut up will you? You're not helping!' She turned pointedly to Diana. 'Anyway, he actually owns the pub, but he doesn't run it himself at all, and he also owns the restaurant next door, which he does run – he's the head chef, and the place is building itself an enviable reputation, and worst of all, he's been on the telly just recently so that everyone – including Jenny – knows that Dorothy has, shall we say, slightly over-reacted, and made a silly fool of herself!'

'Hang on a minute – I think I may have seen him. He was part of that series they did on Cornwall, one of the last episodes I think I remember – they visited his restaurant, and he goes out on a motor bike sourcing his own food – that the one you're talking about? He's Cornish enough for anyone!'

'Mawgan Angwin. Yes. You liked him, then?'

'I found him entertaining, but he's a bit out of my class as a cook. Kim thinks he's brilliant.'

'And she's right. He made a big hit, he's a real charmer as well as a brilliant chef – which is odd really, because he's no looker – not like your man there.' She nodded towards Francis, and added, 'Although, come to think, he may have more charisma! But anyway, back to the story – it now turns out that they're giving him his own series this autumn – it starts next month and runs until Christmas. This morning, Madame Carruthers set out to make poor Dorothy look a great big fool in front of all her friends on the Committee, laughing at her and pointing the finger the way she does so well – I backed her up of course – Dorothy, I mean, not Juggernaut Jen. She wouldn't have liked it for a daughter of hers, after all, if she had one!'

'Well d-d-done,' said Francis. He had put his mug of tea on the top of the stove and had his eyes shut as he gently stroked the cat; he looked as if at any minute he would fall asleep but Diana, who was beginning to think she knew him better these days, wasn't convinced.

'Anyway,' said Bennie, 'I managed to rally some of the troops and we got her to back off – but she'll be back on the attack as soon as he's back on the telly, you can bet your boots – the stupid woman never knows when to shut up, give up, and bugger off!'

'Somebody should set about that bloody woman!' said Ernest. 'Jenny, I mean, not Dot. She's a total pain in the arse. Fancy the job, Francis? She's a friend of your mother's, isn't she? You could sort her out for us, or Mary could.'

'N-n-no,' said Francis, still without opening his eyes. 'To b-both, in case you're w-w-wondering.'

'She thinks she is,' said Benita. 'She's always boasting about, she and Mary are bosom pals.'

'N-no.'

'A man of few words,' said Ernest, 'or just one word, come to think.' He reached out to put his mug on the table and then got to his feet. 'Well, some of us have work to do, so I'll leave you all to your gossiping. See you later, Tamsin?'

'Depends what time you get back in. We're off out for fish and chips this evening.'

'Good gracious!' said Ernie. 'Well, have fun – no doubt we'll be seeing you tomorrow then, if I don't see you again tonight.' The back door closed behind him with a thump. Benita looked at Diana.

'Sorry – I was holding forth a bit there, but that woman really winds me up! Let's change the subject – if you're off to London on Thursday, why don't you and Kim come over here for supper tomorrow night? We'd love to meet her, and if she isn't working at the pub any more…?'

'I have to ask her, of course, but it sounds a lovely idea. Thank you.'

Benita got to her feet and began rounding up the scattered mugs. 'Now tell me, I'm dying to hear – what did you think of Burnthouse?'

X

Fortunately, there was to be a brief period of calm before the next act in the drama was due to unfold.

On a Tuesday evening at the very end of September, the bar at the Two Pigeons wasn't crowded, even at half-past eight, There were one or two drinkers up at the bar, a couple with two teenagers sitting eating burgers at a table, and a group of men around the pool table making enough noise for twice their number, and that was about all. Of Kim, there was no immediate sign, so Francis got the drinks while Diana studied the menu board up behind the bar. On a weekday, and at this time of year, this was not exactly spoiling them for choice: on the other hand, one could only eat one thing at a sitting, and one of her favourites was duly displayed up there.

'I'll have scampi and chips,' she said, and Francis settled for a rare rump steak. They placed their order and then carried their drinks to a table and sat down to wait. Nobody took any notice of them; they were strangers here so they were left in peace, apart from one of the pool players, on his way to the bar for a refill, who stopped briefly to say, 'Hullo Kim, given you a night off, have they? Like the new hair, but that's a nasty bruise you've got there!' Diana smiled at him, and he moved on with a nod to acknowledge Francis. Even without the help of her favourite hair-straightener – she had lost the habit of using this at the cottage, where there had been no power to run it – her hair was shorter than Kim's, and more stylish than Kim's practical ponytail.

'I take it, you're not a regular in this pub,' she said, making it a statement, not a question, and immediately wished that she hadn't; it was perfectly possible, she now realised, that the last time Francis had been in this bar was the night on which his father died in a road accident outside the fated cottage. Francis, thank goodness, made no comment beyond. 'I g-generally use the R-Ravenscourt Arms,' and the conversation, if you could call it that, foundered. Well away from the Sailing Club then. Diana had to remind herself that it was his suggestion, not hers, to come here.

'Kim doesn't work the bar unless it's busy,' she said, after a moment or two, as much to break the silence as anything. 'She'll be out at the back – probably serve us, and drop the plates with shock!' This was what people called "small talk", she realised. Francis was looking tired again, she noticed with compassion, he had drifted off somewhere with his eyes on some far horizon. It was going to take him more than a night and a day to put the recent past behind him and get used to the present, and today hadn't been exactly restful. She decided she had better find something that was actually interesting to say before he nodded off with a thud onto the table, but unfortunately, the only thing that came into her head was, 'You look as if you could do with an early night,' which thankfully had the effect of making him burst out laughing and look at her instead of into outer space.

'Sorry, T-tamsin. Y-yes, I am a bit t-t-tired – I only s-s-seem to s-sleep properly when I should b-b-be attending to s-s-something else. I w-was wide awake half l-l-last n-night.'

'To be fair, I feel a bit jaded myself,' said Diana, and even thinking about it made her want to yawn. 'It's all that fresh air and exercise, I think. Perhaps we'd better talk about something that will keep us awake until our dinner arrives.'

'OK. Y-you think of s-s-something then. M-my brain has c-c-crashed.'

'All right then – try this. Assuming your biological bonanza isn't going to cover the entire Mediterranean, which I don't see how it can, exactly, where particularly did you have in mind?'

That brought him back into focus properly, she saw thankfully. Their night out hadn't looked too promising so far.

'I'm w-w-working on it. D-do you have any f-f-favourite places? You m-m- must have spent m-m-more t-time out there th-than I've had a ch-chance to th-these years p-past.'

'That's a good question.' Diana thought about it, mentally revisiting all the places she had been to with her parents, but they wouldn't do, not really; they tended to be a bit too Monte Carlo for a marine biologist. But they had occasionally visited quieter places too. She thought about those, and finally came up with, 'I loved Greece. And Italy – but Greece has all those lovely islands, they must have loads of seaweed and swimmy things in all those rocky little bays. Would that be a good place?'

'S-spot on, I should s-s-say. Would you l-like to be b-b-based out there?'

'I'd love it. It's a great country.' She added, proudly, 'I even speak a little Greek – but it is a little, just ordering things in tavernas and stuff.'

'You'll n-n-need to brush up on it a b-bit, if that's the l-l-limit,' said Francis, laughing.

'Kim was going to work as a translator if she'd gone back to New Zealand,' said Diana. 'That's one reason why she was back-packing round Europe, but she got side-tracked. We're supposed to be identical.' She sounded doubtful. 'Perhaps I could go to classes?'

'M-m-maybe Kim could t-t-teach you,' he suggested, and right on cue Kim came out from behind the bar, carrying cutlery and condiments for their table, and came across to them, and Diana had said, before she had thought, 'He thinks you could teach me to speak Greek. Could you?'

'No,' said Kim, not missing a beat. 'French, Italian, Spanish, take your pick. Not Greek. Sorry.' She might have added more, but at that moment the pool player returned on his way from the bar carrying three drinks in his hands, saw the pair of them and nearly dropped the lot. He looked from Diana's fashionable bob to Kim's curly pony tail and shook his head.

'I knew I'd been hitting the bottle a bit! Didn't realise it was that much to be seeing double! Twins, are you?'

'You guessed!' Kim smiled at him. 'This is my sister Diana, Ronnie.'

'Pleased to meet you,' said Ronnie, and escaped before he really did drop the drinks on the carpet.

'Now then.' Kim pulled out a third chair at the table and perched herself on it, poised to jump up in an instant. 'I can give you about three minutes! Did you have a good day, what was the farm like, why Greek?'

Diana rose to the occasion. 'Yes, a complete tip right now but with promise, he wants to go and spend serious time out there on a boat.'

'Oh God, you can't fill me in on all of that in two and half minutes! It'll have to wait.' She got to her feet again. 'I'll be back!'

When she had left, Francis said. 'W-w-what were you p-planning for tomorrow? I should g-g-go and check on m-my cattle some time, and I expect you w-w-want to spend s-some time with Kim if she's n-not working. I have another appointm-ment with the architect about th-the b-barn conversion in the aftern-noon, b-but I can m–meet you for lunch s-somewhere if you l-like.'

Diana considered this. It fitted in with her own plans well, although she would have binned those without a second thought if he had wanted to spend another day with her, as she well realised. She said, 'Really, I ought to march Kim back to Embridge to do a bit more shopping – she has nothing at all that's fit to go out for a posh meal in London, just one nice summer dress and even that's a bit casual for my parents. Why don't you meet us in Bordens at, say, one o'clock? Would that fit in with your appointment?'

'F-fine. OK, we c-can d-do that.'

'And you'd better smarten up too,' said Diana, eyeing up his present casual sweatshirt and jeans. 'If you pass the test, my parents will want to take us out to celebrate. They've been longing for me to bring home a really eligible suitor for the last eight years or so!'

'Am I r-really eligible?' He looked at her seriously. 'I w-w-would have th-th-thought they m-m-might th-think me a b-b-bit too old for you. And th-that's just f-for s-s-starters.'

She hadn't realised that this was an issue with him – if it was; it could be a simple observation. Luckily, the answer to at least part of it was readily to hand.

'They haven't a leg to stand on if they do! My father is eleven years older than my mother.' She didn't add that his name, and his putative millions would also weigh in the scales. 'Considering what I've taken home in the past, they ought to fall on their knees and give thanks.' She changed the subject, hoping it wasn't too abruptly, but it seemed safest. 'And in the evening, we're both, that's me and Kim, invited out to Shortlanesend. And on Thursday, we're off the the Big City. And by the time we get back on Monday, it'll be less than a week before Burnthouse is yours.'

'Ours.'

'Yes. Ours.' It felt strange, saying that. 'If you really mean it, that I have a say in what we do with the house, can I run an idea I had past you? I thought about it when I saw the house this morning, and if you're going to see an architect, you could ask him about it, couldn't you? If you agreed it was a good idea, that is."

'D-d-depends what it is. I t-t-told you w-we had to be c-c-careful, and we'd n-need permission for any ch-changes we wanted to m-make.'

'Yes, you did, which is why an architect would be needed, I think. But it's only a tiny one, not seriously structural or anything – the two bedrooms over the drawing room – how much alteration would we be allowed to make, do you think?'

'Why, w-what did you have in m-m-mind?' He looked interested.

'I wondered if we could perhaps divide the smaller one at the back into two, and put two doors through into the front one. Then we could have an ensuite, and a walk-in-wardrobe too, and we needn't clutter up the other room with big cupboards. I've got an awful lot of clothes, in case you hadn't guessed!' She waited while he considered this before answering.

'Sounds like a plan – if they'd l-l-let us,' he said, finally. 'W-we m-might n-not be allowed to b-block up the door onto th-the-p-passage.'

'That wouldn't matter. We could always keep it locked, and anyway, it would look odd on the landing without it. It would be a shame. But four bedrooms will be more than enough for us, wouldn't you agree?'

'You d-d-don't want t-t-ten children, then?'

'You must be joking!' It felt really strange, she found, talking about the house they would share and children, a life that they were really going to spend together. Less than a week ago, she had thought she might never see him again – whoever was responsible for that tree, they had really done her a big favour and perhaps they should thank them, not sue them. What would have happened if that hadn't happened? She had a sad little feeling that the answer might be, nothing at all.

'N-now what're you th-thinking?' Francis asked, but fortunately before she had to reply, Kim reappeared bearing their order, which she placed in front of them with a flourish, before pulling out the spare chair again and sitting on it.

'Bess said, take ten minutes off, we're not busy unless someone else comes in,' she said. Bess was the landlord's wife.

'Are y-you allowed to d-d-drink on duty?' Francis asked, making a move to get to his feet and head for the bar, but Kim said, 'It's on its way. Eat your steak while its hot. And while you're eating it, you can both tell me what you've been up to. And start with why you want to learn Greek, before I die of curiosity. What's all this about a boat?'

'I told you he wanted to buy one,' said Diana, 'at least, I think I did. But anyway, he does. And he wants to keep it out in the Med part of the time.' She didn't give any reasons, that must come later; it was all too complicated for ten minutes in a pub, but to Kim, the idea itself was enough reason.

'Sounds wonderful. Will you have time to go out and sail it, with the farm and everything?'

'He's going to put in a manager.'

'Whoo!' said Kim, impressed. 'And live a life of leisure in the sun? Sounds good.'

'Well, not exactly that, but you get the general plan. Oh, I'll give you all the details later, but isn't it just a great idea? And you and Val can spend holidays out there with us.'

The landlord interrupted them then, coming over to the table with a glass of white wine for Kim. He greeted Francis and looked at Diana critically.

'Make a scar, that will, if you don't watch it,' he said. 'But you looks a lot better than when I last set eyes on you, that's good. Enjoy your meal.' He turned away to go back to the bar.

'In a way, I shall miss working here,' said Kim, with just a touch of regret in her voice. 'It's been fun – and they've been so good to me, but if I'm going to live here permanently, I shall need to find a proper job.'

'Any ideas?' asked Francis. 'T-T-Tamsin said you were planning to w-work as a t-translator. You c-c-could try the University, th-they might f-find a use f-f-for you, if you're g-g-good enough.'

'Oh, I'm good. But I don't have more than an MA, they might want more than that.'

'W-worth asking.'

'Or I suppose I could free-lance. Put something up on the net, offering my services – it's a small world, these days.'

'The University would be more fun. Lots of people round you.' Diana said.

'N-not n-n-necessarily a blessing,' Francis suggested. Diana speared one of her scampi on her fork and held it up.

'Not everyone prefers talking to these,' she said, and Francis grinned at her.

'They d-d-don't nag at you s-s-so much when th-they're fried,' he suggested.

Kim looked from one to the other of them, and took a sip of her wine, but made no comment. Diana's glass was empty, Francis reached across and picked it up, together with his own, equally empty, pint glass. 'I'll j-just get in a r-r-refill,' he said.

While he was up at the bar, Kim looked at Diana, thoughtfully.

'Who's that man you're with tonight?' she asked. 'He looks like Francis, well, sort of, but he sure as hell doesn't behave like him! What've you done to him?'

'Oh – it's all sorts of things, I think – not that I've done, exactly. What's happened. What's happening. What will happen. All of that. I haven't really taken it in yet.'

'Do I get to be told about it?'

'Yes, but not here. When we get back home, I'll fill you in.'

Kim looked at her steadily for a moment, then she said, 'I could always take the bunks for tonight, if you wanted. The caretaker was in to collect the laundry this morning anyway, so the sheets are clean.'

Diana thought about this for a minute.

'It's a nice idea, but – no, I don't think so. Not tonight. He needs to get some sleep, I expect he'll go home quite early – but thank you for the suggestion.' They exchanged a look, which both of them understood perfectly, and Diana added, 'I don't think you need to worry about him, you know. I doubt very much if he's exactly led the life of a monk.'

What Kim might have replied to this would remain unsaid, as Francis came back with the refills before she had a chance to say anything at all. She got to her feet as he sat down.

'I think my ten minutes must be up,' she said, and Francis raised an eyebrow at her but made no comment. 'I'll see you both later, I expect, unless you've gone to bed,' and immediately wished she had phrased that more happily.

'I'll s-say goodnight, th-th-then,' said Francis. 'I sh-sh-all g-go straight back to Sh-Shortlanesend f-from here.'

'Do we see you tomorrow, or are you busy?'

'He's meeting us for lunch in town,' said Diana. 'We can have a girls' day – he's off with his cows or something in the morning, and then he has an appointment in the afternoon – but we're both invited over to Shortlanesend for supper tomorrow, so that'll be something to look forward to. It's a great place – you'll love it. And if you're good, I expect he'll show you his chickens – you've never seen anything like them! Like little feathery snowballs running around! Benita introduced me this afternoon while he was resting his eyes by the Aga…' she caught his eye, and giggled. Kim, watching her, thought that she had never seen her twin so happy since they had first met just a few months ago; she hoped that her happiness would last and last.

A group of customers had just come in through the door, it was time to get back to work. Kim said, 'I'll see you later then. Goodnight Francis, and I hope you sleep tonight! You look as if you could do with it.' She left them with a wave and took up her position on the other side of the bar.

It would be interesting to talk with Diana alone tonight, come to that; whatever had happened today had been seminal, she felt it in her bones. Meanwhile, there were pints to pull.

Diana and Francis were gone just before ten, giving Kim a wave as they passed the bar on the way to the door, but there was no chance to speak to her, a late-night influx when a meeting at the Village Hall came to an end was occupying most of her attention. She managed a brief wave back, no more.

'I'll w-w-walk back to R-romans with you,' said Francis, when they were outside. 'I c-c-can come back for the c-c-car, there's no p-p-point in taking it for th-th-that distance.'

'I wouldn't get lost on my own, if you want to get on your way,' Diana told him. 'Look – you can actually see it from here,' but he only laughed at her.

'J-j-just qu-quit arguing and g-g-get walking,' he said, and putting an arm around her shoulders, turned her in the right direction. They walked entwined together as far as the gate, then he kissed her and said goodnight before walking back to the pub: she stood on the doorstep and watched him all the way, right up until she saw the Discovery leave the car park, before she went indoors. It had been an amazing day, full of interest and information – and long, she felt as if it had lasted at least forty-eight hours and it wasn't over yet. She had yet to run it all past Kim, she knew she wouldn't sleep until she had, however tired she felt. Probably Kim wouldn't sleep either if she wasn't filled in on the details. She settled into the corner of the sofa, switched on the television, and prepared to wait.

Kim got back from the pub shortly after eleven, to find Diana yawning in front of a talk show that was failing to hold her interest. She switched it off as soon as her twin appeared, and sat up from where she was lolling against the sofa cushions.

'I wasn't expecting you until midnight!'

'They'd pretty much gone home by half-past ten tonight. Just locals this time of year, they have homes to go to. There was only Ronnie and his crowd left, Bess and Harry said they'd deal with that and clear up, so I could come and talk to you. After all, they'll have to do it without me anyway from now. Cocoa?'

'Sounds good to me.'

'Then straighten up that sofa while I make it, so there's room for me to sit there too. It looks as if you've been having an orgy!'

'Alas, no. He went home too. Not that he has a home right now, but Shortlanesend anyway.'

Kim made no comment on this, but took herself into the kitchen to put some milk on to heat. Diana swung her legs to the floor and began obediently to shake cushions and put them straight – Kim had been right, loneliness and boredom together had made her restless and unsettled; the state of the cushions showed this all too clearly. By the time Kim came back with a steaming mug in each hand, order was restored and they sat down side by side, slightly turned to face each other, and sipped their cocoa. Kim let out a long sigh.

'That's good! I thought tonight would never end, and they were all so nice to me too, saying how much they were going to miss me.'

'No doubt you will be back in a different capacity from time to time. We both will – we all will, I daresay.'

'That's probably true. Now tell me about your day. What was the farmhouse like? And the farm? Tell me everything!'

So much had happened since she left Burnthouse with Francis at lunchtime, that it felt as if it had been yesterday rather than this morning, but Diana did her best, painting a moving picture of the manure heap and all the rubbish, and describing in gruesome detail the state of the farmhouse kitchen. The bathroom deserved a chapter to itself, she became quite lyrical on the subject. Kim listened with interest and some amusement, and asked pertinent questions now and then, but even a topic as diverse and fascinating as this one ran out of steam eventually. There was a short silence as Diana came to the point where they drove out of the farmyard and headed for the downs, for this was where the day had become really surreal.

'OK,' said Kim, when the pause became noticeable. 'So tell me the rest.'

'Rest?' said Diana, hedging.

'Something happened – didn't it?'

Diana gave up. You couldn't deceive an identical twin, as she had already learned. She said, 'The thing is, Kim, I thought I was getting a farmer, and that was fine with me – but it turns out that I'm not.'

'He looks like one to me,' said Kim. 'I know you told you me last night that his cousin said he was more the estate manager, but that's rather splitting hairs, isn't it?'

'Well, it would be, but it turns out he's not even that either, when you get down to the nitty-gritty.'

Kim thought about what she had thought she knew about Francis Chillingworth, and about the…well, the stranger she had met this evening for the first time, and found that she wasn't as surprised as she might have been yesterday. It wasn't just the walls at Burnthouse that were falling down, something similar seemed to be happening between Francis and the outside world.

'Tell me,' she said curiously, but Diana's response surprised her. Her hands clenched on the mug and she said, in a tight little voice, 'Oh Kim, I'm so angry! I can't believe—' She broke off, took an ill-judged swig of her cocoa, and choked on it. Kim removed her mug from her hands and placed it in safety on the coffee table.

'Count up to ten, and try again,' she suggested, although she already had a good idea of what her twin would say; she had half-reached a similar conclusion herself, and she only had part of the story – so far, she only had part of the story. When Diana stopped shaking – which she was – she might get the other half too.

Finally, Diana pulled herself together and apologised.

'I'm sorry – it just came over me – all the years that have been thrown away, just because our mother was a spoilt little tart and his father was weak and gullible – all Francis's young manhood and ambition, all his mother's love – she did love him Kim. She does. They've both of them lived a nightmare and nothing that happens now can ever give the years back to them. They were made to think the very worst of each other just because two silly people thought they fancied each other – and if they had actually got to New Zealand, how long do you think it would have been before the whole thing was history, and she was off with a younger man?'

'That, we can't know,' said Kim, trying to keep this on track. There's no point in speculating, it didn't happen so nobody can know. But what brought this on? You still haven't told me.'

Diana pulled herself together. She said, 'Francis.'

Kim considered this. Certainly Francis had shown an unfamiliar approachability tonight, together with a sense of humour and a relaxed warmth towards both her twin and herself, but that didn't entirely explain Diana's outburst, even if she sympathised with it.

'You'd better tell me,' she said. 'What's he done now?'

'Nothing – yet. It's what he's done in the past, and what he plans to do in the future that's breaking my heart.'

'You'd better tell me,' said Kim, again, after a pause, and Diana pulled herself together and took a deep breath.

'It's the marine biology thing – I already told you, he has two degrees in it, but what I didn't tell you, because I didn't know until this afternoon, is that he never gave up his ambition…his dream, if you like. I thought it was just an interest – something he kept up with to pass the time – like you and me doing crosswords, but a bit cleverer of course. But it wasn't. Now that he's been given his life back, that's exactly what he intends to do – be a practising marine biologist, do his own research in the field, write about it for other people to study. He never gave up on the dream.'

'Hence, Greece,' said Kim, after a pause to take this in. She didn't make it a question.

'Exactly. Now you see why I feel a bit…well, stunned is the word, actually.'

'I see that, but it doesn't explain why you over-reacted the way you did just now. Most people would call that a happy ending.'

'But it hasn't ended.' Diana spoke soberly. She reached out for her cocoa and took a mouthful, this time without choking on it, holding the mug between her hands thereafter, and staring into its depths. 'It's not just the terrible waste – he intends to redress that anyway, at least as far as he can. It's the damage, Kim. What was he thinking about – Francis's father, I mean? He didn't just wreck his family relationships, he wrecked their whole lives. I don't know about you, Kim, but it breaks my heart.'

It was the second time she had said that in as many minutes; Kim heard the grief, as well as the fury, in her voice and chose her words carefully. 'It wasn't our fault though, you can't take that burden on yourself. We were too young to know anything about it. And everybody who needs to knows the truth now, it will heal. Give it time.'

Diana said, without looking at her, 'I met his mother, Kim – not just in passing like before; properly. She's putting a good face on it, but you can see that it's breaking her up inside. She couldn't take her eyes off him, and she was doing everything he would let her to take care of him and see that he would be all right. Come to that, they both were – he was making sure that his cousin had everything to hand to take over smoothly and take care of things for her, and she was going out of her way to make sure he would be properly w-w-warm in the caravan—' Her voice broke, and she bit her lip. 'I just hope this Cosmo is a kind person. He's younger than us, Kim, only in his very early twenties.'

'Francis chose him. You have to trust him.'

'Francis hasn't even seen him properly for years. He chose him for his skills and his availability, not his caring personality!'

'You'll have to explain,' said Kim, having thought about that for a minute. Diana did.

'He's the younger son of one of his – Francis's – cousins, he grew up on the family farm but his brother inherits. Francis says Cosmo is worth two of the brother. End of.'

'His mother must have had some say, she must know him too. He's her cousin, too.'

'She seems happy with it. I don't know more than that.'

'So what's going to happen when Francis eventually inherits Vachells – I assume he will, one day?'

'No,' said Diana. She shouldn't really be discussing this with Kim, but Francis hadn't asked her not to, and she knew that her twin wouldn't pass anything on, even to Val unless she was given the OK. She said, 'There's no entail on Vachells, Mary can leave it to anyone she chooses. Francis doesn't want it anyway, but what he's doing now is setting up a Trust for the maintenance of the house and the buildings to take the pressure off the estate income, and that will be in perpetuity. Cosmo will inherit, he's a Vachell, not a Chillingworth so that's fair. But he won't be stuck with the upkeep of a historic house on top of the estate, it'll be taken care of. All he'll have to do is to see the job is done.'

Kim thought about this, and when she had done so, she said, 'Lucky Cosmo, then. Let's hope he deserves it.'

'I'm sure he will, really, but you can't help wondering. I have to trust Francis's judgement, when it comes down to it, just like you said.'

'Hmm. Don't get carried away, will you?'

Diana said, half-shamefacedly, 'It's just that I worry a bit about Mary. She's an old woman, Kim. A lonely old woman, and she has been for too long, if you want my opinion.'

'Her own choice, from all accounts.'

'No. It was wished on her. And on him too – Francis. Someone should do something, but I can't think what. Or who, come to that. Maybe one of the family…' She sounded tired. Kim looked at her, knowing what needed to be said, unsure how to say it. Finally, she said it anyway, 'I think that might be down to you, actually.'

'Me?' Diana sounded startled, but she didn't convince Kim; Diana had thought this one out for herself.

'Yes, you. You're the link – or you can be. If you can make a friend of Mrs Vachell-Chillingworth, then the rest will follow as the night, the day. Think about it.'

'It's knowing where to start that's the problem,' said Diana, yielding the point without argument. 'She keeps everyone at arm's length – him, included. Come to that, they're both good at that.'

'Then duck under her armpit,' Kim advised.

Diana said nothing for a moment; it had been a long day and this was a step too far into the unknown. She got to her feet and gathered up the mugs.

'I'll just put these into the sink, and then I'm going to bed. I don't think I can take one more thing today!' She paused as she reached the kitchen door, and said, over her shoulder, 'and tomorrow, we'll go to Sophia and find you something fit to wear to a posh London restaurant in the evening. Sleep on that happy thought, and leave the rest for another day.'

Except that might be easier said than done, Kim thought as she did a last tidy round the room. Tomorrow would be fine – shopping sounded good, so long as there was still enough money in the float, and supper at Shortlanesend would be interesting. The problem that might keep her awake tonight was that after Wednesday, which was tomorrow, came Thursday, and a whole new can of worms would be broken open – probably all over London. Diana's parents would be fine with herself, or at least probably they would be if they could take the New Zealand accent and her more casual approach to dress and behaviour, but what would happen in the Chillingworth camp? There was a whole nest, not so much of worms as of potential serpents, in that area. She hoped that the new, more relaxed Francis would cope with it, but he was bound to find it a strain: by the time he came face to face with Diana's parents, he could be already overwhelmed. You have to trust him, Kim thought. Diana does after all. But let's face it, we don't seem to know him as well as we thought we did, so anything might happen! Oh well, what will be, will be...she called through to the kitchen, 'I'm going up. You have the bathroom first before you come up, and good night!' As she made her way up the stairs, the most unsuitable recollection, given the circumstances, drifted into her head and out again.

She had never asked Diana about the "little feathery snowballs." A farmer's daughter herself, she had an idea she knew what they would turn out to be, but it would have been nice to have it confirmed, you really couldn't trust Diana on livestock! Moreover, if she was right in her guess, they seemed unlikely tenants for a big working estate.

Oh well, tomorrow was also a day; no doubt all would be revealed then. Time for bed...

The twins set out for Embridge soon after breakfast, with Diana driving her own car for once; it seemed a long time since she had last done so, although that had only been the morning after the tree disaster. She had done that pretty much on auto-pilot, she remembered, and neither of them had said a word during that brief drive. Today, their trip into town was enlivened by Kim arguing that she already had one posh frock, and surely nobody needed two just for a few nights in London!

'It's not that posh,' said Diana firmly. 'It's only casual-evening-Embridge posh. My parents have elevated notions of what constitutes a suitable place to eat in. And heaven only knows what the Chillingworths consider suitable!'

'Are we going to meet the Chillingworths, though?' Kim asked. They had not yet been mentioned in connection with their London spree, except in so far as Francis was going to visit his grandmother.

'I wouldn't be surprised,' said Diana, darkly. She had already met two of them, as Kim knew; she wasn't sure about meeting the rest of them but it would have to happen sometime.

This morning, driving along this road, it was inevitable that they should pass the cottage, or what remained of it, and although both of them tried not to look at it, they neither of them succeeded. It was virtually a heap of large pieces of rubble with a large tree lying on one end of it, surrounded with tapes that flickered in the wind and DANGER, KEEP OUT notices, and couldn't fail to attract attention on both counts.

'Funny,' said Diana, as they sped past. 'It doesn't look like home at all.'

'It wasn't,' said Kim.' It was a cheap place to stay, that's all. Poor little house, nobody loved it.'

Diana could have said that wasn't surprising, but didn't. Instead, she said, 'Did you mention your passport to Francis?'

'I haven't had the chance,' said Kim, knowing that she could have made one if she had tried. 'I'll ask him over lunch. But I'm sure it must have gone for ever.'

'You should probably tell the Police, or someone,' said Diana. 'Ask Val's Dad, he'll know.'

'The Police seems a bit extreme,' said Kim, doubtfully.

'You'll have to run it past someone, before long.'

Kim said nothing to this. Truth to tell, the loss of her passport worried at her, like a thorn in your finger. She couldn't retrieve it, and had no idea what she should do about it beyond contact the appropriate Embassy. Presumably New Zealand had one in London somewhere? She had no idea, but Diana's father would no doubt be able to tell her.

They drove into the centre of Embridge, and by a small miracle managed to find a parking space in one of the streets just off the central square. Diana looked at her watch.

'It's nearly eleven already – we didn't exactly set out early, did we?'

'It won't take two hours just to buy one dress,' said Kim, dismissively.

'It might. You don't know that. But how about if we start with coffee somewhere?'

The default activity when life got away from you. Kim agreed with alacrity.

Bordens was the obvious place; they planned to go there anyway, and while they were drinking their coffee, Diana returned to the subject of the missing passport.

'I'm pretty certain that it says in mine that you should report a loss to the local Police,' she said. 'We could find the Police Station and do it, and then your conscience would be clear and you would stop brooding!'

'I'm not brooding,' Kim denied, but she knew that she had been.

'Yes, you are. Ask Francis when we see him, what's happening about clearing the site, and then go and own up before someone arrests you as an illegal immigrant.'

It might make her feel better, Kim admitted if only to herself. She had never been asked to show her passport since she arrived in England, but not having it to hand was making her feel vulnerable. She might be asked at any moment, and if she didn't produce it, would she be arrested? Or what? Deported, maybe? It wasn't even as if it was lost, exactly. She knew pretty well exactly where it was last seen, and it couldn't have gone far with half a house and a large tree on top of it. She just couldn't produce it on request.

'You could be right,' she admitted, reluctantly.

'I am right, and if you've finished that coffee, let's go and see what they've got in the women's clothing department.'

They ended up back with Sophia; Diana insisted that there was still money in the kitty, and although Kim didn't entirely believe that, recalling their last shopping spree, she decided not to argue. It was Diana's idea that she needed an extra dress, after all, let her do the arithmetic. In any case, a little to her surprise she had to a admit that she was rather enjoying herself. Shopping for new jeans and a pair of trainers simply wasn't in the same street.

They arrived back in Bordens' restaurant ten minutes after the appointed time laden with goodies, and there was no sign of Francis anywhere.

'One thing you can be certain of,' said Kim, musingly. 'He won't be buying himself a dress...'

'Let's choose our lunch anyway. He can catch up with us when he gets here.' Diana was already running a hungry eye over what was on offer. 'Soup and a sandwich, if we're eating tonight? And a slice of that lemon cake, it looks good...'

By the time that they had chosen their lunch, found a table and sat down, there was still no sign of Francis. Diana was slightly perturbed by this, but Kim took it calmly.

'Anything to do with farm animals, you can never tell,' she told her twin, knowledgeably. 'I know he said he was only going to check on them, but he could just as easily be wrangling a cow in a muddy field – I wouldn't put anything past him these days, he's a total unknown quantity.

Just like my father, actually – when Dad gets in among the sheep, time goes out of the window.'

'At least splashing about in rock pools and stuff will be cleaner,' said Diana, her eyes and half her mind still on the entrance door.

'Don't you believe it. 'Haven't you ever taken a small child to the seaside? It'll be just the same, except on a larger scale, you just wait! Sand everywhere, and buckets of murky water with things lurking in them. Eat your soup, it'll get cold.'

Diana obediently picked up her spoon, but she was halfway through her bowl of mushroom soup before Francis made an appearance. He didn't have the look of a man who had been wrangling cows, she noted with relief, and he spotted them immediately and came straight over to their table, apologising as soon as he was within earshot.

'S-s-sorry. M-Merlin was home, we g-g-got talking – I didn't n-n-notice the t-time—'

'Find yourself some lunch, now you are here,' said Kim, forestalling him as he was about to sit down and join them. 'Go on – you can make your excuses after that, and it'll save you time – you won't want to be late for your next appointment, too.' She grinned at him to take the sting from that comment. They both watched his progress back to the service counter, and Kim said, 'How will it feel, being married to a man who makes every woman's head turn when he crosses a room?'

'Not every woman,' said Diana, defensively, and then laughed. 'There were a couple of pensioners over at that table over there who didn't even notice him.' She added, thoughtfully, 'I expect they think they might have seen him on the telly – he does rather have that look.'

'I don't think you need worry though,' Kim went on, 'I get the feeling he'd only notice them if they walked on four legs or had fins. How he ever spotted you, God only knows.'

Francis returned with a pasty on a plate and cast a knowing look at the pile of shopping bags beside Diana's chair as he sat down beside her.

'Th-th-that's not just a dress,' he said.

'Of course it's not, did you expect it to be?' Diana asked, with a shade of indignation. They both had a lot to learn, Kim reflected in amusement. She said, 'It needed shoes to go with it, she said, and a clutch bag to look elegant for the evening. Were the cows all right in their cow hotel?'

'F-fine.' He took a bite of his pasty, which prevented him enlarging on the subject, and Diana said, 'Which reminds me, have you sorted out your hotel yet for tomorrow?'

'Don't n-n-need to,' Francis told her, through a mouthful of crumbs. He swallowed them, and said more clearly, 'M-m-my c-c-cousin M-Michael rang l-l-last night. I'll s-s-stay with him and his w-w-wife.'

'And where does he live?' asked practical Kim, and he said, 'H-Henley.'

This meant little or nothing to Kim, who had only the vaguest idea where Henley-on-Thames was, apart from being on the river obviously, but Diana said, after brief consideration, 'That sounds good, but you won't want to drive all the way into the middle of London and out again – you'd better put us on a train when we get there. We can easily get a taxi at the other end.'

'I d-d-don't mind.'

'Well, I do! Have you ever done it?'

'N-no, but Satn-nav w-w-will g-g-get us there.'

'You have a lot to learn,' Diana told him, echoing Kim's earlier thought. 'No, there'll be a train into town from Henley – I think we might have to change, but it can't take much more than an hour, and Daddy will arrange to have us met at Paddington. We can check on your computer tonight – and don't argue!' she added, as he opened his mouth to speak, and he meekly closed it again.

'You drive all the way,' Kim ventured, which she knew to be true.

'But not halfway back again, it would stick at least three hours, maybe even four if the traffic was bad, onto his journey! And not via Henley-on-Thames. And I know where I'm going, anyway.'

'We'll t-talk about it later,' said Francis.

'No we won't. Now let's talk about Kim's passport instead.'

Francis looked surprised, as well he might.

'What about Kim's p-passport?'

'It's still in the cottage,' said Kim. She went on to enlarge on this. 'I keep it – kept it – in one of those sort of purse things you wear round your waist, but I was afraid of it falling out, so I put it in with my camera. I had pushed that pretty much under the bed, as I remember. So it still is, probably, except that now it's under a lot of other things as well, and probably lost for good.'

'Have you t–told the Police? Francis asked, immediately, and Kim said, pleased that she could do so honestly, 'I plan to do that this afternoon. I don't suppose I'll ever see it again.'

'Oh, I w-w- wouldn't say th-that. Is the b-bag w-w-waterproof? If it is, it m-may b-b-be OK. D-don't give m-m-much for the c-c-camera's ch-chances though.'

'It's waterproof in so far as it won't let water in if I'm wearing it in the rain. Not sure what being left out in a storm like that one will do to it.'

'Th-the site should b-b-be cleared s-s-some time f-f-fairly s-soon, it's d-d-dangerous so it's a p-priority. I'll ask th-the c-contractors to l–look out f-for it. W-what colour is it?'

'Black,' said Kim, gloomily. It would be: just the colour not to show up in a sea of mud.

'I'll m-m-mention it. B-but r-r-report it anyw-way.'

'Who pays for the clearance?' Diana asked, with interest.

'The C-Council – th-their insurers th-that is. Th-they didn't r-r-really have a l-l-leg to stand on. Their "expert"'s report is still on file.'

'You got that sorted quickly,' said Kim. He gave her a cynical look.

'M-money talks,' he said.

'But it's not down to you,' Kim objected.

'Th-that isn't. W-wait until you s-s-see Burnthouse.'

He left them shortly after that, with an apology for such a brief stay, to keep his next appointment.

'S-s-see you th-this evening,' he said. 'W-what t-t-time did B-bennie say t-t-to be there?'

'Seven o'clock,' said Diana, and he said, 'Oh, I'll b-be b-back by then,' gave her a brief kiss on the cheek, and was gone.

'And if you believe that, on present form you'll believe anything,' said Kim, and Diana made a face.

'So what now? The Police, I suppose, then what?'

'I'm for going back home and chilling for a bit, if we're out tonight. Tomorrow might turn out to be a long day.'

'There'll probably be some nice football on the telly,' said Diana, without enthusiasm. She began to gather up the shopping.

'Not on every channel,' Kim comforted her. She got to her feet. 'Come on then. We can ask them at one of the counters downstairs about the Police Station – they're sure to know.'

Only one short scene to play now before the curtain went up on the next act. Kim and Diana turned up at Shortlanesend, as instructed at seven o'clock, to find that, a little to their surprise, both the Mercedes and the Range Rover were home, so presumably Francis was too, and found Benita in the farmyard, just setting out to shut up the chickens for the night, so they went with her so that Kim could meet the snowballs.

'He's in the shower anyway,' Bennie told them. 'He and Ernie have been disembowelling the innards of a rather dirty tractor, so supper may be a bit later than schedule. Be thankful for it, they looked like a couple of tramps when they came in!'

The chickens – these chickens anyway, there were others in a big enclosed run somewhere else, were housed in a small, divided henhouse – 'to stop them cross-breeding,' Benita said, and added that the henhouse was not normally a semi-detached property as now. 'Generally, we don't use it much, not unless Ernie decides to enter a few for the County Show, when they're put in here and pampered for a bit. But all these belong to Francis.'

There were two different breeds, as was immediately obvious since one half of the henhouse was occupied by neat little brown birds, and the snowballs were, as advertised, pure white. As Kim had already guessed, these were a breed known as "Silkies", and she knew they came in black as well, but she was still bewildered why Francis should have them – have bantams at all, come to that – until Bennie explained the mystery.

'He's had them for years,' she said. 'Well, not these exact birds, but their ancestors – his mother gave them to him for his eighth birthday because he was keen to have some livestock of his own – or that's how the story goes, and I believe it although I was only about two at the time, so I don't actually know of my own knowledge.'

'And he's still got them?' asked Kim, in wonder.

'Well, you can see he has – the cockerels have been swapped around a bit with other breeders from time to time, of course, but they're basically descendants of the same birds. Although I doubt if he actually mucks them out himself these days, not got the time. But he's fond of them – which I find rather touching, really.'

Kim, and Diana too, found it astonishing, but a little bit sad too. He must have cherished these absurd little birds for thirty years because his mother had given them to him as a child, and that gave out a message that both of them found uncomfortable to think about. Moreover, there was another side to the coin, too; he had been away from Vachells for four years in his early twenties; his mother must have seen they were cared for then. More food for thought.

'They lay little tiny eggs,' Bennie was saying. 'These fluffy ones lay white ones – the brown ones lay brown ones, funnily enough.' He had given them some when they were at the cottage, Kim remembered. She hadn't given it a thought at the time, but of course they had been bantams' eggs.

'Well, you're certainly not going to need an alarm clock,' she told Diana, who for a moment didn't get her meaning. Then she looked at the two cockerels, each strutting with his own hens, and gave a rueful laugh.

'See what you mean...'

The last chicken having been persuaded to go to roost, the three of them made their way back to the farmhouse, where they found Ernie in the kitchen breaking open a can of beer, Francis operating on a bottle of wine, and Maisie and Clive playing games on an ipad on the un-laid end of the big table. Both the men looked well scrubbed, the children, not so much. These last two leapt to their feet, abandoning their game, as soon as they saw Diana, and then stopped abruptly when they also saw Kim before rushing over anyway to greet them both impartially and with exuberance. Benita went through into the scullery to wash her hands, and then went over to the stove where a large pan was giving off an enticing scent, and took the lid off to poke around in the contents.

'Pretty much ready,' she said. 'You two, take yourselves off upstairs now, you can come down to say goodnight later – and don't argue, Maisie, please. The rest of you can sit yourselves down, and Francis can pour the wine while I dish up. Unless you're teetotal, Kim? Diana isn't, I know.'

'Definitely not,' said Kim. She immediately liked both Bennie and Ernie, and was glad to feel that they were going to be in Diana's new life, even if only in the background. She would be needing a bit of moral support in the strange, unfamiliar world that awaited her in the future.

'So has Diana told you the horrible truth about Burnthouse, Kim?' Ernie asked, when the children had finally been despatched upstairs, not without argument, and they had sat down to plates of chicken casserole and vegetables. 'She's one brave woman to take that lot on! And I'm not just referring to the house here!'

'I'm sure she'll be equal to it,' Kim said, returning his grin.

'You've not seen the house yet?'

'Not yet – but I will.'

'All low beams and sloping ceilings – quite often together,' said Bennie. 'Francis will spend his whole time ducking and diving – particularly upstairs, that's unless it's changed a lot since I last saw it.'

'It hasn't,' said Diana, recalling it now with affection. 'It's stuck in a listed time warp. You knew it before?' She didn't specify before what, but they all understood what she meant.

'Oh, many years ago now,' said Benita. 'It was pretty old-looking then, but at least it was standing up straight. I'm not sure if I'm looking forward to seeing it now. It sounds as if it may have got a bit too organic for my taste.'

'I'll be picking your brains,' Diana told her.

Ernie then asked what time they were planning to leave for London tomorrow, and without being prompted Bennie added, 'And I hope Francis isn't planning to go all the way into town and out again—' and was interrupted by Francis and Kim both speaking at once, the one to say 'Of c-course I shall,' and the other to say, 'No way, it wouldn't be fair on him. We can get a train from Henley, I'm sure.'

The resumed argument ended with Ernie grabbing the ipad that the children had abandoned on the table and immediately checking for trains, departure times, and arrivals at Paddington. He said, 'You have to change at Twyford, but it's an easy one – it'll take you just over an hour, Henley to Paddington, if you time it right, driving could take twice that – I'll write down some times for you, just let me find a pen – you'll want to avoid the rush hour—'

'Finish your supper first, for goodness' sake – the train isn't leaving until tomorrow!' Bennie said, and turned to Francis, who looked about to enter an objection. 'And you're outnumbered, so you can just concede victory for once! They're two fit young women, they can carry a suitcase across a platform. You've got enough to think about this weekend without adding getting lost in the middle of London to the list!'

'Who s-s-said anything about g-getting l-l-lost?' he demanded indignantly, and Diana said, placatingly, 'And I promise to ring you and let you know when we arrive at my parents'. Will that shut you up?'

'That's settled then,' said Ernie, before Francis had a chance to reply. He winked at Diana across the table. 'You have to be firm with this one – he tends to think he's God if you don't cut him down to size occasionally, he gets it from his mum. Now, have some more wine…'

When they finally left for home at the end of the evening, both Kim and Diana felt that they were firm friends with Francis's cousins, not just Bennie and Ernie but the children too, who had come tumbling back into the kitchen to say goodnight. It was a warm feeling; Kim put it into words as they drove back to Emberton.

'It's good to make friends of our own – not just Val's Sailing Club crowd – it makes me feel at home.' She hadn't realised, until she said it, that this was an issue. It silenced her, allowing Diana to say, 'I wonder if the rest of the family are the same? It'll be great if they are.'

'From what you tell me, they've had their little beady eyes on us from the start,' said Kim, smothering a laugh. 'Well, that's one river crossed. Two left.'

'My parents won't drown you,' said Diana, understanding her perfectly. 'Not sure about the Chillingworths. The next few days are going to be interesting...' They drove for a while in silence, and then she said, 'He was a bit quiet tonight, I thought.'

'I take it, you don't mean Ernie?' said Kim, grinning into the darkness. She had liked Ernie, he had been a good ally.

'Certainly not.'

'Well...' said Kim, after some thought; it was important to call this one correctly. 'He's got a lot of ground to cover this weekend, and it isn't going to be roses all the way.'

'I know,' said Diana. 'The problem is, so does he. I wouldn't want to be in his shoes, Kim. It's not just his family, it's mine too.'

'It's got to be faced though. Just stand by him. It's all you can do.'

'It's all such a tangle, it makes me wonder what will happen next. He must feel a bit like it's a visit to the dentist, but on a giant scale!'

'And on that happy thought, here's home. Sleep on it, Di. It'll all look better in the morning. It's the depressing effect of alcohol that's getting to you.'

'I didn't drink that much,' said Diana, as she pulled into the parking slot, and they went indoors laughing.

XI

Sir Charles Carey had done his homework, and was at first mildly pleased with the results. Yes, there had certainly been a Chillingworth son, and yes, he did reputedly have a son of his own, but although Christopher Chillingworth had worked briefly in the family business, his son had never done so. And yes. The son's name was certainly believed to be Francis. Good so far.

'He must be quite a bit older than she is,' Eloise said, wrinkling her nose. 'The Chillingworth cousins, as I understand it, are all grown men with children of their own, and Christopher wasn't the youngest of his family, or so you say.'

'You and I both know that age is immaterial,' said Sir Charles, smiling at her.

'What worries me,' said Eloise, 'is that nobody seems to know any more about him than his name. You would have thought that there would be more information, if the family really are his cousins.'

As it happened, this was exactly why Sir Charles was mildly pleased rather than wholly delighted with his findings. He had run into Peter Cox-Hamilton at his Club, and also run up against a brick wall. Yes, he had a cousin Francis. No, he knew nothing about him. 'Not seen him for years, I'm afraid,' had been Cox-Hamilton's exact phrase. He had then noticed an acquaintance with whom he had to speak urgently, over on the other side of the room, and that had been that. Sir Charles hadn't told this to Eloise. He did wonder, however, if his impulsive daughter had done it yet again. She had never, he reflected gloomily, been a good picker where men were concerned, and it was distinctly odd that nobody at all seemed to know anything more about this man than his name. Unless the family did, but if they did, why weren't they saying anything? Cox-Hamilton had practically run away!

It was therefore with some uneasiness that Sir Charles awaited his daughter's arrival with her twin sister – another unexplained enigma – on that Thursday evening. He had sent his car and driver to meet the train from Twyford at Paddington, and he and Eloise awaited their arrival with mixed emotions in their comfortable drawing room, with its beautiful view over the Thames.

'She could just be an impostor, taking advantage,' said Eloise. 'She certainly seems to be making very free with Diana's car, and I wonder who was paying for that cottage they lived in?'

'Diana said they were identical,' said Sir Charles.

'You know Diana – that could simply mean that they both had red hair.'

'Certainly, New Zealand seems an unreasonably long way away.' Sir Charles hoped they could trust their daughter not to be that stupid, but she had done sillier things in the past. Impulsive, that was the word he was looking for. Well if there was any doubt, these days DNA tests told the truth. They went on waiting in silence, Eloise turning the pages of a magazine so quickly that she couldn't possibly be reading it, and Sir Charles staring out at the darkening sky beyond the window. They had left the front door on the latch, and when they heard the sound of the opening door and laughter in the hall, they both jumped to their feet and nearly collided in the drawing room doorway, arriving in the small hallway almost simultaneously with Diana, Kim and their luggage. One look, and Sir Charles realised that one mystery was solved, but another one had raised its head to replace it. How? Eloise simply held out her arms and gathered both girls in together. Diana hugged her back and then threw herself into her father's waiting arms.

'Daddy! There's so much to tell you, it's lovely to see you! This is Kim!'

'I can see that she is.' Sir Charles gave Kim a kiss on the cheek, and stood back to look at them both. 'There are certainly some explanations to be made! This is unbelievable! And what on earth happened to your poor face, my darling, while we're at it?'

'A bit of broken glass hit it,' said Diana, dismissively. 'It's OK, don't fuss, Daddy! Just imagine how I felt, when she opened the door of that cottage.' She picked up her case. 'We'll just get rid of these, and have a quick wash, and then we'll come and talk properly – we seem to have been travelling for ever!'

'Did you come the whole way by train? However did you end up in Twyford?'

'We came most of the way by car – Francis drove us, but he's staying with a cousin in Henley–on–Thames. He would have brought us the whole way, but we wouldn't let him—' Diana was already halfway to her bedroom door, in the wake of their luggage and their parents' man, who had silently appeared to carry it for them. 'Come on Kim – we can explain when we've tidied up a bit.'

'I'll ask Annie to make you a nice cup of tea,' said Eloise. 'You must be exhausted!'

'Not them,' said Sir Charles. 'Tea, girls, or something stronger? It's way after tea time!'

'Tea is fine.' They escaped into Diana's bedroom, which had twin beds – originally for the use of school friends, but those days were long gone. 'This one's mine,' said Diana, throwing her suitcase onto it. 'That one's yours. The bathroom is through that door.'

'En suite, my goodness,' Kim observed. She looked around her at the expensively furnished room. 'Hmm. Romans also ran...'

'My world,' Diana told her. 'Yours is but a grisly memory here.'

'Burnthouse, to you,' said Kim, and they exchanged a grin.

They had a quick wash and tidy-up, which gave them time to think. They had already realised that they could only tell the truth, however distressing it might be, but there had to be a cut-off point. Certain things, only Francis could legitimately tell Diana's parents, and he had already agreed, without much enthusiasm, that he would do that – the bones of them, at least. But the background, yes, they could fill that in for him.

The problem, right from the start, had been, how far could they go after that?

Sir Charles and Eloise had been discussing much the same thing, but with less to go on.

'There's a story here,' had said Sir Charles. 'I wonder how much of it we're to be told?'

'They are certainly very alike,' said Eloise.

'Oh, I think they are twins, not a doubt of it. The question that we need to have answered is, how on earth did it happen that one of them ended up beaten half to death in a house beside a Dorset highway, and the other ended up in New Zealand?'

'I'm sure they'll tell us.'

'I hope they do.'

As they did, of course, over the tea brought in by Annie, the housekeeper. Sir Charles and Eloise already knew the bare bones of the story of how the twins had met again after all those years, but now they were to be filled in properly on the details. Once Annie had left the room, they looked expectantly at the two of them, sitting there, Eloise couldn't help thinking, as if butter wouldn't melt in their mouths.

'Now, tell us,' said Sir Charles, without any preliminaries. 'And tell us how you come to know, while you're about it.'

'It was when I met Kim,' said Diana. 'You know that, of course, and you know too what was in my adoption papers. What you don't know is that we had only just been separated when that happened – probably only days before.' She hesitated there, for this was the first stumbling block. Kim stepped in to help her.

'My own adoptive parents' – she called them that, although she wasn't certain now that it was actually true – 'were friends of the friend our mother ran to when her husband – allegedly – began to beat her up. She knew him already, she seems to have had a bit of a schoolgirl crush on him.'

'Oh dear,' said Eloise, sympathetically, after she had thought this out. 'How difficult for him, poor man, and how dreadful for her, too.'

'In all fairness, I don't think it was quite like that,' said Kim, and Diana then took up the tale again.

'He was a bit smitten too, we think – he had a much older wife, and there she was, all young and luscious – and from the little we've been able to find out about him, he wasn't exactly the strongest character in the line-up. But anyway, he made a plan to get all three of us out of the country and away from possible violence – the friends of his Kim mentioned, they ran the garage in Emberton then, but they were planning to emigrate to New Zealand, he got them to take Kim with them...' She hesitated there, but neither of her parents were fools.

'Forged papers, presumably,' said Sir Charles, and Kim said, 'Yes,' and immediately thought about her missing passport and found herself hoping that its replacement, if that became necessary, wouldn't start a hare that would be better left undisturbed in its form.

'Oh dear,' said Eloise.

'Anyway,' said Diana, picking up the thread again, 'He and our mother were going to follow with me – they had thought we would be less conspicuous separately, or so we were told – only her husband found her first, before they could get away, and the Police know now that it was he who killed her...so we know that threat was genuine. The caretaker for the cottage found her body lying on the path...and I was inside.' She didn't add that it was Francis, not the caretaker, who had found her dying on her little bed, they had agreed that he had to be the one to fill in that part of the story, it raised too many questions that Sir Charles would undoubtedly ask, and to which they didn't really know the answers.

'Yes, we knew that bit from your adoption papers,' said Eloise. She turned to Kim. 'Did your parents ever tell you any of this when you were growing up?'

'No,' said Kim. She added, 'I knew I was adopted.' If she was...

'But didn't you ever wonder? You must have been at the least three years old, Diana was. Had you no recollection at all of having had a twin sister? I can understand why Diana didn't, she had severe shock and head injuries, but you didn't.'

Kim thought about this, for in a way, she had. She said, 'I used to dream – I thought I was dreaming – about another child who was like another part of me...an imaginary friend, my mother told me when I asked. She said I was too imaginative, and laughed at me. I grew out of it in the end...I think I did. You see, the imaginary friend never grew up, and I did.' She had never realised the significance of that before. She exchanged a glance with Diana and then looked down at her hands. Sir Charles brought the conversation back on track.

'So, what took you to Emberton?' and Kim was happy to answer honestly.

'I studied European languages at Uni – I took a gap year, and came to Europe to polish them in the field, before going back to be a translator. My mother has sisters in England, I went to visit them and they told me where my parents used to live, so I went there, just out of curiosity to see what it was like. It's lovely down there, so I took the cottage because it was cheap, and planned to get myself a job so that I could spend time there. It's a great place to spend a summer, and my visa was OK.'

'Reasonable,' Sir Charles allowed, and turned then to his daughter. 'So what took you there?'

When she had originally mentioned her meeting with Kim, Diana had glossed over this bit: it had been easy, because her unexpected discovery of her adoption had filled the immediate horizon. That wouldn't do this time, she realised. She took a deep breath.

'I was going down for a weekend sailing with a friend,' she said. 'It was all arranged, but at the last moment he couldn't make it, so I went on my own – I was restless, I wanted to be away from town…' She stopped there to think about how very odd she had felt that weekend, as if she had lost something…lost someone…odd. Kim had been in London earlier that same week, almost within touch. She didn't say this, which was maybe a pity as it allowed her mother to jump in.

'"He"?' Eloise asked, raising her eyebrows.

'Oh, just a friend,' said Diana, in as throwaway a manner as she could manage, but her mother was undeceived.

''So long as it wasn't that predatory Clive Ward-Jones,' she said, with a sniff. 'He sails, doesn't he? I hope you wouldn't be such a fool!' Diana made no reply to this, for it had been Clive, and her mother gave her a dark look.

'Don't change the subject, Eloise,' said Sir Charles. 'Even if it was Ward-Jones, apparently he didn't go. Go on, Diana. What happened next.'

'I already told you that,' said Diana, relieved to be back on safe ground. 'It was foggy – I went off the road in the fog and ended up outside Kim's cottage. I knew it would be stupid to drive on, I was on the wrong side of the road by then anyway, and you couldn't see a thing. I went to the cottage to see if they would give me shelter until the fog lifted, and Kim opened the door.'

Sir Charles looked at them both, seriously.

'All right, I accept that, so far it sounds reasonable. But how did you find out that you actually are twins? I'm presuming that you did.'

Kim and Diana exchanged a glance, which wasn't lost on Sir Charles.

'The truth, please,' he said, and it was Kim who said, 'We met Francis down at the Sailing Club. He knew.'

There was a silence, broken by Eloise. 'Explain, please. How did he know?'

'We've talked about this,' said Diana. 'The three of us, that is, and we think that it would be better if Francis told you that bit, because he's the one with all the background knowledge.'

'Is he, indeed. And when are we to be allowed to meet him?' asked Sir Charles.

160

'He's tied up with his own family tomorrow…there's history, he's not seen them for years. Oh Daddy, don't ask me, he'll tell you himself, he's said he will. It's all been a terrible tangle of misunderstandings, but he will tell you.'

'I seem to remember asking "when?",' said Sir Charles.

'He's coming up to London on Saturday morning – he's spending Saturday night with Val so we can all meet up – they'll come over before lunch, and Val will take Kim out of the way and Francis can take you through the whole thing.'

'And Val is?'

'My fiancé,' said Kim, holding out her left hand to show her ring. 'He works in London.'

Eloise smiled at her; it was, in any case, time to change the subject she had decided.

'Why don't you ring him, Kim, and ask him if he would like to come and have dinner with us tonight? Then you needn't wait until tomorrow to see him.'

'That's very kind of you,' said Kim. She thought about this, and then exchanged a glance with Diana. It might distract Diana's parents, which would be a good thing. 'Are you sure?'

'Of course we are! Give him a ring and ask him – I'm sure you have his number.' She smiled again, and said almost what Kim had been thinking. 'It will give us all something else to think about.'

'It's on my phone,' said Kim, giving in. 'It's in my bag – I'll go and do it now, shall I, and then we'll know if he can make it?'

'What a good idea,' said Sir Charles, beaming. Kim left the room, which, unfortunately Diana felt, left Diana alone with her parents.

'Well then,' said Sir Charles, and caught an old-fashioned look from his daughter which made him smile. 'It's all right, Diana, we're not going to put you back under the grill! If Francis Chillingworth is going to give us a full tale on Saturday, we'll accept that and enjoy getting to know Kim. What are the two of you planning for tomorrow, if this Val is working? I shall have to be in my office, I don't know what Eloise has planned.'

'Kim was going to come with me to help pack up my things in the flat,' said Diana. 'We can go out to lunch together – Julie might come with us, if she's there – and bring it all back here in a taxi afterwards – if that's OK with you, of course? But before we do that, we're going to go and see her Aunt Rose, who lives in London and would never forgive her if we didn't.' And try not to think what Francis might be doing, but she didn't add that bit. Neither did she say that Kim's Aunt Rose was in for a bit of a shock — or maybe she wasn't. There was no telling what Rod Ford might have told his sisters just lately.

There was a pause, then Eloise said, 'So, you've definitely decided you're not coming back to live in London?'

'Francis lives in Dorset,' said Diana. 'His whole life is there — his friends, his family his farm, everything. Of course I shall live there.' She tried not to sound confrontational, but knew that she had. She looked down at her hands.

'This Francis is important to you,' said her father. It wasn't a question.

'Yes,' Diana muttered, not looking at him.

'So does he really mean to marry you?'

'Of course he does. It's one of the things that you need to talk about with him. And before you ask, the answer to your next question is yes, he can afford to keep me in the style to which I am accustomed.' She knew she had sounded defiant, and bit at her lip.

'I had imagined that would be the case, with his name and antecedents,' said her father, drily. 'It wasn't what I was going to ask, as it happens.' He glanced at Eloise. 'Your turn, darling.'

'You love each other, until death does you part? He's your final choice? — you must admit you've had a few trial runs in the past.'

'Not this time. This time it's the real thing.'

Sir Charles knew an impulse to sweep his daughter up in his arms, kiss her, and wish her very happy, but he held back. There was something a little ephemeral about Francis Chillingworth so far, he thought. How could a man from such a prominent financial background exist without anyone ever having met him — in most cases, hardly having heard of him? Why would his family not talk about him? He said, 'Perhaps you shouldn't do anything irreversible in too much of a hurry. Perhaps you should leave the status quo in place until we've had a chance to meet him.'

'I shan't be going back to the flat. There's no point. And I shall need my clothes in Dorset, if I'm living there. I've only got summer things, and it's getting colder now.'

'You've clothes here,' said Eloise, quietly.

'Only good ones. I shall need more casual stuff down there.' She nearly added, "you haven't seen the place he's buying!" but decided it was the wrong moment just in time.

'You've made up your mind,' said Eloise, a little sadly. Diana looked at her; she tried to speak gently but feared she hadn't succeeded.

'Perhaps you should wait and see on Saturday, before you make up yours?' she said.

'And that's enough,' said Sir Charles, firmly, and fortunately, right on cue, Kim returned. She felt the atmosphere as soon as she came through the door, and immediately elected to behave as if she had noticed nothing.

'That's all sorted,' she said. 'He can get here by about half-seven, if that's all right. I said I'd ring him back if it wasn't – oh, and thank you very much, he looks forward to meeting you.'

'Half-past seven is perfect,' said Eloise, smiling at her, 'I'll go and have a word with Annie in a moment.' She patted the seat beside her. 'Come and sit down, and tell us all about him. What does he do in London?'

'He's an accountant,' said Kim.

'A family firm?' asked Sir Charles, genially.

'No. His father is a Police Superintendent down in Embridge. He – that's Val, not his father – he's hoping for a partnership with a local firm so he won't have to commute when we get married.'

'You wouldn't want to live in London?' asked Sir Charles. Kim decided there was only one way to deal with this sort of conversation: up front. She said, 'No way – I grew up on a sheep farm deep in the hills, London has far too many people for me. Although it is an interesting city. I'm looking forward to Val showing me a few sights on Saturday.'

'Goodness, did he say he would?' asked Diana, before she could stop herself. She glanced at her watch, thank goodness it was already a quarter-past-six. 'I think, if you'll excuse me, I'll go and get a shower and put something more formal on if we're having a guest to dinner – even if it's Val! Then Kim will have time to do the same afterwards.' She got to her feet as she spoke so nobody could argue with her. When she had gone, Sir Charles looked at Kim.

'Don't look so worried. We're not going to interrogate you.'

Kim met his eyes; she felt a certain amount of sympathy with Diana's parents. She said, 'Just one thing, and then we can talk about the weather – or sheep, or something. Francis. Don't lose sleep over him, he's turned out

163

to be a star. One of the bravest and most generous men I think I have ever met. And probably one of the cleverest, too, come to think. End of lecture.'

'Thank you,' said Sir Charles, after a pause, and Eloise nodded her head before looking down at her clasped hands in her lap.

'Now then,' said Sir Charles. Enough was enough, it was time for a complete change of subject. 'Tell us, how does Merrie England compare with New Zealand?'

This uncontroversial topic lasted for twenty minutes, and then Kim looked at her watch.

'She must have finished with that shower by now – I'd better go and tidy up, or Val will land up on your doorstep before we're even dressed!'

Eloise smiled at her. 'I'm not sure we actually have a doorstep – but you're right, off you go. Tell Diana we won't bite her if she comes back.' When Kim had gone, she looked at Sir Charles and made a rueful face.

'I know it's stupid, but she's so like Diana, I can't help feeling that she's another daughter. What a lovely girl!'

'I think I know what you mean.' Sir Charles looked thoughtful. 'I daresay her own parents will feel the same about Diana, how odd! They must have known her before we did.'

'So what about Francis Chillingworth? Any conclusions?' She looked serious now. 'I think she's been badly bitten this time, our scatterbrained daughter! On past form, I'm not sure whether to shout for joy or cry with despair.'

'We shall just have to trust in Kim's judgement and see what comes next – at least for now. But yes, I shall be interested too to meet this mystery man that nobody will talk about.' He got to his feet and headed for the drinks cabinet in the corner. 'Drink, my darling? To get up your strength before the children descend on us?'

'What a great idea,' said Eloise, and smiled at him.

Kim found Diana lying on her bed talking on the phone. As Kim came in, she said, 'That's good then – I shall be thinking about you tomorrow, and be sure and let me know how it goes.' She blew a kiss into the phone. 'Goodnight then, my darling. Sleep well.' She tossed it onto the bed and sat up. 'That was Francis. I rang him, just to make sure that all was well.'

'He is a grown-up,' said Kim, with a grin, and Diana looked sheepish.

'Silly, isn't it? I just wanted to hear his voice. Henley feels like on the moon from here.'

'So does he have a plan? And did he fill you in on it?' Kim picked up her clean underwear, but sat on the end of Diana's bed with it on her lap.

'He'll go and see his grandmother tomorrow as planned, and in the evening, his cousin Ros and her husband will be going to have dinner with them in Henley. I don't know where they actually live.'

'"Them" being?'

'His cousin Michael and his wife – Erin, her name is. They have kids too, but they'll have gone to bed, they're quite young still. And on Saturday, he'll leave his car there and come up here on the train like we did, and join Val wherever Val lives. He'll ring me when he gets that far.'

'That sounds as if the family are rationing themselves to start with – good. It would have been a bit much if they had decided to throw a party.'

'Apparently, his Aunt Clara wanted to do that, but they all talked her out of it.'

'Then good for them. Now I'm going to have that shower, or Val will be here while I'm still half-dressed.'

'He won't mind that,' said Diana, with a grin. Kim got to her feet, but then hesitated.

'Diana – there's something you haven't told your parents, and you ought to before they come face to face with Francis. It's not fair if you don't – not to any of them.'

'I know,' said Diana, apparently studying her feet with interest. 'It's how to say it that's the problem.'

'I see that, but it ought to be said. I've noticed before, under stress he can be half-way to incoherent sometimes – and he's having a lot of stress this weekend.'

'He sounded all right on the phone – maybe it'll be all right, so long as he doesn't try to say "anemometer",' said Diana, with a reminiscent smile to herself. 'All right Kim, I'll warn them. In fact I'll do it as soon as I've finished dressing, before Val gets here. Get it out of the way.'

'Then, good. And don't chicken out at the last moment.' She vanished into the shower room, and shut the door behind her. Diana got to her feet and reached for the dress she had selected from her large wardrobe. If it had to be done, it had to be done – but she really, really, didn't want to do it!

She found her parents sitting quietly in the drawing room, sharing a quiet drink together; when she appeared, her father got to his feet.

'Diana! What do you drink these days?'

'A simple glass of white wine, if you've got one handy,' said Diana, taking a seat where she would be able to see them both. 'I find gin a bit depressing these days – maybe I always did, come to think, and that's why I was such a burden to you!' She gave them a smile, which her mother returned; her father had his back to her, opening wine that stood ready in an ice bucket. When he turned back, he held out a glass.

'There, try that one. And if it's not part of the plot, tell us about this farm that your young man is buying.'

Diana shuddered. 'I really don't think you want to know just before a meal! It's a beautiful house – listed, even – but it's in great need of a bit of TLC. But anyway, there's something else I must tell you first.' She stopped there, and her father raised an enquiring eyebrow.

'That sounded very portentous, my daughter. What have you been hiding from us this time?'

'Nothing, Daddy. I just hadn't worked out how to tell you, but as I'm going to have to anyway…'

'You're not pregnant!' said her mother, in a horrified voice. Diana couldn't help a smile.

'No chance, unfortunately. So far, I seem to be dating the perfect gentleman! But it is about him – what I have to tell you.' She hesitated there.

'Then tell us,' said her father, when the pause had gone on too long. 'What've you done now?'

'Nothing. This is nothing to do with me.' She took a breath and the plunge together. 'It's about Francis – no, it's nothing terrible,' as her mother opened her mouth to speak. 'It's just, I wasn't the only one to get hit over the head in all that drama. He was too – not at the time, several years after. He'll tell you how it happened, I expect, when he talks with you, but what you need to know is that he was hit a lot harder than I was, and he had a brain injury that has left him with a bad speech impediment. It doesn't seem to have done anything else, but he stammers quite badly sometimes. I thought you ought to be warned…' she ended, lamely, and looked down at her glass.

'Probably a good idea,' said her father, dryly, and her mother said, 'Poor man.'

'So,' said Sir Charles, 'do we conclude that there is a lot more to this drama than a simple attack on an unfaithful wife by a betrayed husband?'

'Something like that. But he knows a lot more about it than we do, so please, Daddy, wait and ask him. I can only play guess.'

'Kim seems to think very highly of him,' said Sir Charles, as if he was thinking. 'Do we trust Kim's judgement? I think we have to. And yours too.' He shook his head at Eloise, who was about to speak. 'All right my daughter, we'll wait until Saturday and see what we learn then. Meanwhile, that was the sound of the doorbell, I think...'

It hadn't been, of course, it had just been a ploy to change the subject, but Val did arrive a short time later, and was admitted by Annie simultaneously with Kim's emergence from the bedroom. They entered the drawing room together.

By the time introductions had been made, and drinks had been poured or topped up, as appropriate, and Diana's scarred cheek and fading, but still blackish eye had been inspected and pronounced improved on its last sighting, the atmosphere was considerably warmer than it had been before his arrival, but Sir Charles couldn't seem to resist returning, like a dog to a bone, to the problem that right now most exercised his mind. He loved his daughter; he wasn't at all sure what she might be getting herself into.

'So, do I take it that you and Francis Chillingworth are friends of long-standing?' he said to Val, with a friendly smile – fishing, he knew it, and was almost, but not quite, ashamed of himself. Diana was his daughter, after all, and it was a reasonable conclusion to draw, he told himself; the man was to stay with him! But Val's reply did little to make him feel better.

'Not really, sir – only since we both got involved with these two.' He nodded towards the twins, entertaining Eloise with a lively account of the cottage they had lived in before the roof fell on them: from the odd snatches that Sir Charles caught, it must have been a steep learning curve for his Diana: he would have been interested to hear more but he had other fish to fry right now. He shut out the background chatter and concentrated on what Val had to say.

'We belong to the same Sailing Club, of course, and up until the end of this season, we raced in the same class, but we weren't more than casual acquaintances until now,' he was saying. 'You know what clubs can be like – people form cliques with their close mates.'

'He would be older than you, too,' said Sir Charles, speculating.

'I don't think that cuts much ice after you get past about twenty-five,' said Val, thoughtfully. 'Apart from sailing our interests are different...if he has a close friend at the Club, I suppose it would be Merlin Ravenscourt. They speak the same language. But on the whole, he's not a mixer – too busy to have the time for socialising, with that big estate to run for his mother.' He realised, as soon as he had finished speaking, that he had been making excuses for Francis, and in the same breath recognised Sir Charles's angling technique. Oops, be careful here!

That sounded a little better, but only a little: Sir Charles approved of the name "Ravenscourt", but in essence, it was the same story again: nobody knew anything – or if they did, they weren't telling. He chose his next words carefully.

'It's a big estate is it – his mother's?'

'About three square miles, I believe, so big enough. It runs right down to the coast.'

'Merlin Ravenscourt would be one of Lord Storre's family?' Sir Charles speculated, as if idly.

'First cousin.' Val took a sip of his gin and tonic, wondering where to go next, he felt as if he was picking his way through a quagmire. He said, 'Merlin ran the Ravenscourt estate until young Robin came of age, so he and Francis have something in common, but he's a partner in the Shipyard at Emberton these days.'

That was something, but at the same time, nothing yet again, Sir Charles reflected. People knew people if they were in the same line of business, but it didn't automatically make them friends: the words "I suppose" said everything you needed to know about that. He tried another cast.

'His mother's family are landowners, are they not?'

'The Vachells? Yes, I believe most of them are – but not on that scale. The big house itself is the main base, although I believe two family members run the farms that belong to the main estate – but you'll need to ask Francis about that. I don't know any of them apart from him.'

It was a signal to close the topic, Sir Charles recognised. He said, instead, 'So, when do you and Kim plan to be married? Will her parents get over from New Zealand to be there for her Big Day?' and Val thanked heaven for small mercies. That had definitely been sticky!

Conversation over dinner was easier, for which Val thanked goodness: earlier on, he had been wondering how he had let himself be persuaded to be here – but then, he hadn't expected to be gently interrogated. He wondered why Sir Charles appeared to be so uneasy over Francis, and wondered also if he could guess. The rift in the Chillingworth family must have cut the communication lines at the London end. He hadn't thought about that, he had to admit, but now that he did, it was obvious.

Poor Sir Charles then. He hoped that Francis meant to explain, for it was obvious that Diana's parents loved her very much indeed, and were both proud of her and affectionately despairing of her waywardness – well, he knew how they must feel: she had given him a few bad moments too, and he was only her sister's fiancé! This beautiful town flat – apartment rather, with it's amazing river view, felt like a very happy home, it would be a shame if it was spoiled for them all. Although he did seem to recall Diana saying that her parents also had a house in the country – the Cotswolds, or somewhere like that, wasn't it? Not his territory, but Francis would no doubt take it in his stride.

He realised at that point in his thoughts that Kim had spoken to him twice, and was looking at him with a questioning tilt to her head.

'Wake up there, Valentine! I just asked you a question – will I see you tomorrow, or will it be Saturday?'

Val came hurriedly back to the here and now. He said, 'I hadn't thought. What would you like it to be?'

'Diana's parents are supposed to be going out to dinner,' Kim told him. 'We're all yours if you want us, but you have to have the pair.'

'No he doesn't – I have friends I can go and annoy,' said Diana, immediately.

'I'm sorry about this,' Eloise said, apologetically, 'But it's a long-standing engagement, and the girls did rather spring it on us that they were coming. It's really a mercy we weren't away for the weekend, we easily could have been!' She was laughing, taking the sting from the criticism.

'That's all right,' said Val. 'I can take them both out for a meal somewhere, or Diana can do her own thing if she prefers. Up to her.'

'No, you have a night on the town together,' said Diana immediately. 'Or I might give Toby a ring, see what he's doing – we could maybe have a foursome and go to a Club or something, show Kim a bit of London nightlife. Unless he's got another girlfriend since I last saw him, that is.' She turned to Val. 'Toby is my cousin. More like my brother, actually – we bail each other out from time to time. He's going to miss me when I retire to the country!'

'Ring him after dinner, and ask,' Eloise suggested. 'That sounds like fun. Kim would enjoy it.'

And for me, it will help to pass the time until Saturday morning, Diana thought, but did not say. She looked at Val. 'How does that grab you for an idea?'

'Sounds good to me. After all, having a good time is what London is all about at your age.'

'Not so much of the "your age", grandpa!'

The evening ended in laughter, no more awkward questions, no more disconcerting information, just normality until Val left, quite early as he had to work the next day. When he had gone, Diana said, to avoid any further difficult conversations, 'I think I'll go to bed, too. It's been a long day, with the travelling and all. How about you, Kim? Coming, or staying up to watch a bit of late-night telly?'

'No I'll come with you. London is a bit of a shock to the system!'

'Then we'll say goodnight to you both,' said Eloise. She kissed Diana and turned to Kim. 'May I kiss you too? You're so like Diana, it feels as if you must be part of the family.' She did it anyway, before Kim had a chance to reply, and then Sir Charles did the same.

'It's good to have you both here,' he said. 'Sleep well.'

But when they had gone, he and Eloise looked at each other.

'Toby?' he asked.

'Don't even think about it! He's just a convenient stopgap.'

Sir Charles said, slowly, 'I almost wish that I didn't agree with you. Well, we shall see.'

'On Saturday,' said Eloise. She hesitated. 'She's made up her mind, Charlie. We won't – we can't – stop her, she's of age. And you never know, it may all be nothing – our imagination. No mystery at all.'

'It's just so odd,' said Sir Charles. 'I did try to see if Kim's Val could add anything but he couldn't, either, or not anything that helped. The only plus there, is that I felt he liked the man, but he doesn't know him well. Nobody seems to.'

'They must do! And Kim trusts him. She seems to think very highly of him."

Then we must hope that Diana is right, and Francis Chillingworth means to explain it all himself – but it's what he might explain that's worrying me,' said Sir Charles.

Saturday seemed to be a very long way away.

XII

Friday was a strange day, a nothing day, Diana and Kim both thought when they came to look back on it: a day out of time, living each other's lives and in limbo, waiting to see what would happen next. It was to begin, as planned, with the flat that Diana had up until now shared with her friends, Julie and Jo. Jo worked, Diana said, rather as if it was some strange affliction, but she would meet them for lunch. Julie, if they were lucky, would help with the packing. If they were not, she would just watch them and chat.

Not, Kim discovered, that there was a huge amount of packing to do; mainly clothes (there was a surprise), and a few books (nothing heavyweight, just novels) and one or two other personal possessions, such as ornaments and pictures. The whole lot fitted into two suitcases, a holdall, and a large cardboard box, then Diana made coffee and they all sat round and drank it, gossiping about people of whom Kim had never heard and delving into Diana's planned new life.

'I never saw you as a country person,' Julie said, looking at Diana as if she had suddenly grown two heads. 'What came over you?'

'I would have thought you might have guessed,' said Diana, laughing at her.

'Oh, I have no doubt there's a man involved somewhere.' Julie obviously knew her friend. 'The only thing is, he must be very extra-special to lure you away from the bright lights of town. So tell! And while you're about it, explain this lady here!' She had taken Kim for granted as a cousin or something when she first saw her, more concerned with greeting Diana after her prolonged absence and the packing, but now she had time to look properly. What she saw was, to say the least, intriguing. 'You could be twins, you're so alike,' she said. Then, of course, explanations had to follow – well, up to a point explanations had to follow. Julie took these in her stride, exclaiming over Diana's discovery that she was adopted, but she watched a lot of reality television, and was more intrigued than shocked.

'It's just like *Docksiders*, she exclaimed, referring to a popular soap. 'What fun – and you met Kim just by chance?' She pulled a face. 'I never thought things like that could happen off the telly. Well, well!' She was not to be sidetracked for long, however, and soon returned to her main objective. 'Now, about this man! Tell. He's got to be either a Mr Darcy lookalike, filthy rich, or you're pregnant!'

'Well, no to the last anyway,' said Diana. It was difficult to find an answer to the other two speculations as, in essence at least, they were both right. Kim came to her rescue.

'He's certainly tall, dark and handsome, if that's what you mean, but he's not a hero from a nineteenth century romantic novel. He's an academic, if anything.' It felt odd, admitting that, but she was beginning to accept that it was probably true.

'Doesn't sound like you.' Julie looked at Diana. 'Are you sure you've got this right?'

Diana decided to join in the teasing session. She said, 'He breeds cows,' and watched Julie's face. This was blank for a moment, then Julie said, 'Good grief! You're jossing me, aren't you? That's not an academic pastime!'

'To do it properly, you need to study it,' said Kim, the sheep farmer's daughter. 'You can't just mate Jim Jones with Annie Brown and then expect to get a fairytale princess. But that isn't what I meant.' She added, wickedly, 'He has three degrees and things – good ones.'

'Oh my God,' said Julie. She looked from Kim to Diana. 'You are having me on, aren't you? Please tell me that you are!'

They had better luck with Jo, who met them for lunch at a sandwich bar near to her place of work, and turned out to be a bit more realistic than her – frankly scatterbrained – friend. Julie jumped in straight away with 'Diana's lost her marbles! She's planning to marry a geek, just because he's a sexy beast as well!'

'Is he?' Jo asked, raising her eyebrows. 'I mean is he a geek? I can believe the rest.'

'No,' said Diana firmly, although by Julie's standards, he probably was.

'And is he sexy – or a beast, come to that?'

'No, again. He's just a nice-looking bloke.' Diana knew she sounded defensive, and it wasn't entirely true either. She pulled herself together:

there was no point in letting Julie wind her up any further. 'Julie just thinks that because he has a degree or three, he must be a dreary bore, but I can assure you, he isn't.'

'Well, it certainly wouldn't be like you if he was,' Jo allowed. 'I shall look forward to meeting him – I'm assuming you plan to introduce us some time? She turned her attention to Kim. 'So, where do you come in?'

Every time they had to explain this, Kim realised, it seemed to become less amazing: they had met by pure chance, had found that they were both adopted, made further enquiries, and bingo! There they were. Simplification: a wonderful thing.

'That's incredible!' said Jo, when she had heard this edited version. 'What a great thing to happen! You must be over the moon, Di – what do your parents make of it? It must be like getting an extra daughter for free!'

'I don't think it's sunk in properly yet,' Diana admitted.

After that, and after Diana's worldly goods had all been safely delivered to her parents' home – they were both out, perhaps fortunately – it was Diana's turn to be the long-lost twin. Kim's Aunt Rose, when they finally reached her later that afternoon had, as suspected, been forewarned via email by her brother in New Zealand, and welcomed Diana with open arms and an equally open heart. They had tea with her – her husband and all Kim;'s cousins were at work – and then returned to the riverside apartment block where Diana's parents lived when they were in London to prepare for their evening out on the town with Val and Toby: yet another new experience for country-raised Kim. Returning home in the small hours after a great evening out, they tumbled into bed and Kim was just drifting off into a welcome sleep, when Diana, who was restlessly tossing from side to side in her own bed, said, 'Only eight hours to go. What do you think will happen?'

Kim forced her reluctant eyelids open and tried to think, but a combination of wine, noisy chatter, music, and dancing close with Val had all befuddled her thinking processes. She said, 'We'll find out,' sleepily.

'That's what I'm afraid of!'

'Just go to sleep,' said Kim, already halfway there herself.

'I can't,' said Diana, but nobody answered.

The following morning, Saturday, breakfast was a quiet meal in the beautiful riverside apartment. Diana, although she was looking forward to seeing

Francis again, was apprehensive, both about what might have happened in the last thirty-six hours and what might happen this morning. Kim was ashamed to find that she was really glad to know that Val would be taking her away from the danger zone before any action took place. Sir Charles and Eloise were not certain what their emotions were.

'There could be nothing in it,' Sir Charles had said, robustly, when Eloise had earlier confessed to a certain amount of reservation. 'Families do drift apart, you know that yourself, Eloise! And Peter Cox-Hamilton may have meant exactly what he said – on both counts.' He didn't think so, not for a moment: Peter Cox-Hamilton had looked distinctly shifty, and he had, so far as Sir Charles had seen, exchanged not one word with the man he had indicated. He had not said that to Eloise, at the time or since, and had tried, with indifferent success, to erase it from his mind. Today, it would have to be faced. He hoped it was all a mare's nest.

So, when they all met at the breakfast table, nobody had very much to say. They didn't even know what time the meeting would take place until Val rang them to say that Francis had arrived at his flat in Isleworth. Altogether, it was enough to give an ostrich indigestion!

Val rang just before ten: to avoid any possible questions, it was Kim that he rang, on her mobile.

'His cousin just dropped him off,' he said. 'We'll be with you within the hour, God and the traffic willing.'

'And how does he seem?' Kim asked, because Diana would ask her.

'Perfectly normal, to me,' said Val, but he was a man, Kim thought: they didn't read between the lines. Val then added, 'His cousin sounds a good bloke. They seem to be good friends,' and she mentally took back her original thought, and said, 'That's good.' For what "good" that exchange really meant, she thought immediately afterwards, for Val, of course, hadn't even met the cousin, and then told herself not to be so cynical.

'I'll tell you properly later on,' said Val, not that there was much to tell, but he knew she would ask. 'We'll be on our own very soon – and tell Diana not to worry.'

Worry about what? Kim wondered, as she slipped her phone into her jacket pocket. She looked at Eloise and Diana, who were in the drawing room with her. They were both watching her expectantly.

'That was Val,' she said, unnecessarily. 'They'll be here in an hour if the traffic isn't bad.'

It must have been, Diana thought afterwards, the longest hour since Creation. Sir Charles remained in his study, "dealing with his post", and Eloise tried to make polite conversation at first and then went silent over a magazine, and Kim wondered, but did not ask, whether Sir Charles had made any enquiries – as of course he had. It would, after all, have been the natural thing for a doting father to do. Only, the attitude of both Sir Charles and his wife struck her as unusual in parents waiting to meet their only daughter's chosen life partner; surely it would have been more natural to ask lots of questions of her, too? She couldn't help wondering about what they might have heard…there were, as she well knew, one or two skeletons in the Chillingworth family cupboard. Diana just fidgeted around the room until her mother said, in irritation, 'Do sit down, Diana, you're making me nervous, prowling around like that! He'll be here when he gets here, not a moment before!' Diana sat down on the very edge of an armchair.

'I hate waiting around,' she said, and began to fiddle with her nails. Fortunately, before either Kim or Eloise got as far as yelling at her to stop, the doorbell rang and Sir Charles appeared magically from his study.

How on earth, Kim found herself wondering yet again, could one man, who wasn't even present, have created so much tension? What did Diana's parents know, or think they knew? Then Annie ushered the two men into the drawing room and Diana's parents saw for the first time who it was on whom their daughter had finally set her wayward heart.

Eloise looked, to put it vulgarly, gobsmacked, Kim thought, but stepped forward anyway as a good hostess should to welcome the newcomers, with what must have been the most unfortunate cliché in the book.

'So, you must be Francis!' she said. 'So good to meet you at last, we've heard so much about you!' and visibly winced at her own ineptitude. Francis, however, rose to the occasion, holding out a hand to take hers, saying cheerfully, 'N–none of it good, I d–d–daresay,' and giving her the full benefit of a smile that would have melted Antarctica. 'It's good to m–m–meet you too, Lady Carey. It's n–n–not before t–t–time.'

Sir Charles stepped forward then, and more hand-shaking ensued. Val took Kim by the arm.

'I'll take Kim out of the way, leave you all to get acquainted in peace – she wants to see Westminster Abbey, would you believe!'

'I missed it when I was here earlier this year,' Kim nobly backed him up. She had no particular urge to see Westminster Abbey, but appreciated it was as good an escape clause as any.

'I'll bring her back around four, and we can decide what we want to do this evening – if you haven't already something planned,' Val said, and dexterously whisked Kim out of the room. He wasn't at all sure if any of the four left behind had heard a word he said.

Eloise, taking the obvious path, said that she would ring for Annie to bring them coffee. 'Then we can all get to know each other in a civilised fashion,' she added, with a smile. The beautiful – well, not young man exactly, but a man anyway, that her daughter had introduced into her home gave her a swift, amused look that left her in no doubt that he was undeceived, and Sir Charles suggested that they should all sit down and be comfortable.

'So how did you find Henley?' Sir Charles asked, to set the conversational ball rolling, and added with deceptive ease, 'I understand your cousin lives there, do you know it well?'

'I've n–not been there b–b–before. I liked it – w–w–what I saw of it. I expect D–Diana told you I went to s–s–see my g–g–grandmother yesterday. She still lives in t–t–town.'

She had heard him sound a lot worse, Diana conceded, and took a more careful look at him than she had done so far. He did look remarkably at ease in this slightly awkward situation, she realised: calmer than she had expected – calmer than she ever seen him, even, she realised. A tautness in him that she had not even recognised before was somehow conspicuous by its absence. So, well done family.

The coffee arrived, and Sir Charles was saying 'Diana tells us that you are buying a farm and an historic farmhouse?' and made it into a question.

'R–r–rather a r–r–ramshackle one at present,' Francis admitted. 'I'm hoping f–f–for her help in putting it to r–rights, while I sort out the farm.'

Sir Charles glanced at his daughter: he had never visualised her as a builder and decorator. He asked, 'Is there much to be done to it?' He looked at his daughter again, with more interest this time. 'Do you know what you're being asked to take on?' Diana said that she did, she'd seen it, and a discussion of the state of Burnthouse took them safely through the next ten minutes or so, then 'And where do you plan to live, while all this is going on? The house sounds uninhabitable!'

'In a m–m–mobile home, on s–site,' said Francis. So the caravan had grown a bit, Diana thought, with satisfaction: better and better, things were looking up.

'And you, Diana? Will you continue to live with Kim?' asked Eloise, and could have kicked herself: there was something about this man that was making her behave completely out of her usual character. Perhaps it was because she already recognised that he was here to stay, she thought then, and they knew nothing about him beyond that he was a farmer – and even that, she was beginning to doubt.

'I hope sh-she will live th-th-there with me,' said Francis, and met her eyes as he said it.

Sir Charles heard his cue. He put his coffee cup carefully down onto its saucer. He said, 'Come into my study, Francis, we can leave the women discussing furniture, fixtures and fittings and have a quiet talk on our own, what do you say?'

'Th-that s-sounds like a good idea.' Francis rose to his feet with Sir Charles. 'I need t-t-to t-t-talk to you anyw-way.' He looked at Diana. 'I'll l- leave Eloise t-t-to you.'

'You want me to…?' asked Diana, disconcerted.

'One of us h-has to,' And probably better not Sir Charles, was the inference behind that, Diana realised. She looked glum. The two men left the room, and Eloise picked up her cue, as Diana had known she inevitably would.

'So what is it that you have to tell me?' she asked.

One advantage to telling things separately, Diana instantly realised, was that her parents couldn't gang up on her – on them, indeed. Francis wasn't being so foolhardy as she had thought – probably he wasn't. She said, 'There's a backstory. You must have wondered.'

Eloise said, dryly, 'We certainly wondered why none of his family or their business associates knew anything more about him than his name.'

They had asked around then. Well, she had known they would, Francis too. Diana took a deep breath.

'We told you the bones of it already – how we met, what we found out, all of that. What we didn't say, is that the man our mother ran to was Francis's father.'

There was a silence, while Eloise took this in. She said the first thing that had originally come into Diana's own head. 'I do hope you are both quite sure that he isn't also your father?'

'Quite, quite certain,' Diana assured her. 'Our mother, we know from Francis's aunt, was the daughter of the Earl of Lochaird. She got pregnant up in Scotland, maybe by a boyfriend her father disapproved of, and ran away because her family were insisting she had an abortion. We know that for a fact, because Francis's father knew it to be so. And come to that, so did his aunt.'

'He was unsuitable then – this man?' The Earl of Lochaird had made an impression, Diana could see. She said, 'Not socially unsuitable, I don't think – or maybe he was, nobody seems to know, really. But there was some sort of family feud between the two fathers, over some land or something – he was banished abroad somewhere to get him out of the way, so obviously she couldn't run to him. If she even would have. And nobody knows for certain if he was our father anyway, so far as we can work out.'

'And did he know she was pregnant? Did his parents?'

'History doesn't relate. Anyway, we're getting off the point. There's nothing anyone can do about it now.'

'Yes, we are.' Eloise looked at her seriously. 'Let's get back to it. The Chillingworths. Why do they none of them want to speak about him – about Francis? He's their first cousin! Explain that, if you will.'

'Well, to some of them he is.' Diana realised that she was splitting hairs to put off the moment when she would have to come clean. She took the plunge. 'It was because of something that his father believed – and Eloise, it is not true! He thought that Francis had killed our mother. He couldn't prove it, but he thought it. And he felt duty bound to tell his father because the cousins were all children still; then, not long after, he died himself in a car crash, and as we now know, that was probably murder too. And his grandfather saw to it that Francis and his mother were effectively struck off the family tree, and he had no more contact with the cousins that he grew up with.'

Eloise thought about this. Her thoughts were not happy ones.

'And are you quite sure that he didn't kill her?'

'Yes,' said Diana. 'For several reasons, actually, not the least being, everyone now knows who did: the ordinary working man she married simply because she couldn't make it on her own, and afterwards seems to have lied about and betrayed so she could get Christopher Chillingworth's sympathy. But most of all, I'm sure because Francis himself always thought his mother did it. So think about that one, too.'

'Oh, my dear!' said Eloise, having done so. 'The poor man! His mother too. Did they never talk about it together?'

'Apparently not – or not until recently, when we turned up. You see, the husband was still in the area and our arrival scared him. He tried to kill Francis, because, as it turned out, Francis held a clue if he had ever recognised it – which he didn't. Now that everyone knows the truth, the rules have changed.'

It did, Eloise realised, explain a lot of things, such as why a man so obviously eligible in every conceivable way had never married – until now, that is. She wondered if she was happy about that, or not. Thirteen years her senior, with a history like that behind him: did money – if indeed he had any – and a respected name, at least in business circles, make him an eligible husband – for anyone, not just her own beloved daughter?

Charlie, of course, would be hearing the same story, but from a different angle. She wondered what he was making of it.

It had taken Diana roughly a quarter of an hour to give her mother the facts of the case, and to discuss them, but over an hour later, there was still no sign of the men returning.

'Whatever can they be talking about?' Eloise worried, and Diana, who had a good idea, said, 'Oh, you know men when they get talking. Leave them to it – after all, we haven't heard any shouting.'

'Oh, don't!' Eloise paused to think about this. 'Does Francis shout a lot?'

'I expect he does, at cows and things that won't co-operate, but I've never heard him do it. I think that, over the years, he's learned to keep his temper.'

'Yes,' said Eloise, after a pause. 'That would figure. Poor man, and his poor mother, too. Whatever was his father thinking of?'

'I don't think that you can blame his father too much.' Diana had given this some serious thought. 'He did what he could with what he knew, and if it had been true, he did exactly the right thing keeping the cousins away. It's so easy to be judgmental, and so very hard to be fair, particularly when his was the original fault – if it wasn't our mother's, she does seem, from what Henrietta Chillingworth said, to have made a dead set at him. But I do grieve for Mary – Francis's mother. She wasn't just betrayed in her marriage, she effectively lost her son over it. Kim says it's my job to reconcile them, but I can't see how.'

Eloise thought about this. She said, 'I think Kim may be right. Why don't you start by taking her to see this farmhouse, and asking her advice? She's more handily placed than me, anyway, and from what you say she's lived in a historic building all her life.'

'I could, I suppose – if Francis doesn't mind, that is.'

'I very much doubt it he feels good about it, either. Go on – it has to be worth a try.'

Eloise, Diana realised, seemed to be taking it for granted that all would be well with her proposed marriage plans, and as it turned out, she was right. When Sir Charles and Francis did eventually rejoin them, Sir Charles was smiling. Diana said, 'So, did he pass the exam?' and everybody laughed, so that any tension remaining abruptly evaporated.

'Alpha Plus,' said Sir Charles, smiling. 'In fact, it we can clear up one small point, I think we can say he passed with full Honours. For once, my daughter, you seem to have hit the jackpot. I just hope you know what you're taking on!' He paused. 'I haven't discussed this with him yet, as I felt you should both be present when I brought it up.' He paused again there, largely, Diana thought, for effect. She said, obligingly, 'So what is it?'

'Your mother and I,' said Sir Charles, 'would be happier, if the two of you plan to live together as you – or Francis, here – says you intend to do quite soon, if the two of you were married.'

There was a short pause. Diana looked to Francis for guidance, and Sir Charles and Eloise waited. It was Francis who finally answered.

'That's f-f-fine w-with me, if T-tamsin is happy with it. W-w-we can get a l-l-licence and g-g-get the job done b-b-by the Registrar in Embridge.'

Then you could have a Church Blessing and a proper reception when we have time to arrange it!' said Eloise, immediately.

'Or we c-c-could do it in one go, in the ch-chapel at Ravenscourt Place. It's r-registered for weddings. What d-d-does Tamsin feel?' He looked at her with a slight lift of his eyebrows.

Diana, thus put on the spot, went with her gut feeling: Francis did not want a big fuss, and in any case, with all the various relations in three different families/areas/social levels, the logistics of arranging such an occasion would be terrifying! She said, 'I vote for a quiet wedding, just a few close family members and good friends, lunch in the Ravenscourt Arms, and then back to work. If you want to throw a party, Daddy and Eloise, you could do it when we've got things sorted out a bit, to celebrate that. Francis has got enough on his plate right now. Me too, if I'm restoring a historic building single-handed!'

'Oh, w-w-we can probably f-find s-s-somebody to do the heavy w-w-work,' said Francis. He sounded relieved, Diana was glad she had spoken up. She didn't want to look like a shrouded meringue at a huge Society wedding anyway. Eloise looked disappointed, but Sir Charles said, 'That sounds a plan to suit everyone, well done my daughter! Maybe you should have been in the Diplomatic Service.'

'Well, we can talk about it, when we've all had time to think' said Eloise, suspecting she had already lost the battle.

'And now that's all settled,' said Sir Charles, firmly, 'I suggest you take this young woman of ours out for a damn good lunch, Francis my man, and I shall fill Eloise in on the fine details over our own beans on toast.' He smiled.

'But just one thing before you go,' said Eloise, smiling in spite of her disappointment: she would have loved to organise a really big wedding. 'Why do you keep calling her "Tamsin"?'

'I asked that,' said Sir Charles, stepping in where angels might have feared to tread. 'It was her baptismal name when she was tiny: unlike Kim's, it was mislaid in the upheaval.'

'How very strange,' said Eloise, thinking about it. She looked at Francis. 'You must know so much about her babyhood that we have never known!' She added, wistfully, 'I don't suppose there are any photos – to fill in the missing bits for us?' But Francis shook his head.

'N-n-not that I know of.'

Eloise said, smiling, 'Then if we can't splash out on a huge wedding for you, can we at least take you out for a really good dinner to celebrate your engagement tonight? Kim and Valentine will be back later this afternoon – we could treat you all! It would be so lovely, and tomorrow, you will all be gone.' Diana looked at her warily, she loved her mother but she knew her well; she wasn't sure of the wisdom of this plan. She was always nervous when her mother gave in too easily, it was perfectly possible that she was hoping to recruit Kim and Val on her team, but everybody else seemed think it was a great idea.

'P-p-perhaps we should g-go steady on lunch, th-then,' Francis suggested, and they all laughed. Sir Charles said, 'I'll arrange for a table,' and Eloise hugged Diana and said, 'Have a lovely day, my darling,' and hesitated over doing the same with Francis, finally standing on tiptoe to kiss his cheek, and finding herself hugged in return.

They escaped eventually out into the street, and Diana indicated left.

'The Underground is that way – or we might pick up a taxi, if our luck's in – where are we going? Do you even know?'

'I'm r-r-relying on you,' said Francis, 'b-b-but a good j-jeweller might be a s-s-start. Your c-call – I'm a s-s-stranger here,' and for once in her life, Diana was silenced.

Back in the big apartment above them, Eloise was looking at her husband, with intent. She said, 'So tell me. It seems very unlike you to be so smug over our daughter marrying a farmer, however rich and influential his relatives, so would I be right in assuming there is more to it?'

'A lot more,' said Sir Charles, with satisfaction. 'For a start, he is not a farmer, he's an Estate Manager, and to go on with, I'm not sure you should even call him that. Let's sit down comfortably, and I'll tell you all about it.'

They sat.

'I'm assuming that Diana told you about the terrible misunderstanding that effectively stopped the poor man's life in its tracks?'

'She did. I was appalled, if you want to know.'

'I imagined you would be, when he was telling me.' Sir Charles looked serious. 'Kim was quite right when she called him both brave and generous, but there's more to it than that. He never intended to be the manager for his mother's estate. He isn't a born farmer, even if half his hereditary comes of farming stock, and he has done his best with it but I don't feel that his heart was in it, not when you get right down to it. What the man actually is, is an academic. He holds three good degrees, two of them in Marine Biology, which is what he intended to make his career before all the trouble blew up.' He paused, thinking how much he should say, for Francis had told him rather more than he had told to Diana. Eventually, he said, 'He is also his father's son – or I suppose, more accurately, his grandfather's grandson, and he is very astute financially. He inherited a fortune from his grandfather via his father, which Christopher Chillingworth placed in Trust for him until he reached his majority, and with the proviso that none of it should go to his mother, which is one of the reasons why he gave her fair and rightful share in his own labour and expertise, and that is generosity beyond the call of duty, as I think you will agree. I say " one of the reasons" – Diana will have already told you the other one.' He looked serious. 'It was damnable, if you want my view!' Eloise opened her mouth to speak, but Sir Charles hadn't finished. 'But more than that, in his mid-twenties, he took his own inheritance and seems to have speculated with it – as much with instinct as experience, from what I could gather, and over the last fourteen years or so has trebled it – and that profit being arguably his own money, he now intends to use some of it – a good deal of it, in fact – to provide for his mother and the family estate in perpetuity, by means of a Trust Fund centred on the estate itself. That way, he says, his mother can't argue with him over it. He is, I think, very angry indeed with his father, who managed not only to leave his mother with nothing but what was already hers, after years of lording it over his fellows on her – very large – estate, while cheating on her in the background, but to ruin his own life in the process.'

'He could have lived his own life, done what he wanted. He would have been entitled,' said Eloise, argumentatively. She heard herself, and winced.

'But he didn't. And very soon after he inherited, he couldn't; the injury he received in that accident Diana told us about precluded it, at least for many years.'

'Did he tell you how that happened? Eloise asked, curiously.

'He doesn't know. The incident was wiped from his memory at the same moment as it happened, as I understand it. And there's one more thing you need to take into account before you pass judgement.'

'There is?' asked Eloise, cautiously, and wondering, a little apprehensively, what it could possibly be; she had heard more than enough already, one way and another, she considered.

'You know it already, or you should if Diana did as he asked her. He thought his mother was a murderess.'

'Oh God!' said Eloise. 'I had forgotten – no, not forgotten, how could I? Just filed it, I suppose, as "untrue". But of course, it would have been true for him at the time.'

'Exactly. But now, everyone who needs to knows the real truth.'

'So what's he going to do? He's buying a farm, we know that.'

'He is. He breeds prize cattle, and he's proud of them – a defence ploy, I suspect, but true nonetheless. But basically, he intends to do what he always wanted to do, and leave the farm to a trusted manager.'

'You mean, be a marine biologist? Surely he's left that a bit late – and anyway, you said...' She let the sentence tail off.

'Maybe not quite as he originally intended, but yes. He plans to specialise in the tideline and the shallows.' He smiled at her. 'And get this – the icing on the cake! The wedding cake, indeed – he means to buy a yacht and keep it out in the Med, and initially to do a lot of his preliminary research out there. So…' He waited, still smiling widely, for the penny to drop. Eloise gave a little crow of delight.

'So we shall be able to meet when we go out there in the Summer! Oh Charlie, how wonderful! And in the Winter, presumably they'll be in this country!'

'That seems to be the general idea: to do the practical work in Summer in situ, and write it up when they come back for the Winter.'

'It's everything I would have dreamed for her,' said Eloise, on a sigh of delight. 'That is, if I'd had the imagination, I would have. If he was just a bit younger, and didn't have that awful stammer, it would be quite perfect!'

'Nobody ever gets perfect,' said Sir Charles, getting to his feet. 'And now – let's splice the mainbrace and drink to it! We've waited a long time for this day, and the sun must be just about over the yardarm…'

XIII

Diana and Francis sat in a coffee bar, facing each other over a small table: they had decided to pass on more than a sandwich for lunch, if they were going out to celebrate this evening.

'So, how did it go with your grandmother?' Diana asked, feeling that she had waited long enough by this time for him to tell her without prompting. Even then, he didn't reply immediately. He sat stirring his coffee, watching the brown swirl following the spoon, and said nothing at all, his thoughts returning to the previous morning, when he had stood, for the first time for well over twenty years, on the doorstep of the familiar old town house and pressed the doorbell.

His Aunt Clara had answered it, and at first she hadn't recognised him, she had thought he was selling double glazing or something. Then, when she realised who he was, she had burst into tears and flung her arms round him right there on the doorstep, and Aunt Henry had to come and rescue him. He was grateful that she was there to do it.

'It was the shock,' Aunt Clara had said, in apology afterwards. 'I hadn't expected you to look so...so grown-up,' and Aunt Henry had said, 'He isn't sixteen any more you know, Clara, the clock didn't stop for the last twenty years,' and then she had invited him in. It had half been funny, and half not. A situation in which a close family member was a total stranger should never be allowed to arise.

'You've gone quiet,' said Diana, watching him. 'Was it so bad?'

'N-no. No, not b-bad. S-s-sad.'

'Not your fault, though.'

'N-n-not theirs, either. B-but it was OK in th-the end.' Aunt Henry had apologised too, later, saying 'I meant to get there first, I had warned her not to do that – but you know how impulsive and sentimental she is, she's always been the same, never been any different, after all.'

Yet another indication that life had continued perfectly well without him. Always…yes, that was true. Then, now, forever…

'You've gone again. What about your grandmother? You don't have to tell me, if you don't want to.'

'I d-d-do want to. I was j-just th-thinking.'

Nothing good, whatever it had been. Diana waited, and finally she was rewarded.

'Sh-she's very old now…over n-ninety. She must be – oh, n-ninety-three, or f-four, even. And f-f-frail, a b-b-breeze would lift her away.' She had been sitting in an upright armchair in the first-floor sitting room with its view over the Square, wrapped in a warm shawl, her slippered feet on a stool and a walking frame and a bell both within easy reach. And he had kissed her cheek, with its skin as soft as thistledown, and tasted her tears salt on his lips. Or had they been his own tears? He wasn't certain.

'But she was happy to see you?' Diana prompted, quietly. He smiled at her.

'S-sorry, T-Tamsin. I'm n-n-not telling this very w-w-well, am I?'

'You don't have to tell me at all, if you'd rather not. I already said that.'

'N-no, it's all r-r-right. Aunt C-Clara brought up c-c-coffee and we t-t-talked.' He paused, and Diana waited. She took a bite out of her sandwich and chewed and Francis took a mouthful of coffee. He pulled himself together.

'Th-they w-w-wanted to know what I w-w-was doing with m-myself these d-d-days. Th-they wanted to kn-know about you.'

'So, did you tell them?'

'I t-t-told them about B-burnthouse. M-M-Mike had shown th-them some photographs he t-t-took.'

And nobody had asked about the past years, she deduced, or even mentioned them in passing. Well, she couldn't blame them, but she did sympathise a bit with his Aunt Clara. It must have been a very moving reconciliation.

She thought she might rather like Aunt Clara when she finally met her.

'N-now you're n-n-not saying anything,' Francis accused her, but gently. Diana pulled herself together.

'Well, Burnthouse should have kept you all occupied for a while. Did you mention your future plans, too?'

'Not then. N-no.'

'So what did you tell them about me?' she persisted.

'Th-that I was going to m-m-marry you, but I hadn't yet m-m-met your p-parents.'

'I bet you didn't mention it was going to be that soon,' said Diana, ruefully. 'I am sorry about that, Francis. You don't have to do it, if you'd sooner leave it a bit.'

'W-would you s-s-sooner l-leave it?' he countered.

'Me? I'd marry you tomorrow if it was possible!'

'You d-don't w-w-want a b-big p-posh w-w-wedding? Your m-m-m-mother w-would like it for you.'

'I just want to marry you, and the sooner the better. I don't care how, or who's there and who isn't. I don't want a big show and a big white dress and flowers, and a six-tier wedding cake tottering on a stand and a veil and bridesmaids and all that. I just want you. And I mean it.'

'Th-then th-th-thank g-goodness for that.' He grinned at her, thankfully himself again. 'I expect B-Bennie's WI mates w-w-will m-m-make us a wedding c-cake, if we ask th-them.'

'Then let's. Now eat your sandwich like a good boy, and tell me about Michael and Erin. You'd met him already, so that wasn't so bad, was it?'

'N-no. M-Michael knows the b-b-backstory anyway – and R-Ros and her husband Andrew c-c-came to d-d-dinner l-last night, and they-they knew it too. M-Mike had t-t-told them. S-s-so it was easy.'

'That's good, then. Did you meet any of the others at all?'

'N-n-no, not yet.' He looked at her gravely. 'You've already m-m-met Ed, I understand. H-he and his w-w-wife have invited us to lunch to-tomorrow on our w-w-way b-b-back to Embridge.'

'We'll have Kim with us,' Diana reminded him.

'Th-they know, sh-she's invited too. And V-val, he'll be d-d-driving us th-there.'

Diana considered this, and immediately found a flaw in the arrangement.

'What about your car? It's still in Henley, isn't it?'

'It w-w-won't be. M-Mike and Erin are invited too: M-mike will d-d-drive the Merc and Erin w-w-will drive her own c-c-car f-for them to g-g-go back in.'

'Quite a family occasion then,' said Diana, but with reservations; it sounded like overkill to her.

'Ed and M-M-Mike and I are old s-s-sparring p-p-partners,' said Francis, with far more confidence than he had earlier applied to his grandmother and aunts. 'It w-w-was good to get t-t-together again with M-Mike and R-R-Ros. Ed w-w-will b-be the s-s-same.'

'Yes, I've met Ed already,' said Diana, although it had already been said, and Francis said, 'I know,' and smiled at her.

Diana said, 'I felt awful, after it was done. It was so interfering of me, and I had no right...'

'I'm v-v-very glad you d-d-did.'

It went fleetingly through Diana's head to wonder if there were any more skeletons in his cupboard that needed to be rattled and hauled out into the light, but she knew that even if there were, she couldn't do it twice. And yet, she did sense a shadow there, she was sure. On the heels of that disquieting thought, there came another; she said, before she could stop herself, 'You're different – I don't know what it is, but something...' She stopped.

'D-d-different, how?' Francis asked, with a lift of an eyebrow.

'You'll think I'm being silly.'

'P-possibly. T-t-tell m-me anyway.'

Diana thought for a moment. To tell the truth, it was hard to put her finger on it, but she thought now that she had noticed it – or felt it, more accurately, the moment he had come into the drawing room with Val, and the brief talk with her parents later had underlined it...whatever it was. And then she had it. She said, feeling her way because it was difficult to define, 'It's as if...well, some barrier has come down. You were always a bit tense – on guard – and I'm only knowing that now, because it's gone, which is a bit strange, really. I suppose I was taking it for granted, that was how you were wired – but this morning, I don't think it is. I'm sorry, I'm not explaining that very well.'

Francis said nothing immediately. He played with the teaspoon, watching what he was doing with apparent intentness. Finally, he said, 'I s-s-suppose it's b-b-because I'm n-n-not used to being the f-f-flavour of the m-month. T-t-to be honest, it f-f-felt odd to m-me, too.'

Diana thought about this. It made sense – almost made sense, that is. She said, 'But you have friends – you mix with a crowd, sailing the Moonraker,' and knew, as soon as she had said it, that she had got that wrong. Yes, sailing in the class drew the participants together, but once ashore...she realised that she had never once seen him actually mixing with the others, except for that one disastrous evening at the Regatta Dance earlier that year, when some bitchy woman had started making snide remarks in a loud voice – and on that occasion, he had walked out – stormed out, more accurately. Was that sort of thing common in his life? And if it was, who was behind it? Somebody must be. What had that woman's name been, anyway? She couldn't remember if she had even heard it, either then or later. Francis said. 'Not f-f-friends. Acquaintances. The only one I c-c-can call a f-f-friend is p-p-probably M-Merlin.'

'And Val,' said Diana, argumentatively, but he shook his head.

'V-V-Val is th-there for K-kim. N-not me.'

'I would argue that point, by this time.'

Diana paused for further thought – about this, and about other things. The Regatta Dance, the request that he resign from the Club at Emberton, and where had that one come from? – one or two other passing remarks that she hadn't really taken any notice of at the time she heard them. He wasn't a mixer, that was true, but she had never wondered, why not? And then it came back to her: something he had once said to her, weeks ago – months even, by this time.

The hardest part about having friends is the losing of them. The inference had been, that he didn't try to make them in the first place, or not any more. Maybe once, in another life, he had been different. She thought about that, too.

'Who is it, doing this to you? What did you do to them?'

'T-Tamsin darling, it w-w-was all a v-very l-long time ago. F-forget it. W-we sh-shall go out t-t-to the M-Med and leave th-them all behind quite s-s-soon.'

'Someone poisoned your dog,' said Diana.

'Y-yes.'

'Do you know who?'

'Y-yes. I th-think so. Forget it. It w-w-won't happen again.'

All the vanished tension was back, she realised. She wished she had never brought the subject up, but she couldn't seem to leave it alone.

'Does all this date back to that fight you told me about, at Sixth Form College? Who did you thump?'

'T-Tamsin, give it a r-r-rest. It's n-not him.'

'You know that for a fact?'

'Yes, if y-you w-w-want to kn-now. Now, c-c-can we talk about s-s-something else?'

Diana was silent for a minute; she had upset him, she could see, and certainly, now she came to think about it rationally instead of just jumping in, up until recently there had been little he could have done about it, his weak and stupid father had left both Francis and his mother as hostages to the fortune of every evil wind that blew. But that had all changed now, surely? She found herself wondering, with a shiver of apprehension, what might happen when her engagement to Francis became common knowledge? It might be interesting to go down to the Club with Val and Kim occasionally, put herself in the firing line…and then she dismissed the thought. Don't meddle! Next time, the result might not be so good. Probably, his own technique was the safest: just walk away and go sailing in the Med.

She might find herself caught in the midst of the action without trying…

'W-what are y-you th-th-thinking?' Francis asked, watching her face.

'How much I love you,' said Diana immediately, which was, in essence, true. She would walk through fire for him – well, come to think, she had done so, more or less, on one memorable occasion, stamping on burning straw and tripping over his dog on the night when Tim Wakeley/Mark Eliot had tried to kill him. She began to feel better. 'Finish that sandwich, and then let's get on to what we're going to do next – whatever that is. I'm assuming you have a plan in mind?'

'I alr-r-ready mentioned it.' He smiled at her. 'I th-thought you could introduce m-m-me to your f-favourite jeweller.'

Diana nearly choked on her last mouthful of coffee. When she had finished spluttering, she said, 'That sounds a good one to me.'

'Put m-m-y m-mark on you,' said Francis, the cattle breeder, with a certain amount of wicked satisfaction. 'W-while we're at it, w-we m-m-m-might as well choose a w-w-wedding r-ring, it l-l-looks as if we m-m-might need it quite s-s-s-soon.'

'You really don't mind that?' Diana still felt slightly guilty about it. 'My parents do like to organise things, but you don't have to do everything they say.'

'I've already t-t-told you. It's f-fine. N-n-now, ch-choke down the r-r-rest of that coffee, and l-let's get to it.'

Going shopping with Francis proved to be a slightly surreal experience, mainly because, even in an expensive West End Jeweller's shop, he seemed to have no interest at all in how much anything actually cost; she had no idea if this was just for her benefit, or if he was always the same; she had no idea, in fact, what he was actually worth. What seemed to concern him the most was what she liked the most, and the assistant who attended to them very soon got the hang of this, and called up a senior member of the staff from some deep den in the back of the premises, who already knew Diana from seeing her with her father and was delighted to hear of her engagement, looking Francis up and down critically. Apparently, he passed the scrutiny; from then on, it was like being in Fairyland, Diana decided; beautiful rings were pulled out from hidden cupboards and displayed for her to choose from, and predictably, there wasn't a price ticket to be seen.

But in the end, the choice was simple, and as soon as she saw it, instantaneous.

'That one,' she said, pointing to a big diamond-cut sapphire, flanked with two smaller diamonds. 'It will remind me of you – of your bright eyes – every time I look at it.'

Francis studied the ring critically. He said, 'I don't th-think they're qu-quite th-that colour, do you?' and Diana said, 'I was talking about the diamonds,' and they all laughed.

'So th-this is the one you'd like?' He picked it out of it's velvet bed to study it.

'I love it,' said Diana, with decision. 'It's perfect!'

The assistant took the ring and slipped it over the measuring stick. He said, with a smile, 'And it appears to be exactly the right size! Perhaps Miss Carey would care to try it on?' He held it out to her, but she shook her head.

'If it's the right size, then it'll fit. I'm sentimental, me. We need a more romantic moment than this!' and he smiled at her.

'Of course. Now, is there anything else that I can show you?'

'W-wedding rings,' said Francis. 'W-w-we're g-going to n-n-need one s-s-soon.'

The wedding ring was selected too, a deep circle of gold with a ring of stars engraved round it, and then Diana looked at Francis.

'Are you going to be all Establishment and refuse to wear a wedding ring, or New Man, and let me buy one for you, too?'

For a moment, he looked totally taken aback. Establishment, then, oh well, she could have guessed. But then he said, 'I'll p-probably lose it in th-the c-cowshed.'

'OK. Then we can dig for it, or I'll buy you another. Or a metal detector, that would work too.' Their eyes met, and for a moment, she wondered. Then he laughed.

'All right, if that's w-w-what you'd l-like. But I'll p-pass on the s-s-stars, th-thank you.'

A plain gold ring joined the other two in its own velvet-lined box in a neat cardboard bag tied with ribbon, and two separate bills were made out and settled. Both assistants and a couple of interested customers wished them well, and they left with the little bag safely in Diana's shoulder bag. Outside on the pavement again, Francis stopped, and turned to her.

'Anything else y-you w-w-want to d-do? Or w-w-would you c-c-come with me to m-m-meet my grandmother? Sh-she'd l-like you t-t-to.'

'Have we time? We should be back home by half-past four at the latest, if you're going back with Val to smarten up for this evening.'

Francis glanced at his watch. 'It's only a q-q-quarter to th-three. We've t-t-time, if we d-don't hang about. We d-d-don't need to s-stay l-l-long, j-j-just l-let her s-s-see you for herself. Sh-she w-w-won't make th-the w-wedding, and I d-d-doubt w-w-we'll have t-t-time to c-c-come up again before th-then.'

'Then what are we hanging about for? Let's go!'

Francis turned out to be one of those people for whom taxis magically appear: her father was another one, so the phenomenon was familiar. Diana wasn't certain that he actually snapped his fingers to create the spell, but one smoothly pulled in beside them, right on cue, and not that long afterwards, they were pulling up outside a tall town house in a quiet Square with a tree-lined garden in the centre, a few expensive looking cars parked, and a general air of wealth and tranquillity. Francis paid off the taxi and they climbed the steps to the front door of the house and rang the bell. After a short wait, during which Diana became uncomfortably aware of butterflies in the stomach, the door was opened by a plump, grey-haired woman, probably in her late sixties, with a welcoming smile on her face and her arms held out in welcome.

'You made it! Mother will be so pleased – come in!' She gave Diana a warm hug. 'You must be Tamsin, the best thing that has happened to our family in years!' She then turned to Francis and treated him to a similar hug, which Diana noticed he accepted with stoicism, before he said, 'T-Tamsin, th-th-this is my Aunt C-C-Clara, I expect y-you g-g-guessed,' and they all smiled at each other in the way of strangers meeting for the first time. Diana thought she was actually more at ease than either of the other two, but at least Aunt Clara wasn't crying, although her eyes did look suspiciously bright.

Grandma, seated in her chair in the sitting room upstairs, was equally welcoming, reaching out her arms as Diana bent to kiss her cheek. 'Tamsin! How can we ever thank you enough for what you did for us all! So very brave and kind!'

Diana said, before she could stop herself, 'I thought we owed you – after all that happened. It was all I could think of to try to put things right. It was interfering, but...'

'No, it was not,' said Grandma. There were tears in her eyes too as she spoke. 'It was justice. Now sit down, and let me look at you properly.' Diana did as she was invited, and received a careful scrutiny. 'You are not so very much like your mother, now that I look at you. Her hair was more gingery, and she had grey eyes, I remember, yours are gold, like a lion's.' She smiled. 'And your sister, so Francis tells us, is just like you. How amazing that must have been, when you met!'

'They always were like two peas in a pod,' said Aunt Clara, smiling. These courtesies over, a silence fell while they all considered this unusual social situation and, Diana suspected, all wondered what to say next. Fortunately, Aunt Clara found the perfect answer.

'Francis tells us you are to be married,' she said, smiling. 'I see he hasn't given you a ring yet – you must make him buy you a beautiful diamond.'

'Actually, he just did,' said Diana. 'Well – not a diamond exactly. I fell in love with a sapphire.'

'Are we to be allowed to see it?'

'Of course.' Diana reached for her bag, but before she had it open, Francis, who had been standing by the window looking out at the Square, stepped forward.

'G-give it to m-m-me.' He held out his hand, and Diana extracted the right little box and dropped it into his palm, wondering what he would do next, but he had obviously missed out on a great career on the stage, for he took the ring out of its box and went down on one knee before her, taking her left hand in his and slipping the ring onto the third finger. He ended clasping the hand in both his.

'Aunt Clara is r–r–right, you are the b–b–best thing that ever happened t–t–to me, too, and th–thank you f–f–for t–t–taking the r–r–risk of promising t–t–to m–m–marry me. I l–l–love you.' He leaned forward to kiss her hand that he still held.

'M–me too,' she said, stooping to return the kiss with interest on his forehead, which was all she could comfortably reach.

Aunt Clara blew her nose and sniffed, then passed a tissue to her mother from a box on the side table.

'Lovely,' she said. 'Francis, you are a gentleman! Now, who would like a nice cup of tea?'

Grandma said, 'It should be champagne, Clara. Nobody is driving. Is there a bottle in the fridge?'

'Actually, there is.' Aunt Clara headed for the door. 'You three talk together while I bring it up!'

When she had gone, Grandma said, 'Francis, get up off the floor and sit beside the girl! So much more comfortable – I never knew you were such a romantic – good heavens, you must share that gene with Clara after all! I thought it had missed all of you.' Her voice trembled a little as she spoke, and Diana said, smiling, 'Oh, he's a great showman – you only need to look at his cows!'

Grandma looked at Francis as if she had only just seen him.

'I find it so hard to associate you with cattle, and farming, those country things, but I suppose you are half your mother's son. So strange.' She looked at Diana. 'But you, you're not a country girl. Henrietta knows your parents, they're very much of the town, she tells me.'

'We do have a house in the Cotswolds,' said Diana. 'I don't suppose that counts – but my biological mother was a country girl, my father too – well, he wasn't a girl, obviously, but he was a countryman. I think. I don't actually know who he was.'

'She never said,' said Grandma. 'I think she felt that he ran off and left her to face the consequences on her own, and despised him for it. How true that is, is open to judgement; I'm sorry to have to say this to you, but she could be a little creative with the truth.' She sounded censorious. It was odd, Diana found, to think that she, and no doubt the whole family too, had actually known the mother they couldn't remember; she thought

Kim might have difficulty with it too. It wasn't that she and Kim had never realised the possibility – probability, even – just that actually meeting the people involved made it...well, real. It had been so much easier when she was just an unknown woman in an isolated cottage. Now, among the Chillingworths, she was slowly taking on flesh and blood, becoming solid, not just mist. Very peculiar, and a little disquieting too, there was a definite suggestion that she had been a bit of a troublemaker. And there were more Chillingworths to meet yet, presumably more impressions with them.

Aunt Clara came back with a tray, four champagne flutes and a frosty bottle, and they drank to the engagement.

'And the future,' said Grandma, raising her glass. 'May it be better than the past!'

'What you want to remember, Tamsin,' said Aunt Clara, 'is that Francis is the last of the Chillingworths – so far. It's up to you to keep the name going! Just don't have lots of daughters like Father did." She smiled.

'L-let us get m-m-married f-first,' said Francis, but he was smiling too as he said it. 'Th-there's a t-t-target for you, Tamsin. F-founding a n-n-new dynasty.'

'You are planning on a family, then?' asked Grandma, wistfully. 'It would be lovely to see more little Chillingworths running about before I die.' She made them sound like puppies.

'Don't be morbid, mother,' said Aunt Clara, briskly, but Francis said, 'W-we'll see what w-w-we c-can do.'

They didn't stay long after that, making the excuse that they had to get back to Diana's home, which was true enough. Sped on their way with more kisses and hugs, plus a spatter of happy tears from Aunt Clara, they walked back to the main thoroughfare and found a tube station.

'Th-that could have g-g-gone w-worse,' Francis said, as they walked.

'I thought they were both sweet,' said Diana, 'but how the same genes produced you, God knows!' She lifted her hand momentarily to look at the new ring shining on her finger. 'Anyway, who's talking? You had your moment, too!'

'Th-they have that effect on m-m-me,' said Francis, apologetically. 'P–particularly Aunt C-C-Clara. It s-s-seems to be infectious.'

'They loved it anyway. Come to that, so did I. So?'

'Hmm. Th-the trouble is, th-th-they r-r-remember somebody that I'm n-n-not any m-more. It's hard t-t-to live up t-t-to.'

'I take it, you don't have that problem with your cousins?' She made it into a question.

'R–Ros gave me a few b–b–bad m–moments.'

'Well, it's a very emotive situation, you have to be fair. They must have been so hurt and upset…' She didn't add, 'What was your father thinking of?' because she already knew. They walked in silence for a while, and then the Station appeared on the right and finding the right train and fighting their way onto it distracted them both, so that when they spoke again it was normally, about normal things. It would need thinking about, Diana knew, but now wasn't the time or the place.

Just tonight, which maybe wouldn't be so bad if they were careful, and tomorrow, which was anybody's guess, to get through. This time tomorrow, they should be on their way home. She had never expected to be looking forward to leaving London, she loved the place, and all her friends here, but "home" was definitely the rolling downland of Dorset now.

There was a song about that – *Love changes everything*. She smiled down at her beautiful new ring, spreading her fingers to admire it properly and Francis, noticing, said, 'And t–t–take care of that, f–for God's s–s–sake until I've had t–time to g–g–get it insured,' and she turned the smile on him.

'How like a man! And of course I shall!' She lifted the hand and held it momentarily against her cheek. 'It's the most valuable thing I have ever been given, and I'm not talking about money.'

He took the hand and held it warmly. 'That's good then.'

The train rattled on.

Diana had felt some misgivings at the idea of a dinner party to celebrate her engagement, although she had tried to dismiss them, and Kim, it now transpired, had a few too. She liked Diana's parents – very much, as it happened – but she had no illusions about them. She listened to Diana's account of the earlier skirmish over her projected wedding plans and came to the conclusion that they were both of them used to getting their own way, and she felt very strongly that the way to prevent arguments was to keep the conversation as uncontroversial as possible.

'We must try to keep off the subject of weddings,' she told her twin, as they got ready to go out. 'Your mother has a taffeta meringue and a mist of veiling and a huge reception in her eye, and the easiest way round that is to keep the conversation firmly on house restoration, accountancy, and cows.'

'That might be easier said than done,' said Diana, who knew her mother well. 'But Francis really, really, doesn't want a big wedding, and in any case, the logistics of it would be enough to try the judgement of Solomon! Daddy mixes with the Mighty, the Vachells till the soil! And that's before you even start on the Chillingworths, who are largely a totally unknown quantity.'

'Oh, I think they would hold their own,' said Kim. 'Of course, I only know them by repute, but they sound far from socially inept to me. You can probably measure them by Francis, come to that.'

'I've only met a handful of them so far, and my encounter with his Aunt Henrietta and his cousin Edward was hardly encouraging – and although I think his Aunt Clara is lovely, she's not exactly what my father's crowd are used to. For one thing, she seems awfully sentimental. She keeps bursting into tears.'

'People do, at weddings,' Kim offered.

'Clara Chillingworth doesn't need a wedding to set her off. She's a sentimental spinster, and I don't mean that to be taken in any way as derogatory. I thought she was a sweetie.'

Kim rubbed the end of her nose thoughtfully.

'I think your mum is a sweetie, too, but I suspect she's a bit too used to getting her own way. Which of them would you back in a fight, is the big issue – your mum or Francis?'

'Actually, I think Francis has pretty much pulled the rug from under her,' said Diana, thinking about it. 'All that about a Church Blessing, and a big reception for our friends – even Eloise must have noticed how he immediately came up with the chapel at Ravenscourt Place. I've never seen it, and if it's a private chapel, it isn't going to be big, but it will be consecrated ground – snookering her on both counts. And I'm pretty sure not just anybody can get married there, which will give it status too.'

'Yes, you said about that. And you said, the Ravenscourt Arms after, but maybe that's not such a good idea.'

'He really, really doesn't need to have to make a speech to a huge crowd of strangers – to a small crowd of anybody, come to that. Can you imagine it?' Diana shuddered at the thought. Kim said, 'I've never been in a private chapel. How big is likely to be?'

'A private chapel is usually just for the use of the family who own the house it's in and their staff,' said Diana, considering. 'So…seating for twenty or thirty, tops? It depends on the size of the house, of course.'

'Ravenscourt Place is big, but it isn't enormous. What do you think?'

'I'd only be guessing. We could ask Merlin, I suppose. He'll know.'

'Even seating for thirty would seriously restrict the guest list,' said Kim, thinking.

'I think that's the general idea.'

'He didn't come down in the last shower, your man, did he? And by the way, I do love that ring he's given you.'

Diana held out her hand yet again to admire her new possession.

'He said, not to lose it until he's had it insured.'

'The last of the Great Romantics! But I see his point. It must have cost him a bomb.'

'I don't know. Price was never mentioned.' She sat down on the edge of her bed and looked at Kim seriously. 'It's something I've begun wondering about, Kim – just who, and what, I'm marrying. Someone – I think it might have been Val – once said that he inherited about five million, but even if that's true, it was almost twenty years ago, and in today's money, it must be a lot more than that. And we know, because he said so himself once, that he's played the Stock Market over the years, just to keep his brain in gear, and with his heritage the chances are that he was good at it. Looked at logically, if he's kept on adding and adding and adding to the original inheritance for all that time, he could be worth fifty million by now. More, even. It's a bit...well, daunting, actually.'

'He wouldn't be unique even if it was true. And probably, it isn't. You're only guessing, after all. And be honest, your own father is hardly a pauper, surely.'

'I know, I know – but that isn't the whole of it. Listen to me Kim, please. There's something going on down there in Dorset. I know it, you must know it. And jealousy is a powerful incentive to spite. If we can work this out, so can whoever is behind all that trouble at the Regatta Dance, the poisoning of dear Sacha, the request for his resignation from Ember Valley – maybe even more that we don't even know about – well, you see what I'm getting at.'

Kim did. She sat down too, to think about it. One thought jumped straight into her head, just as it had into Diana's.

'So, what do you think will happen when you announce your engagement?' she asked.

'That's just what I've been wondering myself,' said Diana, and met her eyes. 'Whoever it is, they poisoned the dog because he loved him.'

'Then don't accept drinks from strangers,' said Kim, hardly believing what she was saying.

'The point is, it probably isn't a stranger,' said Diana.

They both thought about this. Kim said, slowly, 'Killing a dog is cruel, but killing a person would be murder.'

Diana said, half to herself, 'I shall have to talk to Ernie.'

'Why Ernie?'

'Because I think Ernie knows something that I wasn't told…although I can't see how a quarrel at Sixth Form would end up in a situation where I'm half-afraid to admit that I'm going to marry the man I love.'

'Maybe that's the whole point of it,' said Kim. 'It wouldn't go that far, but you might think that it would…'

'But whoever it is can't know what we're thinking now.'

A knock fell on the door, making them both jump, and Eloise's voice called, 'Are you two about ready? The car will be round in a moment, we should be on our way. We don't want to be late!'

Diana jumped to her feet.

'Five minutes – I'm just putting my face on and Kim's looking for her shoes – we'll see you in the drawing room in two ticks!'

The tense atmosphere shattered like glass. Hustling round to do rather more than apply lipstick and find a pair of shoes, the conversation they had just had faded into fantasy. They arrived in the drawing room, slightly breathless and after only eight minutes, and almost on the moment, the front door bell rang to announce that Sir Charles's driver had arrived to take them to the fashionable and famous restaurant where Sir Charles must have pulled several strings to get a reservation at such short notice. Or maybe he had planned it in advance? Who knew? Who cared? The evening was going to be good – that is, it was going to be good if the conversation at the table could be kept under control!

Val and Francis were to meet them at the restaurant, and from the moment they arrived it was obvious that whether they were friends in the strictest sense or whether Francis was right, and they were just acquaintances, they were definitely in collusion. The subject of weddings was bound to come up, given the reason for arranging the dinner in the first place, but discussing it with those two around, Kim said to Diana later on, as they were finally getting to bed, was like talking to a couple of wriggling snakes! Or a football, during a rather fast game, Diana had agreed. But that was later.

Eloise introduced the subject, after a suitable interval of greetings and social conventions, over the dish of superb assorted canapés that kicked off a memorable meal. She made the mistake of approaching from the rear, thus affording Val the perfect opportunity to take control of the field.

'So, when are you planning to get married, you two?' she asked Kim and Val, with polite interest. 'Will you be going back to New Zealand for it? Kim will want her family there, I expect, and her friends.' She smiled, but Diana recognised a sly shot in her own direction. She waited with interest for Kim's reply, but in fact it was Val who picked up the ball and ran with it.

'Her parents will come over here for it,' he said. 'In the Spring – that's Autumn over there, and the sheep will be doing their own thing up in the hills, so Kim tells me. Her cousin – her mother's nephew – will be keeping an eye on them. But her father's family are all in this country, and so, obviously, are mine, so the event will be staged at the Queen's Hotel in Embridge where there is plenty of room.'

'Won't that be a bit difficult for her parents to arrange?' asked Eloise, becoming interested. 'They can always call on us for help, you know, if they need it – Kim already feels like an extra daughter!'

'That's very kind of you, and thank you for the offer – actually, my own mother is carrying the can on this occasion, to the accompaniment of numerous emails, phone calls, and when all else fails, actual letters, but if she needs back-up it will be good to know you're there to call on.' He smiled at her, and Eloise said, after thinking about it, 'How unusual – but logical, I suppose, in the circumstances. Will it be a church wedding, or is it one of those hotels where you can get married in situ, as it were?'

'Well, it is, but we won't be taking that option. The actual wedding is to be in the church at Emberton – her parents lived there when they were in England, and Kim lives there now, she won't have to establish a residential qualification. It seemed the obvious choice.'

Eloise looked at Diana, smiling, and said, with intent but an innocent expression, 'You will be living there too by the spring. You could have a double wedding, that would solve all the problems!' Diana winced; she wanted her wedding to herself, thank you very much, Eloise! Probably Kim felt the same, they were twins after all. Fortunately, support was at hand.

'Actually sh-she w-w-won't,' said Francis, snatching the ball before Val reached it. 'B-Burnthouse is in a d-d-different p-parish. And w-w-we shall be g-getting m-m-married before th-th-that, in any c-c-case.' He exchanged a quick glance with Diana, and smiled slightly. Eloise and Sir Charles had scored an own goal with that one earlier on.

'Anyway,' said Val, snatching the ball back, 'they're not like sisters who've grown up together, although it sometimes feels like it – they're two different people, with different parents, different friends, and different tastes. It would be complicated beyond belief to arrange! And Diana and Francis, I know, want a quiet affair with just their closest family and friends. They're going to be too busy for anything more elaborate, anyway, with that house and the land to fix up.'

'And you and Kim want a full-scale "do"?' asked Sir Charles genially, stepping up to the line, 'not like these two, here!'

'If you're dragging people across whole oceans to be there, you need to make it worth it,' said Val, smiling.

They could have rehearsed it, Kim thought in admiration. Perhaps they had. An answer for everything, and the opposition left without a leg to stand on! Magnificent! To mix the metaphors a little, between them Val and Francis had trumped every ace. And now, right on cue, here came the waiter to clear the plates ready for the next course, and by the time that was done, and the wine topped up, the subject would probably automatically change itself.

As of course it did. Even Eloise could accept when she was beaten, and anyway, she consoled herself, there was always the party she would give when all the work was done, they had at least agreed to that – well, in principle, Diana had, she wasn't certain about Francis. She hadn't quite got his measure yet, she recognised. She said, 'So where will you be living, once you get married, Kim and Valentine? Here in London – that will be a bit of a change for you, Kim, won't it?' and answering this question, with all its options, cleared the air nicely and the evening continued in harmony.

At least there was plenty to talk about, Diana thought, not without relief: she knew her mother with a bone in her teeth! There was Val's impending job interview, with all it might portend, there was his and Kim's new house to describe, there were the plans for Burnthouse to discuss, there was Kim's plan to find work as a translator, which Sir Charles found very interesting.

'If you go free-lance, I can probably slip work your way – if you're good, that is.' He smiled at her, and she said without conceit that yes, she was good.

'Very good, in the main European languages. I plan to add Greek, and maybe Russian, to the mix – I already have a smattering. And Mandarin is going to be the coming one to learn.'

'I believe it is already taught in some schools over here,' said Sir Charles.

Nobody seemed interested in what she might plan to do, Diana thought, a little disgruntled. Probably took it for granted that she would be a farmer's wife and make cheese or something. She realised that she had no idea whether Francis's beloved cows were beef cattle or a milking herd, and knew a moment of shame. No doubt she would find out – or no, come to think, wasn't there a milking parlour at Vachells? And somebody had mentioned a milk lorry, although she couldn't remember who…or even why. She felt a momentary qualm, and quickly squashed it. She was at least as bright as Kim, she would catch up.

Only, Kim wasn't exactly stepping out of her comfort zone…

Francis, sitting beside her, leaned towards her and spoke quietly in her ear. 'If you k-keep t-t-twisting that ring round your f-f-finger, you'll end up d-d-dropping it on th-the floor.'

She turned her head to smile back at him.

'And it's not insured – I know! But we could scrabble round and find it, under the table.'

'Actually it is. I s-s-saw t-to it th-this evening, before w-w-we came out, on m-my laptop. B-b-but still b-b-better not t-t-to throw it around.'

She wondered if he had guessed what she was thinking; she had a feeling that he might have. This was confirmed when his hand slipped over hers under cover of the tablecloth and gave it a comforting squeeze. It emboldened her to say, to the company at large, 'And I shall be taking up interior decoration – a bit of a difference there, wouldn't you say, for identical twins!'

'You wanted to learn Greek too,' Kim reminded her. 'We can go to evening classes together – or do they have classes in Greek in Dorset? It's a bit of a fringe requirement.'

'You need Oliver Nankervis,' Val told her, 'but unfortunately, he's emigrated to Cornwall. Pity, he'd make an interesting teacher!'

'You know Oliver Nankervis?' Sir Charles asked, with interest. 'This is the artist, we're talking about?' and Val admitted that yes, he did, and come to that so did Francis, and yes, he was the increasingly famous marine artist, and the conversation moved on to more general subjects. Both Val and Francis had scored Brownie points there, Diana saw. The atmosphere was relaxing by the minute – but that might be the wine, come to think. She caught Kim's eye, and received a wink in return. Weddings had slipped into oblivion.

The evening finally came to an end on a note of friendship and approval, and Sir Charles offered the services of his driver to return the two men to Isleworth.

'I'll ask them here to call us a taxi – it isn't far. And Adam will bring the girls to you in the morning, no need to come and pick them up. It will save you time and give you a few minutes more to enjoy their company!'

'That's very kind of you, sir,' said Val, replying for both of them.

'And th-thank you for a g-g-great evening,' Francis added. There were hugs and kisses and hand-shakings and goodbyes and then the driver arrived and the evening was over. Without a major incident, too, Diana thought thankfully, leaning back wearily in the back of the taxi. One or two sticky moments at the start, plain sailing thereafter. Amazing! She felt as if she had been put through a wringer, but they had survived to fight another day. And come to think…

Just tomorrow to get through. She closed her eyes in relief.

XIV

A good night's sleep on top of the unexpectedly pleasant evening they had spent, not to forget to mention the superb meal they had eaten, had given both Kim and Diana time to think a bit more rationally about the situation back in Embridge. It was unlikely, Kim said as they were packing their things ready to leave for Isleworth and points south after breakfast, that anyone would murder Diana just out of spite, not after all this time. They hadn't murdered Francis, and he was the one whoever it was felt strongly about.

'It's a bit more subtle than a simple gunshot-in-the-woods job,' she said. 'Meaner, somehow. It feels more like bullying at school to be honest – make the victim miserable to amuse your admirers, but keep your own standing unassailable – you know the kind of thing. It goes on everywhere.'

'So what you're saying,' said Diana, thinking about this, 'is that our perpetrator is someone people will listen to, and possibly respect?'

'Not exactly that, no. Just that maybe he – or she, presumably a sixth-form college over here is co-educational – is a person a bit full of themselves who has, at some time, been knocked off his perch and made to feel humiliated, quite probably by Francis, and was basically insecure enough to turn spiteful over it. All mouth and no backbone, you must have met them.'

'Seems a long time to bear a grudge to me, you'd have thought they would have outgrown it by now! And anyway, Francis is quite certain about its not being the one he thumped to hell and back.'

'Pity he didn't give you a name – I suppose he didn't?'

'No, he didn't. But he claims he knows who poisoned Sacha, so...I don't know, Kim. He just plans to sail away, and I can't say that I really blame him. To be honest, I don't think he's that bothered, one way or another, except about the dog.'

They neither of them realised it, but both of them had in fact been given a name, although on different occasions and in contexts where it had carried no particular significance.

'He didn't resign from the Club when they asked him to,' Kim said, thinking.

'I think that was more a matter of principle. And he hasn't been back since, anyway, so he might as well have done.'

'It might be interesting to see what happens next,' said Kim. 'You say, you think Ernie may know something?'

'They were at college together. Presumably, he was there at the time Francis took up assault and battery. At the very least, he'll know who it was he thumped, and that might be informative.'

Kim rubbed her nose thoughtfully. 'Well, you could ask, I suppose, but if Francis says it isn't his victim who's responsible, he's probably right.'

'I'm pretty sure it's someone at the Sailing Club, though,' said Diana. She flung the last garment into her case and closed the lid. 'Breakfast? Eloise will be sending Annie for us if we don't get moving!'

'OK.' Kim had finished her own packing some moments earlier, being more practised at it than Diana after her trip around Europe. 'But remember, something similar happened at the Yacht Club's Regatta Dance as well. A clue, do you think?'

'A lot of them seem to belong to both clubs,' said Diana, without defining who she meant by "them". 'Come on then, if you're ready.' She opened the door, standing aside for Kim to pass.

For Eloise, at least, breakfast was over too quickly.

'It's been so lovely having you both here, and getting to know Kim and meeting Francis and Val. Don't leave it too long before you come again, will you?

'Or you can come to us,' said Diana, immediately. 'We can't exactly put you up right now, but there's a rather good hotel in Embridge called the Langland, you could stop there. And then we can show you Burnthouse, you'll be surprised, I think.' She paused, thinking she had picked the wrong word there, but left it anyway. 'Francis completes on the sale on Friday, just give him time to clear away the world's biggest dungheap and about twenty skips of rubbish, and then I'll give you both a conducted tour. I could use your input, anyway – he's leaving the house for me to sort out!'

'Brave man!' said Sir Charles, smiling, but the goodbyes could be prolonged no longer, Adam the driver was waiting to take the luggage, and they had been instructed to be in Isleworth by ten o'clock at the latest. There were hugs and kisses all round, promises for an early visit to Embridge in the future, and then they all took the lift to the ground floor, and there were more hugs and kisses before the twins got into the car and the driver closed the doors on them, promised Sir Charles he would take care of them, and slid into his own seat. The engine purred into life, and the big white apartment block and the flowing river passed out of sight behind them.

'Isleworth is moderately posh,' said Diana, approvingly, as they sat together on the rear seat. 'Not as posh as Chiswick, but OK. Have you seen Val's flat yet?'

'I spent most of yesterday afternoon in it,' Kim admitted.

'Before or after viewing Westminster Abbey?' asked Diana, with a giggle, and Kim, ignoring this with the contempt it deserved, said, 'It's nice enough, but I hope I don't have to live there, it's far too urban for me, I don't think I would feel right there. But he's got some good furniture. Not a lot, and not very imaginative, but good quality.'

'His, or rented?'

'He rents unfurnished, so it must be his.'

'That could be handy. You need to think seriously about furnishing that bungalow, if you're going to live in it. We could explore a few shops, to pass the time.'

'You too. Francis seems to have mainly bookcases, from the sound of it. And a grand piano, of course.'

Diana gave a rueful laugh. 'It's going to be a while before hunting for furniture is on our to-do list. You just wait until you see it!'

'Not so long now, and you can show me!'

As they neared Isleworth, Kim rang Val on her mobile, so that he was waiting on the pavement ready to switch their luggage from Sir Charles's car to his own as expeditiously as possible, and then Adam drove away after wishing them a good journey home, and they all went into the tall terraced house where Val had his flat on the first floor – two bedrooms, a bathroom, a sitting room and a kitchen/diner, all pleasantly furnished in a masculine kind of a way and slightly untidy. No dust, however, so Diana deduced that somebody probably cleaned it for him regularly, she had no opinion of men's housework – or perhaps Kim had done it yesterday, but she doubted that. They found Francis lounging about in an armchair reading the Sunday papers, which he set aside as they appeared to get to his feet to greet them, enfolding Diana in a hug that almost knocked the breath out of her. He looked, she noticed with interest, perfectly at ease, a friend rather than a guest. She filed the fact with all the others she had garnered during this brief break to consider later on; there was a lot to think about already, and it wasn't finished yet.

They left for Esher quite soon, after coffee that Kim brewed up in the kitchen and Diana helped her wash up after – there was a definite nuance to this flat, which Diana felt needed looking into! Since Esher wasn't exactly just around the corner, Kim and Diana ended up in the back together again, allowing Francis to stretch his long legs out a bit in the front passenger seat.

'You would pick on a giraffe,' said Kim, as they climbed in. 'It's entirely your own fault that you can't have a romantic snuggle back here, and all I can sit and gaze at lovingly is the back of my beloved's head!'

'You two sound just like sisters,' said Val, half-listening as he re-set the Satnav. 'That looks about right—' He looked at it critically. 'Right – let's get the show on the road!'

Diana had already driven to their destination once, but from a different starting point so that she couldn't be of much help, but Satnav Lady brought them safely to the road in which Ed lived, and she was at least able to indicate the right house, and Val obediently turned in at the gate. There were no other cars in the drive as yet, so he parked tidily outside the double garage, and they unloaded themselves into its courtyard. At which point, Ed came round from the front door, looked at Kim and Diana in momentary astonishment, and then seized on the correct one to give a welcoming hug.

'I saw you turn in at the gate,' he explained, as he did so. 'Tamsin! Good to see you again, and this time on a happier occasion! And you must be Kim – my goodness, it's a good thing you do your hair differently, the two of you!' He greeted Kim too, with slightly more reserve as they had never met before, and then turned his freed attention to the men for the first time. His jaw dropped in astonishment, a phenomenon Diana had read about but never actually seen before.

'Good God, Frank, what the hell have you been doing? Standing in the compost bin? You were quite a normal size the last time I saw you, what happened?'

'I g-g-grew up,' said Francis.

'I can see that you did! And not just "up", come to that! God, but it's good to see you again – every bloody inch of you!' He grasped his cousin's hand in both of his, as if he couldn't bear to let go, but then released it to extend his own hand to Val. 'And you must be Val – you will notice, that at least I could tell the difference between you two!' They all laughed, as much with relief that the difficult initial greeting was now behind them as with amusement, and Ed said, 'Come inside. We need to break out the alcohol – this is a great occasion! Mike and Erin will be here at any moment, they're on their way.' He led the way indoors and into the kitchen, where his wife, whom Diana hadn't met on the previous occasion, waited tactfully to greet them when the emotional initial meeting was safely behind them. Her main reaction to all of that, Diana realised as she followed the others inside, was shock, and for a slightly ridiculous reason; she had never heard anyone call Francis "Frank" before.

Like Grandma and Aunt Clara before them, Ed and his wife Amanda had considered this to be a champagne occasion.

'Just remember our men have to drive home,' Diana said, accepting a glass appreciatively. 'Kim and I are OK – we can get as tipsy as we like!'

'By the time you've eaten Amanda's roast pork and all the fixings, you'll have soaked it all up,' Ed told her. 'Erin is providing the pudding course – God knows what that'll be, but hopefully not something really heavy like treacle pudding and custard. These crisps are just the hors d'oeuvres – try one. Cheese and Onion or Original, the dog ate the rest while we weren't looking—'

'You have a dog?' asked Kim, looking around her in surprise.

'She's gone to Amanda's parents' for the day, together with the kids,' said Ed. 'This is a purely grown-up occasion – was that a car I heard?'

'You must have ears like a bat,' Diana told him; she had heard nothing. He grinned at her and headed for the door.

'I'll just make sure he hasn't scrunched your car, Frank!'

Michael and Erin came in laughing, and accompanied by the scent of freshly baked pastry. Erin put a carefully covered dish on the worktop and said, 'Lemon meringue pie. That way we can cut the slices to suit everyone's appetite, it seemed like the best idea,' before turning to greet the three strangers: she had already met Francis of course. 'So which is Tamsin, and which is Kim? I can guess which is Val!'

Introductions over and more champagne poured, Michael lined up Amanda, Erin and Diana and stood back. Amanda was a tall, slim blonde, Erin a smallish curvaceous brunette, and Diana a middle-sized and shapely redhead.

'We've done that rather well, don't you think, fellas?' he said. 'You'd think we'd been consulting each other!' and they all laughed. There was no tension in this meeting, Diana realised. More a feeling of joy, and not a little relief that they were all reunited once more. She hadn't realised fully how close the three boys that the three men had once been had been... that thought had become a little convoluted, and she smothered a smile, which Michael saw, and smiled back. He raised his glass.

'Here's to old times and times yet to come,' he said, and they all drank to that. Then Amanda said, 'And now you can all clear out of here because I need space to carve the joint and serve up. Take everyone into the dining room, Ed, get them sorted out. And if one of you girls cares to volunteer to lend a hand, it would be appreciated – we gave Robert the day off, this is Family Time!'

'I'll help,' said Kim. 'You certainly don't want Diana, she's about as much use in a kitchen as the family cat! And Erin has been driving half the morning.'

'We could be shifting the luggage over,' Val suggested.

'No you couldn't! It's not going to be that long, it's all good to go.' Amanda shooed them all through the kitchen door, and turned to Kim, laughing. 'Men! What are they like?' She picked up an oven cloth and opened the oven door. A delicious smell came surging out and Kim sniffed appreciatively. 'I just hope nobody's vegetarian,' said Amanda, lifting out the roasting dish onto the table where a wooden board and a carving knife already waited.

'That looks good,' said Kim, admiring.

'Rolled, stuffed and amazing loin of pig. It's dead easy to carve, and done this way it's absolutely delicious, the stuffing stays moist and the crackling is to die for! If I give you the cloth, can you haul out the spuds and put them in that dish on the hotplate? The healthy stuff is all ready in the hot cupboard with the plates.' She picked up the the carving knife and fork. 'How did you and Tamsin come to meet up with Francis, anyway? They'll all be through with Chapter One before I get there, I'll need to keep up!'

'He and Val belong to the same Sailing Club,' said Kim, taking the easy way. It was true anyway – as far as it went, it was true. She put the tray of roast potatoes on the hotplate and began to shovel them across to the serving dish that sat ready.

'Handy – so they knew each other before they met you two?'

'From way back, I imagine – we haven't actually asked.' Kim hadn't realised this, she thought about it now. 'They raced in the same class, but Francis packed that in at the end of the season. He's upgrading to something bigger.'

'Hope Tamsin likes yachting then.' Amanda sliced thick rolls of meat from the joint, laying them neatly in an overlapping row. 'I take it, if it's a sailing club, you two sail too?'

'I don't. Diana's done a bit I think, and her father has a yacht, but it's more of the gin palace variety. He keeps it out in the Med somewhere.'

'Nice! The plates are in the hot cupboard – there.' She indicated with the knife. 'Could you get them, please? This is ready to serve now.' Kim fetched the plates and spread them out; Amanda began to lay out the slices; two for the men, one for the girls. 'If you look over there, there's a bowl with some little slices of apple in it, to garnish – they're in lemon juice, so they won't go brown. Put them in a sort of fan shape and add a sprig of that watercress, there...' With what appeared to be an enviable gift for doing two things at once, she went on with scarcely a break, 'Ed says the two of you were adopted separately as children and met pretty much by accident. That must have been an interesting moment.'

Kim thought back yet again to that night, the darkness and the fog, the stranger who wasn't a stranger standing on her doorstep, and thought "interesting" was a bit of an understatement. She said, 'You could say that. But we sorted it out in the end. Francis knew us both when we were tiny, he told us. That's why he calls Diana "Tamsin", it was her original name and he still thinks of her that way.'

'Yes, Ed does that, too,' said Amanda, without adding any comment. 'There's a little jug of gravy – yes, there – I'll just put a swirl on the plates for the look of the thing, if anyone wants to drown it, they can do it themselves...' She suited the action to the word, and Kim watched her.

'Perhaps you should teach Diana to cook,' she said. 'Francis would be grateful – at the moment, her pièce de resistance is a fried egg sandwich.'

'I went to cookery school, I wanted to be a chef – but then I met Ed, and it never happened.'

'Do you regret it?'

'Not really. He loves entertaining people anyway, friends or clients, and I keep my hand in that way. I cook, and we get people in to serve – Robert, our…well, our houseman, I suppose, runs the show out here, and I sit there smiling and listening to the compliments for the chef.'

'Do they know that's you?'

'Only if we tell them.' Amanda smiled at her. 'Right, that's all ready.' She reached for her apron strings. 'Let's get the show on the road – or the table, rather. I'll take the plates, you bring the veg. It'll take a couple of trips.' She picked up three of the plates, deftly balancing them, and Kim picked up the dish of roast potatoes and obediently followed her to the dining room, relieved that she seemed to have weathered that without tripping over herself. Not knowing how much anyone knew was a bit like going downstairs in the dark, she decided. Risky. It would be a relief when she was back with her allies; the one thing she did not wish to do was to drop Francis in it, and she had no idea how much Michael or Ed knew; Michael rather more than Ed, she had a suspicion. Michael was the one who had finally made the link, and he had caught Francis unprepared; it was quite possible that he had learned a few things that even Diana didn't know.

'Don't forget the apple sauce – it's over there,' said Amanda when they returned for the second load. 'One more trip and it's done – you sit down when we get in there, I can manage the last load on my own. And thank you, best kitchen assistant I've had in years!'

It was inevitable, once everyone was seated around the table and the vegetables were doing the rounds, that the subject of weddings should come up, but it was a totally different discussion to the rather awkward one at last night's restaurant. This was a crowd of the same generation, most of whom knew each other well, and the general atmosphere of celebration lightened the mood halfway to euphoria.

'So, are the four of you going for a double wedding?' asked Amanda, smiling. It would always be Amanda, Kim suspected, who rushed in where angels feared to tread but she did it with such style and enthusiasm that you couldn't criticise her for it. She wanted to know – well, so did everyone else round this laden table, and there was only one way to find out.

'Certainly not,' said Diana instantly, but laughing as she said it. 'The mechanics of it would frankly be quite scary, so many different families and friends, we'd need St Paul's Cathedral to house them all! Anyway, Francis and I want small and simple and soon, and Kim and Val have to wait for Spring, when the sheep over in New Zealand will be put out to graze, or something – or no, isn't it Autumn out there? – something, anyway, and her parents can get over here. Don't ask me!'

'Can't you wait that long?' asked Ed, smiling with a lift of his brows.

'W-w-we have our orders,' said Francis. 'I have to m-make an honest w-w-woman of her as s-soon as we can ar-r-range it, s-since we'll be sh-sh-sharing a caravan on s-s-site.' It had gone back to being a caravan, Diana noted with a small sigh. Oh well.

'Fair enough. And will this shotgun marriage take place in London, or where?' asked Michael.

'And how small is "small?"' asked Erin, more pertinently.

'Very small. He wants to borrow a private chapel that seats about twenty people,' said Diana, with a mischievous glance around the assembled company.

'That small?' asked Ed, amazed. 'Goodness! That's only about ten guests each.'

'It m-m-may b-b-be big enough for th-thirty,' said Francis, fairly.

'Gracious! Go steady, won't you? How on earth will you pick and choose who to ask, with all the families involved? There's us, there's loads of us, and there's your mother's family, loads of them, too, and Tamsin's family, and presumably Kim's family, those in this country anyway, will be involved – and that's before you even start on friends—' Ed broke off. 'I begin to see where you're going here.'

'Right,' said Michael, holding up a hand to count on his fingers. 'Let's have a serious look at this. There'll be you two, but you won't get the chance to sit down, so that leaves ten to fifteen guests for each of you. Presumably you'll have a best man, Francis – will he be married?'

'He w-w-will. If he'll d-d-do it, I haven't asked him y-y-yet.'

'That's a potential two on your side, then. Eight more, ten maybe if they can squeeze up a bit.' He considered for a moment. 'Your mother, of course – representing the older generation.'

'And your Aunt Clara,' put in Diana, immediately. 'They can keep each other company.'

'Aunt Clara?' asked Ed. 'You're a brave woman, Tamsin! She'll drown you in her tears.'

'I think she's lovely,' said Diana firmly. 'And your Aunt Henry has already played a leading role. It's Aunt Clara's turn!'

'Fair enough, but what about his Aunt Ellie – my mum? And Aunt Letty? You mustn't forget them.'

'They can come and stay with us for a holiday, and we'll treat them to dinner at Mario's to make it up to them – it's the best restaurant in town. They'd only get the local pub at the wedding.' She caught Francis's eye, he looked amused but he made no comment.

'All right,' said Ed. 'We're up to four. Val and Kim, presumably, will be on the other side of the aisle. Now this is where it gets a bit dodgy, Frank old son. Who gets the last seats?'

'Y-you four, I sh-should th-think,' said Francis. 'And m-my cousin Ernie and his w-w-wife.' There was a silence for a moment.

'Definitely dodgy,' said Michael. 'You'll start a family feud, you do know that?'

'If th-there-s more seating, th-th-they can come. B-but th-they were a l-lot younger than us.'

'This is true. Let's hope they grasp that principle.'

'Ros won't,' said Ed.

'We'll make it up to her, too' said Diana. 'She must understand that you can't get a quart into a pint pot.'

'You could choose a bigger venue,' suggested Amanda.

'That w-w-would d-d-defeat the wh-hole object,' said Francis.

'I see.' Ed was obviously thinking about this. He turned to Diana. 'And how about you? Can you fit your prime suspects into such a small place?'

Diana counted off on her own fingers, laying down her knife and fork to do so.

'Daddy and Eloise. Kim and Val, Kim will be my attendant, of course, and Val's Mum and Dad. My closest friends Julie and Jo and their boyfriends. My cousin Toby. Job done.'

'Sounds like a wrap to me,' said Michael, grinning, and Ed said, 'We can always hope the place is just a bit bigger, of course.'

'We'll check it out,' promised Diana. 'Merlin can tell us. We haven't even got a date yet, so there's plenty of time.'

'Who on earth,' asked Ed, 'is "Merlin"? He'll need to be a magician to keep this train on the rails!'

'He's a friend of Francis's,' Diana explained. 'Merlin Ravenscourt.'

'I hope he w-w-will agree to be my b-best man,' added Francis.

'Well, that shut everybody up,' said Michael, after a pause to absorb this information, and everybody laughed.

'So, how about you, Kim?' Erin asked, turning to her. 'Are you planning to get married in a shoe box too, or have you got bigger plans?'

'We shall be married in a little country church,' Kim replied. 'That's not to say we shall fill it, but it will need to hold a lot more than twenty. The logistics are a bit complicated; Val's mother is doing most of the work, or will be doing it I should say, because my parents are in New Zealand. Hooray for the internet!'

'Maybe you'd have room for some of Tamsin's spares,' Ed suggested, with a grin. 'The two of you are so alike, maybe nobody would spot the difference?'

'The V-Vachells w-w-would,' Francis suggested.

'Is all your father's family in New Zealand, or do you have relatives over here still?' Amanda asked, and Kim listed her aunts, uncles and cousins remaining in England. It was a respectably long list, when all the nephews and nieces and grandchildren were added in.'

'But apart from those I've made this year, all my friends are over there,' she added. 'I don't know if any of them will make it, it's a horrendous trip – twenty-four hours on a plane!'

'Yes, they'd have to be pretty good friends to undertake that,' Ed conceded. 'Still, you never know – if they've been planning a trip to England anyway, for instance, they could combine the two.'

'Not sure that they have,' said Kim.

'Put the idea into their heads,' Erin suggested. 'Anyway, by the time Spring comes, you'll probably have made a few more. And Val will have some. Probably.' She smiled at him across the table.

'One or two,' he admitted.

The subject of weddings having been wrung dry, Ed looked round the table and said, with satisfaction, 'This is good – like old times, almost. Remember them, Frank?'

'N-not r-r-really like them,' Francis contradicted. 'T-t-too many g-g-girls,' and sparked off a game of "do you remember?" that lasted until there was nothing left of the first course but a spoonful of fried cabbage, a smear of apple sauce and a roast potato. Diana and Kim listened with amusement, having nothing much to contribute, and Val added the odd comment but was mainly just listening like the twins. His silence, Kim thought, finely tuned to his moods as love had made her, had a different quality to theirs. Why? And what, come to that?

Amanda began to gather up the plates and stack the dishes together. She looked round the table; the three Chillingworths were all so busy exchanging reminiscences that it would be a shame to interrupt them. She said, 'Val darling, could you just bring those dishes through for me? That pile will be quite heavy to carry – man's work!' and smiled at him.

'Of course,' said Val, rising to his feet. He picked up the pile of vegetable dishes and followed Amanda through to the kitchen.

'Just put them there, I'll see to them later.' Amanda indicated the draining board. 'And don't just run off, Val – I've hardly had a chance to speak to you yet, and the trouble with being the hostess is that you spend so much time in the kitchen that you miss out on the fun.' She smiled at him. 'We can talk without that lot shouting over us, while I get the pud organized, and then you can help me to carry it in.'

'Of course,' said Val politely, but Amanda didn't seem to be in any hurry. She looked at him seriously, and said, 'It must be hard for you, being the stranger, and when the other three haven't been together for so long – they don't mean to exclude you.'

'They're not. It's perfectly natural they should want to talk with each other, it's why we came after all.'

'It isn't just that, though, is it? I've been watching you.'

Val said nothing for a moment. He hadn't realised that he had made his private feelings so obvious, and wondered what he should say. After a moment's consideration, he settled on the truth. 'If you want to know, I'm just so angry that I don't trust myself to say anything at all! Those three – they're like long-lost brothers! What the hell was his father thinking of? And when I think of what—' He broke off. 'Sorry. I'm ranting.'

'No you're not. What were you thinking of?'

'Look,' said Val, after a pause, 'it's not really down to me to say this, but I'm going to anyway. That man in there—' he jerked a thumb roughly in the direction of the dining room – 'is somebody that I don't recognise. He is not the man that I have known for the last ten years or so, and neither was the man who just spent time in my flat. It's something that I've been wondering about just lately anyway and this is the final straw. You'd think he'd just been let out of prison…and I rather think, that's exactly how he's feeling. And the thing that's really making me angry is this: he has to go back. It's all waiting for him again, down there in Dorset.'

'But—' Amanda began, but he cut her short.

'You know that old saying – "give a dog a bad name?" That is exactly what we have here. And I don't have any idea what can be done about it! Or even what set it off. And that is what is making me so angry.'

'He's chosen to stay there,' Amanda pointed out.

'He has. I think that he feels he should stay near to his mother for the moment until he knows she's OK with this cousin – and also, I think that maybe his roots run deep, and he loves the place. But he is steadily disassociating himself from all the people and activities that made up his life and planning to spend half his time abroad anyway. And that looks to me like a very uncomfortable compromise, I don't know how it looks to you.'

'It could be simply a lifestyle choice,' Amanda pointed out. 'He's free to do what he likes now, or so I understand. Couldn't he just be doing that?'

'Well, possibly. But something doesn't feel right. I can't tell you what, I don't know. But it's there. And if Francis is involved – and he is, it's about him somehow – then Diana is, and if Diana is then Kim is, and if Kim is then I am – and I haven't a clue where to look for answers. I don't even know where to look for the questions, come to that! Anything I can guess at simply boils down to gobbledegook!'

'So what do you guess at?' asked Amanda, curiously. She turned to open the fridge, but stood there with her hand on the door, waiting for his reply. He thought for a moment, trying to get this right.

'He doesn't go out of his way to make friends – and that would be out of character in the man I've just seen back in there – and some group of idiots at the Town Regatta Dance back in the summer started getting at him loudly behind his back, so that he walked out and didn't come back, which would also be out of character on present form. And not all that long after, the Sailing Club in Emberton took a Committee decision to ask him to resign because of, and I quote, "conduct unsuitable in a senior member of the Club." By which we can assume they meant his walking out on his mother and leaving her in the lurch – which in fact, is not what he actually did and none of their business if it was.' He paused for breath. 'I do not know who instigated that. I have asked, but nobody names names. All I do know is that it was a majority decision, but not a unanimous one, to send that letter.' He shrugged his shoulders. 'Doesn't sound like much, does it?'

Amanda said, trying to pour oil on these troubled waters, 'You do realise it's early days? He's not had long to get used to the idea that his father was totally wrong about just about everything, and there must be a lot of leeway to make up down there, he must have been on the defensive for years, that can't have helped.' She hesitated. 'You probably don't know the answer to this but I'm going to say it anyway. How much of that stutter of his do you think is down to injury, and how much is down to the situation you've just described? He never had it when they were young, that I do know.'

'God knows, but I suspect it may be mostly down to injury.'

'Shame. He's a lovely man.' Amanda opened the fridge at last and took out the cream that would go with the lemon meringue pie. 'The plates are over there. If you can take them, and this, I'll bring the pie. They'll be wondering where we've got to.'

'Not them – they're too busy talking!' Val picked up the pile of waiting plates anyway, and Amanda put the cream on top.

'You didn't mind me ambushing you like that? Only I could see you were simmering.'

'God – I hope nobody else noticed!'

'I suspect Kim may have.' She smiled at him. 'I'm glad we talked. And you keep your eyes open down there, won't you. Call up the reserves, if war breaks out!'

They went back into the dining room, and nobody asked where they'd been, although Kim did give Val a questioning look. Amanda, who missed little of what went on, noticed this. She said, before Kim could ask questions, 'Sorry we took so long – I couldn't remember where I'd put the cream! And there's cheese on the sideboard there, if anyone prefers it to this luscious-looking pie.'

'I expect we can manage both,' said Michael. 'Shame to waste good food...'

'I haven't noticed any of you doing that!'

The meal drew to its merry close, spun out with coffee and a continuing exchange of news from the years passed since the last time the cousins had foregathered; it was noticeable that Francis added little to this catalogue, beyond a few words on County Shows and sailing races, ably supported by Val.

'Sounds as if Tamsin is going to be kept busy polishing trophies,' said Ed, as they finally, reluctantly, had to call a close and get up from the table.

'As if I didn't have enough to do, rebuilding a ruin!' said Diana, laughing. It was no good, unfortunately, trying to prolong the occasion: the road home was beckoning, quite loudly by this time, and Francis was stealing a surreptitious look at his watch. She heaved a sigh of content. 'That was all lovely, and it's been great to meet you all – and the lunch was amazing, I don't think I shall ever need to eat again! But his lordship is fidgeting, and I suppose now, at last, we have to let Val sort out that luggage!' and everyone laughed with her.

They all went outside to the cars, and Michael put his arm round Diana's shoulders.

'It's been great to meet you all, and make sure that you bring him again – it's been too long!'

'Don't worry, I will – if we ever get the time! And you must come to us, see what we're doing out at Burnthouse – after all, you saw it at its worst!'

'I did indeed. He's a brave man, that one of yours! But then, he always was a one-off.'

Val slammed down the boot lid on the Mercedes, and said, 'Everything aboard and accounted for.' He took Kim in his arms. 'I'll see you on Friday, my darling, and take care! How are you planning to spend the week, with no job to go to?'

'Sizing up furniture, if Diana has her way.'

'And exploring antique shops, and reclamation yards,' Diana added.

'Sounds great. Wish we could come and help,' Erin sounded wistful. 'Right up my street, that sort of shopping.'

'Come down for a few days and help us,' Kim offered. 'We can squeeze you in and it would be fun.'

They had to leave in the end, of course, but it was reluctantly, with much waving both on the doorstep and from the car, as they slid off down the drive.

'What an amazing weekend it's been!' said Kim, heaving a sigh of content, although she was sad at leaving Val behind.

'It had its dodgy moments,' said Diana, thinking about it, 'but yes. It all went far, far better than I expected it to. And your family are great, Francis!'

Francis said nothing at all, and the road home began to roll away under the wheels.

XV

After the social whirl of London and its environs, Emberton seemed very small and quiet. Francis dropped the twins and their luggage at Romans in the evening, and went straight on to Shortlanesend without stopping for the coffee and the beans on toast which Kim offered, promising to be in touch the next day, sometime.

'Whatever "sometime" means, said Diana disconsolately, as they watched his tail lights retreating towards the pub and the main road. She felt flat and sad, as one does after something good comes to an end. Even the beautiful new ring on her finger couldn't console her. Kim glanced at her, knowing how she was feeling as she felt the same herself.

'We're hungry, that's all. I'll get some supper, then you'll feel full of beans!'

'Oh, ha-ha!' said Diana, following her indoors. 'Anyway, after that magnificent lunch, I don't think I can eat another thing.'

'Yes you can. That was hours ago. Come on, you can make the toast – it will give you something to think about. It's got to be something on toast, the bread must be like shoe leather by this time, a sandwich would break our teeth!'

'It's a shame he couldn't stay,' said Diana, as she lifted the bread out of the bin. 'It would have been nice…'

'He just wanted to get somewhere where he could shut himself away and not need to talk to anyone,' said Kim, wisely. 'He'll be here tomorrow – which is more than Val will. Anyway, I don't think he's a beans on toast kind of a man.'

'I know, I know, you don't have to tell me. It must have been a pretty stressful few days for him – but I'm still allowed to miss him, now he isn't here.' She dropped two slices of bread into the toaster, and said, confrontationally, 'Anyway, I bet making toast is more complicated than heating beans! All you have to do is open the tin and keep stirring, I shall have to put it in, take it out, butter it—' She saw Kim's face and her own broke into a grin. 'Got you! Now, let's not quarrel. Shall I put the kettle on, then we can have some cocoa with it – real comfort food.'

'Good idea. And we can sit in front of the telly – there must be something on, with all those channels to choose from these days.'

'Or we could just talk,' said Diana. Kim looked at her. After a moment, she said, 'OK, so we can do that instead. Sunday night telly is pretty crap on the whole, anyway. Unless you want to be educated. Or watch sport and game shows.'

They laid up a tray between them with the beans on toast, the cocoa, and two apples, and settled themselves on the sofa with the tray on the coffee table. When they each had a plate of beans and a knife and fork deployed, Kim said, 'All right then, what did you want to talk about? Or shall I guess?'

'It's just that I feel a bit confused,' Diana admitted. 'That was a very... instructive weekend, wouldn't you say?'

'I would,' Kim agreed. She took a mouthful of beans and toast. Diana poked her fork into her own slice and pushed a few beans around.

'It's peculiar,' she said, finally. 'It's as if I've promised to marry two different men. I love them both – I think I do, I hardly know the Mark II model – but which of them is the real one? I don't think I know.'

'Does it matter – if you love both sides of him, and you say you do?' Kim could see the dilemma, to a certain extent she shared it and she thought Val might, too.

'Well actually, I think it does. Because I don't think he really has a split personality.' She paused to think about what she said. 'One of those two is the real one – and I have a horrible feeling that it's the one we met over this weekend, and it's breaking my heart, to be honest. The way they all interacted, as if they'd never even been apart...'

'Oh, I don't think that's quite true,' said Kim. She thought about it. 'Yes, I agree with you up to a point – but there's a lot of years gone by between the teenager he once was and the man he is today, and they haven't been what they could have been if—' She broke off. 'I'm confusing myself now! But you know what I mean. The basic person is that one, but the one you're marrying is the one that life has made of him, and they're both the same person really. And I agree that it's a bugger, but that's what you've got.

And it applies to everyone, one way or another, it's just that you picked yourself an extreme case. And another thing you need to bear in mind, in the context of the last few days, is that old saying "blood is thicker than water". They're all three of them wired up the same, they talk in the same language – even if Francis is a little rusty these days.'

'I suppose so…' Diana finally took a mouthful of her supper. She spoke through it, muffled. 'I never saw him as a Frank, did you?'

'I think that was just a gang thing when they were kids,' said Kim. 'Frank, Ed and Mike – Ed and Mike still get called that in the family they were all kids with, but I bet they're Edward and Michael in business. What did his grandmother and his aunts call him?'

'Francis. I see what you mean.' She munched another mouthful. 'I think I prefer that, anyway.'

'There you are then. You call him what you like.'

'He didn't talk much on the way home. Just listened to CDs.' She added, direfully, 'And he has a very dodgy taste in music.'

'He never does say much if he's driving, you can't read anything into that. And did you really expect he would, anyway? His mind must be going round in circles right now!'

'True. I know mine is.'

'Just go with whatever happens next,' Kim advised. 'It should be interesting, don't you think? They're not going to go away, that lot up there.'

'Rather the reverse, I suspect.'

'Do you mind?' Kim asked, curiously.

'I don't think so. I think I'm looking forward to it. In fact, when we get that far – which won't be tomorrow! – I might even ask Erin to come and go round antique shops with me.'

'You'll get Michael and the kids in the package.'

'That's all right. He can take them on the beach – the kids, I mean. It'll probably be warm enough again by then!'

'That much of a job, is it?'

'I really don't know.' Diana was glad of the switch in subject, although she had set the initial ball rolling herself. 'To be fair, until I've had time to look at it without a house agent breathing down my neck, I have no ideas on it at all. It's a two-thousand piece fifteenth-century jigsaw, still jumbled up in its box. But the first thing has to be to prop up the walls again and fix the roof. Probably rewire it, too. Then we can think what to do next.'

'You think Francis will think – about that? Or was that the royal "we"?'

'Actually, I was thinking of you when I said that. I've got to bounce ideas off somebody!'

'Fair enough – unless you expect me to be useful, that is! It's way outside my field of expertise!'

'Mine too, so we'll make a good partnership.'

Kim had finished her beans, she set the plate back onto the tray and picked up her apple. 'What about Benita? Would she have any useful input, do you think?'

'She might. But their house is a lot better maintained, it looks as if it always has been. I wouldn't really know. Actually…' She looked at Kim slantwise, from the corners of her eyes. 'Actually, I was thinking his mother might have some useful ideas.'

Kim took a bite of her apple and chewed it while she thought about this. Finally, she said, 'That might be a plan…would you ask her yourself, or get Francis to do it for you?'

'I thought, when the sale is actually completed, I'd ask him if he minded if I asked his mother over to see the place – that is, if he doesn't do it for himself. He may well. And then, I can take it from there. Even if she doesn't want to get involved herself, she might well know somebody who can advise me. And I have less than a week left to finish getting used to the idea, and then it's crunch time!'

'There'll be a builder involved,' Kim comforted her. 'He must have done things like this before, or Francis would never have picked him. Believe me, he isn't stupid!'

'Except in appointing me the Clerk of Works,' Diana pointed out. She picked up her cocoa. 'I don't think I have the energy left to chew that apple, I'll have it for breakfast.' She smothered a yawn.

'Know how you feel. Drink your cocoa, and then we'll clear this away and crash out in front of whatever's on the telly to unwind for an hour. And then, I'm off to bed, I'm shattered!'

Diana put her mug down again, onto the tray. 'This has gone cold while we've been setting my world to rights, I'll bung it in the microwave, I think.'

'Tomorrow, things will look better,' Kim said, gathering up the plates.

'They don't look bad, exactly, now. Just different. And rather exciting, I think. One thing we can be sure of, life isn't going to be dull!'

The following morning, however, proved that this wasn't necessarily so. Francis had said that he would be in touch "sometime," and whatever time he had meant by that, it certainly wasn't early. By mid morning, Kim, already restless after being cooped up for four days in London, was pacing round the small house like a captive lioness.

'Why don't you just go out for a walk?' Diana asked, not kindly. She was equally on edge, although for different reasons. 'Or take the car and go into town, find a Greek class or something. Use up some of your energy!'

'I'm sorry, am I getting on your nerves?' asked Kim, and Diana said, violently, 'Yes!'

Fortunately they both laughed, the tension broken now it had been acknowledged.

'I can't take the car,' said Kim. 'What if he wants you to go out to Shortlanesend again? But I might just go for that walk. You could come with me – you can bring your mobile.'

'And how will that help, if he just rolls up outside the door?'

'It will still work, outside the house. Mine does!'

'And what help will that be, if I'm halfway to Studland? Knowing you, I could well be!'

'Not with you with me, I couldn't. But I see what you mean. Will you really not mind if I just go and leave you? I'm getting claustrophobia in here.'

'I had noticed. And if you take your phone, I can ring you if he does turn up. And if he does, and wants to haul me off somewhere, I'll leave you the car keys.'

'Life was never so complicated, when it didn't have men in it!' said Kim. 'All right, then, but what will you do if he doesn't get in touch – "sometime"?'

'Probably just go to sleep. I'm still shattered, after our wild weekend!'

'No stamina, you townies,' said Kim. She went over to the hooks by the door to find her coat, there was a chilly autumnal wind today. 'I won't be that long, anyway. Just work off a bit of energy.'

'You go and do that,' said Diana, settling down on the sofa, but when Kim had gone she found that she didn't feel like being quietly on her own after all. It was lonely, and she couldn't help wondering what Francis was doing, looking at the ring he had given her to reassure herself that he would materialise eventually, or phone, or something. Perhaps he was asleep? He had looked as shattered yesterday evening as she still felt this morning.

He wasn't asleep, as it happened, but she nearly was when she was disturbed by the sound of a heavy engine grinding to a halt outside the house. Galvanised back into life, she leapt to her feet and ran to the window – and yes, there was a cream-coloured Discovery parked outside the house. Hooray!

She had become used, she realised, to being able to work out what Francis was planning to do on any particular occasion by the way he was dressed – more formal to go into town, or see his solicitor or the architect, scruffy if he was off to do something on a farm, particularly if it was Burnthouse. This morning, she couldn't get a fix. Informal: decent jeans, a sweater and trainers: a halfway point that she couldn't interpret. Well, one way to find out – she opened the door to greet him, and almost fell into his arms.

'S-sorry I d-d-didn't get to you earlier,' he said, catching her. 'It's b-b-been a busy m-morning.' He gave her a hug, which she returned.

'I thought you'd overslept, or something,' she said, and he laughed.

'N-not with C-Clive and M-M-Maisie around. N-no.'

'Come in.' She held the door wide. 'Kim's gone for a walk. Coffee?'

'N-n-no thank you. I'm s-s-sorry, b-but I need to d-d-drag you off to the c-c-cottage. The d-d-demolition men st-started this m-m-morning, th-they want to kn-know w-w-where they should b-b-be looking out f-f-for Kim's p-passport.'

'Oh.' Diana was taken aback; the last place she wanted to visit was the wreck of the cottage. 'Couldn't you tell them?'

'I d-d-don't know, d-do I?' He looked at her face, and read it correctly. 'I'm s-s-sorry,' he said, again.

'Oh well. If it's got to be done, it's got to be done.' She shrugged her shoulders. 'Just let me text Kim to tell her I'll be out when she gets back, or she'll wonder where I am.'

'And f-find a coat. Th-that wind is ch-chilly this m-m-morning.'

Diana sent her text, found her short waterproof jacket, and followed him out to the Discovery with very mixed feelings. Unbelievably, it was only just over a week since that cottage had collapsed on top of them and come close to killing them both, their narrow escape was still too recent to be comfortable. She thought that Francis probably realised that, but he hadn't had any options so she couldn't really blame him.

They set off up the road past the pub, and Diana said, not wanting another silent drive with this destination in mind, 'Was Sacha pleased to see you last night? I bet he was! And your little cat?'

'B-B-Bennie and Ernie w-w-were quite pleased too,' he said, smothering a grin. 'And y-you forgot t-t-to m-m-mention the chickens. Th-they clucked.'

'I'm sorry,' she said. They seemed to have done nothing but apologise to each other so far. Her hand went, without her realising it, to the thin red scar that ran under her left eye, surrounded by a rainbow of fading bruises: her parents had been very distressed to see it, which hadn't helped. Francis hadn't turned his head, but he said, 'It'll h-h-heal. The b-bruises w-will disappear, and th-the s-s-scar will hardly sh-show,' and she wasn't entirely certain that he was talking about her eye. 'Anyw-way,' he went on, 'You m-m-may find this v-v-visit int-t-teresting in more w-w-ways than you expect.'

'Interesting, how?' asked Diana, but he wouldn't tell her. He just said, 'W-wait and see.'

Things had been moving fast at the cottage already, she saw immediately as they pulled onto the verge outside. The fence had been rolled to one side to allow heavy machinery on to the site, and the tree had already been lifted away with a big crane, and a man in a boiler suit and a hard hat was cutting off the branches with a chain saw. A big lorry emblazoned with the logo GARY FANCOT *Demolition & Site Clearance* was parked on what had been Kim's raspberry patch with three men, similarly clad, standing in a group, talking, beside it. When the Discovery pulled up, one of them turned away and came towards them. He was a big man, not so tall as Francis but more heavily built, with powerful shoulders and a darkly bearded face; a few dark curls peeped out from under the hard hat, mostly round the ears. He seemed pleased to see them.

'Francis! You made it then! And this is the lady who's going to show us where the loot is buried?' He smiled at Diana. 'Awkward for you – being parted from your passport. Never mind, we'll dig it up for you if the luck's on our side.' His pleasant, deep voice had a distinct Dorset burr to it.

'Th-this isn't Kim,' said Francis. 'Th-this is her t-t-twin. This is T-Tamsin.'

The man's face changed: where it had been casually friendly, it now broke into a huge grin.

'So this is the girl who's finally got you! Good work, girl!' He seized her hand and pumped it up and down in a warm clasp. 'Very glad to meet you – we'd begun to think he'd manage to dodge the column for ever!'

'Give over, G-Gary,' said Francis, but he was smiling too. Gary – his good friend, Diana realised with surprise – picked up her left hand now and turned it to admire the ring.

'Nice. You have good taste, Mr Chillingworth, sir,' and Diana was left unsure as to whether he referred to the ring or to herself. 'So, when's the wedding to be?' Gary went on.

'W-we'll let you know,' said Francis, which made Diana wonder: there had been no mention of a Gary in yesterday's discussion. He would stick out like a sore thumb among the Chillingworths, her own parents, and the Ravenscourts, as well as taking up more than his fair share of the limited space available. She found herself hoping that Francis meant what he said, this burly rough diamond of a man had genuine warmth.

'Right then,' he said now, 'We'd better go over and you can show us where you think this passport might be. You'll have to put on hard hats – Health & Safety, you know – sorry about that. There's a couple of spares in the lorry.' He raised his voice and called to the men still waiting beside it. 'Col – fetch out a couple of toppers, would you!'

The hats duly put on, the three of them walked across to the toppling remains of the cottage; Diana found she had to blink away unwanted tears at the sight of it close up. Poor little house, it hadn't deserved this! She pulled herself together, leading the way over to the left and stopping short of what had once been the bedroom wall.

'This is the end of the house where we slept. Kim had a camp bed at this side of the room, the tree fell right on it.'

'Lucky she wasn't in it at the time,' said Gary, sounding alarmed.

'No – she was over the other side with me. We got into the same bed, we were scared. It was a humungous storm!' She bit her lip; neither Gary nor Francis made any comment, so she went on. 'She had put the passport in with her camera so she wouldn't drop it in a shop, or something, she says she thinks she had kicked it out of the way under the bed when we got in that afternoon. If she's right, the bed will have collapsed on top of it, and it might be OK. It's black,' she added, belatedly. 'The camera case, that is.' Gary rubbed his bearded chin.

'Not the best colour to hunt in a sea of mud and rubble, but if your sister is right about where she left it, there's every chance it will still be there. I'll tell the digger man to go careful on that side. Doubt we'll get down there today, but I'll let you know. Francis tells me you're in his cousin's holiday let, is that right?'

'Romans. Yes.'

'Then I'll bring it along if we find it. It's on me way home.' He clapped her on the shoulder, nearly making her stagger. 'Don't you worry, if it's there to find, we'll find it. And now, I should be getting back to work – oh, and what d'you want done with this tree, Francis? The farmer says he never wants to see the damn thing again, we can cut it into logs and take it out to Burnthouse when we come, if you want.'

'You're coming out to Burnthouse?' asked Diana, surprised.

'You seen the place? You must've – it needs us, wouldn't you say?'

'It hasn't fallen down quite yet,' said Diana, laughing at his cheeky grin.

'There's an awful lot that has! And can you see this gentleman here, shifting that there dungheap on his own? Take the heavy mob, that one will. Francis, about these logs?'

'Yes please,' said Francis. 'We c-c-can stack them in a loose box to dry out – they'll c-c-come in handy wh-when we f-finally g-g-get into the house. And I d-d-do have a m–m-mechanical shovel, I w-wasn't p-p-planning to do it w-w-with a s-spade!' They grinned at each other, good friends.

Gary walked with them back to the boundary and collected the hats when they reached it. Cradling them in one arm, he shook hands warmly with them both using the other.

'See you around – let's hope, sooner rather than later. Take care of this lovely lady now, Francis my man!'

Back in the Discovery, Francis looked at Diana.

'W-what would you l-l-like to do? I d-d-don't need t-t-to g-get back until l–later.'

'I don't know – to be honest, I'm still recovering from our wild weekend!' She looked at her watch. 'It's well past twelve o'clock – how about a nice pub and a sandwich?'

'F-f-fine.' He started the engine and they moved off. Over by the ruined cottage, Gary waved and Diana waved back.

'I do like your friend,' she said. 'How did you come to meet him? Did he do some work out at Vachells, or did you meet at Shows, or what?'

'We were at Sixth Form together,' said Francis, neutrally. For a moment, Diana didn't quite take this in, then she said, 'Oh...'

Her brain had gone into overdrive, suddenly full of wild speculations and suspicions. But surely...? The one thing there hadn't been in that brief encounter was animosity, very much the reverse; what was she thinking about? But in the end, she had to say it.

'He wasn't the one...?'

'I t-told you, you w-w-would find it int-t-teresting.'

'You can tell me over lunch,' said Diana.

'M-maybe.'

She wondered if he would, when it came down to it, or if she really needed him to do so anyway. The man she had just met had been a friend – a good friend, if she wasn't mistaken. Francis was right, he had to be; the root of his troubles didn't lie there, and for more than one reason. One thing was becoming increasingly clear, the answer, if there was one to find, lay with the sailing crowd, both in Emberton and in the town itself. Gary didn't fit in either place. If he played a sport at all, it would be football – or rugger, that was more likely; the man was built like a tank! She suppressed a smile, but Francis didn't see it as he was driving.

'It must have been quite a fight,' she ventured. 'He's built like a Sumo wrestler.' She was looking at Francis as she said this, and she saw the corner of his mouth twitch in amusement. He said, 'Oh, he c-c-could hold his own.'

'But you won,' said Diana. He didn't reply to this, he had signalled to turn right and was watching the oncoming traffic. When there was a space, the Discovery slid across and down a narrow lane that looked vaguely familiar. Searching her recent experience, Diana came up with an answer.

'This is the way we came up from the seafront, isn't it?'

'Y-y-yes. B-b-but we're not g-g-going there.'

'Well, thank goodness for that! I thought for a moment there you were taking me to the Duck Inn!'

'Dock Inn,' said Francis, automatically. 'N-n-no, I w-wouldn't inf-flict that on you.' He bore right onto another lane that she didn't recognise, heading towards the coast now.

They ended up at an old inn right on the clifftop, some way out of the town, with spectacular views over the sea and along the coast, and an oak-panelled bar with a log fire smouldering in an old fireplace that had a huge beam, black with age, running across the top. Predictably, this had horse brasses hanging against it.

'Y-you can s-s-sit outside in the s-summer, and see r-r-right along the J-j-jurassic C-coast,' Francis told her, '—but I d-don't think we'll t-t-try th-that today.'

They ordered a toasted cheese sandwich each at the bar, and then sat down with their drinks at a table that had a good view of the sea. For a few minutes they sat in silence, enjoying the view, but it couldn't be allowed to last, Diana realised. She had to grasp the nettle eventually, maybe now was a good moment? She set the ball rolling as neutrally as possible.

'I hope you meant what you said, and your friend Gary will be invited to the wedding,' she said. 'I know he'll take up the space for two, but so what? He felt like a really good friend'

Francis didn't reply immediately, he swirled his beer round in its glass and watched it revolving for a long moment. When he finally did speak, it sounded like a complete change of subject.

'L-l-look, T-tamsin,' he said, 'I kn-know you're c-c-concerned about all that b-business at the Yacht Club and at Ember V-valley, b-b-but it's g-g-gone on for a long t-t-time. It d-d-doesn't b-bother me, I'm used it b-by th-this time.'

'You shouldn't be. It's nasty – spiteful! Are you telling me you know who's behind it?' She heard the indignation in her voice, and bit her lip.

'Of c-c-course I do, I'm n-n-not stupid.'

'So why did you put up with it?' That hadn't sounded good either; she took a deep breath. Francis raised his eyes from his beer and looked straight at her.

'I d-d-didn't have m-much option, d-d-did I? M-m-making a big th-th-thing of it would only have m-m-made people ask q-q-questions. Y-you kn-know w-w-why that w-w-wouldn't have b-been a g-g-good idea. Th-the only other option w-w-was to g-give up doing s-s-something I l-love, and wh-why should I?'

Diana appreciated all of this, of course, but it only made her angrier. She said, 'It hardly seems fair.'

'Th-that's how it l-l-looks n-now. B-but th-that's only v-v-very recently. Th-think about it.'

Diana thought. She said, for the second time, 'It's so unfair!'

'It's over. F-forget it.'

'Will you?' Diana asked. 'Can you? You know the truth now, but nobody else does. Most of them don't even know what it was all about in the first place!'

'Oh, th-th-they do. B-b-but T-T-Tamsin, you d-d-don't. You only kn-know w-w-why I let it p-pass for so l-long. And they don't know th-th-that, and they m-mustn't.'

It was all too complicated. Diana said, 'So what will you do now?'

'Y-you kn-know that already. I'm f-f-free t-to go. I sh-shall d-do that.'

'It's so unfair.'

'L-l-life is. L-live with it.'

At that convenient point – convenient for Francis, that is – their lunch arrived, and by the time it had been set out with its knives and forks and paper napkins, it seemed impossible to re-open the subject. Diana knew that she couldn't let it rest there, but she also realised that she would learn no more from Francis. He obviously intended to screw that last... what, dozen or so years of his life, since he came back to Dorset? – into a ball and throw them away, and then walk off and start again. Well, that wasn't on, not in Diana's book. He'd done something similar once before, although not from choice that time, and it hadn't been a great success. The last few days had proved that.

What it came down to, was this: someone had, for some reason as yet unknown, launched an underground spite campaign against a man who had, for reasons that the perpetrator couldn't possibly know, felt unable to defend himself. Soap country. *Docksiders* et al, here we come! She must have that chat with Ernie.

She turned her attention to her toasted sandwich. It looked delicious.

At the same time, a good many miles to the north, Ed, Michael, and their cousin Peter Cox-Hamilton were also enjoying a quiet, possibly to-be-extended, lunch together in a favourite venue. Peter had been surprised by their unexpected news, but after he had got over his indignation at not being told earlier and included in the initial reunion, he did admit that he was happy to hear it. He and Tom, he said, had used to wonder what had gone wrong there, but they grew up and – well, had not entirely forgotten about their much older cousin but accepted that he had, for whatever reason, gone out of their lives. Finish. It happened.

'So how is the old boy, after all this time?' he asked, with interest, when he had absorbed the surprise, and yes, the shock of the unexpected news.

His cousins had given him – almost – a full tale, and not before time, he had told them. Ed raised his eyebrows.

'Old boy?'

'Come on Ed, he must be knocking forty by this time!' Peter was almost six years younger than his re-discovered cousin, his brother Tom even younger – Francis had been exactly twice Tom's age the last time they had met.

'No he's not, he's only a year older than me,' said Michael.

'I suppose…' Peter thought about this, and grinned. 'I tend to forget you're knocking on a bit too, seeing you pretty much every day. Anyway, you didn't answer my question. How's he doing? He must have had a pretty rough ride of it these years past from what you say, so now everyone knows whodunit, what's the score?'

'I don't think anyone but the family was ever told he did it,' said Ed. 'Or even that he might have done it, come to that.' He paused, wondering how far to go. He and Michael hadn't discussed this on Sunday, with their wives present it had been the wrong time: there had been no opportunity since.

'Grandad said he did, you say. And Uncle Chris,' said Peter, watching him.

'Well, they were both wrong. And anyway, Francis knew he didn't.'

'People must have wondered,' Peter persisted. 'The woman who found Sarah's body – she knew the connection, she did the cleaning at that cottage, if I remember right.'

'I don't know if they did or they didn't,' said Ed. 'Francis has been looking after his mother's estate. He's getting a place of his own because he's getting married, and a cousin is taking over.'

'That's not what he planned to do,' Peter objected. 'Wasn't he going on from Winterbourne to uni to read biology, or something?'

'Well, he didn't go,' said Michael. 'He had a breakdown after his father was killed like that, and then…' He stopped. Deep waters ahead.

'So what's he like these days? He was a bit of a hero when we were all kids.'

'Tall, dark and handsome,' said Ed, grinning.

'The swine! Well, he always was a bit of a film star.' Peter ran his hand over his own too-fast-thinning hair. 'I bet he's not going thin on top, like I am!'

'He's not. Face it, Pete, your Dad was totally bald by the time he was my age, you and Tom hadn't a chance.'

'What happens now?' Peter asked, returning to the main point of their discussion. 'Is he intending to keep in touch now you've all met up? It must feel a bit odd to him, after all this time.'

'Believe me, it feels a bit odd to us, too,' said Ed. 'Since you ask, I think we shall see quite a bit more of him. For one thing, we all have a standing invitation to visit with our kids, like we all did way back.' He added, thoughtfully, 'That's when he's propped the house up a bit. Apparently it's in a bit of mess.'

'That'll be good. Does he have a yacht, like Uncle Chris did? My boys'd like that.'

'He will, he says. He's been racing a Moonraker up until now.'

'Good God – those things are scary! I remember them, charging up and down the harbour in clouds of spray.' A far-away look came into Peter's eyes, recalling those long-ago times. 'Those were the days, eh?'

'They were. And it seems they're going to come again, for our own lot.'

'He's getting married, didn't you say? Left it a bit late, didn't he?'

'Oh, he was busy with the estate and all that,' said Ed. 'Never had time, I don't suppose.'

'We're busy, but we managed it,' said Peter.

'Look, Pete,' said Ed. It was going to have to be said, if they were all going to meet up – as they were. He wondered how to put it without giving too much away; he and Michael had both decided that the Cox-Hamiltons needn't know too much – apart from Ros, that is, but she was different. More of a Chillingworth; she took after her mother, his own Aunt Letty

'I'm looking,' said Peter, after the pause had grown too long.

Michael said, quietly, 'What Ed is thinking how to tell you, is that Francis had a bit of an accident when he was in his early twenties. He got a serious head injury and had...well, a sort of a stroke, I suppose. It's left him with a bad speech impediment, and it changed him. He's still recognisably Francis, but he's less outgoing than we remember him – more difficult to know. Life's not been that good to him since we all last met.'

'That's bad,' said Peter, thinking about it. 'Poor old Francis. But apart from that...?'

'He's still too bloody clever to be true,' said Michael. 'Doctor Chillingworth, would you believe, with three first class degrees to his credit! Nothing changes there!'

'So he did go to university, in the end?'

'I believe he did it by distance learning, between ploughing fields and herding cows.'

'That's good then,' said Peter. 'So when do the rest of us get to meet him – and what's-her-name? Tamsin?'

'Whenever you like. You can go down when you want, but you'll need a hotel, I should warn you – Francis is lodging with some cousins, Tamsin and her sister are in a holiday let, Aunt Mary might take you in, I suppose, but your three hooligans would be a bit much for her. She wouldn't do it twice! We've got Francis's mobile number, all you have to do is ring him to say you're coming.'

'I'll do that. Does Tom know all this?'

'He will, when we get a chance to tell him.'

'So, we're all rallying round the family flag, then?'

'We certainly are. And Tamsin is the heroine of the hour.'

'I look forward to meeting her then. Is she pretty?'

'Very. Beautiful, even. And hands off, Pete! She wouldn't even look at you anyway.'

'I wouldn't dream of it,' said Peter, indignantly, and without specifying what "it" might be; they all knew anyway. He hesitated. 'It's a funny feeling, isn't it? Like putting the clock back a quarter of a century, near enough. But you know what, it feels good. I hadn't realised how much I missed him, to be honest.'

'We all missed him,' said Michael, quietly. 'He missed us too, and he had it harder – in every way. At least we still had each other around.'

'Well, we can change all that!'

'Believe me,' said Ed, 'we will.' He picked up his glass – it only had lemonade in it, because this was technically a working lunch, but he raised it anyway. 'Here's to the future!'

The other two clinked their own tumblers against his. Michael added, 'And here's to holidays in the Med on our cousin's yacht, when he has one!' and Peter choked on his glass of spring water.

'What?'

Ed and Michael explained.

XVI

The next day or two continued to be strangely quiet, after the eventful long weekend the twins had just spent. Val was in London, Francis was out at Shortlanesend during the day giving Ernie a hand on the farm – to earn his keep, he said – and at Romans, nothing much happened at all.

'It's as if time has stopped,' Kim complained. 'And it's raining too – we can't even go for a walk!'

Diana didn't necessarily consider this a bad thing. She said, 'We could go into town, I suppose. Look at a few antique shops. Although I doubt if we'll find anything as old as that house.'

'Don't be so defeatist! And at least it would give us something to do.'

Diana had wandered over to the window, and was looking out at the rain splashing down on the village street. She said, 'It's so quiet, it's getting on my nerves – like the calm before the storm, sort of. Except,' she added, with a touch of venom, 'that the storm seems to be here already.'

'That's not a storm. It's just a bit of rain.' Kim didn't add that they had lived through worse than this, although the thought was in her mind.

'Anticlimax,' said Diana. 'That's the word. I knew there was one.'

'Oh, for goodness' sake!' said Kim, suddenly impatient with her. 'Get your coat, and let's go on an antique hunt! And while we're at it, we can look at stuff for the bungalow too. Then, if we see anything, I can take Val in to show it him on Saturday. Life is going to go on, you know, one way or another – even if it is raining!'

They realised simultaneously that they had each of them changed sides in their…well, it wasn't quite an argument, not really. But close. They caught each other's eye and burst out laughing.

'All right,' said Diana. 'Let's do that. And we can have lunch in town and pick up something nice for supper. Cheer ourselves—' She broke off before the final word, as her phone started its ringtone. 'Goodness, action!'

She snatched it up, but it wasn't Francis, had she really expected it would be? It was the next best thing, however: Bennie.

'What are you two up to in this filthy weather?' she asked, sympathetically. 'You must be bored to tears, not even in your own homes with your own things round you.'

'Just about to go out, because we couldn't bear it any longer,' said Diana, laughing. 'You just caught us – Kim was reaching for her coat! We though we'd go and check out a few antique shops.'

'Good idea. But if you find anything you like, have you thought what you would do with it, meantime?' Bennie was instantly practical. 'It'll be weeks – months even – before that house is fit to live in. A shop won't store things for ever, you know.'

'Oh, we'll cross that bridge when we come to it,' said Diana. 'I suppose we can always put it in store – Francis has done that with his stuff already. Anyway, I won't be buying anything today, not until he's seen it too, even if I find something.'

'You think Francis will go looking at furniture?' Bennie laughed. 'I should think again, if I was you! He's about as domesticated as the farm cats. Anyway, that's not why I rang. I wanted to say – ask, I suppose – has Francis told his mother that you're now officially engaged, do you know? Because I don't think he has, and you wouldn't want her to read it in *The Times* or something.'

'Oh God,' said Diana, who hadn't given this a thought. 'I see what you mean about the farm cats. What do you think I should do, then?'

'Well, somebody's got to break it to her. And really, it ought to be him.'

'Oh God! I shall have to catch him first.'

'That's not a problem, you can catch him this evening – I rang too, to ask if you and Kim would like to come to supper to help with your frustration. But whether you will convince him, remains to be seen, he's in a funny mood since he came back from London.'

'I know, I've encountered it myself. We had lunch with his family a couple of days ago.'

'Well, come and have supper tonight, and we'll see what we can do with him between us.'

'That sounds great. I'll just ask Kim—' She took the phone away from her ear. 'Supper at Shortlanesend?'

Kim looked doubtful. She said, 'Sounds great, but do they really want me? I feel a bit of a spare part with Francis's lot, to be honest.'

'I heard that,' said Bennie, so loudly that Diana heard her even though the phone was a foot from her ear. 'Tell her not be an idiot! Or put her on, I'll tell her myself.'

'OK.' Diana handed the phone to Kim. 'She wants to speak to you.'

Kim listened to Bennie for a moment, and then laughed. 'Oh, all right then, if you insist. And I really do appreciate it, you're right – an evening sitting here on my own would be pretty grim—' She broke off for a minute to listen. '—yes, I could, but even when I know people, I always feel a bit…well, odd, I suppose, in a pub on my own. So thank you, I'd love to come. What time d'you want us?…that's fine, we'll be there.' She handed the phone back to Diana. 'She wants to say goodbye to you.'

Diana said a brief goodbye and thank-you to Bennie, and then switched the phone off. 'Right – let's go on an antique hunt! I feel better already!'

The unexpected invitation had cheered them both up, they went out to the car with renewed enthusiasm for their furniture hunt.

'It's that contact with the outside world,' said Kim, as they climbed in, and Diana said, more accurately, 'What it is, is we're both missing our blokes, and there's only one cure for that! We shall have to marry the buggers.'

'Have you discussed a date yet?' Kim asked, as they drove off past the pub.

'Not exactly, no, just ASAP. Daddy and Eloise will come down as soon as he's cleared away the dungheap, we'll talk about it then. No doubt.'

Kim did not assume from this jumbled statement that Diana's father was going to attend to the dungheap, although a picture of him doing so in his smart London suiting did sneak into her head. She said, 'And is he going to talk to Merlin? – Francis, I mean, not your father.'

'Francis, right now, doesn't seem to be talking much to anyone. But I assume so.'

'He must have had a very testing weekend.'

'He's certainly been acting very strangely since,' said Diana, but didn't specify in what way this had taken place; she was still trying to sort that out in her own head, never mind Kim's. She changed the subject; they were just turning onto the major road. 'Take a look as we go past the cottage, it'll make you feel better.' It had done this for her, she had realised as she lay awake last night. In some strange way, clearing away the debris of the tree and the cottage was clearing some of the debris from her own mind with it, putting past events firmly in their rightful place; the past. Kim shuddered.

'Do I really want to?'

'Probably not, but do it anyway. If you're anything like me – and you are – it'll do you good.'

She slowed as they approached the site, which was looking rather different today; more of a mess, but less of a pile, was the way she described it to herself. The tree had almost gone now, turned into a huge pile of logs, and the cottage itself was unrecognisable as such, although a fair pile of rubble still remained. Then they were past, and Kim heaved a sigh – of relief? She thought so.

'So that's history,' she said, and Diana made no reply.

Shopping for furniture rather than clothes was a novelty. They started in Bordens, a shop that sold absolutely everything including soft furnishings, linen, and kitchen equipment of every description, and had a therapeutic exploration of every department, which took them comfortably up to lunchtime, when they took the lift to the top floor restaurant and sat down, with a plate of salad and a cup of coffee each for company, at one of the tables.

'Of course, people like to give you saucepans and things for wedding presents,' said Diana, thoughtfully, 'Only, as you hope to be moving in several months before your wedding, that isn't going to help you much. So that's something you need to think about.'

'You too,' said Kim. 'Or do caravans come fully equipped with that kind of thing?'

Neither of them knew.

'And of course, the same goes for china and stuff,' Kim said. 'And you need to get it sorted pretty quickly too, or you'll find yourselves eating out of the dog's bowl. How long will it be before the dungheap is cleared and you can move onto the site?'

'I don't know, but it can't be as difficult as clearing up after a whole house falling down, so that will give us a guide.'

'Not long then, if what I saw today is anything to go by.'

They considered this as they began on their salad. It seemed unlikely that Francis would have anything useful to contribute on the subject of saucepans, plates, or cutlery, but he was the obvious starting point, as they both recognised.

'You're going to have to speak to Francis about it,' said Kim, putting the dilemma into words. 'You can't manage without saucepans – not even

238

you, you need a frying pan to fry an egg. Or without bed linen and stuff, come to that.'

'Oh, we've got that,' said Diana, happy to be able to say something positive. 'His mother gave us some, it's up at Shortlanesend.'

'That's a bonus then. Then there's food. You'll need to see to that, too, before you can move in.'

'We've got the chickens so we'll be all right for eggs. I can get a sliced loaf in the village shop,' said Diana, and they grinned at each other.

'You'll need a bit more than that. Perhaps we should go into the book department while we're here, and buy you a cookery book for beginners?'

'Actually, all joking apart, that might be a good idea.'

A silence fell between them while they ate; when it became a bit too long, Kim asked, 'What's the matter?' because something quite obviously was. Diana didn't answer immediately; she picked up her bread roll and began to pull it into pieces, her face thoughtful. Kim watched her for a minute, then she said, 'You're making the table all crumby.'

Diana put the roll down abruptly, and folded her hands in her lap. 'Sorry.'

'Don't apologise to me – I won't have to clear it up. So what's bugging you?'

'Nothing, really. It's just that talking like this is bringing it all nearer… living in a caravan with Francis, and talking about saucepans and stores… I don't know what's the matter with me, really. It's silly, anyway. It isn't as if…' She stopped, unable to find the right words. Kim looked at her thoughtfully. When she first met her twin, they had exchanged several ideas, about life, love, men…there had been confidences about a man called Rupert; she had been slightly shocked, she recalled, and look at her now? After a moment, she ventured, 'You're saying you're not happy about buying into the new model without a test drive?' It seemed unlikely, but she couldn't see any other options.

'Not exactly, no. After all, there hasn't been an opportunity, has there? But…I told you it was silly!'

Kim said, forthrightly, 'If you're worrying that he might turn out to be a middle-aged virgin after all, I think it's fairly obvious that you're worrying about nothing. That is a man who knows his way around, and don't ask me how I know. It's just a vibe I get.'

'I know. Me too.' Diana sighed. 'I wish I knew what was the matter with me, but I've never felt like this about anybody before…I just love him so much. It's so…important, I suppose.'

'Well, that's all good,' said Kim, bracingly. 'You'll just have to wait and see, like everyone else.'

'You haven't.'

This was too true to deny, so Kim simply said, 'You know what I mean. Anyway, this time there's no options available – unless, that is, you want Maisie and Clive for an audience?'

'Heaven forbid!' Diana was laughing now, her unusual introspection dismissed. She picked up the roll again, this time to butter it, 'Now let's just eat our lunch, and then we can go on an antiques crawl! I'm looking forward to that.'

'Good plan. And while we do that, I need some bite cream – something was holding a party on my thigh last night, the itch is driving me mad!'

'There's a chemist in the Square, I saw it. And Boots.'

'First come, first served then,' said Kim. 'Then we can concentrate on furniture. This is turning out rather fun, isn't it? I do hope we aren't turning into staid old housewives!'

'I think,' said Diana, considering, 'that in order to do that properly, you need a staid old husband, and I think we both missed the boat there.'

'What, an accountant and a farmer? Perfect casting, I would say.'

'Except that mine isn't – a farmer, that is. Which I still find very, very, strange…' She paused there. 'And as accountants go, Val is not representative of the breed as I have always imagined it.'

'Oh, he has his stodgy moments,' said Kim, smiling happily.

They finished their lunch and made their way down through the various levels to the street. The first thing that met their eyes when they emerged on the pavement was the chemist Diana had mentioned, over to their right, so they began their afternoon there.

Straws in the wind, drops in the ocean…there was a woman at the counter, talking to the assistant, but she turned and stepped aside when the twins came in and stood waiting their turn.

'I'm just waiting for a prescription,' she said, smiling. 'You go on.'

'Thank you,' said Kim, returning the smile, and opened the subject of bite cream. She was just paying for it, when the pharmacist emerged from his lair in his white coat, with the made-up prescription in his hand. He stopped when he saw the twins, and a grin came over his face.

'Why, hello girls! Fancy seeing you here, Millie looking after you all right?'

'Yes thank you,' said Kim, wondering where she had seen him before – she definitely had, she realised. And then she remembered; he was the man at the Sailing Club who had made that disparaging remark about the Vachells and then walked away with a slimy smile on his face. What was his name again? He was on the Committee or something…but no, it had gone. All she remembered now was that she had instinctively disliked him.

Out on the pavement again, Diana said, 'Who was that? He seemed to know us, but I don't remember him.'

'Oh, he's on the Committee at the Club,' said Kim, dismissively. 'Val knows him.'

'On the Committee?' said Diana. If she had been a cat, her whiskers would have twitched: it was the Committee who had vilified Francis and tried to make him resign. She put out the human equivalent of a feline paw. 'Is he a friend of Val's, then?'

'I hope not,' said Kim, briefly, as she led the way down the street. 'Come on – I think I remember seeing an antique shop this way.'

Antique shops kept them busy for an hour or so; there were several down the side streets of Embridge, plus the one big one in the Square itself.

'I'm really only testing the water,' Diana explained. 'For one thing, I'm pretty sure that if we kept to the right period, the stuff would be too rare and valuable to use for every day, and for another, I don't know what – if anything at all – Francis has in mind. One thing I'm sure of, though, is that we don't want modern stuff. No Formica or bent steel, or plastic. It's got to be wood, and my gut feeling is, dark wood. I could be wrong about that, but I am pretty sure they didn't use a lot of pine in those days.'

'What are his bookcases made of?' asked Kim, ever practical, but Diana had no idea.

'I've never seen them, we'd need to ask.'

'You'll be wanting comfortable chairs to sit in, though.'

'Yes – they might have to be a bit more up-to-date.' Talking like this about the home she would eventually be sharing with Francis was making Diana feel a little bit strange. When she had lived with Rupert for a brief, not particularly happy, interval, it had been in a very smart modern flat. Oak furniture and comfortable sofas had a settled feel about them. Odd.

They returned to Bordens with their heads full of impressions but no fixed ideas, and had a cup of tea in the restaurant before heading for home. 'And we'll look in the china department again when we go down,' said Kim. 'We're both going to need some eventually, even if the caravan does have its own.'

'He called it a mobile home once,' said Diana, a little wistfully. 'It's gone back to a caravan now, but I'm hoping that's only a figure of speech. We could be in it for months, all through the winter!'

'Take heart. He doesn't look to me like a man who's used to roughing it.'

'I don't know about that. He wants to live on a yacht out in the Med, and it won't be that big. I've seen the one he's set his heart on, believe me, I know!'

'Well, you know what they say – if you can't take a joke, you shouldn't have joined.'

They took a second look at the china department when they had drunk their tea, and then made their way back to the car; it had almost stopped raining by this time although the clouds did look as if there might be more up there.

'But at least we don't have to spend the evening alone with the telly, listening to it rattling on the windows,' said Diana. 'I don't know about you, but I quite like the idea of real people for the evening.'

'And a lovely warm Aga to cosy up to,' Kim added.

They neither of them looked at the diminishing wreck of the cottage as they drove past.

As it turned out, both Bennie and Diana had been misjudging Francis; almost the first thing he said to Diana after their initial greeting was, 'Have you and K-Kim any plans f-f-for tomorrow? B-because I sh-sh-should go and see my m-mother, and I think you sh-should come too.'

'Nothing we can't change,' said Diana. She caught Bennie's eye over his shoulder, and Bennie nodded her head vigorously.

'G-g-good. If I p-p-pick you up a-around half-past t-t-ten, w-w-will that be all r-r-right?'

'Sounds good to me. Kim can have the car, if she wants to go anywhere while I'm away.' She looked at Kim, it was only polite to ask. 'That OK with you?'

'Fine. I can go and see Valerie, she wants to know about the weekend, too.'

'Give her a ring first,' Bennie advised. 'You never know with Val – she plays tennis quite often.'

'At this time of year?' asked Kim, surprised.

'Indoor court, at the Sports Club. She meets friends for coffee there and has a quick knock-up.' She went over to the Aga, where Ernie sat in his favourite chair with Sacha lying on his feet. 'Shift over you, both of you, I want to get in the oven.'

'Is life that bad?' asked Ernie, grinning, but he shifted his feet anyway. Sacha got up reluctantly, and then came over more briskly to say hello to Kim. It all felt very cosy and domestic. Diana found herself thinking "Make the most of it. This could all change by next week!" and rather liking the idea, or one aspect of it, at least.

Bennie took a pie out of the oven and set it on the hotplate, where the delicious smell of it woke up the cat, who was sleeping in the other armchair, and brought Sacha's attention abruptly away from Francis. Both animals sat hopefully at Bennie's feet, and to add to the confusion, Maisie and Clive came tumbling in through the back door with a second collie in their wake and for a few moments, total confusion reigned. Maisie flung herself on Diana, and cried, 'Tamsin! Lovely Tamsin! Francis says he's going to marry you, hooray, so you'll never go away!' and Clive just grinned in a pleased way, and said 'hello' to Kim, to even things up.

'Oh family life, don't you just love it!' said Ernie, without moving from his chair. 'Haven't you two got some homework you should be doing?'

'I said they could stick around until I started to dish up,' said Bennie, as if she might be regretting it. 'Why don't the rest of you sit down? Francis is blocking out the light.' Since he was positioned quite closely behind her there was some justification in this; he pulled out a chair from the end of the table and obediently sat down, pulling Diana down beside him, and Ernie waved Kim towards the cat's vacated chair, with the advice to sit down quickly before Maisie spotted it.

This was one thing about Francis that neither she nor Diana had fully realised, Kim thought, watching the cheerful family gathering sort itself out as directed, and it wasn't necessarily something new. Apart from down at the Sailing Club, or that night at the Yacht Club, he gathered...well, affection, fun and laughter, actually, around him. As Diana had already done, she began to wonder. It wasn't just a family thing, Diana had told her about Gary the demolition man too. She began to recognise what her twin meant when she said it was like being engaged to two people: at the time Diana had said it, she had thought it was wishful thinking that had brought her to her conclusion, now, suddenly she wasn't so sure. It was a bit like having a splinter in your thumb, she found herself thinking; remove the splinter and the sore spot healed over. The question here was, what, or who, was the splinter? One thing was obvious, there was going to be no chance for Diana to sound out Ernie tonight, but she did find herself now beginning to wonder if Francis, released from the restriction of a terrible family secret might, whatever he said now, hit back.

Interesting, thought.

Maisie came over and sat herself down firmly on Kim's lap. She said, 'You mustn't feel left out, we love you too,' and planted a smacking kiss on Kim's cheek, and the evening continued on its merry way.

The following morning was less exuberant, although, Diana admitted later, interesting in its way. Francis picked her up, as arranged, at ten-thirty in the Mercedes, and they drove to Vachells without discussing anything more exciting than the weather – which was still wet.

'L-l-looks as if it's s-s-set in f-for the week,' Francis said. It was about his only observation until they drew up in the enclosed courtyard outside Vachells, when he said, 'Th-this m-m-matters to m-me, T-T-Tamsin, th-there are a l-l-lot of f-f-fences to m-mend. Take it s-s-steady, w-w-won't you?'

'Of course. I know.' She paused, meeting his eyes. 'And it matters to her, as well as you. Don't doubt it.'

He met her look but made no comment, opening the car door to climb out, and she did the same. They walked together up to the front door.

Mary had been crossing the hall as they arrived, she had heard the crunch of wheels on the gravel and the sound of the doors slamming, and had gone to the window to see who it was. When she saw the familiar car, and Francis and Tamsin crossing the courtyard together, for a moment she felt that her heart had stopped. Then, pulling herself together, she opened the front door just as they reached it, which Francis at least was relieved about; he had been uncertain whether to ring the bell or just walk in; under the circumstances it was a good question to which he had found no answer.

'This is a very pleasant surprise,' said Mary. 'Come in, both of you.' She held the door wide, greeting Diana with a quick kiss on the cheek, but not knowing quite what to do with her son. She would have to stand on tiptoe to kiss him, and she wasn't sure it would be welcome anyway, but he solved her problem by taking the initiative and bending down to kiss her first. The kiss, and the slight hug that went with it, held more warmth, she realised, than she had felt from him for a long, long time.

'Come into the drawing-room, and sit yourselves down,' she said. 'I'll ask Mrs Fairburn to bring us some coffee, and then you can tell me why you're here.' She smiled as she said this, and turned to lead the way before either of them could reply. Francis knew it already, of course, but she was uncertain of the reason for this unexpected visit and didn't want to make a fool of herself: she would love it to be friendly, a family visit, but feared it might be business. Like Francis with the front door, she had nothing to go on; there was too much history to jump to conclusions. She showed them into the drawing-room as if they were strangers and left briefly to speak to her housekeeper. On her return, she saw they were both standing at one of the windows, looking out at her beautiful garden. Francis had his arm around Tamsin's shoulders, they both turned as she came into the room. They were smiling, and she began to feel better; the smiles didn't look businesslike.

Diana had already sussed out that neither of the Chillingworths was sufficiently at ease with the other to make this easy for either of them, she knew that if someone didn't take the initiative this would be the stickiest family reunion in history, and there was only herself to do it. So when Mary said, a little stiffly, 'Coffee is on its way, then you can tell me why you're here. Do, please, sit down,' she jumped straight in. Mary had tried to make it sound an invitation rather than an order, but had dismally failed. It simply wouldn't do.

'Oh, our news won't wait that long!' she said, stepping away from the window and dragging Francis after her. 'We came to tell you that we're now officially engaged to be married – and to ask for your help, and some input on things like weddings, and restoring old houses, and lovely stuff like that! We both want you to be part of it all – don't we, Francis?'

Francis didn't say anything, but his smile told Mary that he was in complete agreement over this. She thought for one horrible moment that she was going to cry, but pulled herself together in time. She said, hardly recognising her own voice because it sounded so light and happy, 'Well, that's wonderful news! And of course I shall be glad to help where I can. I'm flattered to be asked, to be truthful,' and she forced a smile of her own.

'Who else would we ask?' Tamsin demanded, and stepping forward, gave her a hug that had real warmth behind it. With her right arm still round Mary's shoulders, she held out her left to display a beautiful sapphire and diamond ring. 'He gave me this, isn't it beautiful?'

Mary admired the ring, feeling as if she was in a dream where a good fairy had waved a wand to make everything right. She then invited them for the third time, to sit down, and this time they did, close together on a sofa where they could see her, and she could see them, and she had never felt such warmth in this room for over twenty years.

Even so, while they waited for the coffee, the conversation stumbled a bit.

'So, how are you managing, Francis?' asked Mary, to which he replied, 'F-fine, th-thank you.'

'Benita is looking after you all right?'

'Y-yes. F-fine.'

Awkward pause.

'So, when is it you finally complete?' asked Mary, struggling.

'I g-g-get the keys, d-day after t-t-tomorrow.'

Diana/Tamsin had had enough of this. She said, 'And when he does, would you come over there with me, and give me some advice? I get the job of rescuing the house, and I've never done anything remotely like it before in my life—' She broke off, as the door opened to admit Mrs Fairburn and the coffee. So far, Mrs Fairburn had only been a name in Diana's life, the supplier of cold boxes full of goodies when she and Kim had lived at the cottage, delivered mainly by Francis's cousin Clare, but also by Francis himself on occasion. Looking back on that time now, it seemed like another life – well, it had been another life. They exchanged smiles now, and when Mrs Fairburn had been introduced and the good news of the engagement told to her and been suitably greeted, the three main protagonists were on their own again. Fortunately, before they could stumble back into the conversational mire, Francis pulled himself together.

'Sh-shall we g-g-go out and c-c-come in again?' he asked, with a grin.

Mary picked up the coffee pot and began to pour. 'Milk, Tamsin? The sugar is just there…' When she had finished pouring, she looked at her son. 'I think that would be a very good idea, Francis. Now, tell me about this house, both of you. And yes, Tamsin, I should like to see it very much, and if I can help you, of course I will.'

Describing Burnthouse, as it generally did, generated lively discussion and a certain amount of horrified laughter on Mary's part. The dungheap seemed to amuse her particularly – again, not new.

'I hope you aren't meaning to shift all that muck on your own,' she said severely, to her son. 'I wouldn't put anything past you!'

'N-no. I'm getting G-Gary in to help c-c-clear the site, there's too m-m-much for one p-person.'

'Learning sense at last. Good, I'm glad to hear it.' Mary gave him a magisterial look. 'This is Gary Fancot, we're talking about? He was always a good friend to you – not that you deserved it.' She turned to Tamsin. 'I expect he's told you how they beat each other up when they were at college together? Disgraceful!' She was smiling.

'He asked f-f-for it,' said Francis. He didn't sound venomous about it.

'And what about the house?' Mary asked, turning to Tamsin again. 'I imagine that won't be much better.'

'It doesn't actually smell, except of damp, a bit,' said Tamsin. She thought about that statement, and added, 'Well, not much anyway. The outside loo was a bit pong-y…' They exchanged a smile, and Mary nodded her head. She said, 'It would be,' and then Tamsin went on. 'The rest of the house is just musty, mostly it smells of neglect, although, come to think, the bathroom was a bit suspect, too. It's all filthy dirty, though, and there's damp patches everywhere, and I think there may be mice. Francis says he's getting in a professional cleaning firm and a ratcatcher before we start on the important bits.'

'A very good idea.' Mary nodded her head. She turned back to Francis. 'What about the structure of the building itself? How much is there to do?'

'The r-r-roof leaks like a s-s-sieve, th-that's the first j-job, before w-we do anything else, b-b-but the m-main structure s-s-seems to be p-p-pretty sound f-f-for it's age. Th-there's r-r-rot in the interior w-w-woodwork, and s-s-some w-woodworm, and some broken w-w-window panes. And it all n-n-needs re-w-wiring, and l–like T-tamsin s-said, a th-th-thorough c-clean. Th-then, wh-when all th-that's done, it's all h-hers. The b-builders will d-d-do w-what she t-t-tells them she wants.'

'You'll see why I need some advice,' said Tamsin, making a face. 'And it's got to be furnished, too, when it's fit to live in. Kim and I looked at some antique shops yesterday, and I honestly don't know where to start!' She turned to Francis. 'This may sound a silly question – it will sound a silly question – but what are your bookcases made of?'

'D-dark oak,' said Francis, and Mary added, 'And I think that is a very sensible question, Tamsin, since they will take up quite a lot of the space. Counting the ones from the office, I believe he has five.'

'S-seven,' said Francis. 'I had two upstairs in th-the flat.'

'And a grand piano,' said Tamsin. 'See what I mean? That's probably dark oak, too.'

Mary found herself laughing, and was amazed at herself. All of a sudden, it was as if the sun had come out and was sucking up the pain and unhappiness of the last twenty years as if it was mist. It would always be there in the background, of course, how could you forget such terrible things just like that? But it would cease to be the colour of her life, she felt that now like the sun's warmth.

'There is still some coffee in the pot,' she said, lifting it. 'Would either of you like another cup?'

Tamsin said that yes, she would, but Francis declined. He asked, 'Is th-there anything you n-n-need help w-with out in the office? S-s-since I'm here…'

'Actually, there is,' said Mary. 'There are a couple of things on that computer that I do not fully understand – and it keeps flashing up messages that I do not understand either. If you could have a look at it, I should be very grateful, the one that I used to use before you were old enough to take over was a lot less argumentative, and it will be three weeks yet before Cosmo is here.'

'I c-c-can do that – if T-Tamsin d-d-doesn't m-m-mind? It p-p-probably w-wants to update.' He looked questioningly at Tamsin, she shook her head.

'No, you go and play. Mary and I can talk furniture, you'd only find it boring.'

But when he had gone, it seemed that furniture wasn't the subject that Mary was primarily interested in. She poured two cups of coffee, from the insulated pot, but did not immediately pick up her own. She said, 'I understand that you were up in London over the weekend,' in as non-committal a way as she could manage.

'We were. We went up so that Francis could meet my parents, and so that he could meet up with his cousins again.'

'And did he do that'

'He did – with some of them, anyway. Ed, and Michael and – Ros, is it?'

'It is. And was the reunion a success?'

'I think you could call it that.' Tamsin smiled at her. 'Since they none of them stopped talking when we were all together, and the atmosphere was like a particularly good Christmas! You'll know, anyway, as soon as you see them again – they all plan to come down here at one time or another. When it's fit for human habitation, they'll stay at Burnthouse, before that they'll probably use a hotel. But they'll come – and they all mean to come to see you, too, so be warned.'

Mary said, slowly, 'I am so very glad to hear that. Francis lost so much, due to Christopher's stupid and selfish behaviour. How could he think such a thing of his own son, Tamsin? He stole twenty years from his life…'

'I know. But they weren't thrown away entirely, Mary, you must never think that. He loves this place, he's immensely proud of his cows, he kept on following his favourite interests – sailing, his passion for marine biology, breeding better and better cattle – he didn't waste those years. You have to remember that.'

'He destroyed our relationship as mother and son, however. We have lived apart in the same house for a long, long time now.'

'Well, take heart. You won't be doing it in the future! Whenever he comes here, you will be together. And when you come to Burnthouse, I promise you, you will be welcome as…as the sun in summer. You will!'

'You cannot un-write the past, Tamsin.'

'True, but you don't have to keep on reading it!'

There was a short silence, while they sipped their coffee. It had gone a little cold in fact, in spite of the insulated pot, but it filled the time while each of them wondered where to take the conversation next. They didn't know each other well as yet: given the territory it could turn out a minefield. It was Mary who finally broke it.

'I have to say this, Tamsin,' she said, and paused. Tamsin gave her a questioning look but did not speak, and finally she found the words to continue. 'I think…I think that you are the best thing that has come to this house for many years. I am so happy that the two of you met as you did, and I hope – and believe – that you will have a long and happy marriage to my son.' She broke off, looking embarrassed. 'There, I've said it, and I hope you will believe it.'

Thank you,' said Tamsin, touched. After a pause, she added, 'I did wonder if you would think I was a bit young for him. Quite apart from anything else...' She let that one tail off into silence. Mary shook her head.

'You have to be twenty-five, surely. That is old enough to be described as properly grown-up. And he has missed out on his youth to a very great extent. I think you will be his salvation.'

'I hope so.'

There was a pause, it was difficult for either of them to know how to follow that. Once more, it was Mary who found the way.

'So tell me; you say you went up to London to see your parents and presumably to introduce them to Francis. Do you have any wedding plans as yet, or is it too early to ask?'

'Hmm. I'm glad you asked that, I was going to run it past you soon, anyway.' Tamsin made a rueful face. 'My father is very Old School. He thinks that Francis is the perfect match – background, money, property, you know the kind of thing. But he doesn't wholly approve of us sharing a caravan before we get married, so he and my mother would like us to marry soon.'

Mary said, musingly, 'I don't think it is quite a caravan that he has in mind,' and smiled.

'I'm very glad to hear it,' said Tamsin, feelingly. 'He keeps calling it a caravan, but he's a bit on the large side...' and they both laughed.

'So, when would your father like the marriage to be? And have you decided where?'

'Francis has. The chapel at Ravenscourt Place. And my father and mother would like, before Christmas. So we shall work from there.'

'The chapel at Ravenscourt Place...' said Mary, musing. 'Not a large wedding, then?'

'I think that's the idea. I suppose we could have a slightly larger reception – the suggested venue for that is the Ravenscourt Arms. I expect they might do us a buffet.'

'It's possible. There might be a better idea.' She became thoughtful. 'Has Francis discussed this with Merlin Ravenscourt? I believe he is still in charge of that side of the running of the estate, for all he is a partner in the Shipyard at Emberton now.'

'That, I don't know. He said he was going to, but he hasn't said anything. I don't suppose there's been a chance since we got back from London.'

'Well, I shall be interested to hear the result when he has done so.' Mary gave a brisk nod of her head.

Tamsin said, 'If you know the chapel, I expect you know how many it will hold, too.'

'Oh yes. I have been there for special services from time to time. It is essentially a room in the house, so it is not big. Five pews on each side, holding three comfortably, four at a squash. There is a font, which takes up space, and a small organ. I believe they sometimes put extra chairs in at the back if necessary. I would say that, at a push, you would get thirty-five or -six people in there comfortably, no more. People don't like to be squashed.' She smiled.

'That's about what we thought.'

'You are not having a big party in the evening for all those that you cannot fit in?'

'I don't think so. The general idea seems to be, get married, have a quick lunch, and strip off the glad rags to get back to work. My mother wants to give a big party in London later on, when we actually have a proper roof over our heads.'

'So, no honeymoon either?'

'Not then, anyway. But Francis has plans…but I'll leave him to tell you about them himself.' She smiled, and Mary, watching her, saw the tenderness in that smile. She said, 'Take care of him for me, Tamsin. He is the most precious thing I have.'

'You may be very sure that I will,' said Tamsin.

'This coffee is lukewarm with all our talking,' said Mary, putting down her cup. 'Would you like me to ring for some fresh?'

'I think I've probably had enough, actually, said Tamsin. 'Anyway, I heard a door bang out in the hall there – I think our favourite man is on his way back.' They exchanged a smile. Mary said, 'You are a brave woman, Tamsin,' and before Tamsin could find an answer, the drawing room door opened to admit Francis, right on cue.

'All s-s-sorted,' he said, as he came in. 'It j-j-just needed to update, and I've c-c-cleared out the inbox of r-r-rubbish. Th-those two emails w-w-will wait till th-th-the end of the m-m-month, they're n-nothing urgent – l-leave them for C-Cosmo.' He made no attempt to sit down again, and Tamsin and his mother deduced from that, that it was time to go. They both got to their feet. Mary said, 'Thank you for that, it was worrying me. I am not good friends with that computer, it's too clever for me! It's been lovely to see you both, I wish you could stay longer, but I know you're both busy people. Just don't leave it too long before you come again – and Tamsin darling, you don't have to wait for him. Bring Kim to see me, I would love to meet her, too.'

Kisses were exchanged, far warmer than the kisses of greeting, and then Mary walked out to the car with them, as if she couldn't bear to part from them a moment before she had to, which, Tamsin thought, was probably true. She stood in the courtyard waving as they drove away before turning back to the house as they vanished through the gateway and down the drive.

She walked back to the house slowly, the residual warmth still with her. That had been a lovely surprise, and not at all what she had expected her next meeting with her son to be. Tamsin was a lovely girl.

The future was looking hopeful, and that for the first time for a long, long while.

In the departing car, both Francis and Diana were quiet. It had been an unexpected meeting, just as Mary herself was thinking. Full of warmth and welcome, rather than awkwardness, they were both thinking that. Finally, Francis broke the silence.

'I'm g-g-glad we went. Th-thank you, Tamsin.'

'I'm glad, too.' She added, because Mary had put it into her mind, 'Have you seen Merlin yet? Your mother was asking about the wedding.'

'Not yet, but I will. I m-m-might make a ch-chance t-t-tomorrow, before th-the s-s-storm breaks on F-Friday.' He smiled at her, briefly, before returning his attention to the road.

'She said the chapel will hold about forty, tops, if everyone draws in their breath.'

'R-r-right.'

Diana relaxed in her seat to watch the countryside flowing past the window. That had been an interesting morning, and heartwarming. She hadn't expected any of that, from the loving welcome to the computer problems to the warm interest in their future.

The cottage falling down, for all it had nearly fallen on them had turned out to be a catalyst for good. Knowing it was slightly absurd, she mentally wished the site well, and then, her thoughts wandering on, she found herself thinking, if she couldn't catch Ernie to sound him out on past events, maybe she would have a better chance with Gary Fancot?

She'd get one of them before she was much older; she was increasingly sure that it would turn out to be important.

Well, the wind was blowing their way, and fair, right now. She settled back in her seat and thought about possibilities.

XVII

On Thursday, the bad weather really set in. Kim and Diana sat gloomily over their breakfast, looking out at the village street running with water and the black skies above, and watching the few people who, for whatever reason, needed to be out, scurrying past as fast as they possibly could, wrapped up in waterproofs and cowering beneath umbrellas.

'Not a good day for going out,' said Kim, as they crunched their toast.

'Definitely not. Possibly, if we lived in the town, but we have to get there first.'

'No way!'

Their problem was, because neither of them lived in the house but only rented it – not even that, really, because Francis had taken over the rent when his own cottage fell on them – that they had no back-up occupations, no bookcase from which to choose a good book, no jigsaws, no board games to pass the time. All they had, effectively, was yesterday's newspaper, two mobile phones, a television set and each other. Kim's precious ipad, which had travelled with her all round Europe, had been a casualty of the cottage incident; she wouldn't be replacing it until the insurance paid out, as Francis had assured them it would – eventually.

'So what do we do?' Diana asked, after a pause, and Kim said, doubtfully, 'I could start teaching you to cook, I suppose.'

'Have we got anything to cook?'

'Not really. Not unless we go to the shop.' The shop was only a short distance along the street. They both of them instinctively turned to the window, and the water streaming down it.

'Forget that, then,' said Diana.

'Sounds like a morning with the telly then.'

'Ugh!' Diana had no opinion of daytime television. Immediately she had spoken, this became irrelevant, as there came a sudden flash of lightning, a huge crash of thunder almost immediately after, and the overhead light, which they had switched on so that they could see to eat their breakfast, went out.

They peered at each other in the gloom.

'Do mobile phones work when the power's off?' asked Diana.

'Of course they do. That's the whole point of them. Well…as long as they're charged up, they do.'

'Mine is. I put it on charge yesterday, when I got in.'

'Not sure mine is. Anyway—' Kim paused to allow for another clap of thunder, '—the interference from this storm would make it nearly unusable, I should think.'

'There's only one thing for it, then. We shall have to wash up these plates.' Diana began to gather them together. She carried them through into the kitchen, and Kim sat and watched her. When she heard the sliding crash as Diana put them into the sink, she got to her feet and followed.

'It doesn't look any better from this side,' Diana told her, looking through the kitchen window. 'All the plants in the yard are bowing their heads down and shivering – I know just how they feel.'

Kim was about to tell her, for God's sake cheer up! when her phone did ring. She hurriedly grabbed it from the worktop where she had left it while she got the breakfast, and subsequently forgotten it.

'Hello?…Val! How lovely!…what? I didn't quite hear that, the connection is terrible, there's a huge thunderstorm—' She paused to allow a noisy roll of thunder to pass. '—yes, I expect you can, it must be right overhead…say that again?…Oh Val! That's ages…oh, I see, do you really think so?…Oh Val, I do hope so. It would be so great…all right then, I can hardly hear you anyway! Love you too!' She switched off her phone and turned to Diana. 'That was Val,' she said, unnecessarily. 'He's just heard from Hetherington Associates. They're going to call the second interviews for the possibles next month – Val's date is the very end of the month. He says, they're probably saving the best until last.'

'They're not hurrying themselves then.'

'Maybe it's a new version of that old saying, "marry in haste, repent at leisure?". That's what he thinks, anyway.' She put the phone, which she was still clutching like a talisman, down on the worktop again. 'Oh Diana, it would be so wonderful if he got it, and there could be a partnership eventually, too! Now, you wash and I'll wipe.'

Diana turned on the tap. 'I wish we could have the light on – it's so gloomy!' She flinched at a brilliant flash of lightning. 'I wonder what they do on farms in weather like this?'

'Spend a lot of time in the barn?' Kim suggested.

'It must be making a real mush of that manure heap,' said Diana, gloomily, placing the first plate in the rack to drain. 'It'll be ours tomorrow.'

'Well, you won't have to clear it up – is that someone at the door?' Kim paused, with the plate and the teatowel in her hands.

'They'd ring the bell, it's just the thunder.'

'No they wouldn't. The power's off, remember?' Kim set down her work and headed for the living room. 'I'll just check – there it is again.'

Diana heard it too, that time, and it was definitely someone hammering on the door, and she didn't blame them; the water running off the roof of the small porch, which she had noticed while she ate her breakfast, would be pouring straight down their neck. She put the mug she was about to wash back into the water and went to see who it was. Kim had opened the door, and she heard a male voice she thought she recognised, saying, 'Miss Ford? I got something for you.'

'Come in a minute,' said Kim. 'You can't stand out in that.' She held the door wider, and Gary Fancot walked in, smiling. He saw Diana immediately.

'Morning, Tamsin. How're you doing in this lovely weather?'

'Bored, thank you,' said Diana, smiling at him. 'As you can see, we're in the gloom – the lights went with the storm. Hello Gary.'

'You two know each other?' asked Kim. She closed the door behind Gary to shut out the storm, and he stood dripping on the mat.

'Sorry girls, I'm a bit wet.' He felt in an inner pocket, and a little stream of water ran off his shiny waterproof jacket and made a small puddle on the floor. 'Oops, sorry about that.'

'Take your coat off, and put it on the hook,' said Diana. 'It'll drip on the floor, but it's stone anyway, it won't hurt it. We can make you a cup of coffee to warm you up.'

'No we can't,' Kim pointed out. 'No electricity.'

'That'll be the trip switch, most likely,' said Gary, slipping off his wet jacket and hanging it on the indicated hook. 'There, now I won't wash you both away – if I just kick these boots off so I don't tread muck all over your carpet, you can show me where it is, and I'll put it back on for you.'

Neither Kim nor Diana had the faintest idea where the trip switch was;

they had not, so far, needed to know. Gary, however, homed in on it like a returning pigeon and lifted a wooden flap above the fridge.

'There you are girls – like I said, it's tripped the main fuse with that lightning.' He pushed the lever back up and the lights sprang back to life. 'Need to remember where that is, you do. Now you can get that kettle on, and I'll show you why I've come.'

'Tea or coffee?' asked Kim, reaching for the kettle.

'Tea, if there's a choice, thanks.'

'Take him in the other room, Diana,' said Kim, smiling at the strange, friendly man who was taking up half the floor space. 'He's too large for in here. I'll bring the tea when the kettle's boiled.'

'Diana?' asked Gary, following Diana obediently back into the sitting room.

'It's my name. I'm adopted, Francis knew me before.' She saw the puzzlement on his face. 'Don't worry about it. He never gets it straight either.'

'Seems to me there's a story here,' said Gary, with a lift of his brows. He seated himself in one of the armchairs; he filled it edge to edge, Diana almost thought she heard it groan as he sat down. She took her own seat on the sofa.

'Well, there is, but let's not go into it right now. Do we take it you have good news for Kim?'

'Might have.' He grinned at her. 'Let's wait for that tea, and I'll show you.'

He looked enormous, sitting there. Without the hard hat, the top of his head was completely bald, with a fringe of black curls around the back and over his ears; he looked like a large and genial imp.

Kim came out of the kitchen with a big mug of tea, the sugar, and two smaller mugs of coffee, and pulled the coffee table where they could all reach it.

'Now,' she said, 'tell me who you are, and why you're here.'

Neither Diana nor Gary had realised she didn't know. Diana said, 'He's Francis's friend Gary, the demolition man at the cottage. He was going to look for your passport in the debris, remember?'

'Oh, goodness yes!' Kim's face lit up. 'Does this visit mean that you found it?'

Gary grinned at her, ladling sugar into his tea. He said, again, 'Might have.' He then laid the spoon aside and felt in the pocket of the zipped jacket he had been wearing under his waterproof, and removed a small booklet. 'This be it, by any chance?' He dropped it into Kim's outstretched hand. 'Got a bit squashed, but I reckon it's still legal. That bag was pretty waterproof, as it turns out. Good thing too.'

Kim was looking at her rather bent passport as if she had been handed the holy grail. Gary felt in his pocket again. 'There's this, too. The camera was squashed flat, not worth bringing, but I did get this, you might still make something of it.' He produced a small rectangular package, wrapped in a square of what looked like soft toilet paper, and handed it over after the passport. Kim looked at it lying in her palm, without recognition, and then unwrapped it. She let out a long breath when she realised what it was.

'Oh Gary, you are a wonderful man!' she said. The little memory card lay in its nest of paper, slightly scratched and battered; if it still held anything at all, it was around one hundred and fifty pictures of her travels in France and Italy, plus a few of her family in London and points north. She felt tears sting behind her eyes, she had thought it gone for good. The rest of her trip should be safely stored onto her main computer away in New Zealand, waiting for the return she wouldn't, now, be making, but she hadn't got round to downloading this last lot.

Gary said, 'It didn't get wet, neither, it may still have something on it. Give it to Francis, he's got all the gear, if there's anything there he'll find it for you.' He reached across to the coffee table for his mug of tea and sat back in his chair. He took a gulp, and said, 'This is good, this is. It's a nightmare out there!'

'Not demolishing anything new today then?' Diana asked, smiling.

'Reckon this storm'd do it for me,' said Gary. 'No, we'll finish with clearing that site today, when the storm goes over, no use trying in this lot, and after that we've nothing much on but a bit of clearing out 'til Monday.' He grinned at her. 'Reckon we'll meet again, then.'

'So I hear.' Diana smiled back. 'You've seen the mess, I imagine?'

'Certainly have. What got into that man of yours, taking that on?' He paused, reflectively, 'Mind you, he always did punch above his weight, nothing's changed there.'

'Yes, we heard that, too,' said Kim. He looked at her, knowingly.

'So you know about all that, do you? Well, bad news travels fast, they say. Who told you?' His eyes narrowed as he asked the question: they both took note of it.

'Francis told me himself, actually,' said Diana. She added, 'And he told me the other day that it was you that he thumped. What really happened? He didn't go into any great details and I'd rather like to know.'

'Any particular reason why?' asked Gary, with a lift of his eyebrows.

'Well, yes, actually.' She hesitated, wondering how much to say, but then said it anyway. 'We — that's me and Kim — think that there's something still going on, and we think it might be connected.'

'Might you be able to tell me why you think that?' asked Gary. He took a draught of his tea, but didn't take his eyes from her face.

'I suppose so. There's an…an undercurrent, I suppose you would call it, down at the sailing club here — the Committee seemed to know things they had no reason, or right come to that, to know, and they misinterpreted them, and "invited" him to resign. And we wondered…'

'Ah,' said Gary. He thought for a moment. 'That's bad, that is. Well, I can tell you what I know, but I don't know as it'll help you much. There's not a lot as you can do against spite.' He paused there, thinking out the best way to present the sorry tale, and the twins waited. Finally, he spoke. 'It was when we was all at the Sixth Form — well, you'll probably know that. There was this spoilt brat who thought he was God, lording it about the place — his mum said she was a friend of Mrs V-C, but really she was a hanger-on — my mum used to clean out there, she knew. They sat on some of the same committees, was all, but she blew it up into a great friendship — my mum knew that because she worked for some of the same charities, not on the committees, natural, but baked cakes and managed stalls at sales of work, stuff like that. Real, hands-on stuff.' He gave a cynical laugh. 'Well, each to his own, and brat-boy looked down on her — and me, come to that — because his mum was one of the bosses. But my mum knew different.' He paused there, thinking where to go with the story next, and the twins waited. When he finally spoke, it sounded like a change of subject at first.

'My mum used to know the caretaker at that cottage you lived in, the one I'm just carting away to the tip.' He gave them a hard look. 'They was both called Mollie, and they both hated the name, said it was old-fashioned, like a doll's name; it made a sort of bond. Mollie Crowe, that was, I daresay you met her. She was killed in a hit-and-run, back in the summer.'

'Yes, we did,' said Kim. 'She was very kind to us. We were sorry.'

'Well, there you go, that's life,' said Gary. He paused for a moment, then he said, 'She was caretaker when Francis's dad was alive too – there was a woman got herself killed out there, she found the body, poor soul. There was a child in the cottage, half-dead too – poor old Francis found that one, he was passing—' he hesitated there, frowning, but then went on, '—or something, so he says, and heard Mollie Crowe screaming her head off, and the body lying on the path. But Mollie Crowe had said to my mum as there was two children, twins. Little girls with red hair.' He looked at them both.

'Yes, that was us,' said Diana. She made no further explanation, and Gary said, 'I did wonder.'

'Let's get back to the spoilt brat,' said Kim, to forestall any difficult questions, but Gary didn't seem to want to ask any. He just nodded his head and went on with his tale.

'Anyway, little Maxie fancied himself something rotten – he was a bit of a looker, I suppose, if you liked that sort of thing – tall and blonde and sunburnt, he spent a lot of his time messing about in his dad's boat he used to fish from, which impressed some of the lads, and the girls at the comp in town had all thought he was wonderful, it'd gone to his head a bit – well, more'n a bit, be honest, he played to the gallery. Put it bluntly, he was a conceited arsehole! Didn't cut so much ice at the college, mind. The girls there had more sense on the whole, and we was all growing up a bit, but he still had a following…first term we was all there, he gathered a bit of a fan club. Us real blokes preferred football.' He made a face. 'That's not to say we didn't take girls out, I don't mean that. Just that they was different girls, with more brains, and sharp enough to know a slimeball when they saw one. We was at college because we wanted to get on in the world outside. He was there to show off.' He rubbed his nose thoughtfully. 'Wanted to be a rocket scientist, or something, he said. It takes all sorts – his dad was a simple chemist, back in the town here. Him too, these days.'

'Get to the point,' said Kim. 'What happened? That's what we want to know.'

Gary gave her a look that she couldn't quite interpret. He said, 'Just filling in the background for you. It makes more sense if you know it, you'll see in a minute.' He paused. 'I daresay you know what happened to Francis? His dad was killed in a car crash, and he was in the car with him – his dad ran into a flat lorry full of iron girders and his head was knocked right off – it was sitting there on the back seat, grinning at poor old Francis, and blood everywhere, like a—' He broke off, but then went on, 'well, I'll say it anyway, like a bloody fountain. All over Francis, and everything. On top of seeing that woman's body and the little girl that was beat up and left to die not that long before, it was one too many for Francis. They said he ought to get back to normal life as quick as possible, put it all behind him, and he had gone back to his Public School – he was at Winterbourne, I expect you know that – but it was a daft idea. He went to pieces, no surprise there, and they shipped him home, said they didn't want him back, thank you. So, the second term at Sixth Form, he turned up there. You can imagine how that went down. You know Francis, he wasn't that far different then, and he had a romantic back-story to make things worse. He didn't have that stammer then, neither. And he really knew how to sail a boat himself, not just messing about on his dad's motor boat that he fished from. And there was Vachells, too. And he knew, if no-one else did, just what relationship little Maxie's mum had with his own. I knew him a bit from way back; when I was a little lad, my mum sometimes took me to work with her, Mrs V-C didn't mind just now and again, long as I didn't get in the way. Me and Francis used to play together in the farmyard, he had a pony and a dog, it was great. He didn't think himself above me, neither did his mum. Vachells are farming folk, not posh people – only a silly snob like Maxie's mum thought that.' He paused for breath, thinking back to that long-ago time. Diana and Kim forbore to say that, whatever the Vachells were, the Chillingworths were a different story, and waited for him to go on. So far, he hadn't told them much that they didn't already know, but now they were coming to the relevant bit.

'Trouble with Francis,' said Gary, thinking back, 'he didn't mix. Well, he'd been through hell, one way or another, and all he wanted was to be left alone, so it was easy for little Maxie to say that he was too posh to talk to the rest of us – which wasn't true. And it was pretty obvious, quite early on, that he was clever enough to really be a rocket scientist, if he had wanted to – which he didn't. That didn't help, neither.'

'I can see that it wouldn't,' said Kim, when he paused to think where to take this story next. When he didn't immediately take up the tale, she prompted, 'So do we take it that this Maxie started a bullying campaign to prove he was still the king of the jungle?'

'Pretty much,' said Gary, considering. 'Whispered about how Francis was a poof, and how he thought himself a cut above the rest of us, looked down on us and wouldn't soil his hands mixing with us, and how he knew, because his mum was a friend of Francis's mum, that he had been expelled from that Public School because he'd gone mad – none of it was true, but it could have been, the way he behaved. Only the reasons was different. And then—' he paused there, savouring the memory, and Diana prompted, 'Then?'

'His best girlfriend, Janet, got a crush on Francis – she didn't have no encouragement, but that was half the trouble; you know how it is. And quite a lot of the other girls had him on their wish list, if only he'd've looked at them twice. Wasting their time, but it did give little Maxie a lever. But when it comes down to it, a poof is one thing, and don't get me wrong, I ain't got nothing against such, you are what you are, but Francis was quite another, and them girls knew it too. Janet wasn't the only one, not by a mile.'

'The lure of the unattainable?' said Diana. She had a bit of a fellow-feeling with Janet, whoever she was; she had experienced Francis's withdrawal and lack of apparent interest herself.

'You could say that. She was always in his way, following him around like a little dog, trying to make him notice her. He didn't. But Maxie was evil, you can't call it nothing else.'

'You can't help a sneaking sympathy with him, though,' Kim suggested, and Gary said, 'I could.' He scowled at the memory. Diana said, to help things along, 'He told me – Francis did – that he – that's Francis – said in the end that he would thump the living daylights out of the next person who said he was either a snob or a poofter or something.'

'Yes, he did. He lost his temper in the end, which was a shame, because it was exactly what our Golden Boy wanted. He set out to provoke him deliberate, which I thought wasn't a good idea – Francis looked all civilised and cool, but I knew damn well he wasn't, he was just...well, still sick. And tired. And unhappy too, but I never knew what that was about, just that I had an idea it maybe was more than the obvious, don't know what, or why come to that. He was just taking it all a day at a time – I'd known him as a child, remember, even though we hadn't seen each other much since I got too old for my mum to take to work with her. Maxie fancied himself as a bit of a boxer, among all the other things he fancied himself as, he meant to show everyone – the girls included – who really was the greatest, but I knew as Francis would wipe the floor with him and jump on the sludge that was left, he'd been to Public School, for God's sake! He'd played all kinds of sport, done it well, too; he'd worked on the farm, hard work too, not playing at it – Mrs V-C used to talk to my mum, proud of him, like, and wanting to share. He was no push-over.' He looked at the twins sideways, half-embarrassed, and said, 'So before he could get his oar in and get himself into trouble that could finish Francis at the college and ruin his future, and probably do some pretty painful damage to himself, I did the job myself. I called him a conceited snob, very loud, to a group of my mates and he did exactly as he said he would do.' He grinned at the memory. 'I have to be honest here, there was a minute or two when I thought as I'd bit off more than I could chew, but I had to put up a bit of show for the audience – we fought pretty dirty for a minute or two; I gave him a real shiner, and he nearly broke my nose, and we both ended up with cracked ribs that we didn't let on about, then I let a punch that I could've handled easy knock me to the ground instead, and that was the end of it.'

'You mean, you lost on purpose?' said Diana.

'Might have lost anyway come to that – but yes, I did.'

'Did he realise?'

'Course he did. He was never stupid, Francis, whatever little Maxie tried to tell us.'

'So what happened next?' Kim asked. 'We know there was a bit of an uproar, after what happened at – what was the place? Winterbourne? We don't know what form it took, not really.'

'"A bit of an uproar",' said Gary, musingly. 'I like that. Yes, Kim, there was a bit of an uproar. We was both hauled up in front of the head honcho, and given a right bollocking, and a warning that if it ever happened again we would be out on our ear – ears. So we promised to be good, and went off and had a good talk together. First we'd had since we was about eight years old.' He looked back, remembering, and a grin came over his face. 'Well, things hadn't changed much meantime, come to that. He thanked me, and meant it – he knew damn well that if he'd gone for little Maxie the way he gone for me, there'd have been hell to pay. And I said, don't mention it. And then and there, we was back as friends. And since we was friends, I give him some good advice on how to handle things in future, which he did take, for what good it did. And friends is what we've been ever since.' He made an expressive face, and took another gulp of his cooling tea. 'So there you have it. Except for one thing.'

'Which is?' said Diana, prompting, when he didn't immediately continue.

'Except for, little Maxie ran home and told his mummy all about it. And Mummy told Mrs V-C, making a good story of it from what I can gather, and my mum lost her job. The End.'

'That was a bit unfair,' said Kim. 'He attacked you, not the other way about.'

'I did more or less say "come and thump me then,"' Gary pointed out. 'And the way as it was told…well, I've said what happened. But I've always wondered if there was more to it than we knew, or he ever told me?' He made it into a question, and Kim and Diana exchanged a glance, which he didn't overlook. 'So?'

Mary Vachell-Chillingworth had thought her beautiful son was a violent murderer; the story of that fight, as presented by an ill-wisher with every reason to exaggerate, must have turned her poor heart to stone. Impossible to say that. Kim said, 'Well, there was, but it's all sorted now so it's a bit late to worry about it. Tell us what happened after that. Francis took his A-levels at Sixth Form, we know that.'

'But he didn't go on to university. He should've. The College advised against it, said he'd be better at home.'

They had known that, of course. Diana said, 'Well, you will be glad to know, it didn't stop him. He has two degrees and a doctorate to his name.'

'Glad to hear it,' said Gary. 'But he ended up on the farm, none the less. That's not what he had planned. Bloody little Maxie!'

'What became of him – little Maxie?' Kim asked. 'Did he become a rocket scientist?' She thought she knew the answer, but it would be good to have it confirmed.'

'You got to be joking! He went to uni all right, read chemistry or something and got a second class BSc, and then ended up in his dad's shop – well, we all knew that was what was going to happen anyway, so it wasn't no surprise.'

'And is he still there?'

'It was sold when his dad died. He's pharmacist there, working for someone else now, bit of a come-down for the heir to the throne.'

Diana said, hardly liking to ask, 'Would that be the one in the Square – not Boots, the other one?'

'That's it. You been there?'

'Yes. I think we probably saw him.' She hesitated. 'Funny thing, he's on the Committee at the Sailing Club.'

'Well, what a coincidence!' Gary drained his mug and set it back on the coffee table. 'Now listen, you girls – Francis is a good friend to me these days. If there's anything you want me to do, just tell me.' He got to his feet, standing towering above them.

'I don't think there's anything you can do, but thank you anyway. Spite and malice and gossip are a bit like bindweed – you never really get rid of them.' Diana stood up too, and Kim began pushing the mugs together.

'I'll see you back at the farm on Monday then.' He unhooked his still damp waterproof and slipped it on. 'That thunder's going over now, but still raining like Niagara. Oh well, I was wet anyway. Thanks for the tea, see you again.'

'Well, that was interesting,' said Kim, when he had gone back out into the storm, banging the door cheerfully behind him. He waved as he strode past the window, back to his van parked outside. She picked up her passport, handling it lovingly. 'What a nice man.'

'Yes, I thought that, as soon as I'd met him. Good thing Francis has one person on his side – a bit of a heavyweight too, if it comes to a fight.'

'Two people. Val is, too. Three, even, there's Merlin as well. Probably quite a few more, if he let them get near him. He does tend to be his own worst enemy, you know. Nothing much seems to have changed since he was at College.'

'Do you blame him? Really?'

'No. But if the whole thing blew apart down at the Club, it might be interesting to see what the outcome was – don't you think?' Kim paused. She said, 'Was that the same tale as Francis told you?'

'Pretty much. A bit more detail, I suppose, and he named a name, which Francis—' she had been about to say "didn't", but Gary's story belatedly triggered a memory that she had unconsciously filed away. She said, 'Yes, he did! I remember now – he said "Max Carruthers".'

'Bingo!' said Kim. 'And funnily enough, so did Val, that day at the Club. Interesting…'

But the recollection had triggered another one. Hadn't Bennie said something relevant too, when she had made that brief visit to Shortlanesend with Francis after she had first been shown Burnthouse? They had gone out for fish and chips at the Two Pigeons that night, she remembered, but before that, they had dropped in at Shortlanesend to get out of the rain for a while, and Bennie had been holding forth about some meeting she had been to. Something about Francis's solicitor's wife...what was her name? Dorothy! There had been an incident with someone called, surely, "Jenny Carruthers"...she wished she could remember the details, but her mind had been too full of the amazing day she had just spent. She must have a word with Bennie before she mentioned it to Kim, but it did sound, in her recollection, as if the tendency to spite and wishing to be top of the heap without challengers might possibly be hereditary. Or learned. Perhaps that was more likely?

At least she wouldn't have to bother Ernie now.

'What are you thinking?' asked Kim, watching her.

'Venomous thoughts.' Diana gathered up the three mugs on the table, anything to change the subject for now. 'Let's wash these – and we haven't finished the breakfast things yet – and then we can sit and be bored, or go out in the rain, or something.'

Kim, undeceived, followed her to the kitchen.

'Any ideas what you want to do next?' she asked, picking up her teatowel again.

'What, when we've done this? Or about Francis? I don't see what we can do about that, do you?'

'Someone ought to do something,' said Kim.

'It seems to me,' said Diana, thinking about it, and stopping what she was doing in order to think better, 'that it's going onto auto-pilot on its own. The brakes are off; you saw Francis up in London, he was a totally different man – you said so, I seem to remember. So did Val.'

'But we're back here now,' Kim pointed out.

'Yes, we are, but the defences are down here, too, aren't they? He knows the truth about what happened at the cottage, so does Mary, there's nothing to fear there. He's moved away from the Sailing Club crowd and into a completely different circle; Bennie and Ernie have no axes to grind with him, and presumably Cosmo and his family haven't either, and there's a whole lot more of them out there too – the Vachells, I mean – then there's Gary, and I don't suppose he was the only one to suss out what was happening when they were at College all those years ago. There'll be others, he's only got to let the barriers down and I bet you anything you like, they'll all come out of the woodwork.'

'But the Sailing Club – and the Yacht Club, too – are still poisoned ground. Don't you think that's a shame, rather?'

'I think I shall be interested to see what happens next.'

'So what you're saying,' said Kim, slightly scandalised at the idea if she was honest, 'is that you think the whole thing is going to spontaneously combust?'

'It wouldn't surprise me, is all I'm saying.'

'Oh God!' said Kim. She put down her teatowel, the last plate was dry now anyway. 'I can't take this! Let's deploy the anoraks and go out and brave the storm for a minute – we can get some local stewing beef and some veggies at the shop, and I can show you how to make a stew.'

XVIII

Friday, completion day for Burnthouse, was still wildly windy and a little showery now and again, but at least the thunder had rolled away to enliven somewhere else and the sun shone occasionally through the flying clouds.

'I have a serious grudge against that thunderstorm,' said Diana as they sat at their breakfast on what had turned out to be what Kim's mum called "the morning after the night before." 'It managed to ruin yesterday completely.' She scowled at her bowl of cornflakes. 'I was really looking forward to showing off my stew last night, and look what happened!'

'Never mind. We can eat it tonight instead – there's probably enough for Val too, if we do a lot of veg,' Kim comforted her.

'If he turns up,' Diana gloomed. She wasn't referring to Val.

'He will. Probably.'

The previous evening, Francis had been supposed to come over from Shortlanesend to take them both out for some food and a drink at the Two Pigeons, and Diana and Kim had decided that instead, they would eat in – it wasn't fit even to walk down the street, in any case – and feed him Diana's beef and vegetable stew, made under Kim's instructions, and of which she was very proud. Then, just before four o'clock, Bennie had rung them to say that he wouldn't be coming at all.

'That thunderstorm set off a migraine,' she told Diana, apologetically. 'He does get them, from that bang on the head – not often, but when they strike, they do a thorough job. He was violently sick all morning, and now he's in bed, asleep with the cat and looking like something she brought in. He asked me to ring you and apologise.'

'I ought to sympathise,' said Diana, sadly, 'I get them too, sometimes, and for a similar reason, but it didn't get me that way this morning. Just made me jump.'

'It was a bad one, wasn't it? But I think, with Francis this time, it was a combination thing – partly the thunderstorm, partly sheer stress, he's had a rough time recently. He'll be OK tomorrow he says, he said he'd ring you in the morning if he was still alive.'

'Oh well, give him my love, and I hope he feels better soon. I'll wait to hear from him, then.'

The end of a perfect day, to use another cliché. They had put the stew into the fridge and dined on the biscuits and cheese that had been meant to follow it, and a couple of apples that lurked in their fruit bowl, and drunk most of the bottle of wine they had picked up at the store to go with – and in – the stew. As a result, this morning they both felt a bit quiet.

'What shall we do today?' asked Kim, trying to cheer things up. 'It isn't raining – we could go into town and do something about cutlery and china and stuff for you? You'll need to get that sorted soon – did you speak to Francis about it?'

'I haven't seen him, have I?' said Diana.

'Yes you have. You saw him that same day, we had supper at Shortlanesend. And you went to Vachells with him on Wednesday too, remember?'

'That was hardly the moment. Neither of them was.'

'You mean, you forgot.'

They glared at each other over the remains of breakfast. Finally, Diana said, 'Well yes, I suppose I did,' and they smiled at each other ruefully instead.

'Well, ask him today,' said Kim.

'If I see him.'

'You will.'

But not any time soon, it appeared. It was almost eleven o'clock before Diana's phone finally rang; she flung aside the magazine she hadn't really been reading and seized it. 'Hello?'

'T-Tamsin! L-l-look, I'm s-s-sorry about yesterday.'

'You didn't do it on purpose,' Diana comforted him. 'I know what it's like, I get them too, sometimes – but are you OK this morning?'

'W-w-wouldn't p-put it that high. B-b-better th-than yesterday anyway, b-but th-that's not hard.'

'Oh, my darling! You poor thing.' She caught Kim's eye, and made a face. 'What are you doing about the keys, then?'

'C-c-collecting th-them, of c-course. At l-least I can s-s-see s-straight th-this morning. W-what are you two p-planning?'

'Well, nothing, until we heard from you. Then we were going to go into town and maybe get some china and stuff for the caravan, at Bordens. If it needs them?'

There was a short pause, then Francis said, 'G-g-good thinking. I n-n-never g-g-gave that a th-thought.'

'So it doesn't come fully equipped?'

'N-n-no idea, b-but I shouldn't th-think so. I can ch-check. L-l-look, how about I meet you in town, and t-t-tell you then?'

'Sounds like a plan. Where, and when?'

'How about B-bordens, about half-past t-t-twelve?'

'Fine. We can have lunch.'

'I d-d-don't th-think so, th-thank you. I m-m-might manage coffee.'

'Well, we can have lunch anyway. After you've gone.'

'G-good idea. S-s-see you then.' He rang off, and Diana switched her phone off and looked at Kim.

'He sounds a wreck still, poor darling. He's going to meet us for a cup of coffee at half-past twelve, and tell us if we need to buy anything. I just hope the smell of other people's lunches doesn't set him off again.'

'Me too, in that case,' Kim looked at her watch. 'It's after eleven. We might as well go straight in now, and do a recce before we meet up. There's no time to do anything much else in just over an hour, and we've got to get there and park too.'

'Come on then, let's go!' Diana was already on her feet, glad to have something to do that took them out of the house, she was beginning to feel claustrophobic after their long confinement between four walls. Her abandoned magazine slipped onto the floor, and Kim picked it up and straightened the pages. Truth to tell, she was feeling much the same as her twin. They grabbed their coats and bags and went out into the windy sunshine.

By the time they reached the town, it was clouding over again and the wind was picking up. A spatter of rain hit the windscreen as they turned into the Square: there was limited parking right here if you were lucky, to either side of the narrow garden that ran down the centre.

'Keep an eye out for a parking space,' said Diana. 'Close to Borden's would be good – oh look, there's one!' She made a dive for it, just beating a man in a very smart car, who shook his head at her and drove on to continue his search in the adjoining streets where he might be luckier. Considering the weather, there seemed to be a fair number of people about. Kim looked at the trees in the Square, bowing and streaming their leaves in the wind.

'At least Romans won't fall on us,' she said, as they got out of the car, staggering a bit with the force of the wind. It wasn't meant as a joke. 'Looks like another squall is coming in – just look at that sky, black as ink!' They made a mutual dive for the doorway to Bordens and stood in its shelter, looking out.

'Ugh,' said Diana, turning away. 'Let's go and look at saucepans. I suppose we shall need some.'

'You will, when I've finished with you,' Kim told her. 'And we'll do the supermarket on our way home, too, and get some more stuff for you to practice on. And an exercise book so you can write everything down, and do it again when I'm not there.'

'You haven't got long to teach me in,' said Diana, as they headed for the china and cutlery department. 'I don't know exactly when the caravan thing is being delivered, but it can't be long now. Have you thought what you'll do when I move out? It'll be a bit lonely on your own.'

'I thought I'd go to the University and see if they have any classes or something that I could sign up for. Or maybe, even a job I could do. After all, I'm pretty well qualified in my own field.'

'You and Francis both,' said Diana, making a face. 'I feel a real waste of space around the pair of you!'

'You won't, once you both get things sorted out. He's got horses, hasn't he? Someone'll have to look after them, you know how to do that.'

'Hardly rocket science though, is it?'

'You never wanted to do rocket science anyway, did you? Unlike the Carruthers idiot. And anyway, I couldn't do it, wouldn't know where to begin, I like riding them, is all and not that great at that. Don't undervalue yourself – he doesn't.'

'He has very high standards for himself,' said Diana, and added thoughtfully, 'I just hope I can live up to them.'

'You will. Now, concentrate! You need saucepans, here they are. How many do you think you'll need?'

'It's more, how many do you think I'll need. Even more, how many do you think can be fitted into a caravan? If it is a caravan…I'm still not sure. It seems to grow and shrink depending on who's talking about it.'

Kim ignored this, she had nothing to add anyway. She picked up a saucepan.

'Question two. Are you going to leave them for the farm manager, or whatever, or take them into the house with you?'

This time, Diana did pause to consider the question. She said, 'Leave them? Of course, if they're moving down here permanently, as I think Francis said they were, they'll have their own…oh Kim, it's all too complicated! The storm seems to have got into my brain.'

'If they have their own stuff, it'll probably be in store,' said Kim, more practically. 'So, reckon you'll leave them, I would. And the plates. Start again when you have somewhere more civilised to live.' She put down the pan she was holding and picked up another. 'These are good quality, but not top of the range. How about three sizes of these? And you'll need a colander—' Diana just stopped herself from asking "What for?" Instead, she said, 'However much cooking do you think I'm going to do?'

'Even basic meals need at least two,' Kim told her.

'Fried egg sandwiches don't.' Diana finally began to show a proper interest. 'Here's a nice frying pan – not too big, not too small.' She picked it up and waved it at Kim. 'Then all we need is a bread knife, and we're sorted!' Kim took it from her and studied the base.

'Good choice. We'll put it back for now, and come and do the job properly after lunch. Then we can put it straight in the car.' Suiting the action to the word, she moved on to the next section. 'Now, cutlery. It wants to be at least half-decent, good stainless steel…' They continued through the department, Kim pointing out various cooking implements that Diana simply stared at blankly, and ended up in the china department. Here, Diana surprised her twin by taking an intelligent interest.

'I don't think we need to have actual china in the van,' she said. 'You can get that hard plastic stuff, that almost is china, Daddy and Eloise use it on the boat for every day. Then we can leave that too. It's pretty, and you can put it in the washing-up machine.'

'I doubt if you'll have one of those,' said Kim, grinning. She thought for a minute. 'But you can probably fit in an electric kettle and a toaster, you'll be needing that, and maybe a food processor. You will have electricity?' She made it into a question.

'So I'm told. And something called a generator to run it when the power is off in the house – as it will be.'

Kim thought it all sounded rather a steep learning curve for her undomesticated twin, but it probably would do her no harm! She said, 'We'll deal with that after lunch, then, it's a different department. Now we'd better go on up, or he'll be here before us.'

'That'll be a first,' Diana muttered, as they headed for the stairs.

It wasn't to be, however; the age of miracles had not returned and there was no sign of Francis when they reached the restaurant on the top floor. They bought two glasses of orange juice to be going on with, found a table, and sat down to wait for him. Outside, the rain had begun to pound down like a waterfall, rattling on the roof garden where they had sat out to eat lunch in the summer. Nobody would do that now, Diana remarked, watching spray leaping out of puddles and the remaining shrubs flattening to the wind – gale, rather, she found herself thinking, and heard herself say, almost as an echo, 'Perhaps he's got blown away.'

'He hasn't,' said Kim, who was facing the opposite way She took a second look and added, 'not quite. He must have got inside just as the heavens opened,' and Diana quickly turned towards the restaurant entrance. Francis had just come in; he spotted them at once – the restaurant was not crowded this morning – and headed across to them. "Dishevelled" would be a good description, Diana decided, and then took a second look.

'God, the poor man looks a wreck!' she said, concern in her voice, but before Kim could say anything in return, he was with them, pulling out a chair to sit down and flopping into it. He hadn't paused to collect any coffee and seemed relieved to be sitting down.

'W-w-what b-bloody weather,' he said. He ran his hands over his wild and wet hair, trying to get it out of his eyes, not altogether successfully. Diana passed him a paper napkin from the table.

'Blot yourself dry with that,' she said. 'I take it, you got caught just as the heavens opened?' She studied his face as he followed her advice, and Kim passed him a second napkin; one was going to be a bit inadequate. He looked, not just wet and tired, but ill, she thought, and caught Diana's eye. He scrumpled the damp paper into a ball and set it carefully on the table.

'Th-thanks. N-now, shall w-w-we start again?'

'You look awful,' said Diana, before she could stop herself. 'Are you sure you're OK?'

'C-c-compared to yesterd-day, yes. It's j-j-just a headache n-now.' He would have dismissed it then, but Kim, after taking a careful look, said, 'We were going to ask you to come to us for a meal tonight, Val will be here by then, but perhaps we should leave it a day.'

'I'll b-be OK t-t-tomorrow. T-today I j-just plan on an early n-night. V-very early.'

Diana said, 'Should you be driving? You look wrecked.'

'S-so you already said.' He made a face at her. 'G-give it a rest, T-Tamsin. I'll live.' He felt in the pocket of his jacket, and pulled out a handful of assorted keys, which he sorted through quickly, placing a small bunch on the table and putting the rest back where they came from. He picked up the small bunch and held it out to Diana. 'Yours. You'll be n-n-needing them.'

Diana took them as if she had been handed the crown jewels, Kim thought, watching. She held them in her hands and sorted through them: one Yale key, one ordinary one, one bigger one, and a fourth one that looked as if it came from a padlock. And a key ring with a small brown and white cow attached to it by a short chain.

Francis, too, was watching her. He said, 'The t-two smaller ones are for the n-new locks for th-the front d-d-door, and the b-b-back into the v-v-vegetable garden. Th-the big one is the d-d-door into the yard, w-which is how we get in f-f-for now, and the other is f-f-for the p–padlock on the garden g-g-gate. The key r-ring is a p-p-present from B-bennie.'

Diana held them against her as if they were immeasurably precious. She said, in a wondering voice, 'I can't believe this is really happening!'

'W-well, it is.' He was smiling at last. 'Y-you can t-t-take Kim out and show her round, b-b-but I w-wouldn't do it today if I w-w-was you. Th-this weather is g-g-going to be even w-w-worse l-l-later this afternoon.'

'We'll do it tomorrow then. Val can come too!'

'G-g-good.' He began to get to his feet. 'I'll s-s-see you out th-there, I d-daresay. N-now I'm g-g-going home, if you'll excuse me.'

'And if you feel better, you can come to dinner tomorrow instead,' said Kim. She added, 'Diana made a stew. We'll save it for you and get fish and chips tonight.'

'G-good God!' He paused in surprise, his hand on the back of the chair, and Diana remembered what she had to ask, just in time.

'Did you speak to the caravan people?'

'Oh – yes, I d-d-did. Th-they s-s-said they'd s-s-supply stuff if w-we wanted, b-b-but I said we'd get our own. N-now I'm r-r-really going, before the s-s-smell of food gets to me and I disgrace myself—' He stooped to give her a swift kiss. 'And d-d-don't hang around – g-g-get yourselves home ASAP.'

'And you go carefully too,' said Diana.

'I sh-shall. I can't r-risk m-missing that s-stew.'

They watched him make his way back across the restaurant. Kim, said, critically, 'Even saying the word "stew" nearly made him throw up. I hope he will be better tomorrow. He'd probably have done better to stay at home and leave the keys until then.'

'I think it's just the tail-end of the migraine. And the weather isn't helping, but probably you're right, he should have stayed at home.' She looked down at the keys, still in her hand, closing her fingers round them possessively. 'I'm glad he didn't, though.'

A heavy gust hit the window at their side and made it rattle. Kim said, 'You know what, I think he was right. I think we should do what we have to do here, go home via the supermarket and stock up, and then go straight home and barricade ourselves in. We can get a sandwich or something with the shopping, and have a late lunch when we get back safely. I don't think I could enjoy food here, with that lot blowing up outside.'

'Right then, I think you could be right. Saucepans, here we come!' Diana finished her juice and got to her feet, Kim did the same. They made their way back to the household department.

'Get six of everything, until you know how things are going to go – you can always add to it later if you throw parties,' said Kim, so they did that.

'But proper china mugs,' said Diana, and they did that too, buying a set of good-sized ones with various farm animals on them, including one with cows. Black and white ones. 'But I expect he'll forgive me,' said Diana. 'At least it's the right sort of dog on that one. And we'll need some glasses – wine, beer, water—'

'Why don't you just buy the shop? It's a good thing you're marrying a multi-millionaire!'

Cutlery followed, pots and pans, kitchen tools, some of which Diana looked at it in blank bewilderment, then a quick sortie into the electrical department for a food mixer, a kettle, a toaster and a small microwave, which Diana added as an afterthought, saying ominously, 'You never know. We may be reduced to ready meals now and then, we can't live on stew.'

'Just hope there's somewhere to put it all,' said Kim. An assistant was deputed to help them carry it all down to the entrance, and Diana brought the car round and it was all loaded into the boot.

'Setting up home, are you?' the assistant asked, and Diana said with a big smile, 'Yes!'

As they finally drove off into the rising storm, she heaved a sigh of deep satisfaction.

'Now, I really feel as if it's going to happen!' She shot a quick glance at Kim, sitting beside her. 'Your turn next – but you'll have Val to help you, lucky you!'

'Good thing, it sounds as if you're going to be too busy quite soon anyway,' said Kim, with a grin.

'For what use I would be – you did most of it today, I just paid the bill.'

'I shall have Valerie too,' Kim added, 'and Penny, no doubt. And we must remember to get you an exercise book when we're in the supermarket. And maybe a simple cookery book for idiots. If they have such a thing.'

'We'll never get everything into the car,' said Diana, happily.

'We'll never get everything into the house!'

'We can stuff it all behind the sofa. It's only for a few days,'

'We've come a long way together, since that night on the doorstep in the fog,' said Kim, thinking, and Diana said, 'Yes.'

'We'll need to stock up your store cupboard, too, before you move over there,' said Kim, in the supermarket. 'Probably not today, though – the poor little car will collapse.'

'When we can take the stuff straight over there would be favourite,' suggested Diana, on a singing note that made Kim smile for her. She paused in front of the sandwich section. 'Bacon and egg, or cheese and tomato? We could get a little pot of soup to go with it.'

'And some doughnuts. Let's push the boat out! I feel like celebrating.'

'Lucky you didn't say "doughnuts" in front of your man,' said Kim, giggling, although it hadn't really been that funny, it was just the mood they were both in. Like a cat, with the wind up its tail, she thought, totally mad. Life was coming together, and it looked good! She could feel the change like the roaring wind outside, and her spirits were rising to greet it.

They left the supermarket well loaded again, but not so badly as the first time, stuffed their final purchases hurriedly onto the back seat since there was nowhere else left, and took off again into the storm, headed this time for home and unloading. There was a rift in the clouds, Kim said, pointing it out. Maybe it wouldn't actually be raining as they put everything into the house, with a bit of luck, and 'I don't care,' said Diana. She could feel the force of the wind against the car as they went along; Francis had been right when he said it was a bad day for house-viewing. But tomorrow – tomorrow her new life would begin properly!

Which the following day, it did. Val had rung the evening before to say that he was staying in London overnight, rather than driving down in the huge autumn gale with heavy rain on the side that was sweeping the country, and would be with them for breakfast, all being well, and true to his word, turned up on the doorstep while Diana was still in the shower. It was a better day, the wind, which had roared for half the night, had dropped considerably and there were rifts of blue in the cloudy sky. The first thing he noticed, after he had greeted Kim suitably, was the pile of bags and boxes behind the sofa. He raised his eyebrows.

'Been shopping?'

'Just some stuff for Diana's new home,' said Kim, following the direction of his eyes. 'It'll be gone by the end of the week, hopefully.'

'Diana too?' He rested his hands on her shoulders, re-directing his gaze to her face. 'You'll be lonely, my Kim. Have you thought about coming up to London to be with me? Just until we know what's happening.'

'I'd still be lonely there, with you at work all day,' Kim pointed out. 'And I'd have no friends there, so I'd be even lonelier – I do have some here by this time. No, I thought I'd try and sort out my own life a bit – since hopefully, we shall be living here eventually.'

'There's no guarantee.'

They were both silent for a moment, thinking about this. Finally, Kim said, 'It isn't easy, is it?'

'But worth it.' He heard the catch on the bathroom door draw back, and kissed her quickly before Diana emerged. 'Didn't you say something about breakfast when I rang last night?'

'It's all ready to go.' Kim turned for the kitchen, meeting her twin in the doorway. 'Look who's here – I'm just going to start breakfast, get dressed and you can come and cook the bacon and eggs.'

'Is that safe?' Val asked, and Diana drew herself up, pulling her dressing gown close about her as she did so to add dignity.

'I've made a stew,' she said.

'Not for breakfast, I hope!'

'Don't worry,' Kim told him, as Diana vanished up the stairs. 'She can fry an egg with anyone, and bacon's not that different. I'm giving her a crash course, so that poor Francis won't starve – or become permanently eggbound.'

'Good point. He's not a man who's had many close encounters with a saucepan himself, I'd say. What was the stew like?'

'We haven't eaten it yet. We're having it for dinner tonight, the four of us – that is, if Francis is fit for it. He certainly wasn't yesterday, just saying the word "stew" nearly precipitated a public incident.'

'I was planning to take you out somewhere.' Val looked disappointed.

'Do that tomorrow, we can have lunch somewhere. We can't keep it in the fridge for ever, and actually, it's too good to waste, I stood over her while she made it. And we need to celebrate their new home, it really is theirs now. Diana is taking us over to see it this morning, if that's OK with you? I'm assuming, in this wind there's no racing?'

'I shall be interested,' said Val. He laughed. 'The fame of that place spread all over the village, or should I say "infamy"? We can drop my bag off at home as we go.'

'You're not staying the night here?' Kim was disappointed.

'I don't think so.' He sounded regretful. 'It was one thing at the cottage, when I was serving a useful purpose keeping off the marauders, but here it seems just a bit unfair on Diana. Next weekend, it will be different. We'll have the place to ourselves, and can concentrate on our own affairs.'

'I expect you're right,' said Kim reluctantly, after a moment's thought. She picked up a couple of slices of bread to put in the toaster.

'Has Francis been ill, then?' Val asked, belatedly.

'The storm gave him a migraine. He said he'd most likely be out at the farm this morning though, so here's hoping he's feeling a bit better – although we had another snorter of a storm in the night, as you know, so who knows?'

'Great – maybe we could all go down to the Club lunchtime and have a drink.'

'He wouldn't go,' said Kim. She was about to add, 'What do you know about Max Carruthers?' when she heard Diana on the stairs, and got no further than 'What—'

'I'll ask you later,' she said hurriedly.

Diana had no problems with the bacon, naturally enough as, if she was honest, she had – only very slightly – exaggerated her lack of expertise in the kitchen and could handle the simple stuff. Stew had been a new venture but she could, she now confessed, grill a chop without accident, and even heat up frozen vegetables. She had, after all, shared a flat with two equally inexperienced cooks, and they couldn't live exclusively on takeaways. Just mostly.

'Although Jo could make a good lasagne,' she told them, with a touch of awe.

'So will you, by the end of the week,' Kim told her firmly. 'A better one.'

'Francis keeps cows. Better brush up on rare rump steak, with proper chips and real vegetables,' Val told her, grinning. 'He doesn't look as if he's ever seen a frozen one – of any of it. And you won't get away with cheese and biscuits every night, it's cheating.'

'I'm teaching her how to make apple crumble this afternoon,' Kim told him. 'We're having it for dinner, after the stew. You can watch, you might learn something too. But we did buy the custard, as it's better than the stuff you used to make.'

'Not me,' Val told her. 'I never made custard in my life!'

'And Bennie said she'd send cream with Francis,' Diana added. 'I spoke to her last night – I rang to see how he was, but he had already gone to bed, she said.'

They cleared away the breakfast things, and then Val looked at his watch.

'It's nearly ten o'clock. If we're stopping at my parents' place on the way, we ought to get going if you've finished this surge of domesticity. You'll want to get back for your next cookery lesson, Diana!' He added, 'And don't take all day to get organised, either, I know you two! Getting you rounded up to go anywhere is like herding cats!'

'Oh, we don't need to dress up for where we're going this morning,' Diana told him, and Kim added, 'I can't wait to see it.'

'Believe me, you'll wish you had waited,' Diana told her.

They packed themselves into Val's car and drove out to Shearwater, and when they arrived at Val's parents' house, Valerie rather agreed with Diana.

'You need to wear protective clothing out at that place, from what I've heard!' she said darkly. 'And don't nibble any tasty-looking leaves – you never know what they might be!'

'They're not rabbits,' Val objected.

'I'm just saying. Will you be here for lunch? I expect I can rustle up something.'

'Don't know – we might go to the Ravenscourt Arms. We'll very likely have Francis with us.'

'He doesn't bite, that I ever heard,' said Valerie, smiling. 'All right then, do we see you this evening?'

'Diana's made a stew,' said Val. 'I'll be in later on, and tell you all about it.'

'The stew, or the farm?' asked Kim.

'Both,' said Val.

'We might have to do Sunday lunch tomorrow,' said Val to Kim, as they went back out to the car. 'I see little enough of them as it is, and fair's fair.'

'I can live with that. I expect Diana will be invited to Shortlanesend anyway, it seems to be the pattern these days.'

'Well, you are separate people, with separate lives,' Val pointed out.

'I know – it's just that this twin thing is still new to us.'

Diana was already in the back of the car, impatient to be on their way. Val opened the front door for Kim and went round to the driver's side.

'Here we go then,' he said, 'into the unknown!' and set the car in motion.

The lane up to the house looked even worse than it had the first time Diana had seen it; the gale had decimated the surrounding field hedges and woodland, and small branches and leaves lay all over the already muddy surface; they crunched over them carefully, emerging finally in the parking space outside the house, and Diana took out her key to the yard door as they climbed out, in case they needed it later.

'Let's just check if Francis is here,' she said, moving to the farmyard gate which, as before, was open while Kim and Val stood taking in the house with bemused expressions. Like the lane, it wasn't looking its best. More tiles had slipped for one thing, and one of the drains was blocked and dripped relentlessly onto the pathway. Judging by the carpet of moss there, it wasn't a new occurrence. Diana came back from the yard gate.

'The Discovery is here, but I can't see him anywhere – or hear him, come to that. He'll turn up when he sees the car, I expect, there's no point looking. He could be anywhere in God knows how many acres. Let's go in.' She led the way to the front door, where Francis had left the big old key in the lock for her, and struggled momentarily with it before pushing the door open with a flourish. 'Welcome to my home!'

Kim and Val stepped in behind her, and stood looking around them.

'My God!' said Val, in wonderment, 'what an amazing house! I can see why he fell for it.'

'I've never seen anything like it,' said New Zealand Kim, which was more ambiguous. She stepped over to the drawing room doorway and peered in. 'There's rats, from the look of it, did you know?'

'They won't be staying,' said Diana. She went to stand beside her twin. 'There's dry rot and woodworm too, to name but a few. And dirt and to spare – as you see.'

Val was walking round the hall panelling, scraping with a finger here and there and then wiping it fastidiously on his handkerchief. 'Did they ever clean it, do you think? The hippies, or whatever they were?'

'The evidence is against it.' Diana went to the back of the hall and drew back the bolt to open the door that she had not previously been shown behind. She could immediately see why; it smelt appalling; the smell seemed to emanate from the narrow door to the right of the small passageway, which presumably was the downstairs lavatory. She didn't investigate. Another door, to the left under the stairs, also presumably gave access to the cellar, she decided to leave that alone too, although Val did open it and peer downwards.

'Needs a torch,' he said. 'Let's leave that, I don't want to break my neck – or yours.'

Kim emerged from the drawing room as they stepped back into the entrance hall.

'The fireplace is beautiful – huge! You'll need half a tree to keep it warm in there. And I love the windows, all those little panes.'

'Some of them are broken,' said Val, critically. 'That'll be a right jigsaw of a job for someone!'

'Come upstairs,' said Diana. 'The bathroom will amaze you.'

'I am already amazed,' said Val, picking his way carefully round the debris on the floor.

They did a tour of the upstairs, and Diana outlined her plan for the two bedrooms to the right of the landing. 'But we need planning permission, Francis said, because of the listing. He's getting an architect in to look at it this coming week. That'll be interesting.'

Downstairs again, she-re-locked the big front door and slipped the big key into her pocket, and then paused at the door of the dining-room.

'I've been thinking,' she said. 'You can see yourselves that this isn't all going to be done any time soon, even when it's been cleaned properly – and that isn't going to be done in a day, even I can see that. I'll run what I think past you as we go, if you don't mind, and see what you think. Starting here.' She pushed the door open and led the way inside. Val and Kim followed, exchanging speaking looks and wondering what was coming now.

'This is quite a big room, as you can see,' said Diana, sounding, even to herself, a bit like a tour guide. 'That door at the back leads into a smaller one, that could be used as a study for Francis, with a bit of TLC, it looks out over the vegetable patch at the back, but he must be used to looking at vegetables in his job. Not,' she added honestly, 'that's there more than weeds and cabbage trees there at present – or they might be sprouts, come to think. But there will be.' She took a breath. 'Bright idea number one. I thought that, to start with, once it's all cleaned up we could leave the other side of the hall and the rooms above it until we know what we can legitimately do with it all, and concentrate on this side for now, make it fit to live in so that we can come in out of the cold. Do the bathroom, sort out a bedroom to sleep in, stuff like that, and turn this room, into a living room, it's plenty big enough. Maybe even keep it that way for everyday, that room on the other side is huge!'

'Plenty big enough for the grand piano,' Kim agreed, although she only half-believed in the instrument, never having seen it.

'The what?' asked Val, but Diana was still airing her ideas.

'We could put a wood burner into that fireplace – we won't need a huge fire when we've got some storage heaters in, which is probably what it will have to be, and there's plenty of wood around. There's room by the window for a table and chairs for posh occasions, but mostly, I thought we'd eat in here—' She pushed the kitchen door open. 'Just look at this!'

Kim and Val looked. Both of them were thinking that this was a cook's kitchen, or could be with a bit – well, a lot – of restoration, and wondered what on earth undomesticated Diana had in mind for it. She stepped into the middle of the floor, and with consummate showmanship, let them know.

'This could be great – first of all, we need to unblock that fireplace—' she gestured towards the one at the far end, '—and put an Aga into it – Bennie has one, she'll show me how to use it – and some decent cupboards beside it – we may need to search the reclamation yards for something suitable, we can't use modern stuff of course. And up by the other fireplace—' she turned, with a wide gesture of her arms, 'a long refectory-style table that we can all eat off for working lunches and big family dinner parties and things, and some good sturdy chairs to go with it, fire dogs and a decent hearth for a fire when it's cold, maybe even a few horse brasses – they'd be in period, even if it did look a bit like a historic pub – in its heyday, it probably pretty much was one!' She paused for breath, smiling at them. 'We might even have a pair of Staffordshire dogs on that beam.'

Val took a breath of his own, to say that he was startled would be an understatement.

'Well Diana, I can only say, you've surprised me! You've really thought this out, haven't you?'

'Of course. Nobody else is going to – Francis will be too busy with the outside for a while yet, you haven't seen it! Probably take a hundred years, it looks as if it's been running downhill for about that!'

'It'll be great when it's all done,' said Kim, looking around her and trying to visualise it, 'but I'm glad it isn't my job to organise it!'

'Oh, I shall simply be the demanding client – the builders will do the hard work. And you haven't seen it all yet!' She turned towards the passage door. 'Come and look at this.'

'You mean, there's more?' asked Val. They followed her through into the passage that led to the yard, and Diana stopped by the first door.

'You'll probably think I'm mad, but I'm going to run it past you anyway. I think we should start with the renovations right here.' She turned to Kim. 'It was something you said yesterday – about laying in some stores. You see, in a caravan you usually spend holidays – you bring what you need for a week, maybe two, you eat out, you picnic on the beach – you don't need a stockpile. There isn't the space, because it would never be needed. But we shall be living in it. And I know people do, but this is a farm. There'll be more than a can or two of beans on the shelf once it gets under way – I've seen Shortlanesend, I get the idea. We'll need a big fridge and an even bigger freezer, just for starters.' She pushed open the door beside her. 'This is the larder, you can see it will give plenty of space for tinned goods and jam and stuff on the shelves—'

'—you plan to make jam?' interrupted Val, in amazement.

'Somebody will have to,' said Diana, smiling at him. 'There's fruit bushes in the back garden, and an orchard somewhere too – we can't waste it. I understand there will be help with that side of things, but it will still have to be stored.'

'God in heaven!' said Val, staring at her. 'What's got into you?'

'Come on,' said Diana, smiling at him mischievously. She stepped back into the passage, pulling the door to behind her, and opened the next one. 'We can put the fridge and the freezers in here, there's plenty of room for good-sized ones – and in here—' she went to the next door, '—we can put a washing machine and a tumble dryer, and there's a sink too, as you can see, and by some miracle, it isn't cracked.'

'You said, you thought you ought to start here,' said Kim; for once, her twin's thinking had left her behind. 'Why here?'

'Because,' said Diana, as one addressing an idiot, 'we shall be living here, in that caravan or whatever-it-is. We shan't be on a proper site, with facilities, and we can't cart all the washing back and forth to Shortlanesend, although Bennie did say we could. We shall need to store food, there's no campsite shop. We shall be producing food, when the place gets under way.' She pointed to the door at the end of the passage. 'That leads into the farm office. That will have to be set up PDQ, and it'll be a whole lot easier all round if it's decorated and clean first. And there's more.' She led the way to the office door and the turning to the yard entrance. 'There's this, too!' She flung open the door to the washroom. 'If this is put in order first off, we shan't need to use the caravan facilities in the daytime, and once the place is re-wired we shall have hot water on tap, too. I think there may even be room, if we move the sink, to put in a shower – it won't be a big one, but it'll be a whole lot better than trying to fit Francis into the one in a caravan. Particularly after a day among the cows…' She stood back, smiling. 'So, what do you think?'

'You mean,' said Val, thinking it out, 'you think you ought to put the engine in order before you start running the ship?'

'Something like that. Yes.'

'Well, you have surprised me!' said Val. 'And here was me, thinking I'd cornered the brains of the partnership.'

'Not sure if we thank you for that, or kick you in the teeth,' Kim told him. She looked at her twin. 'What does Francis have to say to it all?'

'I haven't had a chance to run it past him. I only thought of most of it while I was lying in bed last night.' She looked at them, her head on one side. 'So, you think it's a plan?'

'It's practical,' said Val, approvingly. 'Getting one half of the house done first, so you can live in it, sounds good to me – if it's possible. You'll have to have it all rewired first, presumably.'

'And the rest. Rot, rats and rain come into the equation, too. I'll have to talk with the builder on Monday, when he comes. But yes, that's what I thought. I don't particularly look forward to spending January and February in a caravan out at the end of nowhere, to be honest. We may have to put up with December.'

'You'll have your love to keep you warm,' Val consoled her. 'Come to that, where is he? You say he's here, let's go and find him, and he can show me the rest of this nightmare. I'm assuming outside is no better?'

'Worse, if anything.' Diana unlocked the back door and held it open. 'Pass, friends, and mind the dungheap!'

Once outside, there was again no sign of Francis, although the Discovery was still parked by the barn. They were standing there, wondering where to start looking, when a loud crash and a yell came from the direction of the stable yard, followed by laughter. At least two people were there, so they headed that way. If Francis wasn't one of them, at least they might know where he was.

He was one of them, although they needed to look twice; overalls, heavy working boots, and a knitted hat pulled down over his thick and wayward hair made an unfamiliar picture. His companion, a young man with the same familiar dark hair and strong, Mediterranean features, was similarly clad but without the knitted hat; he had shorter hair. Both of them were filthy. A collapsed pile of rotten wood at their feet explained the crash and the shouting, they appeared to have pulled down the framework of one of the stable doors, whether accidentally or on purpose remained a question; either way, it looked as if it hadn't been difficult. A big skip stood in the yard behind them, with the now familiar Fancot Demolition logo. The younger man spotted them first.

'Goodness, human beings!' he exclaimed, and Francis turned round and saw them too. He and Diana walked straight towards each other without words, and he gathered her into his arms.'

'I'm f-f-filthy,' he apologised, unnecessarily; it was obvious.

'Did you mean to do that?' Diana asked, indicating the woodpile.

'N-n-not quite s-s-so ab-bruptly, no.' He turned to the others, his arm still round her shoulders. 'Hello K-Kim, V-V-Val. N-no r-r-racing this morning?'

'Cancelled. Too much wind still, so we came with Diana to have a look at your new desirable residence. Bit of a car-crash, isn't it?' Val looked about him in amazement. 'You are one brave man to take this on, Mr Chillingworth!'

'You c-c-could say that.' He made a rueful face. 'Or an idiot. Oh – th-this is m–my cousin, M-Matt. He's g-g-giving me a hand over th-the w-w-weekend.'

'Tidying up the stable,' Matt explained, unnecessarily. 'He wants to put horses in it, or chickens, or something.' He was grinning, obviously having a good time.

'Funny way to set about it,' said Val, and they all laughed.

'We were going down to the pub for some lunch,' said Kim. 'Can you knock off for an hour and come with us? Matt too, of course.'

Francis and Matt looked simultaneously at their extremely grubby hands.

'Th–they'd throw us out,' said Francis.

'You could wash. There seems to be plenty of water about.'

'My mum gave me a flask and some sarnies,' said Matt. 'Tell you what, you lot go and I'll eat mine out here in the sunshine and then get this lot into the skip.' He gestured at the heap on the ground. 'Got to earn my keep somehow. You can wash properly in the gents,' he added, to Francis. 'They got hot water and soap down there. But get those overalls off before you go. You look like a navvy.'

'And the boots, would be good,' said Kim, looking at them. 'They'd never call you "posh" again down at the Club, if they could see you now.' She immediately wished that she hadn't said that, but Francis just laughed.

'I can k-kick 'em off in the p-porch,' he said. 'OK th-then, w-w-we've earned a break. You sure you w-w-won't come, Matt?' But Matt wouldn't be persuaded, he said his sandwiches would suit him fine. Francis dumped the knitted hat and the overalls in the stable, revealing slightly more respectable jeans and a sweatshirt, and the four of them left Matt to it and took themselves to the pub in Val's car.

It had been a strange morning, Diana thought, as they sat, drinks in hand, waiting for lunch to arrive. Without the agent there, the house had felt completely different, as if it was their own – well, it was their own, of course, but she knew what she meant even if nobody else would. It was their responsibility to bring it back to the lovely old farmhouse that it should be, and now she had laid out her plans in front of Kim and Val, she could feel her enthusiasm for the task growing. It would work beautifully, she would see to the inside, Francis would see to the outside, and between them they would create a miracle. Val had been quite impressed with her programme, which was flattering since she had never done anything like it before and was planning mainly by common sense and instinct. She had never suspected herself of having common sense.

'You're very quiet,' said Kim, in her ear. She had a good idea what Diana would be thinking, and in a way, she envied her. The bungalow that she would share with Val was lovely, of course, and right down by the sea, but Burnthouse…it had a feel to it. Very old. Interesting. Things had happened there, they would again.

'I just feel…well, at peace,' said Diana. 'Yes, it's going to be hard work, harder work than I've ever done, in fact, but it's going to be such fun.' She added, 'He was right, he looks completely better this morning, doesn't he?'

Kim felt that Francis, much like Diana, was lit up by the anticipation of what was to come now the place was really his. He was like a flame, talking to Val and laying out his own plans for the place, burning full of energy, yesterday not even a memory. He was as different from the man they had known at the Sailing Club as it was possible to be, she wondered what Max Carruthers would make of him now.

Formidable…the word came into her mind and was gone again. She turned her attention back to Diana.

XIX

Val didn't hang around for the cookery lesson: after dropping Francis back to the farm and being given a whistle-stop tour of the continuing disaster that was the Burnthouse farmyard, he drove the twins back to Romans and announced that he thought that, while they were busy, he would just slip down to the Club and check that his precious Moonraker was all right after all the storms they had just had, which the twins correctly translated as ducking out from domesticity to have a quick drink with his mates before the bar closed. Which, said Kim, when he had driven off, was fair enough. Watching someone peeling Bramleys, even if it was a ham-fisted amateur like Diana, wasn't greatly entertaining, and he had been at work up in town all week after all.

'We'll probably do better without him,' was her verdict. 'Anyway, he needs to get over the dungheap!'

'What on earth are you going to do with all that?' he had asked, in horror at the sheer size of it, and, 'Spread it on the f-fields,' Francis had answered, and Val had said that he was glad he wasn't a farmer, and headed as quickly as was polite back to the car and escape.

'He wasn't impressed, was he?' Diana asked now, grinning at the memory, and Kim tolerantly excused him, saying, 'Well, he's a white-collar worker, bless him. What do you expect?' She paused, the potato peeler poised over the first apple. 'Which would you sooner have?'

'The muck-spreader, obviously,' said Diana.

'So we aren't completely identical,' said Kim, setting blade to peel. 'I'm rather glad actually – sometimes, I feel as if I'm losing my individual identity- I suppose we came to this twin thing a bit late in the day. It takes some getting used to.'

'I know exactly what you mean,' said Diana, considering. Then she gave a smothered giggle. 'But we both settled for tall, dark and handsome, didn't we? Come to that, they both have a connection to finance and mathematics. Ugh! What came over us?' Kim smothered a laugh at her expression.

'And has your model remembered that he's expected for a meal this evening?'

'Who knows? But probably – he may not be on time, of course, he's going to need a pretty thorough scrub after all that!'

'That's very true – for what sort of an excuse that is. There's a song – I forget who sings it, but it goes "Love isn't always on time…" It could have been written for Francis!'

Val, meanwhile, had headed down to the Club, where he found several kindred spirits, ostensibly on the same mission but also with one eye on the bar, and had found himself caught in a situation which he might have expected, but hadn't.

The news of Diana's engagement to Francis had, of course, been announced in a couple of the more upmarket newspapers that listed such things and had been showcased in a posh society magazine as well, and Merlin Ravenscourt knew of it because he had spoken to Francis recently, which most people hadn't. Perhaps unfortunately, but probably inevitably, Max Carruthers' mother had heard Bennie Vachell congratulating Mary Vachell-Chillingworth on the unexpected good news at an Autumn Market in aid of some charity, at which they had all three been present. Jenny had naturally passed the news on to her son, with suitable comments, and Max had spread it around at the Club among his close associates, with his personal spin on it. Val walked, unprepared, into the fallout. The reactions were mixed, showing more clearly than he had realised that the members were divided into two, albeit unequal, camps on the subject of Francis and of his position in relation to the Committee and their well publicised request for his resignation. Perhaps for the first time, he found himself wondering how that request had become common knowledge. It shouldn't have done so, surely?

He was only a step behind Diana and Kim by this point. That was about to change.

It began quite innocently, when his crew, Rob Lambert said to him, laughing, 'The grapevine has it that you're about to get Francis Chillingworth for a brother-in-law! Is that true?'

'More Kim's brother-in-law,' said Val. 'But yes. That's the general plan.

Obviously we all have to get married first,' and they both laughed, and one or two friends standing near to them smiled too.

Max Carruthers, who was leaning against the bar with a couple of his own friends and hangers-on, overheard this and laughed with them.

'Amazing what women will do if they think there's money around,' he observed. 'I hope she knows what she's taking on.'

'Why, what is she taking on?' Val asked. Closer acquaintance with Francis had made him begin to wonder – about a lot of things, to only some of which had he found an answer. He now understood his reserve towards other people in the past, he didn't quite understand why it still seemed to be in place now. There was nothing to stop Francis coming down to the Club with him and starting again without the understandable reservations, but he didn't, and it had become obvious over the past few weeks that there were some club members who were neither surprised at his absence nor cared about it, rather the reverse. They couldn't possibly know the real reason for his past attitude, so what was their reason?

'Oh, come on Val,' said Max, smiling. 'The Club threw him out. That wasn't over nothing.'

'Actually, we didn't.' Merlin had appeared at Val's shoulder, glass in hand, apparently at ease. 'He's still a member. The Committee have accepted that they asked for his resignation – not on a unanimous vote, I would remind you – on grounds that did not, in fact, exist. Or were any of the Club's business if they had existed, come to that.' He gave Max a cool look. 'You know that, you're on the Committee. Perhaps you should back off a bit?'

'Come on, Merlin!' said Max, as he had said to Val and still with that smile. 'He's sold his boat, he never comes near the place, his mother has thrown him out and he's bought some old wreck of a house in the middle of nowhere which nobody else would touch, and which went for peanuts!'

'You would know all about that, of course,' said Merlin, who did: it had been he who had drawn Francis' attention to Burnthouse in the first place.

'Everybody knows! Without his mother's support, the man's got no money behind him and no standing either! Ask around, why don't you? My mother is a friend of Mary Vachell-Chillingworth, I hear things that seem to have missed you!'

'Oh, I never listen to fairy stories,' said Merlin. 'Outgrew them years back. Where did you pick up this rubbish anyway? His mother never said it. And more, what gives you the right to spread it around for the whole Club to hear? You can get yourself in serious trouble, doing things like that.'

'You can't be penalised for telling the truth.'

'Not sure about that, even if it was true.'

'It's true he was expelled from his Public School,' Max countered.

'No, it's not. That is a misrepresentation of the real truth.'

'How would you know? You lived on the other side of the world at the time and had never even heard of any of us. And – you can't argue with this, because I was a witness – he was also nearly thrown out of Sixth Form for beating up another student, and it was only his mother's influence that saved him! Defend that now, why don't you?'

Val, by this time, had heard all about the return of Kim's passport and the interesting story that had accompanied it, although he had been given no name for the ringleader; he had been identified simply as "another student who had a bit of a grudge". Kim hadn't been ready at that moment to point the finger directly, possibly because she could visualise the uproar it might cause. He thought he might guess the culprit now, however, and took the lead from Merlin. By this time, he realised, the argument was attracting attention, people were beginning to listen: better get this right. How certain was he? Ninety-eight per-cent – worth a shot.

'That's another lie – he wasn't nearly thrown out. I know this story from both sides, and I don't mean from Francis before you jump in, so don't try to pull the wool. He was deliberately provoked – by you, I'm thinking now – and yes, there was a row about it but nobody was threatened with expulsion. The other man started it. He's quite open about it – he started it so that you wouldn't get the chance and cause real trouble, apparently, and the two of them have ended up good friends to this day. So back off, like Merlin told you!'

'Gary Fancot is a good friend of Little Lord Fauntleroy? Pull the other one, it's got bells on!' Max was derisive, although, Val realised, he must have known how the fight ended at the time. He narrowed his eyes a little; this was becoming interesting, and on many fronts. Max met the look impudently – Val chose the word deliberately. Max Carruthers was a bit of a case; he had never noticed that before, although come to that he had never had much to do with him either. Not his first choice for a friend.

'Anyway,' Max went on, 'What makes you so partisan all of a sudden?

Francis Chillingworth was never a friend of yours – of any of us, come to that.'

'He's a friend of mine,' said Merlin, quietly, adding, 'and Bob's. And Julie-Anne's too.'

'And mine,' said Val, 'whatever you choose to think.'

'And mine,' said Rob, who had been listening with interest. It wasn't entirely true, but given a choice between Max and Francis, he would take Francis every time. There was a small, encouraging murmur behind them.

'So you say now,' said Max, ignoring it. 'I didn't see any of you rallying round when the chips went down with the Committee.'

'You just weren't listening,' said Merlin, adding, 'You never do.'

Max shrugged his shoulders. 'Val's bound to stand up for him now, if he's going to marry Diana Carey – if. Her parents might have something to say about that when they hear the truth.'

'They already know more of the truth than you apparently do,' Val told him.

'You don't think his own mother doesn't know it?' asked Max, with a lift of his eyebrows.

'I certainly don't think yours does.'

Max shrugged his shoulders, turning back to his own group, saying, 'Well, don't say I didn't warn you, when the shit hits the fan.'

Val, Merlin and Rob were left looking at each other in slight bewilderment.

'So, what brought that on?' Rob asked, with a shake of his head. 'Oh, I know Francis doesn't mix very easily, but that was real malice! Whatever did he do to deserve it?'

'From what I have observed of Max Carruthers over the years, probably not very much,' said Merlin, with a shrug. 'Quite probably, it was something as simple as pinching his girlfriend when they were at the College together – which I understand he actually did. The cause doesn't matter now, but the continuing effect is slightly disturbing if that was a symptom of it.'

'Oh come on – Francis wouldn't have taken any notice, if that was all it was about. And he definitely did, you know – does even. He hasn't resigned, no, but he doesn't come here any more either. So what's been going on, that none of us seem to have noticed?'

Val hesitated, but it wasn't his secret. He said as much as he felt he could. 'Well, I know Francis a bit better than I did these days. He's sold the Moonraker, yes, but he has plans to get something else. And has plans about what to do when he's got it, too, which don't include this Club. Francis hasn't simply moved out – and by the way, that was by mutual agreement because of changed circumstances and sensible discussion, he wasn't "thrown out" – he's moving on. And good luck to him, I say.'

Merlin looked thoughtful. He said, 'That fits, I suppose. He's certainly changed, these last few weeks. Or perhaps he hasn't. Maybe he was always like that.'

Rob said, forcefully, 'Someone ought to do something about Max Carruthers! He's a pernicious little creep! Why did I never see it before?'

'Because he sells himself well,' Merlin told him, cynically. 'Golden boy, good organiser, sails something safe and slow in the handicap class and wins on handicap – smiling, happy face. Everyone likes old Max. Or perhaps they shouldn't.'

'Going on that performance, they certainly shouldn't! Can't we show him up?'

'Probably not without descending to his level,' said Val. 'Although, I must admit, the idea is tempting.'

'Have another beer – the bar is closing in a minute.' Merlin brought the discussion to an abrupt end, this wasn't the place for it. 'Rob? We can drink to the confusion of our enemies!'

At the other end of the bar, Max Carruthers was laughing at some joke with his friends, tipping his head back with mirth. Val, watching him, felt an unexpected crawling sensation up his spine. He caught Merlin's eye, but Merlin simply shook his head, and said quietly, 'Not now, Val.'

Val wanted to say, "What better time?" but he didn't. He gave himself a mental shake and picked up his beer.

'Well then, here's to us!' he said, and pushed his misgivings out of his mind.

Back at Romans, the crumble was in the oven, and Kim was showing Diana how to create a starter out of what they could find in the store cupboard and the fridge, which, so far as Val could make out, had been tinned tuna chunks, fresh cream and lemons. The result looked interesting; it appeared to have some vegetable content too, possibly spring onions Val decided, peering into the bowl. The good thing about it, in his view, was that Diana didn't have to cook it, although there were disquieting murmurs in the background about Melba toast, he could just imagine what she might do with that!

'Shove it in the fridge for now,' Kim was saying to Diana, when he appeared. 'We'll chop the parsley for the garnish later – we can take a break, and make Val a good strong coffee. I've no doubt he's been hitting the bottle down there with all his mates!'

'Not to any great extent,' said Val. 'The bar was about to close, for one thing, so I hardly need sobering up. But coffee would be good anyway.'

'Then sit down out of the way, and we'll make some. We can have a break too, before we hit the washing-up, and you can tell us what's been going on down there since we last saw them all.'

Diana's got engaged to Francis, that's what's been going on, Val thought, and wondered how much, if anything at all, he should say. In the end he simply said, 'Merlin and Rob and Co. send their congratulations,' and sat himself in an armchair out of harm's way. He hadn't liked the sound of "washing-up".

When they were all sitting down, coffee mugs in front of them on the table, he raised another subject that had occurred to him as he waited. Toothache or headache, small choice in rotten apples.

'When Diana leaves,' he said, 'which will be quite soon, I gather – sometime next week, or early the following week from what Francis was saying – when she goes, your means of transport will go with her. So how are you planning to get around, Kim? You were talking about looking for a proper job, you won't find one to suit your qualifications in Emberton.'

'There's a thing called "the bus",' Kim told him, kindly. 'I don't suppose you remember them from your schooldays as its been so long, but they can be very useful if you haven't a car, you get on at a bus stop, pay the man at the wheel a small sum, and it takes you where you want to go – well, more or less, it does – remember them now?'

'They don't run that frequently from out here in the sticks,' Val argued.

'They get people to work. And to school. Not every one drives their own car, you know.'

'If it comes to that, I can leave the car here,' Diana told him. 'Francis has two of them, for heaven's sake – he can spare me one now and then, I expect.'

'Yes, I can just see you parking that enormous Merc in Embridge Square,' said Val, grinning.

'Don't be such a man,' Diana told him. 'I've driven it before, and I didn't hit anything.'

'In an emergency. And late at night when there's not so much traffic about,' Val reminded her, pushing his luck.

Diana gave him a cold look. She said, 'Do you really want to marry this man, Kim?' and fortunately, they all laughed, Val included.

'Sorry Diana. But face it, it isn't the handiest form of transport in the catalogue, and anyway, it must have cost him a small fortune, he won't want it scrunched in the supermarket car park. You've got to be practical here.'

'A bus is very practical indeed,' said Kim.

'Well, if it comes to it, I suppose. You might be better to look for something secondhand and cheap, just to tide you over.'

'It'd have to be very, very cheap indeed,' Kim told him. 'About ten quid.'

'You could maybe get one of those little moped things?' Diana suggested. Val ignored this.

'I can probably put a bit towards it,' he offered. 'We've got to pay the balance for the house too, of course, quite soon now, and get a bit more furniture, but I could scrape up a small contribution, if that would help.'

'Not a great deal, I don't suppose. No, the bus is fine. When we live in our own house, if we work the same hours we can car-share.'

She was taking it for granted that he would be offered that job with Hetherington Associates, he noticed. He wished he shared her confidence: there was a lot at stake here, and it would be six weeks at least before anything was decided, and no telling which way it would go then. He said, 'Come to that, you could give this place back to Francis's cousin, and go and live with my mum and dad, they'd be up for it. Then you could car-share with Penny until we get things sorted out.'

'She'd be safer on the moped,' Diana told him. 'Don't fuss, Val, people use buses all the time and survive to tell the tale.'

'I don't like to think of her on her own here,' said Val, pushing his luck.

'Hardly on her own,' Diana told him. 'The neighbours are just the other side of that wall.' She gestured towards the fireplace. 'We share a chimney, for heaven's sake! When they turn it up, we can hear their telly.'

Val knew that he was being unreasonable, it must be a side-effect of that disquieting encounter at the Club, but he couldn't let it go.

'That's not the point,' he said, 'and anyway, if they had it that loud, they wouldn't hear if she screamed!'

'Why would I scream?' Kim asked. 'Look, Val, I got myself across the world and all round Europe without needing to scream, or a car, or a man come to that, or anything more than a bus or a train and sometimes my own feet!'

Val gave up, his heart wasn't really in it by this time anyway. He said, 'That's the first I heard they ran a train from New Zealand to Europe,' and laughed.

'That's better,' said Kim. 'Now, are you going to tell us what's upset you? Something certainly has!'

'Nothing has,' Val denied, unconvincingly. He met their twin sceptical gaze and said the first thing that came into his head. 'I just had to get up rather early this morning to get here for breakfast, and I didn't sleep well anyway, not with that storm going on.'

'So now it's our fault,' said Diana, nodding to Kim. 'Come on Val, what's going on? It can't just be the dungheap, although I could see that stopped you in your tracks a bit. You don't have to get up close and personal with it, after all.'

'I just told you. I'm a bit short of sleep.'

Kim began to pull the coffee mugs together. She gathered them into one hand and passed him the remote control for the television with the other.

'Here – there's some nice, soothing football on the telly, you can go to sleep in front of that, then maybe when you wake up you'll sound more like a human being! We're going to wash-up.'

'Have fun,' said Val, with a lazy smile. He switched on the television, and under cover of the football commentary, Kim and Diana repaired to the safety of the kitchen.

'What got into him there?' Kim asked, as she put the mugs onto the draining board with everything else. She turned on the hot tap. 'He was fine this morning. He was fine when he left for the Club, come to that!'

'Something happened down there?' Diana offered.

'Then why didn't he tell us about it?' Kim demanded.

'Perhaps he's saving it until Francis gets here, so he doesn't have to tell us twice?'

'Or perhaps it was about Francis,' said Kim, darkly, and more accurately than she realised.

'I would have thought they had already said everything they had to say about him,' said Diana, on a note of bitterness. She picked up a teatowel.

'Get some water in that sink, let's get this lot out of the way. Then we can sit down, too.'

'What, and watch football? Thanks a bunch!'

'You suggested it.' They both paused there, caught each other's eye, and laughed at the same moment.

'There we go again,' said Kim. 'We really must stop this bickering! He'll tell us in the end, I expect.'

'And if he doesn't, we won't be any worse off.'

Kim plunged her hands into the soapy water and fished out the dishcloth. She gathered up the first pile of cooking implements. 'And when we've done this, we'll see to the Melba toast and the vegetables. Then we can sit down too. The match might be over by then.'

It was a quiet afternoon. Diana and Kim finished up in the kitchen, and Diana successfully made perfect Melba toast although she did peer into the oven rather more often than Kim said was necessary. By the time they had finished clearing up and organised plates and cutlery ready for this evening, the football was over and Val was, as predicted, asleep, so perhaps he really had been tired, Kim thought, but wasn't convinced. The wind had dropped considerably too by four o'clock, but the clouds were gathering ominously outside the windows.

'So, no point even in going for a walk,' said Kim, and Diana agreed. She had considered no such option, but she knew how Kim felt; after the busy morning and the cookery lesson in the early afternoon, the remainder of the afternoon looked very blank and rather boring. Diana threw herself onto the sofa, a bit like a spoilt child denied a treat, Kim thought. She sat down more decorously in the empty armchair.

'So, what do we do?' Diana asked. 'Go to sleep as well?'

Kim reached for the remote and turned off the game show that had followed the football, she wasn't interested in watching grown adults making fools of themselves doing things that nobody in their right mind would normally even consider. She said, 'I don't know. Read a book?'

A spatter of rain, or it might even be hail, against the window echoed Diana's despondency. She knew what her trouble was, of course; she was missing Francis. On a weekend, you expected your partner to be free to spend time with you, not be demolishing rotten stable doors and slinging rubbish about several miles away and in the rain. She said, 'Next time we go to town, we must remember to buy a pack of cards. Or a scrabble board. Or something.' She paused. 'Do you think he'll even remember we invited him to dinner?'

'This weather might remind him,' said Kim, without needing to ask to whom she was referring. It was really hailing now, battering so hard against the window that it woke up Val. He yawned and opened his eyes.

'Sorry, did I go to sleep?'

'Yes. Welcome to this exciting afternoon!' said Diana. He looked at her more carefully.

'Something wrong? Burned the toast, or something?'

'The toast is perfect, thank you,' Diana told him, with dignity. 'I'm not a complete idiot, you know. I can put bread into the oven and take it out again with anyone!'

Val pushed himself upright in his chair, he had slumped a bit in sleep. He said, 'You know what? You need something to do,' and Diana gave him a look that could have shrivelled stone.

'It's Saturday. Saturday is a fun day.'

'You shouldn't have turned off the telly, there's bound to be something on that to keep you entertained.' He reached for the remote, but Kim put her hand firmly over his and stopped him.

'No thank you. How about you tell us what really happened at the Club at lunchtime?'

There was a short, electric silence, broken only by the rattle of hail on the windows. Eventually, Val realised that he had kept silent for too long to be able to deny that anything had happened at all. They were both watching him, waiting for his reply. He chose it carefully, feeling a bit as if he was picking his way through a treacherous bog without a map. He said, 'Oh, there was a bit of an upset with one of the Committee members. He had the wrong end of the stick and seemed to think your engagement might be a mistake, Diana. Merlin trod on him.'

'Well, good for Merlin,' said Kim. 'Are you going to tell us which member of the Committee?'

'Would it do any good, if I did?' Val asked. 'He won't do it again.' Probably won't, he added, in his own head. Or not in front of me or Merlin, anyway. Kim and Diana exchanged looks.

'Shall we guess?' Kim asked.

'You can try if you want, I can't stop you. I don't have to answer, after all.'

'Oh, I think you do,' said Diana. She hesitated, then went on, 'Francis said he was pretty certain who it was who poisoned poor Sacha. He didn't name names, either, but a pharmacist might have access to all kinds of things that us ordinary folk don't, and wouldn't want to either. Like arsenic, for instance. Chemists don't sell it these days, I don't suppose, but a man like that would have contacts. Isn't there a pharmacist on the Committee?'

'There might be,' said Val, disconcerted if he was honest. 'But you can't prove anything, and neither can Francis – which is probably why he didn't say, and why I'm not saying either.'

'But you say there was an incident today, with witnesses. That's not the same thing at all.'

That was true, of course, but Val still didn't want to get too involved. Hopefully, Max Carruthers had read the warning signs and would shut up in future, the last thing the Club wanted or needed was open warfare on such a tender subject and Francis certainly wouldn't welcome it. He said, 'Oh, that was just something and nothing. A bit of spite and petty jealousy, made a bit too obvious. Like I said, we shut him up pretty smartly.'

'But you still aren't telling us who it was,' said Kim.

'No, I don't think so. Least said, soonest mended.'

'You'll run out of platitudes in a minute,' Kim told him.

Silence. Diana made a mental note to have a word with Merlin if opportunity offered. She got to her feet.

'We can't sit here annoying each other for the rest of the afternoon. It's only about four, who's up for a trip to a reclamation yard to look for something that might be useful in my house renovation experiment? I could do with a man's opinion, and there's no way Francis will find time to offer one. That hail is starting to ease off now.'

The change of subject broke the tension, as she had meant it to do. Val stood up too.

'Good idea, There's a big one out at the back of town, that might be a good place to start.' He raised his eyebrows at Kim, who hadn't moved from her seat. 'Coming, Kim?'

Kim felt that they hadn't fully thrashed out the subject of what happened in the Club bar at lunchtime, but she could see she was going to get nothing more out of Val. She stood up too.

'Of course I am – sitting here on my own would be even worse than sitting here with you two!' and fortunately, all three of them smiled.

The trip to the reclamation yard, which was a good one, and extensive, cleared the air as Diana had hoped it would. Val shared her opinion that they were unlikely to find any old cupboards or panelling of the right period, but agreed that it probably wasn't critical. After all, the house must have had some attention in other centuries than the one in which it was built, to keep it running.

'So long as it isn't earlier, I suppose,' he said.

'Unlikely,' said Diana. 'Pre 1400, or whatever, would be dangerously antique! Not that I know anything about it – do you?'

Val shook his head. He admitted, 'Only as common sense applies. You don't want anything blatantly modern either, after that it's a matter of... well, what's available, really, and suitable. I think. There must be an expert somewhere you could consult – your solicitor's wife is a bit of a one for historic buildings, I believe.'

'I don't have a solicitor. Not down here anyway.'

'Francis's, I meant, Jerry Nankervis. The house will be home to both of you if you can stop it falling down first. Presumably similar will apply to the solicitor.'

'Why, is he likely to fall down?' Kim asked, with interest, 'I don't quite see how Diana could stop him—' and Val punched her on the upper arm, quite hard.

'You know what I mean!' He looked at his watch. 'Come on then, girls, if you've seen all you want to we should be getting back – believe it or not, it's heading for six o'clock, and the man will want to close up.'

'No hurry,' the yard owner said, easily. He had been favourably impressed by the amount of notes Diana had taken as the three of them explored round his very varied stock.

We'll be back,' Diana assured him. 'We've got to get back now and cook the dinner, but thank you for your advice and help. I'll try and bring my fiancé next time, he'll have more idea what you're talking about!'

'You think,' said Val, with a grin. 'He didn't have much idea this morning, tearing the place apart!'

'I think that was largely unintentional,' said Diana.

There was no sign of Francis when they got back to Romans, but then, none of them had really expected it, but by the time seven o'clock had passed into memory and there was still no sign, Kim began to worry about the stew, simmering gently in the oven. 'We don't want it to dry up,' she said anxiously, 'Not after all your hard work. You can only keep things warm in the oven for so long.'

'Did you give him a time?' Val asked, but neither of them had. He shook his head at them. 'What organisation! Give him a ring, Diana, see what he's doing – and just hope he's not still demolishing Burnthouse.'

'I could, I suppose,' said Diana. She took out her mobile and looked at it, hesitating. 'I don't want to hound him, poor darling He's got enough wolves on his tail.' She didn't enlarge on that.

'Just ring him,' said Val, 'then we'll all know what we're doing.'

'Oh, all right.' Diana had her hand poised over the phone when it rang anyway. She held it to her ear. 'Hello?' There was a short pause, while a distant voice could be faintly heard, talking, then Diana said, 'Oh my God! What happened? ...oh, my God, how did he manage that?...oh God, Bennie is he OK?' Then a much longer pause, during which Diana winced and made a face and tried, without success, to interject questions. 'Oh, my poor darling,' she said, after what seemed to be quite a long tale, '...no, he needn't do that, I can probably be there before he gets out of the shower, and Val can run him back later on his way home...no, they'll probably be quite glad for half an hour to themselves! Poor Val has had both of us under his feet all day...no, it's stew, we can just turn the oven off and it'll all keep hot. I expect.... yes, that's what Kim said...yes, OK, I'll be with you in twenty minutes or so, and do thank Ernie for the offer – no, I won't.' She switched off the phone and looked at her two companions, waiting expectantly on the sofa.

'Now what's happened?' Val asked, resignedly.

'There was a bit of an accident out at Burnthouse this afternoon, after we left – you saw they were getting all that rubbish out of the stables, and accidentally brought the doorframe down to one of them?'

'Yes. His cousin was going to clear it into the skip.'

'And he did, and when Francis got back they went on clearing out the rubbish, and from what Bennie says, Francis picked up a great load of it and dumped it in the skip, and it slipped and so did he, and one of the pieces of wood was lying in the way with great rusty nails sticking up, one of them went right through his hand.'

Val and Kim both winced, much as she had herself.'

'Ouch,' said Val, in sympathy. 'Is he OK?'

'Obviously not,' said Diana, tartly. Then she relented and went on with the sorry tale. 'Matt has a driving licence, fortunately, although he went there on a motor bike, so he drove the Discovery to A&E, where they did X-rays and things, and by some miracle it had managed to miss anything really important, although there was a lot of blood. So they stitched him up and pumped him full of antibiotics and painkillers at the hospital and sent him home after about two hours mucking about, with orders to leave the rest of the rubbish for another day – or better still, for somebody else, and Matt took him back to Shortlanesend. That was when he remembered he was meant to be here for dinner.' She shrugged her shoulders, helplessly. 'Well, you can't blame him really. It must have been hideously painful.'

'So, do we take it that you're going to collect him?' asked Kim.

'Seems so – apparently he said he could drive perfectly well as it was his right hand, not his left, and he could still change gear and use the brake and stuff, but Ernie said no bloody way, and he'd drive him. And you know the rest.'

'How's he managing a shower, with one hand out of action?' asked Kim, imagining it. 'Mind you, I'm glad that he is – it sounds as if there was a fair amount of blood, sweat and probably tears involved, and he wasn't exactly spotlessly clean when we last saw him, either.'

'I don't think he actually cried,' said Diana, 'and in answer to your question, Bennie said with the aid of a plastic bag and an elastic band, and Ernie on standby in case of emergency.' She slipped the phone back into her jacket pocket. 'I'll be off then. We should be back here in about three-quarters of an hour, I expect, all being well.'

'I expect we shall manage without you,' said Val, lazily.

Diana left, and Kim and Val looked at each other as the door shut behind her.

'Poor old Francis,' said Val.

'Careless old Francis, more like.' Kim had less sympathy, she considered that Francis had brought quite a lot of that on himself. 'He'd already brought the doorframe down, going at it like a madman, he should have learned from that to be more careful. Although,' she added, after a moment's thought, 'I don't think "careful" is a word in his vocabulary at present. Perhaps it's a good thing if it slows him down a bit.'

'It certainly might not be a bad thing – if it does, that is, I wouldn't bet on it. It might give him time to listen to Diana for one thing, they need to work on this together, and he's certainly not listening at the moment.

She's got some bright ideas about that house of his, your twin. They should be able to discuss them. They're both going to live there, after all.'

Kim was surprised at this speech; it was all true, but she hadn't thought that Val would notice. She said, 'They arranged it that way between them. He does the farm, she does the house.'

'I know that, but she takes an interest in the farm.'

'Not to the extent of talking it over with him, don't try to tell me she does.'

Val looked at her. He said, 'Not like us, you mean? But they're different people from us, Francis certainly is. I wonder sometimes if the age difference between them, and the life he's led, are more than she will find she can handle.'

'Oh, I think she'll manage,' said Kim, distantly. He looked at her.

'Love conquers all, you mean? I hope you're right. I like Francis, now I'm beginning to know him a bit more, it's way past time something went right for him. Now, since we have a precious few minutes to ourselves in this very peculiar day, shall we file them both for now and concentrate on us?'

'It's the weather,' said Kim. She slid into the armchair with him, half on top of him, half beside him, snuggling up. 'It's making us all quarrelsome. Kiss it all away for me. There isn't time for anything else and I've only had a peck on the cheek all day...'

Even so, it was quite some time before they heard Diana's car turning into the parking slot outside, and Kim had not just had rather more than a peck on the cheek, but had also put on the vegetables and laid the table for dinner. She was chopping parsley to garnish the starter when Diana and Francis finally came through the door together, and Val had been deputed to opening the wine, which he was doing in the kitchen, getting in her way on the worktop. They were not quarrelling about this.

'Sorry we took so long,' Diana said, breezing in. 'We all got talking, you know how it is.'

'We certainly do with you,' said Val. He came forward, the wine bottle in one hand and the other held out to greet Francis, who held up his heavily bandaged right hand in apology and offered his left for a high five instead, which they exchanged with a mutual grin.

'You should be more careful,' said Val.

'I kn-now.' He looked rueful. 'It w-w-was a stupid thing to do.'

Kim came out of the kitchen to add her own greetings; she looked at Francis critically. He looked a bit pale, she thought, and no wonder.

'You need a keeper,' she told him, and Diana said, 'He's got one. He can't drive for the next few days, so I shall have to. Keep him out of more trouble – I hope.'

''Good luck with that,' said Kim, smiling. 'Dinner is almost ready to go on the table; sit down, Francis darling, before you fall down, and Val, get some wine circulating – can you drink alcohol, Francis? If they've given you antibiotics and stuff?'

'N-nobody s-said not,' said Francis. 'L-let's risk it.'

'We can always scrape you off the floor,' said Val cheerfully. 'Red or white?'

Diana and Kim left the men to it and returned to their normal workplace for the day; the kitchen.

'But don't worry about transport,' Diana said, to Kim. 'If you can drive me over to Shortlanesend after breakfast, you can have the car all day and I'll drive the Discovery back here in the evening, ready to face whatever happens on Monday. He grumbled about the lack of space for his legs – you just can't please some people!'

'You're spending the day out at Shortlanesend tomorrow?'

'They've invited me, yes. Bennie thought you and Val would like the chance to be on your own for a bit, and I agreed with her. Come to that, I shall like spending time with Francis when he can't get away, for once, although heaven knows what we shall do. Count chickens, or something. He's not fit for much else right now, although he may feel a bit better in the morning. Here's hoping.' She gave Kim a quick look. 'Next week may be a bit odd. We haven't discussed it properly yet, but he's going to need to be able to get about, and I shall have to drive him, there's nobody else around to do it. I think I may be about to learn a lot about muck spreading; he said he'd have to teach me to drive the tractor, if he couldn't do it – not sure if he really meant it.' She looked thoughtful.

'That's all right. If I have use of the car, I can job hunt. I need to, anyway, I can't live at other people's expense for ever, and Francis has done enough, with this house and all.'

'Actually, that was Ernie, but I see your point.'

'Get that fish out of the fridge, and let's dish up. This parsley is OK now.' Kim put down her knife and began spreading plates. 'I've put the toast into a basket, it's over there.' She nodded towards it, but Diana didn't see because she had her head in the fridge. As she withdrew, the bowl of tuna in her hands, she remarked, 'It's a good thing that the whole meal can be eaten with a fork, isn't it? We might have planned it on purpose.'

'Don't be surprised if he doesn't manage to eat much of it,' Kim warned her. 'He looks to me as if he should have stayed at home. And he's right-handed, too.' She caught Diana's eye. 'It's been a very peculiar day, hasn't it?'

'I hesitate to stick my neck out here, but surely tomorrow can only be better?'

'I wish!' Kim picked up two of the plates in one hand and the basket of Melba toast in the other. 'You bring those last two, let's get this meal on the table. Poor meal, it's waited long enough…' and she led the way into the other room. 'On your feet, you two, time to sit at the table! Grub's up!'

XX

It was a quarter to ten before the twins left for Shortlanesend the next morning, they had started the day lazily. The dinner party had ended earlier than planned, but Val had said, as he and Francis left, that he would come over at around eleven the next morning, so there was no tearing hurry.

'I ought to spend a little time with Mum and Dad, I suppose if you two are off to Shortlanesend.' He pulled a resigned face. 'If you get back in time, Kim, we can go down to the Club before we go back for lunch. And Diana, I don't know what you have planned, but Mum said if you want to join us for the roast beef and Yorkshire pudding, there's plenty to spare.'

'I'm invited to Shortlanesend,' said Diana, 'but thank her from me, anyway.' She didn't add that a traditional Sunday Lunch was possibly her least favourite meal, and Kim, who knew her pretty well by this time, winked at her; she might well be getting it anyway. Francis had said nothing at all. Looking at him, Diana wasn't even sure that he had been listening. This morning, however, sitting over a late breakfast with neither of their men present, they could be a bit more open with each other.

'That was a slightly…' Kim paused, looking for a suitable adjective, and ended up with 'unusual evening last night, wouldn't you say?'

They had not discussed it before they went to bed, but both of them had been thinking about it. Diana said, 'A bit quiet, on current form, but I think they both enjoyed it. They were very nice about my maiden stew.'

'Yes, they were.' Kim considered this. 'About everything really – although I noticed that Francis didn't exactly eat much of it. I was sitting opposite to him, watching him get whiter and whiter as the evening went on. He really shouldn't have come, I think.'

'I'm glad he did, though,' said Diana. She knew this was selfish, at least in one way, but she would have been very disappointed had he stayed at home and missed her first attempt at serious cooking.

'Yes,' said Kim. She understood that, and she thought that the fact that he appreciated it too was why Francis had been there. She added, 'He's not very handy with his left hand, though, is he, your man?'

'No.' Diana began gathering the remains of breakfast together, using the action for an excuse to say no more. She hadn't fully realised how much it would hurt her to see the man she loved hurting. He had put a good face on it, but it had been obvious he was at the very least experiencing considerable discomfort. Not all of it physical, if she didn't miss her guess.

Kim shot a quick, sideways glance at her twin's face, sympathising. She said, 'It was a pleasant evening though, I thought. Quiet, yes, you're right, but friendly.' She paused. 'What are you planning for today, if you aren't joining us with Val's lot for the roast beef?'

'I shall wait and see what Francis has to say. I might just drive myself back here after lunch for a quiet afternoon with my thoughts, if he wants to be quiet – you'll be in Shearwater anyway. Let's play it by ear.'

'Then we had better clear away and get to Shortlanesend, so I can get back in time for Val.'

They threw the dishes into the sink for attention later on, and went out to the car.

'How do you think you'll get on with the Discovery?' Kim asked, as they set out. 'It's pretty big, compared to this.'

'You sound like Val,' Diana told her. 'I shall get used to it – quite quickly, if I got the picture correctly! I think I'm now to be temporarily employed as chauffeur, secretary, and the slave who chops up dinner into small bits.'

'Does he really mean to teach you how to drive the tractor, like he threatened?'

'Who knows? I think he was just snatching at straws, but we shall see. He's had a bit of time to think things through properly now.' She added, 'Which isn't to say that he's done it.'

They parked the car at Shortlanesend, and as they crossed the farmyard to the back door, Bennie opened it with a welcoming smile on her face.

'Morning Tamsin, good morning Kim! Come in out of the weather, before it rains again. But at least that horrible wind has gone—' She shut the door and added, 'Coffee? I'm just getting the dinner in the oven.' It sat on the table waiting, a large leg of pork with crisscrossed, shining skin, and onions sitting round it. Hard luck, Diana!

'You'll need to cut that up for him,' said Kim, looking at it speculatively. 'Or better still, mince it. Yes please, I've probably just about got time.'

Bennie didn't ask who "him" referred to. She laughed, and went to push the kettle onto the hotplate. 'Maisie has already pointed that out, after his performance with the breakfast bacon. He just picked it up in the end, and ate it in his fingers. He asked me to put the egg on a piece of toast, and ate that as if it was marmalade; I had to restrain Clive from doing the same, he thought it was a great idea.' She added, 'He passed on the cereal, I think it was beyond his skill at present.'

'He was able to face the idea of breakfast, though?' Diana asked, trying to keep the anxiety out of her voice and sound casual. Bennie looked at her, undeceived.

'Good heavens, yes,' she said. 'He's OK this morning – he didn't sleep that well, I don't think, and you can see that it hurts him still, but he hasn't let it spoil his appetite, not now the shock has worn off. This morning, he's more concerned with dung.'

'That sounds about right.'

'Where is he now?' asked Kim, as Bennie gathered mugs onto the worktop.

'On the phone in the office, pursuing his current obsession,' Bennie told her. 'He's trying to track down someone with a couple or three days to spare to spread muck for him, early in the week, although I very much doubt he'll find anyone who can start it tomorrow. He's obsessed with getting that dungheap out of the way as soon as possible. To be honest, I can't say that I blame him.' She reached for the milk. 'Ernie phoned round a bit after Val took him away last night, he came up with a few "might do"s. One of them phoned back about ten minutes ago. One of the million cousins, I think, don't know which.'

'Couldn't they just load it into skips and cart it away?' asked Diana, and Kim and Bennie both looked at her. 'What have I said?'

'You have a lot to learn, if you're going to make a farmer's wife,' said Kim, hiding a smile.

'But I'm not, am I? I'm going to be a marine biologist's wife.'

'Not immediately,' Bennie reminded her. 'He's got to sort the mess out first,' and then she relented and took pity on Diana's ignorance. 'Lovely, well-rotted manure? You can't waste stuff like that – from the size of the heap, as Francis describes it, those fields can't have had the benefit for at the very least, three years, quite possibly more! Of course it needs spreading, it's rrripe for it!' She spoke the word "ripe" with relish, as she handed Diana a mug of coffee. 'Sit down and drink that. It'll make you feel better.'

When they were all seated, Diana immediately asked the question at the front of her mind.

'So, how is he really, this morning? I know you said he ate some breakfast, but really.'

Bennie considered this while she sipped her coffee. Finally, she said, 'Grumpy? Frustrated – to be honest. And worried, you can see. He hasn't said anything, but it won't have done that hand any good, it's the one he drops things with anyway on a bad day.' She paused. 'You're going to have your work cut out finding him things to occupy him for the next few days, or he'll go mad – and so will the rest of us, come to that.'

'Has he told his mother what's happened?' asked Diana.

'He rang her this morning, but she knew anyway.' Bennie looked at her sympathetically. 'Bad news travels fast on the Vachell grapevine, and he had Matt with him, remember. '

'He should have done it yesterday, when it happened.' Diana was upset for Mary, hearing the news at second hand.

'Well, there you go, that's families for you. And you saw him last night anyway, he wasn't up for discussing it. Still isn't, come to that.' She paused. 'I've invited Mary for lunch, anyway, so she can see for herself that he's OK. He will be, you know. It's the time between then and now that's going to be hard. Not just for him, if I don't miss my guess.'

Kim looked at Diana. She said, 'Maybe this would be a good moment for your mum and dad to come down here to sort out your wedding? It would give him something practical and optimistic to think about, and he'll have the time on his hands to pay attention, too.'

Bennie looked at her with approval.

'Good thought, Kim! Do you think they could do that at such short notice, Tamsin?'

'I can but ask. If I explain, they'll probably find a way. It's something that's got to be done, after all. And their idea, come to that.'

'Work on it, then.' Bennie put her mug down on the table and got to her feet. 'Time that joint went in – I was about to do it when you got here, and I just noticed it still sitting there – one of those days.' She opened the top oven of the Aga and slid the roasting tray in with its burden. 'There!'

She shut the door on it and picked up her mug again, but didn't sit down. 'I think I heard the office door – stand by!'

Francis came into the kitchen about two minutes later; Diana, looking at him, thought that he still looked a bit rough, but at least he wasn't scowling.

'Find someone?' asked Bennie, and almost in the same breath added, 'Coffee?'

'Please.' He crossed to Diana and swept her up for a quick kiss. 'And y-yes. N-not the best d-d-deal in the book, but g-g-good enough. S-Simon can give m-me T-Tuesday and Wednesday; if w-w-we go at it, th-that should work. Someone else m-m-may step up after th-that.'

'I take it, that was the royal "we"?' said Bennie. 'You won't be going at it.'

He did manage to smile at her – just. 'I sh-shall have to be ar-round – in f-f-fact I sh-sh-shall have t-t-to be there first thing t-t-tomorrow m-morning, to l-l-let Gary know w-w-what's happening.' He gave Diana, who was still in the curve of his serviceable arm, a quick hug. 'H-hope you c-c-can get up that early.'

'I'll see that she does,' Kim promised, and then, seeing that Diana was going to let the opportunity slip, she went on, 'And while you're both there, and since you can't do anything practical, you can go over the house with her and the builder, and she can tell you what she'd like to do, and how she'd like to work it.'

To do him justice, his hesitation was so brief that it was almost undetectable. He accepted the mug that Bennie had handed him, releasing his hold on Diana to take it in his good hand, and said, 'Yes, th-that s-s-sounds a g-g-good idea. W-when I've w-w-worked out a Plan B w-with Gary.'

'Just don't take all morning,' Bennie told him. 'You've a hospital appointment at 11.30, remember. Just see he doesn't forget, Tamsin, and keep your eyes on the clock! I know this man.'

'I'm not l-l-likely t-t-to forget,' Francis objected, with a touch of irritation, but Bennie shook her head at him.

'Yes you are. And I don't mean the appointment – the passage of time is what you'll overlook.'

'Nothing new there, then,' Kim murmured, so quietly that only Bennie heard her. They exchanged a swift smile, and Kim said, 'Isn't Simon Cosmo's brother? Or have I got that wrong?'

'No, you've got it quite right.' Bennie sipped her coffee, looking thoughtful. She finally sat down, beside Kim. 'I imagine he's volunteered – or their father volunteered him, more like – because the whole family are so over-the-moon about the chance he's given Cosmo. Something they can do in return, sort of. I wouldn't be surprised if there are more offers before the end of today, even if it's only just a couple of hours here and there. The Vachells stick together.' She paused, and then nodded towards the other side of the big table, where Diana and Francis were sitting together, talking quietly. 'She's going to have to think of something to stop him going bananas over the next few days, so I hope she's working on it.' She paused. 'I don't suppose for an instant that he's told Tamsin, but yesterday, after the accident, he couldn't move his fingers. They told him at the hospital that there was no obvious nerve damage, and that given his medical history, it was just the shock, but it's preying on his mind a bit, I think. He needs distracting.'

'I can see that, it's one reason why I thought it might be a good moment to sort out the wedding plans,' said Kim 'If her parents can come down for the weekend, it would at least give him something else to think about. Meanwhile, she'll probably tow him round reclamation yards.'

'Well, that won't hurt him, he might even be interested. Not so sure about wedding plans, but it's worth trying.' She paused. 'Has he spoken with Merlin, do you know?'

'He said he had.' Kim sounded doubtful.

'Then he probably has. Tell Tamsin, she should have a word herself to be safe, academics are very unreliable when it comes to being domestically practical. She'll learn.'

'Oh well. She chose him – and actually, I think she made a good choice.' Kim put down her mug. 'And now, if I'm not to upset my own equally good choice, I should be making tracks. Thank you for the coffee.'

'It's a pleasure – oh, and if he doesn't tell Tamsin about that hand, I didn't tell you, OK? I probably shouldn't have, and anyway, he probably will, but…well, you know.'

'My lips are sealed unless she opens the subject herself,' Kim assured her. 'And if she does, I'll pretend I don't know. But I'm glad you did tell one of us, even if it was the wrong one. Forewarned is forearmed, and all that.'

She said her goodbyes and left for her rendezvous with Val, and Bennie looked at the two who were left.

'So, what do you two plan to do? If you want to go back in the office,

Francis, I can teach Tamsin how to make bread-and-butter pudding and how to peel sprouts. Up to you.'

'If T-tamsin is OK w-w-with it, I thought I'd have a g-g-go at Kim's memory c-card. I can d-d-do th-that with one hand. P-probably.'

'Is there anything left on it?' Tamsin asked – without Kim around, she was definitely more Tamsin than Diana.

'Th-that's what I m-m-mean to f-find out.'

'Off you go, then,' said Bennie. 'That should keep you out of mischief for a bit. OK with that, Tamsin?'

'Fine by me. I like bread-and-butter pudding.'

'So does he, so it'll be a useful thing for you to know.'

'I should have brought my book, to write it down. Kim said I should start a personal collection.'

'And Kim is quite right – look, I'll write it down on the back of this old bill, and you can copy it in when you get back...'

Francis vanished back to his computer, temporarily installed in Ernie's office, and Tamsin embarked on her third cookery lesson to date, and the morning slipped quietly and pleasantly by.

'It's very quiet,' Tamsin remarked at one point. 'What have you done with the children?'

'They were going wild, after being cooped up by the weather, so Ernie took them out with him to see to the horses. They have a pony, between them at the moment, but we'll soon have to be getting Maisie one of her own, and there are a couple of others too.'

'Francis has horses.'

'I know. Do you ride? You could go out together, round the fields.'

'You know I do. He let me ride his mare, remember?'

'So he did.' She reached for a loaf that was sitting on the worktop. 'Now, this is how you do it – it's very simple. Some people put sultanas in, but I like fresh blueberries, you can always get them in the supermarket, or you could grow them yourself come to that. I do, and you'll have the space.' The cookery lesson began.

Mary arrived when the pudding was safely in the oven, the roast potatoes had joined the pork, and they were considering whether to lay the table in the kitchen as usual, or to do it in the dining room, as a concession to Mary's more organised lifestyle. Tamsin was interested – and to be honest, surprised – to find that she was sufficiently familiar with the place to come automatically to the back door and enter without knocking; she would have expected Mary to be more formal. Bennie greeted her with a hug.

'Mary! How are you? And great you could come at such short notice, I'm just giving Tamsin a cookery lesson.'

'It was kind of you to invite me. I was worrying about him, to be honest, such a silly thing for him to do!' Mary turned to Tamsin. 'And you, you poor girl!' She put her arms round Tamsin and gave her a hug, too. 'How is he this morning, our careless and irresponsible man?'

'Quiet, sore and touchy,' said Tamsin, which seemed a fair description. 'He's playing on his computer, probably as an alternative to throwing things.'

'Go on through, and see for yourself,' Bennie invited. 'He's in the office, you know the way.'

'Thank you, I will. If you think he won't mind?'

'For goodness' sake, why should he mind? You're his mother!'

'We aren't on such easy terms, Benita.'

'Go and see him – he won't bite, you know.'

'I wouldn't be so sure of that, this morning,' said Tamsin, as Mary left the kitchen. She looked at Bennie. 'Bennie, can I say something that might sound odd – or even rude? Particularly as it's a snap judgement.'

Bennie looked at her, raising her eyebrows. Tamsin took a breath first, and then the plunge. She said, 'That was only a five-minute meeting, but Mary was…well, different just then. Without the big house and the estate and the huge, manicured garden around her, she was immediately…well, different.' She tailed off there, running out of words and also wondering if she had put her foot in it. Bennie, however, took it calmly.

'Mary is a Vachell, you have to remember. This is the kind of family she grew up with, her mother and father weren't posh: they were hardworking landowners, yes, but country people just like the rest of us. She would never have inherited Vachells, even, if her older brothers hadn't died in the war- right at the end too, such rotten luck and they were so young too. That was never intended to happen – Mary was the baby, just a sort of afterthought. Little baby sister, for fun.' She pulled an expressive face. 'But it's the Chillingworths that put her off her stroke, from what I've heard. She felt she should live up to them, but really, I think it was only Christopher who set any store by it.' There was dismissal in her voice, and something else. Scorn?

'You didn't like him?' Tamsin ventured, feeling her way.

'I didn't know him. I'm only a Vachell by marriage: by the time I met Ernie, Christopher Chillingworth was long dead. But I don't feel I would have had a lot to say to a grown-up spoilt brat who married an older woman so that he could swan around on her country estate and not have to do a stroke of work himself, and then betrayed her for a silly infatuated girl about half his age who had her eye on his money and thought he was a safe bet to get her out of the trouble she had got herself into. Neither of which she got, as things turned out, but she would have if her much-to-be-pitied husband hadn't killed her first, make no mistake. And neither did Mary get anything – the conceited idiot left her with no more than he found her with – less, he took all her pride and self-respect – and alienated her from her only child and set the two of them at loggerheads. Why should I like him?'

'This is the family version of what happened?'

'I suspect it is also the true one.'

There was a pause, while both of them wished that they hadn't started that. Eventually, Tamsin spoke. 'I'm surprised that any of you have a word to say to me.' She sounded mortified.

'We speak as we find, Tamsin. And what we find, is two lovely young girls who have done anything in their power to put the record straight, and restore her only son to poor Mary. And when it comes down to it, it's only justice that Francis should reap some of the benefit. Let's face it, he's had most of the stick!'

'Oh God...' said Tamsin. She looked at Bennie. 'Do you know what she said to me? "He is the most precious thing that I have"...'

'Then take care of him,' said Bennie, gently. Mary had said that, too.

There was a silence, while both of them laid out the knives and forks on autopilot, on the kitchen table. Then Bennie said, out of the blue, 'You and Kim should both remember, Tamsin, that it isn't just your mother who made you, you weren't an immaculate conception. You had – probably still have – a biological father, too. And I know that nobody even knows who he was, but looking at your mother's record, and then looking at you two, I would be very interested if I ever met him. And now, I'm going to shut up.' She wasn't to be allowed to.

'We both of us have adoptive parents, too,' Tamsin pointed out, argumentatively.

314

'I know you do. But you two seem reluctant to give them any credit, you just beat yourselves up over your silly spoilt brat of a birth mother. And you should – not just you, Kim too – sit down and think about it all seriously some time.'

'I don't suppose we have a snowball's chance in you-know-where of ever meeting with our biological father, so what is there to think about, really? There was some sort of family feud, he's down as "father unknown" on Kim's birth certificate – which her parents do have, by the way.'

'That could be a clue in itself. Your birth mother's own parentage isn't a secret, is it? Even if her family won't come across, someone must know about a feud on that scale, even this late in the day.'

'We each have a full set of parents that love us, and that we love in return. Don't stir, Bennie. The custard is cooked.'

But Bennie, since she had been re-started, hadn't finished. She said, 'Do you think that Francis might know? He seems to have been in his father's confidence.'

'We haven't asked him. Nor will we. Give it up, Bennie.'

There was a whole lot of muck floating to the surface since her engagement was announced, Tamsin reflected, a little uneasily. She suddenly realised what they had been doing. She looked at the table. 'So, have we decided on the kitchen table?' and Bennie instantly realised the same thing.

'Oh God!' She gave a slightly scandalised laugh. 'Oh well, it might be the best option anyway, with the kids. They won't be exactly Sunday-smart after mucking out stables, even if we wash them.'

'Which we shall have to do.' They looked at each other and burst out laughing – reaction, Tamsin thought, to the last few minutes.

'Mary isn't posh. Not at heart anyway. She won't mind,' said Bennie, and Mary came back into the kitchen, right on cue.

'I see what you mean, Tamsin,' she said, but she was smiling, in relief as much as anything. 'A man that grouchy is sure to survive; I was half-afraid I would find him ready to give up. But that's more bad temper than distress, in my opinion.'

'No chance!' said Tamsin, and Bennie said, 'From my experience so far, "giving up" isn't a phrase he understands. This is more like Clive and Maisie when they can't go out to play.'

Also right on cue, at that instant the back door burst open and Clive and Maisie came crashing in. Bennie took one look, and let out a roar –

"Don't touch a thing! Upstairs, right away, the pair of you, and get clean – dump all those clothes in the washing basket – now!'

'Can't we just say a proper hello to Tamsin?' Maisie pleaded, dancing up and down ready to pounce.

Bennie opened her mouth to reply unequivocally "No!" but to Tamsin's astonishment, Mary stepped in first.

'Don't you worry, Benita, I'll see to them.' She adopted the tone of a strict headmistress, 'Upstairs, both of you! Tamsin will forgive you, you can say hello properly when you're clean and decent,' and rounded them up expertly and had them out of the kitchen before they had time to do more than draw breath. Tamsin stood with her mouth open.

'Did I just see that, or was I dreaming?'

'Oh, Mary's great with the kids – she loves children, she's like an extra grandmother to those two.'

Tamsin closed her mouth. She felt as if her heart was breaking, as she played that little scene back in her head. She said, unevenly, 'And her own child…' and stopped.

'He was a teenager at the time. But yes. Now you see why I have nothing good to say about Christopher Chillingworth.'

Tamsin was silent for so long that time that Bennie began to worry about her, but eventually she said, 'And this Cosmo – will he be kind to her, or just an employee?' and Bennie knew exactly what she meant.

'Cosmo is a perfectly normal young man, who owes her – or will owe her, one day – a great deal. He'll behave accordingly. And they already know each other well anyway, there are no axes to grind between Mary and his family. They're a good crowd, the Mayfield lot – well, you'll meet his older brother on Tuesday, you can judge for yourself.'

'That's good, then.'

'Oh, Francis isn't stupid – well, most of the time he isn't. He had it all worked out, have no fear. And as for the rest, there's too much history to cure everything in a day, probably even in a year, but with goodwill on both sides, it will happen in the end. Quite probably when the two of you have children of your own.' She hesitated, watching Tamsin's face. 'Try not to be angry about it, Tamsin. It wasn't your fault you know, and neither was it theirs; we both know whose fault it was. Just give it time. Now, go and see what that man of yours is doing in there – lunch will be on the table in half an hour or so, and you know men when they get onto computers, it can be worse than cowsheds! And don't worry.'

Easier said than done, Tamsin thought as she left the kitchen, and Bennie could almost read it on her retreating back. She shrugged her shoulders; well, she had done her best. Up to Tamsin, now.

Tamsin went into the office feeling completely disorientated by the steep learning curve of the past half hour, and was immediately brought back to the here and now by finding Francis considering a computer screen covered in tiny pictures.

'Oh!' she cried, in delight, 'you found them safely!' and he swung round on the office chair to face her; she had made him jump, she saw.

'You sh-shouldn't c-c-creep up on a bloke l-like that,' he told her, but he was smiling as he said it. 'Yes, I f-f-found them; th-there was no p-p-problem. Th-the thing now is, w-w-what d-d-do I do with th-them?'

'She emailed the rest to her own compute in New Zealand, she said, to deal with when she got home,' Tamsin told him. 'Only now, of course, she isn't going home.'

'And d-d-do you have her em-mail address? I d-d-don't suppose you d-do,' he answered himself.

'Well, no. I've never had to email her, obviously, and she wouldn't be there to read it if I did! But she'll know it, and I expect her parents will email them to her on her laptop when she's got one, which she means to do so you could even leave them where they are.' She looked at the mosaic of little pictures critically. 'At least she can look at them on this. That's something to be going on with, for now.' She hesitated. 'Can you print that out? Just so that she can get an idea, she'd love to see them.'

'Of c-c-course I can, if you th-th-think sh-she'd like that.'

'I know she would.'

'OK.' He reached out to switch on the adjacent printer.

'Dinner's nearly on the table,' Tamsin warned him.

'Th-this won't take t-t-two minutes.' He was pressing keys with his left hand, obviously disconnected for the moment.

'Keep dinner in mind then,' she told him, and went back to the kitchen to rejoin Bennie. Ernie had just come in, very little cleaner than his children had been and closely followed by Sacha; he passed her in the doorway

'She just told me where to go, in no uncertain terms,' he said, as the dog vanished swiftly under the table Possibly he had been told, too.

'I'm not surprised. You smell like a horsebox,' Tamsin said, wrinkling her nose.

'Francis will love me, then.' He grinned at her. 'See you in a while.'

'Not more than twenty minutes,' Bennie called after him, adding, 'I don't suppose he heard me. Oh well.'

'Family life, don't you just love it?' said Tamsin. 'Now, what can I do?'

Diana drove back to Romans in the early evening, leaving the Vachells to spend a family evening together. Mary had left soon after lunch and Francis had gone upstairs for a rest, looking, to be fair, obviously in some pain and as if a period of quiet was what he needed. He reminded her to be on the doorstep at eight o'clock tomorrow before he kissed her goodbye.

'You're OK, though?' She scanned his tired face carefully.

'Y-yes. It j-just hurts a bit, it t-t-takes it out of you. And I d-d-didn't sleep m-m-much l-last n-n-night.'

'I may be gone when you come down later. Val will be going back to London, and I can't leave Kim on her own all evening, it wouldn't be fair.'

'Th-then we'll m-m-meet at dawn.'

After an afternoon spent playing Scrabble with the children, since Francis had not reappeared Tamsin took her leave; in any case she wasn't enthusiastic about driving a large, strange car down the narrow Dorset lanes in the dark. Ernie had brought the Discovery round to the front for her, and showed her how to adjust the driving seat and the mirrors and sent her on her way, with Kim's photographs on the passenger seat beside her. She had explained again that Val would be going back to London, and Kim on her own for the evening, and although the children had pressed her to stay, Bennie and Ernie had understood.

'But we shall see you tomorrow,' Ernie told her, as they all crowded on the doorstep to see her off. 'At dawn, on the doorstep!'

'I wish you two wouldn't keep harping on about dawn,' said Diana, laughing, and he laughed too. He stood, still watching, as she negotiated the gateway, and in the rear-view mirror she saw him nod, and turn back to the yard gate. She hoped that the nod was one of approval.

The Discovery was bigger and heavier than she was used to, but fortunately, on a Sunday evening, there wasn't much traffic about and she negotiated the lanes safely without having to reverse or perform any complicated avoidance manoeuvres, arriving back in Emberton with her palms sweating slightly, but pleased with herself. Of course, it might be different on a Monday morning. She parked outside Romans, behind their neighbours' car and as close to the kerb as she could judge; Romans, being on the end, was the only house in the terrace that had a parking bay, but Kim would be using that.

She wasn't yet back. Diana let herself into the house and put the photographs in their plastic folder on the table and then stood, a little bit lonely and uncertain what to do with herself. There was so much to think about, and she wasn't sure that she was ready to do that. She wished that Kim would come.

After a few moments just standing there in the living room, she pulled herself together. If Kim wasn't there to talk to, her parents might well be at this time on a Sunday, and discussing the wedding plans would keep her occupied, however much like goblin gold her projected marriage to Francis seemed at this moment, and it would stop her brooding, at least for a while. She took her phone out of her jacket pocket, and finally sat down. If only they hadn't gone out…

They hadn't. Eloise picked up the phone after only three rings; she had read the number on her own phone.

'Diana! This is a lovely surprise, darling! Is everything all right with you?'

There was such a choice of answers available to this question, including a straight "no", that Diana settled on the easiest one. 'Yes, I'm fine,' which was literally true, but disingenuous. She hurried on. 'I wanted to talk to you about the wedding plans. There's been a development, and I – we – wondered if you could possibly get down at the weekend.'

'That's a bit sudden, darling. I'm not sure that your father…anyway, isn't Francis very busy right now?'

'He wishes.' Diana took a breath. 'Actually, Eloise, he's had a bit of an accident, he ran a big rusty nail right through his hand, and he can't do anything practical until it heals. So he'll have time to listen properly, which makes it a good moment, if you and Daddy can manage it.'

'Oh, poor Francis! Is he all right – apart from that, I mean?'

'Well, he only did it yesterday, so it's a bit painful—' She broke off, as Eloise interrupted.

'Here comes your father now – you had better speak to him about the weekend, he knows what he's got planned. I'll talk to you again when you've finished.' There was the sound of murmuring, and then her father's voice said, 'Diana? What's all this about an accident?' and Diana had to say it all again.

'Poor man, I expect that's painful, but so long as it hasn't done any serious damage…Eloise says you think it's a good time to discuss wedding plans?' He made it into a question.

'Well yes. He can't do anything constructive, so he'll have time to listen. But I know it's short notice.'

'Hmm. Just let me get my diary, let's see what we can do.' There was the sound of someone walking across a room, and then of a door opening and the scuffle of papers, so presumably he had taken her with him into his study. Then he said. 'Yes, I think we could manage that, there's a couple of small things Saturday morning, but they can be postponed, I think – we can come down late on Friday, if Eloise isn't doing anything important then, and leave on Sunday afternoon, so long as nothing unavoidable crops up in the meantime. I have to be back in the office on Monday morning. That gives us all of Saturday and Sunday morning to get things sorted out, that should be long enough if there are no snags. Did Francis ask about that private chapel he mentioned?'

'He says so. Yes. We can maybe get his friend Merlin to show it to you.'

'That would be good. Now I'll hand you back to your mother and you can talk to her. We shall be needing a good hotel, you can sort that out between you I daresay.'

'The Langland is the best one, that I know of. It's on the harbour front in the town. But Francis may know something even better, I can ask him. Or his mother.'

'Talk about that with your mother, and I'll look forward to seeing you on Friday evening, all being well. You can both of you join us for dinner, maybe. And tell Francis how sorry we are to hear about his accident.'

Short, but practical. Talking to Eloise was a bit more drawn-out, but finally, Diana had to put her mobile back in her pocket and throw herself down on the sofa to think – or rather, to try not to think. She wondered whether it was a good moment to ring Mary about hotels – she had no great faith in Francis on the subject, in spite of what she had said to her father – but decided that tomorrow morning might be better, when they had gone round the house at Burnthouse and been to the hospital. Maybe they could drive out and see her? Francis would need something to do!

Thinking about Mary breached the protective layer that she had been deliberately building between herself and this morning, and the flood water broke through. When Kim arrived home half an hour later, she found her twin sitting on the sofa with tears running silently down her cheeks, staring at nothing.

'What's happened?' asked Kim urgently, her thoughts immediately flying to Francis, but Diana replied, 'Nothing new. Just everything.'

Kim slid off her coat and tossed it into the nearest armchair; she sat down beside her twin.

'Tell me.'

Diana wiped the palms of her hands across her wet cheeks and sniffed. She said, 'Mary came to lunch.'

'She wasn't nasty to you?' Kim asked, quickly, 'She didn't blame you—'

'No, of course she didn't, how could she? It was nobody's fault but his own, I wasn't even there! It was…oh Kim, she was so lovely. Quite different from at Vachells…with the children, and everything and Bennie said…she said…' The tears began to run down her face again, she couldn't seem to stop them. Kim got up and went into the kitchen for a handful of kitchen towels; she sat down again and pushed them into her twin's hand.

'Blow your nose, wipe your face – not necessarily in that order – and take a deep breath and tell me what happened,' she ordered. Diana did as she was told, and made an attempt to pull herself together.

'I am so ashamed of our mother!' she burst out, without quite meaning to, and stopped. Kim said nothing. After a moment, Diana went on. 'Do you remember, Kim, me telling you about that photo album that Ed showed me, that first time we met? All of them on holiday, playing in the yard at Vachells, and on the beach together, and on the farm wagons, and Mary leading one of the little girls around the yard on the pony? She loved them all Kim – Christopher's family – and she lost them because he made up lies, and she never saw them again – and Kim, oh Kim, she lost Francis with them…and I watched her with Maisie and Clive this morning, and I saw…I saw someone I don't know. But someone I have seen in a photo album. And yes I know, over time they will all come back, those grown-up children that she loved all those years ago…but those years won't, Kim. They're lost under a pile of wicked lies told by two utterly selfish people who only cared for themselves and nothing will ever be the same for her again!' She ended on a rising note that was almost a howl, and bit her lip, hard. 'Sorry. But I've been sitting here thinking about it, and it was so cruel. They neither of them cared for anything but themselves! Probably not even for each other, not like you care for Val, or I do for Francis.'

'Well, said Kim, trying to pour oil on these troubled waters, 'that's been obvious for a long time, so there's no point in beating yourself up about it now. Although I do know what you mean.' She did, she realised, and anger stirred in her own heart. She shut it down quickly. So long after the fair, it was pointless.

Diana said, simply, 'She loved Francis too, and whatever happens now, those years won't come back. And I'm not sure that the gap can ever be bridged.'

'Did you say any of this to Bennie?' asked Kim.

'She said a lot of it to me, first. She never knew our mother, but you can tell she thinks she was a waste of space.'

'Well, they do say that onlookers see most of the game,' Kim reminded her.

'She got her opinions from what other people said. Which made me wonder how the Vachells saw you and me, to be honest, but it seems that we're the heroes of the hour.' She gave a dreary laugh. 'I'm not sure that we deserve that, Kim. It wasn't us, really, it was just a bomb that was ready to go off, and we tripped over the fuse.'

Kim said, 'Then be thankful that we did. The Vachells and the Chillingworths have made it quite clear that they're still in the game, and not just as onlookers either. Build on that. And now tell me, how is Francis?'

'Frustrated. Tired. Hurting. And if I read the signs right, rather dreading a hospital appointment I have to drive him to tomorrow. Otherwise OK, I suppose. Oh, and you have to wake me up and get me on the road before eight o'clock tomorrow. That's a.m, not p.m.'

'Ouch! Well, I can try.' She gave Diana an affectionate slap on the knee. 'Now snap out of it, please! There's some wine in the fridge, I'm going to rout it out, and we're going to raise a toast to tomorrow and all the days that will come after it. And then you can tell me something positive, to cheer us both up!'

'Such as what?' asked Diana, but managed to smile as she said it.

'Anything you like. Think about it, while I fetch the bottle.'

She fetched the bottle, and some glasses to go with it, and sat down beside Diana again, placing her trophies on the coffee table. 'So, have you thought?'

'Sort of.' Diana paused to assemble her thoughts. 'Bennie was talking about our parents, yours and mine, and how we mustn't undervalue them.'

'We don't,' said Kim. She handed Diana a glass, and added, fairly, 'but I do see what she means. We are rather concentrating on Sarah Eliot, to their exclusion. We have her genes, but they gave us our upbringing – I suppose that's what she's trying to say.'

'Not just that,' said Diana. 'She said that we shouldn't write our biological father out of the equation.'

'So, how did she suggest we wrote him in? We don't even know his name! All we know about him is that he buggered off and left silly sexpot Sarah to carry the can.'

'But do we know that?' Diana had been thinking about this. 'There's nothing in the story as we know it to tell us that he actually knew she was pregnant.'

'Of course there is! His parents packed him off to America PDQ, so he couldn't rush in and marry her out of hand.'

'Not exactly. Because they didn't want them going out together, yes. Not necessarily because she was pregnant. Maybe he didn't know, like I just said?'

'That's a hypothetical question if ever I heard one,' Kim told her.

'I realise that. But it does make one wonder, doesn't it?'

'Nothing we can do about it, however. Unless you plan to go up to Scotland to do some detective work among the natives? My guess is, that wouldn't get you anywhere, not after all this time. And if you're planning to ask Lord Lochaird – well, I just wouldn't.'

'I wasn't,' said Diana, 'He'd probably have me run out of his castle on a rail. And Bennie didn't mean that, anyway. She just meant that two people made us, and maybe we shouldn't dismiss the boyfriend as negligible. Because we aren't. I think that's what she meant.'

Kim considered this; it made sense. She said, 'But I still don't see what we're meant to do about it.'

'Just bear it in mind, I think she meant.'

'Have some more wine,' said Kim, deploying the bottle over both glasses. She raised her own. 'All right then, here's to him, our unknown father. May his shadow never grow less, wherever he is!'

The toast was drunk, and then Diana put her glass down on the coffee table and got to her feet.

'Oh, I nearly forgot – I've got something for you.' She picked up the folder from the dining table and handed it to Kim. 'Get an eyeful of these.'

Kim took the folder and gave its contents a casual glance, but a moment later she was sitting up straight, her face alight with pleasure.

'Oh, they were still on the card! Oh, how wonderful!' She ran her eye over the pages of tiny photos, delighted. 'I would have hated to lose these, I hope you thanked him properly – although I'll do it myself when I see him, of course.'

'I told him you'd be over the moon,' said Diana. 'He wanted to know what you wanted him to do with them now? He'll email them to your computer if you give him your email, or they can stay where they are until you get it over here.'

Kim clasped the folder to her breast as if was a favourite cat. 'We can talk about that when I see him. I can give him my email then, he won't want them cluttering up his computer. And now, shall we find something to eat before we both get sloshed on this wine?'

'Let's do both – eat and get sloshed.' Diana picked up the bottle and poured another refill for them both. 'Not necessarily in that order. Oh, and I can make a bread-and-butter pudding! I must copy the recipe into my book before I lose it.' They smiled at each other.

'And can you also open a tin of sardines?' Kim asked her. 'Come on – I'll make the toast!'

They headed for the kitchen, good humour restored.

XXI

Early mornings and Diana had never been close friends, but Kim did manage to chase her downstairs in time for breakfast at seven o'clock, and to be fair, the necessity to help Francis had been a powerful incentive too.

'He's going to drive you bonkers, until he gets the use of his hand back,' Kim warned her, over the toast and marmalade.

'Do you think I haven't grasped that? And what really worries me, is what is it going to be like when we're actually living together? I just hope he can use it by then, or it'll be a steep learning curve!'

'Second thoughts?' asked Kim, knowing that there weren't any.

'Definitely not. It's a high price, but the goods are worth it.'

'I'm dying to see this caravan everyone keeps on about. You can never tell with large outdoor men. It might be only the size of a largish tent, a lot of them are.'

'Let's hope not.' Diana picked up her coffee mug and gave it a sip. 'Everything seems to have gone very quiet since we got back from London, it's beginning to make me nervous. What d'you think?'

'Apart from Francis trying to cripple himself, and Val scowling over hidden meanings, you mean?'

'Exactly. Those are just normal things that happen—'

'My God!' said Kim. 'I hope they aren't! But I know what you mean, our usual huge upheavals seem to have gone off the screen. Nothing has fallen on us for ages now!'

Diana smiled at her and glanced down at her watch. 'Oops, I'd better get organised, or it'll be Shortlanesend that falls on me, with Francis pushing it!' She drained her mug as she got to her feet. 'I don't know when I'll be back. Hospitals can take for ever, and I don't know what he's got planned after that, if anything at all. He might just go to bed with the cat again.'

'Come on, he's a big, strong man, and he's had thirty six hours – more – now to get over it! But don't worry about me, I've got the car and I shall keep busy. I plan to go up to the university to suss out my chances there, and then to look at normal furniture, for a normal-sized bungalow. Valerie said she'd meet me for lunch and help me.'

'That's all right then.' Diana was already heading for the door, snatching up the keys to the Discovery from the coffee table as she went. 'See you this evening – it'll be my turn to wash up then.'

Kim forbore to remind her that technically, it already was, and simply waved goodbye, with the adjuration to have a nice day. She finished her own coffee at a more leisurely pace.

Diana drove to Shearwater with no hitches other than an unexpected meeting with a bus, which she managed to negotiate without incident with the help of a convenient field gate, and arrived safely at Shortlanesend feeling quite proud of herself. Bennie greeted her with a smile, and Ernie said, 'So how many dents have you made in that enormous vehicle? Or in the walls in the lane, come to that.'

'None at all,' Diana told him, with dignity. Where's Francis? He told me to be here at eight, so what's he doing?'

'He's here,' said Francis, from behind her, and she jumped, and swung round. He was just coming in through the back door, both of the dogs at his heels and his damaged hand in a neat padded sling, where it should have probably been all weekend. She was relieved to see that he looked a lot more like himself this morning.

'Well d-d-done,' he greeted her. 'Ernie and I had a b-b-bet on w-whether you'd m-m-make it or not.'

'And where did you put your money?' Diana asked him, coldly. He simply gave her a quick kiss on the cheek by way of a reply.

'R-right, let's get on the Wall of D-d-death, shall w-we?'

'Any idea when you might be back?' asked Bennie, without hope. He shook his head.

'S-some t-t-time.'

'Well, thanks for that. Take him away, Tamsin, and ring us when you can answer me, Francis, there's a good man. You might end up with just a sandwich if you leave it too late.'

'Oh, it w-w-won't be th-that late,' he told her, and swept Diana back out through the door, Sacha on their heels. She turned and waved to Bennie as they passed the threshold, and Bennie smiled back with a sympathetic waggle of her fingers.

Diana had been a little apprehensive about driving Francis in his own Discovery, but he passed no comment, sitting relaxed in the passenger seat and watching the scenery go past the windows. He did, however, make a comment on the CD she had swapped into his player.

'W-w-what on earth is th-th-this row?'

'Live with it,' she told him. 'Kim and I suffered God knows what all the way back from London!'

'You d-d-don't like C-c-classic Rock?'

'Not my favourite. No.'

'Hmm. S-so, w-w-what's your choice? A-p-part from th-this cacophony?'

'You really don't want to know,' said Diana, grinning to herself. 'We have a lot still to learn about each other, don't we?'

'D-doesn't everyb-body, when they s-s-start out?'

'That's probably true. Val certainly gave Kim a surprise or two over the weekend.'

He made a sound that might have been a laugh, and fell silent, and Diana concentrated on her driving and tried not to wonder what he was thinking.

Burnthouse, when they reached it, was more crowded than Diana had yet seen it. Gary's truck was in the yard, and a flatbed kitted out for shifting skips, and outside the double garage that lurked in the woods opposite to the side wall of the house there was a builders' truck, with men shifting ladders off the roof. There were men everywhere, in fact, Diana began to feel a little outnumbered as she drew up behind the builders. Two of the men made an instant beeline for them. One of them was Gary; he took a long look at Francis, as he climbed out of the Discovery, and said, 'I wondered why that skip was all bloody! Thought you might have found something that had died an unnatural death in the stable and a fox or something stole the body in the night, but I see I was wrong. So what have you been doing to yourself?'

'M-misunderstanding with a r-r-rusty n-nail.'

'Yes, I could see you had a bit of an accident with that doorframe.' Gary grinned at him. 'You should leave the serious stuff to us experts, eh Steve?'

The other man stepped forward and held out his hand to Diana. 'You must be Tamsin. Stephen Postgate, I understand we shall be seeing quite a bit of each other in the near future.' And he smiled at her in a friendly way. She smiled back and shook his hand. It seemed slightly over-formal against the backdrop of chaos that was the farm at present.

'Right,' said Gary. 'Business. Where do you want us to start, Francis? No point starting to shift that muck if we can't get rid of it, and I imagine you're not up for tractor driving this morning.'

'Th-there'll be someone h-h-here t-tomorrow m-morning to deal with that.' He gestured towards his bandaged hand. 'We d-d-didn't get clearing the stableyard f-f-finished yesterday, m–maybe you could do th-that first?'

'Sounds a good place to start. Let's give it a look, shall we?' The two of them moved off, leaving Diana and Stephen Postgate looking at each other.

'Francis said you'd talk me through what you want done,' he said, and the easy use of the forename told Diana that here was yet another good mate of the Vachells. She felt herself smiling at the thought, and he smiled back in a friendly way, and said, 'Probably take all day, state the place is in, but we have to start somewhere. The men are on the roof for the next couple of days, and the cleaners will be in later today I'm told. We can get going downstairs as soon as they're done, if you can tell me how you want it.'

'Well, I will, of course, but Francis did say he'd walk through the house with us. He has no idea yet what I have in mind.'

'But you do have something? Well, perhaps we can start without him?'

'I should think we could.' She stopped him as he automatically turned to the gate into the front garden. 'No – we need to start at the yard door, if you don't mind.'

He raised his eyebrows, but obediently followed her into the yard. The back door was still locked, but she had the forethought to bring the key and soon had it open, with a bit of help from the builder.

'Could do with a bit of oil, that,' he said, pushing the door open with a groaning creak. It seemed an understatement. They stood in the dank, dark passage; the cold struck right through to the bone. Diana pushed open the door that led into what seemed to have been used as an office.

'Start here,' she said. 'As I see it, the farm is going to be up and running long before the house is fit to live in, so making this room fit for use before it is used has to be a priority. At least, I think so.'

Stephen Postgate looked at her in a mixture of surprise and approval, she thought.

'Sounds like a good idea – not what I expected, but good.'

'Why, what did you expect?'

'Not sure, now I think about it.' He kicked at the floor. 'This is stone, so no woodworm or dry rot. Just a bit of repair work here and there, and the skirting board. Walls need re-plastering. One or two "ooh, nasties" in the door frame and the door. We can see to them.' He looked at the window pensively. 'That'll need a glazier, fortunately we've got one lined up. At least this bit is a later addition, so there's none of that fiddly stuff.'

'That's good.' Diana turned back to the door. 'Next – this one.' She pushed open the door to the rudimentary washroom. 'Can we put a shower in here, and turn it into a proper wash place? First off, it will keep the amount of muck tramped through the house to a minimum, but also, we can use it while we live in the caravan thing, and keep trips to the septic tank to a minimum.'

'Actually,' said Stephen Postgate, 'the "caravan thing" is scheduled to be connected to the main drains as a priority. But yes, we can probably do that, I'll have to measure up a bit. I take it you don't want it posh?'

'Just practical.' Diana was surprised – pleasantly so – about the drains, but made no comment then. She led the builder along the passage, outlining her plans for the various rooms and her reasons for making them a priority, and he nodded in agreement. Francis caught up with them at the pantry, just as Stephen Postgate said, 'So the re-wiring needs to start in this bit, we'll need to look into that. Should be possible.'

'Diana said, 'It needs to start in this half of the house, full stop. I thought we could just clean up the other side of the hall and the landing, get rid of the woodworm and stuff, and shut the doors on it, and concentrate on getting this half habitable so that we can…well, inhabit it. Then we can think about the posh end.' She was privately amazed to hear herself talking with such authority. Stephen looked over her shoulder at his approaching friend.

'This isn't just a pretty face you've got here,' he said, approvingly. 'She's full of sensible ideas, most of which will probably work.'

'Well, g-good. I th-thought she might be.'

'Did you?' asked Diana, slightly amazed.

'Kim w-w-would b-be. You're id-d-dentical twins.'

'I think that might be a bit of a rash conclusion to draw,' Diana told him, but she was pleased anyway.

The tour of the house continued. Diana looked, more carefully this time, into the room at the end of the dining room, and to her delight it met her remembered specifications.

'This can be your study,' she told Francis. 'You can put all your books in here, and keep your proper work separate from the farm.'

'S-s-some of the books,' he corrected, measuring it up with his eye. 'So you don't w-w-want it for a s-sewing r-r-room, then?' But he looked quietly pleased, and she laughed with him.

'You have to be joking! And the bookcases that won't fit in here can go in the other room, so you can get at them easily. They'll look nice there.' She turned to the builder, standing by listening to all this with amusement. 'And I thought, a wood-burner in that big hearth – would that be allowed?'

They continued the tour upstairs, where the immediate problem, apart from the wiring, was the bathroom. It would have to be modernised, Diana said firmly, but it needn't be actually modern. You could get reproduction baths and sinks and things in specialist shops and tuck a shower in the corner where it wouldn't be noticed. 'I expect we'll have to leave the fireplace, but we can put seashells in it, or something.'

'We might get away with that,' said Stephen. He looked at Francis. 'What do you think?'

At which point, Diana noticed the time, and they had to make a dash for the Discovery

'We'll do the rest tomorrow,' she called over her shoulder, and Stephen raised his hand in acknowledgement.

When they reached Embridge, she automatically headed for the big general hospital, but Francis re-directed her to another large building on the opposite side of the road with its own car park adjacent.

'Th-this is w-w-where the p-p-private patients come,' he told her.

'You mean, posh people like you?'

'Am I p-posh?' He looked slightly surprised. 'I s-s-see it more as p-p-people who can afford to p-p-pay and not b-b-burden the NHS even further.'

Diana considered this – all of it – as they walked together to the entrance. Was he posh? She supposed that depended on how you defined the word: probably he wasn't. He was reputed to be rich, but he didn't put on airs about it even if it was true. He was frequently noticeably scruffy, and he was obviously a hands-on farmer as well as a manager. His

Discovery wasn't top-of-the-range for a 4x4 and was frequently slathered with mud, although the Mercedes always shone. He did not have a valet or a chauffeur or any of the usual trappings of wealth. So what was he? An enigma, that's what!

She had been right: there was still a lot to learn.

She was to have plenty of time to ponder the question. Even paying customers, it seemed, did quite a lot of waiting about and it was twenty minutes before Francis was summoned from her side, even though they had arrived slightly late. They hadn't talked much in the interval; she had a feeling, that she didn't follow up, that he was deeply worried about the coming examination and had been for some time, and while he was gone, found it impossible to concentrate on the glossy magazines provided for her entertainment in the waiting room. Finally, the receptionist at the desk, who had been talking on her phone, put it down and came over to her.

'Mr Simmonds says, would you like to go through and speak to him?' she said, with a smile. 'I'll show you the way, if you like to follow me.'

Diana's heart leapt, and fell with a great thump; a conviction that Kim's breakfast foreboding had come home to roost swept over her, and she followed the receptionist with her heart banging against her ribs, but she needn't have worried. Mr Simmonds, the Consultant presumably, and Francis were sitting easily together, while a nurse rinsed her hands at a sink in the corner. As Diana came in, she finished what she was doing, and headed for the door with a smile to Diana as she passed her. She and the receptionist left together, and the consultant rose to his feet, holding out his hand, and Diana took it, hoping her own wasn't shaking, but then she saw Francis smiling at her and began to feel better.

'Miss Carey, how do you do?' said Mr Simmonds, waving her to a chair. Then he, too, smiled at her. 'No need to look so frightened – Mr Chillingworth said that if I told you the good news myself, you would probably believe it. He said that you had been worrying.'

'That's true. I've been doing that a lot, to be honest. So is he going to live?'

'Oh, definitely, I would say. Particularly if he can manage to avoid close encounters with rusty nails. No, there is some infection, from the dirt of ages he tells me, which is causing him some extra pain, but it should clear up with the antibiotics, and the District Nurse will be in each day to do the dressing and to keep an eye on it. He still has feeling in his fingers, and should regain the use of his hand without any after-effects. Does that make you feel happier?'

'Lots,' said Diana, with feeling.

'He'll probably need a bit of practical help for the next couple of weeks, but I think there's no doubt he will recover fully, if he does as he's told. He tells me you'll be living together shortly, and you will be the principle carer?'

'That's the plan, yes.'

'I wish you joy of it. My feeling is that you may have your work cut out keeping him under control, but do your best.' He smiled, warmly. 'I'll see you in a week, then, Mr Chillingworth, take care meanwhile; our receptionist will give you the appointment details on your way out. And I wish you both the very best of good fortune in your impending marriage. I have a feeling that one of you, at least, may need it!'

'Thank you,' Diana said, and Francis made a murmur of acknowledgement. They all rose to their feet, the brief interview over, and Diana and Francis made their way back along the corridor to the reception area to collect the appointment card and reach the door to the outside world.

'What a nice man,' said Diana. She added, 'And thank you.

'I th–th–thought you m–m–might believe it b–better f–f–from him.'

'I did! You're a big, macho man, and I don't trust you an inch further than I could throw you – which wouldn't be far! Now I feel as if someone had rolled a stone off me, that I hadn't even known was there.' They were back at the Discovery, she paused with her hand on the door. 'So, what shall we do to celebrate?'

'I thought we m–might g–g–go and buy Kim a c–c–camera.'

Diana stopped halfway into the driving seat.

'I'm sorry?'

He smiled at her, sliding into his own seat.

'Sh–she likes t–t–taking photos, she t–t–t–takes g–g–good ones, and m–my holiday let s–squashed her old one. The insurance c–c–covers th–things like that, b–but even if it d–d–didn't, I'd replace it.'

Diana was safely aboard and had started the engine before she found an answer to this. Then she said, as they drove away, 'The Square, then?'

They drove for a while in silence, negotiating traffic and traffic lights and turnings with growing aplomb on Diana's part, then she heard herself ask, out of nowhere, 'Why did you do that?'

'D-do what?' This was disingenuous, as he knew perfectly well; he hoped she would leave it there, but she didn't.

'Ask me in so that the doctor could tell me himself what was likely to happen.'

More silence, when she thought he wasn't going to answer. Then he said, 'I c-c-could see it was w-w-worrying you.'

'It was worrying me, because it was worrying you,' Diana told him. 'I thought you knew something I didn't.' Which he had, of course, according to Bennie. They went a little further in silence, and she waited, wondering what he would say. The truth? Or some soothing half-truth?

She got the truth.

'I w-w-was afraid that I had d-d-done something irreparable. I c-c-could hardly m-move my fingers, although I c-c-could f-f-feel when they w-w-were stabbed w-w-with a pin. I th-thought that m-my l-l-life was g-g-going to b-be snatched away, j-j-just as I had g-g-got it b-back, and th-then b-b-be a hundred t-t-times worse.' Pause. 'That d-d-do you?'

Diana found herself lost for words; no wonder he had been such a grouch over the weekend. She wanted to ask "why didn't you say?" but retained enough sense not to do so. She made the final turning into the Square, found a parking space, and switched off the engine.

'Right, where do we go for this camera? Bordens again? Kim and I seem to spend half our life in there,' she said, and felt his relief. 'Come to that, she's probably there now – she's having lunch with Valerie.' She was babbling for the sake of it, still shaking inside from what she had just learned.

'N-no. Th-there's a b-b-better place d-d-down that turning.' He indicated with his left hand, as glad as she was to let the subject go. They set off in the indicated direction, both of them suddenly silent.

Choosing a camera to suit Kim's roving lifestyle, which Diana felt would not change too radically in the future, husband or no, allowed a soothing interval between that disturbing confession and the here and now, and they came out of the shop with their feet, metaphorically speaking, back on solid ground.

'What now?' Diana asked, as they paused outside on the pavement. 'Borden's for lunch? Or what.'

'N-no,' said Francis, thinking. 'I c-c-can't face Borden's, and K-kim will be th-th-there with V-Valerie, you said. Act-t-ually, I'd like somewhere qu-quiet. I'm n-n-not that bothered about l-lunch, to be t-t-truthful.'

Diana looked at him measuringly; he was looking a bit pale. OK, she was the "principle carer", was she? – she would start right here.

'All right then. Do you want me to take you back to Shortlanesend?' She hoped he didn't, time with just the two of them was precious. Fortunately, he said, 'N-no. C-c-can't we just g-g-go back to R-Romans, if Kim is out?'

'We could.' She took his arm and turned him in the direction of the Square and the Discovery. 'But you can't not eat. We'll stop at the supermarket – you can stay in the car if you want – and I'll slip in and get a pot of that ready-made soup, even I can deal with that, and some rolls to have with it.

'N-not sure about s-soup. I'm not too g-g-good with m-my left hand, I'd m-m-make a m-mess.'

'We noticed, the other night,' Diana told him, smiling up at him. 'I can put it in a mug for you. You can manage that.'

They followed this programme, or at least Diana did and Francis came along for the ride, and ended up parked outside Romans. Diana had added another box of doughnuts to the soup and rolls, and had every intention of seeing that he ate enough to keep body and soul together; she led the way indoors with a firm step. Pointing to the sofa, she said, 'Sit there – and don't go to sleep! This won't take ten minutes.'

'I'm n-n-not sleepy,' he disclaimed. 'J-just had enough for the m-m-moment.' He smiled at her. 'W-w-we don't d-d-do that well for t-t-time to ourselves, do we, between K-kim and V-val and the k-k-kids at Shortlanesend? B-be a shame t-t-to waste it.' As this was more or less what she had thought for herself just now, she returned the smile warmly. Not, she thought sadly, as she went into the kitchen, that anything exciting was going to happen, not between his sore and painful hand and the fact that Kim might appear at any moment. Oh well. Roll on the caravan. That plumbing had sounded hopeful.

She heard Francis call her name as she unpacked the supermarket bag, and returned to the living room with a packet of ham in her hand.

'Sir? You rang?'

He grinned at her from his collapsed position on the sofa.

'Yes. S-sorry, I s-s-seem to have r-r-run out of steam. There's s-some painkillers in the p-p-pocket of my c-coat, c-c-could you g-g-get them out for me, p-p-please, and liberate a couple? It's impossible w-w-with one hand. And m-my phone, if y-you c-can find it. I n-n-need to make an ap-pointment for us w-w-with J-Jerry Nankervis.'

'You do look a bit pale.' She looked at him critically, and then belatedly realised what he had said. 'Us?'

'Yes.' He gestured to his bandaged hand. 'If I c-c-can't s-sign things for th-the n-next c-c-couple of w-w-weeks, and it l-l-looks as if I w-won't, we n-need to give you a t-t-tempor-rary Power of Attorny, or something, s-s-so you c-c-can l-legally do it for me.'

'You can't do it all on your computer?' Diana wasn't sure about this proposal.

'N-not everything, n-no. And I'm n-n-not too handy with th-that, w-w-with just one hand, either, so I'll be c-c-calling on you th-there, t-too. W-w-will you m-mind?'

'No, of course I won't. It just hadn't occurred to me.' She fetched the phone and the packet of tablets and popped out a couple for him. 'Not the most convenient packaging for someone with only one hand,' she commented. 'Hang on – I'll get you a glass of water to swallow those with.' She put the tablets carefully on the table and went back into the kitchen. When she came back, he was already on the phone, so she put the glass beside the tablets and was about to return to the kitchen, when he gestured to her to stay where she was, so she waited until he put the phone down.

'Now what?'

He extended his left arm across the back of the sofa and jerked his head towards it.

'C-c-come and s-s-sit down for a m-minute. Th-there's n-no hurry f-f-for lunch.'

She sat obediently, and his arm immediately tightened round her shoulders and drew her close: they sat like that without speaking for a few minutes. Then he said, 'I'm s-s-sorry, T-Tamsin – I k-keep saying that, d-don't I? Th-this isn't at all w-w-what I had in m-mind.'

It wasn't quite what Diana had had in mind, either, but she decided not to labour the point.

'At least my parents will be relieved,' she offered. He turned to look at her, half-smiling and bright-eyed.

'They will? You sh-should be ashamed of yourself, M-Miss Carey.'

'I'm afraid that today's young people are a disappointment to them. But you – you're old enough to know better!'

'You th-think so?'

'Not really. I'm assuming that at your age you must have been round the block a couple of times. To be fair, I think I'd be more worried if you hadn't.' She paused, realising that she didn't actually know that, she was making an educated guess. 'I am right, aren't I?'

His arm tightened further round her shoulders and he bent his head to kiss her, very slowly and thoroughly before he answered her. Then he said, 'Of c-c-course you are. Do you m-mind?'

So long as it wasn't Barbara, Diana thought, but refrained from saying out loud. Barbara had been a friend, from her own point of view dangerously near him in age; years back, his mother had once thought that he was planning to marry her and knocked the idea on the head, hard, as she knew, because at the time she had thought…but all that was over, and a long time ago. She realised that the silence had gone on for a bit too long, and turned her head to look him straight in the face.

'But you didn't marry her, whoever she was,' she said, stating an obvious fact.

'Th-there w-w-was never any question of th-that.'

'Just good friends?' asked Diana.

'A l-l-little more th-than that. But m-m-marriage d-didn't enter into it, f-f-for s-s-several reasons. You m-must kn-now one of th-them.'

She did. He, in his turn, had believed his mother was a murderess. Her heart clenched with pity for both of them.

'Well, I hope she was beautiful, kind and generous, and you parted as friends a long time ago.'

'All of th-those. And t-t-ten years older than m-m-me.'

Not Barbara, then.

'Do you still see her?' She shouldn't have asked that. She bit her lip, but he answered easily enough.

'Occasionally, in th-the distance. We d-d-don't m-m-meet up on purpose.'

They sat for a few minutes longer, simply enjoying the quiet closeness of each other, and then Diana reluctantly pulled herself away.

'I should see to the lunch. Did you get Jerry Nankervis?'

'His s-s-secretary, or whatever you c-c-call them th-these days. We're s-s-seeing him at three o'clock th-the day after t-tomorrow.'

Diana nodded, and went into the kitchen to see to the lunch. Soup that she didn't even have to make, and ham rolls, followed by doughnuts, and apples from their fruit bowl shouldn't be beyond her capabilities. She stuck her head round the door once, to ask him if he liked mustard; he looked as if he might have fallen asleep after all, lying back with his eyes closed, but then she saw the tightness around his mouth and realised that he was simply fighting pain. She stepped back into the kitchen without saying anything, and put the mustard in anyway.

Kim returned towards the end of the afternoon, and found Francis lying on the sofa with his feet up and his head and shoulders propped on the pillows from the spare bunk bed, and Diana sitting at the dining table writing lists in a notebook. They both looked very relaxed and peaceful, talking quietly together, but they broke off as she came through the door, and she felt a bit like an intruder. She realised, for the first time, how awkward it must have been for Diana sometimes, in the cottage.

'Hello Kim, had any success with your hunting?' Diana asked, looking up as she came in. 'You look a bit laden.'

'Sheets and things, Val won't want to give an opinion on those and he says his own are pretty ancient.' Kim heaved her parcels onto the table; there was one bag of something already there, she noticed. She smiled at Francis. 'Hello. You're looking better than last time I saw you.'

'Not difficult,' said Diana, under her breath. She reached out and pushed the small extra parcel in Kim's direction. That's for you. A present from your ex-landlord.'

'Really?' She picked it up, and glanced at Francis. He was smiling at her, and moving himself into an upright sitting position at the same time. 'Don't get up for me,' she added hastily.

'I have t-t-to anyway. We've got to be away soon.' He glanced at his watch. 'V-v-very soon, in f-fact.'

'Shame. You looked very comfortable on that sofa.' She glanced at Diana with a wicked grin. 'Have you shown him what's behind it?'

'No. He just flopped onto it, and hasn't moved off it since.'

'Why, w-w-what is?' He peered over the back. 'Ah – I s-s-see what you m-m-mean.'

'Pots, pans and paraphernalia for our camping interlude,' Diana told him. 'Nothing posh, so we can leave it there for the next tenants. Melamine, mostly – apart from the pans, of course.'

'S-sensible. It'll p-p-probably end up as a holiday home for the f-f-family in the summer.'

'Do you have planning permission to leave it there for some time, then?' Kim asked, practically.

'Of c-course.'

'It's going to have proper drains, the builder told me!' Diana added, gleefully.

'And electricity and m-mains w-w-water,' Francis told her.

'It's sounding better every minute!' Diana rubbed her hands together happily; she had had her doubts about that caravan.

Kim remembered the small bag in her hands, and peered inside it. Her face was a picture when she saw what it contained.

'Oh Francis! Oh, you star! But you shouldn't have, it wasn't your fault it got busted!'

'You c-c-could argue w-w-with th-that,' he pointed out. 'B-but it's the Insurers you sh-sh-should thank, n-not me.'

'Have they paid out, then?' asked Kim surprised; it seemed rather prompt.

'N-not yet. Y-you'll know w-w-when they d-d-do.' He finished getting to his feet, and Diana shut her notebook.

'Right, are we off?' She turned to Kim. 'I have to run him to Burnthouse so he can check with Gary and the builder and so forth, see what they've been doing and things. Then I shall take him back to Shortlanesend and come back here for supper. If that fits in with you?'

'Sounds great,' said Kim, who had thought she would be spending the evening alone. 'But don't you want to spend the evening together?'

'He'll only go to bed early,' Diana told her. 'No, I shall see him tomorrow – all day again! A girl can only take so much punishment.'

They left, and Kim took her shopping upstairs in a thoughtful mood. She hadn't asked about the hospital appointment, she realised, but she had sensed a deep joy in her twin and a new relaxation in Francis, and felt it safe to assume that all would be well in the end. It was good, looked at in one way, that the accident had happened; it was giving the two of them time to get to know each other properly, and they were probably learning things they had never suspected. Just like she and Val had over the weekend. She made a face at herself in the bedroom mirror and went back downstairs to see what there was for supper. The short answer to that, seemed to be "eggs". And a couple of doughnuts in an opened box that seemed to have held four originally, she had no idea where they had come from, she would have taken oath that she and Diana had eaten them all. Then she chucked her last bit of shopping, which was a Bordens' bag containing a Scrabble board and a pack of cards, onto the coffee table and sat down to explore the workings of her new camera while she waited for Diana's return. She didn't expect that to be soon.

The following day was a lot more lively, and full of unexpected events – good ones, which made a change. It began well, so far as Kim and Diana were concerned, in that they didn't have to rise at dawn; Diana didn't have to report to Shortlanesend until 9.30, due to the visit from the District Nurse to see to the dressing on Francis' hand. It had turned out that she was a cousin of Bennie's – was everyone in the immediate area related to the Vachells? Diana wondered – and had promised to try to make Shortlanesend her first visit if there were no emergencies. She was just leaving when Diana rolled up outside, but even so, they arrived at Burnthouse an hour later than they had the previous day, and things were well under way. There was an unfamiliar tractor in the home field below the house, busily mowing, and another one, which Diana thought she recognised as Francis's own, parked out in the yard with richly rotted dung being loaded with a mechanical shovel into the muck-spreader behind it. The builders were up on the roof, the cleaners' van was parked behind Stephen Postgate's outside the garage, and a man was busy pressure-washing the stable yard. Gary was standing talking to a young man, whom Diana had not seen before, beside the tractor in the yard. Obviously yet another Vachell; he had curly dark hair almost the same length as her own held back by an elastic band, bright brown eyes and the family's trademark sturdy build and striking good looks. Simon, presumably.

But no. Apparently not.

'What th-the hell are you d-d-doing here?' Francis said, striding up to greet him warmly with a slap on the shoulder. 'Sh-sh-shouldn't you be up in th-the M-Midlands, w-w-working out your s-s-sentence?'

The greeting was as warmly returned, and the stranger said, 'Simon rang me on Sunday night, he told me what you'd done. I had a couple of days' holiday owing, which I wasn't intending to take, but when I told the boss what you'd been doing to yourself, he told me to take them anyway and threw in another for luck. So I have to be back on Friday morning for the weekend, but in the meantime, I'm all yours.'

'Th-that's good news, w-w-we can do with you – as you can s-s-see.'

'Thought you might.' The stranger turned to Diana. 'And you, lovely lady, you have to be Tamsin.' He held out his hand. 'I'm Simon's little brother, Cosmo.'

'I haven't met Simon yet, either,' Diana told him, and he grinned.

'He's over yonder, mowing the wildflower meadow the junkies left for you.' He pointed to the home field. 'Seemed like a good place to start – he left me with the dung pile, that's an older brother for you. We borrowed the other tractor from the neighbours, so we could work twice as hard to get it done for you.' He waved an arm in the general direction of Ravenscourt Place, and turned back to Francis. 'So, what did you think you were doing? You should know better than to be that careless, at your age! Or were you just ducking the dung?'

'You g-guessed,' said Francis, and then Stephen Postgate arrived to join them.

'Morning Francis, morning Tamsin. So are we up for finishing the conducted tour while you're here, so we all know what we're doing?'

'J-just l–let me fill C-C-Cosmo in on what n-n-needs t-t-to be done here,' said Francis, already turning aside as he spoke, and Diana and Stephen exchanged a look.

'Let's just get on with it,' Diana suggested. 'He can catch us up – or maybe he won't. He's got more important things on his mind.'

'That's farmers for you.' He turned and led the way.

They had reviewed the bathroom, with the help of a catalogue that the builder had brought with him, and settled on the corner bedroom, which was the largest, for first position on the decorating list, and were heading for the far side of the landing when Francis did, in fact, catch up with them. He and Diana between them then outlined their plans for the two remaining bedrooms, and Stephen asked about planning permission.

'It's a listed building. You can't just do what you want,' he pointed out, and Francis said he had an architect on the job, and when the plans were drawn up, permission would be sought.

'W-which is another g-g-good reason for l-l-leaving this end of the house until l-l-last.'

'Well, that all seems pretty clear,' Stephen said, as they went back downstairs. 'We'll do the job in the order we've discussed, and if all goes well, I reckon you may be able to move in, at least to the planned living area and the one bedroom, by Christmas. You may have to use the downstairs washroom for a bit.' He caught Diana's eye. 'We'll make the service passage a priority, as we discussed, but at least there's a separate loo at the end of the upstairs passage, and we can sort that out quickly, I daresay. It's a bit poky, but better than a gazunder.' He grinned.

'W-which bedroom did you s-s-s-settle on, for now?' Francis asked, as they went back outside, and Diana told him, 'The one on the corner, with the funny little window down by the floor. It's not got the best view, but it's the biggest at that end of the house.'

Francis looked into space for a minute, and then came abruptly back to earth.

'Eight or n-nine weeks, t-tops, then. We'd b-b-better g-go and find some f-f-furniture, while we've got the ch-chance.'

Diana had not expected that he would be that interested in furniture, she had thought that would be down to her, and maybe Kim, but it seemed that the rusty nail had done her a favour – a rather backhanded one, but still a favour. He needed a distraction – OK, let's have an antiques hunt!

Cosmo was over by the tractor, watching as the digger loaded up the muck-spreader; he turned as they emerged through the back door and came over to them.

'Take him away, Tamsin,' he said. 'This is no place for a man who already has one infection from this pit of Hell, and I can see in his eye that given half a chance, he'll find an excuse for sticking around. There's nothing you can usefully do, coz – get thee hence!'

'It's all right, we're going,' said Diana, giving Francis a push as she spoke to start him moving towards the Discovery. 'We're going to look at furniture, he says.'

'Good hunting, then.' He waved them towards the car.

They didn't get away that easily, because Gary waylaid them with a question about the carpenter scheduled to repair the woodwork in the stable block, but eventually they were safely aboard and heading back to the road. As they drove away, Diana was thinking; her thoughts were taking her into uncomfortable places: there had been a warm friendliness to that brief and unexpected encounter, not just Gary, and Stephen Postgate, whom she had already placed as old friends, but his young cousin Cosmo too had displayed a warm, casual affection that must have deep roots. It was the Chillingworths all over again – except that the Vachells had never withdrawn their support, as witness the warm and instant welcome given to him by Bennie and Ernie when he left Vachells, and the way the family had rallied round in the present situation. It set her thinking, not for the first time, about that other situation down at the Sailing Club and to an extent, at the Yacht Club too: the more she learned about Francis, the more it began to feel that the cold-shouldering and mockery he had to put up with in both those places was actually also limited to them, and it was becoming more and more like being engaged to two separate and distinct people, as she had once said to Kim. She put that out of her mind, now wasn't the moment.

'He seems a nice young man – Cosmo,' she said, to distract herself; no use worrying at it like a dog with a bone. Francis shot her a glance.

'W-w-why do you th-think I chose him?'

'It was a good choice, why ever it was.' She negotiated the end of the farm lane and went on, 'Does your mother know he's here?'

'Ab-bout as m-m-much as I d-d-did, I imagine. She w-w-will. He's p–planning to ring her t-t-tonight, he'll t-t-try to slip over before he l-l-leaves on Th-Thursday.'

'Good, she'll like that. She's lonely, your mum.'

'I kn-now. B-but at least the d-d-dust is b-b-beginning to settle n-now.' He spoke this time without turning his head. 'L-l-largely d-d-due to you. So th-thank you.'

'I like your mum,' Diana told him, and he said quietly, 'M-me too.'

Despite the continuing pain from his unusable right hand, Francis seemed to have bounced back this morning – possibly, Diana speculated, because of the weight that had been taken off his mind yesterday morning, but partly too, she realised, because things were beginning to move now out at Burnthouse, thanks to his two good friends, his two young cousins and two distinct teams of cheerful and busy workmen. The only fly in the ointment was that he couldn't be there with them right now, but he made up for that by conducting her on a whirlwind tour of antique shops and auction houses, some of which she and Kim hadn't even found on their previous trip. Francis claimed to have enough bedroom furniture already in store for their immediate needs, but they would be needing other things. They ended up in a pub at lunchtime, and Diana flopped into a chair clasping the lunch menu in a state of total amazement, the proud co-owner of a long farmhouse kitchen table together with eight, slightly assorted kitchen chairs, a couple of big antique wardrobes for their eventual bedroom, the prospect of going to an auction on Friday to try their best to secure an antique four-poster destined for the same place, and an equally antique and very beautiful sideboard for their temporary living room. The afternoon was to be devoted to the purchase of an Aga for the kitchen, after that, she thought, assessing him critically, it might finally be back to Romans, or maybe Shortlanesend, to let him chill out for a bit. Personally, she felt as if she had been hit by a hurricane; he already seemed to have the whole thing organised in his head, she had no doubt that it would become reality.

'W-we can sh-shove it all in th-the d-drawing room, when th-the w-wood has been t-t-treated, and it's c-c-clean,' he told her, when she had wondered aloud where they were going to put it all until they were ready for it. 'If y-you p-plan to l-leave it until n-n-next year, we can use it as a s-storeroom. In f-f-fact, we c-c-can get all the rest of m-my stuff out of st-store too, and have it where w-w-we c-can keep an eye on it – and c-c-come to that, where I c-c-can g-get at my books.'

'Even the grand piano?' asked Diana, who still only half-believed in it.

'M-most of all, the g-g-grand piano,' he told her, laughter in his eyes. He knew exactly what she was thinking, the thing was a myth to tease her.

'Then you can play it to me,' she told him, and re-directed his roving attention to the menu. 'Come on, you can't live on soup and sandwiches – there must be something here that you can tackle one-handed! If it has chips with it, you can just pick them up in your fingers. People do.' Now, Francis Chillingworth, we'll see how posh you really are! But if she had expected horror at the mere suggestion, she was to be disappointed.

'Good thinking,' he said, and settled on scampi and chips. Diana chose the same, it was one of her pub lunchtime favourites anyway, although she wouldn't necessarily eat it with her fingers. She went up to the bar to order it, and he entrusted her with his wallet to pay for it.

'Easier than fumbling ab-b-bout myself,' he told her. 'And I'll have a b-b-beer while you're about it, t-too.'

He managed the scampi and chips easily, partly with a fork and partly with his fingers, and seemed to enjoy them too, which was an improvement, although he did turn down the idea of sticky toffee pudding on the plea that he was sticky enough already from the dipping sauce, thank you, which Diana did not allow to stop her. They left the pub eventually in a lighthearted mood that she didn't recognise, but felt she could get used to, and headed for the Aga shop, where Diana settled on a bright red one, and Francis didn't argue about it. By that time, she noticed, he was beginning to go a bit quiet, so she said, 'Romans or Shortlanesend?'

'Where's K-kim?' he asked.

'Having lunch in Shearwater with Valerie, so far as I know. Why?'

He didn't answer that question, but merely said, 'R-romans then. And you c-can slip across to th-th-the yard and have a word with Merlin ab-bout the w-w-weekend, while I p-p-put m-my feet up. I'm starting to feel as if I've d-d-done ten rounds with Henry Cooper.'

'Probably time you popped a few more pills, then.'

'Y-yes, teacher.'

She left him on the sofa, and walked across the road to the yard and in through the big gates. The last time she had been here, she reflected as she walked, was the day after Clive had let her down over the weekend they were supposed to be spending on a "yacht". She had just met Kim, and they had come down to see if there was any message from him, and while they were there, they had looked at the…well, yes, it was a yacht. Just. The smallest that Diana had ever seen, and the accommodation was very cosy indeed. A near miss, that one, and how glad she was now!

Merlin was working in one of the big boatsheds, but he was perfectly happy to be interrupted. He knew what had happened, of course, partly because Simon and Cosmo had told the tale when they borrowed the tractor for the day, and partly because bad news always travels fast, and he agreed that while Francis was thus immobilised more or less in one place, it was probably a good time to sort out the wedding plans. He placed himself at their disposal for Saturday morning and went back to work, sending his sympathy to Francis, and Diana went back to Romans for a quiet afternoon, which by this time Francis wasn't the only one to need. When Kim returned, later, they were quietly watching afternoon sport on the telly, and it was Diana who was practically asleep.

Sir Charles phoned that evening, while Kim and Diana were addling their brains in front of a game show.

'Right,' he told Diana, when the preliminaries were over. 'We shall aim to be at the Langland Hotel on Friday evening, perhaps you can slip over later for an after-dinner drink and a chat?'

'Well, I can,' said Diana. 'I can't answer for Francis without speaking to him, but I can let you know. He isn't here at the moment.' She had taken him back to Shortlanesend, after a cup of coffee with Kim so that his departure didn't look too pointed.

'Right, we'll leave that pending for now, there's plenty of time.' He paused. 'Now then, can you arrange for us to have a look at this chapel on Saturday morning, and then we can maybe fix a date and arrange a small reception at – where did you say? The Ravenscourt Arms, was it? We shan't be able to get down again much before the day if it's to be soon, so we need to arrange everything we can while we're there.'

Diana told him that the inspection of the chapel was already arranged, and confirmed that the pub was the Ravenscourt Arms. 'It's a very nice pub. Quite classy.'

'Your mother is a little disappointed that the wedding reception will be so small, but we would both like it to be a memorable occasion none the less.'

'The Ravenscourt Arms has a very good reputation.' She caught Kim's eye and smothered a grin, that in any case her father could not see. 'They can shut off part of the restaurant to make a separate functions room for private parties, if they're not too large, that is.'

'Which it seems that it won't be,' said her father, drily. 'Now, your mother would like a word with you. I'll leave the arrangements for you?' He made it into a question.

'I've already got Francis's friend Merlin lined up for Saturday morning,' she told him, pleased that she had been so prescient. 'He's the one in charge of all that. He'll take the morning off from the boatyard for you.'

Sir Charles voiced his approval of her forethought, and then Eloise came on the phone.

'Diana darling! How is everything going down there on the farm? Is the house as dreadful as it sounded?'

'It is at the moment,' Diana told her honestly. 'It will be beautiful, when I've finished with it. We've been out all day sorting out some furniture for when we can move in, and tomorrow we have to measure up the utility rooms and order freezers and fridges and a washing machine and stuff. We could be in by Christmas, the builder said! Well—' she paused, and ended more honestly, '—in that half of the house, anyway. It'll be a while longer before it's all finished.'

'When *you've* finished with it, darling? What can you possibly know about renovating historic houses?'

'Believe me, I'm learning fast,' Diana told her. 'Actually, it's fascinating – I hadn't thought it would be so…so satisfying, I suppose. Poor old house, it should never have been allowed to fall apart like it has.'

'So, are we to be allowed to see it?'

'Of course! The dung heap should be gone by the weekend, and the cleaners have been in the house today, and tomorrow too. It already smells a lot better out there!'

'Oh darling, it sounds dreadful!' But Eloise was laughing. 'Will you both be free to have dinner with us on Saturday, at the hotel? Perhaps Francis's mother would like to join us, what do you think? We should obviously like to meet her before the wedding day, and I expect she feels the same way!'

'I'm sure she would, I can ask her for you. But I'm not sure if Francis will be up for it. He's having a bit of trouble, having to use his left hand all the time – he's not terribly good at it.' Understatement of the Year.

Eloise and Sir Charles had, of course, heard about the accident, but Diana had played it down a little, not expecting them to arrive on the scene so promptly. Eloise said now, 'But surely, it will be getting better by the weekend?'

'I wouldn't put money on it,' Diana told her. 'He's got an infection in it, it's giving him hell, and he's not very dextrous with his left hand, to be honest. He might not be up for demonstrating his ineptitude in public.' She enlarged on the subject to give Eloise a clearer picture. 'Last night he dined on a mug of soup, a ham roll and a doughnut, all of which he can just about manage OK. Breakfast was a fried egg on toast, eaten in his fingers, or so Bennie told me, and he did manage scampi and chips at lunchtime, but only because he could pick it up in his fingers again, while no-one was looking. So far as eating with just a fork is concerned, he's probably limited to things like shepherds' pie, or macaroni cheese – and even that might be pushing it.'

'I'm sure the Langland will be equal to the challenge, if we ask them. It does have four stars, after all.'

'Can we leave it pending, maybe? It's only Tuesday, there's four days yet – he might get the hang of it by then. Only don't get your hopes up too high – that isn't very long.'

They spoke for a few minutes more, and then Diana switched off her phone and looked at Kim.

'It's all suddenly getting very close,' she said, not sure if she liked the idea or not.

'Cold feet?' asked Kim, grinning at her.

'No – well yes. Not about marrying, about the actual marriage. It seems to be suddenly sweeping in on us as fast as a spring tide with an October gale behind it!'

'But you're still sure, in your own mind?' Kim narrowed her eyes. 'He's given you a bit of stick this last couple of days, one way and another.'

'Not really. And yes, I am sure. Surer than ever, actually. I've been seeing another side to him, and…well, I like it. Life isn't going to be dull – well it isn't being dull, certainly not right now. '

'Then that's all right, isn't it? And now, shall we watch the end of this programme, see who wins? Then you can give me the lowdown…'

XXII

By the time the weekend came round several things had changed, most, but not all of them for the better. The dungheap had virtually disappeared, spread out over the fields by the two hard-working Vachell boys, and neat piles of plastic-wrapped bales of slightly dubious silage occupied corners in a few of the fields, under equally neatly trimmed hedges. The ditches still had to be cleared and the stone walls that formed some of the field boundaries needed to be checked and repaired, and in some cases rebuilt: Matt's Dad was a drystone walling specialist, the perfect man for the job, Cosmo said – although Matt was heard to say that he was tearing his hair a bit at the prospect of working under the eye of a frustrated, picky, and unfortunately also knowledgeable second cousin once-removed, with insufficient to distract him! There was still a good month at the very least of hard, backbreaking work to be done yet, Francis had estimated, before the place would be even halfway fit for use, and God knew how long before it was in tiptop condition again, but he may have been being a bit pessimistic: All of this present work on the fields, of course, was what he had reckoned on doing himself with just the help of young Matt, and his enforced role as a mere onlooker was quite obviously sending him distracted, which probably accounted for Matt's Dad's hair problems. The only bright spot in the overall picture right now, as he saw it, was that the additional fields to be rented from Ravenscourt Place were already immaculate and in good heart. Cosmo vanished on Thursday evening, back to the Midlands to work out his notice, but Matt and his father would be there on Friday to take over from Simon and to make a start on the walling, and the work would go on. Gary had pressure-washed the farmyard and removed eight huge skips of very assorted rubbish, and still counting, from the premises; he reckoned he should be finished and gone early the following week. A competent carpenter and his mate were reconstructing the stable doors.

By the end of the following week, Francis reckoned, being positive for a change, the stable might be half-way fit for horses, but he didn't say that he was going to import any just yet.

Francis himself was beginning to recover his energy and spirits as the infection gave ground to the antibiotics. By this time he had a little use in his damaged hand, although nothing impressive: he was, said Diana, to Kim, about equal to a soup spoon, but she wouldn't trust him with a dinner knife. Unfortunately, as he began to feel better, he also began to lose his patience, and finding things to keep him safely occupied and away from the centre of operations became a primary consideration. Diana found herself spending quite a lot of time with him in Ernie's office at Shortlanesend, Sacha under the desk and the little black cat, Birdie, sitting on top of the filing cabinet, typing letters and emails on Francis' computer with the haphazard fingering and sometimes creative spelling that she employed for emails on her own laptop and Francis practically breathing down her neck, putting her own legible signature to documents connected with the Planning Permission for the main bedroom and other side issues, and helping to keep the ship of farm management on course – a job for which she was in no way qualified, but maybe something of Kim's competence was rubbing off on her. Or possibly, it had been there all the time, just undiscovered? She began to acquire a vague idea of what was involved in running an estate, but there was also another side-effect, that she tried to explain to Kim on Thursday evening, when she had spent two whole days in her new role.

They had waved Cosmo off at the end of the working day, and she had returned from taking Francis back to Shortlanesend feeling unexpectedly flat; one thing you could say for Cosmo, it was never dull when he was around. She wondered privately what Mary would make of him when he joined her at Vachells at the end of the month, but on the other hand, she had known him from a child so she would probably be at least half-prepared and able to cope with the excitement.

As she had coped with her own son, and all his many cousins. As she coped today with Clive and Maisie.

There was a lot more to the Vachell family than she had initially supposed; she had thought the Chillingworths were the dominant gene, the interesting ones; now she wasn't so sure.

'What's the matter now?' Kim asked her. 'You're sitting there like a thundercloud; for goodmess' sake, cheer up!' She was privately a little concerned about her twin: Cosmo had left that evening, she knew, he was dark, handsome, and full of energy and charm, he was only about a year younger than Diana, not thirteen years older, and the situation could have been – maybe had been – potential dynamite. But Diana's answer put these fears to rest.

'I was just thinking,' she said.

'You looked as gloomy as sin! I wondered if everything was OK?' Kim ended on a questioning lift, but to her relief, Diana relaxed her pensiveness and laughed.

'Don't sound like that, everything's fine – well fine but peculiar. You see, I hadn't realised…' She tailed off and sat thinking out what she wanted to say. Kim said, 'Realised what?'

'You'll think I'm wool-gathering! You see, I love Francis very much, I think he's amazing and I'm so very, very glad that he loves me too, and all the rest of it – but until this week, when we've been thrown together practically from dawn until dusk, and I hadn't realised this, but I didn't actually know him that well. Not like you know Val. I hadn't shared his life until now, or met his immediate family or his friends – I don't mean the Chillingworths, they're different anyway – or had any…well background, for him, I suppose. They've been very educational, these last few days.'

'I thought you told me he was being a pain in the arse,' Kim reminded her.

'Oh, he has been, quite often. He wants to be off playing with his new toy, but nobody will let him because of the risk of infection in all that muck and mess, and anyway, he'd only get in the way, he couldn't do anything useful! He behaves sometimes as if he's about four years old, to be honest, but it's understandable. And it is only sometimes.'

'So explain, I know Gary Fancot was a bit of an eye-opener, but how are the Vachells so different from the Chillingworths? They're all family, just the same.'

'No, not just the same.' Diana considered this for a minute, and then tried to explain sensibly – not easy, when she was going largely by instinct. 'The Chillingworths have been off the stage for years, it's great that they're all reunited, but it's different from…well, I suppose I'm trying to say, the Vachells have always been there. They've all been in regular contact, they all do the same job, they're countrymen and they're all friends. They know each other well, and in a crisis, they all rally round – as they've just demonstrated. Are demonstrating, in fact. And they are as different from the Chillingworths as chalk is from cheese, socially, financially, the lot really. And Francis is far more like them, come to that.' She paused, reflecting on this, and then added, 'and he can be a real slave-driver when he sets his mind to it, too.'

'Do you good,' Kim told her, unsympathetically, 'You chose him – and anyway, what you've just told me should have been obvious, shouldn't it? After all, he grew up with them, not just saw them for holidays now and then.'

'I know, I know. It's just that I never saw it that way before – at the Sailing Club, he never mixed anyway, and when he met with his London cousins it was great, of course, but somehow…well, I suppose it was holiday time again, and that's different from every day. For goodness' sake, he and Ernie were at Sixth Form College together!'

'And he and at least one of his Chillingworth cousins were at Public School together,' Kim pointed out.

'I know that – but you know what I'm trying to say.'

Kim did, of course. It was amazing how many things were obvious, once someone pointed them out. She said, hesitantly, 'I wonder how they all felt about the situation over the past few years – it must have been obvious, if they're all that close, that something was seriously wrong.'

'I'm sure that it was. I get the impression that they were all sitting back and keeping an eye on things, they didn't know anything after all, it was just obvious that there was something to know. And if they didn't know, there was nothing they could do either – but now that there is, there they all are.'

'That's families for you,' Kim offered. 'Real families, I don't think there are so many of those around these days.'

'It's positively feudal!'

'Don't complain about it. It's saving your man's sanity.'

'They've been farming these same acres for hundreds – possibly more than a thousand – years, it makes me feel quite strange to think about it. They've been here far longer than the Ravenscourts. Did you know, Burnthouse is about two hundred years older than Ravenscourt Place?'

'Good heavens, did that belong to the Vachells too?'

'No, of course not, although the land it's on may have – but Burnthouse was originally theirs, years and years back, and that land was certainly the Vachells' then. I think that must be one reason why Merlin drew it to Francis's attention, he certainly wouldn't have noticed it on his own, the state it's in! And it wouldn't be big enough for him either, without the Ravenscourts' contribution.'

'State it was in,' Kim corrected. 'It's getting better now, so you tell me.'

'It's getting cleaner. I wouldn't put it as high as "better" yet. Neither would Francis.'

They exchanged a speaking look.

'What are you planning to do with him tomorrow?' Kim asked. 'Back to the office, or are you going to be allowed some fresh air?'

'We shall do our morning inspection, of course. Then he has to talk to the architect on site after that, he'll be coming over there at ten – we have to talk, rather, since it was my idea originally. And in the afternoon, we're off to an auction. So yes, I shall get some fresh air. If the forecast is right, a bit too much fresh air.'

'And are you going to the Langland in the evening, like your dad suggested?' Kim had wondered about this, and as it turned out, Diana had wondered too. She said, 'No. I told them it was too late, too far, and too dark. They had no idea of how long the circular tour from here to Shearwater to Embridge and back would be until I explained, they thought we could just drop by, so we'll be meeting at Ravenscourt Place on Saturday morning. But we couldn't duck out of dinner that evening as well – not that I wanted to – so Francis is just going to have to lump it.'

'Is Francis going to inspect the chapel with you, then?'

'No, he's seen it before. He's going to check on his cows while we do the inspecting, and then we'll have lunch at the Ravenscourt Arms, so the parents can check that out.'

'Of course, he's still got them up there. I'd forgotten.' Kim thought about this. 'Do they move in when you do, or what?'

'God knows, but I don't. Probably not, the state his hand is still in. Unless Matt or someone comes to live with us, which I am not in favour of!'

'I doubt if Francis would be, either,' said Kim, hiding a smile. 'The pair of you haven't had much time alone, have you?'

Diana gave her a look that was hard to interpret, even for a twin. She said, 'No. Or not in the right circumstances, anyway.'

352

Kim knew that this had been hard on her twin, and probably on Francis too. She made no comment, deeming it not to be her business, but she did sympathise and because they were twins, Diana felt that unspoken sympathy. She shrugged her shoulders.

'C'est la vie, don't they say? And at least Eloise and Daddy are happy.'

Kim didn't answer this directly, but she did say 'When does this caravan arrive, then?'

'Next week sometime, so I'm told. They need to lay some gravel first, or something, because of the mud. We don't want to tread it all over the floor, Francis said, and you know what field entrances can be like.'

Kim did, but she hadn't realised that Diana would realise it. She made no comment, merely saying, 'Roll on next week, then,' and Diana replied, 'Amen to that!'

Friday went much as planned; architect in the morning, auction in the afternoon. The architect agreed that Diana's plan was probably workable without doing any serious structural alterations to the old building, since the dividing wall was already there, and took some measurements for his drawings, promising to make the application a priority as it might well take some time before a decision was made.

'Too many people involved,' he said, shaking his head. 'There's English Heritage and God knows who else with a listed building of this age. But I think we can swing it, with time and patience. It isn't a radical change, and it's sensible. And after all, the house has been updated many times already over the centuries! We shall see.'

The auction was equally successful, they acquired the four poster bed and the sideboard, even if at a cost that made Diana blink, and were able to add to their haul a lovely old antique oak dining table and six matching chairs, and the auction house agreed to store all of this for them for a week or so until the floors at Burnthouse had been treated for rot and woodworm.

'But when it comes to soft furnishings, we won't be going antique,' Diana told Francis, firmly, as they returned to the Discovery. 'Obviously, we shall choose something that doesn't look too out of place, but it will also be modern and comfortable. After all, it's our home, not a museum.' She sounded challenging, and he turned to grin down at her.

'I t-t-totally agree, you needn't b-bite me,' he told her, and she said, without thinking, 'And we won't be having an antique mattress, either!' and caused a sudden silence while they both thought about that.

That evening followed the now-established weekend pattern: Diana stopped for the evening at Shortlanesend when she took Francis back after the auction, and Kim drove out to Shearwater to spend time with Valerie and Val's sister Penny while they waited for Val to return from London and his father to return from Embridge, when they would all have dinner together as a family. The only slight change in the normal routine was that the four of them, Val and Kim, Francis and Diana, had arranged to meet at the Ravenscourt Arms instead of Val's more usual choice, the Sailing Club, for a drink together later in the evening. Quite possibly, Penny would come too, if she was at a loose end.

It was while they were in the pub later on that Diana's parents rang her on her mobile to say that they had arrived safely in Embridge, and that the hotel had more than come up to expectation.

'We have a lovely room, with a view over the harbour and the sea,' Eloise told her, happily. 'It's so lovely to be out of town for a breath of fresh sea air! And the food here is amazing, quite up to London standards.'

'I told you it was good,' said Diana.

'And you were right. And I told them about Francis, and they said the chef would work out a few things that he could manage with one hand, or eat with his fingers without attracting attention, and give me a list for him to choose from when we meet tomorrow. So that's all sorted.'

'That's very nice of them,' said Diana, slightly surprised. She hadn't expected such consideration from Embridge's top hotel, which just showed that you should never pre-judge a four-star establishment.

'Will you be able to come over in the morning, so that we can all go to Ravenscourt Place together?' Eloise then asked, predictably, but Diana told her they wouldn't.

'Francis wants to go over to the Place anyway, to check on his cows, and I shall have to drive him. And if I then drive to Embridge and go back with you, it will take a lot of time and the car will be in the wrong place to take him back to Shortlanesend, and it would all be too complicated. But if we're all going to have lunch at the Ravenscourt Arms when you check that out, you'll see plenty of us. And we'll be with you for dinner.'

'We wondered if Kim would like to come too? We wouldn't like to think of her all on her own.'

'She won't be. She'll be going out with Val. But Mary said she'd love to join us, and thank you for the invitation.'

'Mary? – oh, Francis's mother. Of course! Oh, that's good. How will she get there, will you be bringing her, or will she have a taxi, or what?'

'Mary is perfectly capable of bringing herself,' Diana told her.

'Then we shall see you tomorrow, darling.'

Diana switched off her mobile and went back to her friends – she had taken her phone outside when it rang.

'Everything OK?' Val asked, as she sat down.

'Of course. They love the Langland, they sound all settled in. And the chef is making a short list of specials that Francis can handle with one hand, and they'll bring it with them tomorrow, so that he can choose, and not make an exhibition of himself.'

'That's nice of them,' said Kim, when Francis made no comment, although he did look slightly relieved: the prospect of tomorrow's dinner engagement, which was obviously unavoidable, had been squatting at the back of his mind like a malevolent toad: although he was a lot more competent with his left hand than he had been at the beginning of the week, there was still room for improvement, and in public, in a four-star hotel, wasn't the best place to practice.

'So you've made up your minds about the chapel?' Penny asked, changing the subject with a tact that was purely accidental; Penny wasn't much into tact. 'It'll be a very small wedding – I've been in that chapel!'

'I think that's the general idea,' said Val. Penny looked across at Diana.

'Not yours, I bet!'

'I'm happy with it, thank you Penny. Not all of us want to make a huge splash.'

Penny looked as if she as about to say that she had thought Diana would, but Kim got in first. 'Her parents are planning a big bash up in London in the Spring, when all the dust has settled on the farm.'

'That sounds better, but it still sounds to me like the waste of the best day of your life.'

'Oh, I hope it won't be that,' said Diana, which was sufficiently ambiguous to bring a smile to her prospective bridegroom's face, and make Penny knit her brows as she sorted it out.

But as it happened, the whole question became null and void the following morning, when Diana and her parents met Merlin.

Diana met up with him first, when she had dropped Francis off at the Home Farm; he was just driving up from the Gate House where he lived with his wife and two children as she parked the Discovery, and pulled up on the drive in front of the big house beside her.

Good morning Diana – not that it is very good!' This was true; there was a stiff, cold, mid-October wind blowing, and fine rain carried with it like mist.

'It's what the forecast said,' said Diana, pulling her coat round her against the chill, and he said, 'Come inside, out of the wind,' and led the way into the house. Diana had half-expected a butler, but there wasn't one visible.

'Parents not with you?' he asked, as they went up the steps together.

'They said they'd meet us here…' she looked at her watch '…in about ten minutes time. And knowing my father, they're probably just entering Shearwater now.'

'Not long, then. Have a look round while you're waiting – I take it, you haven't been here before, if you haven't seen the chapel?' Ravenscourt Place was open to the public, the gardens all through the Spring and Summer, the house on specific days throughout the holiday season, but Diana had only ever seen the garden. The house was a lot bigger than Vachells, this was a true stately home. She was glad she wasn't responsible for the housework, but then, they probably had a fleet of servants, being Lords. Merlin took her round the hall and its beautiful pictures to pass the time while they waited, explaining who they were by and how long they had been in the family, and pointing out the main features, but then he caught sight of a car pulling onto the drive beside his own.

'I think they've just arrived, your parents,' he said. 'Let's let them in, and spare them the ordeal by butler.'

'So you do have a butler?' Diana went with him to the door.

'Not me personally, no. My cousin does. It's kind of expected in a house like this.' He was opening the big front door as he spoke and stepping out onto the top step to welcome the newcomers with a friendly "Good morning" and a warmly outstretched hand. They all exchanged greetings and introductions, and then Merlin said, 'So shall we go and look at this chapel, then?' and they all set off down a long passage with arched doors to either side, suggesting huge rooms, and with more pictures hanging on the walls between. Diana heard Eloise mutter to Sir Charles, 'Whatever do they do with all these rooms? And this is only one wing!'

They came to a halt outside the last doorway, wider than the others and with double doors. Merlin paused with his hand on the latch.

'This is the chapel – as you will see, it has been built as a wing on the end of the house, to give it length. Purpose built, some time in the seventeenth century. The then Lord Storre was a deeply religious man, from all accounts, and he put a lot into it.' He pushed the door open and they stepped inside.

It was like walking into a small church. The far end was rounded, with beautiful stained glass in its high windows, casting a rainbow light over the plain wooden altar before them. There was a small organ to one side, and as they had been told, a font to the other. Simple dark oak pews to either side, a vaulted roof with oak beams, and religious statues in alcoves around the walls. A couple of stone tablets on the walls listing those members of the family and the household who had died in the two World Wars of the last century, a smoothly polished wooden floor.

'It's…amazing,' said Eloise, after a moment. 'So simple…and so beautiful! I can see why Francis thought of it.'

'I think Francis may have had an ulterior motive,' said Merlin, who knew his friend well. 'However, you're right. It's the perfect place for a simple wedding, which I gather is what you want?'

'And anyone can get married here?' asked Sir Charles, looking around in admiration 'This is a private family chapel, that's obvious.'

'Not anyone,' said Merlin, smiling. 'As you say, this is a private chapel – but it is licensed for weddings, and in special circumstances, it is used for occasions outside the family.'

'And do we qualify?' asked Eloise, looking at him.

'That's why you're here. Francis is an old friend. His family and ours have worked this land for centuries side by side – and I don't include myself in that, necessarily, because I'm Canadian by birth as you can probably hear, but you'll get the picture.'

'The Ravenscourts are aristocracy,' said Eloise.

'They are – we are, I suppose I should say. But the Vachells were here a long way before us.' He gestured to the room with his hand. 'So, what do you think? Will it do?'

'I think it's beautiful,' said Diana, immediately before her mother could speak. 'I should love to be married here.'

'It's just a shame it's so small,' said Eloise, reluctantly. She had fallen in love with the chapel too, and she realised that for Diana to be married here would be a privilege not accorded to everyone. 'How many will it hold?'

Merlin told her what Mary had already told Diana. 'About thirty – thirty-six at a push, and we can put chairs at the back either side of the door, too. Say, around forty.'

'That's still not very many,' said Sir Charles, doubtfully.

'There could be a way round that,' said Merlin. 'Diana tells me that you were planning a reception at the pub down the road, but let me show you something before you make up your minds. This way—' He turned, and led the way back into the passage. Sir Charles, Eloise and Diana obediently followed, wondering what would be coming next. They followed Merlin back down the passage a short way, to the door to the room adjoining the chapel; he pushed it open and gestured them inside.

'Take a look at this,' he said, and they stepped through.

The room beyond the door was square, and therefore not enormous, and furnished with comfortable chairs, a coffee table, and a big rectangular television screen across one corner at just above eye level. There were a few additional folding chairs leaning in a stack in one corner. Sir Charles and Eloise looked around them with surprise, and then Sir Charles said, 'And? So what happens in here?'

'It's a kind of ante-room to the chapel,' Merlin explained. 'Back in the old days, when the family had a resident priest, it was the study where he wrote his sermons and stuff like that. Now, it serves a different purpose. I don't suppose you noticed, because you aren't meant to, but up on the wall behind the altar there is a small camera, lurking behind a religious statue. That is connected to this big screen, so that when there is an occasion where the number of people who wish to be present exceeds the number of seats in the chapel, they can be in here and watch the proceedings in comfort. It gets used at times like Remembrance Day, and family weddings and significant anniversaries, and sometimes at Christmas, and of course, it would be equally available for your own wedding. If you wanted. You can fit about fourteen people in here, if they squash up a bit. Ten would be more comfortable.'

Eloise and Sir Charles exchanged glances, and turned to Diana.

'What do you think?' Sir Charles asked. 'It would accommodate a few more of Francis's cousins, if they didn't mind being put in here, and one or two more friends of our own that we would like to be able to include. But it would send the numbers up, and you said you wanted it kept small.'

'I don't think that fifty or so people is actually large,' said Diana. 'We can ask Francis – but I think it's a great idea. And at least the overflow would get a ringside seat, and most of them in comfort too!'

'That's not all,' said Merlin. He gestured towards the door. 'Come with me, and take another walk.'

This time, after a slightly longer walk, they stopped outside a door on the corridor at the other side of the entrance hall. Merlin said, 'Take a look at this, too,' and pushed it open. 'This used to be the family dining room, although heaven knows how many family members and hangers-on there were to fill it.'

Sir Charles and Eloise stepped through the door, Diana on their heels. They all stopped dead just inside.

'Good heavens!' said Sir Charles. 'It's a banqueting hall, not a dining room!'

'We have one of those as well, sir,' Merlin told him, with a grin. 'Bit big for your needs, but we do use this one for smaller parties, although not, these days, for family dining. You can see why.'

They could. The room was big, although not enormous, and presently furnished with a long table, placed across one end, and more comfortable chairs arranged in groups with small tables around the walls. A piano stood in one corner, raised up on a small stage with room for more players, or a singer maybe, and there was a sound system rigged around the room.

'As you can see, it's all set out as a small party room these days,' Merlin said. 'And a small party is just what you'll be having. People – like me, for instance, can make their speeches on the stage. What do you think?'

Eloise's mouth had dropped open. She closed it to say, 'You mean – we could have the use of this room for the reception?'

'Don't see why not. Robin's up for it so there's no problem there.'

'What about catering?' asked Eloise, doubtfully. She was unable to believe in this miracle.

'Oh, we can fix that too,' said Merlin cheerfully. 'There's a very good chef down the road in Embridge, he used to work for Mawgan Angwin down in Cornwall, but now he and his mother run an outside-catering business in the town. He does the food, with help of course, and she does the arrangements and sees to the office work. They provide their own staff to do the serving. And because he worked with a top chef, he's pretty good at his job.'

'He wouldn't be free at such short notice,' said Eloise, disbelieving in this miracle.

'Well, actually he would be – for us. I rang him this morning to check, just in case you were interested. He can do you a slot just before the end of December, but you must decide quickly. It's right in the middle of the Christmas period, and it's only there at all because of a cancellation.'

'Ring him,' said Sir Charles. 'We've decided – haven't we, Diana?'

'It's a Friday,' Merlin said, by the way.

'Friday is good.'

'Ought we to ask Francis first, before we decide?' Diana said. It seemed only fair.

'Francis will do what he's told,' Merlin told her. 'Seeing as it seems I'm elected Best Man, I hereby make the decision for him. But we will ask him, when he comes back from the cows.'

'So who will be conducting the wedding?' asked Sir Charles. 'We should perhaps speak with him before we go home tomorrow.'

'The vicar of the local church is the usual choice. I had a word there, too.' He looked at Sir Charles apologetically. 'I know this is all a bit high-handed of me, but I knew you would be pressed for time, and anyway, notice is short so there was a risk in waiting until you were here – Christmas again. I can give you his card before you go, remind me. It's in the office. We can talk about the cost at the same time, I imagine you'll want to know that.'

'We're very grateful to you for your forethought,' Sir Charles told him. 'You're a very efficient young man, sir. Any time you want a job, just call me!'

'I don't suppose many boats need building up in Parliament,' said Merlin, grinning, 'but thank you. I was glad to be able to help.'

They walked back to the main entrance hall, where they found Francis and a young man, casually dressed in scruffy jeans and a sweater so possibly a cowhand, just coming from the opposite passage; they all met in the middle, under an impressive chandelier.

'How're the cows?' Diana asked, 'I have to tell you, we've had an amazing morning!'

Sir Charles and Eloise, who of course had not yet seen Francis, greeted him warmly although slightly inhibited by not being able to shake hands properly, and Merlin introduced his companion.

'This scruffy object is my cousin Robin,' he said, 'believe it or not, the current Lord Storre, but you don't have to curtsey,' and they all laughed, any ice instantly broken, by surprise as much as anything.

'We have to thank you, sir, for the offer of your amazing facilities for our daughter's wedding,' said Sir Charles, shaking the offered hand warmly.

'It's a pleasure, Sir Charles. There's not a lot we wouldn't do for this man here.' Robin Ravenscourt smiled across at Francis, who looked expressionless. Something here, Diana thought, she had caught a whiff of it earlier, listening to Merlin. A connection...not livestock or farming, the Ravenscourts knew all about those. Money, then? It was the only other option, although it seemed equally unlikely. Not her business, but she found herself looking at Francis with slightly different eyes.

Merlin took Sir Charles along to the Estate Office to give him the caterers' card and the vicar's address, and some other relevant information about costs, dates and arrangements, and Diana and Francis took her mother out into the sunshine. Diana looked at her watch.

'We had better leave Burnthouse until after lunch, or we'll have left it too late to get any by the time Daddy's finished gassing,' she said, and smiled at her mother. 'That's good, because you can have a stiff drink to prepare yourself!'

'As bad as that?' asked Eloise, laughing. She had no real idea of what the place actually would look like, even after a week's hard labour; her innocence was disarming.

'W-wait and see,' Francis told her. Contact with his precious cattle seemed to have cheered him, he looked brighter than he had done all week, Diana thought, eyeing him critically. There was a lot of farmer in there with the marine biologist, it might be interesting, over the next few years, to see who won. It was quite possible that not being able to study them freely had made the sea creatures more enticing. Anybody's bet, really; she didn't know where she would put her own money.

'What you should do,' said Robin, who had come outside with them, 'is to get yourselves down to the pub – you've got two cars here, and you won't want to hang about in this wind. You could sit indoors, of course, but the pub would be more fun.' He grinned at them. 'Not that you wouldn't be welcome.'

Eloise was looking around vaguely for Diana's car. She said, 'Where have you parked, darling?' and Diana indicated the Discovery.

'There. It's Francis's, he claimed he couldn't fit his legs into mine.'

'I c-couldn't,' said Francis.

'But surely, you can't drive,' said Eloise, looking at him doubtfully.

'But I can,' Diana pointed out. 'That was a good suggestion, Milord – thank you.'

'Get away,' said Robin, his friendly grin widening. 'You're practically family.'

Eloise still looked doubtful, but Robin offered her a hand into the back of the Discovery and helped her with the seat belt, while the other two got into the front and Diana performed the same service for Francis. Diana started up the engine, and they moved off, Robin waving after them.

'What a charming young man,' said Eloise, by the way. 'But he looks very young to be a lord.' She might have added Merlin's "scruffy" to that, but didn't.

'He's b-b-been one s-s-since he was twelve,' Francis told her.

'Oh dear. Poor boy.'

'M-M-Merlin was his g-guardian. He r-r-ran the estate for him until quite r-r-recently.'

Maybe that was the close connection, Diana wondered, they had been in the same job. Or maybe it wasn't.

'So what does he do now – Merlin, I mean?' her mother was asking.

'He's co-owner of the old Shipyard in Emberton,' Diana told her. 'He's a boatbuilder – yachts and dinghies, that is, wooden ships are a bit out of date these days.'

'Good heavens,' said Eloise, half to herself.

It turned out to be an excellent suggestion of Robin's to go down to the pub; it was a good half hour before Sir Charles joined them, and they would have been very bored hanging around at the Place, outdoors or indoors, with nothing to do but look at each other. In the pub there was a cheerful background of company and talk, and they were able to sit comfortably with a drink. Eloise looked around her critically.

'Well, it's a very nice pub, I agree with that, but so much better up at that lovely house.' She smiled across the table at Francis. 'It nearly makes me forgive you for insisting on a small wedding!' She changed the subject, they had had enough of weddings for the moment. 'Now tell me all about this house we're visiting after lunch.'

Burnthouse was a wide subject, and even when edited kept the conversation going until Sir Charles appeared. He sat down with them, beaming, and reached for the lunch menu lying on the table.

'Well, that was an amazing morning,' he announced, casting a cursory glance down the menu. 'This looks reasonable for a pub! Have you ordered?'

They said they hadn't, yet, and a swift discussion ensued; they were eating again tonight so nobody wanted anything heavy. When they had done, Francis picked up the list that Diana had scrawled on the back of an old envelope she found in her bag and got to his feet.

'Th-this one is on m-m-me, if you're p-paying tonight,' he told Sir Charles, before he could object, and headed off for the bar. Eloise watched him go.

'That accident has really taken it out of him,' she said severely, as if it was Diana's fault. 'He looks so weary, just asking for a bit of TLC, darling.'

'You should try offering it, if you want your head bitten off,' Diana said, but smiled as she said it. 'But truly, I think it's more frustration than pain now, he just wants to get his hands on the place and haul it into order, and he has to leave it to other people.'

'He doesn't look well.'

'He isn't. He got an infection in the wound, not surprisingly; there's a long red streak of inflammation all the way up his arm still, and he's on all kinds of pills and potions, all of which seem to make him disagreeable.' She caught her mother's eye. 'But before you say anything, I still love him.'

Eloise gave her an old-fashioned look, and changed the direction of her...well, grumbles really, Diana thought, not wholly amused.

'I really don't like the idea of you driving that big, heavy 4x4,' her mother said next.

'Why not? Lots of women do – Mums on the school run, or just because they want to—'

'It's not what you've been used to, darling.'

'I haven't had to be. It's different now. And I shall give it back as soon as he can drive it himself, so you needn't worry.'

'But if he can't fit into yours...'

'Then he'll do the driving, mostly. Blokes do. Anyway, he's got another car as well as that one.'

'And is that any easier for you to drive?'

'It's the same as the one Daddy has. And the Discovery isn't difficult. Not when you get used to the size.'

'Now stop it, you two,' ordered Sir Charles. 'Where's your own car, Diana? You can still drive that, I don't know what your mother is on about.'

'At the moment, Kim is using it,' Diana told him. 'She's trying to find a job, as she's obviously staying in England, so she needs to get about, and I'm not using it right now after all.'

'Then perhaps you should just give it to her, and we'll find you something a bit more suited to your man's long legs,' said Sir Charles, making the first reasonable suggestion of the discussion, and Francis, returning right on cue, said, 'I intend t-to, if that's all r-r-right with you.'

Diana looked at him open-mouthed for a moment, and then Eloise said, 'Shut your mouth darling, the flies will get in. And I think that's a really sensible suggestion, you can give it to her for a wedding present. Much better than a diamond pendant.'

'More practical, certainly.' Sir Charles looked at his prospective son-in-law with approval, but Francis looked at Diana with a slight lift of his brows as he sat down.

'S-so, which w-w-would you prefer? The d-d-diamonds or the c-car?'

'The car, every time. Now I don't have to worry about parking and car thieves and heavy traffic, maybe I can have something a bit more exciting to drive at last. Not that I haven't had fun with the old one.' She turned to her father. 'Did you mean that about Kim? Because I think she'd really like it, but it was a present from you originally, so...'

'Of course I meant it, it seems very appropriate if Francis here is planning to give you another. And now, if you've finished quarrelling with your mother, how about we discuss your wedding plans now that you actually have some?'

The wedding plans lasted them safely until lunch arrived, although Diana was noticeably silent; it had never entered her head that Francis might give her a car although, of course, she did know that he was reputed to be a wealthy man, and the suggestion had taken her breath away, she needed time to get used to the idea – and to all the other ideas that couldn't help following on behind. Fortunately her parents seemed so impressed, with Merlin and the Place about equally, that nobody noticed. And then Sir Charles said something that brought her attention immediately back to the present moment.

'They seem to think a great deal of you up at that house,' he said, looking at Francis. 'I got the impression that they wouldn't have gone to all that trouble just for anyone?' He made it into a question, but Francis was non-committal when he replied.

'M-Merlin and I have kn-known each other for a w-while. We s-s-sailed in the s-same class up t-t-to the end of the season.'

It seemed inadequate to Diana, who knew the situation down at the Sailing Club, but her father accepted it without question. He said, 'It's always good to have friends in high places,' and they all smiled politely.

Burnthouse was a different story. After lunch, they returned to their respective cars and Diana led the way to Burnthouse. In a way, she was sorry that they weren't all in the same car so that she missed her parents' first reactions: by the time they all climbed out in the now swept and clear farmyard they had had time to pull themselves together. Cleaned up, the yard did look a little better, but still dilapidated. Sir Charles ran an experienced eye around it, he had a small country house of his own.

'Needs a lot of work, but it has possibilities,' he said, fairly.

'You should have seen it with the monster dungheap and all the rubbish,' Diana told him. 'It was horrendous — he's one brave man, this one of mine!'

'C-come and see the stable,' said Francis, moving to lead the way there. 'It l-l-looks a lot better, it'll g-g-give you an idea how it m-m-may end up.'

Sir Charles approved of the stables, clean, orderly and with repairs proceeding on the woodwork. Even the bushes that overhung the walls from the fields beyond had been trimmed back until they looked merely ornamental. Eloise, however, was anxious to see inside the house.

'It looks so sad and run-down from the road,' she said. 'If you're going to live here, it's going to cost a fortune to put even just the outside in order!'

'Just wait until you see inside,' said Diana, she was afraid gleefully. 'You've got the key, Francis — let's go!'

'Although still shabby and in places obviously rotten and worm-eaten, the inside of the main hall at least smelled clean — mainly of disinfectant, which was understandable.

'Th-they'll start working on the electrics this c-c-coming w-week,' Francis told Sir Charles in answer to his immediate question. 'After th-that, T-tamsin has s-some g-g-good ideas for the r-rest.'

'You still call her Tamsin,' said Eloise. She had noticed it already during their lunch together, and it saddened her a little.

'It's h-h-how I kn-knew her f-first.' He looked at her in apology, realising what she was thinking; it distanced her daughter for her. 'Th-think of it as nickn-name. N-nobody else uses it, except my m-m-mother, n-n-not even K-kim.'

'It seems so odd that you knew her before we did.'

'B-but n-n-nothing like as w-well.' He smiled at her and she smiled back, a little hesitantly. She didn't know this man who was going to be her son-in-law that well as yet; there was a wide gap to close. She still found herself wondering occasionally if Diana hadn't been carried away by the film star good looks and ignored the more obvious disadvantages. Impossible to ask, or even to guess. She turned to Diana.

'So, take us through it – tell us these good ideas of yours!'

They did the guided tour, and although her parents were concerned with the amount of work, they could see that something rather special could replace the mess eventually and approved, with some surprise be it said, their daughter's practical plans for it. They then emerged once more out through the front door – no yard doors for Sir Charles and Eloise – and Eloise looked round the garden, seeing it consciously for the first time; Eloise was fond of gardening, and her head was still reeling from the amount of work to be done in the house. This garden didn't impress her.

'This is a total mess, it looks as if nobody has touched it for years!' she said. 'Will you have a professional gardener to put it in order for you?' She eyed the tangled undergrowth in what passed for the borders askance.

'Actually, I thought I might give it a go myself,' Diana told her. 'I shall need something to do if I can't go shopping! I might need help getting those big overgrown bushes out, but I expect someone will give me a hand with that, it won't take long. Then I shall start again, and plan it from scratch. Replant it next autumn, when all the builders and things have gone away.' She didn't mention archaeologists in this context, that might be a step too far for her mother right now.

'There's certainly nothing here that can be rescued,' said Eloise, looking around her. The men had moved off, back to the yard. 'So how many acres are there here, altogether?'

'Where – in the garden?' Diana was laughing at her. Eloise pulled a face at her.

'Don't be ridiculous, my darling! On the farm.'

'I've no idea. A hundred? You'll need to ask Francis that one, but I do know it's not enormous.' She paused, hugging her coat to her against the wind; it was chilly out here, and there was beginning to be some rain in the wind. 'I take it, you don't want a guided tour of the whole property? It's quite interesting – some of it is. There's a big prehistoric Barrow or something in the field by the road. There's going to be an archaeological dig up there in the summer, that should be fun.' There now – her mother couldn't say she'd kept things from her, even if, in fact, she had!

'It'll be a completely different life for you.' Eloise thought about it. 'You are quite, quite sure, my darling?'

'Quite, quite sure. Now let's get back to the men before we get rained on!'

Sir Charles had arranged for them all to see the vicar at three, and it was getting on for that time now. Time was short, and there might not be another opportunity.

'Such a rush job,' said Eloise, regretfully, ignoring the fact that this was largely down to herself and Sir Charles. 'And for goodness' sake, put a comb through your hair before you get out of that monster,' she added to her windswept daughter. 'And do the same for that man of yours, too – he looks as if he's been out in an Atlantic gale! You don't want to shock the vicar.'

'Oh, don't fuss, Eloise!' Diana told her. 'I have a complete repair kit in my bag – well, for me anyway. He's irreparable, I'm afraid.'

'Then use it!' Eloise turned away to where the two men stood talking.

'All aboard, you two!' Sir Charles called. 'We're going to be late if we don't hurry, which wouldn't be fair as the vicar has made a special effort to fit us in!'

It was half-past four before Diana and Francis were on the road back to Shortlanesend. Eloise had pressed them to go back to the Langland with her and Sir Charles for tea and a chat, but Diana had refused the invitation. She could see that Francis had had enough for now, and come to that, so had she by this time. Much as she loved her parents, on some occasions – and this was one of them – a little went a long way.

'We ought to get back and think about getting tidied up for tonight,' she said. 'I could kill for a hot shower, and Francis could do with a rest – we'll see you at half-past seven anyway, and I expect you could do with a rest too, we've had a busy day.'

'It's just that we see so little of you these days,' said Eloise regretfully, 'and there's so much to talk about.'

'We can do that over dinner,' Diana told her. 'Mary will want to hear it all too, and we don't want to have to do it twice.'

'It's been such an...an amazing day,' said Eloise, who still had difficulty in believing in it all. The small, unexciting, swept-under-the-carpet ceremony that she had wondered how to explain to her friends had turned into fairytale this morning.

They escaped eventually, and headed back to normality.

'Well, that went off all right,' said Diana, as she drove along the lanes. 'I think Daddy and Eloise were quite impressed, they'll feel better about it now.'

'Th-that's good,' said Francis. He was leaning back against the headrest with his eyes closed; Diana stole a swift look at him and then looked back to the road.

'Merlin did you proud,' she said. 'Well, us proud I suppose, it's going to be the perfect compromise; small still, but quite impressive enough for Eloise, she'll dine out on it for weeks!'

He shot her swift look. 'Th-that's important t-t-to her?'

'She likes to impress her friends, but she's a sweetie really.'

'Sh-sh-she's not sure about m-m-me,' Francis told her, opening his eyes to look at her properly.

'Do you blame her? But I am, and that's what counts.' Diana smothered a laugh. Then she spotted a lead, and ventured, 'She was very impressed with the way Merlin pulled out all the stops for you. You must be really good friends – I hadn't realised. You never seemed to be, particularly, down at the Club.'

Nobody had ever accused Francis of being stupid. He smothered a laugh. 'Are you f-f-fishing, b-by any ch-chance, s-s-sweetheart?'

'Could be,' Diana admitted, but added, 'It's not my business, of course,' hastily, in case he thought she was prying. His answer surprised her.

'I th-think it p-p-probably is, actually, s-since you're g-g-going to marry m-me. B-but wait until w-w-we get back to Sh-shortlanesend, and I'll explain th-then.' He closed his eyes again, turning his head away again and to all intents and purposes asleep, and Diana finished the journey with a huge question mark taking up her attention: fortunately, traffic wasn't heavy at this time of day

Bennie and Ernie were both out when they arrived at Shortlanesend, Ernie out on the farm, Bennie collecting the children from a day out with friends, so they had the kitchen to themselves. Diana was by this time quite at home here, she pushed the kettle onto the hotplate, took down a couple of mugs from their hooks, and sat down at the table opposite to Francis.

'All right,' she said. 'Now tell me. What's the big secret?'

'It's n-not a secret,' Francis told her. 'It's j-j-just s-something that isn't g-generally known.'

'Don't quibble,' said Diana. 'Just tell me without all the beating about the bush!' and he did.

'B-Bob and M-M-Merlin had decided to g-g-go into p-p-p-partnership when Robin c-c-came of age, and c-could r-r-run the Place himself, he grew up th-th-there, he w-w-was p-p-perfectly able to. Th-they b-b-both of them know b-boats, Bob was a boatbuilder anyway, b-b-but they n-n-needed bigger p-p-premises, pref-f-ferably down by the w-w-water. W-when the Sh-shipyard c-c-came on the m-market, it w-w-was the perfect p p-p-position for wh-what they w-w-wanted to do – build y-yachts, n-n-not just d-dinghies – B-bob built quite a l-l-lot of the M-Moonrakers d-d-down at the Club. Including m-m-mine. He w-w-was good. B-b-but th-they didn't have enough c-c-capital, even b-between them.' He paused for a break, it had been a long speech for him. Diana had already worked out where this was going, but she didn't prompt him. Instead, since the kettle had now boiled, she made two cups of coffee and set one of them in front of him before sitting back down with her own. Only then did she say, 'Go on, then.'

'I heard about it, of c-c-course. Everyone had, it w-w-was hardly a secret, it w-was obvious, everyone kn-knew wh-what they wanted to d-d-do.' He paused, looking at her seriously. 'F-forget the Club, th-that's another st-story. Th-think about it; M-Merlin and I were in the s-s-same business. W-we met at shows, at s-sales, all over the p-p-lace. W-we got t-t-talking at the C-County Sh-show, and you c-c-can w-w-work out wh-what happened next.'

'You put up the money,' said Diana. He took a sip of his very hot coffee and put the mug down again, hastily.

'N-n-not all of it, th-they c-c-could r-r-raise a l-lot of it themselves. B-but I own around forty per-cent of the b-business – and n-now, you kn-know that, b-b-but nobody else n-n-needs to.'

'So, you're a sort of sleeping partner?' said Diana, thinking this out.

'S-something l-l-like that. S-s-sometimes I w-w-wake up and give f-f-financial advice.' He smiled at her. 'H-happy now?'

'So today was just about returning the favour.' It was a statement, not a question. He didn't answer, but took another, more careful, sip of coffee. She said, 'Are there any more skeletons in your cupboard, or have we covered them all now?' The Sailing Club was at the back of her mind, but he said 'P-probably,' which wasn't any kind of a lead – probably deliberately. They drank their coffee in silence for a minute or two, and Diana's mind, as it often did, flew off at a tangent – a rather uncomfortable one.

'I was going out with Bob when you came back on the scene,' she said, uneasily. 'I dropped him like a hot coal, I remember…'

'He d-d-doesn't hold it against me,' Francis told her.

'I'm glad.' She hesitated. 'Will you be asking him to the wedding now there's more room?'

'P-probably. If you d-d-don't m-mind.'

'No I don't, not if he doesn't. It will be odd, but nice – I liked Bob. *Like* Bob.'

They drank in silence again for a minute, then Diana said, 'Does my father know? About the Shipyard?'

'He w-w-will, when I t-t-tell him.'

'You didn't tell him up in London?'

'N-no. It w-w-wasn't r-relevant until th-this morning.'

He hadn't thought it was relevant to a lot of people, Diana thought. And Merlin and Bob had said nothing either, but then, why should they if it wasn't anybody's business but that of the three of them? And then she found herself thinking about the Club again, and wondering.

XXIII

Kim was still out when Diana returned to Romans on Saturday evening: the dinner party at the Langland had been pleasant, but had ended quite early. Mary had not wished to be too late getting home, and Francis had obviously had enough by ten o'clock, and come to that, Sir Charles and Eloise were ready to retire after their long drive the previous evening and the busy day today. They had all parted on a positive note, and Diana had headed off to Shortlanesend with Francis, but she hadn't stayed, in spite of Ernie's invitation to come in for a nightcap. She had already taken quite enough alcohol on board, she considered, and she certainly didn't want coffee or hot chocolate, most of all she wanted to sleep! So she said she would see them all tomorrow, kissed her man goodnight, and headed off into the dark lanes.

She was almost relieved that Kim wasn't back, her mind was so full of unfiled information that she needed time to herself in which to sort it all out: it had been a very unexpected day in just about every way, she couldn't think of a better word to describe it. She left a note for Kim on the table where she would see it, and took herself upstairs. She fell instantly asleep and never heard Kim come back; so much for thinking things out.

In the morning, however, she had pulled herself together, waking early and refreshed, and looking forward to telling Kim all about it. For once, she was downstairs first and had the kettle on and the breakfast laid before Kim came downstairs, heavy-eyed and yawning. Complete role reversal, Diana thought, looking at her.

'I heard you crashing about,' said Kim. 'I hadn't realised it was this late.' She glanced at the clock on the shelf above the fireplace. 'Except that I see that it isn't. What's the matter with you, getting up at this hour?' She smothered another yawn with a hand.

Diana grinned at her and said, 'I take it, you had a good evening?' and Kim yawned again behind her hand.

'Coffee – give me coffee!'

'Black?'

'It's not that bad, but strong anyway. Just give me time to have a quick shower, and I'll take it upstairs while I get dressed. Then you can tell me why you're looking so smug while we have some breakfast. I'm assuming it's not the obvious reason.'

'I should be so lucky!' Diana reached for a mug. 'Get in that shower, and then I'll tell you.'

Twenty minutes later, Kim came downstairs for the second time looking a little brighter, but still with shadows under her eyes. She took the second mug of coffee that Diana immediately handed her and collapsed onto the sofa. Diana took the armchair that gave her a clear view of her twin.

'So what kept you? I wasn't late back, but I was fast asleep before you showed!'

Kim yawned and took a gulp of coffee. 'God, I need that! I didn't get home until nearly midnight, and poor Val still had to get back to Shearwater!'

'I hope he was sober enough to drive.'

'He wasn't too bad, I've seen worse. He's pretty level-headed, Val. It comes of being an accountant, I think.'

'You sounded almost as if you regretted it, there,' said Diana.

'Oh well, we all have to grow up sometime I suppose. And I'd sooner that than being an idiot like Rob…and even that's not entirely fair, because if Rob had been completely sober, Val and I would never have met.' Rob, Val's crew, had been taking his turn at driving Val's car, and towing the Moonraker they sailed together back from an Open Meeting, when they had done what Diana had already done some days earlier, and come off the road outside the fated cottage, in their case flattening the fence and ending up on what passed for the lawn.

The rest was history. Diana hid a smile. Kim took a more ladylike sip of her coffee. 'Now tell me what you've been up to. You look all lit up. I take it, yesterday was a success?'

Diana told her about it; the chapel, the reception plans, the interview with the vicar, a blow-by-blow account that left Kim smiling too.

'What it is to have friends in high places,' she observed. 'That all sounds amazing – particularly the caterer! I shall look forward to it.'

'But that's not all,' Diana told her. 'You haven't heard the best bit – Francis is planning to buy me a car that he can fit into, and Daddy said I should give mine to you.'

'What?' Kim stared at her, her mug halfway to her mouth. 'You can't do that ! It's only a couple of years old!'

'Yes I can. It was a present from him anyway, and he thinks it would be a nice idea to keep it in the family. That's you. Family.'

'Oh my God,' said Kim. She finally made contact with her coffee and took a long swallow. 'What was in the air yesterday, for heaven's sake? I had phone call from my Mum and Dad that took my breath away, too.'

'Well, tell me about it then,' said Diana, when Kim fell silent.

'I'm not sure where to begin,' Kim admitted, but told her anyway. 'They had an email from Francis. He wants them to be at your wedding.'

'What?' asked Diana, after a blank pause.

'He said he'd pay the fare because he wanted them to be there, he thought they should be, what with us being twins and history and so forth, and maybe they would like to stay on a bit with me here over Christmas, and get to know Val too, before he married me.'

Diana took a moment to get her breath. Then she said, cautiously, 'And what do you think?'

'I think it sounds wonderful, and I told them so. And if you're not getting married until the very end of December, although I didn't know that at the time, maybe they *could* stay for Christmas, which would be… even more wonderful.'

'And are they coming? I think it's a great idea!'

'They'll have to make arrangements – the sheep and everything – but I think they will. Whether they'll let him pay the fare or not is another matter.'

'Tell them they should. If he wants to, let him, he can afford it and they probably can't, if they're coming over again next year – as they will be. That long flight will cost a bomb – twenty-four hours, isn't it, God knows how many miles?'

Kim got to her feet, she had finished her coffee.

'I'll put the toast on, I see you've got it all ready. You can polish your halo while I do it.'

Diana grinned, and followed her into the kitchen anyway.

'Daddy and Eloise want to see you before they leave – they invited us both for coffee at the Langland about ten, then they can be off before lunch. What do you think? You could ring Val, and I can drop you off in Shearwater on the way to Shortlanesend.'

'The men are not invited, I take it?'

'I think they just wanted the two of us, so no. It must feel very odd to them – like getting an extra daughter, Daddy said.'

'That was sweet of him – well, in that case, you watch the toast and I'll give Val a quick ring before he sets out to pick me up. Then he can spend the morning with his parents if he wants to, they'd like that.'

'The toaster does a pretty good job of watching the toast,' Diana pointed out, and Kim said, 'Good thing too, with you around!' and went off to the living room to make her call.

'Are you having lunch at Shortlanesend?' Kim asked as they sat down to their breakfast.

'Not this time. No. Mary has invited us to Sunday lunch at Vachells. I shall just pick up Francis and Sacha and we'll head off there, and then in the afternoon we shall take her out to see Burnthouse. But I shall be at Shortlanesend for the evening, so you and Val will have time to yourselves before he has to start back for London.'

'I think,' Kim said slowly, considering, 'that it's about time that we all had some time for each other, actually. Couldn't you persuade Francis to come with us to the Club one lunchtime, maybe next weekend?'

'I very much doubt it.'

They looked at each other.

'You'll have to do something about it,' said Kim, after a pause. 'As things are, he might just as well have resigned when they asked him to and spared all the fuss. It's not fair.' She didn't specify to whom.

'I honestly don't think he can be bothered any more,' said Diana. 'It was one thing when he wanted to race his Moonraker, but now…well, it's something he can spare from a life that actually seems pretty full these days. I hadn't realised…' She paused.

'Realised what?' Kim prompted, after a few moments.

'Exactly what he is,' said Diana. 'I thought I had, but yesterday was a bit of an eye-opener, to be honest. And he'll buy a yacht and take it to the Med, and sail it and live his life and be happy, and leave all the backbiting and squabbling to get over itself. And I can't say that I think he's wrong, because I don't think I do. He has plenty of friends without that lot down there, as it turns out.' She stopped, and Kim looked at her.

'Friends are friends. He – and you – might be surprised at how many people have asked after him.' But Diana shook her head.

'He's had enough. That last nasty incident with the Committee just put the lid on it, he won't go back. Anyway, where were they all when they could have been of some use? Sitting on the fence, that's where!'

'You know who's behind it, of course,' said Kim. It wasn't a question.

'Yes. That nasty little chemist. So does he, obviously, but he can't do anything about it without descending to the same level. So maybe he's right to just walk away. It's his decision, anyway.'

Kim said slowly, 'Max Carruthers has a very charismatic personality when he chooses to turn it on. That's why he's the Sailing Secretary, he presents himself as amusing and likeable. And people need a leader to take sides if there's no obvious reason.'

'And you know why Francis didn't step forward, or step *on* him, even. And he's right, you know – it's too late now. After the fair.'

Kim said, thoughtfully, 'I suppose…well, he – Francis, that is – must have wondered how much his mother had told her friend – I am right, that the little creep's mother is a friend?'

'Not sure that you are, but I understand what you're saying. But I doubt she'd been told who she supposed to have killed our mother. Not in a thousand years.'

'Rumours start. And Mollie Crowe must have had some ideas. She had a ringside seat a lot of the time, being the caretaker.'

'So you see what I'm saying – what Francis is saying, the way he's behaving. Least said is soonest mended. You can't blame him.'

Kim had to admit that she couldn't. 'But I still think it's a shame. It would only take a tiny push to open the door again and let him back in.'

'It's what might come out that's the problem,' said Diana.

They left it there, there was nothing useful to add although each of them could see the other's point. But time was getting on, and they had to smarten up and be at the Langland in half an hour.

'At least we don't have to worry what to have for lunch,' said Diana, as they washed up. 'I'm presuming Val's Mum and Dad will offer you some?'

'They're hardly going to sit and eat while I look on,' Kim pointed out. 'I don't know, maybe Val has other ideas. We may end up down at the Club with a sandwich.'

Then it was time to set off for the town, so they locked up, climbed into the Discovery, and set off, arriving at the Langland a little later than specified, to find that Sir Charles and Eloise were waiting for them in reception. They were not desperately late, however, and Diana explained by saying 'Kim overslept. She didn't know we were supposed to be going out.'

Eloise smiled. 'Couldn't you have woken her up? I don't suppose she bites.'

'I might have, this morning,' Kim admitted, as they all seated themselves round a small table. Sir Charles had stopped to order their coffee at reception and fallen into chat with the receptionist; he had waved a hand towards the door of the main lounge and smiled at them; he would no doubt be with them shortly.

'You do look a bit tired,' said Eloise, looking at her critically.

'Say "hung over" and be done with it,' Diana suggested, and they all laughed together although it wasn't necessarily that funny, and the residual ice between them due to the strangeness of the occasion shattered with the laughter. Eloise looked at the twins happily, and said exactly what Diana had predicted she would say, 'It's just like gaining another daughter, right out of the blue!' just as Sir Charles arrived in time to hear, and to nod agreement as he took his seat.

'It's nice of you to look at it like that,' said Kim, smiling back at them both. 'Some people might have thought it rather a nasty shock.'

'Never! Oh look – here comes our coffee, then we can really talk!'

As they did, once the coffee was served and the waiter had left them. Eloise and Sir Charles wanted to get to know the unexpected addition to the family, they asked questions about her life in New Zealand, her parents, her mother's relatives out there, her ambitions, and Kim answered them as best she could. The subject of the car inevitably came up before the end.

'It's a huge present to someone you hardly know,' said Kim, who was having trouble getting her head round it.

'Rubbish!' said Sir Charles. 'Look at you both, sitting there like peas in a pod! You're part of the family, young Kim, whether you want to be or not, and I'm entitled to treat you that way – and you, young lady, are entitled to accept. Diana isn't going to need it, as soon as Francis takes that big 4x4 back, as he very soon will, he's planning to buy her another car anyway. You can call it a Welcome gift from Eloise and me.'

Diana looked at Kim, feeling it was necessary to restore some balance to this conversation. 'I wonder what your parents will make of me?' she speculated.

'They won't give you a car, that's for sure. They might name a sheep after you,' Kim said, relieved at the turn in the conversation. She was feeling a bit overwhelmed, if she was honest. 'Anyway, they had some warning, not like your poor parents here. At least they knew you exist. They'd even seen you, years ago.'

'I look forward to meeting them,' said Sir Charles, genially, and Eloise nodded her head in agreement. Kim pulled herself together, not before time, she realised.

'I can only thank you from the bottom of my heart for such a generous gift,' she said. 'It will make such a difference if Val is still working in London, and it means we can afford a bit of extra furniture, too, if we don't have to worry about transport for me,' and they all laughed.

'And now the subject is closed,' said Sir Charles, firmly. 'You must arrange the transfer of ownership between yourselves when you're ready.' He looked at his watch. 'And now, if there's none of that coffee left, and you two have eaten the last biscuit, Eloise and I must be on our way, I'm afraid. We've already loaded the car, so if you want to make a last pitstop before we leave, Eloise…?'

Diana went with her mother to the cloakroom; they looked at each other over the washbasins as they washed their hands.

'Poor Kim was a bit overcome, wasn't she?' said Eloise.

'Do you blame her? It was so generous of you both.'

'Well, we shall hope to see a lot of both of you in the future, so she might as well get used to it,' said Eloise, smiling. 'You know your father – generous to a fault to those he loves.'

'He can't love Kim – not yet, anyway. He hardly knows her.'

'She's the other half of you,' said Eloise. 'Come now, your father will be pawing at the ground!'

They all went out to the cars together, and there were hugs and kisses all round before Sir Charles and Eloise got into the Mercedes that was the twin of the one Francis owned. The twins stood waving as they drove away, and then turned to the Discovery.

'They hardly mentioned Francis at all,' said Kim, as they climbed aboard. It had worried her a little.

'They don't know what to make of him, that's why,' said Diana, and Kim could have replied that they weren't the only ones, but didn't. Instead, she said, 'Well, they'll get used to him I expect, when they've seen a bit more of him.'

'I'm sure that they will. The farm threw them a bit yesterday, I think – it crunched rather painfully with all the business at Ravenscourt Place, and the fact that he's a Chillingworth.'

'Oh well.' Kim leaned back in her seat and prepared to grit her teeth as Diana erupted into travel mode. 'Time cures everything, so they say, you'll just have to explain to them that he needed a project – as he did – does – and do you have to stamp on the brake like that?'

'Sorry, I'm a bit wound up after all that.'

'Me too,' Kim admitted. 'But calm down now – this road up the hill out of town is quite narrow.'

They drove past the Dock Inn, and Diana pointed it out to Kim, who was unimpressed.

'It looks like a dive,' she said, and Diana said, 'Francis says it is.'

'He knows at first hand, does he?'

'So he told me.'

'Well, rather him than me.'

'I don't think he's exactly an habitué,' Diana said.

She dropped Kim off in Shearwater at the end of the short road that led to the Harries' house and drove on to Shortlanesend to pick up Francis and Sacha, mentally psyching herself up for the next stage in this remarkably social day – the second in a row, she had become unused to things like that, down here in the country. She liked Mary – very much, as it had turned out – but she was slightly uneasy about them all surviving a whole lunchtime together, let alone an afternoon with the joys of Burnthouse. She didn't think Francis was entirely happy at that last idea either, but as it had been her suggestion in the first place, there was no option but to go with it.

She needn't have worried. For a start, Mary and Mrs Fairburn had designed a menu that could easily be eaten by a man with only one serviceable hand and had not stuck slavishly to a traditional Sunday Lunch. Francis had no trouble at all with the chicken casserole with tiny roast potatoes and cauliflower florets, although he did need assistance with the spinach, which had got a bit tangled in its dish, and neither did sticky toffee pudding and custard put pressure on his left-handed skills.

'Not quite as fancy as the Langland,' Mary said, 'but Mrs Fairburn is very good.' The Langland had provided him with little shortcrust pastry boats filled with Lobster Thermidor and accompanied by buttery asparagus spears – and chips, which had been a bit of a let-down in Eloise's opinion, even if they were described as "French fries", but all delicious and eminently manageable with a bit of surreptitious help from his fingers. He had called no unwelcome attention to himself, much to his mother's relief.

'It's fine,' Francis told her, and she smiled at him.

'We did our best.'

'It's a pretty good best,' Tamsin told her. 'Mrs Fairburn is a great cook, he's going to miss her when he's stuck with my fried egg sandwiches and stew.'

'Oh, I expect you will have someone to help you,' said Mary kindly, adding as an aside, 'Just try not to get too sticky with that pudding, Francis dear.'

Burnthouse was the next hurdle. They put Sacha, who had been enjoying himself outside with his old mate, the cowman's dog, in the familiar farmyard that he hadn't seen for so long, into the back of Mary's car, where he settled down with the air of a dog who was on familiar ground, and she drove them all out to Shearwater.

'Then you can come back here for a cup of tea before you leave,' she told them, 'and we can talk in comfort.'

Tamsin had expected Mary to throw up her hands in horror over the farmhouse, but she took it calmly, merely remarking that it would need a lot of work to bring it back into order. She had expected the rot and the woodworm of course, having been warned, and seemed more concerned with the height, or lack of height, of the ceilings.

'You'll be hitting your head on these beams,' she told Francis. 'Are you sure you've thought this through properly?'

'He's all right down here,' Tamsin told her cheerfully. 'There's two inches clearance under the lowest ones, we measured, he'll just have to stop wearing his high heels! It's a bit different upstairs though, because of the sloping ceilings. He'll have to duck – but then, so will I, to a certain extent anyway.'

'That's all right in daylight, but what about going to the bathroom in the dark? He shouldn't keep on banging his poor head.' She looked disapprovingly at the huge black beams that crossed the ceilings.

'We've thought of that – if we get the permission,' Tamsin told her. 'Come upstairs, I'll show you.'

They climbed the stairs, and Tamsin explained her grand plan and Mary nodded her head in approval. 'But make sure you have the window side of the bed, if that's the way you place it,' she instructed Tamsin. 'He shouldn't take unnecessary risks and that slope down to the window goes quite low.' It had never occurred to Tamsin that this might be a problem, but now she thought about it, it was a bit of a no-brainer: Francis had already had enough of a bang on the head to last him a lifetime – as it would. Not for the first time, fury towards the man who had set up the situation that had caused the problem in the first place twisted her gut and made her feel slightly sick. She changed the subject – she was getting good at doing that, this weekend.'

'Come and see the bathroom – it's amazing!'

They finished the tour and returned to the farmyard; to Tamsin's private surprise, Mary wanted to inspect the barns and stables, but then she realised that it shouldn't have surprised her at all; this kind of thing was Mary's heritage. She followed mother and son – and dog, Sacha had been let out of the car to join them now – around quietly, listening to them talking about storage bins and silos and milking sheds while Sacha sniffed after rats, and her view of both of them re-aligned itself yet again. She had a lot still to learn, she realised, and that in many ways.

They ended up at the field adjoining the vegetable garden, and inspecting the proposed site for the "caravan" – or whatever it would turn out to be. Mary, ever practical, immediately said, 'So what will you use this field for? You can hardly put cows in it, if people are living here. Cows have no discretion at all about where they do their business, you won't want cowpats on your doorstep.'

'W-we'll use it for exercising the horses,' Francis told her. 'We'll put some j-jumps here, and it's handy f-f-for the stableyard. They needn't b-b-be in here all the t-t-time, and the f-field can just stay like that w-w-when we m-move into the house.' He didn't add that horses had no discretion either, so Tamsin was surprised when Mary nodded her head, apparently in approval, and merely suggested putting up a fence round the caravan. They moved back to the car, that was the end of the tour.

What with one thing and another, it was nearly six o'clock before Diana and Francis returned to Shortlanesend, but it had been an interesting day, particularly the afternoon, Diana thought. But it had underlined a problem that was going to have to be addressed, and soon. She felt as if she was leading a double life with this Diana/Tamsin thing, and it wouldn't do. The Vachells called her "Tamsin" as a matter of course, it was the way Francis always referred to her, and it would be a mammoth undertaking to get them all to stop, it came so naturally. It was obvious already that she was going to see a lot of them, whereas she wouldn't be seeing the Sailing Club crowd, who knew her as "Diana", at all as things had turned out. Kim and Val, who were the link between the two, would just have to get used to it, as would Merlin and Bob, and Val's family. She didn't think any of them would find that a problem if she explained properly. When she went back to London for visits, she would just have to revert to her old name for the duration of the visit. And she would have to be married as "Diana Louise" of course. But that would be it.

Oddly, she felt more at home with "Tamsin" herself, and she thought that Kim might too. Old memories? How much did you remember from when you were three years old? She only knew that the name felt both familiar and comfortable. She parked the Discovery outside the farmhouse with her mind made up and walked into the kitchen with Francis as Tamsin.

Bennie was there, predictably, getting the children their tea, and Birdie the cat was curled in her now-accustomed chair beside the Aga, it all looked very homelike. Distant yells from upstairs announced that Maisie and Clive were playing some exciting game on their shared computer. Unusually, The Boss was in the kitchen too, snuggled up by the Aga and looking smug.

'He brought me a present,' said Bennie, not looking too pleased about it. 'On the whole, I wish he hadn't bothered.'

'Why, what was it?' Tamsin asked, curiously: mice, and even rats, were commonplace, she had never heard Bennie bother to mention them particularly.

'Half a rabbit,' Bennie said. 'God knows where the other half is – I found the first half on the stairs, just where everyone would trip over it.'

'R-rabbit pie for supper, th-then?' asked Francis, with a grin, and Bennie gave a shudder.

'No – you can't tell where it's been, and anyway, there wasn't enough. I just skinned it and took the guts out and boiled it up for the dogs.'

Francis saw Tamsin's face. He said. 'Ah, c-c-country life! D-d-don't you just love it?'

'If you'd been here, and had the use of both hands you'd have been the one doing it,' Bennie told him, firmly. She looked at them both properly for the first time. 'Good day? You both look pretty smug.'

'Very interesting,' said Tamsin, pulling out a chair to sit down, before asking belatedly, 'Can I do anything?'

'It's all done and in the oven,' Bennie told her. 'Francis – if you go into the office, there are a couple of messages for you on your desk, one from Gary Fancot, he'd mislaid his cell phone, that had your number, and the other from Kim, who didn't have it anyway.'

'What did Kim want, did she say?' Tamsin asked, as Francis headed for the door to the passage.

'Something about, her Dad wanted him to ring, about nine o'clock tonight.'

Oh.' Tamsin thought about this. Probably, it was about the wedding – and hopefully, about Christmas. Kim must have rung home at some point during the day and persuaded him: she wondered what had been decided in the end. Bennie put the lid on the saucepan she had been stirring, and pulled out another chair to sit down herself. She said, 'Tell me about your day, while that cooks,' and settled down to listen.

Tamsin told her about it, a much abridged version of the morning, where Bennie didn't know the full cast of characters, but a more detailed account of the afternoon's events. At the end of it, Bennie said, 'I'm glad that the two of you are making friends with Mary. She's had a hard time over the years – Francis too, but he had more options. In a way, he did.' She smiled, unexpectedly. 'So what did she make of the house?'

'She was very concerned about the height of the ceilings,' Tamsin told her. 'And it's true, he probably shouldn't keep banging his head, but then, who should? Anyway, it's to be hoped he's got the sense to duck.'

'So what are the plans for next week?'

'I'm not really sure. We have to go to Burnthouse tomorrow to meet with the electricians and talk about the re-wiring, and at some point in the week, I suppose we shall have to go out and buy a fridge.'

'At least, a fridge,' said Bennie.

'And on Wednesday, I have to drive him to the hospital for another appointment in the afternoon. Hopefully, they're going to take the stitches out, so at least it should be less painful after that. Whether or not he will have any use in it yet, remains to be seen.'

'Not for a while, I wouldn't think, certainly not full use. I think you'll be needing your chauffeur's cap for a while longer.'

'That's another thing. He means to buy me a car. As a wedding present.'

'Nice one! I take my hat off to him, the man is inspired! What will you do with the old one, sell it?'

'My father said, give it to Kim – it was a present from him originally. She'll find it useful, even if Val does get this job he's after. He'll still be at work all day, and the bus is very erratic from Emberton. I've been watching for it.'

'Do you think he will get it?' asked Bennie.

'Anybody's guess. They start serious interviews at the end of next month, he passed the preliminary.'

'It sounds like sitting for a degree.'

'I think there is a bit of that. There's maybe a partnership involved for the right applicant, so there's a lot at stake – on both sides.'

'Then let's hope he passes the final.' A sudden noise outside the door announced the imminent arrival of Clive and Maisie, in search of tea. 'That's the end of peace and quiet. Look – there goes The Boss!' A streak of tabby and white shot across the floor and vanished through the door as the children tumbled through it. 'He has bad nerves, that cat.'

'Don't blame him,' Tamsin told her, flinching a bit herself as they came charging across the kitchen and rushed to greet her with enthusiastic hugs, and in Maisie's case, a smacking kiss.

Tamsin didn't stay late after supper: Francis was obviously tired, and back at Romans Kim would be on her own once more feeling lonely for Val, who would be on the road back to London. It would be so much nicer, she reflected as she drove herself through the lanes back to Emberton, if he got this job in Embridge with Hetherington Associates, or whatever they were called, and could be at home in the evenings all week, like a normal person.

Kim was lounging on the sofa with the television for company when she got back; she sat up and turned it off as Tamsin came through the door.

'Human life! Why is Sunday telly such rubbish?'

'I think it's just the mood you're in,' Tamsin told her. She hung up her coat and came to sit beside her twin. 'What time did Val leave?'

'About six o'clock.' Kim smothered a sigh. 'I don't know what we'll do if he doesn't get this job – we were talking about it. It might be a better idea to live in London if he ends up having to stay there, but I really don't want to, and anyway we've already exchanged contracts on the bungalow.'

'There are other jobs,' Tamsin pointed out.

'I know, I know, it's just that I'm missing him. I'll get over it tomorrow.' She pulled herself together. 'Did Francis get my message?'

'He did, and he rang your Dad, and your Dad said he would ring you around nine o'clock, our time, tomorrow morning.'

'Did they sort something out?'

'Presumably. He didn't say.' She had been relaxing lazily on the sofa, but now she sat up. 'Fancy some hot chocolate, or something, before we go up to bed?'

'I was just about to get up and make some when you came back. I thought it might cheer me up.'

'Then let's hope it does.'

They went out into the kitchen together, and Tamsin collected the mugs while Kim put the kettle on, and while they waited for it to boil, Tamsin explained her decision to adopt her original name while in Dorset.

'It gets so complicated, having two names. And I'll never train all the Vachells, there are too many of them. And…I don't know. I feel at home with "Tamsin"…I think it's because since I met you, there's a …well, a connection, I suppose.'

'Won't your parents mind?'

'Oh, I shall be "Diana" when I go back up there.' She didn't realise that she had avoided saying "home", but Kim did. She made no comment, but merely said, 'I suppose that would work. But won't you find it confusing?'

'I already do, so what's new?' Tamsin told her. They were silent for a minute, considering this, and then Kim said, 'How did it go with lunch? Did you manage to stop them fighting?'

'They didn't even try.' Tamsin pondered this for a minute, and then said, on a wondering note, 'And come to that, they went all over Burnthouse, the barns and everything, with only a slight disagreement about beams – and most of that was me and Mary.'

'Beams?'

'He's quite tall. The ceilings, as you know, are not very high – and I suppose, there's more risk than there would be for you and me, for instance, and I don't mean just because he's taller than us.'

'But in general, you got on all right?'

'Yes…it's amazing how different people can be when they're happy, she was like a different person – just like she was with the children. It will take a while, Kim, but I think they'll get there in the end. They just need some common ground to get their balance on – and this afternoon, I think they found some.'

'So that's one happy ending,' said Kim, with satisfaction.

'I wouldn't go that far. The possibility for one is there.' She paused. 'How about you? Things OK?"

Kim considered: the answer to that question was probably best described as "on hold". She temporised. 'There's so much going on, it's hard to be answer that: the waiting is going to be hard – it could just be the thought of living here on my own that's getting to me, and with nothing settled… anyway, I shall miss you, you know, while it all sorts itself out.'

'I thought you said you had been invited to live with Val's lot.'

'I have been.' She didn't enlarge on that, and didn't have to. Living with Val's family would inevitably curb her freedom, and Tamsin wasn't just thinking about sex. She said, 'I know you've exchanged contracts and all that, but when can you actually move into that bungalow?'

'Some time in November. There was a hitch in their purchase contract which held things up for a bit, but it's all cleared up now. I suppose I shall just hang on here, it won't be for long after all. That's if Ernie doesn't mind.'

'Valerie will be hurt.'

'I've never definitely said I'd go there.' Kim yawned, and set her empty mug aside on the coffee table. 'Life is full of problems, but I've noticed, a lot of them sort themselves out. We shall just have to go with the flow.'

'It's like ploughing our way through a bog, isn't it?' said Tamsin. 'One damn thing after another. You look about ready for bed.'

'After last night, are you surprised?' Kim smothered a yawn. 'How's the caravan going?'

'Imminent, by this time, I should think. Nobody's put a date to it.'

'I see.' It might be easier if they had, Kim thought. She would have to come to a decision then. She got to her feet, gathering up both mugs to take them to the kitchen. 'You go and finish with the bathroom, I'll just rinse these out.'

It had been a good weekend, Tamsin thought as she did what she had been told, and some good things had come out of it, but she wouldn't mind if there wasn't another like it for a while. Families were great, but you could have too much of a good thing.

Kim probably felt the same about Val's family. Oh well, it would all sort itself out.

She reached for her toothbrush. Bedtime. Electricians tomorrow.

But how would Kim pass the time? It must be hard for her, and right now, she herself was the lucky one; Francis' exploit with the rusty nail had thrown her into his life and out of her twin's. She made a face at herself.

Problems, problems, problems. They never seemed to come to an end.

XXIV

The chilly wind had dropped by Monday morning, but instead, it was raining. Hard. Kim looked out through the kitchen window with deep gloom as she made the toast for breakfast, contemplating a day on her own where she couldn't even go for a walk on the cliffs with any enjoyment. Shopping on her own simply to pass the time lacked charm, even if she had any spare money to shop with, but now she had no job she needed to be careful. She was lonely, in fact. It was a new sensation. Diana/Tamsin didn't make it any better by asking cheerfully, 'What have you got planned for the day?' and Kim answered with uncharacteristic force, 'Sod all'

Tamsin looked at her carefully, that hadn't sounded like Kim. She thought before she answered: a new idea.

'I have to go with Francis to see this electrician and talk about where we want the sockets and things, but I don't know what he wants to do after that. If it's going back to Shortlanesend and working in the office, perhaps I can leave him to it, and we can go and look at freezers and things. I doubt very much if he will want to, and it's got to be done sometime.'

'It's all right,' said Kim slamming the toast into the toast rack. 'You don't have to worry about me! My father will be ringing me anyway.'

'At nine o'clock,' Tamsin pointed out. 'I shall barely have left the house by then.' She sounded so reasonable that Kim felt ashamed of her brief outburst. She picked up the butter dish and the toast and carried them to the table before she answered, to give the dust time to settle. When they were finally sitting down, she said, more reasonably, 'Francis needs you, he can't do things for himself.'

'He can in the office, if he just takes a little more time and patience, and he's got the first, at least, to spare at the moment, although he is a bit short on the second. And it isn't fair that you should be all on your own all the time. After all, it was his own silly fault in the first place.

'I said, it's all right,' said Kim, trying to make light of it.

'No, it isn't. And your input will probably be more useful than his anyway. He's about as domesticated as the farm cats – Birdie excepted, of course.'

'Even so, he should come first – under the circumstances.'

'I'll ring you, when I've talked to him,' said Tamsin, firmly. She pushed the toast towards her twin. 'Eat your breakfast, and stop pining.' She paused, narrowing her eyes, as a new thought struck her. 'Everything is all right with you and Val, isn't it?'

'Of course it is!' Kim realised she had spoken with too much emphasis the minute the words were out of her mouth. She went on, hurriedly. 'Oh, it's just that he's so set his heart on this job, and all the waiting is getting to him a bit, he must be at the very bottom of the list – it isn't a good feeling. And the weather's been so awful these last two weekends that he hasn't even been able to work it off sailing.' She looked at her twin, and made an expressive face. 'He's a bloke, after all. You know the score.'

'All too well. And mine is fretting over whether he'll ever have the full use of his hand again, and he won't know that for sure for a couple of weeks yet either, so really, we need each other quite as much as they need us.'

'Even more, what do we do with the pair of them?'

'God knows! I hope He does…' They caught each other's eye, and Kim gave a reluctant smile. Tamsin said, 'And cheer up, they could just be saving the best until last.'

'I wish I believed that. Far more likely, they're doing it alphabetically, and all the others are called things like Anderson and Evans.'

'Then just hope that Mr Anderson and Mr Evans are rubbish,' Tamsin told her, and finally made her smile. 'That's better. Look on the bright side and pass the marmalade, please.'

They finished their breakfast, and as it was Kim's turn to wash up, Tamsin left her with it and headed off for Shortlanesend. Francis was in the bathroom with the District Nurse seeing to the dressing on his hand when she got there, so she placed her quandary in front of Bennie, who listened sympathetically.

'I see your problem, but you can't be in two places at once,' she said. 'Tell you what, give Kim a ring and invite her over here for lunch, that'll give her a bright spot in the day to look forward to, and we can sort something out between us then. I'm sure Francis will be quite glad to be spared the fridge-and-washing machine shift, and taking Kim with you is a good plan, it'll give all three of you a break.' She paused. 'And whichever of them you end up with, don't forget to take some measurements with you. Things have got to fit. Or fit under worktops, in some cases. And be sure to include a good tumble drier. And a decent microwave, the house may be fifteenth century but you don't have to live back then. And an electric stove, so you can let the Aga out in a heatwave. He can afford it all.'

Tamsin looked thoughtful. 'I hadn't thought about most of that – really, Kim would be much better as a companion on this trip, I'm nearly as undomesticated as he is. The pair of us together would be a recipe for domestic catastrophe.'

'There you are then. I'm pretty sure he'll agree with you, anyway. Why don't you give Kim a ring about lunch, while they finish in the bathroom?'

'Good plan.' Tamsin took out her mobile and keyed in the number, but it was engaged.

'Probably talking to her dad,' she said. 'Heaven only knows how long that will take!'

'Leave me her number, I'll ring her later on,' Bennie suggested. 'She's got transport – and if there's anything urgent she needs to tell you, she can ring you.'

Francis and the District Nurse entered from the passage at this point, the District Nurse said that everything was healing cleanly, smiled reassuringly at Tamsin, and bustled off to her next appointment, and Francis said to Tamsin, 'R-ready, then?'

'Certainly am. Electricians, here we come!'

'See you both at lunchtime,' said Bennie, waving them away.

Tamsin had wondered how to approach the subject of Kim and the afternoon, but fortuitously, once they were on their way, Francis forestalled her. He asked, 'G-got any plans f-f-for w-when we've finished out h-here? I n-need to be on the c-c-computer, but it's not any th-thing I need your help f-for, unless you're offering. I c-can manage with t-t-two fingers. It w-will pass the time, and I c-c-can't take up your whole l-life.'

Was there a note of bitterness there, Tamsin wondered. She wouldn't blame him if there was. She said, 'I'll help you if you need me.' She slowed for a tractor lumbering down the lane ahead of them before adding, 'If you don't, I had thought I might take Kim with me and look at electrical goods. I can't see you wanting to do that.'

'Th-that sounds a good idea, we n-need to get that s-s-sorted soon.'
He paused. 'I had b-been thinking about K-Kim. Sh-she must be a b-bit
lonely, with V-Val in London, and me t-t-taking up all your time.' He
sounded remorseful, and Tamsin thought she heard a warning bell. She
therefore answered carefully.

'She is, of course. Particularly when it's pouring down like today and
she can't even go for a hike along the cliff, but she understands, we neither
of us hold it against you. But to be fair, her input might be more valuable
than yours anyway, today.'

'It w-w-will be.' They drove along at a dignified speed for a bit, and
then the tractor turned off and Tamsin was able to put her foot down
again. As they sped away, Francis spoke.

'You m-m-must both be f-finding me a p-p-perfect nuisance.'

'No. I'm finding you an interesting challenge.' She shot him a quick
look, but he wasn't smiling. Bother the man! While they were driving
along the lanes was not the time for this kind of conversation. She added,
with her eyes back on the winding road, 'Get it through your head, I love
you. I've loved this chance to get to know you well, I'm only sorry for
the reason for it. And Kim understands. After all, with all her travelling all
over the place, she's used to being self-sufficient.'

'It's hard f-f-for her, when the t-two of you have only just m-m-met.
F-for you, too.'

'Francis! Stop beating yourself up, what's got into you?'

'F-frustration, probably.'

And depression, Tamsin thought, but did not say. And stress; that self-
inflicted injury and its problematic outcome must be hanging over him
like a black cloud right now. She switched back to where the conversation
had begun, hoping to restore normality.

'If you're happy with the computer on your own, we can run the plan
past Kim when we see her. Bennie's inviting her to lunch.'

'G-good.'

There was something about the way he said it, that made Tamsin finally
certain that all was not well. There was a small passing place just ahead,
she slid into it and switched off the engine.

'So, tell me,' she said, with unwonted force. 'What's eating you this
morning?'

'N-nothing.' He didn't look at her.

'Now pull the other one, it's got bells on! And don't say "Kim", that may have been true, but it wasn't the truth. It was a diversion! You can't kid me, Dr Chillingworth, so give!'

There was a pause, while Francis said nothing and Tamsin wondered if he ever would. Whether he did or whether he didn't it would be a measure of his trust in her, one way or the other. She was all at once acutely aware of the thirteen-year gap between them: would he treat her like an irresponsible teenager, or as an adult?

The silence spun out until she felt like gritting her teeth, but finally he did speak.

'If th-this hand is p-p-permanently d-d-damaged, it w-w-will louse up m-my life all over again – f-f-for g-good, this time.'

Tamsin kept her calm only with a huge effort. She spoke as levelly as she could manage. 'Does anything make you think that it will be? Did the District Nurse say something this morning?'

'N-no.'

'Did you ask her?'

'N-no. She w-w-wouldn't know anyway. Or have t-t-told me if she did.'

This was like pulling teeth! Tamsin said, 'So what makes you think so?' and waited.

For quite a long time.

Finally, when she had almost given up hope, he spoke. 'It s-still hurts like hell, it's b-b-badly inflamed, and I c-c-can't close my fingers.'

'You shouldn't be trying,' Tamsin told him. 'Look, you were told it wouldn't heal overnight, it would take time – and patience! You've more than enough of the first, nearly eighteen months before you need to start worrying and it certainly won't take that long to heal – and you just have to work on the second. Nine days is not "time". It's the blink of an eyelash. And the inflammation is at least in part due to the infection. That will clear up but you have to give it a chance'

'You would know, of c-c-course.'

'Well actually, yes. My mother cut her hand on a piece of glass in the flowerbed, and she had the same sort of thing. Took three weeks before it finally cleared, and she hadn't skewered her whole hand either.'

He said nothing to this, but just sat there chewing his lip and staring into space. After a while, he spoke.

'S-sorry, Tamsin. I'm b-being a p-pain in the arse, I kn-know. But j-j-just when I th-thought that I things w-w-would go w-well for once, th-this happens…I d-d-don't think I could bear it, if I l-lost everything again, j-j-just for a moment's carelessness.'

Tamsin refrained from saying that it would teach him to be more careful, this wasn't the moment. She said gently, 'It won't. Stop imagining nightmares.'

'If I c-c-can't use my r-right hand…you know what I'm l-l-like with the left. It w-w-would cripple me for the p-p-practical stuff.'

'OK,' said Tamsin. She had to think on her feet for this one, for she could see that he was quite possibly right. 'If it happens – and it's a ginormous "if" – then I shall just have to give up lying in the sunshine on the beaches of Greece and be your assistant – your hands, if you like. And we shall have to have a paid hand to help with the boat – you said we'd need one for the crossing anyway. Just pick him carefully, and keep him on.' She stole a sideways glance; he looked as if he had been carved in stone, staring at the lane. She said, gently, 'It won't happen, Francis.'

He took a deep breath and turned towards her at last.

'T-Tamsin, you are s-s-something else. W-what d-d-did I do to d-d-deserve you?'

'Would it work, do you think?'

He didn't answer that, and she twisted, rather uncomfortably, in her seat so that she could get her arms round him, and he turned towards her and returned the compliment, hard. They stayed like that for a few minutes, then Tamsin began to get cramp in her spine, and drew back. He let her go reluctantly, and when he spoke it sounded like a complete change of subject, although she thought that it actually wasn't.

'You have n-n-no idea how much I envy V-Val.'

For a second, Tamsin had no idea what he was talking about, but then it dawned on her. She laughed, as much as anything from sheer relief that the drama seemed to have taken itself off.

'Me too – envy Kim, that is. But we could always go and have dinner in that lovely pub you took me to up on the cliff, and stay overnight.'

'Y-you liked th-that pub that m-m-much?' He looked surprised; knowimg it so well he probably took it for granted.

'I thought it was amazing. And the views were breathtaking.'

He smiled; she was relieved to see it. The last few minutes had been a bit gritty.

'Th-then m-maybe we should spend our w-w-wedding n-night there. W-w-would you l-l-like that?'

'I'd love it. But what about the animals? Someone would have to look after them – I presume there will be some on the premises by then, even if it's only Sacha and the cats.'

'Hedley w-w-will see to them f-f-for one n-night.'

Hedley? Tamsin decided not to pursue that one for the moment, this was neither the time nor the place. She started the engine and put the car into gear.

'Time for the electrician. We're late already.'

They were back on the lane, heading for Shearwater and Burnthouse, and after about a mile she spoke again, curiosity getting the better of her. 'Would it work?'

'Would w-what work?' He sounded surprised – confused, even.

'Me being your hands. I know sod all about marine biology,' and to her relief, he laughed outright; she had wondered if she would be treading on a sore spot.

'You'd have t-t-to learn a bit about it. I c-c-can teach you on the l-l-long winter evenings.' He gave her a wicked grin.

'Actually,' said Tamsin, having thought about this, 'I think I might rather like that. After all, it's a major part of your life – or it will be. It would be nice to be able to talk sensibly with you about it.'

'J-just give me t-t-time to get the b-books out of storage.'

'Is that a threat, or a promise?'

'W-which would you like?'

She didn't answer that, as they were approaching Burnthouse, but as she made the turn, her heart was lighter than it had been all morning. If he could laugh about it, things weren't so bad.

It was still tipping down with rain; as they drove into the spring-cleaned yard, empty now but for a large yellow skip: they could see Stephen Postgate and another man sheltering in the doorway to the back premises. They both waved as the Discovery pulled up, as close to the back door as was possible. Tamsin waved back, and she and Francis tumbled out onto the cracked paving and made a run for it.

'Sorry we're a bit late,' said Tamsin, breathlessly. 'We were a bit held up – the District Nurse left late when she came to do his dressing.' It was pushing the truth a little, and Francis shot her a quizzical look, but the nurse had been running late, come to that. Stephen nodded his understanding and introduced his companion. 'This is Will Gates, he's the head of the electrical team.' Everyone said hello and then Stephen said, 'So shall we get on with it?' and gave Tamsin a smile. 'I'm sure you've got it all worked out.'

You hope! Tamsin thought, as she accompanied the men inside, but she was underselling herself, she discovered; faced with the reality of the empty rooms she found herself mentally furnishing them, and imagining freezers and fridges and television sets, reading lamps and computers, all in their relative places and was happily conscious of Francis looking at her with surprised approval and, except for when they were in what would be his personal study, leaving her to it. In what would eventually be the drawing room, she was pleased to see men already working on the floor, lifting the rotten boards. This morning, the whole house seemed to have come alive, it was even possible to believe that they would one day, in the not-too-far distant future, be living here.

They left eventually, with Tamsin carrying a list of measurements and recommendations for suitable electrical appliances for her utility rooms, and got back into the Discovery. Amazingly, it wasn't even eleven o'clock. Tamsin looked at her watch and then at Francis.

'So, what shall we do now? Or do you want to go back to Shortlanesend? We've got a couple of hours until lunch.'

The constructive interval seemed to have calmed him down, thank goodness, or maybe he felt he owed her one after that uncomfortable interlude earlier on. He leaned back in his seat and said, 'L-let's g-g-go and f-f-find a car showr-r-room.'

Tamsin had thought that he would have in mind a sensible hatchback, much like the one she had at present but a size bigger to allow for his own long legs, and she had been happy with that; it would be practical for their immediate new lifestyle. It turned out that he had no such idea in mind, and when they finally pulled up outside the showroom to which he had directed her, the first thing that happened was that she went completely silent. He gave her a quizzical look.

'B-Birdie g-g-got your tongue?'

Tamsin responded with a stutter to match his own. 'I th-thought you'd j-j-just up-size…'

'Why? W-w-we've got enough s-s-sensible models already, l-l-lets have some fun!' He opened his door and prepared to jump down. C–come on, l–l–let's see what w–w–we can find.'

Tamsin followed obediently into the sparkling showroom, wondering if he classified his own beautiful Mercedes as "sensible", and if so, why had he bought it in the first place? and finding no answer. He certainly wasn't being sensible this morning.

They emerged an hour later, Tamsin with her eyes like stars, the prospective owner of a Mazda MX5 convertible in bright scarlet with pale coffee upholstery, to be collected at the beginning of the following week when all the paperwork would be done.

'It'll w–w–work out well,' Francis had told her, watching her face. 'You c–couldn't k–k–keep it in the s–s–street in Emberton. It c–c–can go straight in the g–g–garage at B–Burnthouse.'

'But we won't be there!' Tamsin had said, unable even to consider being parted from such a wonderful gift, and Francis took her breath away yet again by replying, 'Y–yes, we sh–should be. W–with a b–bit of l–l–luck and a f–f–fair wind.'

Tamsin considered this, and everything else, in silence as she drove them away. She had to concentrate in the unfamiliar streets in which she found herself, but when they were back on the main road she found her voice again, and said, 'When are they delivering the caravan, if we'll be in it next week?'

'Th–Thursday, with l–luck.' He turned to smile at her, and although she was concentrating on the busy road and didn't see it, she could almost feel the warmth like the sun on her skin. 'Th–then they'll have to c–c–connect the p–plumbing and the w–w–water and electricity, b–but that shouldn't t–t–take m–more than a d–d–day, the groundwork is already d–d–done. W–w–we should be able to m–move in over the w–w–w–weekend.'

'Whoo!' said Tamsin. She drove for a few minutes in silence, her mind teeming with all sorts of thoughts, some of them so wonderful that she had trouble keeping her attention on the road, and when they arrived back at Shortlanesend it turned out that Kim had experienced an equally amazing morning of her own, which was only fair.

Arranging about the Mazda had taken up quite a lot of time, so that Kim was already at Shortlanesend when they got back, sitting in one of the chairs talking to Bennie in the kitchen, with The Boss curled up comfortably on her lap, purring. Bennie was ironing, on a board set up in the corner, and seeing her Tamsin was immediately reminded of yet another electrical appliance she would need to be buying. Such was her euphoria at their recent purchase and the marvellous and unexpected news that they would be able to be together properly at long last by the weekend, that she took out the electrician's list and a pen, and added it without a qualm. Francis looked over her shoulder.

'D-d-do you know how t-t-to use one?' he enquired with a lift of an eyebrow.

'It can't be rocket science. And I know damn well that you don't wear minimum-iron cotton polyester shirts, or not all the time.'

'I'm only s-s-s-surprised that you even kn-know the word,' he said.

Kim looked at them. Tamsin had gone off that morning in a cheerful enough mood, making plans for the day and wondering how she would get on with the electrician, but now she was on cloud nine. Kim was her twin, she could tell. As she was in a similar mood herself, she was glad: there had been one point during the morning when she had wondered if all was well with her twin. They did have this link, she knew, but it seemed to have played her false this time.

Bennie said, 'Do I take it that you two had a good morning? You look very cheerful.' And a good thing too, Francis had been under a bit of a cloud when they had left, she had thought. No sign of it now.

'He bought me a car,' said Tamsin, happily.

'A nice one? Or a boring workhorse?'

'A lovely one!' Tamsin pulled out the brochure that the salesman at the showroom had given her. 'Here it is – have a look!'

Kim and Bennie poured over it together, jealously.

'What came over him?' Kim wanted to know. 'I expected him to get you a jeep, or something practical,' and Bennie said, 'That is the most inefficient, and the most beautiful, farm workhorse that I have ever seen. You lucky, lucky girl!' She looked up and smiled at Francis, who was watching the three of them with amusement. 'And talking of horses, you're a dark one! I agree with Kim, I expected something quite different.'

Francis just grinned back at her, and Tamsin said, changing the subject, 'And did your Dad ring, like he said?'

'He did.' Kim's reply sang with happiness. 'They'll be over for your wedding, and they'll stay over Christmas, although they'll have to be back at New Year. But then it will be only three months before I see them again anyway, and they can stay a bit longer that time.' She paused. 'Francis, I can't even begin to thank you enough – it's going to be so good to have them here, it's almost a year since I saw them! It's the most wonderful gift that you could have given me – given any of us – and if ever you need anything translated, just call me!'

He laughed, and headed for the passage door. 'It w-w-was a p-pleasure. It'll be good to see R-R-Rod and Ann again. It's more than t-t-twenty years since l-l-last time.' He had his hand on the doorknob when Bennie noticed what he was doing.

'Just don't get stuck into that computer, you!' she said. 'Lunch will be on the table as soon as Ernie gets in, and hopefully that's any minute now.'

'J-just going to ch-check the emails,' he said. The door closed behind him, and Bennie gave a loud sigh of despair. 'That's him gone, then.'

'There's another thing,' Tamsin said, wondering how Kim would take this one in view of their morning's confidences. 'He says the caravan – or whatever it is – will be delivered on Thursday and we can be in it by the weekend.' She hesitated. 'Not sure that's good news for you, Kim.'

'No, that's brilliant!' said Kim, with simple delight for her twin. 'You'd better start taking some of those saucepans and things out of their packaging, then the dustmen can take it away.'

Oh, practical Kim! 'There's a big skip on site,' Tamsin told her, but Bennie agreed with Kim.

'You don't want to be unpacking bags and boxes and all that unnecessary packaging everyone uses now, in a small space, not while you're trying to get everything else straight. Ernie will find you a box. You can put all your stuff in that and ditch the rubbish like Kim says. And I expect Francis and Co. can fill that skip without your help.'

'There's another thing,' said Kim, and Tamsin looked at her; something in Kim's voice told her that this, too, was good. What was it about today?

'Tell me then,' she said, when Kim didn't immediately do so.

'I dropped in on Valerie for coffee on my way over here – there was nothing else to do in all this rain. And I don't mean that how it sounded,' she added hastily. 'You know what I mean – company and all that. And she asked me what I was planning to do when you left, because it would be very quiet on my own after all the excitement. And she must have seen that I wasn't that enthusiastic about being there on my own, although I could have stood it if it came to it, and I thought she was going to invite me to stay with them, and it would have been awfully difficult to refuse. But she didn't.'

'So what did she do?' asked Tamsin, when Kim paused for breath.

'She said, how about if Penny came over to sleep there occasionally during the week, if I was to be on my own all day, and kept me company. Not over-exciting, but she would be someone to talk to, or to watch telly with. She said Penny wouldn't mind, she had mentioned it herself after the last time Val and I were over there but she thought I would think she was interfering. But I don't. Penny works all day, so it would only be the evening, and it's the evenings that can be lonely. I can entertain myself quite happily most of the time, but it would be nice to have company to call on now and then. If you know you only have to ask, you needn't feel so lonely.'

'That sounds like a good suggestion,' said Bennie. 'It wouldn't crowd you, but the offer would be there. What do you think, Tamsin?'

'I think it sounds as if Valerie is a bit more streetwise than Val has been giving credit for,' said Tamsin, honestly, and caught Kim's eye.

'Caravans, to you!' Kim retorted, and they all laughed. Right on cue, Ernie came through the back door, Sacha and his own dog running at his heels, and the conversation came to a fortuitous end. Bennie put the iron down for the last time, folded the shirt she had been ironing, and headed for the fridge.

'Lunch. Tamsin, go and rout out that man of yours please, and don't listen to excuses. Ernie, go and have a wash, you're filthy, and Kim, would you mind getting out the cutlery?'

'Yes, ma'am,' said Ernie, heading for the door. 'I can do Francis on the way, is he in the office?'

'Don't you dare!' Bennie told him. 'That would be the two of you gone!' She opened the fridge door. 'Home-cured ham and salad, and the bread is in the bin...'

Nobody at Shortlanesend had time to sit over lunch so it was quickly over, and Ernie was heading off outside again with his own dog at his heels, Sacha preferring to stay with Francis.

'You don't have to hang around and help with the washing-up,' Bennie told the twins. 'It's all going into the machine anyway, you two get off on your shopping expedition, and I'll just clear this away in two minutes.'

'I'll see you later then, Francis,' said Tamsin regretfully, she had become too used to his company, she needed to break herself of the habit. Having observed Ernie, she knew that farmers in general didn't hang about being cosy with their wives during the day, and she was quite sure that marine biologists didn't either. 'I'll get back in time to run you back to Burnthouse to check in with the workmen.'

'I w-w-wouldn't bother, not t-t-today,' Francis told her, and seeing her surprise, enlarged on the statement. 'They'll be c-c-clearing the verges d-d-down the drive th-th-this afternoon, w-w-we probably w-wouldn't get up it. And it's f-f-far too wet to walk. Th-they'll manage without us.'

'Then I'll come and see you when I bring Kim back to swap cars,' said Tamsin.

'You're not taking the Discovery?' Bennie asked.

'No need. The most we'll bring back with us, if anything at all, is the iron,' Tamsin pointed out. 'Mine – Kim's – is much easier to park.'

'We'll see you later then. Have fun!'

'More like a very steep learning curve,' Kim told her. 'And thank you for lunch, I expect I'll be seeing you again.'

'I daresay you will,' said Bennie, smiling, and waved them off.

'Lovely girls,' she said to Francis, who was heading off back to the office, but he only said a brief "yes" and vanished. She looked after him thoughtfully, and spoke to The Boss, who was still curled up on the chair. 'I wonder if that girl has fully realised what she's taken on?' she said to him. He blinked at her and tucked his head down to sleep. 'Exactly,' Bennie told him. 'Should I warn her, do you think, or would it be interfering?' but The Boss was already in dreamland.

She hoped that Tamsin wasn't.

It proved to be an instructive afternoon for the twins, and that in many ways, some of them unexpected. Bennie had drawn them a map to find the retailer recommended by the electrician, and they had found it without getting lost more than once; it was on a business estate on the outskirts of town, where Tamsin had been once with Francis, looking for antiques, and was unexpectedly large. Plenty of scope in there, Kim said, eyeing it up.

'Let's go and see what they can do for us,' said Tamsin. She got out of the passenger seat; she and Kim had had a brief argument about which of them should drive, she had won. It had felt very odd to be a passenger in what was arguably still her own car – Kim had argued it, anyway –

particularly after chauffeuring Francis all over the place for the past week. Restful, though.

Armed with the electrician's comprehensive list, they went through the double glass doors into the store. An assistant came forward to offer his help and Tamsin gave him the list, it seemed simplest. He ran his eye down it, took a measuring reel from the nearest counter, and led the way into the enamelled metal jungle.

What followed was a very educational half hour, full of advice and surprises, one of which Tamsin thought was rather uncanny: if the measurements they had been given were correct the washing machine, the tumble drier, and the dishwasher would all fit under the allocated worktops.

'It's spooky,' she muttered to Kim. 'They didn't have stuff like this in the fifteenth century – and they're supposed to have been shorter than us anyway, the worktops would be too high for them, and too low for these.'

Kim looked at her in mock despair. She said, 'Do you ever stop to think before you open your mouth? I don't suppose they had worktops at all, back then! They'll have had cupboards and dressers and things.'

'They had sinks,' Tamsin objected.

'But not fitted cupboards. I bet you! And come to that, I'm not at all sure about sinks, either, not that far back, or not as we know them, with plumbing.'

'Those worktops and stuff look pretty old. And they're slate, not Formica.'

'They are not six hundred years old, not by a mile! And I daresay it's all been replaced a time or two over the centuries, anyway.'

'I suppose…' Tamsin sounded reluctant to believe her. The assistant, who had been listening with amusement, said, 'This is a pretty old house we're fitting out, is it?'

'You could say that,' said Tamsin, giving her sister a telling look. 'So how about you show us a medieval fridge?'

'Be glad to.' He grinned at them. 'Step this way!'

Francis, unexpectedly practical in this domestic context, had directed them to choose a fridge-freezer and a fairly large chest freezer; they wouldn't be needing the latter for a bit, but it would be sensible to install everything at the same time: since neither of these items needed to fit underneath anything, this was easier. Neither he nor Tamsin had thought about a vacuum cleaner, but Kim did, and they added a neat rechargeable cordless one to their list, which was growing by the minute. 'It'll do for the moment,' Kim said, 'and it'll be easier to use in the caravan,' and Tamsin looked at her askance. She hadn't given housework a thought, but of course someone would have to do it. It was unlikely to be Francis, which only left one candidate.

'Have we forgotten anything else?' she asked, looking at the list anxiously. 'Oh – yes! We need an electric stove, didn't Bennie say? Oh – and an iron.'

The store could supply an ironing board too, it turned out, which seemed like a good idea.

'I'm sure we've forgotten something,' said Tamsin, uneasily.

'You have. A microwave.'

'I already bought one – remember? It's behind the sofa.' She caught the assistant's eye, he looked as if he wanted to roar with laughter and was having difficulty restraining himself. She said, defensively, 'Well, we had to put it somewhere!'

'That was a smallish one, for the caravan,' Kim reminded her. 'You want a bigger one for the house. And anyway, that one will still be wanted outside, didn't you say someone was moving in when you moved out? A manager, or something?'

'That's true. All right, we need a microwave then – and that must be it!'

They then had to explain that none of these things could be delivered until sometime the following week, or even the week following that, but the assistant took this calmly. It could all be stored, he assured them, just ring when they were ready. He then totted up the bill and Kim nearly had a heart attack when she heard the final total. Tamsin, however, took it in her stride, a rare indication of the social and financial gulf that lay between them now, and paid with her credit card, as she had arranged with Francis, without blinking an eyelash. They returned to the car unusually silent for them, and they were on the road back into the town before Kim spoke, and when she did it was to say something that she immediately wished she hadn't.

'Will Francis be paying you back for all of that?'

Tamsin shot her a swift look.

'No, why should he? It'll be our home, not just his, when we live in it. It's only fair I should put something towards the cost of fitting it out.' She had argued this one out with him, too, but he had seen the sense of it in the end. She hoped that Kim would as well, although she feared that wasn't the aspect of the case that was bothering her twin. Money, she reflected, was a curse as well as a blessing, and strangely, it now seemed quite as much when you had it as when you didn't.

She remembered the vacuum cleaner, that was the other side of the coin, another straw in the wind. It had, for different reasons, made her feel much the same for a moment as she guessed that Kim was feeling now. They couldn't discuss it, the waters might run too deep: she had been made to feel inadequate, Kim to feel inferior. Both of them were probably being ridiculous.

'Let's go and find a cup of tea, after all that,' she said, and Kim said, 'OK. Good idea,' and each of them felt relieved, although for different reasons.

They didn't go to Bordens, they neither of them was in the mood for its temptations; instead they went to a small but pretty teashop down one of the side streets, that they had always meant to try but never had. It turned out to be an instructive choice.

They picked themselves a table near the window, and gave the waitress their order – it was the sort of place where they still had proper waitresses – including two slices of carrot cake to cheer themselves up, and sat looking around with interest as they waited for it to be brought. Tamsin had her back towards most of the room as they had a corner table, but Kim had a clear view. The place wasn't crowded, but it was by no means empty either; mostly women, obviously on a shopping spree much like themselves, but on the whole older than they were. Housewives, Kim thought to herself, Tamsin will be one of those very soon now, and me not long after if I can't get a job here – how odd! And then she realised that one of them was looking towards their table and nodding as if she knew them. She returned the smile out of politeness, but she had no recollection of seeing the woman before; a solidly built, well-dressed woman of middle age, with short, well-cut dark hair streaked with grey and a strong face, a woman who knew her way around, quite obviously. But why was she smiling at them? And then the waitress went over to the woman and handed her a piece of paper that was obviously the bill, and the woman got to her feet. But she didn't immediately go over to the till to pay, she came over to their table.

'Good afternoon,' she said. 'Forgive me for interrupting you, but haven't we met?' and she smiled, although she didn't seem an essentially smiley person. Kim said, 'I don't think so,' and again smiled back.

'I know that I've seen you both somewhere, you're very noticeable, the pair of you.' She frowned, it seemed to fit her face better, although she didn't look bad-tempered, particularly. Serious. Strong. The words came into Kim's head and sat there. Tamsin had said nothing, but she looked as if being accosted by a stranger like this was making her uncomfortable, but then the woman's face lit up as recollection came to her. 'I know where it was – the Regatta Dance, down at the Yacht Club, back in the summer! Weren't you with Merlin and Julie-Anne Ravenscourt's party? I think that must be where I saw you both.'

The Regatta Dance wasn't one of their happiest memories. Kim said, 'We were at the dance, yes.'

'I remember now.' The woman nodded her head. 'One of you is engaged to the Police Superintendent's son, am I right? And the other...' She paused, thinking back. There had been a bit of an incident, caused by that total fool, Jenny Carruthers and her lot of course! Francis Chillingworth had slammed out of the door and not come back, and there had been a lot of talk, mainly instigated by Jenny. And that tied in with something else that she had heard recently, and not quite believed, although she had wanted to believe it. She said, 'May I sit with you for a minute?'

That is the kind of request to which it is virtually impossible to say "No", so both the twins made a murmur that might have meant anything, and the woman pulled out a chair and sat down with them.

'I should introduce myself,' she said. 'My name is Marie Law, I am a friend of Mary Vachell-Chillingworth, whom I believe you both know?' Another murmur. She went on. 'I understand that one of you has become engaged to her son, do I have that right?'

'That would be me,' said Tamsin. She held out her hand with the beautiful ring, and Marie Law looked at it.

'Very nice. And so long as you know what you're doing, I congratulate you on your choice. Francis Chillingworth has had most of life's cards dealt from the bottom of the pack so far, but you will know that. He deserves a break now.'

'We do know,' said Kim, seeing that Tamsin was speechless for the moment. She didn't know what to say after that, how much did this woman know, anyway? How good a friend of Mary's was she? But Marie Law, whoever she was, was no more prepared to discuss it than they were. She said, 'That's good,' and gathered up the bag and gloves she had temporarily placed on the table. She said, 'Here comes your tea now, I'll leave you in peace. I'm pleased to have met you, I'm sure we will meet again.' She smiled as she got to her feet, looking directly at Tamsin. 'Francis Chillingworth is very brave, and extremely clever: he can also be very temperamental and highly-strung, but I won't need to tell you that. He has caused some of his troubles for himself, although I believe not all of them. You will need to support him and try to guide him along the safer paths of life, rather than through the thorns and pitfalls – although that may be a bit like trying to direct a whirlwind. I wish you good fortune in your enterprise!' She smiled at Tamsin. 'And happiness. I'm sure you will have it but I won't need to tell you that.' She was turning away, but then she turned back, opening her bag and taking something out. 'And if you should have any trouble with Jenny Carruthers, here is my card. You needn't hesitate to ask for help, and it would give me great pleasure to sink her ship for good!' She did leave then, with a smile for each of them, leaving Tamsin clutching the card. The waitress put the tea and the carrot cake on the table, and they were left staring at each other.

Marie Law went over to the till to settle her bill feeling pleased, not necessarily with herself but with the way things had played out. Francis Chillingworth needed some allies and she was happy to volunteer as one of them and offer support to the troops. The fact that, in her opinion, he also needed some sense kicking into him was another matter entirely.

Kim and Tamsin were left staring at each other.

'Who on earth was that?' Kim asked, even though she knew that Tamsin knew no more than she did.

'Someone prepared to fight on the side of the angels – which is a first,' said Tamsin. She thought about it. 'She obviously knows Francis quite well, she had him bang to rights, but then if she's a friend of Mary's, I suppose she would. And she has no opinion of this Carruthers woman who keeps cropping up – I suppose she may be Max Carruthers' wife, or something. Or perhaps his mother, if she calls herself a friend of Mary.'

'That's an odd way to put it,' said Kim, quietly.

'It's the way Francis put it.'

'He's mentioned her, then?'

Actually, I think it might have been Bennie. I don't remember – it was just in passing.' She picked up the teapot – it was that kind of a café. 'That cake looks good, let's just put it all out of our minds for now and enjoy this. It will all wait for us.'

They finished their tea and cake – the cake was amazing, home-made and meltingly delicious, they bought another couple of slices to take away with them – and made their way back to the Square, where they had left the car. Thankfully, the day's torrential downpour had gone away for the moment, it was still spitting a bit, and the sky was a dramatic sooty grey, but they could walk at a reasonable pace without getting soaked to the skin.

'What now?' asked Kim. 'I'm all shopped out after that lot, and you must be all spent out!'

'For today, anyway,' said Tamsin, with a grin. 'I tell you what, you take me back to Shortlanesend and I can spend a bit of time with Francis if he's not working, and then I'll come back to Romans and have an evening with you for a change – he has plenty of company out on the farm, and he's in a bit of a mood today, anyway. We can get some fish and chips in the pub, and eat them in front of the telly with that gorgeous cake.'

'Won't Francis want you with him?'

'He'll understand – probably, anyway. We talked about it a bit this morning, and anyway, by the weekend, he'll be having more than enough of me – a caravan, or whatever it is, isn't going to be big enough for us to get far away from each other.'

They drove back to Shortlanesend without saying much to each other. Tamsin sat in the unfamiliar passenger seat watching the world go by for a change, instead of the traffic, and Kim was unwontedly silent. The woman in the café was occupying her thoughts; there had been something there that had triggered that twitch of foreboding that kept invading her peace, that feeling that something was just waiting to happen. She couldn't see how a total stranger could be part of that, but nevertheless, the feeling was strong. Perhaps Tamsin would need her help, maybe in the near future, but she couldn't pin it down. She wished that she didn't get these flashes of…well, not insight, exactly. More like second sight, but she didn't want to think about that.

Back at the farm, Bennie was outside, just come back from feeding the chickens; she waved when she saw the car drive up, and came over to speak to them.

'Had a good afternoon? Did you get everything you needed?'

'Yes. Plus a vacuum cleaner,' Tamsin told her, and she smiled. 'You must be about ready for a cup of tea after all that! Come inside, and I'll put the kettle on.'

They explained that they had already had one, and Kim said that she ought to get back to Emberton anyway.

'You don't have to,' Bennie said. 'You're always welcome here, you know. Stay and have supper with us.'

Tamsin said, 'I thought I'd just see Francis and then go back too. We thought we'd get some fish and chips from the pub and have a quiet evening in,' and Bennie looked at her seriously.

'That might be a plan. Francis is tired, I think, he went up for a rest shortly after you left, and he hasn't come down yet, a quiet evening and an early night might be just what he needs, too – I think it's all getting to him a bit.'

'It is,' said Tamsin, feelingly.

'When do you go back to the hospital?' Bennie asked.

'Not until Wednesday afternoon.'

'That'll be it, then.' Bennie nodded her head wisely. 'He always has let things wind him up – too much imagination, and too much knowledge too. He's afraid, I suspect.'

Tamsin thought so too, but didn't say. Instead, she asked, 'Do you know someone called Marie Law?'

'Oh God, yes! The Empress of Embridge! Her husband is a retired Admiral, she commands the fleet excellently herself. But good as gold underneath – why do you ask?'

'Oh, she came up and spoke to us while we were having our tea – she'd seen us down at the Yacht Club – on Regatta night.'

Bennie, of course, would know nothing about the evening of Regatta night, unless Francis had told her, which was unlikely. She said, 'Then hope that she's fighting on your side.'

'She seems to be,' said Kim.

Kim left them to drive herself home, and Tamsin and Bennie went indoors out of what had now developed into a drizzle. Birdie, Tamsin noted, was not in her favourite chair by the Aga in spite of the rain outside.

'She'll be sleeping with Francis,' said Bennie, seeing the direction of her look. 'Go and wake them both up – if he sleeps any longer, he won't sleep tonight and he has trouble with that anyway at the moment. Go on up, I need to start the children's tea, they'll be back in a minute.'

As it turned out, neither Francis nor the cat was actually asleep: he was lying on his back stroking the cat, who was sitting on his chest, and the cat was purring happily. The cat looked perfectly relaxed and happy, the man didn't. Tamsin sat down on the edge of the bed.

'Hello there. I got everything done, and Kim made me buy a vacuum cleaner. And an ironing board. I'm hoping she will also show me what to do with them.'

He smiled at her; he looked weary and strained, but he hadn't lost his sense of humour.

'G-good, there'd be no use asking m-m-me.' He took his hand away from the cat and held it out to her; she took it and leant forward to kiss him.

'You look a mess! Bennie asked Kim and me to stay to supper, but I think I'll go back and spend the evening at Romans, if that's OK with you. You look as if you could do with an early night anyway.'

'F-for what use it w-w-would be. B-but you're probably r-r-right.'

'I'll be over in the morning, to take you to Burnthouse.'

'N-n-no need to m-make it too early, th-they can always ring if they w-w-want me.'

'Then try and have a bit of a lie-in for once.' She wondered whether to mention their meeting with Marie Law, but decided not to. 'I'll be off then, unless you need me.'

'I sh-shall always n-n-need you, but off you g-g-go, then, you've p-p-probably had enough of me t-today anyway. Have a g-g-good evening.' They exchanged another kiss, passionate enough to make the cat jump to the floor and stalk off in indignation, and Tamsin went back downstairs in her wake thinking, roll on the weekend! She had no idea what Francis might be thinking, she never could second-guess him.

The children were back from school, the kitchen was full of chaos. They begged her to stay, but she said no, she was spending the evening at home with Kim.

'Kim could come here,' said Maisie, hanging on to her hand, while Clive stood to one side, grinning.

'Maisie, let her alone!' Bennie told her. 'She's entitled to a bit of time off, and you'll be seeing her again. Run, Tamsin, before they get you!' She laughed. Tamsin ran, waving goodbye.

Escape was just what it felt like, too. It had been a long, worrying sort of day, she had had enough of it. Fish and chips with just herself and Kim looked like a glimpse of heaven...

XXV

Next morning came, as it inevitably does, and had to be faced. Kim and Tamsin sat over their breakfast, discussing its possibilities.

'I have no idea what Francis has in mind, if anything at all,' Tamsin said. 'The only thing he said last night was, don't bother to be too early. I get the impression that he's running out of things to fill the empty hours, he must have killed the office work stone dead by this time, even with only one hand, with the farm not really running yet. I'm not sure what I should do with him.' She glanced at the window. 'And it's raining again, which doesn't help.'

'Take him to see his horses,' Kim suggested. 'He hasn't been out to the stable, at least since he had his misunderstanding with that nail. It might do him good to be among his own animals, and sensible people.'

'Are you saying I'm not sensible?'

'Don't be so touchy. Of course I'm not.'

'He needs something to think about, not just passing the time. He's scared of what Mr Simmonds might say tomorrow.'

'Well, you can't blame him for that.'

'That woman was right, you know,' said Tamsin, thinking about it. 'He is a bit highly strung, although you wouldn't guess it unless you knew him well, which nobody outside his family seems to round here, and he does quite often make the rod for his own back.'

'So bad luck for the shrimps and plankton, then.'

'I think they may calm him down, actually. I think they're half the trouble. He lost his way, or more probably, he got derailed.'

'He just doesn't seem to know how to deal with people. But I suppose that's inevitable, after all he's been put through.'

They looked at each other, and each simultaneously pulled a face. Tamsin said, 'It's this weather. It's depressing, all this rain, I hope it stops by the weekend.'

'Keep hoping. It looks to me as if it's set in for ever.'

'Let's hope you're wrong.' Tamsin started gathering up the breakfast plates. 'And it's my turn to wash up, before you tell me. Put the telly on, we might just catch the weather forecast.'

Kim was about to do so, when Tamsin's phone rang and she put the plates down again to answer it. Sighing, Kim gathered them up herself and headed for the kitchen and Tamsin gave her an apologetic look as she picked up the phone. Kim heard one end of the conversation while she resignedly ran the water into the sink. It sounded promising.

'Hello…yes, it's me…oh Erin, how lovely to hear from you!…yes, of course we would…yes…no, don't do that, just let me speak to Kim a minute.' She came to the kitchen door, the phone in her hand. 'Kim, how would you feel about having the spare bunk for a couple of nights, and letting Michael and Erin have your bed? He has to come down to Dorset on business this afternoon, they're going to dump the kids with Erin's parents so that they can stay over and come the rest of the way down here to see Francis and the farm on the side.'

'When?' asked Kim, practically.

'Tonight and tomorrow night, they'll have to leave at dawn on Thursday, for Michael to get back to work, he can only steal one day. Erin said, a hotel, but it seems a shame when we have a double bed we can make spare.'

'We'll have to sort out about clean sheets. The caretaker does all that.'

'Bennie will arrange it,' said Tamsin, with all the confidence of someone who was used to being waited on hand and foot, and Kim smothered a laugh.

'All right then. It would be fun. We all need a bit of distraction.' And how true that was!

Tamsin went back into the other room and the conversation continued, but she had gone over to the window and Kim didn't hear it. She was putting the plates into the draining rack when Tamsin came back into the kitchen.

'Oh, you needn't have done that, I was going to do it!'

'You can do it next time.' Kim dried her hands on the kitchen towel and turned to face her. 'Well, are they coming?'

'They'd love it. Erin said they'd take us all out to dinner somewhere tomorrow night.'

'That'll cheer things up a bit.' Kim thought for a moment, and then said, 'Well, don't just stand there! Get yourself over to Shortlanesend and talk to Bennie about sheets!'

Tamsin hesitated. 'What will you do?'

'Twiddle my thumbs.' She saw Tamsin's face, and laughed. 'I shall go into Embridge and maybe go up to the University again. They said they'd contact me, but there's no harm in reminding them. And I have nothing better to do.'

'Well, one good thing has already happened today. Maybe we can make it two?'

'Let's hope.' Kim paused, as a thought struck her. 'Does Michael know what Francis did to himself?'

'Erin didn't ask about it, so I assume not.'

'That'll be a surprise for them then.' They looked at each other.

'And there's the hospital appointment tomorrow afternoon,' said Tamsin, but Kim thought that might be a bonus.

'It'll give you some moral support if they tell him something awful, if Michael is here,' she said.

'Do you think they will?' Tamsin sounded apprehensive.

'How would I know?'

'You feel things...'

'All I'm feeling right now is frustration – with you!' but she said it kindly. 'We need to organise about that room. And clean towels, come to that.'

'I'll ring Bennie,' Tamsin reached for her phone again. 'I can ask her how Francis is and find out when he wants me over there at the same time. And it'll be quicker anyway.' She punched in the number and listened to the phone ringing out at Shortlanesend. It was a minute before it was picked up, and she had begun to wonder apprehensively if something dreadful had happened, but eventually Bennie said, 'Hello?'

'Bennie! I was beginning to think...you were out,' she ended lamely, her fears had immediately seemed empty and foolish the moment she heard Bennie's cheerful greeting. The things love did to you! She made a face, which only Kim saw, of course.

'I just got in from feeding the chickens when I heard the phone ringing,' Bennie explained. 'What can I do for you? Is everything all right? You sound a bit odd. You'll be over here soon, why the phone?'

Tamsin explained about the visitors and the bed, and Bennie said that she would arrange it. She said, 'You could have asked when you got here, you didn't need to phone. There's plenty of time before tonight.'

'Francis said not to bother to come over too early. I wondered how he was, and if he had decided what he wanted to do, so I knew what I was doing.'

'Answer to the first, quiet. Answer to the second, I doubt it. He's a bit... low, I suppose, is the best description, this morning; I think you should ignore his instructions and get over here and cheer him up. And if you can think of something positive for you both to be doing, then make him do it.'

'Kim suggested, visit the stables and see the horses.'

'Not in this weather, I wouldn't think – although it's not a bad idea in itself. He needs to keep away from too much muck right now, and that yard will be filthy – well, by hospital standards it will be filthy.'

'I've run out of ideas, then. Except I was thinking in the night, I probably ought to get a broom and a dustpan before the weekend.' She sounded doubtful, as if she wasn't quite sure what they were, and Bennie laughed.

'The idea might make him laugh, coming from you, but I doubt if the deed would hold his attention. You can get those at the village shop where you are. And while you're at it, don't forget dusters. And tea towels, they'll have them too, I expect, and – oh, take Kim with you, she'll tell you how to equip a household. And then get yourself over here, it won't be too early by then, if that's what he wanted. Did you want to talk to him? He's only in the office – I thought he was, but he may be in the bathroom if he didn't answer the phone. Not far, anyway.'

'Yes please, I can tell him about Michael and Erin coming, it might cheer him up a bit.'

It might have done, but she wasn't really sure. He said, 'Th-that's one g-g-good thing, th-then,' but he sounded really depressed, she thought. She tried to think of something to cheer him up.

'I'll be over in half an hour or so, if that's OK? I'm going to the hardware shop with Kim now, to buy a broom.'

To her relief, he burst out laughing. 'I always s-s-suspected you were a witch! I'll have a w-w-word with Birdie, put her on s-s-standby, she needs something to do. You c-c-can cast a spell for me, w-while you're at it.'

Tamsin said, severely, 'And a dustpan and dusters and things. Someone's got to do the housework!'

'Th–this, I c–c–can't wait to see! I'll s–s–see you in about an hour, th–then?'

Tamsin switched off her phone and looked at Kim.

'Well, I got a laugh out of him – a snigger anyway – but Bennie's right, he sounds really down.'

Kim said, wisely, 'He needs something positive to do. Seeing to the paperwork and just visiting isn't enough, and I don't blame him for that. He needs to be involved, it's his project, after all.' She added, after a pause, 'And what's all this about buying a broom?'

Tamsin explained, and Kim, like everyone else, broke into a giggle. She said, 'Your mother will be horrified at the bare idea! OK then, let's get our coats and go and see to it.'

Kim agreed that Crowe's would be more practical than the village shop, she had never noticed a broom in there, just food and stationery and washing powder and the odd T-shirt and things, so they dashed across the road through the rain to the hardware store and Kim guided her twin through the domestic jungle of buckets, mops and brooms and cleaning aids. They emerged with Kim carrying a bucket with the latter items in it, and Tamsin with a broom, a squeezy mop, a cobweb brush, and a plastic bag with a dustpan and brush, a packet of dusters, and six tea-towels in it. All this, too was stowed behind the sofa.

'Goodness knows what Michael and Erin will think,' said Tamsin, looking at the heap ruefully.

'Goodness knows what the caretaker has already thought,' said Kim, and they grinned at each other. Kim then added, 'And there's another thing that you need to think of. If you're going to be living out there at the weekend, you need to lay in some food. I'd better give you a hand with with that as well, maybe Thursday? Preferably something you know what to do with it.' And she smiled mischievously.

'It all feels so strange,' said Tamsin, wonderingly. 'I suppose it will really happen?'

'Oh, it will. And now, once we've stowed all this, you'd better get organised and go to Shortlanesend, your bloke will be wanting to see what's been happening out there on his farm.'

The pile of stuff behind the sofa was by this time beginning to show over the top. Tamsin said, optimistically, 'But it won't be for long now. And Erin and Michael will see the joke.'

'As well,' said Kim, suppressing a smile. 'On your way, then. I'm off to Embridge and I'd better get something for all of us to eat this evening, while I'm there. Will Francis be joining us, do you think?'

'I would think so, but I'll ask him. Do you need to know? I can ring you.'

'Don't bother, I'll count him in anyway, if he doesn't come there'll just be more for the rest of us.'

They parted on their separate ways and Tamsin drove out to Shortlanesend, where she found Francis trying to read a newspaper he had spread out on the kitchen table, Sacha at his feet, and Bennie about to go out.

'I'm glad you got here,' said Bennie, smiling at her. 'I have to go to a committee meeting, and Ernie is out in the fields somewhere.' She didn't add that she hadn't wanted to leave Francis alone, but it was somehow implicit in what she had said.

'Have fun then,' said Tamsin, and Bennie scowled.

'Maybe – if Jenny-bloody-Carruthers will leave poor Dot alone. And if Dot doesn't kill her this time.'

Tamsin saw, out of the corner of her eye, Francis raise his head at the sound of the name "Jenny Carruthers" and then look down at his newspaper again. She said, 'It sounds like something out of *Docksiders*.'

'Believe me, it often feels like it too!'

Francis looked up properly this time, and said, with interest, 'W-which would you back in a f-f-fight?'

'Dot, on present form, but you can never tell. And now I'm off – Tamsin, if you want to come back for some lunch, there is enough, and can you ring me if you both decide to do something else? – and now I'm gone!' She vanished through the back door, waving goodbye. Francis looked at Tamsin.

'W-w-what time are M-M-Mike and Erin g-getting here?'

'Mike has to see a man in Dorchester this afternoon, Erin reckoned they'd get to Emberton somewhere between six and seven at the latest.' She paused. 'Oh bother! I should have told Bennie you'd be out for dinner this evening – that is, we assumed you'd want to be with us?'

'Th-thank you, I'd l-like that.'

'And tomorrow, they want to take us all out. We could maybe book a table at Mario's – what do you think? Do they like Italian food?'

414

'Who kn-knows? P-probably, but you can ask them tonight.' He began to fold the newspaper, clumsily with one hand, and Tamsin itched to offer to do it for him, but didn't. 'W-we'd better get ourselves t-t-to B-Burnthouse. Steve s-s-said he had something to sh-show us.'

'Good or bad?' asked Tamsin, apprehensively.

'G-good, I think.'

The first thing that struck Tamsin as they reached Burnthouse was the lane up from the road. It was about twice the width that it had been when she last saw it. All the brambles and other tangled undergrowth had vanished, the muddy residue had been mown flat, and it was now possible to see rather than to guess that the lane, too, had stone walls to the adjoining fields. She was so surprised that she stopped the Discovery to stare at it.

'What happened? I never even suspected it was this wide!'

'It hasn't b-b-been, not for years. But it's going to n-n-need to be now. Anyway, it was a m-m-mess.'

That was too true to argue with, and Tamsin had to concede that it would certainly look better once it had been tidied up. It gave more status to the house itself, too, not to be approached by a narrow lane with tangled hedges of brambles and weeds brushing the doors of your transport. Maybe for the first time, she caught a glimpse of what Francis was ultimately aiming for, and liked it. This house, she suspected, would one day, perhaps quite soon, look as if it deserved its listed status. Ensnared by this pleasant thought, she failed to read between the lines, and also failed to notice Francis smiling as he realised this, and then they had reached the house.

Steve came out to greet them when he heard them arrive, also smiling. He shook hands with Tamsin and clapped Francis on the shoulder, saying cheerfully, 'Come with me, I have a surprise for you – several surprises, in fact,' and they followed him in through the yard door.

The first thing that was noticeable was that the walls to the passage were no longer stained with mould and cracked but smooth, clean and white. Then Steve led them through into the office, where a carpenter was working on the doorframe and had to move aside to let them in, and made a sweeping gesture with his arm. 'So, what do you think?'

Like the passage, the room was clean and white; an electric flex with a light bulb hanging from it dangled from the beamed ceiling, and several short rows of electrical sockets snuggled into the skirting board or sat along the top of the panelling that covered the bottom half of some of the walls. This panelling was clean and repaired, no trace of rats or woodworm remaining.

'Still needs a bit of spit and polish to bring it back,' said Steve happily. 'And what do you think of the window?' This, which had been severely cracked and letting in the rain, was now bright and clean and undamaged. Steve said, 'I reckon you can probably move your stuff in here by Thursday, or maybe we should say Friday to be safe. The power is connected to everywhere at this end of the house, so it can be put into use. There's just that doorframe to finish, and a bit of titivating, and then it's all yours. So?' And he stood back, his smile broadening as he watched them.

'It l-l-looks great,' said Francis, in a wondering voice as if he didn't quite believe in it. He wandered off inspecting the walls more closely, and Tamsin said, 'Do you actually have any office stuff? I thought all of that stopped at Vachells.'

'It d-d-did. It w-w-will.' He stopped in front of her. 'W-w-we shall have to go sh-sh-shopping again, and s-s-smartish.'

'Start with the floor,' said Tamsin practically, startling both herself and him yet again. 'With this stone floor, it will be freezing in here in the winter, you need to cover it with something. Preferably a nice Persian carpet, with a bit of style to it – well, not a real one, that would be ridiculous! You know what I mean...'

'W-w-we can see t-t-to that at the s-s-same time.' He was cheering up by the minute, she was glad to see.

'Will said he'd leave you a convector heater if you wanted – one of those big ones that churn out plenty of warmth,' said Steve, and Tamsin said immediately, 'He does want. Tell Will thank you, and yes please.'

'And that's not all,' said Steve, smiling even more widely. 'Come with me...' He led the way back into the passage. 'Ignore that—' he gestured towards the door of the washroom. 'That's a major undertaking, but at least they got it clean and it works as what it is now. But look at this—' and he flung open the door to the putative freezer room with a flamboyant gesture. 'What d'you think of this, then?'

The room was effectively just a bare square, but under the window had been put a narrow counter with cupboards beneath it.

'For your freezer packaging and stuff, and cleaners, that kind of thing,' Steve explained. 'You can see we've put the doors centrally, so you can get your big freezer in here and still be able to open them, and a big domestic fridge, and there's still room for another freezer if it isn't too big. What do you think?'

This was now Tamsin's department, so it was Tamsin who answered. 'It looks great.' She noted the row of sockets alongside the worktop, and the central light fitting. 'Power in here, too?'

'Oh yes, all along here. We made it a priority.' He was still smiling, as much at her pleasure as with his own at watching her reaction. 'This is what you said you wanted done first, to live here comfortably while the rest was done, so this is what we've been concentrating on. Come next door.'

Next door was the utility room, similarly laid out but with space under the worktop for the utilities and the necessary pipework in place for the washing machine, and it had the big Belfast sink already, of course, with another cupboard beneath it for washing machine capsules and such things. There was ample room to set up an ironing board, Steve pointed out, and Tamsin agreed with a shudder that she kept to herself, and a hook on the wall to take a washing basket. Again, it was all shining white and scrupulously clean with gleaming, uncracked windows.

'We had to push a bit to get it all done,' said Steve. 'It should be all ready to roll by Friday, then you can get your stuff in and we can get on with the rest. That will take a lot longer, I'm afraid, there's so much wood needs replacing, and all the new wiring to do, and of course it's on a much grander scale in the main house. We replaced all the shelves in the pantry, it was quickest – and most hygienic – come and see. I think you'll approve.'

Tamsin did approve, it all been grimy and rotten and there had been mould on the walls when she had first seen it. All gone now. White walls, the big stone main shelf that ran round three sides repaired and smooth, new slatted shelves above, everything necessary to run the supply line to a big country house. Tamsin admired it, and then realised that somewhere along the tour, Francis had disappeared. Steve noticed her looking round in surprise.

'He left us around the washing machine bit,' he told her. 'I think he went back to the office. I've shown you everything now, so we can go and check.' He led the way and Tamsin followed, asking as they went, 'So it's all good to go, and we can get the utilities in, and food and things?'

'Any time you're ready. It's all yours, and the electrics are all wired in to the new fuse box.' He indicated this on the wall at the end of the passage.

'It's all working and good to go. Just here, of course, not anywhere else yet. That'll take time.'

'You must have gone all out on it to get it done so quickly,' said Tamsin. 'It will make such a difference, we do appreciate it. Thank you.'

He laughed. 'It's been a challenge – here we are, I told you so!'

Francis had hijacked the carpenter's services, since he couldn't write anything legibly for himself right now, to make him a list on a scrap of paper the carpenter must have found in his box; there was no horizontal surface available apart from the stone flagged floor, so he was having to write against the wall. They were just about coming to the end now, and Francis was saying, '...and a c-c-couple of f-filing cabinets. Th-that should d-d-do it for now.' He added, 'Sh-show it to T-T-Tamsin, she c-c-can double-check for me.'

'For what that will be worth,' said Tamsin, obediently accepting the list. She ran her eye down it: shelving of some kind, two large desks, chairs, printer inks and stationery and a cupboard to put them in, a shredder... two cork boards for the walls...filing cabinets. She said, 'You've forgotten filing baskets and a wastepaper basket – at least one, probably two, one by each desk.' She held out her hand to the grinning carpenter. 'Give me the pencil, I'll put them on.' She added them, with difficulty against the wall and handed the finished list to Francis. 'And don't lose it!'

Steve said, 'This room is all ready to use, you can get it all delivered on Thursday if you want. The electrical stuff too, for down the passage. Get it all set up before you move across at the weekend.'

'And stores,' said Tamsin, remembering Kim. 'Kim and I can see to that and bring the stuff over.' It felt slightly unreal, saying that. She looked at Francis, he must be feeling the same, only more so. At last, he would be able to be involved in the site, at the heart of his own affairs even if he was largely confined to the office. Just the prospect of it was already having its effect, she could see he had come alight again for the first time for over a week, so about time too! It might not last, tomorrow afternoon was still hanging over him, but even a temporary improvement was a plus, at least it showed the flame hadn't entirely blown out.

'Right, l-l-let's go and see to all th-this,' he said, with a lift in his voice that she hadn't heard for a while. 'L-l-let th-this lot get on. And th-thank you, S-Steve – thank all of you. You've w-w-worked a miracle!'

'And we've only just begun,' said Steve, grinning. 'Isn't there a song about that? Off you go then – take him away, Tamsin, we'll see you tomorrow I daresay.'

'You will,' Tamsin assured him. 'Some of his cousins are coming for a couple of nights, they want to see the place.'

'I'll look forward to meeting them – unless they're Vachells, when I shall probably know them already.'

'They aren't. They're part of the London lot,' Tamsin told him, and his grin widened.

'Should be educational for them, then.'

'They've known him all his life, it shouldn't surprise them.' She returned the grin, but as she walked with Francis back to the Discovery, she found herself thinking, but they hadn't known him all his life. They had known him for only part of it – the best part. It might be interesting to see what they did make of all this.

They set off on their shopping expedition, ending up on the same trading estate as she had been to with Kim for the electrical goods – which was handy, said Tamsin, as they could arrange for a delivery on Friday for the fridge and stuff too. She had thought Thursday at first, but Francis had said 'M-make it F-Friday – we'll need to be out th-there anyway th-then.' She noted the "we", and felt an unexpected shiver of excitement. Roll on Friday, then!

The office suppliers to whom they took their custom had everything on their scrawled and in places illegible list, or something that would do the same job – for "shelving", read two wide, waist-high bookcases for instance – as if they didn't have enough bookcases already, Tamsin remarked. They completed the tally, Francis settled the bill with his credit card, and delivery was arranged, again, for Friday.

'What next?' asked Tamsin, as they emerged once more into the windy sunshine that had – temporarily – replaced the rain.

'Sh-Shortlanesend, when you've s-spoken to the freezer lot. Enough is en-nough.'

Tamsin shot a swift glance at him; he did look tired, his burst of energy was waning now the job was done – but to be fair, so was her own energy waning. The thought of going home was enticing. She said, 'Let's get it done quickly then. If we drive across to the place, I can slip in and do it, and you needn't even get out of the car.'

'I n-n-never was good at sh-shopping,' he confessed, but without shame, she noticed.

The electrical store was happy with a Friday morning delivery, and that arranged, they headed back for Shortlanesend, where Bennie was once more in the kitchen.

'You must think I live in here,' she told Tamsin, smiling. 'I don't – it's just that you always seem to turn up at mealtimes – and I didn't mean that the way it came out! Did you have a good morning?'

'We had a bonanza with the office equipment. It's all being delivered on Friday, with the fridge and stuff too – it's beginning to feel as if we may even be living there one day. They've done a brilliant job with the utility rooms.'

'Saturday, according to Francis,' said Bennie. 'By the way, what have you done with him?'

'Sacha met us in the yard,' said Tamsin, which was explanation enough and they both smiled.

After lunch, Tamsin returned to Romans to give Kim a hand, promising to pick up Francis around six, and Bennie said, eyeing him up, 'Good plan. It will give him time for a rest. It sounds as if this evening may be a bit of a party!'

'On previous form, "may" is a bit of an understatement.'

'Good, then. It'll do him good.'

'Am I such a m-m-misery?' Francis asked, with interest, and they replied in unison, 'Yes!' and made him smile, but not apologise.

Tamsin drove back to Romans, where she found Kim stuffing a chicken, and about to make something called a "Strawberry Japonais", which, she explained, was in effect two giant almond macaroons sandwiched with strawberries and cream and topped with coffee icing. 'You diddly up the strawberries a bit,' she explained. 'It always goes down a storm at dinner parties, so I thought we'd put push the boat out. Life is taking off!'

Tamsin looked at her thoughtfully, refraining from any clever comments about pushing the boat out in a storm. There was a note in her twin's voice that had been missing just lately. She said, 'So, did you have a good morning?'

'I did.' Kim smiled happily. 'The university said they could give me part-time work as a translator up until Christmas, and if that worked, would I be interested in teaching the odd class, maybe? And I said "yes" to both. It's what I'm trained for, after all. So I start as an assistant lecturer after Christmas if I pass the test, and all we need now to make everything perfect is for Val to get that job! How about you?'

Tamsin told her about the kitchen passage and the office, and their imminent move out to the wilds around Shearwater, and Kim recognised the same note in her twin's voice as her twin had heard in hers. She asked, 'Any sign of the caravan yet?' and Tamsin said thoughtfully, 'I think it may be due for delivery on Thursday – Francis arranged all the goods deliveries for Friday. But we shall see.'

'Didn't he say? Didn't you ask?' Kim sounded surprised.

'Well…no. I just took it for granted, perhaps I shouldn't have. But Bennie said we should be living there on Saturday, so…well, work it out for yourself. I did!'

'We'd better lay in some stores for you on Thursday then. It sounds as if you've actually got somewhere to put them.'

'Things are picking up speed, aren't they?' said Tamsin, happily.

'They are. Oh, and by the way, I bought you a present. It's on the dining table.'

Tamsin went to investigate; the present turned out to be a book called *The Hamlyn All-colour Cook Book*, and was packed with recipes, all helpfully illustrated in colour; it was quite an old copy although it did survive with its original and only slightly battered cover. Kim stood at the kitchen door, watching her. She said, 'I saw it in a secondhand bookshop I was poking around in – my mother had a copy when she first married, and she swears by it still. It's simply written, and the recipes are really good. I thought you'd like it.'

'I do,' said Tamsin, riffling through the pages. 'It looks easy to follow, and the pictures are great too. At least you know what you're aiming for!'

'We'll pick out a couple of recipes that you can do over the weekend, and add the ingredients to our list for you,' said Kim. 'Now put it down, you can look at it properly later, and come and scrub the potatoes for me, then I can be making the macaroon. It'll need time to cool before I ice it.'

'Do we know what time Michael and Erin are coming?'

'They reckoned anytime after five, all being well. Michael's appointment was for two o'clock, in Dorchester. That's not all that far.'

'Then you're right. We'd better get the show on the road.'

In fact, their guests hadn't yet arrived by the time Tamsin left to pick up Francis, but they did arrive almost the minute she had vanished over the horizon, pulling their car into the vacant space she had left, and Kim went out to greet them.

'No Tamsin?' asked Erin, when the hugs and kisses of greeting were over, and Kim explained that she had gone to Shortlanesend to pick up Francis, wondering as she said it where they would park the Discovery on their return. Oh well, that was their problem: Francis would no doubt find a solution for them.

'Pick him up?' asked Michael with a lift of his eyebrows, and Kim explained.

'He had a misunderstanding with a rusty nail, he ran it right through his hand.'

'Ouch!' Michael winced. 'I hope it was the left hand, then.'

'It wasn't. Sod's Law. Come on, let's get your stuff indoors and upstairs, then I'll make a cup of tea or something while we wait for them. They'll be a while yet, she only just left and it's a good twenty minutes to Shortlanesend from here.'

'There's a couple of bottles in here somewhere, we could open one of them,' Michael suggested, opening the boot. 'Tell us about Francis.' He heaved a holdall out onto the pavement and reached for the small case that still remained. 'If he's not driving, presumably it was quite bad? When did he do it?'

'About ten days ago. And yes, it is quite bad, he got an infection in it from the dirt, but I think it's more the frustration that's wearing him down most. He can't do anything practical, and there's everything to do. It's a bit like giving a child a new and exciting toy and then telling them they can't play with it. If he was young enough to bawl his eyes out, I suspect that he would.'

'Poor old Francis, then. It's a good thing we came down to cheer him up.' He shut the boot and picked up the cases, handing the bottles to Kim. 'Right, lead on.'

Kim showed them to their bedroom and returned downstairs to open one of the bottles and find some glasses, checking in the fridge to make sure there was some grape juice cooling for Francis, who couldn't drink alcohol with the medication he was on. Another cloud on his horizon. She hoped very much that tomorrow's appointment would bring good news, or the poor man would shoot himself – if he could hold a gun, that is, which he couldn't…she pulled herself up abruptly. That was no way to think, even as a joke!

Erin came downstairs first, on a search for the bathroom. 'Just a quick wash and brush-up,' she explained. 'I feel a fright She didn't look it, but

Kim showed her anyway, and when she came out into the kitchen, poured them both a glass of wine. Right on cue, Mike joined them and the three of them sat down round the cheerful glow of the electric fire to talk while they waited.

'So, what's this place really like?' Michael asked. 'Tamsin made it sound like the pit of Hell when she described it to us.'

'She wasn't far wrong,' Kim told him. 'It's getting better now though – it improved out of all recognition the moment the dungheap had gone.'

'Ah yes, the dungheap. She was quite lyrical about that, I remember.'

'I think they're actually moving over there at the weekend,' Kim told him. 'Francis will tell you more, I expect, but Tamsin thinks that may be the plan.'

'You'll be lonely without her,' said Erin.

'A bit, but I have a part time job at the university as from next week, and Val will be here at the weekends. It won't be so bad. And it won't be as if Tamsin has gone to the moon, or anything. She'll still be around.'

'What do you think she'll make of being a farmer's wife?' Mike asked. 'She seems a bit...urban for the position. I hope they both know what they're doing.'

'Oh, I think they do. And she's my twin, I'd manage.'

'True. Well, I'm looking forward to seeing it all – was that a car I heard?'

Kim had heard it too, but it hadn't stopped, not that there was anywhere to stop, come to think. However, five minutes later Tamsin and Francis came through the door, shaking raindrops from their coats like a pair of dogs – and talking of dogs, they had one with them.

'It's started again,' said Tamsin, slipping off her damp jacket. 'We only came across from the Yard and we nearly drowned!'

'The Yard?' Kim queried.

'Merlin and Bob said we could park one of the cars over there. The night watchman will keep an eye on it.'

'That was nice of them.'

Tamsin finished helping Francis with his coat and they came into the room properly to say hello, where Michael and Erin were already on their feet, greeting Sacha while they waited for them. Michael automatically held out his hand to his cousin, saw the bandages and altered the gesture to a cousinly slap on the shoulder. He said, 'You should learn to be more careful, coz,' and then enveloped Francis in a man hug. 'Keep him on a lead, I would. Is this his guard dog?' and he bent to give Sacha, who was prancing round his legs, another friendly pat. 'Didn't do a very good job, did you, young fella?'

'Take no notice of him,' said Erin, to Francis. 'Hello, lovely to see you again, and we were so sorry to hear about your accident, although you wouldn't think it to listen to Michael.'

'Sit down all of you, while I get a drink for these two,' said Kim: the small room felt a bit overcrowded with them all standing and the dog scudding around their feet. 'I'll check on the dinner while I'm at it—' she headed for the kitchen, and Tamsin said, belatedly, 'Do you need a hand?'

'Not yet. I will when I start dishing it up.'

It was a pleasant evening, Kim had kept the meal simple if they were all going to Mario's tomorrow night, serving the chicken with jacket potatoes and salad, and the japonais, being an all-in-one dessert, was quick and easy to serve. Francis was getting quite dextrous with his left hand by this time, and with a little help cutting things up managed without calling attention to himself, and Erin and Michael tactfully pretended not to notice anything. They had plenty to talk about to distract them anyway, wanting to know all about the old house and the plans for it.

'We're only doing half of it this time round,' Tamsin told them. 'When we have enough house to live in – round about Christmas, hopefully – they're going across the yard to convert the old tithe barn, and by the time that's done, we shall be preparing for an invasion of archaeologists, so the other half of the house will wait until Autumn, and the builders will go off and do something else in the meantime.'

'So what's the plan for the tithe barn?' Michael asked, with interest, and Francis replied, 'Th-there'll be a m-m-manager living there. His w-w-wife will help in the h-h-house.'

This was the first Tamsin had heard of this part of the plan, and it was good news. She would have given it a go, but she didn't think housekeeping was really her specialist subject.

'So what's this about archaeologists?' asked Michael, and Francis explained about the pre-arranged dig on the Barrow that he had inadvertently taken on along with the farm. Michael commented that it should be interesting, but since none of them knew anything about archaeology there was no follow-up.

'I expect you're looking forward to moving in, even with only half a house,' said Erin, smiling at Tamsin. 'It'll be exciting too, watching it all take shape.'

'And at least he'll be able to get all his stuff out of store,' said Tamsin. 'I suspect that he's been pining for his books this past week, and they'll give him something to do, at least.'

'I hope b-b-by that time, I sh-sh-shall have plenty to d-d-do anyway,' Francis said.

'Eventually, of course you will,' said Tamsin, more cautiously, 'but don't try to tell us you won't be glad to see them.'

He only smiled at that, and Erin said, 'Do you have much in store, or just books? Anything useful to help furnish the house? It sounds as if it's quite big.'

'S-s-seven bookcases and a d-d-desk,' Francis told her, and Tamsin added, 'and he tells me he has a grand piano, but I'm not sure if I believe him.'

Michael considered this. He said, 'Well, he could have – he did play the piano, back when. I remember him doing it. But it wasn't a grand piano, just an upright.'

'The Merry Peasant, and all that stuff?' asked Kim, remembering her own piano lessons as a child – which had not lasted for very long, she had shown no talent for it and her father had called a halt to protect his ears, or so he said. Michael caught Francis' eye and grinned. He said, 'Not exactly, no.'

'Oh God, tell me the worst!' said Tamsin.

'Shall I tell her?' Michael asked Francis. 'She's going to find out anyway, perhaps she should be warned.'

'Wall-to-wall chopsticks?' Kim suggested, but Michael shook his head, still watching Francis.

'Sh-she won't like it,' said Francis, but he sounded amused.

Michael turned to Tamsin. 'Are you ready for this? For a start, he was pretty good at it, way, way past the Merry Peasant by the time we were all in our teens, which is when we're talking about.'

'Brahms and Beethoven?' Kim asked, with a mischievous grin. She didn't have her twin down as a classical music fan.

'Definitely not. Jazz, rhythm and blues, hard rock – all the current stuff at the time.' He broke off laughing, as Tamsin buried her face in her hands with a groan.

'I could have guessed it,' she said. 'He has that stuff in his car, we had it all the way back from London along with a bit of rather highbrow classical.'

'Not to your taste?' asked Erin, laughing at her expression.

'Definitely not. But I suppose I shall have to learn to love it. It could be worse.' She didn't sound too sure about that.

'Just tell me, so's we know,' said Kim, turning to Francis, 'Is there anything you can't do?'

'He's pretty crap at sewing,' Michael offered. 'And I don't believe he can cook, either.'

'That'll make two of us then,' said Tamsin, and they all laughed.

'But seriously,' said Kim. 'There must be something, or he's too good to be true!'

Michael thought hard for a minute, and came up with, 'He was always better at figures than words. Useless at crosswords. Will that do?'

'Better than nothing. Anything else?'

'Don't know of anything. To be honest, he was always pretty sickening.'

They all laughed once more, and the conversation moved on, leaving Tamsin still uncertain whether the grand piano was a fact or a joke.

The meal over, they dumped everything in the kitchen and sat round the fire, finishing the wine and talking about this and that, until Tamsin noticed that Francis had gone very quiet and rather white, and got to her feet.

'Come on, my darling it's time I took you home. On your feet!'

Michael got to his feet too, saying, 'I could do that for you, you must be tired yourself.'

'You couldn't, you know,' said Tamsin, grinning. 'You'd get there OK – if he stayed awake long enough to direct you – but you'd never find your way back. Not in the dark. And anyway, you've done a lot of driving already today. It won't take me long – I'll just wake up the dog, and we'll be off and you can all go to bed.' And she wanted to say a proper goodnight to Francis, without witnesses, but she didn't add that, just unhooked their coats so that there was no more argument.

When they had gone, out into the still falling rain, Kim headed off to the kitchen to deal with the heap of dirty crocks in the sink, and Erin followed her.

'I'll give you a hand with that. You must be tired, too.'

'There isn't much, I planned it so that there were no saucepans and things. Just plates, and they can sit in the draining rack all night.'

'It was very kind of you take us in.' Erin picked up a tea towel anyway, and stood waiting as Kim ran water into the sink.

'You make yourselves sound like stray cats. We were happy to, anyway, we see much more of you this way.'

Erin picked up the first plate as it came out of the sink and began to dry it. She said, 'Francis doesn't look so good. Is that hand bad, then?'

'Bad enough. The main problem, I suspect, apart from the infection which is a bugger, is that he can't do anything constructive out at the farm, and the rest is, because of that he has too much time to think about it, and he's convincing himself he's done some permanent damage. Plus, it hurts him, of course.'

'Ouch! Do you think he has? Done any damage?'

'I don't know, do I? Half of it is just over-reaction, I think – he does let himself get a bit wound up about things, I've noticed. But that's just my opinion.' She was thinking of the Club as she said that, more than the injury maybe.

'Michael says he was always a bit of firework,' said Erin, meditatively, and Michael said, from the doorway, 'He was. It seems to go with the territory somehow. When will he know?'

'Hopefully, tomorrow afternoon. Tamsin has to take him to the hospital at about three, she said. Then, if there's any worst to know, we'll all know it.'

'Not so long, then.' Michael added, but without moving from the doorpost, 'if I knew where it went, I'd put that away for you.'

'Don't worry, it won't take a moment.' Kim smiled at him. 'You two have had a long day, why don't you just take yourselves up to bed? I can wait up for Tamsin, I'll put the telly on – low, so it doesn't keep you awake.'

'Will she be long?' Erin asked, but Kim didn't know.

'It depends if they're all still up at Shortlanesend. Don't worry about me, if she's too long I shall just go to bed too. It isn't as if she doesn't know her way around.'

Erin smothered a yawn. 'I could certainly do with getting my head down! And there's tomorrow to get through yet – I'm looking forward to that farm, it sounds…' she paused, for it sounded a lot of things depending on who was telling about it. In the end, she finished…'full of possibilities.'

'If Tamsin is going to the hospital with Francis, perhaps we should go and see Aunt Mary after lunch,' Michael suggested. 'I haven't seen her for… it must be over twenty years. Do you think she'd like us to do that, Kim?'

'I think she'd like it very much.'

427

'We'll do it, then. Come on Erin, if we get out of the way, Kim can have a bit of peace before she comes up.'

Nice people, Kim thought, as she put the carefully dried plates away. Kind and friendly, and she was glad they were behind Tamsin, she might need them. She put the last plate in place and threw herself down in front of the television, reaching for the remote as she did so. Today was nearly over, tomorrow still to come. It felt strange to have the house full of people…she'd give Tamsin half an hour, and then she'd just leave the door on the latch and go to bed.

The house settled down, quiet around her.

XXVI

Breakfast the next morning was livelier than usual, even Tamsin had managed to wake up properly instead of yawning over her toast and marmalade. There was a lot to talk about.

'Poor old Francis has really taken a hammering,' said Michael. 'I've never seen him so low – he doesn't even seem to have the energy to fight back. Not like him – he always used to go off like a rocket when things upset him.'

Tamsin had a sudden vision of Francis erupting out of the Yacht Club on Regatta Night; Michael's comment was a perfect description. She said, 'He was really wired up over the prospect of sorting out Burnthouse and getting it back on its feet – he's desperately frustrated because as it turns out, he can only watch other people doing it.'

'And give orders, no doubt,' said Michael, grinning.

'Well…yes. But that's hardly enough, is it? He's a hands-on sort of person, he doesn't make a good onlooker.'

'And talking of hands,' said Michael, 'what's the story there? Has he done any permanent damage?' He sounded concerned. Tamsin shook her head.

'Ask us that when we've been to the hospital this afternoon. Hopefully not, the Consultant he saw last time seemed optimistic, and I do think it's mainly the antibiotics that are making him feel so lousy – that, and the frustration. But I'm not going to guess.'

'OK, I won't make you. So what's the plan for this morning, then? We're off out to see this famous farm, yes?'

'If you've the stomach for it,' said Tamsin, smiling. 'Mind you without the dungheap it's just an ordinary mess, not an actual health hazard. Francis said last night to pick him up at about ten, and we'll meet you out there around half-past. Kim will show you the way.'

'We could all go in our car and pick him up on the way,' Erin suggested, but Tamsin shook her head.

'We don't know what we shall be doing afterwards, and you won't want to come and wait hours at the hospital. Better if we travel separately, you wanted to go and see Mary this afternoon anyway.'

'True.' Michael had almost forgotten this. 'I'll ring her when we finish breakfast – I presume you have her number?'

'Of course.'

'We could all have lunch somewhere, when we've done the tour,' Michael suggested. 'Francis took me to a rather good pub in Shearwater the last time I was down. We could go there, just have something light if we're going on the town tonight. Save Kim the trouble of feeding us.'

Kim grinned at that, and exchanged a glance with her twin. Michael had got the domestic situation bang to rights in the short time he had been with them. She said, 'It wouldn't be a trouble, but lunch out would be nice. You mean the Ravenscourt Arms, I take it?'

'That'd be the one.'

'But this one will be on us,' said Tamsin, with decision. 'You're taking us all out tonight, so this is our turn. And don't argue!' as Michael opened his mouth to speak. He closed it again and then said, meekly, 'I was only going to say "thank you".'

'And that reminds me,' said Kim, 'we ought to book a table for tonight.'

'So, where's the best place round here?' Michael took out his cell phone and waited expectantly.

'Mario's, so long as you like Italian,' said Tamsin, instantly. 'But there are some posher or more traditional places, if you prefer.'

'Italian sounds good to me. Got the number handy?'

Kim had it on her own phone. While Michael was making the booking, Tamsin got to her feet and began to clear the table. Kim caught her eye and said, 'You've just about got time to wash up before you go off for Francis,' and Erin said, predictably, 'I can do that.'

'No, let her,' said Kim. 'I'm trying to domesticate her, and she's ducked it twice. But we can dry.'

With three of them doing it, the job was done in a flash and Tamsin prepared to leave.

'Give me half an hour to get over to Shortlanesend and pick up Francis,' she said, glancing at her watch. 'If you leave here just after ten, we should arrive more-or-less together.'

When Tamsin had gone, Michael turned to Kim. He said, 'So, how is it with those two? Tamsin seems to have been rather thrown in off the deep end, as things have turned out.'

Kim considered before she replied, recognising the genuine concern behind the question. Eventually, she said cautiously, 'She seems to be a good swimmer.'

'She must have landed with rather a splash,' Michael commented.

'I think they both did. The circumstances have thrown them together, but pushed them apart at the same time. I think, maybe when they have a place of their own with no-one else around, and can just be quietly together, things will sort themselves out.'

'Imminent, I understand.' He narrowed his eyes at her.

'Saturday seems favourite for moving day, as I understand it.'

'Forgive me for being inquisitive,' said Michael, although she wasn't blaming him. 'I get the impression that it can't come too soon.'

'I think you may be right.'

'There's great stress on their relationship with all this, not just on Francis.'

'Tell me about it!' said, Kim, with feeling.

Erin said, looking at Michael, 'Your gorgeous cousin is like a bomb waiting to go off. I hope it all goes right for them.'

Kim admired her percipience, and she only knew the half of it! She said, 'I'm sure it will. I put my faith in that old chestnut "love will find the way".'

'You must know Tamsin pretty well,' said Michael, taking comfort from the thought.

'Not really, we've not long met. I can only judge her by myself, and even then it's only half a picture. We know about our mother, who now I've had time to think about it, I think was possibly as much sinned against as sinning, but we haven't even got a name for our biological father, let alone a character reference, or even a general background that we can rely on.'

'I can't help you there,' said Michael, but with regret. There was a pause, and then he said, 'I have to say this. I feel guilty – I think we all do – that we didn't come a lot sooner.'

'It wouldn't have helped if you had,' Kim told him, quietly. 'It wasn't until we came on the scene back in April and brought it all to the boil again that there was anything anyone could have done. Now, it's different – and here you are.'

'I wish that made me feel better about it,' said Michael, making a face. He glanced at his watch. 'What time do you think we should leave? How far is it?'

Kim looked at the clock on the mantelpiece. She said, 'We should probably start getting organised in about ten minutes. It's not far as the crow flies, but the lanes are a bit twisty.'

'I remember them well,' said Michael, pulling a face. 'We cycled down them – risking our lives quite often – and Francis used to ride a horse along them. Rather him than me!'

They left for Burnthouse after nearer twenty minutes than ten, and Michael drove circumspectly along the narrow country lanes until they came out onto the slightly more civilised road that ran through Shearwater itself.

'Right, here,' Kim told him, 'and then, just beyond the village, there's two turnings on the left, take the second one – it's a bit jungly and narrow, but you can get down it. The gate is falling off.' Tamsin hadn't mentioned the transformation, and from this description, Michael nearly drove past it altogether, and Kim had to yell, 'Stop! Turn here! Oh goodness, what's happened to it?' She was almost unsure that she was in the right place, but there was the Barrow hill rising up on the left, and distantly across the fields to the right, she could see the roof of the house. 'My goodness, they have been busy!'

'I thought it was just another lane,' said Michael, apologetically. 'It doesn't fit your description, and there's no gate at all...oh goodness, is this the house?' They pulled up by the garage, alongside the Discovery, and Tamsin came to meet them.

'You got here! I was beginning to think Kim had lost you in the lanes.'

'What's happened to the drive?' Kim asked. 'I nearly didn't recognise it – and oh goodness, doesn't it all look different!'

'I'm almost disappointed,' Michael admitted, looking around him. 'It's a bit scruffy, but it's not exactly a heap of horror.'

'Th-that's gone,' said Francis, coming up behind him from the stableyard and making him jump and turn round. 'N-n-not far. We spread it on the f-f-fields as t-t-top dressing.'

'Where would you like to start the tour?' Tamsin asked, swinging the house keys in her hand. 'Inside or outside?'

'Let's start inside and work outwards,' Michael suggested. 'It looks almost as if the sun will come out later if we give it a chance, it's hardly raining at all now.'

They entered through the front door, and did the tour of the house in the same order as the estate agent had done: drawing room, upstairs, potential dining/living room, and out through the kitchen, saving the good bit until last. Michael and Erin were impressed by the drawing room, rat-and-rot free now with its flooring and panels cleaned up and the floor repaired, although there was obviously a lot of work still to do, and Tamsin explained that they were leaving this part of the house until last.

'We can put dust sheets down and get everything brought here, and use this room as a furniture store instead of paying someone else to store it, now that they've mended the floor – all Francis' books and things, and the four-poster we bought at auction and stuff,' she explained. 'This room is the least essential for now, so it can be left until the very last of all, when all the stuff has found its proper place. It will probably also end up the most beautiful, the proportions are great, so we don't want to rush it.

'What will you use it for?' asked Erin, looking about her in wonder. 'It's far too big for a sitting room for two.'

'Show, and large parties,' Tamsin told her, and added, with a chuckle, 'and the mythical grand piano. It'll look well in here.'

The tour continued: Michael and Erin were half-impressed, half-horrified by the antique bathroom, and in the bedrooms planned for immediate use they had to step round two electricians.

Tamsin explained her grand plan for the two bedrooms above the drawing room yet again, then it was back downstairs to the putative living-room, the study for Francis, and the kitchen, which was a scene of noisy destruction as two more men were un-bricking the far chimney to accommodate the proposed Aga. Then the show piece, the kitchen passage. Kim knew about it but had not seen it yet, the cousins hadn't even been warned. The contrast between the storerooms and the rest of the house was startling.

''I've shown so many people round this house, I'm beginning to feel like a tour guide,' Tamsin confessed, as they reached the end room. 'This is the farm office, or it will be. We got everything for it yesterday for delivery on Friday, so it will soon be up and running.' She realised something then. 'Oops! We forgot a carpet for the floor! Oh well, Kim and I can get that tomorrow with the stores. There was a cheap furniture warehouse out on that trading estate, I noticed it when we were out that time.' She took a deep, happy breath. 'I can't believe it's all happening at last! Only a couple of days, and we'll be living out here!' and Francis gave her arm a quick squeeze with his serviceable hand.

Then it was outside, and more surprises, the first being that the sun was actually shining, although there were still clouds in the sky, waiting for their cue. The main yard looked shabby still in its light, but workmanlike, and the stables were practically finished, just needing a bit of cosmetic work on the walls and woodwork, but there was also something else that Tamsin had missed on her previous visits. The first one, of course, they had been interrupted by the estate agent, the second had been cluttered up with Gary Fancot and his Merry Men, and after that it had been generally raining as well as thick with muck due to the shifting process, and she hadn't realised that behind the wall to the stable yard and alongside the farmyard there was another yard, with two more big old stone barns at right angles to the two she had already seen, making a compact square of sizeable farm buildings adjacent to the house, covering in total roughly twice the area she had envisaged. She began to understand that this was a more serious enterprise than she had realised, and went very quiet while she thought about it.

Yet another surprise was to be found in the field behind the vegetable patch, which they came to last of all, where the caravan (or whatever it turned out to be) was to go. A wide, shallow rectangle about four inches deep had been cleared by the wall just inside the gate, and Matt was hammering narrow planks of wood edge-on into the soft earth around the edges to line it and keep it squared off. A trailer stacked with large sacks of gravel stood to one side, waiting its turn. Tamsin saw Kim narrowing her eyes, measuring the area. It was quite large: she caught her twin's eye and they shared a smile but made no comment. Then she saw Francis watching her face and smiled at him as well. She said, 'Can I have tubs of flowers in the corners?' and he smiled back.

'You c–c–can have whatever you 'l–l–like, but wait until the f–fence is up, or the horses will eat the f–f–flowers.' He added, his smile deepening, 'And w–w–when did you last l–l–look at your v–v–vegetable patch?' Tamsin looked at him for a minute, blankly, and then walked over to the gate into the back yard. She stopped in astonishment the moment she had the gate open. The whole area had been cleared and dug over, and from the look of it, enriched with its share of the dungheap, and the greenhouse had been cleaned up and repaired. She turned to look at Francis, standing grinning at her back.

'I th-thought you'd need something to d-d-do, once we g-g-get into the house,' he told her. 'You c-can start things off in the g-g-greenhouse, and plant th-them out in the Spring. L-like it?'

'Oh yes!' Tamsin was privately surprised at her own reaction, which if she was honest with herself, had been excitement. 'I just wish it was Spring now.'

'Th-the ground can do with a r-r-rest,' he told her. 'J-just keep an eye on it th-through the Winter, s-s-so the w-w-weeds don't t-t-take over again.'

She turned right round then, and gave him a hug. 'You are the most amazing man!' It was true, she realised; this simple act had shown her, more clearly than ever before, that she was to be a working partner here, not just an ornamental housewife.

'I'll like that, too,' she said, and he gave her a hug and released her, just as Kim and the cousins came out of the adjoining field to see where they had got to.

'Sorry, are we interrupting something?' said Michael, with a grin, and Tamsin felt herself blush, although Francis showed no sign of embarrassment, merely saying, 'N-no, we'd f-f-finished, thank you,' and returning the grin.

The tour was now complete, and it was chilly standing in the cold wind, in spite of the intermittent sunshine. Erin said, 'It's getting on for lunchtime, how about we go down to the pub and have a drink, and see what they've got on offer for us to eat? We can talk over all of this more comfortably there.' She shivered a little, pulling her coat close round her. 'It's a bit October-y this morning for just standing around.'

They walked back to the cars and Tamsin said, 'You go first. We'll follow you,' as they reached them, but when Michael had pulled away and his car had vanished down the widened lane, she didn't immediately follow. Instead she turned to look at Francis, sitting beside her.

'Thank you,' she said, and he looked surprised.

'W-w-what for, p-p-particularly?'

Making me a part of it all. Having faith in me,' said Tamsin simply, and he gave her a serious look.

'You are p-part of it all,' he said, and she felt ridiculous tears start behind her eyes and had to blink hard to get rid of them. He saw them though, and reached across with his left hand to cover hers on the wheel. 'D-don't be an ass,' he told her, but kindly. 'You c-c-can't have thought you'd b-b-be left out of everyth-thing.'

'I'm not sure what I thought,' Tamsin admitted. 'You just surprised me. Took my breath away, to be honest.' She sniffed, and he squeezed her hand and then let it go, sitting back in his seat.

'L-let's get down to the-that pub, and d-d-drink to it,' he said, adding, with a wry grin, 'in lemonade,' and thankfully, they both laughed. Tamsin started the engine.

Lunchtime on a cold October weekday wasn't a prime time for custom at the Ravenscourt Arms, and the landlord greeted them warmly, asking Francis how things were going out at Burnthouse and welcoming the twins with a smile; they were almost counted as locals these days, living so near, and rumour had it that they wouldn't either of them be going far away, either.

'You met those two in the cottage yet?' he asked Francis, as he assembled the drinks for them, and when Francis said that he hadn't yet had the pleasure, he shook his head.

'Weird, they are,' he said. 'Friends of that same lot as run the place down the way it is. They lived right here one time, them and their little girl, but they was given the cold shoulder and run out the village for the things they got up to. Seances, stuff like that. Weird, like I said, and the local kids was learning about stuff as they shouldn't. Some said she was a witch, and I wouldn't like to say what he was.' He shook his head. 'People like that, what gets into them? You want to get rid of them, and quick.'

'I sh-shan't be renewing the l-lease in September, I n-need the cottage,' Francis told him. 'B-but th-they haven't d-d-done anything to me, I can't j-j-just evict them.'

'Shame. Well, you keep an eye on them. Up to no good, they are.' He pushed the filled glasses together for Michael to start carrying to their table, and reached for an empty one. 'Still on the fizzy stuff, are you?'

'Unf-f-fortunately.'

'Shame about that, too,' said the landlord, making a sympathetic face. 'Going OK is it?'

436

Thankfully, before Francis had to find a reply to that, Tamsin appeared at his shoulder to help with the last two glasses, since realistically he could only manage one of them. 'And can we have a couple of menus?' she asked. 'I'll bring them back with the order in a minute, promise,' and the landlord smiled and handed the menus over together with a piece of paper and pen.

'Th-thank you,' said Francis quietly, as they moved away to their table. Tamsin glanced at him quickly, and then returned her attention to the two glasses she was carrying.

'I had a feeling you might be getting into deep water,' she said. 'You had that look.'

'Th-th-the trouble with villages, everyone kn-knows your business,' said Francis, but without enlarging on it. They rejoined the other three, and in the business of choosing what to eat the subject was dropped – or was allowed to slip away, Tamsin thought. Instead, their talk became mainly about the farm, and his plans for it.

'You've taken on a big undertaking, even a layman can see that,' said Michael, considering. 'How long before you get back into milk production, or whatever, do you think?' and Francis said, 'I'm a c-c-cattle breeder, primarily, not a dairy f-farmer. That was at V-Vachells. Here, m-m-milk will be just a b-by-product, th-there's not the acreage for a b-b-big commercial herd. T-Tamsin can make cheese w-w-with it.' He didn't sound as if he was serious, nor did he mention the necessary sale for slaughter of surplus bull calves, although as a breeder he did keep the best of them to rear and sell on for their designed purpose. These were things Tamsin had yet to learn.

'This, I must see,' said Kim, grinning, and Erin said, 'I'm glad you're not a beef producer. It seems so cold, somehow, to rear animals just to kill and eat them.'

'Don't tub-thump, Erin,' Michael told her, but kindly. 'Anyway, it's hypocritical. You enjoy a good steak as much as anyone.'

'I know, but I sometimes think I shouldn't. And the emissions from the big herds are destroying the planet.'

'Along with a lot of other things,' said Michael, dismissively. He looked at Francis apologetically. 'Ignore her. She gets this way sometimes.'

'Sh-she has a point,' Francis said, and Tamsin thought of his own concern about marine pollution but decided not to mention it, this wasn't either the time or the place for an ecological argument. She said, instead, 'What did you think of the show so far, anyway? Looking promising, wouldn't you agree?'

'It's going to take a long time to get it all done,' Kim suggested, and Michael joined in with obvious relief to add his own opinion, and the subject lasted them until they had finished their lunch, and Tamsin all at once realised that Francis had gone very quiet again, a sure sign that enough was enough. She glanced at the clock over the bar, not quite two o'clock. Time for a quick improvisation. She said, 'What had you got in mind for this afternoon? I shall have to get Francis back to his computer in a minute, and there's the hospital at half-three. What time are you going to Vachells?'

'Aunt Mary asked us for tea, so about half-past three too,' said Michael. He gave Francis a measuring look, obviously undeceived by her ruse, but to her relief he took her lead. 'If it's all right with Kim, we'll just go back to the house and put our feet up for a bit. It's been a busy morning, and we had a long drive yesterday. Will you be joining us later? We aren't due at the restaurant until eight.'

'I don't know. I'll be back at some time though, to get changed. I can't go to Mario's dressed like this.' She glanced down at her warm sweater and jeans. 'They're fairly informal there, but Mario'd throw me out. It's not that they'd mind the jeans, it's the decorative splashes of mud they wouldn't like.'

They said a temporary goodbye in the car park and got into their respective cars, and Tamsin headed off for Shortlanesend with Francis, in the absence of any other instructions. He didn't make any comments during their brief journey and she was glad of this, as she had a lot to think about. Every day now, it seemed, she was learning something different about him; his past life, his fast-expanding present, his future ambitions. His natural temperament, which he must have been suppressing for years. The two huge extra barns, that she hadn't even noticed, how unobservant was that? It was only an excuse to blame the weather, and the fact that they were hidden behind the stableyard wall. She had let preconceived ideas blind her to a lot of things, she now realised. From Rock and Roll to breeding cattle, he was a gilded box of surprises, and when she stopped to think about how much she loved him she turned into a shaking mess, so perhaps better not to do that while she was driving. Finally, however, his continuing silence began to unnerve her, and she said, 'Did you really mean that, about me making cheese with the spare milk?' and was glad to hear him laugh, he had been too quiet.

'N-no. We can s-s-sell it on l-l-like we always did,' he told her, and stealing a glance at him she saw that he was looking at her and smiling. He added, 'Unless you w-w-want to, of course. There's a d-d-dairy out the b-b-back – if we put it in order, th-there can be.'

'I'll give it some serious thought.' Then the silence fell again, but it was an easier silence, and soon after they arrived at Shortlanesend.

For once, Bennie wasn't in the kitchen, but she heard the car arrive and came round from the yard to greet them.

'Hello, had a good morning? I wasn't expecting you back until later.'

'We had lunch in the pub, and thought we'd take a break before we go to Embridge,' Tamsin told her, and Bennie nodded understandingly.

'Good idea. Would you like some coffee, or did you have some at the pub?'

'I'd love one,' said Tamsin. 'Francis?'

'I've g-g-got some st-stuff I can be getting on w-w-with in the office,' he said. 'But yes p-p-please, if you're m-m-making it.'

Bennie and Tamsin exchanged a look once they were alone in the kitchen.

'It's getting to him,' Bennie diagnosed, with accuracy.

'That's why I brought him back from the pub. I thought he might bite someone,' said Tamsin. 'The first person who said "you've gone very quiet, are you OK" would have been for it, and I could see Erin was on the verge of it. She kept looking at him.'

'Oh well. We just have to hope that they tell him everything is marvellous this afternoon, and then you can enjoy the evening.'

'Hmm.' Tamsin picked up one of the mugs of coffee when Bennie had finished making it and took it to the office, where she found Francis not so much working on his computer as sitting staring at its blank screen, with his chin supported on his left fist. She put the mug down beside him and kissed the back of his neck. 'I'll come and tell you, when it's time to go,' she said, and he said, 'Right,' without looking round. She went back to the kitchen, where Bennie had put the other two mugs by the closed lids of the Aga, within reach from the two wing chairs.

'Just push the cat off,' Bennie advised. 'She's far too possessive over that chair – like a permanent furry cushion,' but Tamsin picked her up instead and sat cuddling the little black cat while her coffee cooled a little – a process which sitting on the warm Aga wouldn't be helping.

'So, how is he?' Bennie asked, when they were all three settled. 'He was a bit tense, I thought, this morning. Not that I blame him.'

'Composing himself,' said Tamsin, which seemed the fairest description.

'That'll be a blast!' They smiled at each other, each of them appreciating the hidden joke, and Bennie said, 'You must have learned a lot about him, these last few days.'

'I have,' Tamsin said, not qualifying the statement. She said instead, 'The landlord at the pub was on about the tenants in that cottage, the one up the lane by the Barrow. He was on about witchcraft or something, he said Francis should get rid of them.'

'Unfortunately, he can't just do that,' said Bennie, which Tamsin already knew from what she had heard in the pub. 'They'd better not put a toenail out of line though, or they'll wonder what's hit them. Francis has no sympathy with hocus-pocus – or druggies, come to that.'

'Oh well, there has to be a serpent in every Eden, I suppose,' said Tamsin, moodily. She felt strongly that right now, Francis could do without one.

'Is it Eden?' asked Bennie, looking at her speculatively.

'I think it has a good chance of it, if all goes well this afternoon. Now it's all cleaned up – well, more or less cleaned up – you can see the potential. But it won't happen tomorrow.'

'He needs a project,' said Bennie, quietly. 'There's a lot of ground to cover, and a lot of fences to mend, and I'm not just talking about Burnthouse.'

'I know,' said Tamsin, and picked up her coffee to take a sip.

'You do know that you're the best thing that ever happened to him?' said Bennie, sipping her own coffee with her eyes on Tamsin. She was not the first to say so. Tamsin said, 'Am I?'

'You must know that you are. You gave him back a future full of love and amazing possibilities.'

'To be honest, I can't see past this afternoon. Suppose Mr Simmonds has to tell him that he won't ever have full use of that hand again? That he'll be crippled for the rest of his life? It would cut the ground from under him, and I don't know what he'd do.'

'Just hope it isn't going to happen,' said Bennie quietly.

Tamsin didn't meet her eyes, but looked down at the little cat that she was absentmindedly stroking. She said, still without raising her head, 'They used to say black cats are lucky. So get working, little Birdie, and don't just lie around purring.'

Michael and Erin returned to Romans just after five o'clock, and found Kim sitting on her own, staring without seeing at Flog It! On the television. She had hoped for Tamsin to be back before this and was starting to worry, so the return of their guests came as a relief – of sorts, anyway. When she heard the door open she had leapt to her feet, and then tried to disguise her disappointment, but nobody was deceived.

'Tamsin not back yet?' asked Erin, watching her face.

'Not yet – but the appointment wasn't until three-thirty, and they're always running late in hospitals,' said Kim trying to convince herself as much as them.

'She hasn't rung?' asked Michael, although the answer was obvious.

'No,' said Kim.

'Well, it's early yet to start worrying,' said Erin, comfortingly. 'She's got to take him home, remember, and I expect they'll all be talking.'

'I'll make some tea,' said Kim, longing for something to do to pass the time, but her guests had only just had tea with Michael's Aunt Mary, and she sat down again, saying brightly, 'So, how did your afternoon go?' and sat listening with half an ear to their account of their pleasantly nostalgic visit, with the other half listening out for the return of the Discovery, but in the end she didn't pick it out from the sound of other traffic turning in and out of the Yard gate, and Tamsin's return half an hour later made them all jump. She came through the door smiling, and they all broke off what they were saying and turned to look at her. Kim leapt to her feet again and went straight over to hug her.

'Tell us what the Consultant said,' she demanded, although it was blessedly obvious from her twin's face that the news was good. 'What happened?'

'What happened was, we waited for ages as usual, and then he was nearly an hour in with Mr Simmonds while I bit my fingernails and tried to read a very dull magazine, and then the Receptionist took me in again, and the moment I set eyes on Francis, the sun came out!'

'Sit down, and tell us properly,' said Erin, taking her arm and leading her to the sofa. 'It's obvious the news is good, so fill us in.'

Tamsin obediently sat down and tried to pull herself together; the release from tension had been a bit like firing a catapult, she thought: infinite recoil. She took a deep breath.

'Well, they took the stitches out, which was a good start. There's a bit of infection left, but it's clearing up nicely, apparently – he's still bandaged up, but a lot less, and they've liberated his fingers and done a lot of tests, and after all that, Mr Simmonds finally told him he can start trying to use the hand, so long as he doesn't get carried away – and he can use it, which is a merciful blessing.' She stopped then, blinking away sudden tears that started to her eyes, and Kim passed her a tissue from a box on the table. She held it in her hand without needing to use it, and went on with her account, but a bit unsteadily. 'They did some X-rays, too, and it looks as if everything may heal up and leave him with nothing more than an occasional twinge in cold weather, so that's good news, too. He can't drive yet, or lift anything heavier than a small bag of feathers, but the prognosis is good, Mr Simmonds told me. It'll just take time – oh, and every time he goes out into the yard, I have see that he covers all the bandages with a surgical glove against dirt and possibly more infection, they gave him a pack of them to take home. I have to take him back in another week, unless something goes wrong in the meantime, and then he'll be told when he can drive a car again. Meanwhile, he just has to be careful, do as he's told, and keep on taking the tablets. The second of those will be the hardest, I suspect.' She stopped there, and choked on what was this time suspiciously close to a sob. 'I don't know whether to laugh or cry, to be honest.'

'You need a drink,' said Michael, eyeing her critically. 'Do we have anything left from last night's binge, Kim?' But Kim was already on her way to the kitchen. By the time she returned with four moderately-sized glasses of Italian Pinot Grigio on a tray, Tamsin had pulled herself together and was smiling at something Michael had said, but she took her glass thankfully, and swallowed a large gulp.

'That's better!'

'So, what have you done with him now?' asked Erin curiously. 'Will he be fit to come out tonight?'

'I should think so. I took him home for a rest now, but he certainly means to be with us. I said I'd pick him up at half-past seven, and Bennie said she'd make sure he was ready, he should have got himself together by then, he'll have had a good two hours to recover in.'

She did not add that, on the way home, she had tactfully ignored the fact that Francis had wept, scrubbing away tears from his cheeks with his handkerchief and looking steadily away from her out of the near-side window. Not for long, he had pulled himself together by the time they were back at Shortlanesend, but it was a measure of the strain he had been under.

'You don't want to be driving that monster in the dark, after the day you've had,' said Michael. 'We'll all go out there in my car, and later we can take him back, you can tell me how to get back here again. Then you can have a proper drink, you look as if you need it.'

'He might want to leave fairly early,' said Tamsin doubtfully, but Michael said that was no problem. 'So will we all, come to that, Erin and I have to be up at dawn tomorrow to get back to London, and however quiet we try to be, in this little house we're almost bound to wake you and Kim too.'

'You'll have to work at it to wake Tamsin,' Kim told them, and the atmosphere, which had been a bit tense up until then, disintegrated in laughter, not at the rather feeble joke, but with relief.

That evening at Mario's, in spite of any misgivings, proved to be a resounding success. The five of them jelled well together and Kim, who had almost wondered if she should stay at home rather than impinge herself on the family party, felt in no way unwelcome, rather the reverse. Tamsin, who had wondered if Francis would be up to it after the stress of the past few days, found that he had bounced back like a tennis ball to the man he had been before he speared himself on the rusty nail, which she realised with both compassion and sadness, was a measure of his previous anxiety, most of which he had kept to himself. Erin and Michael were just out to enjoy themselves and, in Michael's case, cementing his restored friendship with someone who had, in the past, been his favourite cousin and closest friend.

'So, when's the wedding day to be?' Michael asked, when they were well away with the antipasti. 'Fixed a date yet?'

'The Friday before Christmas,' Tamsin told him.

'As soon as that?' Michael sounded surprised, but then he looked at them both, sitting side by side on the other side of the table and said, 'I see. Well, why wait around, after all? Neither of you looks to be going anywhere.'

'My mother wanted us to be married before we moved in together,' Tamsin explained. 'This is the nearest compromise we could agree on. So keep the date clear – or clear it, if it's already booked. That's an order, by the way, not a request.'

'Oh, you couldn't keep us away,' Michael told her. 'Nor Ed and Amanda. Nor Ros, and probably not Peter and Tom either, so I hope you're planning on inviting us all.'

'Well, we are, but the arrangements may seem a bit…well, unusual,' Tamsin told him, happily. 'We're getting married in a rather small private chapel at the stately home in the centre of the village – Ravenscourt Place. It only holds about thirty people, forty tops if they put some extra chairs at the back, so some of the guests will have to spill over into the room next door. There's a CCTV camera in the chapel, so the overflow can watch it all on wide screen telly.'

'Unusual.' Michael sounded amused.

'Yes, but it means we can invite more people – around fifty plus, instead of just thirty-odd,' Tamsin told him, 'so all of you can come, which you couldn't if we didn't use it.'

Michael looked at his cousin. He said, 'You're being very quiet about all this.'

'S-safest way,' Francis told him, with a grin.

'So what about his grandma and the aunts?' Erin asked, but Francis shook his head.

'G-G-Grandma is too old and f-f-frail to come,' he said, but with regret. 'Aunt Henry w-will stay to look after her, and Aunt C-C-Clara is coming for all three of them. I'm hoping T-Tom can be persuaded to bring her.'

'He will,' said Michael, firmly. 'I'll see to it personally. If it gets him a seat in the chapel, he probably won't argue.'

'Oh, it definitely will,' Tamsin assured him. 'I love your Aunt Clara.' She paused. 'Well, I love your Aunt Henry too, but we have to draw a line, or the pews will collapse!'

'And the other aunts and uncles?' Michael asked. 'Mind you, they haven't seen you in years, and it sounds as if you can't fit everyone in anyway. I expect they'll forgive you if you send them a bit of wedding cake – and anyway, someone will have to stay in town to run the business, so the uncles will be tied up. Erin and I can explain when we see them, or when you can actually write, you could do that Francis. But I should warn you, they will almost certainly turn up to see what's going on down here now that communications have been re-opened, so better be prepared.

Funnily enough, we've all missed you.' He gave his cousin a direct look, but Francis made no reply beyond a slight shrug of his shoulders that could have meant anything.

'So where will you have the reception?' Erin asked, briskly bringing the discussion back on course. 'At that four star hotel we nearly stayed at? Or the pub in the village where we had lunch yesterday? That looked as if it could be quite good.'

'Neither,' Tamsin told her. 'We shall have it in the old dining room up at the Place, with catering by a top chef who trained under Mawgan Angwin!'

'Then Tom will definitely be there,' Michael told her. 'He likes his tum, does Tom.'

Kim glanced at Tamsin briefly, wondering if she was getting the same feeling as she was getting: doors opening, friends and family support flooding in, hope and sunshine and the future, blossoming like a flower too long in the bud. She said, 'I suspect he's in luck,' as much to dispel the feeling as because it was true.

'So, who are you calling on to be best man at this amazing ceremony?' Michael asked his cousin. 'Kim will obviously be chief bridesmaid.'

'—only bridesmaid,' Tamsin interrupted, and Michael grinned at her.

'No room for a regal half dozen? Well, I get that. But Francis only needs one supporter, so how is he going to choose from the wide field now available without treading on people's toes?'

'He's already chosen,' said Tamsin, 'hence the incredible venue.'

'Really?' Michael raised his eyebrows. 'To whom falls the honour, then?'

'A g-g-good friend,' Francis told him. 'M-M-Merlin Ravenscourt,' and Michael looked thoughtful.

'I don't remember a Merlin, back in the day,' he said, and Tamsin explained.

'He's a cousin, from Canada. He came over as guardian for his young cousin when his father's brother died, and forgot to go back. He's one of the partners in the Shipyard over the road from us, where we've been parking the Discovery.'

Michael thought about this for a moment, then he looked at Francis.

'Good to know you've got one good friend outside your immediate family, then,' he said. 'I was beginning to wonder,' and Francis gave him a scowl and flicked a piece of bread at him across the table. Tamsin giggled at this display of doubtful etiquette, and said, 'Actually, he has at least three, apart from the family,' and they all laughed. Kim counted on her fingers. 'Val, Pete Lawson, Gary Fancot, the builder, I make it at least five,' and felt the atmosphere unravelling still further.

The tone was now set for the rest of the evening, and the five of them laughed and joked their way through it, leaving the restaurant just after ten o'clock in a happier mood than the Dorset contingent had known for some time now.

'What a lovely evening,' said Kim, as they headed off for Shortlanesend in Michael's car. 'I don't think I remember when I laughed so much — thank you so much, Michael and Erin.'

'Like old times,' said Michael, with a quick glance at Francis in the passenger seat beside him. 'You OK, coz? You've gone quiet.'

'About t-t-time one of us d-did,' said Francis, with a lazy smile at him. 'I'm j-j-just a bit tired, th-th-that's all. It's been a l-l-long day.'

'So, what time do you want me to come for you in the morning?' Tamsin asked, from the back. 'You could probably use a lie-in — I know I could.'

'You'll be lucky,' Erin observed, and Francis said, 'Actually, you n-n-needn't bother t-t-tomorrow. Ernie said he'd come with m-m-me to Embridge with the truck. I w-w-want to get a couple of b-b-boxes out of store — just a bit of s-s-stuff for the office, and a few books.'

'Just don't put them on the office floor then, until Kim and I get there with the rug,' said Tamsin. 'Put them in the utility room, or something, for the minute, there's plenty of blokes around to move them later.'

'Yes, b-boss,' Francis murmured, closing his eyes and shifting into a more comfortable position. Tamsin looked at the top of his dark head over the seat and smothered a smile. 'So, what time did you want me over there to take you on somewhere else, or home, or whatever, or will you go back with Ernie?'

'G-get your housekeeping d-d-done, and have lunch out with K-Kim, and get over mid-afternoon-ish, I'll be OK. You can put your shopping s-s-straight into the larder, then.'

'Good thinking. If you'll be all right.'

'I s-s-said so.'

They dropped Francis off at Shortlanesend, and Tamsin walked with him to the back door, not because she didn't trust him to find the way on his own but because she wanted to say a proper goodnight, without an audience. Standing there in the dark, with his arms around her and his cheek resting against her hair, she felt deep peace stealing over her.

'It's all moving on at last, isn't it?' she said thankfully, 'I was beginning to think we were stuck in the doldrums for ever.' He smothered a laugh.

'You j-just w-w-wait and see,' he said. They kissed again, more slowly and thoroughly this time, and then he went indoors and Tamsin picked her way back across the yard to the car.

'Everything OK?' asked Michael, as she slipped into Francis' vacated seat.

'Oh yes!'

'Home, James, and don't ask personal questions,' said Erin, from the back seat, and the car moved off, headed for the lanes and the end of the long day.

The next morning started early, as Michael and Erin were up at six to be away by seven, and Tamsin and Kim both got out of their beds to say a proper goodbye.

'It's been a lovely couple of days,' said Erin, kissing them both goodbye warmly. 'Thank you so much for having us, I suppose we'll be meeting next at the wedding – it seems incredible!'

'It's been lovely having you,' said Tamsin, returning the kiss. 'Come again in the Spring, and bring the kids, they'll love it and we should have somewhere for you all to sleep by then.'

'Oh, we will, and thank you!'

Michael came back from putting the bags in the car, dangling the keys from his fingers.

'Turn the volume down, you women! You'll wake the whole village!' He kissed the twins and took Erin gently by the arm. 'Come on girl, London's calling. We need to be on our way, or I'll be getting the sack!'

When they had gone out of sight up the narrow street, the little terrace house, as the twins returned to it, felt very quiet and empty. At a loose end all of a sudden, Kim wandered into the kitchen on auto-pilot. 'Coffee?'

'It always feels so flat, somehow, when people leave,' said Tamsin, wandering disconsolately in her wake. 'It's too late to go back to bed, but it's far too early to be up.' She yawned.

'We don't have to rush. We can have a long, hot, leisurely shower each, and dawdle over breakfast, Francis said there was no particular hurry. As a matter of fact, I wondered what he wasn't saying, how about you?'

'Yes, me too.' She smothered another yawn. 'Actually, it will be nice to have almost a whole day together, I don't suppose there'll be that many more.'

'Then let's make the most of it.' Kim handed her a mug of steaming coffee. 'Get that down you. Let's go and sit down comfortably and plan our day.'

They dawdled through the next two hours with the aid of breakfast and early morning TV, but when the hands on the clock showed nine o'clock, Tamsin pulled herself together and reached for her phone.

'I'll just ring Shortlanesend and see how Francis is making out after last night,' she said. 'I can check if he's thought of anything else we need at the same time, and then, I suppose, we had better hit the road to Embridge.' She found the number on her phone and held it to her ear. 'Nobody there,' she said, after a moment or two, and then, immediately after, 'Oh, hello Bennie! It's me, I just wondered how Francis was after all the excitement yesterday…was he? That's convenient for him!…the swine, how dare he?' She was laughing. 'Yes please, I'll hang on.' She covered the phone with her hand and turned to Kim. 'He wanted to speak to me anyway, but he said I wouldn't be up yet!'

'Normally, he would have been right,' Kim pointed out.

'Not at nine o'clock, he wouldn't – oh, hello my darling!' She hurriedly returned the phone to her ear. 'Just ringing to see how you are this morning, and if there's anything else you've thought of while we're in Embridge…a what? …what kind of a clock, one to stand on the shelf or a wall clock? …we can probably get that when we get the rug, somewhere on that estate anyway…me too, and you take care. Tell Ernie to bully you if you get above yourself…take care, my darling.' She took the phone from her ear and switched it off, then looked at Kim. 'As you will have gathered from all that, he wants a clock for his office. An electric wall clock, big enough to see.'

'He sounds on form, then,' said Kim.

'He sounded quite different from any way I've ever heard him,' said Tamsin. She slipped the phone back into her pocket and looked at her twin. 'Full of…well, of joy, I suppose…I just hope he doesn't come down from his high too hard.'

'He won't,' said Kim, with conviction. 'He'll level off when he gets used to it all, and be…well, himself, I suppose. Whoever that turns out to be.'

'Are you soothsaying again, Madame Arcati?' asked Tamsin, narrowing her eyes.

'I think it's obvious,' said Kim, begging the question.

Shortly after that they walked across the road to collect the Discovery from the Yard, and ran straight into Merlin, who came out of the office the moment they appeared in the gateway.

'I'm glad I ran into you two,' he said, smiling. 'I wanted to ask you, how did Francis get on yesterday. Will he be OK?'

'If he behaves himself, and does what he's been told,' said Tamsin, returning the smile. 'Not sure what the chances are of that, but we're hoping.'

'Oh, he's got sense, has Francis. He'll be good – probably drive you mad in the process, but he will. Are you off out there now?'

'No. We're going to buy some essential office supplies, like a rug for the floor and a clock, and then we're going to stock the store cupboard. After that, who knows? He doesn't want us over there until later this afternoon, so it'll probably be lunch and a bit of browsing.'

'Well, when you get over there, say Hi from me – and tell him that people have been asking about him down at the Club. Sensible people, with genuine concern, the news of his little misadventure has spread around a bit.'

'I bet that twit Max Carruthers isn't one of them,' said Tamsin, and Merlin gave her a long look before he answered, 'Well no. He had a different take on it.'

'What did he say?' asked Tamsin, but Merlin hesitated.

'You might as well tell us,' said Kim. 'Somebody will, you can bet your boots. It might come better from you.'

'He sniggered a bit, and said words to the effect of, now you see what the incompetent nincompoop gets up to when he's away from his Mummy,' said Merlin, adding, 'I don't think many people actually listened.'

'Well, good for them! Isn't there something can be done about that nasty little man?'

'He's too clever to go too far, and he's entitled to his opinions, I suppose, just like the rest of us. But fear not, we're all watching for an opportunity. I think a lot of people have had just about enough of the asshole, and not just for that. He won't be voted on the Committee again, of that you may be sure. The AGM is in February, not that far away, just watch this space.'

'That's good news, anyway.' Kim tried to speak lightly but she felt a shiver run up her spine as she spoke, something to do with cornered rats, maybe. 'Well, we'd better get on our way, I suppose – and you'll need to get back to work. But we'll see you soon, I expect.'

'Oh, you certainly will – oh, and Tamsin, you can go on leaving that thing over here until you move across, it isn't in the way this time of year, and it's probably safer than parked out in that narrow road. For everybody,' he ended, on a grin, and walked off with a wave, back to his office, although, as Kim remarked, he wasn't exactly dressed for office work: scruffy jeans and a sweater with pulled threads in it told a different story.

'Off to build a boat, from the looks of it,' she said. 'Or repair one, maybe – and now, let's go and build a store cupboard,' and Tamsin reversed out of their parking space and headed for the gate to the outside world.

'That was nice of Merlin,' she said, after a while, as they drove along the road to the town.

'Merlin is nice. And I found what he said very interesting, didn't you?'

'I did. I should just love to see the little snerp get his come-upance!'

'What on earth is a "snerp"?' Kim asked, and Tamsin answered, 'Max Carruthers.'

Having visited it three times now, Tamsin had no problems in finding the Trading Estate, and the furniture store was exactly where she remembered it, which was a bit of miracle given her bump of location. She took the piece of paper on which she had written the measurements from her bag, and they went inside to see what they could find.

'What you need,' said Kim, as they made their way through other departments to the carpet and flooring section, 'is a very large, bristly doormat to go in the doorway, with PLEASE WIPE YOUR FEET on it in very large black letters. Since the place opens almost directly onto a farmyard.'

'Or a large basket, and a notice saying PLEASE REMOVE YOUR BOOTS,' Tamsin agreed, 'but we had better settle for an ordinary one. Farmer Chillingworth might not see the joke.'

They found a suitable doormat easily enough, and proceeded to the carpet department, where they settled on a large mock-Persian rug with a dark red background and enough pattern on it to help disguise any trodden-in mud from the yard, and then Kim said, 'And if it's a stone floor, you should put a bit of underlay under it, to smother the cold a bit more, it'll strike up through stone like the Arctic in Winter!' So they bought some of that, too. Then, when they had paid for it all, there was the problem of fitting it into the Discovery. The underlay was no problem, as it would fold fairly easily into the back, but the only way the rug itself would go in and still leave room for further essentials was to roll it up, put the seats on the passenger side down, and shove one end under the dashboard, leaving Kim with the offside rear seat, and the stores to manage as best they could in the back

'After all that, I need a coffee!' Tamsin said. 'Let's go and bother Bordens, and then have a look round there to pass the time until lunch. We can get the stores in the supermarket afterwards, and then be at Burnthouse during the afternoon, as requested. How's that for a plan?'

'Depends how much looking around you want to do,' said Kim, glancing at her watch.

'Why? What's the time?'

'Not quite half-past eleven.'

'Good heavens! I thought it was mid-day at least!'

'That's getting up early for you. Better get used to it.'

'Oh, shut up, you!'

Tamsin parked the Discovery in the Square without trouble on an off-season Thursday, and they made their way across to Bordens.

'At least it isn't raining,' said Kim, looking up at a sky that was mid-grey with blue patches. 'It looks as if it might even turn out to be fine, later on.'

'I'll believe that when I see it. Come on, step it out – coffee is calling!'

They dawdled over their coffee, and then did a leisurely tour of the store, checking if there was anything they might have missed, or forgotten, and, coming away with two new toilet brushes with holders and a large, curled up sleeping cat made out of polished greenish stone, that Tamsin had fallen in love with. 'Just like little Birdie,' she said, stroking it lovingly. 'It can go in our sitting room – there may even be room for it in the caravan for now. It won't get knocked off easily, after all, it weighs a ton.' She hefted it in her hands.

'Just don't let Mr Careless drop it on his foot,' advised Kim.

They took their purchases back to the Discovery and locked them in, then went back for lunch, over which they dawdled. Marking time, Kim thought, watching her twin as they ate. Tamsin couldn't wait to get on to the next stage, but she was trying to hide it. There was no point in hurrying, mid-afternoon was still a long way ahead.

'What are you thinking?' she asked, after a while.

'That he kept me away for some reason. Like the delivery of our first home together.'

'Oh, I think that's a certainty,' said Kim, smiling at her. 'They've got to plumb it in and everything before you can live in it. That won't be done in under a day, I shouldn't think.'

'It's exciting, but daunting at the same time. What do you think it will be like?'

'A lot more luxurious than that cottage,' said Kim. 'Maybe even larger. How would I know?'

'That's what I think, too. Hope.' They exchanged a smile.

'Have you got that list safely?' asked Kim, changing the subject. She looked at her watch, not for the first time that day: they had dawdled to some purpose. 'Come on then – let's go and fill the store cupboard. Then, by the time we've had yet another coffee, it will be about time to get out to Burnthouse and see what really is going on out there.'

'We'll never sleep again,' Tamsin objected.

'Drink something else, then. Come on.'

They left the restaurant and headed for the supermarket, where they spent a happy hour arguing over what constituted essential stores and buying some big storage tins for things like flour to discourage the mice. They couldn't, said Kim, leave everything to Birdie and The Boss. 'But you'll have to do the frozen stuff on Saturday morning,' she added. 'The freezer won't be cold enough before then if it's only delivered tomorrow – we can make a list, and you can call in here on your way over,. Same with chilled stuff, like those prawns you're looking at.'

'Suppose I have to take Francis over?'

'Then you'll just have to come away again.' Kim slammed the boot shut. It was time to go.

This time, into the unknown...

XXVII

'Oh my God!' said Tamsin, as they drove up the unfamiliar wide lane to the farm, and Kim looked at her in surprise.

'What?'

'We – I forgot the clock!'

'So what? You can always get one tomorrow – he won't be needing it immediately.'

'He'll kill me!'

'I very much doubt it. It's hardly a life or death matter, is it?'

'He said he was going to ring me specially.'

'Only because he knew you were going into town anyway.'

'It was all that business with the rug put it out of my mind,' said Tamsin, remorsefully. 'I should have written it down—'

Kim shot her a sideways look: it seemed to her that her twin was over-reacting over a triviality that could be easily rectified, probably the measure of her present tension. Well, Kim couldn't find it in her to blame her for that, she had a lot ahead of her, not just her first sight of her temporary new home. There were all the things that would go with it; getting it all organised, moving stuff in, finding places to put it…Saturday night, when she and Francis would finally be alone together. Taking that huge, final step into a new and unfamiliar world. It would have been amazing, really, if Tamsin had remembered every last small thing. And come to that, Francis had a perfectly good watch – two of them, indeed, at the last count. But she said none of this, deeming it to be useless, and they parked up outside the house in silence.

Francis must have had someone keeping a lookout for their arrival, for before they had more than opened the doors to climb out, he appeared from the farmyard and came over to them, gathering Tamsin into his arms as she slid to the ground.

'G-good day?' he asked, cuddling her.

'I forgot the clock,' said Tamsin, tipping her head up to peer into his face, but he took this earth-shaking admission with the calmness that Kim had hopefully expected of him.

'I d-d-don't suppose it's the only th-thing that's been f-f-forgotten,' he said cheerfully. 'C-come and s-s-see what I've got for you, b-b-before you unload. You too, K-Kim.' Without removing his arm from her shoulders, he propelled Tamsin towards the farmyard, and Kim followed, in some curiosity.

It wasn't a caravan, precisely, although it did appear to have little wheels, tucked up now like the legs of a flying bird, so that it stood firm towards the back of its gravelled yard on eight stout steel supports, but neither was it big enough to be termed a mobile home, or not in Kim's view, even though the field gate and the short fence to either side of it had needed to be removed to let it through. But nobody would have towed this monster behind a car, if anything it was a hybrid between the two. "A tiny bungalow on legs" was the best description Kim could come up with. Tamsin, less objective, simply stared at it in amazement. The first comment that leapt to her lips was, absurdly, 'How on earth did they get that up the lane?' to which Francis replied 'V-v-very carefully, on a flat-bed l-lorry.'

'I can see why you needed to clear the lane,' said Kim, eyeing the little home measuringly. 'How wide is it?'

'Sixteen feet. And th-thirty-six l-long.' Francis handed them both up the four shallow folding steps that led to the door and stepped aboard after them, and the twins looked about them with interest. They found themselves in a kitchen/diner area with openings to each side, and a window at each end; the one behind them had a blind to wind down for privacy, the other one, straight ahead of them beyond the dining area, had cheerful red curtains. There was a fitted table here, with two leather benches, one to each side, just about big enough to seat three people each, if they minded their elbows. On the near end of each of these seats was a low bulkhead, against each of these was a square worktop with, on the left, a small fridge beneath it, and on the right, a single drawer and a cupboard. Above the fridge was a double electric socket, one of them with a plug already in it: the fridge, no doubt. Behind them was a wide worktop with a small electric stove set into it and another row of sockets along the back, and at the far end, a corner sink and a small draining board against the inside return wall. More cupboards and drawers underneath, the whole arrangement suggested nothing so much as the galley of a yacht, carefully designed to make the maximum use of a small area, and with adequate safe passing space behind whoever was doing the cooking.

'Nice,' said Kim, when she saw that Tamsin had been struck speechless. 'Easy to work in.'

'N-n-not if you were preparing a b-b-banquet,' Francis observed, with a grin. 'It'll w-w-work for fried-egg s-s-sandwiches. S-s-see, you can even plug in the t-t-toaster,' and he gave Tamsin a squeeze round the shoulders, before moving her through into the far end. Here, there were windows all around, with more of the dark red curtains, and centrally beneath them, the fitted equivalent of a comfortably upholstered three-piece suite, although it was actually in one piece, covered in a greenish-brown tweed effect fabric. To either side of this were low cupboards in light pine with drawers below, and opposite, against the dividing wall, was what was effectively a sideboard, also in light pine, with more wide drawers and another cupboard in the centre, and shelves, deep and high enough to take books, or games maybe, at either end. Above this was a rectangular panel of decorative smoked glass to borrow light into the dining area.

'It's d-d-designed for two people to l-l-live in comfortably,' Francis told them, 'but p-part of the seating pulls out to m-make a d-d-double bed, if we n-need it.'

'Nice,' said Kim, looking around – although two thoughts had leapt immediately into her head. One of them was "coffee table", and the other one was "cushions", but if Tamsin had to buy a clock tomorrow, that could be seen to. Tamsin's reaction was less – or maybe more – practical. 'So, where do we sleep?' she asked, and could have bitten her tongue out immediately afterwards. Francis raised an amused eyebrow at her confusion, but took them to the other end of the little home. Here, the kitchen opened onto a short, narrow passage, which actually had a door to it, unlike the living area which hadn't. Opening off this was, at the end, a shower room with a sink and lavatory, and a small window facing over the wall to the vegetable patch: it was a bit cosy, but Kim had seen worse on her foreign travels, and the shower looked an adequate size – although possibly not for Francis. A second door, in the centre of the passage, was to the bedroom; this had a wide end-window alongside its fitted 4'6" wide double bed – no footboard, which was probably a good thing given the cramped circumstances – with a small bedside table to either side that filled the available space wall-to-wall, and two overhead reading lights above the headboard, and facing that, against the front wall, a reasonably sized wardrobe with a mirror on its nearer door, and a high chest with deep drawers, that filled the space under a second small window. Red curtains again. It was a bit of a jigsaw puzzle from end to end, but as a temporary home, surprisingly adequate. Kim thought that Francis had done well, or come to think, maybe Bennie had, or even whoever had designed it, but whichever way, the end result was good.

'Th-they'll be c-c-connecting the utilities tomorrow,' Francis was saying to Tamsin. 'After th-that, we can g-g-get our stuff over on Saturday m-morning, and m-m-move in.'

Tamsin looked at the wardrobe sceptically. She said, 'We'll never fit it all in!' and Francis laughed.

'We can leave what we don't n-n-need immediately packed up,' he said. 'It's d-d-dry in the utility room, and r-r-reasonably handy if we want anything, and th-there's enough space if we're tidy about it. I d-d-don't suppose you'll be doing m-m-much ironing.'

'I think it's lovely,' said Kim, 'but now I'm going to see to that carpet. Is there anyone around could be spared to give a hand to get it out of the car, Francis? We can probably manage after that.'

The three of them went back to the Discovery, scooping up a passing electrician on the way. They had to get the bags of stores out first, setting them on the ground alongside, and then Kim and the electrician between them hauled out the carpet and carried it through to the study, coming back for the underlay while Tamsin, with some one-handed assistance from Francis, began to shift the eight bags of stores along to the larder. Their way in and out of the back door was slightly impeded by not two, but three tea chests stacked against the wall, but Tamsin decided it would be unwise to comment. At least they hadn't found their way into the office itself, and since Francis could manage as many of the bags with one hand as she could with two, it took only two trips anyway. The bags were dumped on the flagged floor for attention later, the electrician took himself off back to work, and Tamsin and Kim laid the underlay and the carpet, under Francis' instructions and, it had to be faced, interference, and that part of the job was done. It had to be laid, he had informed them, as some of the furnishing, such as the desks, would need to sit on top of it, and Kim ordered him to organise a dust sheet before large men in dirty boots tramped all over it. He left them after that, which was a relief, Kim said, and she and Tamsin went along to the larder to unpack the fruits of their mammoth shopping spree.

'So, what do you think of the show so far?' Kim asked her twin as they unpacked the bags and put the contents onto the marble lower shelf of the larder, where they could see and assess them.

'I'm speechless, actually,' said Tamsin. She paused with a tin of evaporated milk in each hand to think about it: so far, there hadn't been time for assessment. 'I'm still not sure whether that's a caravan or a mobile home, to be fair.'

'It's definitely not a caravan,' Kim told her. 'You'd never tow that behind a car, even if you were Francis – and I'm beginning to think I wouldn't put much past him.'

'He does seem to be coming out in his true colours just lately,' Tamsin agreed, thoughtfully.

'The big question there is, do you like what you see?' Kim shot her a quick smile as the answer was obvious, and Tamsin heaved a deep sigh and said, 'Most of it – nobody is perfect.'

'Well, men aren't. But I don't envy you, living in a small space with that!' and they both laughed, and Kim went on, 'and you're putting that flour in the bread bin.'

It didn't take long to arrange their purchases on the shelves – well, Kim arranged them, Tamsin followed instructions – and they rolled the bags together and set them to one side, and Kim asked, 'Did we buy a swing bin for rubbish?'

'You would remember if we had – it would be behind the sofa,' and they both laughed.

'Another errand for tomorrow, then.' They went back outside into the unfamiliar sunshine of the late afternoon, but there was no sign of Francis anywhere. Steve came past from the house to fetch something out of his van and saw them looking around them. He said, 'If you're looking for Francis, he took the surveyor's report over to the honeymoon suite, to scowl over it in comfort. You'll find him there,' and he grinned at Tamsin. 'Like it over there, do you?'

'Very much. Compact, cosy and convenient, but I may trip over him occasionally.' They exchanged smiles and Steve went on his way and the twins went back to Tamsin's temporary future home, where they found Francis sitting at the dining table, scowling over a small heap of paperwork. He looked up as they came in, obviously with relief.

'You're d-d-done, are you?' he asked.

'For now,' said Kim. She looked around her. 'When Tamsin brings you over tomorrow, can she bring all that stuff from behind the sofa and stow it away? Or would that be in someone's way?'

'I don't see s-s-s-why it would be, m-m-most of the heavy work to be done is outs-s-side now. But she d-d-doesn't need to c—c-collect me tomorrow, Steve said he'd g-g-give me a ring when the office s-s-stuff arrived, there's n-n-nothing I can do here until then.'

'But how will you get over here?'

'B-bennie's g-g-got to go int-t-to t-town. She s-said she'd d-d-drop me on the way, it d-d-doesn't m-matter what time.'

'Then it won't matter either if I'm not here until late morning? I have to buy a clock.'

'So you do.' He grinned at her, shuffling the papers on the table together; Tamsin and Kim both noticed that he used both hands – just. 'Th-there'll be no hurry, I d-d-doubt th-they'll be early. T-take Kim with you and have some t-t-time together, it'll be your last ch-chance for a bit.'

'You'll be all right?'

'Yes. B-but take your phone, and I c-c-can yell for help if I n-need to. I w-w-won't, though.' He got to his feet and sidled out from behind the table. 'C-can we go, if you've f-f-finished what you had t-t-to d-do?'

'Come and admire our day's work, before we leave,' said Tamsin, taking his arm. 'You can tell us if we forgot anything vital that you like – not that I think for a minute that tins and packets are your normal grazing ground.'

Francis duly admired the larder, still fairly sparsely stocked for its size, and said they'd done a good job.

'But it's not just that,' said Tamsin, her eyes sparkling, 'it's another big step towards really being here – I'm just beginning to believe it may really happen, when I look at all this.'

'Oh, it w-w-will really happen.'

They went back down the passage to the door, negotiating the three tea chests as they went, and Kim said, 'How are you going to unpack these, with just one serviceable hand?'

'S-someone will help me, I expect.'

'If it can wait until Saturday, I expect Val would. Then I could help Tamsin move all your personal stuff into the…whatever it is.'

'Steve called it the honeymoon suite,' Tamsin reminded her, smiling.

'I d-d-don't think we'll stick w-w-with that one,' said Francis, but he smiled too as he said it. 'S-Saturday w-w-would be fine, if Val w-w-wouldn't mind. And I expect T-Tamsin could use some help, too.'

'We'll have to ask Val, of course, but I'm sure that he'll be up for it. Oh – if he's not racing, I suppose. I hadn't thought of that.'

'Tide's not until th-three o'clock. They w-w-won't be s-s-starting early.'

'Well, we'll ask him.' They were back at the Discovery by this time: Steve saw them preparing to leave and came over to say goodbye.

'All sorted? I'll give you a ring in the morning when they get here then, Francis—' He paused, as Kim opened the rear door, and said, 'Oh shit! I forgot about that!' when she saw the seats, still folded down to accommodate the rug.

'I'll give you a hand with that,' he said, and did so with masculine efficiency. Kim, who could perfectly well have managed it for herself, thanked him with a smile, and they all climbed aboard and set off for Shortlanesend. Steve raised a hand in farewell as they pulled away, and walked off back to his own affairs.

At Shortlanesend, the children had just got back from school and chaos reigned in the kitchen. Maisie ran straight across and threw herself at Tamsin, and Sacha made straight for Francis, who narrowly missed tripping over him, and then bent down to fondle his ears.

'N-n-not long now, b-boy,' he told the dog. 'S-stick it out one m-m-more day, th-then we'll be home.'

'I wish you weren't going,' said Maisie, peering wistfully up at Tamsin. 'Must you go?'

'We're not going far,' Tamsin told her. 'You can come and see us – we hope that you will, don't we Francis?'

'Of c-c-course.'

'What about darling little Birdie? And The Boss ? Will they be going with you too?'

'N-not for a d-d-day or two – when we've got settled in.'

Maisie ran across to fondle the little cat, asleep in her usual place, crooning, 'We'll miss you, lovely little Birdie,' and making kissing noises.

'And the chickens?' said Clive. 'Will they go too?'

As s-s-soon as we've b-built them a chicken house. Yes.'

'They're so sweet,' said Maisie, pushing out her lower lip. 'Like little fluffy snowballs.'

'Then perhaps we can rear some chicks and give you some of your own – if Mummy is up for it,' Tamsin suggested, exchanging a look with Francis. 'We could do that?'

'Of c-c-course. W-when they go broody, in the S–S-Spring.'

'Mummy?' asked Maisie, bouncing hopefully.

'So long as you promise to look after them properly,' said Bennie, who privately liked the little white snowballs herself. 'We can go against you at the County Show, Francis – show you what chicken rearing is all about!' She turned to the children. 'Now off you go, both of you, and get your school uniform off before you have your tea. Shoo!' Reluctantly, the children ran off and Bennie shouted after them, 'And fold it tidily!' before she turned to the twins.

'It's early yet, but would you like to come back over for supper? There's plenty, and we won't be seeing so much of you after the weekend, I don't suppose.'

Kim and Tamsin exchanged a glance, and Kim said, 'We'd love to, if you really mean that—'

'—of course I do—'

'—but tomorrow, we'd like Francis to come and eat with us, if that's all right?' She added, on impulse, 'You and Ernie too, if you can find a child-sitter. Val will be there too, it will be a sort of Last Supper before we separate.'

Bennie looked at her for a minute. She said, 'Now it's my turn to ask if you really mean that.'

'Yes, I do. I hadn't thought of it until this minute, but it would be great – after all, you're going to miss them too when they go solo. Please come.'

'I'll have to ask Ernie,' said Bennie, but she resolved to twist his arm until it fell off, if necessary. 'I'm sure we can get a sitter – my mother will come, if we ask her.' She moved over to the Aga to give the kettle a shove onto the hotplate, asking automatically, 'Cup of tea, before you go?' but Kim and Tamsin, after exchanging another look, said they would pass on that and go home, if that was all right?

'We need to get tidied up a bit, and maybe put our feet up – we seem to have done an awful lot of hard labour today,' Tamsin explained, and

Kim added, 'And it will be wonderful not to have to think about getting a meal this evening. We can just chill for a bit.' They said goodbye, and Tamsin and Francis exchanged a kiss – a fairly moderate once since they were in company – and the twins left.

'It felt so odd, when you said that about a last supper,' said Tamsin, as they drove away. 'So…so imminent, somehow. I hadn't really thought that it was going to happen. Does that sound silly?'

'Well, it is going to happen, so get used to the idea.' Kim smiled at her briefly, and then looked back to the lane ahead. 'Mind that bird—' The bird had flown off even as she spoke, but Tamsin made no comment. Then she said, with only a slight change of subject, 'I'm glad that it'll be the weekend. Val will be here with you.' She didn't qualify that remark, and they drove on to Emberton in silence, both of them aware that, however golden their separate futures, they were going to miss their brief few months together.

The following morning, Tamsin drove out to the Trading Estate on her own, Kim saying that she would drive her own car and meet up with her twin for lunch at Bordens, and then travel to Burnthouse in convoy.

'There's stuff I need to do in town,' she said. 'Building Society, and a couple of extras for dinner tonight if there's going to be six of us. We'll get through it all quicker if we go separately, and you don't need me to buy a clock and a bin, after all, and then when we've unloaded and I've helped you stow it all, I can get back to see to tonight's dinner – but I'll help you get all the stuff into the Discovery now.' She glanced towards the sofa. 'It's going to look empty, when it's all gone,' and felt a faint pang of imminent loneliness, which she swiftly quelled. Life went on, after all; hers would too, when Val had got himself sorted out. It was no good thinking, as she nearly was, that her time with her long-lost twin had been too short.

Tamsin brought the Discovery from the Yard car-park to just outside Romans to load up, there was too much to keep carrying it over the road. They packed as carefully as they could so that it wouldn't rattle about, and then Kim shut the rear door and gave it a pat. 'There you go, all loaded. I'll see you at Bordens around half-twelve,' and stood to wave as Tamsin drove off before going into the house to sort out her own rather later departure.

So it was that Tamsin was on her own when she went into the furniture store to complete her errands, and had an unexpected and disquieting encounter.

She had found everything she needed under one roof, which was a plus: six fat and squashy velvety cushions in shades of dark red and gold that would go nicely with the upholstery and curtains, and a not-too-large swing bin, which sat in her trolley rather precariously on top of the cushions, and had picked out a small bamboo table with a glass top, which would have to travel to the check-out, and probably to the car park as well, separately with the aid of an assistant later on, and was looking at the wide selection of electric wall clocks that the store had to offer, when a woman came round the corner of the aisle and stopped when she saw Tamsin, crying, 'Kim! What a lovely surprise!'

Tamsin had never set eyes on her before. She was slim and suntanned, with a mop of fair curly hair bleached by the sun, and dressed in old jeans and a thick sweater as if she had just come off a boat, and she carried a basket in which there sat a frying pan, and not much else. Seeing Tamsin looking at it – for clues as much as anything – she went on cheerfully, 'Oh, don't look at this! We lost the old one over the side off Finistère, and Donald does love a good fry-up, he was missing it like a lost dog! How are you? – it's been ages since we last saw you!' and she waited, smiling, for a response. Tamsin was just searching for the right words in which to reply, when a thin dark man with equally curly hair came round the corner after the woman, he also looked as if he had just come off a boat. The woman turned to him immediately.

'Don, look who I've found!' She turned back to Tamsin, smiling happily. 'Can we assume from your shopping that you and Val have actually completed on a house somewhere, and are going to move in? What fun!' and then the man – presumably Donald – said, before Tamsin could get a word in, 'This isn't Kim, Shona,' and then, to Tamsin, 'You have to be Diana, surely?' He sounded Irish – looked it, too, come to that. Tamsin said, with relief, 'Yes.' Short-lived relief. Shona said, 'Oh, my God!' and looked as if she could have bitten her tongue out immediately after. The man changed the blanket wrapped in plastic that he was carrying to his left hand and held out his right.

'Donald Moran. This is my partner, Shona, we know Kim through the Sailing Club in Emberton, and of course we know of you from the same source.'

Tamsin took the hand, not sure if she was shaking hands with the enemy or a friend, but prompted by the good manners she had been taught from childhood. She said, 'And you obviously know who I am – Diana Carey, Kim's twin – also known as "Tamsin" these days.'

Shona said, as if impulsively, 'You are Kim's twin?' and looked as if she could have bitten her tongue out immediately afterwards, and Donald said, 'Shut up, Shona, and use your eyes!' and Tamsin thought, if anyone struck a match now, the whole store would go up! She said, trying to smile, 'We haven't actually done a DNA test, but as we have history and witnesses to confirm it, I think I can say "yes" to that.' She didn't want to say the next obvious thing, but it came out almost without her own volition. 'What made you ask – ask like that, I mean, as if I might be just pretending?'

Shona opened her mouth to reply, but Donald interrupted her. 'Not right here and now, Shona, for goodness' sake!' He turned to Tamsin. 'Is this all your shopping? Why don't we take all this to the checkout and get it out of the way, and go upstairs for a coffee? I think we need to talk.'

Tamsin thought that too, but she wasn't sure that she wanted to. She said, 'I just have to choose a clock and pick up a coffee table – or get someone else to do that for me, even better,' and she smiled, although she didn't feel like smiling.

'I can do that for you,' said Donald, handing the blanket bag to Shona, 'just show me where it is.'

Tamsin picked up the nearest clock and put it in her trolley, and the two of them followed her to the furnishings area, and thence to the checkout. All the while they were doing this, her mind was whirling in confusion. Friends? Enemies? They knew Kim, they said, but she herself had never seen them before, or heard them mentioned. She felt a bit as if she was under arrest, with the two of them following her so closely, but surely that was ridiculous! She thought she might be able to escape once she had been through the checkout, but Donald said, 'Hang on while I pay for this, and I'll carry the table out for you and help you get it in your car,' and since she would obviously need further help with the table, it would be rude just to call up an assistant and walk out. So she waited, and she was to be glad that she had.

'So, which is your car?' Donald asked, as they stepped out into the courtyard. Tamsin couldn't point to it since her hands were full of cushions, but she nodded towards the Discovery and said, 'That one,' and caught – thought she caught – Donald and Shona, obviously recognising it, exchanging a look.

★

'Right, let's get your stuff aboard,' said Donald, stepping out towards it with the table.

'It'll have to go on the back seat,' Tamsin told him, hurrying after him. 'The back is full already.'

Donald had reached the Discovery, he paused, looking in through the window. He said, 'You're not joking, are you? What are you doing, moving house?'

'Not exactly, but near enough, I suppose. Moving in.'

Neither Donald nor Shona had any comment on this, either, Shona crossing over to a nearby jeep with their own shopping, and Donald shoving the table, with its legs in the air, along the back seat of the Discovery.

'Give me the bin – it'll fit between the legs, I think,' was all that he said.

Loading complete, the three of them walked together back to the store, which had a café on the top floor as Donald had said, serving tea, coffee, sandwiches and cakes. They ordered a latte each and took them to a small table, and when they were sat down, Shona said, 'You must think we're behaving like a pair of kidnappers – but we aren't. It's just that something happened last night, and we think you should know about it,' and Tamsin's heart sank. It never meant anything good when people said that. She said, 'You said you were down at the Sailing Club,' and waited.

Donald said, sounding as if he was choosing his words with care, 'We've been away cruising a good bit of the summer – we went down to the Azores, not racing or anything, just to take a look round and stopping here and there going and coming back. We didn't do the Med this time, but we explored round Spain and Portugal and looked in on Brittany, and we got home mid-morning yesterday. We need a bit of work done on the rigging after all that, so we pulled into the little dock up by the Yard for a couple of nights, and Merlin – you'll know Merlin of course – came over to check on what we needed doing, and quite naturally, after all that time, we got talking.' He paused, and Shona took up the tale.

'Of course, we wanted to be filled in on what had been happening while we were away, had anything exciting happened that we had missed? And he said it had been quite an eventful summer, one way and another, and were we asking about racing results and who had won the Moonraker Championship, or what? But we knew about that, because Donald got it up on the computer, so I said, give us the local gossip – and he did.' She paused then, and Tamsin said, 'I can imagine!' in unintentionally heartfelt tone, and Donald looked at her and then away again.

'He said – Merlin said – which did we want first, the good news or the bad?' Shona continued, 'And we said we'd start with the good news, please, and he grinned at us and said, "Well you're never going to believe this one. Val Harries has got himself hooked at last!" and then he told us who to, of course, and we remembered that we had seen her around with him – we don't go down to the Club that much, even when we're home, which isn't that often, actually.' She added, by way of explanation, 'We live on the boat and work from it – I write sentimental novels, and Don puts them up on Kindle for me, along with other people's, and we tend to move around a bit during the good weather because we really only need internet contact and a mobile phone, and spend the winter holed up in the Marina, working a bit more seriously. But we do know Kim, although we never met up with you. We did know you existed, of course. You didn't always come down to the Club with them.'

'Three's a crowd,' Tamsin explained, and Shona nodded sympathetically.

'I can see that. And then, Donald asked, what was the bad news, then? And he said…we couldn't believe it…that the Club Committee had requested that Francis Chillingworth resign his membership. And when we asked "why, for God's sake?" as obviously we did, he said it was because of some apocryphal story put about by someone who listened at keyholes, and he sounded really disgusted as he said it. Which is understandable.'

'But he didn't resign – he hasn't resigned,' said Tamsin.

'So Merlin told us,' said Donald. 'But he hasn't been back there since, Diana, which isn't the best move he ever made – if you don't mind me saying so.'

'He's had a lot to do,' Tamsin said, knowing it sounded lame.

'Surely not so much that he couldn't spare time for a drink with his mates occasionally?'

'I think he feels a bit as if he hasn't any – not down there, anyway,' said Tamsin, wondering as she spoke why she had said it. It wasn't their business, was it? But for some reason she instinctively trusted these two, she got the feeling they were playing on the right team.

'That, if you'll forgive the vulgarity, is bollocks,' Donald told her. Tamsin gave him a steady look. She said, 'If that's true, then they didn't declare themselves.'

'They didn't realise that they needed to,' said Shona, returning the look. 'We didn't, and we've known him for years.'

'But you weren't here when it all went pear-shaped,' Tamsin reminded her. 'You were living it up in the Azores. And if you hadn't been, I doubt if you would have realised what was going on either. After all, nobody else did, not until the storm broke.'

'We damn well know now, after last night!' said Donald, with some force, and a silence fell. Tamsin broke it.

'You do know that he and I are engaged? Merlin did tell you?'

'Yes, he did.' That hadn't sounded exactly congratulatory. Tamsin made no comment, however, but waited to see what happened next, and Donald and Shona exchanged a look. Shona asked, 'Will you tell her, or shall I?' and Tamsin's heart sank. That hadn't sounded good.

'You start. I'll interrupt.'

'That sounds about right.' Shona picked up her teaspoon and began to fiddle with it, looking at Tamsin rather than at what she was doing. 'Last night, we went down to the Club. This time of year, it isn't open on week nights usually, but there was a talk or something so the bar was open, and as we hadn't seen everyone for months, we thought we'd just drop by when the talk was over, see who was there. Quite a lot of our crowd were, as it turned out.' She paused, and Donald said, 'Rob Lambert – you'll know him, and Val's sister Penny. Pete, who used to crew for Francis. Max Carruthers and his mates, although they're not exactly bosom pals of ours, some others we know well.' He hesitated. 'Merlin hadn't given me any clues. We accidentally trod in the wasps' nest.'

Tamsin made no comment. Shona took up the tale, but as if she did so reluctantly. 'Obviously everyone was ready and willing to tell us the news – Val's engagement was top of the list, that was Penny, of course, and then someone else said, had we heard that Francis Chillingworth was going to be married at last, too? They said it as if they were pleased about that as well, should you be interested, but Max Carruthers sort of snorted, and said, "Yes, to some little tart from London who says she's Kim's long-lost twin, although how she makes that out, who knows? Kim's from New Zealand!" And Pete said, "Steady on, Max," and Max said, "She's just an opportunist, Pete, make no mistake – and she heard that Francis is supposed to be a multi-millionaire and made a dead set at him. Although that's a bit debatable since Mummy threw him out at last! First off, he sold his boat to raise some ready cash to live on, and have you seen that place he's bought for himself? It's a tip, even the house is falling down, and the buildings, and there's no land to speak of and what there is, is just a wilderness! It's a miracle he even got a mortgage." Words to that effect, it's not a direct quote.'

Tamsin said, painfully. 'Some of that is true. Not all of it, not by a long shot.'

'That's what we thought,' said Donald, watching her.

'We thought it was probably true about the place he's buying,' Shona offered. 'After all, that's provable – people only have to go and look.'

'It's a project,' said Tamsin. 'He needs one…it's a listed building that's been allowed to fall into neglect, it will be beautiful when he's finished with it. But it's not true about his mother throwing him out – he left by mutual agreement.'

'I'd like to believe you, but it's not good enough,' said Donald, watching her. 'He's run that place for her for years now.'

'It's hard to explain – it's not my story to tell.'

'Let me help you,' said Donald, not moving his eyes from her face. 'There's a tale that used to go around that he murdered his father's mistress and it was all hushed up because of the money and the connections. Although presumably he didn't, or at least it was never proved since he was never arrested.'

'And we all know where that rumour began!' Tamsin retorted. 'And it has been proved, anyway – disproved, rather.' She hesitated. She didn't know these people, it was a difficult one to call. Finally, she said, 'When Kim and I met each other again after all the years, it sort of stirred things up. The Police found the real killer, and it wasn't Francis.'

Donald gave her a ruminative look. He said, 'The woman had red hair, I remember someone saying that once. And a child.'

'Two children,' said Tamsin, woodenly.

'Twins?'

'Yes. And please, don't ask me anything more. Just believe me, Francis didn't kill her. He just found the body, and he didn't even find it first. So…'

'Oh, I believe you. He never struck me as the murderous type anyway.'

Tamsin could have kissed him. She said, 'Thank you. And you can work some of the rest of it out for yourselves, I expect. But just to clear up a few points, he sold the Moonraker because he wants something bigger now, and he doesn't come to the Club because bloody little Max Carruthers won't get off his back! He…well, I think he just can't be bothered any more. He's moved on. And finally, although it isn't really your business, there is no mortgage on Burnthouse!'

She could almost read the thoughts in Donald's mind, he was an intelligent man. He would add two and two and make four, no doubt of it, but she thought he wouldn't say anything, and she was right. About his conjectures, at least. The only clue he gave was to say, 'This discovery of the real killer – was it reported in the papers?'

'I never saw anything. He was dead anyway, it was old news. The reporters wouldn't have been able to make anything of it, where would have been the point? His death was reported – it was quite spectacular – but nothing more. I think – I don't know – that Francis and his mother may have asked the Police to play it down. They'd had enough, I think.'

'But if, for instance, someone asked the Police for confirmation of what you just told me, they would give it?'

'No reason why they wouldn't. But why ask at all? It's history, and only gossip ever accused Francis of anything anyway.' Not absolutely true, but they needn't know that. 'I just wish the whole thing would die a natural death – and it would have, long ago, if it wasn't for your friend Max Carruthers.'

There was a silence then, that drew out until Tamsin began to feel uncomfortable. She saw Donald exchange a quick glance with Shona, and then look down at his coffee cup, playing with the spoon as if his mind was occupied elsewhere. Shona said, 'We have to tell her, Don. It might be…well, relevant.'

'I know.' He raised his head at last and looked straight at Tamsin. 'This may mean nothing at all – it might be just blether, like everything else the man says. But…' he paused, and Shona said, 'Go on, you can't stop there.' Donald said, not moving his eyes from Tamsin's face, 'When we left, we walked back along the foreshore to the Yard – there was a good moon and the tide not long turned, we could see our way and it's quicker than going by the road. As we passed below the car park, we heard someone talking, quite quietly. He said, "…but you can't argue, if it's true, a man who committed such a foul murder and got away with it just because his family were rich, should be in jail for the rest of his life!" And then he paused, and added, "Or dead." And he sounded really vindictive as he said it.'

'It doesn't have to be taken too seriously,' Kim said, but she sounded guarded as she spoke. 'It's the sort of over-statement that people make when they want to be dramatic – or prove a point, come to that. And Max Carruthers is a master of the genre. Also, you don't know, and neither does Donald, that it was him speaking. It was dark. It doesn't even have to be Francis he was speaking about.'

'I know that,' said Tamsin, not sounding as if she believed in it.

The two of them were sitting at a small table in the banal environment of Bordens' rooftop café, with a glass of orange juice and a sandwich each to keep them from starving before tonight's dinner, and Tamsin had effectively destroyed both their appetites by telling the tale of her morning encounter, with its disquieting postscript.

'Little Maxie dislikes Francis, we know that anyway – but he wouldn't kill him, why should he? What happened – or didn't happen – was nothing to do with him, after all.' Kim was talking as much to convince herself as Tamsin. Anyway, she wouldn't have said Max Carruthers would have the guts, it was all too Agatha Christie to take seriously, surely.

'I know, I know. I just hate even the thought that someone would say that about Francis. I know it's only words, but…well, it's nasty. It wasn't a joke, it was a declared opinion. Probably not a statement of intent, but even if it never gets that far…' She paused there, considering. 'Do you know Donald Moran?'

'I've met him – only a couple of times, if he's who I think he is. He's an IT man, he and his partner live on a boat. Yes? Am I thinking of the right person?'

'Yes.' Tamsin picked up her sandwich, looked at it, and put it down again, and Kim asked, 'Why does Max Carruthers dislike Francis so much, do you think? What did Francis ever do to him?'

'As to that, you know as much as I do. According to Gary, he pinched Max's girlfriend but didn't actually want her. Not sure who to blame there. I wasn't around at the time.'

'The girlfriend, from what I understood. And he thought Francis was a public school snob. Is he, do you think? He is a bit quiet in company, but he doesn't look down on people – or seem to, anyway. But I never met one, only read about them in books.'

'For heaven's sake, he only went to Winterbourne! It's a Public School, yes, and a good one – but it's not exactly Eton or Harrow! Lots of people have probably never even heard of it.'

'Max Carruthers obviously had.'

'His mother is a friend of Francis' mother – or likes to think she is, from what I gather. So I suppose she would know what sort of school it was. And that was another thing – according to Gary, when his mother worked at Vachells, he and Francis were great mates – still are, in fact. But he never played with Maxie, even though, at least according to the two of them, his mother was a close friend, not an employee. Although I have some doubts about that.'

'Well, so what? Francis was presumably at a boarding school quite early on, and anyway, there must be a good two years between them, and that's a lot when you're young. And come to that, Gary is very likable. Max was probably a spoiled brat even that far back.'

'Whatever, Max obviously does still think Francis is a crashing snob.' Tamsin looked gloomy. 'And his mother thinks Mary is Dorset's answer to the Queen.'

'I can't see why. The Vachells are just farmers, have been for centuries as far as I can work out.'

'The Chillingworths aren't.'

'They're not aristocracy though. What's the matter with them both?'

'Plain envy, as far as I can work out, for Max anyway. The big house. The money.' Tamsin sounded weary. 'Max Carruthers seems to have implied that there wasn't any left – how much was it? Five or six million that Francis is suppose to have inherited, didn't Val say? He'd have had to work at it to get through that!' She was scornful now, but Kim looked thoughtful.

'Unlucky investments could have done it, I suppose – except Val doesn't think he made any.' She looked at her twin, reluctant to put her next question but asking it anyway. 'Would it make any difference – to you – if it turned out that he had?' and Tamsin gave a snort of laughter.

'Now you sound like little Maxie! He didn't – he hasn't – and I wouldn't care if he had.'

'You know that for a fact?' Kim asked, curious now for there was something in her twin's assertion that carried with it conviction.

'My father does. Fifty million, at the last count, according to Eloise. But you don't know that. And officially, neither do I. I'm not even sure that I quite believe in it. So...'

Kim said nothing, and after a minute, Tamsin said, 'I find it difficult to take in too,' and they both relaxed. Kim said, 'Don't blame you. I take it, your father has checked?'

'I take that, too. Double-checked, I expect, aren't I his precious daughter? But it doesn't make any difference, I'd still marry him if he only had fifty pence! And I hate the idea of some jealous little twerp wishing him dead because of it!'

Their conversation had come full circle. Did either of them really believe that Max Carruthers would have the bottle to kill someone? Kim wondered. Or to get someone to do it for him, that would maybe be more like him. She thought not, but that was just her opinion; she had him down as a boastful weakling, all spite and showing-off and no follow-up action, but she could be wrong.

Assassins cost money. She had no idea of the going rate, but it wouldn't be cheap. She pushed the ridiculous thought out of her head, and said instead, 'Eat your sandwich, you'll need to keep your strength up. We've all that stuff to unpack yet.'

'Oh God, yes, so we have!' Tamsin picked up her own sandwich and took a bite out of it, chewing thoughtfully. 'You said you'd met Donald Moran. What did you make of him? Is he…well, reliable as a source of information, do you think?'

'He's Irish. He has a bit of a reputation.' Kim considered these statements, and moderated them. 'People like him, and he's supposed to be good at what he does. But he's a bit of a wild card, from what I heard.'

'But trustworthy?'

'I never heard anyone say that he wasn't.' Kim paused. This was a hard one. She said, 'If you want to know what I think, I think that if he and Shona really did overhear what he said they overheard, he was quite right to mention it to you – since he ran into you. It's too much of a coincidence, almost as if it was meant…' She tailed off, and shrugged her shoulders. 'People don't usually say things like that. Not nice people. And I'm not saying that I believe Max Carruthers would actually kill someone. If it was him, he was most likely just sounding off.'

'Should I tell Francis, do you think?'

'I think he's probably heard it all before,' said Kim.

'If he hurt Francis…' Tamsin let the unthinkable end to that sentence die on the air, and Kim gave a rueful laugh.

'So far, the only person round here who has managed to hurt Francis, is Francis. Let it rest, Tam. It's just words, and you don't know for certain it was even Max Carruthers that said it.'

The unlikely idea that it might have been someone else, some unknown person bearing a grudge of his own, was even worse if anything. They finished their lunch, unusually subdued for them, and made their way back to their respective cars, neither of them able to decide what would be the right thing to do. To tell Francis would only stir up possibly unnecessary trouble, and Mad Max would deny it anyway. Not to tell just might be taking an unacceptable risk. Deadlock. They were both of them relieved to reach the comparative sanity of Burnthouse.

There was no immediate sign of Francis, but as Tamsin noted with grim humour, there were no Police cars either, so he hadn't been murdered in their absence. There was, however, the electrical retailers' van, with a man unloading the washing machine: from a quick glimpse into the back of the van, this seemed to be the last item.

'Let's go and check it out. He might be there,' said Tamsin, heading for the back door, and Kim followed, if she was honest, with equal curiosity. The first thing to strike them both was the absence of the three tea chest blocking the passage, and Tamsin pushed the office door open with curiosity, as well as to see if Francis was lurking within. He wasn't. The three tea chests were now sitting on a dust sheet in the middle of the rug, and apart from them, the office appeared to be fully furnished: shelves along the opposite wall two filing cabinets just inside the door, the desks and their chairs in position. One or two items intended for the walls leaned against the empty shelving.

'Looks promising,' said Kim, as they withdrew, carefully closing the door again behind them. 'Come on – let's investigate.'

In the freezer room, the big freezer and the upright fridge-freezer were both in place, with red lights shining and a gentle hum to show they had been switched on, and more important, were in working order.

'Be able to put stuff in them by tomorrow,' said Kim, with approval. 'Come on – what's going on next door?'

Next door was the seat of the action: two men already had the dryer in place, and were just shifting the washing machine into a position where they could connect up the water pipes.

'Hello girls,' said the electrician, whom they had already met. 'Nearly done in here, so you can wash your smalls tomorrow,' and he gave them a grin.

'It almost looks as if we might even be living here tomorrow, too,' said Tamsin, who somewhere at the back of her mind still found this hard to believe.

'You better be, after all our hard work,' the plumber told her. 'All connected up, you are, and good to go. ''scuse me, miss, I need to be working just there…''

The twins withdrew out of the way with sounds of appreciation, they had work of their own to do. Back at the van, Steve was waiting for them.

'Hello girls! What do you think of the show so far?'

Diana opened the back of the Discovery and gave him a happy smile. 'It all looks great – is Francis over in the mobile home?'

'No, I just stopped by to tell you. He went home. Young Matt was going that way, and there was nothing much he could do here, so he went home to pack – or that's what he said. He said he'd see you tonight.' He grinned at her. 'Moving in tomorrow, he tells me. Would you like a hand with that lot?' He was looking in the back of the Discovery, with raised eyebrows.

'We can manage, thank you, none of it's heavy – but if you're going that way, this clock needs to be in the office.'

'OK, I'll drop it in as I go past.' Steve took it from her and turned to move away, saying over his shoulder, 'Come and have a look at the kitchen when you've stowed that lot – tell me what you think.'

It took some time and a certain amount of effort to transfer everything to the mobile home and pile it onto and under the dining table, and once there, it looked as if it couldn't possibly fit into the cupboard space available.

'Take it one step at a time,' said practical Kim. 'Plates and things can go in the cupboard next door, there won't be room to put them in here, and after all, it's quite normal to keep your china somewhere out of the kitchen.'

'Yes – in the dining room,' said Tamsin. 'This is the dining room, technically.'

'You know what I mean,' Kim told her, lifting a pile of Melamine dinner plates. 'You bring that lot – let's get the job done. We can leave the mugs in here, on those hooks.'

For the next hour, they worked hard – fortunately, Kim had the forethought to bring a roll of bin bags with her to take the discarded packaging – putting the small microwave above the fridge, where it could be plugged in and turned on and off easily, and arranging saucepans in the cupboard beside the cooker, and the Pyrex dishes for cooking in the cupboard opposite to the fridge. Cleaning things and a bucket under the sink, cutlery and cooking tools in their respective drawers. Somehow, it all fitted in, with kettle and toaster on the side of the worktop farthest away from the sink. Finally, Kim beat the last cardboard box flat, and they stood back to admire their work. Tamsin heaved a deep sigh.

'I'm just starting to believe that we might even be living here tomorrow,' she said, and Kim shot her a glance.

'Collywobbles?'

'A bit. It's a big step to take. Let's go back and get all that stuff on the back seat, shall we?'

'You lived with that man – Rupert, or whatever his name was, that you told me about.'

'That was different. I didn't love him, there was nothing at stake.'

They brought in the cushions and the swing bin, and went back for the coffee table, which they could manage easily between them, it wasn't that big, or even heavy; just awkward. When it was in place and the cushions flung on the seats, Tamsin collapsed on the widest one.

'Phew, that's done! And it'll be even worse for you and Val, the house is so much bigger.'

'Oh well, if we're going to talk about bigger houses...' said Kim, grinning, and saw her twin wince.

'Ouch, I see what you mean! Just let me get these cushions arranged, and then let's go and look at the kitchen before we go home – before we go back to Romans.' She caught Kim's eye and they both dissolved into giggles. 'It's going to take some getting used to.'

Kim looked at her watch, still smiling. 'We need to get back anyway – we've got dinner to cook for six people!'

'We?' asked Tamsin. She distributed the cushions and stood back to admire the effect. 'That looks better, doesn't it?'

It looked to Kim as if her twin had a real knack for home-making. She said, 'It all looks great. What about bed linen? You said you had some.'

'We have. So I'm told, anyway. We have all the stuff from Francis' flat out at Vachells, but I don't know what it consists of. Enough to make up a bed, I daresay. It's at Shortlanesend, he said he'd bring it over tomorrow so I hope he remembers.'

'Then let's go and look at that kitchen.'

In the kitchen, the end wall had been completely unblocked, and work was going forward on repairing the brickwork at the back of the old fireplace and the stone archway that framed it. It already looked quite different, and the kitchen looked bigger for the clearance, too. The twins admired it: with the new Aga within the arch, and cupboards and worktops to flank it, it would look amazing: there was even another old bread oven revealed by the devastation. It would be a real showplace when it was finished, Kim said, and the carpenter, who was busy unscrewing the battered old oak doors from the cupboards under the windows and stacking them into a heap to take to his workshop for renovation, grunted and said, 'You ain't seen nothing yet, lady,' and gave them both a grin. Everyone seemed to be smiling at them today, Tamsin thought. A good omen? She did hope so, after her earlier encounter she could do with one!

'Right,' said Kim, as they headed back to the cars, 'Time to go home and think about dinner – and come to that, Francis isn't the only one who needs to pack. You do, too.'

'I can do that while you cook the dinner,' Tamsin suggested, but without enthusiasm. The thought of packing made her feel a bit desolate for some reason, she had enjoyed her time with Kim, she didn't want it to come to an end, even if something even better was beginning…she realised she was getting her thoughts in a tangle and came back to the here and now to hear Kim saying, '…do that later. You're going to do the pudding first! There's a brilliant recipe in that book I gave you for Lemon Flan, that even you can't screw up – and it only takes about five minutes actual cooking.'

'I've never—'

'—I know, and it's time you did. That poor man of yours will starve to death unless you pull yourself together.' Kim paused with her hand on the door of her car; she knew what Tamsin was feeling because she was feeling it herself. She said, more gently, 'I know it seems like the end of everything – but it isn't, it's the beginning. You know that, and you wouldn't have it any other way, be honest.'

'It's just that it's been fun,' Tamsin said, trying to excuse her momentary wobble. 'And before you say it, I know – all good things have to come to an end.'

'So they do. But tomorrow – and the days that follow it – will be good too. So get in that monster, and follow me home – it's time for a cookery lesson!'

XXVIII

After a highly successful dinner party that had gone on for longer than either expected or intended, both Kim and Tamsin overslept, and unusually, it was Tamsin who had woken first. Kim staggered out blearily and went to bang on her door, only to find the door ajar and Tamsin, only half-dressed, sitting on the edge of her bed in the bottom bunk staring with blank eyes at an open suitcase, half-filled apparently with underwear, and with a large pile of miscellaneous sweaters and other garments piled beside it.

'I don't know how it's happened, but yesterday afternoon I put all my summer things into the bigger cases that Daddy and Eloise brought with my winter stuff, like you told me – ordered me, rather! – and I thought there'd still be some space because it would take up less room than sweaters and things, but there wasn't – and now, I can't get all of this into the case that's left and my holdall. It's kittened, or something.'

'Or something,' Kim agreed. 'Would it be anything to do with all that shopping you've been doing all summer, do you think?'

'It just could be,' said Tamsin, thinking about it. 'Yes, it definitely could be, now you come to mention it. Do we have any black bags? I could perhaps put my shoes into one. That might help – it would free up the holdall, at least.'

'I'm just going down for a shower, I'll find you some. Finish dressing and come down, I'll put the kettle on. You look as if you could do with some strong coffee, and I know I could.'

'I already had one,' said Tamsin, yawning. 'A shower, I mean. Coffee would be good. Black, like the bags. Strong, ditto. I seem to have an awful lot of shoes.'

'Get some proper clothes on,' Kim advised her, and headed downstairs to see to the kettle, the shower, and possibly some toast. It was already well past nine o'clock.

They re-convened a bare quarter of an hour later over two mugs of powerfully strong coffee, Tamsin looking a bit sheepish.

'I think I must have drunk rather more wine than I intended last night,' she confessed. 'My brain doesn't seem to be working properly – did we decide on a programme for this morning, or what?'

'Well, sort of.' Kim took a sip of her coffee and looked pensive. 'To be honest, I'm not very clear on that myself, but I think it went like this: Francis is going out to Burnthouse with someone called Ronnie, but not that early as they have to clear all his stuff out of Ernie's office first. Val is going straight up there from home when Francis rings to say that he's there, there's no point in him coming out here and back when he'll be only just down the road.'

'Who's Ronnie?' Tamsin asked. The name was new to her.

'I don't know, but everyone else seemed to. I think he might be some sort of local computer geek.'

Tamsin nodded wisely. 'That figures. We shall be needing one of those.'

'You will today. But I suspect, not after Francis gets his hand back; I think you may be about to marry one. But after that, which was clear enough, it all got a bit blurred.' She paused to consider. 'Bennie was involved somewhere – I think she's going to bring Francis's stuff and the bedding over some time in the farm truck – but then there was something I lost track of, involving Val going back with her. I was out in the kitchen fetching more wine at that point – as if we needed it by that time!'

'The Merc?' Tamsin hazarded. 'Someone will have to drive that over, sometime.'

'Could be. It would make sense.' Kim smothered a yawn. 'That leaves you and me. If we put all your stuff in the Discovery – when you've finished packing it, that is – we can do the fresh and frozen stuff at the supermarket on our way over, and sort everything out when we get back to the farm. Toast?' She pushed the rack across to Tamsin, who took a slice but did not immediately butter it.

'I suppose we ought to ring and check that there's nothing that's been forgotten, that we could get on our way round. There's bound to be something. There always is.'

'We could, I suppose. It might be a plan.'

They both fell silent after that, each of them knowing they had been talking for the sake of it. Tamsin buttered her toast with unnecessary concentration but made no attempt to eat it, and Kim went on sipping her coffee. Finally, Kim broke what had turned into a fairly long pause.

'Don't you feel as if someone had stolen a whole lifetime from us? One that we should have shared and can't get back because it's too late?'

'Yes. We've had just four months, when we should have had almost twenty-six years...it doesn't seem fair, does it?'

'We did have the first three years,' Kim said, fairly.

'We don't remember them. I don't, anyway.'

'I think I do – a bit.' Kim frowned. 'I think I can remember what our mother looked like...and I think I remember another child, or did I dream it?'

'I don't. For me, life began with Eloise and Daddy. But then, I did get a bang on the head...just like Francis did, later on. It was all so violent—' She broke off.

'Very strong emotions often are.'

They both fell silent, then Tamsin yawned, smothering it with her hand. 'I feel as if I was awake all night – that's wine for you! I should sleep like a log tonight, that's one thing!' and Kim laughed.

'That I doubt, somehow. Chance might be a fine thing.'

'Not all night,' Tamsin said ambiguously, and Kim said, 'Eat your toast. You've got to finish packing for your adventure yet.'

Tamsin's phone rang just as they were clearing their breakfast things into the sink. It turned out to be Bennie – Francis, it seemed, had been thought-reading.'

'He said, when you go to the supermarket today, could you get...' she paused. 'Hang on a minute, I wrote it down – oh, I've got it. Paperclips, drawing pins, a stapler, a good pair of scissors and some Sellotape – he's been using Ernie's stuff, but it's a bit far to come for a drawing pin. And A4 paper, 80 GSM, whatever that means, and some envelopes – A4 and just ordinary eight inch ones.' Tamsin made wild writing gestures to Kim, who came over with an old supermarket receipt and a pencil. Tamsin deployed these on the table and said, 'Can you just read through that again slowly, while I write it down – I'll never remember it, not this morning.'

'That bad, is it?' Bennie asked, sympathetically. 'I know I woke up with a thick head – it was a good evening, wasn't it?'

'It did take off a bit – not sure it was a goodbye party or a hello one, though.'

'Sort of, one door closes and another one opens, you mean?'

'Exactly that. Now, give me all that again…' She scribbled frantically as Bennie repeated the list. 'Right, I've got all that down. Anything else?'

'Better get him some pencils and a rubber while you're at it. And a packet of ball-point pens. His mind isn't really on the job this morning, and they're bound to come in useful.'

'Neither is mine,' Tamsin admitted.

Bennie made no comment on that. She said, 'I'll be over with the bedding and stuff around lunchtime, I expect – I imagine you've got plenty to do to fill the time.'

'You imagine right. What's he doing? Has he gone over yet?'

'He and Ron are dismantling things in the office. Did you want to speak to him?'

'No, leave him in peace. I'll see him later.'

'I don't think "peace" is the right word, exactly,' said Bennie, laughing. 'Make sure you've got some heating on to air the mattress.' She rang off, and Tamsin carried the list through into the kitchen.

'Fortunately, we can get all of it in the supermarket,' she said, studying it.

'Then just add bog rolls and kitchen roll and put it in a safe place, and go up and finish your packing,' Kim told her. 'We need to be off soon – there'll be masses to do when we get to Burnthouse. It's moving day, remember!'

'I'm remembering.' Tamsin unexpectedly gave her twin a hug – unexpected to herself as well as Kim. 'It's been great fun – and I'm so, so glad I ran off the road that night.'

'Me too,' said Kim, returning the hug. 'Now scram! There's only twenty-four hours in a day, and we've wasted nearly ten of them already!'

By the time the twins had raided the supermarket and completely filled a large trolley, balancing the bag of toilet rolls precariously on the top of the heap, it was well past eleven o'clock. The Discovery was already groaning under the weight of Tamsin's worldly goods, which included a cardboard box of pictures and ornaments and two more of books that her parents had brought from her bedroom and her flat in London, so quite a few of the shopping bags had to be piled onto the back seat.

'We should have put the back down,' said Kim, ruefully, trying to fit the packet of toilet rolls onto the floor. 'I sort of forgot that we were starting from scratch here – and Francis didn't help, with all his office stuff!' She gave one last push and slammed the door quickly, before the toilet rolls could bounce out again. 'There, that's it! Now, let's hit the road to the next chapter of your already interesting life!' They grinned at each other.

'I've got collywobbles in my tummy,' Tamsin admitted, as they climbed aboard. 'It's a huge blindfold step into the rest of my life, and I'm not quite sure what I might tread in.'

'A large quantity of assorted dung?' Kim suggested. 'And a steep learning curve leading, let's hope, to a sunny blue sky.'

'How poetic!' Tamsin engaged the gear and pulled out of the parking space, but she was laughing as she said it. 'Wish I had your faith in a sunny sky – I think I might be throwing in my lot with a hurricane.' She didn't sound as if she minded.

Burnthouse, when they reached it, was busy. Val's car was there, and Ernie's truck, and an unfamiliar red van with its rear doors open on emptiness. Also, the builders' truck, parked in the yard rather than outside the house, but fortunately leaving enough space for Tamsin to reverse the Discovery right up to the field gate, restored to its position since she had last seen it. Beyond this, Matt was hammering fence posts into the ground surrounding the gravel, and the door to the mobile home or whatever you wanted to call it, stood open. Apart from Matt, who raised a hand in greeting, and the traffic, there was no other sign of human life.

'Bennie must be already here, then,' said Tamsin, as she slid to the ground and stood looking around her. 'Where do we start?'

'Let's get rid of the stationery first, and say hello to our men,' said Kim, going to the back and opening it. 'Come on – we can do it all in one trip of we load up carefully. Then we can come back for the cold box. You take that—' She thrust the two packets of A4 paper into her twin's arms. 'I'll stack the bag with the envelopes on top, that doesn't weigh anything, and I can bring the other one – which does. Come on, let's go.'

The office, when they reached it, was looking completely different, although not necessarily improved. The tea chests had vanished from the floor, as they already knew since they had almost tripped over them in the passage, and their contents were stacked anyhow onto the carpet, plus a pile on the smaller of the two desks together with a heap of files, and a further overflow that had spilled onto the top of the shelving. The larger desk held a computer, a printer and scanner, and a wide computer screen, none of it connected to anything, and a digital radio which was playing loud music. Also a cardboard box, full of printer inks and two filing baskets, the top one of which was full of yet more paperwork. Val was kneeling on the floor, transferring the books onto one of the bookcases where Francis sorted them out, with one-and-a-half hands by this time: Sacha was curled comfortably under the bigger desk, he thumped his tail when he saw them, which was more than either of the men did; they neither of them heard the twins arrive until Kim asked, in a loud, clear voice to drown out the music, 'Where do you want us to put this lot?' when they both jumped and swung round. Tamsin said the first thing that came into her head.

'I hope you've done what you were told and covered that hand! Those books are all dusty!' and Francis grinned at her and held it out, neatly encased in a surgical glove from which the fingers had been cut so that it protected only the bandage.

'Yes, ma'am,' he said, and put down the book he was holding in order to gather her into his arms as Val scrambled to his feet to greet Kim with a kiss.

'So you got here at last,' Val said.

Once she had got her breath back, Tamsin looked around her. Three hooks had been drilled into the wall above the shelves, and the two cork boards hung there together with the randomly chosen clock; Tamsin was pleased to note that it looked all right. One of the bookcases was already nearly full, the remaining shelves would presumably accommodate the small army of box files that marched along the top in tottering piles. There was still a fair few un-accommodated books, however. Francis saw her looking at them, and correctly read her thoughts.

'N-not all of those are reference b-books,' he told her. 'S-s-some of them are novels, they c-c-can g-go in the house. You might like to r-r-read them.'

'Depends what they are,' Tamsin told him. So it was a "house" was it? Well, it was as good a name for it as any other. 'Just leave a bit of room for some of mine – there's two boxes full in the car.'

'So long as it's not another tea chest,' said Val, grinning. He released Kim and got back onto his knees by the bookcase. 'Good you've arrived, but we've all got work to do if we're ever going to finish – I don't suppose there's any chance of a cup of coffee, is there? We're getting parched in here, with all the builders' dust flying about.'

'Give us a chance to unpack the milk, and we'll see what we can do,' Kim told him. 'Come over in twenty-minutes or so – OK? Oh – and you'll find the vacuum cleaner in the utility room. It's all charged up. Dusters in the cupboard under the sink.'

'It's a date,' said Val, ignoring the last part of this speech. He glanced at his watch. 'Twenty minutes. OK.'

The twins went out to the Discovery again, where they found Bennie quietly unloading the back seat and carrying the stores inside, piling the bags onto the dining table.

'I didn't know where you want everything put,' she said. 'Hello there!'

Kim seized the cold box. She said, 'Bennie, you're a star, but we can manage if you need to get back – probably.'

'I don't mind helping, if you can use me, but three of us might be one two many in this small space,' said Bennie. She saw where Kim was heading, and added, 'You'll find some stuff in the big freezer. I just dumped it there, I didn't know where you wanted it. Mary dropped it over this morning, "just to start them off." I think she's afraid Francis might starve.'

'As he well may,' said Kim, darkly. She made her way with some curiosity to the freezer room and opened the lid of the big freezer with interest.

Three chickens, and what looked like a brace of pheasants, a box marked "Rabbit" with some pink little joints in it, Tamsin would love that! Two medium-sized rounds of beef, three packets of steak, rump from the look of it, a bag of stewing steak already cut into chunks, a duck and a couple of pounds of sausages. No lamb or pork, apart from the sausages, so presumably it was mostly home-produced or locally sourced, and as all of it was neatly labelled and dated, Kim assumed it was from a store kept at Vachells. Well, he certainly wouldn't starve with this lot, but Tamsin might need a bit of help and advice to deal with it. Their own frozen store was more things like frozen peas, chips and various manifestations of fish, from breaded prawns, through fishcakes to fish in batter, all with simple cooking instructions on their packaging. Oh – and vanilla ice cream. Tamsin had added that at the last minute. She stowed these in the empty drawers of the fridge-freezer, placed the empty cold box in a corner, and returned to the centre of activity at…well, "the living accommodation" was as good a compromise as any, failing "the immobile home". On the way, she met Tamsin, towing a large suitcase on wheels.

'I'm just dumping this in the utility room for now,' she said. 'Bennie said she'd put quite a lot of Francis' stuff in there already, although it can't live there for ever. We certainly can't fit it in the caravan thing, so we're going to have to do some thinking. There's one more to come, if you could manage it – then we can concentrate on sorting out indoors.' She gave a theatrical shudder. 'It looks a bit like a battlefield at the moment – you should just see the bedroom!' She added, over her shoulder, 'Take a look, if you dare – but don't trip over the dog's basket! He just dumped it in that little passage. Oh – and there's a man in the sitting room, I haven't looked to see what he's doing, perhaps we should make him some coffee too?'

Kim assumed that it was Francis, rather than Sacha, who had dumped the basket, and went to inspect the back of the Discovery. Apart from Tamsin's second suitcase, it appeared to be pretty clear, just the toilet rolls remaining behind the back seat. She lifted the pack out and placed it beside the steps before hauling out the suitcase, shutting the doors, and heading off in her twin's wake.

It turned out that "quite a lot" was a bit of an understatement. Just inside the door to the utility room there was a medium-sized, old-fashioned steamer trunk with two large cases and a holdall piled on top of it, and on the hooks opposite, meant for things like laundry baskets and ironed shirts, there hung three suit-bags containing, from the look of them, jackets and trousers of various kinds including what appeared to be a dinner jacket and trousers. He wasn't short of clothes, wasn't Francis – but then, neither was Tamsin. Her black bag of shoes slumped beneath the suit bags and her suitcase sat beside it, it looked quite moderate compared to Francis' stash – but then, she probably had her more formal clothes still in London. Tamsin herself was standing looking thoughtfully at the heap.

'We shall have to do something about it,' she said, as Kim slung the second suitcase beside the first. 'Although I don't know quite what – you can hardly move in here. There's certainly not room to deploy the ironing board.' She gestured to where it stood, folded up and leaning against the wall. She added, confirming Kim's previous conclusion, 'And there's still quite a lot of my stuff up in London.'

Kim shuddered at the thought. 'We can't do anything about it now, it'll just have to stay as it is until we think of something. Let's go and see if we can find the milk – I think I remember where we put the coffee. I need time to draw breath before we do anything else.'

Back at the mobile home – for want of a better description – Bennie had already found the milk, put the kettle on, and was preparing to leave. She said, 'There's a couple of builders in the house kitchen, but they've brought their own flask. They'll be leaving soon anyway.' She smiled at them. 'Have fun! And you know where we are if you need us – now I'll just pick up Val, and I'm on my way – I'll see he gets some coffee before I send him back.'

She left, and Tamsin picked up the cardboard box containing her knick-knacks and carried it out of the way into the sitting room area, where she found a thin, dark man on his knees before the sideboard, fiddling with a wide-screen television screen and a couple of black boxes that fitted underneath it. A cardboard box of DVDs stood on the shelf where Tamsin had planned to put her own box, so she put it on the nearest sofa rather than pick her way around behind him past the coffee table to the other side. She hadn't expected the television set, and was pleased to see it; presumably it came from Francis' flat at Vachells.

'Hello,' she said. 'You must be Ronnie. We're just making some coffee.'

'Sounds like a plan.' He smiled up at her. 'I'll just test this is working OK, then I'm finished in here and can get out of your way – you've got Freeview and the DVD player, there's no Sky or anything – no dish for it either, out here. Don't think he spent much time sitting in front of the telly.'

'We can change that,' said Tamsin. 'And Freeview is good, I can live with that – for now, anyway.'

'That's all right then – I'll check it and make sure it'll work for you, like I said, and then I'm off to battle with the office computer when I've had that coffee you mentioned. I'll leave the remotes on the table.' He grinned at her. 'Your first home together, I understand. How does it feel?'

'Very strange, right now,' Tamsin told him.

'And congratulations on your engagement, by the way. You're a brave woman!'

He wasn't the first to have said that. Tamsin thanked him and went thoughtfully back into the kitchen. It was becoming increasingly obvious as she became drawn into his life that Francis wasn't short of friends at all when he was away from the Sailing Club; on the contrary, he seemed to be generally very well-liked: she was beginning to understand why he had elected not to go there any more. It needed thinking about, when there was time for thinking. Added to what she had learned from Donald

Moran, it was beginning to make her uneasy. There was starting to be something…well, focussed about it all.

Kim was putting out the mugs on the worktop: there was no sign yet of Francis, and of course Val was gone to Vachells. She said, 'I shoved your cases on the bed for now, there's just about room. Bennie said she'd hung some of Francis' stuff in the wardrobe to make it look better. Not a good omen.'

Tamsin went across the passage and peeped through the bedroom door, catching her foot on the dog basket as she came back. She gave it a shove further along until it was more-or-less directly under the little passage window: it would just about fit there if it was turned a bit slantwise, and Francis was right in one respect, there was nowhere else to put it. Where the cats would sleep when they got here was another question; probably on the furniture. They had both of them lost the habit of sleeping in barns.

'It could be worse,' she said, as she re-entered the kitchen. 'Those really enormous black bags are probably the bedding and stuff. That'll disperse naturally when we make the bed.'

'There'll be more than one set of sheets and towels, presumably. And I see no linen cupboard.'

'Oh, we'll manage,' said Tamsin, optimistically. The thought of making the bed had made her feel a bit strange. Bed, not beds. Um.

They worked throughout the remainder of the morning, sorting out the kitchen and dining area and tidying up in the sitting room after Ronnie, leaving the bedroom to wait until after lunch. At least they could shut the door on it.

'Although what we're going to have for lunch, who knows?' Kim asked. 'It's not that there's not plenty of food now, it's just what.'

'There's bread. And cheese. And apples.'

'That might do for us, but those men are probably starving. Men generally are, in my experience.'

'Beans on toast?' Tamsin speculated. 'We could put an egg on top.'

Kim eyed her in disbelief. She said, 'Are my ears deceiving me, or are you trying to be domesticated?'

'Well, it's a thought. And we bought a fruit cake – I think we did.'

'That's true.' The proposed menu had its merits, Kim had to admit, simplicity being one of them. 'We'll see what they say, shall we?'

Predictably, what Val, who had returned by this time with the Mercedes, and Francis said was 'Let's go down to the pub,' Val adding that they needed to wash away the dust.'

'So long as you dusted it away, as well,' Kim told him, and Val said, 'I did. Francis was busy with Ronnie and the computer – a fine excuse, as I told him.'

'Would Ronnie like to come with us?' Tamsin asked.

'No. We did ask him, but he said he'd finish here and go home to his wife. We told him to put the latch down and shut the back door after him if we weren't back. The builders have already gone, about ten minutes ago. They said they'd be back Monday morning.'

'What were they doing?' Tamsin asked. 'I didn't have time to look.'

'T-tiling the floor in th-the chimney recess, ready for the Aga,' Francis told her. 'Th-that's being d-d-delivered on T-Tuesday.'

'Oh goodness!' said Tamsin, and fell silent. Things were beginning really to gallop along.

Val drove them to the Ravenscourt Arms, they would all fit easily into his car; Sacha was left on guard in his basket with a rubber bone to chew on. Once they had ordered lunch, they sat at a table in the window with their drinks to discuss what would happen after it.

'What have you two got planned for this afternoon?' Val asked, when they were seated. 'We've about done everything I can help with in the office department, how about you Kim? It might leave more room to sort the rest out if we just took ourselves off, unless there's something we can do to be useful – that super-van is a bit small for us to work mob-handed.'

Tamsin had been considering this as they drove along and had reached a similar conclusion. She said, 'If Kim can just help me make the bed, you're right, I can unpack better on my own. It probably won't take that long, anyway. You might as well go and enjoy yourselves – aren't you supposed to be racing, anyway?'

'Not on your life!' Val nodded towards the window, where the clouds were stacking up again, iron-grey. 'The forecast is, pouring with rain yet again later and blowing a hooley by tonight. I rang the Club earlier. It's cancelled. But we might drop by for a drink and a chat with everyone. Or then again, we might not.' He had suddenly recalled that he and Kim would have Romans to themselves for once. 'It's probably going to be a good afternoon for curling up with the fire and the telly.'

Tamsin looked at Francis. She asked, 'What have you got to do? I shall be doing our unpacking, and then I shall probably do what Val said – crash out with the telly.'

'Th-then I shall probably go on p-p-putting things away until you've finished, and j-join you.'

'You don't need my help with that?' Val asked.

'N-no thank you. P-paper isn't heavy, and anyway, I shall n-need to th-th-think about it.'

'Fair enough.' Val looked at Kim. 'Then when you've finished with the bed, we can be off. OK with you?'

Kim caught Tamsin's eye and nodded her head. She said, 'Fine. I expect they'll be glad of some peace and quiet anyway.' She left out the word "together", although it trembled on her tongue. It occurred to her that Francis and her twin had not had a great deal of time just quietly alone together. Probably, the sooner she and Val took themselves off, the better.

When they got back to Burnthouse, the first thing that Tamsin and Kim did was to take the four cases into the kitchen/diner and stack them on the seats. They then undid the sacks and tipped the contents out onto the bed. A duvet, feather-filled, not more than about 4tog, Kim estimated, and a bit wide for the bed here. Five fat, soft feather pillows. Three sets of bed linen in plain colours, very masculine and probably designed to show every mark, not a flower or a leaf in sight to break the monotony. Three double sets of thick white cotton bathroom towels. Six tea towels, assorted, two bath mats, two pedestal mats. Two thick woollen blankets, one brown, one pale yellow and a plaid rug. Two striped towels, presumably for the kitchen, and better and better, a plastic bag full of miscellaneous coat hangers; Mary, or possibly Mrs Fairburn, had done them proud. While Tamsin was counting all of this into piles, out of curiosity Kim opened the wardrobe – it was fairly wide, and the absence of a linen cupboard of some kind had been bothering her slightly in such a well-appointed dwelling. To her delight, she found what she was looking for.

'There's shelves all up one side in here,' she said. 'Not very wide, but quite deep. You can get all the spare household linen in here and still leave room for the odd thick man's sweater – or perhaps I should say man's thick sweater – that won't fit in a drawer, or some of your shoes and stuff, on the rest of the shelves. I thought there ought to be some provision for household linen somewhere.'

'Great! Get stacking, while I put these in the kitchen.' Tamsin had sorted out some plain, dark blue sheets and pillowcases and shoved them aside to make up the bed; she picked up two tea towels and a stripy kitchen towel and headed off. Kim watched her go pensively: not so hopelessly domestically disorganised as she made out, Tamsin – fortunately for Francis, who definitely was! They might just survive together, on present form. She sorted out two sets of towels and some bath mats for the shower room from the remaining heap and began to stack the remainder in the wardrobe as economically as she could. One of the blankets, she rolled up and put in the bottom of the wardrobe part, the other, they would need. There were already three or four hangers in use on the rail, as Bennie had told them: Francis' beautiful dark grey suit, his navy blazer, a tweed jacket and a couple of cotton shirts, one striped, one plain. Pure cotton, beautifully ironed. Hey ho, that just might be her twin's Waterloo.

Tamsin returned, swept the set-aside towels onto the top of the chest of drawers, and grabbed the nearest pillow.

'Right – let's get this job done!' She was making herself be deliberately brisk, although there was a distinct flutter under her ribs at the thought of what she was actually doing. It wasn't that she had never shared a double bed with a man, certainly not, but she had certainly never done so with a man like Francis Chillingworth, whom she loved and wanted so much that if she thought about it too hard, she actually felt sick, and that was even before she addressed the question of why he had needed a double bed in the first place, for these sheets, she already knew, were from the bed that had been in his flat at Vachells. Best not go there, maybe…she caught Kim's quick glance and knew that her twin had her bang to rights. It hardly made her feel any better, she simply felt immature and stupid and wished that her heart would stop thumping. Kim would hear it at this rate – Francis would hear it, over there in the office. He would hear it over his radio if she didn't pull herself together!

'What's Val doing?' she asked, to distract herself. He wasn't in this van-thing, that was for sure.

'Probably getting in Francis' way,' said Kim. 'They went off together.' She tossed the pillows she had been attending to onto the floor and reached for the duvet. 'Where's the cover for this?'

With both of them on the job, it didn't take long to make up the bed. Fitted sheet, a bit big for this mattress, it needed tucking in, top sheet, duvet, blanket, sling the pillows aboard, plaid rug folded at the foot, job done! Kim picked up the pile of towels.

'I'll just put these in the shower for you, and then I'll go and rout out Val, and we'll get out of your way and leave the two of you to finish sorting yourselves out. If you're sure there's nothing else?'

'No, I'll be fine. It doesn't take that long to unpack stuff, it's the packing that causes the problems.'

'And anyway, you want us gone.' Kim grinned at her. 'Oh, don't look at me like that – been there, and done that—'

'—and you couldn't get rid of me,' said Tamsin, returning the grin. 'I lived there. At least you two have a home to go to.' She paused. 'It's silly to feel the way I feel, and I know it, so you don't have to tell me. It's… well, a rite of passage, I suppose. I feel like an inexperienced teenager on her first date.'

'It'll be all right on the night,' Kim assured her. 'And take courage – at least you won't be fumbling about in the dark – not either of you, is my guess!' And she ducked out of the door with the towels, laughing.

For all that it was quite true that she had wished them gone, Tamsin found the tiny home very quiet when Val and Kim had left. Francis was still in his office, every step she took on the hollow floor seemed to echo and re-echo. She should have hijacked the radio, Tamsin thought, trying not to tiptoe across the floor, except that he was probably listening to it himself. She wondered if he did that all the time, there was much that she had yet to learn about him. No use brooding about it, however. There was work to done.

She began in the sitting room area: there was less to be done there and it would be one more job out of the way. She took Francis' DVDs out of their box, riffling through them as she did so: at least he wasn't a James Bond afficionado but apart from that, the play list looked pretty gloomy. A lot of it was recordings of various non-fiction programmes, often associated with water and what went on, in or under it in places such as the Great Barrier Reef. She arranged them tidily on one of the bookshelves, tossed the cardboard box that had contained them to one side, and dug into her own box for some more congenial recorded entertainment of her own: between herself and Francis they had filled two of the small shelves with DVDs which, so far as she could see, they would probably never watch together. Oh well, no doubt they would discover a middle road somewhere – when they knew each other better, and where had that idea come from?

Thoughtful now, she arranged a few bits and pieces on the top shelves alongside the television, thrust a handful of miscellaneous plates that she and Jo and Julie had used for parties – how had those got here? – into the cupboard, and put the two pictures onto the kitchen table, pending. They would have to be stored somewhere, yet another problem to be addressed. They were already running out of space, what with all the suitcases – full or empty, they would take up the same amount of room.

One last item remained; she didn't know what Francis would make of it, but he would have to put up with it. She tucked her worn old teddy bear that she had cuddled through good times and bad since she was four years old under one arm, put the smaller of the two empty boxes into the larger one and picked them up with her free hand; at least the boxes could just go into the skip. She was half-tempted to toss the suitcases after them! But no, that wouldn't really help. Looking around the little room, she was surprised to see the difference that the television, the DVDs, the books, and the few ornaments had already made. It looked like…well, home, actually. Hiding a smile, she moved on to deal with the problem of the suitcases.

It felt strange, unpacking Francis' unfamiliar male clothing; men's shirts, jeans, underwear, socks…he didn't seem to own any pyjamas, hmm… Thick sweaters, pullovers, a couple of down-filled gilets, one blue with the Yacht Club logo on it's left breast, the other plain dark maroon, that would have to hang on the hooks in the passage over the dog's basket, at least for now, they were so plump and thick. Three or four neatly folded cotton shirts in white and pale blue, rather more brushed cotton work-shirts in various checks, a few t-shirts, sweat shirts…it was liking getting to know him on a far more intimate level than any yet, she fingered the clothes tenderly as she stowed them in the drawers and on the shelves. And there was better yet to come…she bit her lip and slammed the last drawer shut with unnecessary vigour. She had given him the bottom three, because the bottom of all was the deepest and would take some of his thick shirts and sweaters: the bag that contained a selection of his shoes she slung wholesale onto the bottom shelf of the wardrobe, he could sort them out himself. Considering that he had a whole trunk plus two more cases in the utility room, the man must have an awful lot of clothes. Even more than she did.

There was just about enough room left to take most of her own immediate needs, she gathered up their respective wash bags to take to the shower room and looked at what was left. Francis' sailing jacket, her own hooded waterproof jacket, her warm winter coat – there were more hooks left under the high passage window for things like this: surprisingly, it looked as if everything had squashed in pretty well – but of course, this was only what they thought they might need right now, the tip of a bigger iceberg! She put the wash bags in their proper place, hung the coats, and sat Ted Bear in his accustomed place on the bed and stood back to look at her work.

Like the little sitting room, it was beginning to look lived-in: she was pleased with the effect, although she didn't know what Francis would make of Ted. He must like animals to be a farmer...she hid another smile, there seemed to be a lot of them about this afternoon, and turned to collect up the emptied suitcases to carry over to the house: it took her two trips, even with her holdall stuffed into one of her cases. She dumped the first lot just inside the door, and listened for sounds of human life before she went back for the second, but all she could hear was the radio. At least that probably meant that Francis was still in his office, she would look in on him when she had stowed the cases in the utility room, see if he'd like a coffee or something. She herself was really thirsty after all that hard work!

Sacha had obviously heard her in the passage, for when she got back with the last two cases, he was sitting waiting for her: he stood up when she appeared, tail wagging, and tried unsuccessfully to push his way through the luggage barrier to get to her. Together with the tea chests already there on the other side of the office door, the passage was now pretty well blocked, and he gave a sharp yelp which brought Francis to the office door. He looked down at the blockage, and then at Tamsin.

'W-what are you p-p-planning to do with all that?' he asked, with a lift of his brows, and Tamsin shook her head and said, 'I have no idea, it just needed to be got out of the van. I was going to put it in the utility room with all the rest, but I don't think there's room.'

'As b-b-bad as that?' He sounded sceptical.

'You obviously haven't looked in there lately.' She lifted one of the suitcases out of the way, fielded Sacha, and stepped past into the passage. 'Come and look, you'll see what I mean.' She led the way, and Sacha and

Francis obediently followed her. They stood together at the door to the utility room and looked in. Even the dog's tail drooped at the sight that met their eyes.

'I s-s-see what you mean,' said Francis, after a moment's pause. 'B-but it isn't a problem, is it? – I m-mean, there's a whole house, m-m-most of it empty, to st-stow it in for now.'

'The men will want room to work in. They won't want to be tripping over empty suitcases,' Tamsin objected.

'N-n-not in all if it, they won't. Th-they won't g-g-get to the far end until S-S-September next year, after the archaeologists g-g-go, so it c-c-can all go in one of th-the end b-bedrooms for now. In f-f-fact, when we get my stuff out of s-s-store, all of th-th-this can go up too, and m-m-most of it could be unpacked and put into m-my wardrobes where we can get at it, th-there'll be heating up there, when we g-g-get round to it. It'll come to n-n-no harm.'

Tamsin thought about this, it hadn't occurred to her before now but now it looked like a good plan. She said, 'I don't suppose we could put the wardrobes in the right room straight away? The one above the kitchen, where we're going to be sleeping to begin with? If they just did the floor, and painted the walls – even just one wall would do – before they went in? The windows and stuff could wait, and surely just doing that wouldn't take them long? It would make things a lot easier in the end, and they'd hardly be in the way if we planned it right.'

'W-we can ask Steve on Monday, but it's certainly a thought. Now, sh-shall we get those cases in the passage out of the w-w-way?'

'I can manage – you're busy.'

'I've j-j-just about finished for n-now. W-we can do it in two t-trips if we d-d-do it together, then we can kn-nock off.'

With no help at all from Sacha, they got the empty cases upstairs and into the back bedroom over what would eventually be the drawing room. Francis said, 'I'll ask M-Matt and one of th-the men to get the r-r-rest up here too, on M-Monday. Then you'll have r-r-room to do the ironing.' And he grinned at her, wickedly. Tamsin chose to ignore this unseemly dig. She said merely, 'That would be great,' and led the way downstairs – well, after Sacha, who ran ahead, she led it. Back at the back door, they stopped, and Francis said, 'I'll just switch everything off in the office and l-lock up, and I'll be home. G-g-get the kettle on!'

Tamsin thought about this as she walked back to the house; it gave her an unfamiliar warm feeling that she rather liked. "I'll be home…" Oh yes!

The cardboard boxes still sat on the dining table; she filled the kettle and switched it on and then carried them out to the skip in the stable yard. It was just starting to rain, and the wind had got up considerably since lunchtime; Val had been right about the weather. She tossed the boxes into the skip and stood for a minute looking at the empty stables, neat and clean and…well, empty. A farm should have animals, not empty barns and stables. Cows and horses and chickens – cats – heads looking over stable doors, hooves stamping in the barns as cows shifted around in their stalls. Did cows have stalls? She had a feeling they might, at least in the winter. No doubt she would find out.

Because it was in the front of her mind, when she met Francis on her way back to make the coffee, the first thing she said was, 'When do we get the horses back here? The stables are all ready.'

Francis slipped his arm round her shoulders as they walked together back to their temporary home. He said, 'When there's something here for them to eat, and some b-b-bedding for them. End of n-next week, probably.'

'Can't they eat that hay that Matt made?'

'I w-w-wouldn't recommend it. It's v-v-very poor quality, f-f-full of weeds and…well, stuff.'

'So what will you do with it?'

'Set fire to it on N-November the fifth?' He saw her face and gave her a hug. 'Compost, p-probably. Let's g-g-get indoors, it's going to t-tip it down in a moment.'

The kettle had just boiled when they got back. Tamsin reached down two mugs and glanced at her watch: nearly five o'clock, she could probably put her feet up for an hour before it was time to get the dinner – whatever that would be. She reached for the coffee jar, and called through into the dining room, where Francis had already dropped onto the centre section of the sofa and was reaching for the television remote. 'What do you fancy for dinner later on?' and he said, 'What is there?'

'Fish and chips, we've got that in the freezer if you fancy it? I only need to follow the instructions on the packets, Kim said. Or beans on toast, I could put an egg on top and I think there's maybe some bacon in the fridge here. Or I could make you a fried egg sandwich, my piéce de resistance.'

A spatter of hail clattered against the windows and began to pick up speed. Francis glanced in that direction.

'You don't want to g-g-go getting stuff from the house in this l-lot. I'll settle for the baked beans. When we're ready.' He held out his hand. 'F-fetch that coffee in here, and s-s-sit down for a bit. You l-l-look shattered.'

'It's all that unpacking,' said Tamsin. She obediently sat down beside him, putting the mugs on the coffee table. Sacha settled himself on their feet, and it all felt very domesticated. Francis slid his arm round her shoulders once more – his right arm, but she felt his fingers close round her upper arm even so. He was getting the use back into his hand and her mind, running ahead on its own volition, thought that he would need to have the inside berth, and she herself the window side: there was less chance that way that she would roll on the injury in the night and hurt him just when he was healing. That poor hand had suffered enough. She heaved a sigh of satisfaction without meaning to, and felt his fingers close tighter on her arm and then relax. She said the first thing that came into her head.

'Do you watch The X Factor? Only it's on tonight,' and heard him smother a laugh.

'I n-n-never have, but I suspect I'm g-g-going to.'

'You could always go to sleep,' Tamsin consoled him. 'Then tomorrow afternoon I can sleep through the football. Fair's fair.'

'I d-d-don't think there is any.'

Tamsin relaxed contentedly against his shoulder, it felt good. She said idly, 'You've made a rather dramatic beginning to your stewardship here – can we slow down now, do you think?' and he smothered another laugh.

'Here's hoping, b-b-but don't put m-m-money on it.'

They drank their coffee in companionable silence after that, and watched the News together: then Tamsin began to get her breath back, ready for her solo performance in the kitchen. Beans on toast and a fried egg each didn't overtax her skills, fortunately, neither did fruit cake and apples. Francis opened a bottle of wine for them to share, after a discussion as to whether red or white went best with baked beans, and Tamsin tried to remember where she and Kim had put the wine glasses. They sat on either side of the table, each of them very aware of the other.

'I'd offer to do the washing-up, if I had t-t-two hands,' Francis said, as they cleared away, and Tamsin said, smiling at him, 'I expect you could dry,' and he kissed her and nearly made her drop the plates. Then they took the rest of the bottle of wine and the glasses next door, and Tamsin watched *The X Factor,* and to her surprise Francis stayed awake and watched it too, cradling her in his arms while she snuggled against him and neither of them really concentrated on the small screen. When it was over, he released her slowly and pushed himself upright from his slumped relaxation. He said, 'I d-d-don't know about you, but I'm going to test out the shower and g-g-go to bed.'

'I'll just rinse out the glasses, and I'll be right behind you, said Tamsin, gathering them up. The idea of bed was enticing, and for more than one reason. He stood up and pulled her to her feet beside him.

'D-do you want the w-w-washroom first? You'll probably be quicker th-than me.'

Their sudden mutual politeness made Tamsin want to giggle. Come to that, this whole evening had made her want to giggle, it spun a weird magic between them, the first believable breath of a future when they would finally be able to share their lives together.

'That would be nice. If you're anything like my Dad, you'll be in there for ever.' And Val, and Rupert too but she wouldn't mention him.

'R-right then. Off you g-g-go, I'll do the glasses and j-j-just let the dog out.'

Letting the dog out allowed Tamsin the time to have a shower too: she felt sticky and tired after her busy day, and the hot water falling on her face and shoulders was pure bliss. She closed her eyes and thought about what might happen next, but she didn't do so for too long as she had no idea how much hot water there was, and the last thing on her agenda was Francis having a cold shower, and that for several reasons of which domestic peace was only one.

Domestic. She savoured the unfamiliar – in this context at least – word as she slipped on her sexiest and most diaphanous nightie, even though she suspected it might be a waste of time, and effort, and headed for the bedroom. Sacha was safely in his basket, he thumped his tail as she passed him, and she found Francis, stripped down to just his underpants and sitting on the edge of the bed, holding Ted Bear and looking at him thoughtfully.

'Who's your friend?' he asked, as she appeared in the doorway.

'Ted Bear. We go back years together.'

'More like Fred Bear,' said Francis, handing him over. 'He l-l-looks as if he's had a hard l-life.' The sight of his muscular sun-browned torso with the smudge of soft dark hair on his chest made Tamsin gulp. She clutched the bear to her own chest and felt her colour rising. Francis stood up, she could tell from the look in his eyes that he had noticed her blush, and the smile that he gave her made her feel dizzy.

'I'll be b–back,' he told her.

When he had gone, Tamsin drew a deep breath and put Ted – or maybe Fred – down on her elected side of the bed and folded Francis' untidily discarded clothes into a neat pile, which she placed beside her own on top of the chest. He had tossed a clean t-shirt and a pair of boxer shorts onto the pillows, which must be his normal night wear; she put them tidily on the near side ready for him, aware even as she did all this that the burst of domestic tidiness was simply a displacement activity. Farmers, she presumed, sometimes, or even often, had reason to get up and rush outside in the middle of the night, so his choice of nightwear was practical when you thought about it, but that wasn't going to happen tonight, whatever else did. She got under the bedclothes and waited for his return, her heart beating until she thought it would choke her, and with Ted clutched to her for moral support.

Or perhaps that should be immoral support?

You're behaving like a teenager on her first serious date, she remonstrated with herself, giggling. What on earth has got into you?

When he returned, damp hair, bright eyes, skin smelling cleanly of expensive shower gel, he tossed his nightwear to the foot of the bed and slid in, naked, beside her. He propped himself on his left elbow, and his bandaged right hand reached across and lay lightly against her cheek: from where she lay, she could see clearly along the length of his bare forearm: the inflammation was noticeably and blessedly much less – and why was she thinking that, at this particular moment? Displacement activity again…

He said, 'Are you up f-f-for this, or are you t-t-too tired?' and for reply, she reached up and pulled him down towards her, so that they slid together right down beneath the duvet, and Ted fell onto the floor.

'It's such bliss to be on our own…let's not waste it,' she said. And then she added, quite without meaning to, 'Please…' on a breath so slight that it could hardly be heard. He reached across her to switch off the bedside light and the darkness fell softly around them.

'Th-then let's s-s-start by getting r-r-rid of this,' he said, suiting the action to the word. The nightie slipped over her head and onto the floor to join Ted, and even that he managed to make so sexy that Tamsin lost her breath. Then his arms were right around her and she felt his breath on her cheek and his lips on her mouth, and then…

She wasn't certain what she had been expecting: previous experience of the rough and tumble she had shared with Rupert, as young, and if he had admitted to it, as unpractised as herself, hadn't prepared her for the gentleness and consideration that she now received. Where Rupert had taken, Francis shared, and he knew exactly what he was about; he could spin out expectation and crown it with ecstasy, not just for his personal satisfaction but for hers as well, and he knew things about women and their needs that Rupert had never imagined – and then she shut Rupert right out of her life for now and evermore, and gave herself up to the present until the amazing climax, the unbelievable fountain of pure magic that concluded their coupling. Yes, she had come to orgasm before, but not like this, never like this! Without even realising that she was going to do so, she gave a long-drawn-out and ecstatic cry of delight, and unintentionally toppled the whole magical moment.

There was a thud outside the door, a crash against it, and a torrent of loud barking accompanied by urgent scratching and banging, and Francis collapsed on top of her with a shout of his own, half of triumph and half of uncontrollable mirth. 'N-n-now you've done it,' he said, when he had got his breath back. 'He th-thinks I'm m-m-murdering you!'

'Then you had better go and tell him that you're not,' said Tamsin, but without releasing her clutch on him; he was still shaking with laughter – or was it reaction? Or both, maybe? He smothered another laugh that threatened to overtake him.

'I w-w-will, if you let me g-g-go.'

Tamsin loosened her hold reluctantly, and he sat up, running a hand gently along her cheek and down to her smiling mouth.

'You are b-beautiful, and I l-l-love you m-more than I d-d-dreamed was p-possible.' He barely got the words out for the emotion with which he spoke them, and Tamsin reached up and touched him in return.

'Me too – you're amazing – and now go and see to that poor dog before he breaks the door down! This is only a glorified caravan, after all!' and he bent and kissed her, swiftly but passionately, and reluctantly went to do her bidding, trying to field Sacha as he burst through the door but not succeeding, so that the dog landed, still barking his head off, on the bed. His tail wagged furiously and his tongue lolled with pleasure at finding them both alive and unharmed, but he was obviously not going to apologise any time soon: rather, he seemed to want to join in the fun. Francis reached for his night clothes with a sigh of resignation.

'I'll just l-let him out for a minute. C-calm him down.'

Sacha, and who else? Tamsin wondered. She said, 'Well put on more than that – put your sweater on at least, I don't want you getting pneumonia.'

'I sh-shan't actually go outside th-the door myself,' he told her with a grin.

'You'll still get cold, just on the steps. You'll come back here like an iceberg!'

'Th-then you can w-w-warm me up again.' He obediently reached for the sweater, chased the dog off the bed, and vanished through the door, closing it behind him to shut out the cold night air when he opened the outside door, and Tamsin lay back and thought about things.

She was still trembling inside, she realised, from that whole experience, the reaction of the dog had fitted perfectly with her own, an explosion of sheer instinct that mixed and matched and, even just thinking of it, made her laugh all over again. She sat up and switched on the bedside lamp; there was no follow-up to that, that wouldn't be an anticlimax, she might as well put her nightie back on, it was cold anyway with the heating turned off for the night. She picked it up from the floor, sat Ted, with an apology, on the bedside table, and when Francis returned was lying snugly with the bedclothes pulled up to her chin. She heard the outside door close, and his voice talking quietly to the dog, and then he came back into the bedroom, still smiling although not actually laughing now. He tossed his sweater untidily onto the neat heap on the chest of drawers and slipped back in beside her. It was like being embraced by a snowman! He almost echoed her own thoughts.

'Th-there's no w-w-way of following that performance. R-ready for some s-s-sleep?'

Tamsin had her arms around him sharing her own warmth to thaw him out. She snuggled her cheek against his. 'Mmm.'

He fell asleep almost at once, men were good at that, she reflected. She herself lay awake a long time thinking about today, tonight, yesterday, the past…this unexpectedly joyful evening…and wondering, not by any means for the first time, just who she was marrying, and if the problems that piled up in his past could ever be resolved and allow him to move on, and if not...what? Life in the Mediterranean with the prawns and the octopuses – octopi – whatever?

She could find no easy answer to that.

XXIX

For one reason and another, not all of them intentional, it was a couple of days before Kim and Tamsin saw each other again. They had planned to spend the weekend separately anyway, both of them feeling the need to be alone with their individual partners for a while; what they had not planned was that they wouldn't see each other until Wednesday. For this, life at Burnthouse was largely responsible, although it hadn't been arranged that way.

Tamsin's new car was delivered on Sunday morning, by the car salesman on his way to church: it was a deliberately chosen and pre-arranged moment, as there were no workmen's vans cluttering up the area and so it was possible to get it into the garage, or it would be when the time came. That wouldn't be quite immediately of course, it had to have a run first to try it out. The salesman's wife drove his own car in his wake, and he handed over the Mazda's keys before joining her to finish his pilgrimage.

'All filled up for you and good to go,' he said, as he dropped the keys into Tamsin's hand. 'Enjoy. That's a good little car you have there.'

'Thanks, Marcus,' Francis said, smiling at Tamsin's joyful expression, although her pleasure didn't stop her wondering. "Marcus", eh? Another friend? They were behind every bush once he got clear of the Sailing Club, and nobody around here ever seemed to call him "Mr Chillingworth", either – they were all either relations or were at Sixth Form College with him. She wondered which category Marcus fell into, because that was another thing. It was impossible to tell because not one of them – and that now seemed to include Francis – could possibly be described as "posh". So where had that come from…? She filed the question for future consideration, for the moment she was too taken up with her beautiful new possession. She stroked the door as if it was a favourite cat, and Francis and his friend Marcus watched her with amusement, Marcus' wife with sympathy, and when the delivery team had driven off, Francis said, 'Th-that settles what you'll be d-d-doing this morning, I imagine,' and laughed at her expression.

'Come with me,' she said. 'It'll be much more fun if you do – come on!'

'Give me t-t-ten minutes to let the dog have a r-r-run, then – I presume he isn't inv-v-vited?'

I don't think he'd fit,' said Tamsin, considering the space behind the seats with a measuring eye.

'Oh, he'd f-f-fit, he'd see to it. He j-j-just wouldn't be very c-c-comfortable.' He turned away, and then turned back. 'F-fancy lunch out somewhere? I c-c-can ring that pub on the c-c-cliff th-that you like unless you have s-s-some exotic dish planned f-f-for us?'

'You should be so lucky!' She returned the mischievous smile he gave her as he spoke. 'I love that pub – that would be great, thank you.'

They left Sacha curled resignedly in his basket in the office, where he seemed to feel more at home on his own, and set out on the maiden voyage with the top down to enjoy the sunshine; this late in the year it necessitated a warm jacket each, but who cared? Just seeing the sun was becoming a rare treat this October. Ending up – eventually – at the pub, windblown, chilly and hungry, they enjoyed lunch by a window overlooking the curve of the beautiful coastline, called in on Mary on their way home to check she was all right and – in Tamsin's case – to show off the car, and returned home to spend the rest of the day with each other, the dog, and the television, and treated themselves to another early night.

Tamsin had intended to take her new toy to show it off to Kim the next morning, but it turned out that it wasn't going to be an option, as the workmen decided that this would be a good day to dig up the top of the lane beside the house, where the double garage was, to lay the pipe for the oil tank that would feed the new Aga. The tank was to go on the patch of waste ground behind the garage, so that effectively sealed off the lane for most of the day, the decorators and the plumbers parking in the home field, climbing over the garden wall with the aid of a stepladder and entering and leaving the house via the front door. By three o'clock in the afternoon, when they finally began to fill in the trench again, Tamsin decided that tomorrow was also a day, took out the cookery book that Kim had given her, and spent the remainder of the afternoon experimenting in her kitchen. It was going to rain again anyway, just for a change. You couldn't show off a sports convertible properly in the pouring rain. You couldn't show it off at all!

Tuesday featured more rain, a threatened thunderstorm, and an official visit from a man who wished to discuss the projected alterations to the layout of the bedrooms above the drawing-room, prior to considering the planning application. He wasn't from the council: since Burnthouse was a listed building he was a qualified advisor on behalf of whatever body it was who looked after such matters. Tamsin thought it might have been English Heritage, but she wouldn't have sworn to it as he showed his card to Francis, not to her. Francis, who looked as if he had a thumping headache this morning, handed him over for Tamsin to look after and retired to his office with Sacha. How like a man! Tamsin thought; she had a bit of a headache herself, come to that: the threatened thunder, probably, and wasn't in the least in the mood for presenting their case to this stranger. But at least Francis wasn't laid out with a full-blown migraine this time… and then she thought about that, and not for the first time, came to no conclusions.

The man – he said his name was Anthony Hargreaves, and this time, for a change, he was a stranger – asked to be taken first through the work that had already been done, so they started the tour at the back door. Tamsin explained their plans for the washroom, and Mr Hargreaves nodded his head in what she hoped was approval, and made a note on a pad that he took from his pocket and thereafter held in his hand, making more notes as he went. He looked into all the utility rooms, stuck his head round the office door, murmured something that Tamsin didn't catch to Francis, and then withdrew into the passage.

'Presumably this leads to the kitchen?' he said, gesturing towards the one remaining door at the far end, and Tamsin, as was obviously expected of her, led the way. Here, he looked at the newly-laid stone floor lining the fireplace itself – it had proved impossible to find tiles to make a perfect match with the kitchen floor, and Tamsin and Stephen Postgate had settle on local stone crazy paving, much like the original but clean and soot-free, with a solid concrete rectangle to take the weight of the new stove – nodded his head at the newly whitewashed rear wall with its old bread-oven door, now cleaned up and awaiting sympathetic restoration, and made another note on his pad – quite a long one this time. Then he asked questions about their plan for the fireplace now that it was cleaned up and repaired, and Tamsin explained about the Aga to cook and to heat the water for the household, and he made another note, and then handed her the pad and pencil and asked her to sketch the layout for the fireplace area, including any extractor fans and the worktops or cupboards that would presumably fill the spaces adjoining the new stove, and Tamsin drew him a picture. He then looked in disparagement at the existing, now doorless, cupboards along under the windows and said, in a neutral voice, 'And these?' and Tamsin, the thunder headache now beginning to thump behind her eyes, lost patience with his patent scepticism as to their intentions and told him.

'They've gone to be renovated of course, anyone could see they were terrible!' She shot him a challenging look that said as clearly as words, "even a silly little thing like me!" and went on. 'We shall try round the reclamation yards to see if we can find anything with some age to it that can be used to replace or patch up the ones that have gone too far, but if we can't do that, we have a carpenter lined up to make a reproduction where necessary – there wouldn't have been fitted cupboards here when the house was originally built, anyway.' She ended on a challenging note, and to her surprise, he smiled at her.

'No, there wouldn't, of course.' He ran his fingers with obvious affection over the old Belfast sink. 'You'll be keeping, this, of course?'

'We may give it a friend, so that we can keep vegetable peelings separate from washing-up,' Tamsin told him. The suggestion had been Bennie's, but she spoke it as her own. It came out like another challenge, which she hadn't intended, and he caught her eye.

'I'm not here to ruin your plans, you know, Mrs Chillingworth,' he said, gently. 'I'm here to see they don't ruin the house – and so far, I see no sign of it. We do recognise that it must be rendered fit to live in, in the present day.'

'Thank you,' said Tamsin, surprised to hear approval in his voice. 'And I'm not Mrs Chillingworth, not yet, I'm Tamsin Carey,' and he apologised and shook her hand.

'You've taken on quite a challenge here, Miss Carey, but so far you seem equal to it,' he told her, and the tour continued, as did his note-taking, ending where Tamsin had expected it to begin, in the two end bedrooms. Here, he took a copy of their architect's drawings from his coat pocket and spread it out against the front bedroom wall, taking her step-by-step through the planned modifications, nodding his head now and then, or asking questions, before thumping his hand against the walls and peering up at the rafters. He made no comments, either of approval or disapproval, and they eventually left the house via the front door just as the heating engineers arrived to install the Aga. Tamsin left him talking to them, and took herself to the office, where she found Francis sitting at his desk with his head in his hands and his computer screen covered with his trademark floating rainbow fish. He looked up when she came in.

'Go OK, d-d-did it?'

'I have no idea. I think so, but he didn't give a lot away. He seemed to like our plans for the kitchen, though.'

'G-good, then.'

'I'm just going over to make a cup of coffee and find some Paracetamol – do you want some? I can bring it over here, if you want.'

'The coffee or th-the Paracetamol? Yes p-please to both, but d-d-don't bother to bring it over, I'll come across in a minute. J-j-just let me close this d-d-down.'

As she left the house, the first rumble of thunder sounded over the distant hills and three heavy drops of rain landed on the path ahead of her. The heating engineers passed her, pushing a large cardboard-enshrouded shape on a trolley, and nodded as they passed.

'Morning,' one of them said. 'I won't say "good"!' and she gave him a smile, which he returned. Francis arrived from the office to the accompaniment of a huge flash of lightning, like the Prince of Darkness in a pantomime, just as the power went off. Fortunately, the coffee had already been made, they sat at the table in a deep gloom that was more like late evening, and drank it without speaking until Francis said, 'I t-t-take it, you're not p-planning to take Kim f-for a run in this l-l-lot?'

'I thought I wouldn't go anywhere. Thunderstorms give me a headache – I rang Kim and she agreed with me.'

He gave her a sympathetic look. 'Kn-know the feeling. Another th-thing we have in c-c-common,' and fell silent, swirling his coffee round in his mug and watching it spin with close attention. Tamsin had no comment to make either: the same chain of events had, in one way at least, seen to them both. She was aware, now that she knew him more intimately, that the thick waves of his dark hair hid a formidable scar going back over his skull on his left temple; less alarming scars lurked under her own hair.

Violence, jealousy, distrust and resentment. The evil that had damaged them both, mentally and physically. She said, 'Why don't you go and lie down and let those tablets get to work? You can't work on a computer without any electricity.'

A sudden shower of rain, mixed with hail, rattled against the windows. Francis gave it a black look. He said, without looking at her, 'I c–c–can't keep g–giving in to it. You d–don't.'

'I don't think I had any actual brain damage.' Tamsin pointed out, 'just basic concussion,' and then wished that she hadn't when she met his eyes across the table. Hers dropped first, to the suitable accompaniment a huge rumble of thunder. The hail seemed to be settling in for the day, they were having to shout to be heard above its rattling on the roof of the mobile home, which hadn't helped her unfortunate remark; right at this moment it seemed about the right sound effect. She almost spoke again, but decided in time that might just make things worse. Francis had also dropped his eyes to study his half-empty mug. He said, 'Well, l–let's n–n–not argue about it,' in a noticeably argumentative tone of voice, before getting up to rinse his mug out at the sink. He had not, Tamsin noted, finished his coffee. She made no comment, and Sacha, obviously sympathising with her mood, came out from under the table and rested his chin on her knee. Francis turned from the sink and looked at them both without expression, and it was he who finally said, 'Sorry,' moving as he spoke towards the door. Tamsin said, before she could stop herself, 'You're surely not going back over to the house in this weather!'

There was a short silence, in which each of them felt they were teetering on the edge of a Grand Canyon of misunderstanding. Once again, Francis was the first to recover his balance. The breath he took was both audible and visible.

'C–c–come over with me,' he said. 'Th–there's a load of clearing up s–still to do, I could do with a hand w–w–with that, and it w–w–won't need electricity. And you'll be on hand if the p–p–plumber wants you.'

'Why, what's he doing?' Tamsin got to her feet, relieved at the break in the deadlock which she had so thoughtlessly created. And Francis said, 'P–plumbing, of course,' and then, as she moved towards the door, 'G–g–get a coat on, I w–w–would.'

Another roll of thunder and a huge bolt of lightning accompanied their helter-skelter passage over to the house – fittingly, Tamsin thought as she ran; the hail was easing off from its first violence, but not the rain, it felt as if she was trying to run through a waterfall. She had nearly not so much put her foot in it, as jumped into the shit over her head just now, she realised, and wondered how many other hidden pitfalls there were to negotiate? She had no idea what Francis might be thinking, and mentally cursed herself for having been so thoughtless and clumsy. They ended up outside the office door, where a row of pegs gave somewhere to hang their coats, drenched even in that short time. She hoped the rain would have eased by lunchtime as she hung her jacket to drip water all over the stone floor and kicked off her soaking wet shoes. They had to go to Embridge after that, hopefully for the last hospital appointment, which might account for Francis' unusual hyper-sensitivity this morning, come to think – although she wasn't sure about that. The District Nurse, who had continued her visits when Francis moved from Shortlanesend, had been uncommunicative on the subject, but Tamsin could see for herself that his arm was almost clear of inflammation by this time, it must be fair to assume that the wound itself was equally clean. All that she had got from the nurse was cheerful chat about how much more convenient the visits were for her now – apparently she lived in Shearwater. It had hardly helped. She hoped that Mr Simmonds might be more forthcoming – oh, within the bounds of his Hippocratic Oath, of course! And equally of course, she wasn't even Francis' wife as yet…the earlier depression returned full force, and she followed Francis into the office in a truculent mood that unpacking cardboard boxes filled with unfamiliar cardboard folders equally full of paperwork, in light so dim she could hardly see what she was doing, and then trying to file them in the correct alphabetical order did nothing to help.

It was only gradually, as the rain began to ease at last and the light to grow, that it dawned on her that most of this pile of paperwork had nothing at all to do with farming, or even restoring old houses. It wasn't until she accidentally dropped one of the cardboard folders on the floor and spilled its contents far and wide that she realised that what she had been handling, in that particular instance, was a detailed report from some university on the catastrophic effects of discarded plastic packaging being introduced into the world's oceans by the dumping, careless or intentional, of general non-degradable rubbish and the erosion of landfill along the coasts. Fortunately, the pages were numbered. She gathered them up without comment and began to sort them back into their correct order, stopping to read occasionally as something particular caught her eye, and then became conscious that Francis was watching her from where he was seated at the desk that didn't have a computer on it, trying to write something down in the still-quite-dim light that came through the window behind him – with his right hand, she noted. That was a first since his accident.

'You sh-should read that properly,' he told her. 'You might f-f-find it int-teresting.'

He must have been watching her for some minutes, to know exactly what she had dropped. She sat back on her heels, clasping the restored file in her arms.

'I just might – but not in this light, thank you. I'd like to know more about what concerns you so much.'

She thought he smiled at her, but what light there was, was behind him and she wasn't sure.

'I'd l-l-like that, too,' he said, and dropped his eyes again to attend to his work.

Tamsin had been so occupied – and getting so frustrated, to be honest – with her file sorting, that she hadn't noticed that the thunder was going over, but now she realised that she hadn't heard any for the last ten minutes or so, and that the light was, by this time, really brightening in the window behind Francis' head. The rain, too, seemed less forceful, and there was no hail rattling the windows. Symbolic, when you thought about it. The storm, both atmospheric and personal, seemed to be over: she set the file to one side and picked up the next box. She had learned something this morning, she realised – quite a lot of things, actually, – and the new knowledge was illuminating one or two other things she had recently learned, as well. She thought it might be interesting, and possibly illuminating, to run them past Kim when she saw her. She could trust Kim to understand what she was trying to say, she knew that. She could also trust her not to repeat anything she had learned in confidence.

It was amazing what you could learn about someone in just three days of living close to them. Far more than you would ever learn just by going out with them. She thought about that too, it cut both ways of course, but before she had followed the idea through to its conclusion, the plumber stuck his head round the door.

'Can't do anything more until they put the power back on,' he said. 'We're knocking off for an early lunch if that's OK with you, and hope it'll be back on when this storm goes over. It's brightening up now.'

'Fine,' said Francis, without looking up, but Tamsin smiled at the plumber and said, 'I'll come and look at what you've been up to, when there's enough light to see. We have to be out by half-past-two, but it should be back on long—' she broke off, as the lights came on, illuminating the scene of papery desolation around her, and they both laughed. 'There you are! Give us a shout when you come back from lunch, and I'll come over. We both will, I expect.'

'Fine. See you later, then.' He vanished, and Tamsin looked across at Francis. He met her look, putting down his pen and flexing his fingers, making a face as he did so but adding no comment. He said, 'Lunch s-s-sounds a good idea. Is th-there any?'

'The fried egg sandwich that we didn't have yesterday?'

'That'll d-d-do. It's t-t-time I tasted your s-s-signature d-d-dish.'

Tamsin shuffled the spread files into a neat pile by the cabinet, with a bit of help from Sacha, who had heard the word "lunch" and come out from beneath the desk, and said, 'I'll finish these later, promise,' as she got to her feet.

'S-s-see you in a m-minute, then.'

Domesticity. There it was again. She made a face, that he didn't see, as she left the office and resumed her damp coat and shoes. She wasn't sure that it really suited Francis, any more than office work suited either of them.

Hang on there – was she saying that domesticity suited her?

Perish the thought! But she found that she was smiling as she made her way back through the diminishing rain to her temporary home.

'Apparently, it's something called a "static caravan" she told Kim, over coffee the next morning. They were sitting by the electric fire in Romans, which felt strange: so quickly had she adapted to her new life. 'I asked Stephen – Francis didn't seem to know. '

'That sounds suitable.' Kim took a sip of her coffee. 'Are you keeping warm enough, in all this cold weather? It'll get worse than this before you move out into the house and join the Aga.'

'There's an electric fire built in, and we've got a couple of loose small convector heaters we can carry about as we need them – there's sockets for them here and there – for something, anyway. So yes. We don't use them at night, of course, but then central heating wouldn't be on then, either.'

There were other questions Kim wanted to ask, but the long weekend seemed to have created a space between herself and her twin, so she left them for now. Instead, she said, 'How will you be heating the house? With the Aga?'

'No, that's just for the cooker, there's to be a new boiler down in the cellar, and of course the hot water tank will keep the chill off the centre of the house – that will be in the hall cupboard. But there's no way of putting the pipes where they won't show and look hideous, there's no cavity walls and a lot of the ground floor is stone tiling anyway, so they can't go underneath except for the bits where the cellar is. It'll mostly be electric, apart from the bathroom: wire is easier to disguise, it can be put behind the panelling and the skirting boards, or upstairs it can go up in the roof – more of those heaters I mentioned, but bigger, and with individual time switches so they go on and off as necessary for where they are. Not those clumsy big storage heaters, thank goodness. And of course, in the living room, there'll be the wood burner, and the kitchen has the Aga anyway. And there's to be provision for an open fire in the drawing room, when we use it – which probably won't be that often. It's huge for just the two of us!'

'Room for the grand piano, then,' Kim observed, with a grin.

'If there really is one. All his stuff is coming out of store to be shoved in there now that there'll be some heating, where we can get at it, so we shall know the truth soon.'

'Has he got a lot of stuff?' Kim asked, idly. 'After all, he lived with his mother, in her house.'

'He had an upstairs flat in the kitchen wing. Apparently he has a bed and some other bedroom furniture, which we can use in our temporary bedroom—'

'A double bed?' Kim asked, before she could stop herself, and bit her lip in embarrassment. Tamsin didn't flinch.

'As it happens, yes. And he's got bookcases of course, and several thousand books to go in them – I'm not joking – and a desk that he had in the flat, stuff like that...' She caught Kim's eye. 'I didn't ask too much about the bed, either. Let sleeping dogs lie...if "sleeping" is the word I'm looking for.'

She had given Kim the opening she needed to ask a question to which she really wanted to know the answer, but which she had no right to ask. She said, as casually as she could manage, 'So, not a middle-aged virgin, then, you think?' and Tamsin replied, in unintentionally heartfelt tone, 'Definitely not!' and they looked at each other.

'I'm sorry,' said Kim, suddenly ashamed of herself. 'I shouldn't have asked that. It just popped out before I could stop it, it's none of my business.'

'No, don't be sorry. I'd have told you anyway – that much, at least. Probably not blow by blow.' Tamsin paused, looking down at her hands. 'Actually, I wanted to...no, not tell you everything, but to run something past you that's...well, relevant, I think.'

'To what?' Kim asked, when she didn't immediately continue, and Tamsin raised her head to look directly at her.

'To Francis. To what we know happened to him when he was a teenager. To how it's affected him – it has, you know. He covers up well, but the scars are there, and not just on his poor head.'

'The one on his head doesn't show,' said Kim, making it almost a question.

'It does, if you look. And so do all the others, the ones on...well, on him. Who he is. What he does. How he behaves. I suspect, the ones that stop him hammering Max Carruthers into the ground, as he has every right to do – metaphorically, at least. It's...odd, Kim.'

'In what way, particularly?' Kim asked, when she didn't immediately continue. 'He's been through a lot, one way or the other – you can't expect an immediate recovery, just because he knows the truth now. It still happened.'

'I know that. It's...oh, I don't know, I can't put my finger on it. He... holds back, somehow, as if...well, as if...oh, I don't know! I can't explain it, I just know it's there.'

'You'll have to do better than that,' Kim told her. 'I mean, I know that he doesn't make friends down at the Club, but—'

'—that's just it!' Tamsin interrupted. 'He could have but he chose not to, and now he just doesn't seem interested. But outside it, he has loads of them – Stephen the builder, Gary, Marcus Rose who sold him my car, Ernie, Matt – his cousins, from both sides, come to that – they come out of the woodwork like...like beetles, or something. Everywhere I turn. The ones here aren't posh people, like the awful Max tries to make out he is, they're...well, friends. And good ones. They care.'

'Probably he was at sixth form college with a lot of them – he certainly was with Gary – so what are you saying?'

'That whatever the problem is, it's only at the Sailing Club – and the Yacht Club, of course, that one time we were there. And that means that the only reason he ever stayed there in the first place, once he knew what would happen there, is simply that he wanted to race his Moonraker – but he always kept the barriers up.' She paused. 'He said to me once, "the hardest part about having friends is losing them"…I found that so sad.'

'So, is what you're saying that the man has been leading a double life for years?' Kim looked sceptical. 'I find that hard to believe.'

'Or that somehow, probably because of Max Carruthers, he's earned a reputation for setting himself above other people at the Club – considering himself to be posher than them, or something – that he can't live up to – or down to – or something. Oh Kim, I don't know! I only know that he isn't entirely at ease with something – quite possibly with himself.' She broke off. 'Am I making sense?'

Kim said carefully, not sure if she should say it at all, 'Actually, I think "posh" is a Carruthers myth. I don't think Francis is any posher than Ernie is, for instance, not when you get right down to it. It was just made up out of jealousy. Because of Christopher Chillingworth and the money and the big house, maybe.'

'You could argue that the big house is a fact even if the money isn't relevant, since it was the Chillingworth family money anyway.'

'Whose side are you on? What if it is a fact? It's just a family home, handed down through successive generations of one farming family, it's not Ravenscourt Place! Come to that, why just pick on Francis, when Merlin is standing right in the firing line too? Anyway, if you want my opinion, if Francis didn't make such a hash of saying a sentence more than two words long, he has quite a bit of the west country in the way he speaks, he's certainly not just pure plum-in-mouth public school.'

'I've wondered about that, too,' said Tamsin, after a pause. 'It would make sense – Mary is a country girl, even if his father was a townie. And his cousins down here are definitely west-country, although his London cousins certainly aren't. I think that he adapts in both camps, and even he isn't quite certain which of them he actually belongs in. He can be posh – he'll get that from his dad, and anyway I suppose he had to be, to survive at a public school – but his deep roots are right here, and he seems to be reverting to them, if I'm honest.'

Kim considered this, and came to no conclusions: she couldn't entirely agree. There must be a lot of his father in Francis, he was an academic rather than a countryman when you got right down to it. She didn't point this out, as she thought Tamsin realised anyway, and it was equally true that he had lived in Dorset all his life so it proved nothing at all. Instead, she reverted to where the discussion had begun, and said, 'You mustn't let it all get to you, though. For Francis, it must be a bit like being let out of prison after serving a long sentence – he'll move on from it. Just don't let it make you unhappy. If he loves you, and you love him back…' She broke off.

'Oh, he does – I do – it's just so bloody unfair – punishing him for being someone that he isn't, or for doing something that hurt the Carruthers twat's pride way back in the past, that didn't matter anyway if we believe Gary – and I do! When he finally buys this yacht that he's planning on, he'll never sail it with either of the local clubs, among people who should by rights be his friends. Don't you find that sad? He loves sailing, he should be able to share that with his friends.'

'You said he was taking it abroad, anyway,' Kim reminded her.

'Not this year. Probably not next, either, from what he said.' She realised that she needed to lighten the atmosphere, Kim was looking concerned. 'Don't look like that, I'm not having second thoughts, just realising things that I hadn't thought of before.' She added, on a laugh that broke in the middle, the first thing that came into her head. 'One of them is, I just wish I knew who taught him the things he knows in bed – he found places that I didn't even know were there myself, and nearly blew me away!'

'Rupert also ran?' Kim looked relieved at the change of subject. She smiled as she spoke.

'And as far, and as fast as he wants to! In the opposite direction to me!' Tamsin had pulled herself together now. She hadn't meant to make that confession at all, not even to Kim, so she hurriedly moved the conversation on. 'So, how was your weekend? I've told you all about mine.'

'You haven't, not really. We can come back to it though. Mine?' Kim paused. 'Well, it was good – missed you, of course, not being here, although it was good that Val and I could have some time together. He's a bit strung-up about this final interview thing – only about three weeks now, but the suspense is getting to him a bit. Me too, if it comes to that – such a lot is riding on it, and there are no guarantees. We should complete on the bungalow at the beginning of the month, and we still don't know…' She broke off and shrugged her shoulders. 'Oh well, that's life, I suppose. Nothing is ever graven in stone.'

'We're a right pair, aren't we?' said Tamsin, with a sympathetic smile.

'We are. Quite literally.' Kim reached out for her twin's empty mug. 'Didn't you say something about giving me a run in this car of yours? I didn't see it pull up, what've you done with it?'

'Parked it over the road, Merlin said it was OK. And I want to go to the supermarket, so we can go there and then decide what to do next.'

'You haven't eaten all that food already!'

'No, no – I want to buy a kettle to put in the utility room – we got stuck in the office in that storm yesterday, and I couldn't even make a cup of coffee!'

'Does he expect you back for lunch?'

'No – in fact he suggested I find something to do that would keep me out until late afternoon. Apparently there's some hay being delivered, which will mean large lorries and some frenzied activity for a bit! He said he'd ring when it was all over and the dust had settled – I think he may have meant that last literally!'

'Hay sounds hopeful. Is the farm about to have some animal tenants, then?'

'Horses. Next week sometime, probably, now. It was going to be the end of this week, but it was postponed because Clare is on holiday – you'll remember Clare? She's coming in each day to see to them like she did at Vachells. I'm looking forward to them, it feels eerily quiet for a farmyard, particularly in the evenings.'

'Just horses?'

'Matt is to build a chicken house in the field behind the tractor shed – the one where we're living, but hopefully not too close because there's at least one, or more probably two cockerels involved. It'll be fenced off like the van is, so that the horses don't try to demolish it, and frighten the snowballs; he wants them to have grass to scratch around on, or something, so they can't go in a barn. He's soft about those birds!'

'So when do the cows come home?'

'Don't know. He was muttering something about doing over the milking

514

parlour before they come in for the winter – there is one, sort of, in one of the outbuildings behind the stable block. And what used to be a dairy. It's all a bit of a depressing, rather unhygienic mess at present, round the back there. The cows are mostly pregnant at this minute, but he wants to get the noise and disturbance over before they move in.'

'Soft about them, too, then,' said Kim. He does like a challenge, your man.' She finally got to her feet and headed for the kitchen with the mugs. 'I shall be interested to see how it all ends up. I'll just rinse these, and then we can be off.'

Kim liked the new car, and Tamsin buzzed around the lanes for a bit, showing it off, before they arrived at the supermarket, where she bought the kettle, four man-sized plain mugs in a pack, some teaspoons, and on Kim's suggestion, a big jar of coffee, a pint of milk, a packet of PG Tips and some granulated sugar. On an impulse that she tried not to identify, she also added a lidded basket for laundry and tried not to see Kim grinning at her. Since it was by this time past one o'clock, they then took themselves to Bordens for some lunch, over which Kim cautiously returned to the subject of their morning talk.

'So, do I assume from all your purchases that you're happy with your new life?' she asked, and then realised immediately from Tamsin's reply that her twin had seen right through her. Tamsin smiled happily.

'Are you asking if I'm having second thoughts?'

'Well, are you? It must be a very different life from what you're used to.'

'It's certainly that,' Tamsin agreed, and Kim said, 'That doesn't answer my question.'

'I'm not certain what your question actually was.'

'OK. Now you have an idea of what you've let yourself in for, do you still want to go through with it?'

'Marry him, do you mean? Yes. Although I'm still not entirely certain what it is I've let myself in for. We met under very different circumstances.'

'You always knew he was a farmer,' Kim objected.

'But I'm not sure that he is, when you really get down to it. One of the filing cabinets in the office is full up with stuff about seaweed and mussels and the Mariannas Trench and things, and Greenpeace reports on floating detritus of one kind or another, even blue whales, and it isn't new. I had to put it all away yesterday, and it filled a whole filing cabinet, so I know. And he's getting in a farm manager before Christmas, when we can move into the house and leave the man somewhere to live in. None of that sounds to me like a dedicated farmer, does it to you?'

Kim digested this information along with a mouthful or two of her lunch. Then she said, 'I see,' although she wasn't certain that she did. But Tamsin hadn't finished.

'There's another thing too, that I'm sure he's considered, although we haven't talked about it – so far. Technically, Francis is the last of the Chillingworths of Chillingworths Bank – at least, he is unless, or until, we have a son. I don't think he's overlooked it. I'm not sure where that thought is taking me, to be honest.'

'So, a real magical mystery tour! And you're still up for it?'

'Wouldn't you be?'

'That's a question to which I don't have the answer,' said Kim, wrinkling her nose. 'Val is a very different proposition, and I love him to bits. But unless I miss my guess, you wouldn't have chosen him.'

'So we're not that identical after all,' said Tamsin, almost with satisfaction. Kim perfectly understood this, she preferred to think of herself as an individual too. She said, 'We are, and we aren't. After all, we had completely different upbringings and we have completely different backgrounds, those things shape who a person becomes – but genetically, we started off as nearly identical as two human beings can get, which is why we understand each other so well. We've just travelled different roads, we never really lost contact in that way. And how profound is that!' She made a face. 'Just listen to me! And now, tell me – didn't you go to the hospital again yesterday? I meant to ask first off, but we got side-tracked. What did they say?'

Tamsin's big grin answered her before she even spoke. She said, 'Good news, at last! The infection has almost cleared up – the tear in his palm is still leaking a bit, he has to keep that covered and keep on with the antibiotics for now, and the nurse will come and dress it still, but it's only got a plaster on it, no bandages, and the back is all dried up and healing. He has to cover it if he goes out into the farmyard to do anything, and he can't do any heavy work, but he can start using his hand again and – oh Kim! Wonder of wonders after the last couple of weeks! He drove the Discovery home! I was with him, of course, but I wasn't needed. So…' She smiled happily, and Kim smiled back.

'So, does he have to go back?'

'He has to go next week, just for a final check-up, but he can take himself that time, now we know he's all right to drive. And if it's all OK then, that's it! The surgery in Shearwater can handle it from there.'

'He'll be scarred for life after all that.'

'Then perhaps it will remind him to be more careful in future,' said Tamsin. 'Hopefully, the fact that it will still hurt him for a while if he doesn't take care will give him time to learn. He really did a good job, Kim, now I can see it. Poor darling, it must have been agony, and he came like a hero and ate that stew I made.'

'He didn't eat that much it, from what I remember,' said Kim. She paused. 'Have you made another one yet?'

'It have it on my to-do list. There's a recipe in that book you gave me for Boeuf Bourguignon, which I thought I might try tomorrow, it'll probably do us two days – Francis thinks that cut-up steak in the freezer is probably chuck, whatever that is, so I took it out to thaw before I came out – and there's another for Chicken Mornay, which doesn't look too taxing. I thought I might try that at the weekend, and invite you and Val to dinner. What do you think? We've cadged enough meals off you.'

'All this domesticity doesn't sound a bit like you,' said Kim, looking at her affectionately. 'I'll have to ask Val, but I'm sure we'd love to come. I'd like to see what you've made of the honeymoon suite.'

'There wasn't a lot to make of it,' said Tamsin, reflectively. 'It's all pretty much built-in. But we have added a few bits and pieces to make it more like home. You'll see, anyway.'

'I'm looking forward to it.' Kim paused. 'When we did that mammoth shop, did we buy a slow cooker?'

'Not that I remember. I haven't seen one around anywhere, and I think I would have noticed.'

'Then let's get one as we go out – it'll be perfect for your Boeuf Bourguignon, and there'll be much less washing up. You can put it in the utility room in the house when you're not using it, so you don't have to fit it in the van.'

'It certainly won't fit anywhere else. And next time we come, we can start equipping your kitchen.'

'Maybe,' said Kim. She twiddled with her knife and didn't look at Tamsin. 'We shall have to see what happens, won't we?'

'But you'll be buying the bungalow anyway?' Tamsin made it into a question, she suddenly wasn't sure.

'Oh yes, but if...we might just equip it with essentials and let it furnished,' Kim finished, adding, after a moment, 'For now.'

'It'll be all right, Kim,' said Tamsin, although she wasn't actually sure about that.

'I try to believe that. I really don't want to have to go and live in London all week, although I would if I had to, for Val.'

'Then let's hope you won't have to. It's not so long now, Kim. It's November next week. Cosmo will be back and living at Vachells, the farm will have horses, by the end of the month we might even be able to live in the house – things are happening, Kim. You can't deny it.'

'I suppose – for you, anyway.'

'For you, too. When's the interview?'

'The twenty-first.'

'That's not so long – barely three weeks. Believe it, Kim, the wind is blowing our way! I'm sure of it!'

'You sound like me,' said Kim, deprecating her own tendency to have strange feelings about things, in which, in spite of confirming evidence now and then, she hardly believed.

'And is that surprising? Have you finished with that sandwich, because if you have, let's go and give the car another run, and you can play with it too – it's insured if I give you permission – and then I promised to go and see Mary, check she's OK. Although I'm sure that she is.'

'She'll want to hear about Francis,' said Kim, getting obediently to her feet.

'He rang her when we got back from here. And believe me, that's a first. Particularly as yesterday he was pretty much under the weather, and biting my head off if I so much as put a foot out of line.'

'Why, what on earth did you do?'

'I made a stupid remark and nearly started a quarrel.' Kim did not ask, and Tamsin didn't say, what the stupid remark was, and they walked together to the elevator. All Tamsin said by way of a clue was, 'It was the weather, we were both feeling a bit head-achy and cross,' and Kim drew her own, not entirely accurate, conclusions.

They played with the car for an hour, which both of them enjoyed, and then went back to Romans for a coffee before Tamsin headed off on her errand. She suggested Kim came with her, but Kim declined: it was important, she felt, to keep their private lives separate until they had settled into them properly, but she felt a bit flat when the little red car had gone roaring off up the village street and she was on her own once more. She envied Tamsin, she realised. Her own life was still on hold, but Tamsin's had gathered speed and overtaken her. She sat down on the sofa and picked up a book, but did not read.

It was only Tuesday! No Val until Friday evening, at the earliest. She opened the book and stared without seeing at the pages. Six months, they had had. Six swiftly-passed months to enjoy their twinship, and now they would be going their separate ways.

Val had to get that job. She didn't want to leave this place, she felt she belonged here and not just because of Tamsin.

Three weeks looked like three years from where she sat now, but Tamsin had survived worse, at least she was sure of Val, as Tamsin had not been of Francis. She herself only had to wait for her wedding day and enjoy the interval, Tamsin had not known if there was even anything to hope for. She dismissed her thoughts and tried to concentrate on the book in her hands.

On Friday morning, out of the blue, there was a phone call from Tamsin.

'I thought you'd like to hear the news,' she said, and Kim could hear the laughter in her voice.

'The news? What...?'

'It's a grand piano. Only a baby grand, but definitely of the species. I'll show you tomorrow.'

'Has he played it for you?'

'He says it will need tuning, and anyway, he can't at present with that hand. I'm not sure that I'm sorry, Bennie told me he favoured hard rock and jazz.'

'Oops! Are you sure you know what you're doing?'

'I told you already, and more than once, I have no idea. Oh – and Matt has asked Francis if there's a permanent job for him here. He doesn't really want to be a stone-walling expert, he likes company – and animals – and us, as it turns out.'

'And is there?'

'The idea is under consideration. Francis doesn't want to upset Matt's dad, he's too valuable – stone-walling is a dying art. But God knows where he'd live.'

Kim switched off the phone eventually, trying not to feel that all-too-familiar these days pang of envy. There was no need: Val would be here tonight, the weekend lay ahead. November was within touching distance, and by the time the month was out they would surely know where their future would lie? She envied Tamsin the security of her own future, but she only had to be patient for a week or so…whatever happened at Val's interview with Hetherington Associates, a whole new beginning in some form or another awaited them both equally – them all, even.

She sat down on the edge of the sofa and thought about it, for it wasn't just herself and Val who would be making a new start: Francis was not only rebuilding an old farmhouse and returning life to the farmland, he was rebuilding his own life – and doing so with great courage, she had to admit, and with Tamsin at his side. She wondered for a moment if he would ever get as far as going back to either of the clubs, or if he planned to let Max Carruthers hold the stage; she wouldn't put money on it either way. Oh well, like her mother always said "what will be, will be" – and if the answer was no, he wouldn't, did that matter so much? Sailing was a hobby, not his whole life.

She pulled herself together then and reached for the television remote control: nothing would be helped by sitting here trying to second-guess the unknown future. Whatever happened, she felt at this moment that it would be good, and nobody got everything they wished for anyway. She and Tamsin had found each other against the odds, they would be living close and would continue to see and get to know each other, each was to marry and start a new life. They were remarkably blessed, when she thought about it.

So, the barometer seemed set to fair, and the winds of change were blowing strong. Bring on November, and quite right, what would be, would be!

www.ingramcontent.com/pod-product-compliance
Lightning Source LLC
Chambersburg PA
CBHW070926100726
47908CB00001B/112